W9-BYU-876

BOB HOPE

BOB HOPE
A Life in Comedy

by William Robert Faith

G. P. PUTNAM'S SONS
NEW YORK

Library of Congress Cataloging in Publication Data

The author wishes to express appreciation for permission to quote from the following
sources:

Doubleday & Company, Inc. for excerpts from *The Last Christmas Show* by Bob Hope,
copyright © 1974 by Bob Hope; and for excerpts from *I Owe Russia $1200* by Bob Hope,
copyright © 1963 by Bob Hope.
Simon & Schuster for selections from *So This Is Peace* by Bob Hope, copyright © 1946,
1973 by The Hope Corporation; *Have Tux, Will Travel*, Hope's Own Story as told to Peter
Martin, copyright © 1954 by The Bob and Dolores Hope Charitable Foundation; and *I
Never Left Home* by Bob Hope, copyright © 1944, 1971 by Bob Hope.
Stein and Day Publishers for an excerpt from *Call Them Irreplaceable* by John Fisher,
copyright © 1976 by John Fisher.

Faith, William Robert.
  Bob Hope, a life in comedy.

  Includes index.
  1. Hope, Bob, 1903-   2. Comedians—United
States—Biography.   I. Title
PN2287.H63F3   1982   792.7'028'0924 [B]   81-22716
ISBN 0-399-12627-9   AACR2

To Bob Hope—
    the man,
    the talent,
    the legend.

Contents

BOB HOPE

. . . I left England when I was four because I found out I could never be king.[1]

CUE IN
"This Is Your Life,
Leslie Towns Hope!"[2]

1

New York, Sunday, November 15, 1970
There had been rain since early morning. It was raw and windy weather but the planes were flying at Kennedy. The Hopes were headed for London where Bob would entertain royalty twice in five days.[3] As usual they were running late, and the passenger agent worked fast to hustle four hefty pieces of luggage, including Bob's theatrical wardrobe trunk, to the plane.

The airline had been alerted. Even before the limo had time to glide out of the Waldorf driveway, an assistant manager standing in the Towers lobby was on the phone asking a BOAC official to hold the London flight. Somehow, they arrived at Kennedy with minutes to spare.

Hope breezed through this barely-making-flights routine with an accustomed nonchalance that could have been irritating to the airlines except that he was a unique customer. After all, for thirty years his benign airline gags ("I knew it was an old plane when I found Lindbergh's lunch on the seat"), and his omnipresence in airports and on regularly scheduled flights (sometimes he racked up as many as 20,000 miles a week), rendered him a cherished unsalaried spokesman.

He was striding now a few feet ahead of Dolores toward the gate, affably smiling at people who stopped in disbelief. He spotted a public telephone, and while the passenger agent escorted Dolores to the plane, Bob called "the boys" on the Coast.

It was one of his celebrated NAFT calls, the writers' acronym for "need a few things" at whatever hour and from whatever place. Usually he called his chief writer and television producer Mort Lachman who, then, called the other six. Right now Hope needed Grace Kelly material because she had, on very short notice, replaced an ailing Noel Coward as compere (British for master of ceremonies) of his Monday night London benefit. Also, he had neglected to tell Mort he would be staying at the Savoy this trip.

The passenger agent hovered over Hope and was visibly relieved when the comedian finally hung up. By now his telephoning had delayed the takeoff. Hope walked briskly into the first-class section of the plane, humming and smiling his way to what was universally acknowledged as "his" seat on any commercial flight—the right-side bulkhead seat. There he could stretch out, put his feet up, work undisturbed. And when he traveled alone, which was more often than one might suspect, the airline thoughtfully left the space beside him unsold.

Soon after takeoff, Bob opened his briefcase, put on his half-glasses and began to look over the London material that Miss Hughes had put in his case. On top were fact sheets prepared by his public relations people describing the royal events and Hope's role in each one.

Dolores glanced down and followed with interest the details of his Monday night benefit performance, extravagantly labeled "A Night of Nights." It was a fund-raiser for Louis Mountbatten's favorite charity, the United World College Fund, for which Bob was sharing the bill with Sinatra.[4]

Two identical performances were scheduled back-to-back for Royal Festival Hall audiences expected to pay £50 a ticket. The first of these two shows would be videotaped by BBC for international distribution, and Hope was concerned that his first audience might be a tougher one to reach. He would prefer BBC to tape the second show—or both, for that matter—because he had some special material he could "try out" on the first sitting.

Following the second performance, he and Dolores, Sinatra, Princess Grace, and assorted other members of the British elite were invited to a buffet supper at St. James's Palace hosted by Prince Charles and Princess Anne.

This event held particular interest for Dolores, as well as a certain amount of disappointment. While she and Bob were dining with the royal family, the rest of her immediate family—daughter Linda and husband Nat, daughter Nora and husband Sam, son Tony and wife Judy—would be lurking at the Savoy and forced to dine wherever they could remain anonymous. Yet, Dolores appreciated the importance of these cloak-and-dagger arrangements. They related to Tuesday night's surprise event.

The Hope children, including son Kelly if he could be located, were being flown to London to surprise Bob in Thames Television's production of "This Is Your Life." Hope was to be the first honoree in a British revival of the American radio-television success show of the early fifties. Dolores was pleased that this secret had been successfully kept from Bob, who generally hated surprises but mysteriously seemed to know everything that was going on. What convinced Dolores that the secret was intact was a conversation she and Bob had a few days before.

"Bob, be sure and have Miss Hughes add the Annenberg dinner party to your London schedule. It's Tuesday night. They're honoring Mountbatten."

"When is it?"

"It's Tuesday."

"What time Tuesday, Dolores? I'm taping a talk show at Thames Television that night."

"It's dinner. I think seven."

"I can join you there. I should be finished by seven-thirty."

Dolores had studied his face; she was positive he didn't know. If the surprise was to be tipped off, it would happen because the Thames producer had arranged, foolishly in Dolores' view, to house all of the "Life" show guests at the Savoy. Program coordinator Alan Haire confidently assured her that precaution had been taken—whatever that meant—to protect Hope and the guests from meeting each other prematurely.

Actually, Dolores felt secure about most of the arrangements for this London trip. This was largely due to the numerous telephone calls she had received in recent weeks from Lady Carolyn Townshend, Bob's socially prominent London press agent, whose sometime royal connections were useful in coordinating these high-level engagements, making wardrobe suggestions and smoothing out questions about protocol.

By this time Bob had removed his glasses, handed the fact sheets to Dolores and dozed. Dolores' eyes fell on the next fact sheet. Bob's appearance Wednesday night was unquestionably the most intriguing event on their schedule. Its distinction lay in the guests, not the performers. Under one roof, a London nightclub called The Talk of the Town, would be gathered most of Europe's royalty for a Gala Cabaret to benefit the World Wildlife Fund, whose cosponsors were Britain's Prince Philip and the Netherlands' Prince Bernhard.

Though the invitation had emanated from Prince Philip, Hope was urged to accept by the show's organizer (and Bob's former British booking agent), Sir Lew Grade. It was a fairly distinguished cast—Rex Harrison, Rudolf Nureyev, Petula Clark, Glen Campbell, Engelbert Humperdinck and George Kirby—with Hope assured of top billing.

The real draw, however, was Princess Beatrix of the Netherlands, the Greek King Constantine and Queen Anne-Marie, Prince Don Juan Carlos of Spain, Prince Henrik and Princess Margrethe of Denmark, the Grand Duke and Duchess of Luxembourg, the Crown Prince of Norway, Prince Albert of Belgium and, with luck, Queen Juliana of the Netherlands. All these would shine beside Queen Elizabeth, Prince Charles, Princess Anne, Princess Alexandra and Prince Michael of Kent in an effort to raise £200,000 ($500,000) for the cause of conservation.

Dolores' eyes were fastened on this note:

> Because of possible jealousy on the part of other people, Mr. and Mrs. Hope *will not* be seated at the Queen's table at the Talk of Town royal cabaret. Mr. Hope will be seated at Prince Charles' table at the request of Prince Charles.[5]

Dolores focused on one particular sentence, "Mrs. Hope will be seated at a table near the Queen." In no circumstances did she intend being separated from Bob at this gala. She would also insist that her children not only have good seats but be introduced to the Queen.

Bob woke up, got out of his seat and went to the toilet. When he came out, Dolores was asleep. He rubbed his eyes, and put his glasses on again. He began to paw through his briefcase for the material that "the boys" had delivered to his Toluca Lake estate. He rubbed his eyes again. Normally he would never admit it even to himself, but he really felt tired. His recent schedule had not necessarily been more grueling than usual, but the activities of the past week had probably introduced some stress. Ever since he had suffered the eye hemorrhage, and had heard the doctors' warnings about stress, he tried to let things that were out of balance wash over him. But that was hard. He wanted things *his* way.

Hope adjusted his pillow and listened as a voice announced there would be an NFL game on film after dinner. His mind turned back to the events of the previous Saturday when he was entertaining at Notre Dame, and especially

his conversation with Father Hesburgh about American troops in Cambodia
and Laos, and he was mystified about the political views of this man he had
always respected so much. Images flickered and then faded as his attention
returned to the material in front of him.

He had to pick gags for his Monday night shows. He had a system which
had worked ever since radio days. He looked at every writer's material three
times. If he liked a joke at first reading he would place a check by the gag.
Next time he would only reread the checked gags and the ones he still liked
the second time got a double check. When he reread the crosshatched gags,
he would circle, and number in order, the ones he planned to use in the
monologue.

> Everybody got nervous when a bearded man in khaki with a sub-
> machine gun got on the plane, but he turned out to be an Israeli
> chaplain.

He liked that one but thought it too sophisticated. No check. The next three
he liked, however. They got checks.

> On the trip over, our BOAC jet was almost hijacked but the
> British are so clever. The stewardess turned out to be a man from
> Scotland Yard.
> Imagine that . . . just when I was beginning to care.
> All that time I'd been whistling at shoulder holsters.

2

London, November 16, 1970

Lady Carolyn and Hope's London gag writer Denis Goodwin were waiting
at Heathrow. Bob was wide-awake, responding brightly to their questions
about his health and reciting to them the frenetic schedule of his past five
days. Dolores was sleepily cordial.

Carolyn, a pretty blonde in the Swedish model tradition, chattered nonstop
during the ride into the city. It now seemed that the BBC planned to videotape both of Monday's "Night of Nights" performances. That pleased Hope.
Queen Juliana of the Netherlands definitely would attend the Wildlife Gala,
as would Neil Armstrong, Clare Boothe Luce and Cary Grant. Grant would
be there as official celebrity spokesman for Fabergé, the cosmetic and perfume firm that had purchased the United States television rights to the
Royal Gala Cabaret. This news interested Bob; it meant that his agent
Jimmy Saphier would be negotiating with Lew Grade for a sizable fee.

Carolyn also announced there would be a news conference for Bob, Princess Grace and Frank at two o'clock on Monday afternoon. Hope asked her
to arrange it for at least four o'clock in the afternoon. She said she would try
but didn't think it possible.

In spite of the late hour, the Savoy's public relations officer Pru Emery
had arranged for porters and a hall maid to be standing by, and after her
welcoming speech in the lobby, she led them up to their suite. Bob asked Pru
to arrange for some cold milk and asked her to find him a masseur. It was

then already past midnight but he said he wouldn't need the rub until one-thirty.

Bob said goodnight to Dolores and set out with Carolyn and Denis for his usual walk. The air was cold and penetrating as they walked at a brisk pace, set by Hope, along the Strand. Hope told Carolyn to make certain the British press, and particularly the wire services, knew the London performances were strictly benefits, and that any television fees were being assigned to the Eisenhower Medical Center. Carolyn said they could cover that and other subjects at the news conference the next afternoon at Festival Hall. Hope asked how late he could arrive for rehearsal and still meet the press. Carolyn said she would find out.

They crossed over the Strand to the BBC buildings and turned back toward the Savoy. Thoroughly chilled, Carolyn and Denis were relieved when Hope said goodnight to them in the lobby.

Upstairs, after he had read some more material from his briefcase and the masseur had arrived and left, Hope put on his pajamas. He wandered around the suite for a while and then went in to make certain the shades were closed tightly over his bedroom windows. He got into bed and tried to sleep. Finally he got out again and took a pill (something he disliked doing) and finally dropped off to sleep about four-thirty.

3

London, Monday afternoon, November 16, 1970

Carolyn arrived at the Savoy just after one o'clock. It was sleeting when she stepped out of the cab and she nearly lost her umbrella in a sudden gust of wind. She pulled off her rainhat and looked around the lobby. The cherubic Denis came to greet her.

"He's not taking calls according to the operator," said Denis.

"The hell," she said, with a desperate look on her face, as she headed for the house phones. The operator agreed to connect her with Hope only after she imperiously announced "This is *Lady* Carolyn Townshend" in her well-bred voice.

Hope responded sluggishly, asking what time it was. "It's one o'clock, Bob," she said. "And we're due at Festival Hall in forty-five minutes."

He told them to come upstairs. Dolores had gone out to shop in Lower Bond Street. Bob was coming out of a heavy sleep. The blackout shades were still drawn and the room was stygian.

"What time is it?" he asked from his bed.

"One twenty-five," Denis said.

"What's the weather?" Hope asked, rising out of the bed and going into the bathroom, leaving the door ajar and relieving himself noisily. Denis told him about the sleet.

Breakfast arrived with amazing speed but Hope was on the telephone speaking in low tones. He hung up the phone and sat drowsily on the edge of the bed pouring coffee. The phone had rung again. This time he spoke soothingly to Charlie Hogan's wife, Pat, in Chicago. Charlie was dying of cancer. Hogan, one of Hope's two or three most cherished friends, was the booking agent who gave him the job that saved his life in 1928, and he had remained one of his agents and a confidant since. Bob told Pat that he would come to Chicago as quickly as he could, probably Saturday night at the latest.

"Denis, ask Carolyn if she wants some coffee."

Denis went into the sitting room and spoke to Carolyn who was on the other phone, then he came back. "She says no, Bob. She just wants you to hurry."

The phone rang. It was Lew Grade welcoming him to London. It rang again. It was Walter Annenberg welcoming him to London. Denis brought in a telegram that had just arrived:

> BOB HOPE SAVOY HOTEL WC2— BOB OF BURBANK
> WELCOME TO LONDON— MOUNTBATTEN OF BURMA.[7]

Hope looked through a few other messages and placed them beside his telephone.

At two o'clock he was still in his pajamas talking to Mort Lachman in Burbank about the monologue for his November NBC special. Then he talked to David Frost, asking him to help with a walk-on gag at the "Night of Nights" shows. He asked David what glamour stars were in London. Raquel Welch? Could he ask her to do the gag with him? Frost agreed to find Raquel, and to meet Hope at Festival Hall for rehearsal at three.

"What time is the news conference, Carolyn?" Hope called out from his bedroom.

"Right now. I couldn't get it changed."

"Well—let's go!" said Hope in a Jackie Gleason-like voice. By 2:35 they were in a car headed across the river to the rehearsal.

4

Monday afternoon, November 16, 1970

Princess Grace, a scarf covering her yellow hair and dark glasses shielding her eyes, arrived at the rehearsal first. Just as she was asking where Mr. Hope and Mr. Sinatra were, Frank arrived. The two of them posed for pictures and answered questions from the media people.

Then they went onstage and worked out some business for Her Serene Highness to use when introducing Hope and Sinatra. After that she waved goodbye and was gone.

At 2:55 Hope, trailed by Carolyn and Denis, walked into the rehearsal. Except for the *Daily Mail* reporter and photographer, the media crowd had departed. Frank was rehearsing. Then David Frost came in. Soon after, Raquel arrived but only, she said, to tell Hope she really didn't think she could do the dance-on bit with Frost that evening. Bob, however, was his most persuasive and she agreed to rehearse the gag while the photographer snapped away. After that the *Daily Mail* pair left.

Hope took Carolyn aside and asked what happened to the news conference. Carolyn said apologetically that it really was more of a photo session. She reminded him that they were late arriving. But Hope, whose media

wisdom stemmed from thirty-five years of top-notch press agentry and ballyhoo, wasn't buying.

He walked away from Carolyn to Sinatra who by then had broken off his
rehearsal in deference to Hope. They walked together over toward Frank's
conductor Bill Miller. Hope and Miller then went over the tempi for a few
songs. Hope told Sinatra a new Spiro Agnew joke, and then Hope said he
had to go.

The ride back to the Savoy was mostly silent. Hope spoke to Denis once,
asking him if those seats behind the stage would be sold. Denis said with a
twinkle that they were called "organ stalls" and they probably would be.

Hope sailed through the lobby as if he was alone, and Carolyn and Denis
barely made it into the lift before the door closed. Carolyn finally broke the
thick chill between them by saying that they would be back to help print
some cue cards. He said, "That's fine," went into his suite and closed the
door.

5

London, Monday night, November 16, 1970

The two performances that night went well enough. Hope was not, as
several friends and critics observed, in prime form but still sufficiently outrageous at one moment and suitably ingenuous the next to satisfy an
audience who had paid high ticket prices for a once-in-a-lifetime chance to
see him, Sinatra and a real live storybook princess together on one stage.

Just before the first performance, Hope was told that Raquel had decided
not to appear. He suggested they find Eric Morely of Mecca Ltd. who ran
the annual Miss World Contest. Morely would help them get Eva Reuber-
Steir, the reigning Miss World, who was in London for this year's contest.
Eva had gone to Vietnam the Christmas before with Hope. As Hope suspected, she was on her way to the show anyway and she agreed to do the gag
with Frost. The *Manchester Guardian*'s Philip Hope-Wallace, expected to
be sharply critical of a high-priced benefit marred by the intrusion of glaring
lights and television cameras, was mellow in his November 17, 1970,
review:

> I can't say why, but Mr. Hope has charm. He clung to a micro-
> phone, ribbed the orchestra, apologized for the prompt cards dur-
> ing his songs, and at one moment danced with David Frost just
> when we thought he was cutting in to dance with David Frost's
> "Miss World" partner, and referred in his immensely good-
> natured way to Sinatra's second wig.

Princess Anne and Prince Charles laughed and applauded from the royal
box at the second performance. At about one o'clock they left the Hall in
order to precede their guests to St. James's Palace. The Hopes left the Hall
just after one-thirty and were among the first to arrive for supper. There was
a lavish array of foods, served exquisitely, and there was dancing to a society
orchestra and polite conversation until Dolores insisted they leave when
Princess Anne retired at three.

6

London, Tuesday morning, November 17, 1970

Mildred Rosequist Brod—Mrs. John Brod—was awake at seven-thirty and dressed by eight-fifteen. Her breakfast tray arrived at eight-thirty. The Thames limousine was to pick her up before nine-thirty. Alan Haire had advised her that it would be a long day of sitting around the studio.

She had come to London alone, which was a big mistake. But her husband was not living with her at present, and when she had agreed to appear on the program she had been told that Bob's older brother Fred and his wife LaRue from Columbus would also be in London for the telecast, so she would have company. Mildred had known the Hopes since childhood days in Cleveland. Mildred was Bob's first sweetheart and his first dancing partner. Bob had proposed to her in front of Hoffman's Ice Cream Parlor on Euclid Avenue. They had dreamed together so many years ago of dancing their way to stardom like the Castles.

Mildred had arrived in London on Sunday, was met at Heathrow by a Thames representative and driven to the Savoy. At the hotel she learned that Fred and LaRue were not expected. As she was somewhat frightened of London, she had remained alone in her room.

Now, while she waited for the telephone to ring and announce her limo, Mildred picked up the *Daily Telegraph* and worked her way back to the entertainment page. There was a review of the "Night of Nights" benefit. She was struck by the way the story seemed to focus on Sinatra and Kelly. Finally, the telephone sounded, her limousine from Thames was waiting. She reached for her raincoat, umbrella and scarf and headed for the lobby.

7

Later that morning, November 17, 1970

In spite of the hour that Dolores finally got to bed, she was up, drank her hot lemon juice, was dressed and had the remainder of her breakfast by nine. She barely glanced at the morning papers on her tray, but she had seen enough to be irked by the inordinate fuss over Grace Kelly and Frank.

She had a full day ahead of her. She had remembered to tell Bob, before she retired, that she would be out shopping and running errands all day. She assured him that she would be dressed and waiting when he returned from his Thames talk show. Secretly she had arranged to dress for the telecast in Nora's room, and the limousine would pick her and the children up at the Savoy between four and five o'clock.

Before she went out, Dolores went to Bob's door and listened, but hearing nothing, she left quietly.

Bob opened his eyes about noon and in the darkened room continued to doze for another thirty minutes. He fumbled for the phone, ordered breakfast and asked to have all the national dailies delivered to his suite. Then he got out of bed, padded to the door of his room, opened it and called out, "Dolores?" No reply.

He was proud of her, the way she was carrying off her "This Is Your Life" smokescreen. She would not like knowing that he knew about it. He had, in fact, known for days. One of his publicity men had asked Miss Hughes and she had said, "You know Mr. Hope hates surprises," and so Bob was told. He had done his best to let Dolores think she was a good actress. He wondered about the rest of the cast Thames had assembled in London, besides Dolores. His brothers Fred and Jim? The children? His relatives from Hitchin? Crosby and Lamour? Benny? If *he* were producing his own "Life" he would get Arnold Palmer and Frances Langford, Colonna and Durante, Merman and Lucy Ball. Of his many writers probably Hal Kantor, Larry Gelbart, Charlie Lee. And he could envision people like Westmoreland and Honey Chile. When he thought about some people who ought to be there, he felt sad remembering they were gone—Doc Shurr and Monte Brice, Charley Cooley and his brothers Jack and Ivor. Now, in Chicago, that beautiful little Charlie Hogan was slipping away.

Breakfast arrived and with it came the newspapers and Denis Goodwin, ready to work on material for his Wednesday, Thursday and Friday appearances.

"Have you looked at the papers yet?"

"Some," said Denis.

"Well?" asked Hope pouring himself half hot coffee and half hot milk. "Were we a hit?"

"Yes—except in the *Daily Mirror* which goes bonkers for Sinatra," Denis said holding up the tabloid and turning to page three of the November 17, 1970, issue:

> The simple happy truth is that, if this really was a "Night of Nights" at the South Bank's Festival Hall, then it was due entirely, well almost entirely, to the indestructible Francis Albert from Hoboken.

At that moment the telephone rang in Hope's bedroom and he went in to answer it. Denis could hear Bob reading excerpts from the *Mirror* article to whoever was on the other end. Hope came back to get more coffee.

"That was Mort. He's going to call back later with more stuff for the Wildlife show."

The day wore on with Hope remaining in his pajamas, nibbling fruit and drinking orange juice, working on material and talking to people in various parts of Britain and America. He brightened considerably when a small, richly wrapped package was delivered to his suite. The stationery crest on the accompanying card had "Broadlands, Romsey, Hampshire" engraved just below it. The note read:

> My dear Bob,
>   I am writing to thank you for your splendid generosity in making the "Night of Nights" such a tremendous success, and particularly for doing two shows in one night under the duress of the Bengal Lancers!!
>   You were magnificent and everybody loved your performance.
>   I am looking forward to seeing you again tonight when I can express my thanks and appreciation in person.

Meanwhile will you please accept this small souvenir of the
"Night of Nights." The box was designed by my son-in-law,
David Hicks.

                              Yours ever,
                              Mountbatten of Burma.[8]

Hope read it aloud to Denis, and then opened the box to find a pair of
exquisite cuff links in gold. He walked over to the window and looked closely
at his gift.

"Who needs the *Daily Mirror?*" he purred.

8

That same night, November 17, 1970

The surprise cast of immediate family, Hitchin relatives, old friends and
casual acquaintances chatted nervously in the Green Room. About 200
people sat impatient and mystified in audience seats facing a living room
stage set. An anxious program host, Eamonn Andrews, had to mollify both
Green Room guests and his studio audience with assurances that Bob Hope
would at any moment walk through a side entrance (they would see it on
studio monitors) and then step into the set believing he was the interview
subject of a talk show.

Mildred Brod had been sitting around Thames studios nearly eight hours
waiting for this moment and she was not particularly thrilled. One by one the
guests had trickled in, but none until early afternoon. First to arrive were the
Hitchin relatives, followed by other British guests, and finally by Dolores,
the children and other American guests. When the room was full and there
seemed a common purpose in the air, even Mildred's excitement rose to the
occasion.

Hope was met outside by a BBC page and led to a particular stage door.
When he opened that door, Andrews was waiting on the other side, a camera
pointed, its red light glowing.

ANDREWS: Bob—you're late. How are you? There's an
             audience waiting for you—
HOPE: What?

Hope sounded incredulous, and stepping toward the brightly lit stage area,
he removed his coat, beaded with wetness from the rainy night outside. One
more step to the set; there was noisy, prolonged applause. He was dressed for
the Annenberg party. He shaded his eyes to search out the audience, nodded
to their greeting. He cut a dignified figure as he walked to the seat of honor.
He crossed his arms over his chest and looked up at Andrews who waited for
the applause to stop.

ANDREWS: Bob, this is a very special week for you, and this is
             a very special time, and we want to make this a
             night you're going to remember for a long time—
             because tonight Bob Hope—this is—*your life!*
HOPE: Come on—you're kidding—really?

Hope looked around. He grinned like a small boy. The audience was once again applauding and a lush, symphonic version of Hope's theme song, "Thanks for the Memory," filled the studio. Andrews opened his big black book. He explained that the first guest was someone Bob would be seeing later that night. The figure who appeared on the studio monitors was Walter Annenberg, ambassador to Britain, being picked up by remote cameras as he stood in the doorway of his Regent's Park residence. Annenberg said his real task was to introduce yet another "surprise guest," Richard Nixon. The President's face, on videotape, loomed large on the monitors.

> NIXON: America owes a great deal to Britain . . . our common law . . . our language . . . and many of our political institutions . . . but we are particularly indebted to England for giving us Bob Hope. Not only because he is a great humorist who has given joy to millions of his fellow citizens and countless millions throughout the world . . . but because he is a fine human being who has never failed to respond in helping a good cause, any place in America or in the world. We are proud to claim him as an American citizen . . . and I am proud to know him as my friend.

Hope seemed embarrassed, touched. This did not seem the time for one of his Nixon gags. Hope sensed the moment needed a laugh, but he was at a loss. Then a slide showing the house at 44 Craighton Road flashed on the screen, and Andrews said it was where Hope was born at Eltham.

> HOPE: And we still owe some rent there.

He had found the laugh he needed and the audience responded. Then Andrews said that the baby born there was christened Leslie but the name was changed later.

> HOPE: Well—I thought—Leslie—you know—might be misinterpreted, Leslie's also a girl's name. I thought Bob was more chummy—and I was going to play a lot of vaudeville—and I might get up on the marquee quicker.

The audience laughed again, and Hope's name-change humor led nicely into Andrews' introduction of Antonio Dominick Benedetti. It was Tony Bennett who walked out and hugged Hope, explaining how much he owed the comedian—for his new name, his career, launched when Bob had put him into his Paramount Theater show in New York years ago. There was enthusiastic applause. Next came Bob's cousins Frank and Kathleen Symons from Hitchin. Other Hope relatives from Hitchin and Letchworth were in the audience. Next came a highly sentimental interlude with the little Anglican priest James Butterworth, known to Hope as "the little Rev," for whom the comedian had done a series of benefits and had raised thousands of pounds to put his war-damaged boys' refuge called Clubland back in business. The audience was effusive. Jack Benny came next. On videotape, because he was opening in Las Vegas that night, Benny said it was "true love" between them.

BENNY: Now, Bob, say something nice about *me!* Bob?
. . . Bob? . . . The whole world is waiting . . . !

The laughter was loud. Then a woman's voice came over the studio sound system.

MILDRED: My mother told me to forget him—he'd never
amount to anything.

She walked through the rear double doors and over to Hope who hugged and kissed her. And she was immediately followed by Dolores whose entrance produced applause so enduring that it nearly covered her line.

DOLORES: Don't let them tell you wives can't keep secrets.

In quick succession came British comedians Tommy Trinder and Ted Ray— inserted for home-viewer appeal—and Ray Milland, a long-time pal of Hope's who happened to be in London. Dorothy Lamour appeared on video-tape from Honolulu where she was opening a nightclub act with Don Ho. General "Rosy" O'Donnell lauded Hope's USO trouping and then British stronglady Joan Rhodes demonstrated how she had dropped Hope on his head during a USO show in Iceland. Denis Goodwin came in and explained the meaning of NAFT. Then the familiar face with a pipe on videotape, and a voice of mock condescension:

CROSBY: I'd be delighted to lend my stature to assist this—
unknown. Exactly what is it that this—Bob Hope—
does? What is his talent?

Crosby's appearance was a true audience pleaser. Next came the parade of children, Linda in a dramatic white ballgown; Nora, often considered by insiders as being especially close to her father; Tony, the successful lawyer, boyishly handsome and still in awe of Bob; and Kelly, becoming the show's biggest surprise, the college student who was flown in from Yugoslavia. There was much applause. And the final guest was Mountbatten who said he had come partly to thank "Bob of Burbank" for his appearance on the "Night of Nights."[9]

That was it. When the stage manager signaled an all clear, Andrews thanked the audience and went to escort the other Hope relations seated in the audience to the stage. All the guests stood up and surrounded Hope.

In the Green Room there were hors d'oeuvres and drinks. The party faltered, however, when Mountbatten, guest of honor at the Annenberg reception, and the Hopes, also expected to be special attractions at that gathering, had to say their thank-yous and goodbyes.

Most disappointed when the party limped to what seemed a premature close was Mildred Brod whose other prospect of the evening was the solitude of her Savoy room and hotel food without even a view of the Thames. Some-one at the party mentioned that near the Savoy was an excellent place to have a typically English meal but there was no suggestion of companionship. Mildred tried the recommended roast beefery and was unimpressed. Walk-ing back to the hotel in a cold drizzle she marveled at coming so many miles to say, "My mother told me to forget him, he'd never amount to anything."

9

London, Wednesday, November 18, 1970

All morning the Hope suite was log-jammed with activity because the children, no longer surprises, could come and go freely, asking questions about the Wildlife Gala arrangements, and deciding on matinee theater tickets.

Mildred Brod called to say goodbye. Tony and Judy also came to say goodbye. Bob slept through it all, almost till noon. When he awoke he remembered he was taping *If It's Saturday It Must Be* with its host, British comic Derek Nimmo. He needed to work with Denis on material for this show, and also for the BBC Christmas Special.

The Nimmo show was fun, and afterwards Hope and Denis drove to Leicester Square so Bob could inspect the Talk of the Town stage setup. He decided he could not use cue cards, so he would not do his new songs and would have to memorize his special gags.

When he got back to the hotel he took a nap until time to meet the royal family. Bob and Dolores went to Buckingham Palace about six-thirty and were introduced to their majesties at an abbreviated cocktail reception. They went on to the nightclub where they joined another receiving line to meet visiting royalty.

At about a quarter to eight, the Queen's fanfare was sounded, "God Save the Queen" was played, and Elizabeth arrived with Prince Philip, Princess Anne and Prince Charles. This ceremony and a speedy receiving line over with, the remainder of the evening was casual. The Queen received guests at her table, and there was continual table-hopping by royalty and commoners alike.

Lady Carolyn's table-hopping had more than one purpose; for one thing she was trying to pick up anything that might be good gag material for Hope. She didn't come up with much except that Princess Anne seemed dreamily in tune with her dinner partner, actor Roger Moore, who was rumored to be the leading contender in the search for a new James Bond, and also that Tom Jones had arrived at the dinner.

Halfway through his meal Hope excused himself and retired alone to the manager's office where he could rehearse his material and not have to review it in front of Prince Charles. He brought with him the elegantly produced souvenir program, and he scribbled the first few words of each gag on the flyleaf to serve as a cue sheet. He planned to take the program onstage with him. Now all he needed was good lighting.

When Rex Harrison introduced him he said, "Thank you, your highness."

> I've never seen so much royalty . . . it looks like a chess game . . . live. . . .

The security here is very tight. They searched everyone but
Tom Jones and we know he's not hiding anything. . . .

And I really have to mind my manners tonight. I'm the only one
here who doesn't have his own army. . . .[10]

10

Thursday, November 19, 1970
When he awoke late Thursday morning, Hope was in a mellow mood.
Things had gone smoothly the night before. And he was amused by the way
the tabloids covered the gala: IT'S THE WEST END'S MOST FANTASTIC NIGHT EVER
screamed the *Daily Mirror* on November 19 in front-page headlines showing
a photograph of Bob and Dolores seated at dinner with Prince Charles. The
coverage was extensive and garish, and his "chess game" gag was repeated in
six newspaper accounts.

As he sipped coffee, Dolores brought him two notes, both hand-delivered
in late morning. The first, brought by a Buckingham Palace messenger, was
encased in heavy vellum. It was addressed in longhand but the body of the
message was typewritten. It was a rather formal, form-letter thank-you from
the Duke of Edinburgh, conveyed through his aid Major Randle-Cooke.
Hope smiled wryly, comparing this note to Philip's uncle Mountbatten's
warm and personal gratitude for the "Night of Nights" benefit.

The second envelope contained a short personal message from Lew
Grade:

> My dear Bob,
>   I cannot tell you how thrilled I was with your performance last
> night at the Talk of the Town. It was superb and everyone said it
> was one of the best performances they have ever seen you do—
> and God knows you have done so many fantastic shows!
>   George Barrie of Faberge was so thrilled he said we must place
> it in the show. Firstly because the cause is so great, and secondly,
> because he said he had never seen you in finer form.
>   I hope you will be able to arrange this. On behalf of everyone
> my thanks and congratulations.[11]

The brief letter had been dictated to a secretary but just above Grade's
signature he had scribbled by hand, "I am proud not only of our association
but of our friendship. With affection, yours ever, Lew."

Hope liked that, even though he knew that Grade's note was also an effort
to cinch his name on the Fabergé telecast. Well, if he had been *that* good,
and they wanted him *that* much, then perhaps the price would go up. He
would call Jimmy to discuss it.

Denis arrived with some changes in the monologue for BBC's "Christmas
Night with the Stars." Hope spent most of the afternoon on the telephone
with Mort Lachman trying to clear dates for taping his November NBC
television monologue, and discussing plans for this year's around-the-world
USO Christmas tour, which would include some European stops and the

accustomed four or five days in Vietnam. Hope was trying to sign Sophia Loren.

At seven he and Denis went to BBC's Shepherd's Bush studios, and when he had finished taping the monologue, he returned to the Savoy. Dolores reminded him there was a family dinner that night with Linda, Nat, Nora, Sam and Kelly in a little Soho spot they had heard about. Hope lay back on his bed in the darkened room and wished that the Miss World telecast was tonight rather than tomorrow night. It seemed like he was wasting time. Yet, if he counted the two performances on Monday, figuring that "This Is Your Life" would be telecast in two half-hour segments, and then counted in the Derek Nimmo show, the Wildlife Gala, the BBC Christmas monologue and tomorrow's Miss World telecast—that was eight. Eight TV shows in five days. That had to be some kind of record.

11

Friday, November 20, 1970
Even if Hope's remarkable antenna system had detected trouble at the Miss World contest that evening, he probably still would have gone to Albert Hall. He had a guarantee from Mecca to have exclusive rights to the winner as an added attraction of his annual USO tour, so remaining in London one more day in order to crown Miss World 1971 was definitely useful. Yet, from other perspectives, Hope ought to be heading back. He was scheduled to appear for the trustees of Brandeis University in Chicago on Saturday. Even more important was Charlie Hogan, slipping away from cancer at River Forest, a few miles from Chicago. Dolores thought Bob should cancel Miss World and go immediately to Charlie. But Hope's rigid sense of obligation to be, in effect, the only name attraction in the Miss World telecast made him reluctant.

Tugging from another direction was "the owl," Mort Lachman. Mort was an exceptionally creative producer whose most aching frustration was not being allowed to put the show together without Hope's constant supervision. Hope exercised total artistic control, functioning as both executive producer and director despite the fact there were highly skilled professionals in these roles.

Hope spent much of Friday on the phone with Mort trying to solve the thorniest problems connected with the Christmas USO tour. Sophia Loren had turned Hope down. So far the cast included Cincinnati catcher Johnny Bench and the Golddiggers—nice, but not enough to fill a two-hour stage show. Mort suggested Catherine Deneuve, which Hope liked.

When Hope arrived at Albert Hall, just after eight-thirty, both Carolyn and Denis were there. The contest had started at eight but Hope would not do his monologue until after nine, and then would go back out to crown the winner before the final curtain. As soon as the audience spotted Hope there was loud and prolonged applause. Hope, with microphone in hand, waited for the applause to subside. He looked around and then faced the people sitting up in the organ stalls, much as they were at the Festival Hall shows.

~~When it was quiet he said, "Who are _they?_ Relatives?" Laughter. It~~
wouldn't have mattered what he said.

> I'm happy to be here tonight . . . by the way, where am
> I? . . . It has been such a social week for me . . . cocktails at
> Buckingham . . . supper at St. James . . . and dinner at the
> American ambassador's . . . Thank heaven I have a drip-dry
> dinner jacket . . .
>
> I'm not used to mingling with that much royalty . . . it was
> the first time I ever had to have a blood test to do a bene-
> fit. . . .[12]

But what happened next was shocking because of its orchestration.
A mannishly dressed woman leaped out of her seat and activated a large
noisemaker which signaled pandemonium. Other women appeared in the
ground floor aisles and in the lower loge areas activating rattles, hurling
stink and smoke bombs, dropping flour bags from the balconies, firing
overripe tomatoes, and hoisting placards reading: YOU ARE SELLING WOMEN'S
BODIES and MISS WORLD IS A SYMPTOM OF A SICK SOCIETY.

There were probably only 15 or 20 women demonstrating but in the ensu-
ing fracas it appeared to be a melee of hundreds. The noise level was painfully high. Hope saw one large woman try to reach the stage. A tomato shot
past him and he left the stage at a near run.

Robbed of Hope as a victim, the women turned toward the judges, shouting, "We are liberationists! Bar this disgraceful cattle market!" The police
moved to protect the judges but not before a heavy noisemaker was hurled at
them and landed at Glen Campbell's feet. Then an ink bomb spattered
actress Joan Collins and the Prime Minister of Grenada who was standing
next to Campbell. Another judge, a Danish singer known simply as Nina,
screamed, and a policeman led them all backstage to safety.

There were a few more profanities as the police forcibly escorted women
up the aisles. Morley went out on stage to restore order and Hope, standing
offstage with a microphone in his hand, said "Is it safe?" The audience
laughed in relief.

"I'm flabbergasted. I've never faced a _whole bunch_ of mad women
before . . . I'll say this . . . it's good conditioning for Vietnam." That
brought a big roar from the audience. With the stink and the smoke puffs
still hanging loosely around the hall, Hope said, "Hey! What do you say?
Are we ready? Let's go!"

Hope walked to the side of the runway as a hand reached up to give him an
envelope. He reached down. "Glen Campbell, folks. Right here!" Audience
applause while Campbell waved. Then, after walking a few steps with the
envelope in his hand, he sensed the suspense was pulled taut, ripped the
paper and announced the winner was Miss Grenada, Jennifer Hosten. Evidently she was not a favorite; touts had placed her at twenty-five-to-one.

There was applause, and some booing. Hope thought it was somehow connected to the previous demonstration. Later he learned that one of the judges
was the Grenada prime minister. Joan Collins, who had been his costar in
The Road to Hong Kong some years before, took him aside and said: "Get

yourself out of this mess, Bob. The contestants are convinced the results were fixed."

Eric Morley then told Hope that the judges' decision was final, that he regretted the disruption but was grateful for Hope's support, and that Miss World 1971, Jennifer Hosten of Grenada, would be thrilled to go to Vietnam with him.

News reporters who had been outside covering the demonstration, and some inside the hall, crowded by the stage door wanting to talk to Hope. One reporter asked, "How did you feel when this thing erupted?"

"On all the fighting fronts I've ever been to, I've never come across anything like this."

Another reporter: "I take it you don't react well to the Women's Liberation Movement."

"You'll notice about the women in the liberation movements, none of them are pretty, because pretty women don't have those problems. If a woman's clever, she can do just as well—if not better—than a man."

Still another: "Don't you agree that there's something inherently immoral about a beauty contest ritual like this one?"

"Immoral? Is Miss America immoral? Is there anything immoral about beauty? All it is, is a pretty girl wins a competition, travels around a lot, goes on television, makes a lot of money. There's nothing immoral about that—"

"Mr. Hope, I've heard it said that your position on Vietnam is that of a right-winger."

"I'm not a right-winger. I'm middle America. I just figure that if you've got a lot to eat and there's a guy next door starving with eight kids you've got to help him. Otherwise he's going to figure out some way to undermine you. That's why America's got to help Vietnam."

A voice from the back: "What's it like to be Bob Hope?"

"I wouldn't have it any other way."

Carolyn interrupted with a statement that there was a plane to catch. Hope looked around and said, "Thanks and I know you understand. With my act I have to keep moving."

Early Years
1903–1928

I was born in 1903 at Eltham in England. Eltham is about ten miles from Charing Cross Station. It's pronounced without the h. When I was about two years old, my father and mother moved to Bristol. My mother was the daughter of a Welsh sea captain. Her name was Avis Towns. My dad's name was William Henry Hope.[1]

1. 44 Craighton Road

WILLIAM HENRY (called Harry by family and friends) showed promise of "getting on" in the world. One of seven brothers and two sisters in a family of artisans, he wanted more from life. He was a stonemason with dreams of becoming an architect. Whenever he, his brothers and his father James traveled away from their home at Weston-Super-Mare to a construction site, Harry spent his free hours reading, mostly books about building and design, but he also enjoyed history.

In the winter of 1890–91, James Hope, a contractor and master stonemason, took Harry with him to join a work crew building the new stone docks at Barry, across the Bristol Channel on the southeast coast of Wales. Harry, just turning twenty-one, was lithe, muscular and handsome. His appearance easily caught the interest of the Barry town girls who came to watch the seawalls going up.

One of those girls was fragile-looking teenager Avis Towns, who was coming home from her music lesson when she stopped to watch Harry. Avis was a sensitive and romantic girl who lived with her foster family, retired sea captain Abraham Lloyd, his wife Mary and their son Basil. She knew very little about her real mother and father and her memories from early childhood were only vague fragments: handsome parents who traveled most of the time; days spent with a governess; a house in Cardiganshire on the west coast of Wales; a small lake in which a black swan paddled lazily. She remembered hearing of a shipwreck in which her parents drowned, and then she was taken to a new home in Barry.

Avis thrived under the Lloyds' loving care. Gifted with a lovely singing voice, she also learned to play the spinet, the dulcimer and the Welsh harp. Still, she was lonely and eager for an intimate relationship when she spotted the handsome and sinewy Harry Hope. She came back every day; they talked, flirted, and fell in love. Harry's father disapproved and, when he was able, moved Harry to another location.

The separation for both was painful. Finally James decided to send Harry home to Weston. On a rainy afternoon, just before he was to depart, Harry went to collect the rest of his tools from the cutting shed near the docks. As always, he looked at every passing couple and every solitary figure for a glimpse of Avis. Leaving the shed he saw her, and she him, and as their eyes met, Avis fell to the ground. Harry ran to her and James, who had followed his son, joined them. As James bent over Avis, Harry lifted her up and placed her in his father's arms.

"Now what do I do, Dad?" asked Harry.

"You take her home where she belongs!"

"But I love her. I want to marry her."

"This is just a baby," said James.

Suddenly the fifteen-year-old Avis, with her Dresden-doll features, recovered from her faint and in a sturdy voice said, "I am a woman, sir!"

At that, James lifted her up, set her on her feet, and turned to Harry. "Marry her and be done with it. We've got work to do."

Their vows were said in nearby Cardiff on April 25, 1891, and the couple went to live in the Stow Hill district of Newport, Monmouthshire, Wales. One year later, Ivor was born. In July the following year Avis gave birth to James Francis II and Emily followed in July of 1895.

Soon after, Harry took Avis and the three children back to live at Barry where they had first met. There, in 1897, a third son, Frederick Charles, was born. He was a fretful baby, so much so that his brothers Ivor and James begged Avis to send him back. When Harry's stonecutting at Barry ended, the family moved again, this time to Lewisham in Middlesex, England. And when Avis said goodbye to the Lloyds, she never saw them or heard from them again.

But life in Lewisham was for the Hope family the sweetest it would ever be, on either side of the Atlantic. Harry worked steadily in good jobs, providing Avis and the children with a big stone house that had sheds, stables and a workshop. There was enough space for Harry to raise prize chickens, and chrysanthemums "as big as footballs," and he kept a pony for the boys.

It was also the happiest Harry and Avis would ever be, with Harry coming home with flowers in his arms, singing:

> I'll be your sweetheart
> If you will be mine,
> All my life I'll be
> Your Valentine.
> Bluebells I'll gather,
> They are all for you,
> And when I'm a man, my plan,
> Will be to marry you.[2]

At Lewisham, Harry began to squander their money and to drink excessively. Avis, who hadn't been entirely well since Emily's birth, worried about Harry but she couldn't stop him. In one of his more expansive moods, Harry was induced by a chum to invest his savings in a stable of horses, but the chum disappeared with the money.

The Hopes moved to more modest quarters in Kent. Remorseful Harry worked hard to recoup their losses but it was difficult. Avis was pregnant again, and while she was carrying this next child, beautiful little Emily, whom Harry idolized, caught diphtheria and died. The birth of her fourth son, William John, helped Avis through this dark period but Harry began drinking even more heavily. He neglected his prize hens, and more important, he stopped reading. He went off on his bicycle and would be gone for days, cutting stone in other towns and only coming home for weekends.

Work was becoming more infrequent for Harry and his skill was less in demand. Cinching their belts tighter, the Hopes moved again, this time to 44 Craighton Road, Eltham, one of the row houses Harry's father James had built. Harry's visits to the "local" were frequent and he justified them with the stonemason's excuse for drinking which was that dust from the stone is constantly inhaled and ale is best to wash it down.

It was not only Harry's drinking that worried Avis, but his wandering eye. She once found a lady's photo crumpled in Harry's pocket, inscribed "To Harry with love." When Avis confronted him, Harry said it was a poor lovesick barmaid, and Avis broke her hairbrush hitting him.

In spite of his drinking, Harry was easy to like. He had more than a suggestion of self-assertiveness in his manner, but he was a gentle man and Avis loved him deeply. She would wait up for him while he closed the pub. He might come home on foot, or in a horse-cab, but often he would be carrying a bouquet of flowers or some candy like a young lover.

On the day that Leslie Towns was born, May 30, 1903, Avis thought it was not quite time, but she did feel she had a touch of influenza. Jim was concerned. "Mahm only has the flu, dear. Nothing to fret about." Even though Avis was sick, the floors were scrubbed. Jim made the doctor go around to the back door. After he examined Avis, the doctor came downstairs and asked Jim for some boiling water and told him to get a neighbor. Leslie came into the world ahead of schedule.

Avis thought Leslie was probably her last try. Soon after his birth the Hopes moved again, this time back to Weston-Super-Mare, the resort town where Harry had grown up. Avis liked this move; it tore Harry away from the temptation of the lady in the photo.

The Boer War had just ended and times were tough. Stonecutting jobs were scarce; the quarries were all but shut down, and there were soup lines in Weston. To save money, the family moved again, this time to Moorland Road, the last street in town, and any Hope who could speak a complete sentence or count to ten was shoved out to find a job. Avis worked as cashier in a tea shop, taking Leslie with her, and supplemented that job by doing housework for others.

Avis tried to keep family spirits high. She played her spinet and sang songs and Welsh hymns, teaching her boys to sing along with her. She took them to watch the boardwalk buskers, the puppet shows, magicians, sword-swallowers, and often on picnics.

In the summer of 1905, Harry severely fractured his ankle and couldn't work. With little money coming in for several months, Ivor got a full-time job at a dairy and then got Jim a job there, too. Both boys kept their previous jobs of selling newspapers in the morning and early evening. Even when Harry's ankle healed, he failed to find work in Weston and the family moved to Bristol, their last home in England.

It was there that new family roles developed, roles that would reshape the pattern of their lives. Ivor, partly because of Harry's inability to find work and his drinking, would become the dependable provider. Jim, on the other hand, protected Mahm. He was her confidant, her Lochinvar; whatever money he could earn was to make her life easier.

Fred idolized and imitated Ivor which annoyed the oldest brother, especially when Fred would hang around him, finding any excuse to spin his top at Ivor's feet just when he was talking to a pretty girl. Jack (William John) was the loner; he wandered off to the woods on long adventurous hikes or got himself lost in Bristol and had to be found by his brothers. Sidney was born in 1905 and replaced Leslie as the baby of the family.

Leslie's personality, at age four, was just beginning to take shape. Jack remembers that even then Leslie was a mimic. When the Hope children were taken to visit their great-great-aunt Polly, who lived nearby, Leslie could make her laugh. She was one-hundred and two and lived alone in a tiny cottage since her husband, a whaling sailor, had died at ninety-seven. Leslie, short-legged and tubby, would imitate someone he had seen by putting his hands into the pockets of his abbreviated pants, and then push them out beyond his stomach. His reward was a cookie and, according to Jack, Aunt Polly would say, "That's right, laddie, I hope you always leave 'em laughing."[3]

Other times, to the surprise of his family, he would try to sing and dance. One time, Ivor recalled, Leslie recited all the verses of "The Burial of Sir John Moore" from memory. Another time he dressed up in Avis' clothes, but his brothers ridiculed him enough to make it the only time.

In the spring of 1906, Harry's thoughts turned to America. His older brother Frank, a master plumber, and his younger brother Fred, a steamfitter, had immigrated to Cleveland several years before and the idea of joining them looked increasingly attractive. While stonecutting jobs were scarce in England, that trade was apparently still practiced in America for churches, schools and public buildings. After much debate with Avis, Harry decided to go over alone and establish himself.

Avis was depressed following his departure; she walked through the house in a daze, sometimes putting on a piece of Harry's clothing to feel his presence. His first letter convinced every one of the Hopes that America was the most wonderful place to be. Harry said the buildings in New York were so tall they had to be lowered to let the moon pass by. Nobody worked hard and everybody was in a hurry. Everything was abundant and there were lots of labor-saving devices. "Believe me, Avis, when you get here, all you'll have to do is sit on the front porch and chew gum."[4]

In a subsequent letter Harry told Avis to begin preparations for coming to Cleveland. It was winter in Bristol and Avis had to cut fuel costs in order to afford steerage passage for herself and six sons. Sadly she consigned her precious spinet and the grandfather's clock from Scotland for sale. What Avis refused to part with was carefully packed and sent ahead to Uncle Frank's in Cleveland.

After tearful goodbyes to Aunt Polly and the other Hope relations, Avis led her luggage-laden brood to the train bound for Southampton and then to their ship. They occupied two steerage cabins directly above the main drive shaft. It was hot and noisy and difficult for sleeping. At night, Avis brought them all into one cabin; she was fearful after the first day out when she returned to her cabin from lunch to find her suitcases rifled and her beloved breast watch and its gold chain gone.

When it was time for the customary vaccination of the immigrants on board, Avis lined up her children, but suddenly Leslie bolted and ran. The four-year-old was cornered, captured and returned to the lineup where, amid his howling, the needle pricked. When Avis reached down to quiet his screams, her hand brushed the tiny bandage aside, and she got some of the vaccine on her left thumb. For the remainder of her life she carried a cicatrix there as a reminder of that incident.

Their ship was delayed in the outer waters of New York Harbor because of thick fog, but when they were finally disembarked at Ellis, they were quickly transferred to an immigrant train bound for Cleveland. The train was filthy and most of the time the restrooms were kept locked, which meant that everyone scrambled for station facilities during stopovers. The only food available was what they could find and/or afford during these stops.

Nevertheless their anticipation was boundless, their spirits indomitable, though clearly it was the thought of seeing their father at the end of the trip that made the cattle car conditions bearable.

Encouraged and sometimes led by Avis, the Hopes sang, until she nearly choked from embarrassment when the boys passed the hat for coins. The boys were embarrassed when Avis washed their underclothes and held them out the window to dry. And all the while she dreamed about the gold-lined streets of Cleveland.

My first day in school in Cleveland the other kids asked me, "What's your name?" When I said "Les Hope," they switched it to Hopeless. It got to be quite a rib and caused some scuffling and a few bloody ski-snoots for me.[1]

2. Doan's Corners

Harry Hope—moustache waxed, pin-striped suit pressed, heart thumping like a compressor—waited nervously with his brothers Frank and Fred at Erie Station. He knew Avis and the boys would be eager to know about America and Ohio and Cleveland. What would he say? The biggest news was Henry Ford's Model T, and the new nickelodeon on lower Euclid. And wouldn't the boys' eyes bug out when he told them the *Cleveland Press* was promising its readers air travel! He would tell them how beautiful the lake and parks would be now that spring was coming. He would *not* tell Avis right away how little he had worked, or that he had joined a labor union for stonecutters.

America in 1908 was not the promised land Harry's brothers had described to him or the haven he had written about to Avis. There was ample evidence of achievement; the nation's ability to produce goods on a magnificent scale was reported the world over. But for people like the Hopes there was disillusionment. Life for immigrants was a 70-hour work week for $10 pay. For skilled artisans like Harry things were a bit better: a shorter week and a pay range from $13.50 to $19.30 a week. Harry's barroom chum Felix, just back from a job in Pittsburgh, had told about conditions there that made

~~him sick: the surplus~~ of immigrant workers in those steel towns that stretch along the Monongahela all the way to McKeesport. People there were clawing for available jobs, jobs that were nothing less than slavery. What was he going to tell them?

When the train finally halted, Harry stalked each exit stairs until he found Avis. The boys hung on his body until he recognized each one. The uncles were hugged as well. Somehow the luggage and people arrived at Uncle Frank's plumbing shop at 2227 East 105 Street. He and Aunt Louisa lived upstairs. She had prepared a meal that the boys practically inhaled, though they were disconcerted by being served kernel corn (reserved for the chickens back in England) and something called olives. Since Louisa's apartment had only three bedrooms, the older boys Ivor and Jim went to stay with Uncle Fred and Aunt Alice nearby. After a few days of doubling up, Avis found a one-family house with three bedrooms and a bathroom at Stanisforth Court near Euclid and 105th. She rented it for $18.50 a month. It was several weeks before she found a church home for them—Euclid Avenue Presbyterian. The minister was a friendly Scotsman, the Reverend McGaffin, who remained her friend until she died.

Avis was not shocked about Harry's drinking or lack of regular employment; the important thing was that her family was together again. Actually she knew the revolution was under way, that hand-cut stone was being edged out by much cheaper materials and methods; the artisan was becoming redundant and Harry was either too stubborn or too proud to attempt other work. So he let Ivor, Jim and Fred find jobs to support the family.

Unable to meet the second month's rent, Avis asked her in-laws for a loan. Fred's wife Alice was cool about the idea. She was not overly fond of Avis, her "brats" or Harry's drinking. Uncle Frank demurred, asking Avis why she allowed her husband to avoid finding some other kind of work. Incensed by these attitudes, Jim earned the $10 needed. Next day, he and Ivor went out and got jobs at Van Dorn Ironworks.

One of Harry's stonecutting chums, James Kier, has chronicled part of the plight of the Hopes trying to weather their first year in America:

> It was an unusually severe winter and the financial panic of 1907–1908 was at its height. Harry had been looking forward to his family arriving, and was anxious to get his home established.
>
> When spring came we were both working at Painesville and Harry felt the responsibility of family and was quite sober for a time. Then we were suddenly out of work but luckily I secured one for two men to go to work at Sharon, Pennsylvania, and asked Harry to go with me and he approved, though he was reluctant to leave his newly arrived family—but he needed the work badly.
>
> I think Mrs. Hope was reconciled to Harry's coming with me because she knew I had no drinking habits and there would be no temptation for me. We worked about two days and one night when we came home and found a telegram for Harry saying his wife was very sick and asked that he come home immediately.
>
> Harry was deeply affected and he said, "Oh, my poor Avis!" He broke down and cried like a child. I have never forgotten the occa-

sion and more particularly the remark he made which I consider worthy of a Shakespeare. He said: "Jim, I am not ashamed to shed a tear. The lower animals cannot weep and only human beings can cry." . . . I met Mrs. Hope and I could not imagine a more gentle and ladylike woman. No matter how Harry neglected his responsibilities, she was always forgiving and held to the belief that someday he would be different. There was a strong bond of affection between them and I'm sure he idolized her. . . .

I have seen Harry in a union meeting with a great group of angry stonecutters debating and arguing in a most violent fashion, and after listening for a while to their remarks, he would rise to the floor and with all the true marks of a born orator, would calm them down and show them the proper and logical approach to their problem.

I surely felt proud of him when he did so. Bob undoubtedly inherited his gift of gab from his father.[2]

That winter was as cold as any the Hopes had known. Harry haunted the employment lists and could be heard to say: "America's a fine place for women and dogs! It's a poor place for horses and men." He managed to form a partnership with another cutter to bid on a Cleveland high school contract. Their bid was low and they got the contract, but they failed to compute the cost of two of the building's towers, and they lost money on the job.

Undaunted, Avis moved her family to a bigger house at 1925 East 105th where she could take boarders. It was an equally bitter winter in 1909 in that new house when George Percy, the seventh son and the first United States citizen, was born to Avis and Harry Hope. But the arrival of George intensified family spirit in two ways. Harry and the boys celebrated by going out in a blizzard and buying a used heating stove and dragging it home in the snow. Also, that year Harry become eligible for naturalization, and with his citizenship the whole family became Americans.

Avis, however, was the core of the unit. Her ability to make ends meet seemed nothing short of miraculous. She took a streetcar miles downtown to the public market and shopped from stall to stall. She made over clothes for the younger boys and devised home medicines to cut doctor's bills; she kept a spotless kitchen and always had snacks for her sons whenever they appeared from a variety of working hours. She saved pennies and finally was able to buy a secondhand upright piano so there would be music in the home.

Harry, on the other hand, was respected but avoided because of his mercurial behavior. But when Harry worked he could be sober for several months and then he was like a young lover, courting Avis with sweets and taking her for rides in the park. And he was a pal to his sons.

Ivor and Jim had full-time jobs, but the younger brothers Fred, Jack, Leslie and Sid sold newspapers at Doan's Corners, at the intersection of Euclid and 105th. Each hawked his papers on a different corner. Leslie liked his Southwest Grocery corner because it was an uptown traffic side and because the grocery stayed open long enough for him to duck inside and warm his hands on wintry afternoons.

Sooner or later each boy had the experience of selling a paper to "that man" in the big black Peerless limousine. Les caught him in the evening

when the hand reached out from the back seat window with his two cents for
the *Press*. His face was wrinkled, Leslie thought, like an old leather coin
purse, and he seldom said a word when he took his paper.

One night he handed Les a dime. Les told him he didn't have any change,
but the man stared until Les said he would go get some. The youngster
disappeared into the grocery and waited his turn at the front counter for his
ten pennies. When he ran back to the side of the big automobile, the man
leaned out slightly and said, "Young man, I'm going to give you some advice.
If you want to be a success in business, trust nobody—never give credit and
always keep change in hand. That way you won't miss any customers going
for it." All Les could think of was the customers he had already lost because
this man was so stingy. When the chauffeur drove the car away, the trolley
starter said to Leslie, "Know who that man was?" Les shook his head. "John
D. Rockefeller, that's who."

The Americanization of the young Hopes happened, as one might expect,
in school. Leslie's early reputation as a scrapper stemmed from his need to
strike out at those who teased him about his clothes and his name. Those who
didn't jeer at his Eton jacket and stiff collar were able to roast him for the
way he responded to roll calls. When his last name was called and he
responded with "Leslie," there was laughter, and when he shortened the
name to "Les" there was even more laughter. "Hopelessly" and "Hopeless"
echoed through school hallways and out onto the playing field. But he was
quick with his fists and could win his own battles.

His favorite class was music. His voice had developed into a strong soprano
and he loved to sing in school and in his church group, The Sambo Minstrels.
But his favorite activities involved footraces. He was very fast on his feet in
spite of thin spindly legs, and his best pal, Whitey Jennings, was also a fast
sprinter. Les and Whitey, and sometimes Jack and Sidney, would compete
for prizes at various parks and picnic grounds around the Cleveland area.
And they devised a racket to double their winnings.

The boys would study the neighborhood activities sections of the newspapers to learn which organizations were planning outings that included 50-
and 100-yard dashes. There were usually several promising events, but they
were often miles apart and scheduled to take place at the same time. United
Grocers, for example, might have an annual picnic at Luna Park at two
o'clock, while the Freemasons were having their outing at Euclid Beach at
the same time.

Les would have Jack, whose voice was more mature, telephone the grocers
association headquarters to find out what time the footraces were being held.
The surprised member of the picnic committee would say, "Two-thirty,
why?" Jack would say he was with the *Cleveland Press* (well, he *was*) and
explain: "We wanted to come out and take some photos but two-thirty is too
late." The accommodating grocers would ask what time would be good for
the *Press*, and they would agree on two o'clock.

Then they would call the Freemasons' outing chairman and go through the
same routine, until it was established that the *Press* would show up at Euclid
Beach at three-thirty.

When the boys got to Luna Park on Sunday at one-thirty, the picnic chairman would be harassed by a chorus of boys to start the races, but he would

insist on waiting for the *Press* photographer. But Jack and Sid or whoever was there would start up a chorus of "Aw, let's get it over with. We want to go swimming." And with that kind of pressure the race would usually start.

Les and Whitey would engage the race official in conversation, asking him how he usually started a race. "How does anybody start a race!" he would say sarcastically, "On—your—mark—get—set—*go!*" The boys listened to the cadence and took their places. As soon as the starter said "Get," the boys were off, and by the time he had said "Go!" they were already a yard in the lead. Sometimes they dug starting holes, and if one of their opponents was the very swift Henry Thomas, they might give him a damaging shove at the start, or bump him hard at the turn to come back. At least one of them would take first or second place. They preferred second because it was normally a cash prize, and first was a cup or a merchandise certificate. The Hope boys always turned over their earnings, however ill-gotten, to Mahm for family expenses.

Fifty years later, at a Boys Club benefit in 1967, Hope would do a monologue about his youth that was, in fact, infused with truth:

> . . . I came from a pretty tough neighborhood. We'd have been called juvenile delinquents only our neighborhood couldn't afford a sociologist.
>
> I guess it's no secret, but I have a record in Cleveland. They nabbed me for swiping a bike. It's a lie. I was walking down a hill when the damn thing rolled under me and we coasted downhill right into a cop's arms . . . fortunately, he knew me and all my brothers . . . so he arrested me.
>
> I pleaded for mercy, but the judge was an ugly, vindictive, cruel man. He turned me over to my parents.
>
> But then came my moment of decision. Like most kids today or any day, I had to make my choice. Was I going to go out and get a job and earn a living, or was I going to spend the rest of my life stealing? I decided to forget the job and stay with show business . . . and I'm not sorry.[3]

What worried the older generation of Hopes about young Les was the way he flitted from part-time job to part-time job. Except for the knowledge that he ought to earn money for Mahm, he really had no stomach for work. He told Fred that when he grew up he had no intention of holding down a conventional job. When Fred asked how he intended to live, Les said he just might be a movie star like Doug Fairbanks.

True, he had scored a neighborhood success with his imitation of Chaplin. In the summer of 1915, Chaplin contests had become a nationwide rage and every kid with an urge to act blackened his upper lip, found a derby and twirled a cane. The Hope brothers rounded up all their pals and took Les out to Luna Park for a Chaplin contest, and when the judge put his hand over young Hope's head, the neighborhood claque took the day with their cheering, winning enough prize money to buy Avis a new stove.

Les tried a variety of after-school jobs like delivering packages for Heisey's Bakery. Overacting lost him that job with Heisey. When he took packages to well-heeled residential neighborhoods, he would say to the lady of the house, "Boy, did I have a tough time finding this place. I spent all my carfare looking for it." Touched, the lady would say, "How will you get back?" Hope would shrug, "Oh, I'll walk." Of course, Les would get a handout for carfare. The scam was lucrative until he pulled it twice with the same lady.

Whatever part-time job he held after school, he couldn't wait till it was done so he could get to the Alhambra Billiards Parlor at 106th and Euclid. He and Whitey both had become quite skillful at pool and Les's specialty was three-cushion billiards. Avis' sister-in-law Louisa said she didn't like to see Les hanging out in a pool hall, but Avis refused to make it off limits because she knew who his pals were and said, "He's just trying to find himself. He'll be all right, you'll see."

Hope's pals were Whitey, of course, and two fellows who were not only pool sharks but talented tap and specialty dancers, Johnny Gibbons and Charlie Cooley. Jennings could sing and dance, too, but he dreamed of becoming a professional boxer. Gibbons was a highly proficient tap and ballroom dancer who had big-time aspirations, but Cooley was clearly not an amateur at anything. He was already semipro as an acrobatic hoofer who had done enough work locally as a performer to be a glamorous figure in Hope's eyes. And Les loved the "acting" assignments he received from his pals when it came time to shill. When a sucker came into the Alhambra, Les would pretend that he didn't know an eight ball from a corner pocket. The sucker, baited by Les's buddies, would soon challenge him to a game and Les would usually win.

Glen Pullen, one-time entertainment writer for the *Cleveland Plain Dealer,* was also a pool hustler in those days. In an article that appeared in the *Cleveland Plain Dealer* on May 17, 1974, he remembered:

> I shilled for a guy I ran around with. He was missing most of one arm but boy could he shoot pool! He'd cradle the cue in the stump of his bad arm. One day we suckered this kid named Hope into a game and he trimmed us both. He pocketed the money, grinned and said, "You guys don't even know how to shill properly." They say he's a millionaire today.

As soon as Les could legally do so, he said goodbye to school. He had never really liked school and he was now thinking of becoming a performer. Johnny Gibbons had taught him some dance steps, and he had begun to frequent Zimmerman's dance hall both to dance and to meet girls. He still loved to sing, anytime, anywhere. When he and Whitey were younger, they had harmonized as a duo, and with pals in a quartet usually on a neighborhood street corner. They liked to sing outside Pete Schmidt's Beer Garden because the drunks got sentimental, and even Pete would encourage them with a quarter. That was just the amount for two tickets to the Doan's Corner movie house (including candy) to watch a swashbuckler named Fairbanks.

Now that they were older they were still smitten with the idea of being entertainers. But on the other hand, Les and Whitey had both given some thought to being prizefighters. As advancing teenagers and devotees of the Fairbanks physique and athletic prowess, they hung around Charlie Marotta's Athletic Club on Seventy-Ninth Street working out and practicing their punches before going to "work" at the Alhambra. One afternoon, over the pool table, Whitey confessed he had decided to enter the featherweight division of the Ohio state amateur matches.

"You're kidding!"

"I'm not either. Here's my entry form."

"Packy West?" Hope asked derisively, but he had to admit Packy was a strong name to adopt because it evoked the charisma of legendary Packy McFarland.

Envy gnawed at Les for a full day and then he, too, went downtown and registered in the lightweight division. When they asked him his fighting name, he said: "Packy East."

> I was sixteen, I weighed one hundred and twenty-eight pounds and the featherweight class had a top limit of one hundred and twenty-six. I just missed getting into it. If I'd taken the apples out of my pockets, I could have qualified as a featherweight. If I had, I'd have made out better. As it was I creamed my first opponent. He was constantly looking over his shoulder toward his corner for instructions. When I hit him, he turned to his second, asked "What'll I do?" and his second yelled back strategy. I finally tagged him while his head was turned.[4]

Winning the preliminary bout at Marotta's meant that he could go on to another elimination bout, and then semifinals. But in Hope's case, or rather Packy East's case, they couldn't pair him up, so he went right to the semifinals at Moose Hall.

All of Hope's pals from 105th and Euclid came to see him fight: Johnny Gibbons, Charlie Shaefer, Perry Caulkins and Kenny Fox. They were astonished to discover Hope's opponent was to be Happy Walsh, a slug-happy "smiling muscle" who later became a local champion. Packy was more than astonished:

> At the bell, I crept from my corner. Nothing happened to me at first, so I threw a terrific left to his jaw and crossed my right to his button. Walsh's hands dropped to his sides. He looked at me in amazement. Then he grinned. I found out later that he always did that when he was hit. We came out for the second. Because Happy slipped a couple of times in the first, I decided to make the best of it. My footwork got fancier. I pranced around on my toes. Then I wound up and threw my right. I never got it back. And that's all I remember.[5]

Hope insists he was the only Cleveland fighter carried both ways: *in* and *out* of the ring.

I planned to take Mildred with me when I left Cleveland to
become Mr. Marvelous of the footlights. But Mildred's
mother was small-minded about it. (Another way of putting
it is to say that Mildred's mother got the notion that I
wasn't the divinity-student type and she refused to trust her
daughter on theatrical tours with me.)[1]

3. East Palestine, Lima and Brazil

Nineteen-twenty was a year of decisions for Les Hope. As a disinterested
sophomore he abandoned East High School. As a boxer he was clearly too
lightweight for the fight game. As a dancer he was good, but not good
enough, so he decided to divert some of his earnings and Alhambra winnings
to dancing lessons from a seasoned black entertainer named King Rastus
Brown over on Central Avenue.

That year he spent a lot of time riding streetcars to and from downtown
Cleveland. He and Johnny Gibbons were butcher's helpers for Fred Hope,
who leased a meat stand at the central market. Instead of working, the two
teenagers would feint and spar like Golden Gloves contenders, tap dance on a
platform built above Fred's stall, or harmonize tunes and mug for market
employees and customers. Fred, who later married Johnny's sister LaRue,
was both exasperated and amused.

Les had an even better reason for riding the streetcar that year. He would
ride downtown, just before lunchtime, and meet his new sweetheart,
Mildred. She was a salesclerk and later a fashion model at Halle's Department
Store. Mildred was a pretty, willowy blonde who (Hope thought)
danced better than Irene Castle.

They had met on a group outing and she was a new face. Mildred says,
"Les was tall and skinny and I thought, *Oh, brother*. We went to a party that
first night and Les got bored, I guess, and took the fellows out to the kitchen
to shoot craps. I got snippy and went home."[2] But Mildred had made an
impression.

Whenever Les came to Halle's to wait for Mildred he would stand near her
cosmetics counter and stare at her. He flirted and tried to make her laugh.
Mildred recalls:

> . . . or he'd come in and lean over the counter and say, "Let's
> get married on your lunch hour." And I would say
> "No" . . . because my mother told me that if I married him I'd
> have to go up and live with his family and . . . well . . . we
> were better off than they were. But he would follow me home
> from work some nights—I mean, he would get on the same street-
> car and I wouldn't even know it. It was one of those dinky trolleys
> and I never looked around to see who else was on it. When I'd get
> off at Cedar he'd be walking right behind me. Then I'd walk in
> the front door and my mother'd ask if *he* was with me again and
> I'd say "No," and then he'd stick his head around the hallway
> door and say, "Oh, yes I am." Most of the time I wouldn't know

he was following me because I was half-asleep anyway what with dancing all night and working behind that counter all day. My mother would say to Les, "Why are you down here eating again tonight?" Les would say, "We're having duck at our house tonight, but I thought I'd come down and eat some more of your tough roast beef."[3]

Mildred cannot recall Les ever having a "steady" job during the time they were dating except for the summer he worked for the Cleveland Illuminating Company as a lineman. He told her he had to earn money for their engagement ring, which he presented to her in front of his second favorite hangout at Doan's Corners, Hoffman's Ice Cream Parlor. Mildred looked at the ring and wisecracked, "Does a magnifying glass come with it?" Les was hurt and went inside Hoffman's. Mildred followed him in and apologized. Then Les slipped down the street to the Alhambra to hustle some money to take Mildred dancing at Zimmerman's.

Some nights after work Les would steal liver or sweetbreads from Fred and go up to Mildred's house, where she would fry him a late supper. When everyone was in bed and with all the doors and windows closed, they would wheel the boxy phonograph into the kitchen and practice their steps, rehearsing some for hours. Mildred says they "wore out the linoleum."

Not satisfied any longer with King Rastus Brown, Hope sought out an old vaudevillian named Johnny Root who taught at Sojack's Dance Academy behind Zimmerman's. Mildred added some of her earnings to what Les could scare up and they took enough lessons to put together a dance act which included, not so surprisingly, an imitation of the Castles.

Their first paid engagement was a three-night stint for the social club in the Brotherhood of Locomotive Engineers Building. Mildred remembers:

> . . our act was in between the other acts . . . I guess we were on during intermission . . . but anyway this was the last night, and when we came to all the hard stuff, the buck and wings which were so fast . . . I just quit, and I said I was tired and I walked off the stage. Bob looked at me with kill in his eyes—he was furious . . . but he ad-libbed . . . maybe it was his first before a paying audience . . . he picked out a little old lady in the first row and said, "See, Ma, you should never have made her do the dishes tonight."[4]

There were other engagements after that. They danced during intermission at the Superior Motion Picture House and at a place on Broadway where there were vaudeville acts along with the movie. Mildred says that Hope in later years loved to tell people that they were paid seven or eight dollars a performance and they split it, but the truth is Mildred never got a cent. He told her they were all benefits or something. "I think he still has a cup we won in a dance contest. I'm told it's on his desk in Toluca Lake and he keeps paper clips in it."[5] (It is, and he does.)

Elated over their show-business success, the Cleveland Castles began to plan their future together. Les wanted to take their act on the road; he was certain some small-time vaudeville circuit would take a chance on them. Mildred's mother had a poor opinion of Leslie Towns Hope's prospects of supporting Mildred; and as for taking her out of town without a chaperone, that was out of the question.

When Johnny Root retired from Sojack's, Les took over his dancing classes and immediately had cards printed: LESLIE HOPE WILL TEACH YOU HOW TO DANCE—CLOG, SOFT-SHOE, WALTZ-CLOG, BUCK AND WING, AND ECCENTRIC.[6] But try as he would, teaching dancing did not lead to financial success. Consequently Les was receptive to brother Jack's suggestion that he take a night job at the Chandler Motor Car Company. His days were still free for hunting down dancing engagements, rehearsing, and pool hustling at the Alhambra. At Chandler he met several other would-be entertainers. He got together with three of them to form a vocal quartet, in which he sang high baritone. Working at night, the boys would take extra liberties. For example, they used to record their voices on the dictaphone cylinders and play them back to improve their tone and blend. One day they forgot to erase the cylinder. An unsympathetic executive heard their efforts, recognized voices and Les found himself out of a job.

In Mildred's opinion Les liked singing as much as he liked dancing. Many nights, when he left her house, after the streetcars had stopped running, he would walk thirty blocks to meet with the guys in his quartet and they would rehearse for a couple of hours right out in the street.

It seemed clear to Les that he and Mildred would continue to be sweethearts but not on the road. He would need a new partner. This didn't upset Mildred who had never really wanted to be a performer in the first place; she just liked Les and liked to dance. So Les picked a fellow he had known slightly around the neighborhood, whose name was Lloyd "Lefty" Durbin. Durbin was a good dancer, had been in Sojack's classes and had obviously "been around," not professionally but enough to create an act. He was light, like Les, and had a slightly unhealthy pallor, but he was energetic and clever and had style. The act they worked up was eclectic, working from tap through soft shoe into some eccentric routines that allowed for humor.

Their first appearance was in August 1924 at a Luna Park amateur contest and they were well received. They continued to break in the act as fillers on vaudeville bills at small houses in and around Cleveland for a few bucks, and one night they even danced in an amateur contest at their own neighborhood's top-drawer vaudeville house, Keith's 105th Street. Les begged his brothers to round up as many of their pals as they could to fill the front rows of the theater. He also worked out a deal with a cute Keith usherette to allow him to play host to a dozen or so of his Alhambra cohorts. "Zick" Zicarelli, one of the crowd, recalled: "Somehow he'd arrange to have the side door left open and we sneaked in and cheered and applauded the act. We figured if he won the five-dollar prize we'd all eat."[7]

Durbin and Hope forced themselves on an agent named Norman Kendall who booked local talent for a small vaudeville showcase called the Bandbox.[8] Roscoe "Fatty" Arbuckle was booked there; he was trying to resume a career destroyed in 1921 by a scandal involving the supposed sadistic coke-bottle rape of a film starlet. Kendall's job was to book a cheap act to flesh out the bill. He decided to take a chance on Lefty and Les who quickly dreamed up a new act. Their finale was a comedy Egyptian dance. In dark suits and brown derbies, they pantomimed broadly against a desert backdrop showing pyramids and the Sphinx, as they pretended to dip their derbies into the

Nile. Later, after several tricky dance routines, they managed to pour real water from their hats. The audience loved it. So did Arbuckle. His show didn't last long, but long enough for him to make good his promise to introduce them to Fred Hurley of Alliance, Ohio, who produced tabloid shows. Tabs were a peculiar genre of entertainment rapidly becoming the rage of small-time vaudeville; they were miniature musical comedies ideal for the audiences along the Gus Sun Circuit. Sun Time meant touring the tank towns of Ohio, Indiana, Pennsylvania, the Virginias, the Carolinas. The likes of Will Rogers, Eddie Cantor and Al Jolson had all worked the Gus Sun Circuit at one point.

But Hurley was not terribly impressed with Les and Lefty; all they could do was dance. Each member of a tab unit had to be versatile, since everyone had to double or triple in parts. However, Hurley trusted Arbuckle's taste, and Frank Maley, who managed Hurley's 1924 tab blockbuster *Jolly Follies,* thought the boys were trainable and he needed bodies. The pay was $40 a week. Les decided to send Mahm half of his and trust he could house and feed himself with the remainder.

There would be little rehearsal time. The boys would have to pick up their cues by watching performances, and by help from other cast members. As miniature musical comedy, tabs could be of two kinds—either an abbreviated book show fully scripted, or a series of independent sketches with blackouts following each punchline. Distributed here and there were specialty dancing, vocal and instrumental offerings. Tabs were marvelously flexible; they fit a bill that included a silent film, or they could be a self-contained vaudeville presentation.

Les and Lefty joined the show in East Palestine, Ohio, and were first assigned chorus parts. Hazell Chamberlain, lead vocalist in the company, notes that Hope's voice was heard publicly for the first time in scripted gags around Thanksgiving of 1924 at Bloomington, Indiana. She says he substituted as M.C. of a Country Store Night, a rube segment of the *Follies,* and "killed" the audience by the way he read his lines. "Frankly we had all thought 'Lefty' Durbin was the more likely of the two to be a comic, but that night Les Hope was as much surprised as the rest of us."[9]

Hurley was unmistakably small-time show business, and if Hope recognized it that way, he was still thrilled to be in it. He was discovering how much he liked the traveling. And whenever the show played close enough to Cleveland, he liked to saunter along 105th Street or Euclid to the Alhambra, believing himself a big-time vaudevillian and playing it that way for his pals. But first stop was always Mildred's, even if his train or bus arrived at dawn. Mildred would wake up and find Les sitting at the breakfast table with her mother, needling her gently about the Hurley magic and the wicked stage. Mrs. Rosequist liked him in spite of herself, and was gradually becoming convinced of his prospects of success.

At home, his family was not impressed. They believed this was a phase he was passing through, and that when he fell on his face he would settle down to a sensible job and marry Mildred. But to prove his life-style had legitimacy, Les would produce a newspaper clipping from the *Springfield Daily Sun* written by the paper's dramatic editor William J. Murty, who said in part:

From the "thing-of-the-devil" class in which it was held by mistaken public opinion only a generation or so ago, it has risen until today it is the most highly commended and most liberally patronized of the arts. Objections to it have disappeared with its development and now the theatre is ranked, as an essential to community life, second only to the church, with which it works in harmony to bring peace, happiness and contentment to its people . . . the Gus Sun Booking Exchange Company is educating the people of the cities in which it furnishes same, to an appreciation of the beauty of good music, the charm of graceful dancing, the worth of keen wit, the artistry of the drama, and the originality of novelties.[10]

Here was tangible support for his passion. If *Jolly Follies* was not class entertainment, it was tuned to the popular taste just as vaudeville had been for twenty years before it. These touring shows were ideal for backwater towns of America, and you wouldn't expect to find Jolson, Ken Murray, Mae West, Burns and Allen or Will Rogers playing Uniontown, Pennsylvania, or Morgantown, West Virginia. Those towns couldn't afford to pay the big-time salaries of $2,000 a week. Hurley paid Frank Maley $500 and Hazell Chamberlain got $300. The others got between $100 and $200, depending on their specialty. Hurley brought his *Jolly Follies* to Lima, Ohio, for a tenth of what it would take to bring the Marx Brothers to the Cleveland Palace.

Conditions they encountered were frequently dreadful. In addition to the cold and foul smells where they dressed, quarters were cramped. Theirs was a small troupe, thirteen in all, and there was the usual doubling up in cheap boardinghouses and theatrical hotels. They often slept together in narrow, lumpy beds in rooms so small they could hardly breathe. But for six dollars apiece double occupancy for the week, there was bowl and pitcher, the same linen and the same facecloth and bath towel for the entire stay, and so "by the end of the week the towels would be so dirty you would usually bypass them and fan yourself dry."

Most of the theaters were small. The backdrops were ancient, and the street scene where most of the bits were performed had buildings painted so tiny they only came up to the actors' knees. There had to be room for commercial messages. But Les and Lefty thrived in this soil.

Late in that first Hurley season Hope's love life quickened. Not that his feelings for Mildred had changed, but she had decided to date other men. Their engagement was "conditional." And Hope was beginning to think that Kathleen O'Shea, who did a piano specialty with the troupe, was nearly the most beautiful girl in the world.

In Bedford, Indiana, at a small theatrical hotel, Hope decided to put his passion for Kathleen before his reason. He knew, as every vaudevillian knew, that hotel managers were a law unto themselves regarding showfolk and morality. Nevertheless, armed with the excuse that he had a bad chest cold, and encouraged by Kathleen's willingness to rub his chest with hot salve, he went to her room and they closed the door.

Then came a loud knock and the manager demanded an explanation for Les's bared upper body, Kathleen's hands sticky with grease. The manager terrified them both by producing a gun and pointing it at Leslie, saying, "Get downstairs!"

"You got me wrong, pal," stammered Hope, fumbling for his shirt. "Get downstairs!"[11]

Several Bible-belt hotels and rooming houses shunned showfolk. In Brazil, Indiana, for example, the affordable hotel in town was a converted store, and as the troupe stood outside on the street they could read Maley's lips as he asked, "Do you—?" and they started to shuffle along main street when they read the other pair of lips.

The impression that entertainers were loose and "fallen" was a condition assigned by curious "others" more often than it was earned by the players. In the main, vaudeville bookers, agents, theater managers and the company managers were Puritanical and became Prussian officers if they sensed infractions. B.F. Keith had notices placed backstage in his theaters that announced: DON'T SAY "SLOB" OR "SON OF A GUN" OR "HOLY GEE" ON THE STAGE UNLESS YOU WANT TO BE CANCELLED PEREMPTORILY.[12] Most theater managers censored their own shows, though small-town managers were less careful about the presence of blue material than big-time managers. Hurley's material was clean; Maley saw to that. Besides, *Jolly Follies* had three married men in the troupe whose wives were along: Maley himself, plus Bud Brownie (the other comic) and Gail Hood.

The only other major problem in touring was finding decent food in the odd hours that actors either want or need to eat their meals. There was frequently graffiti on the walls of their dressing rooms to help them decide what places to avoid, but inevitably the scrawled message "Terrible food at the Savoy, flies in the soup" didn't help because the Savoy was the only place open after the show and *it* closed at eleven.

Tainted food was blamed for a tragedy that threatened to put Les Hope out of show business. One night in Huntington, West Virginia, Lefty Durbin collapsed onstage and by the time he was carried to a dressing room there was blood oozing from his mouth. Earlier Lefty had complained of stomach pain and had blamed his discomfort on the coconut cream pie he had eaten earlier that day.

Durbin remained in bed the following day in excessive pain, and by evening Hope made the decision to take him home to Cleveland. Les rode the whole distance in the baggage car with Durbin. It was clear to the Cleveland doctor examining Lefty that tainted or poisoned food was not the only trouble. The young dancer had what they once called consumption. He had contracted this months before, and neither man had recognized the symptoms, the cough, occasional fever, loss of weight.

Durbin had lost more blood than anyone had suspected and he died three days later. This was a blow to Les. Also he worried that this trip to Cleveland had cost him his *Jolly Follies* job. As he was leaving Huntington, Maley had said, "Don't worry, we'll fill your spot."

Then we got a job dancing with Daisy and Violet Hilton, the Siamese Twins. At first it was a funny sensation to dance with a Siamese twin. They danced back to back, but they were wonderful girls and it got to be very enjoyable in an unusual sort of way.[1]

4. *Sidewalks of New York*

When Les stepped off the train at Parkersburg, he learned that Maley had hired a new partner for him, George Byrne from Columbus. Hope would later say: "George was pink-cheeked and naive. He looked like a choirboy. He was real quiet. Real Ohio. He was a smooth dancer and had a likable personality. We became good friends. And later on his sister married my brother George."[2]

Byrne and Hope, as the alphabetical listing might have read (but Hope and Byrne, as the company billing was soon established), worked hard to become a unit, and in a matter of weeks were overall a smoother dance team than Hope and Durbin had been. They got a featured spot in the 1925 edition of *Jolly Follies* and later that same year in a revue called *Smiling Eyes,* subtitled "a real production of youth and class—luxuriously staged." Occasionally, if Les begged hard enough, Maley would work him into comedy bits but was generally not bowled over by the results. In the *Cincinnati Inquirer* of February 11, 1942, Hazell Chamberlain remembered:

> Hope was a swell guy . . . we all thought he was like most amateurs who think they'll make the grade. We all hoped he would . . . but I doubt if any of us thought *he* would make it any more than we had . . . and I do remember that he wasn't trusted much with bits, and I think the answer was that he was supposed to feed the comic laughs, but was so much of a comedian himself—even though perhaps he didn't know it—he just couldn't get the right idea to put the laugh over for the comic.

But Hope and Byrne as "dancers supreme" were noticed. They loved the entertainment reporter for the Newport News, Virginia, *Times-Herald*:

> But for the premier honors of the entire bill, Hope and Byrne came through with flying colors in the eccentric dance. Friends, it was a regular knockout. There has never been anything better in this house of this kind. They easily take first place without a contest. They tore the house down and came back for more and they got it.[3]

With every good review the team itched to be heard as well as seen. Once they decided to surprise Maley by adding a comic song to their dance spot. When the orchestra picked up their introduction music they charged on, waving their straw hats and then, as their patter song music was being vamped, they leaned on their canes and weaved back and forth. Someone in the audience shouted, "Ye Gods, are they going to jump?"[4] Hope swears it wasn't that bad. But the next day the Uniontown reviewer wrote: "Hope and Byrne had better stick to dancing."[5]

Lester Hope (Leslie had become Lester—"it sounded more masculine"),[6] second tenor, was better suited to doubling in "Four Horsemen—A Real Harmony Quartet," as they were known in one town and as "The Frisco Four—Four Horsemen of Harmony" in another. The foursome were Hope, Maley, Hood and a guy named June Hoff. Hood was a bit deaf and never knew when the quartet went sour. The other three would look at each other accusingly and get a laugh. But Hood would go right on singing. This struck Hope so funny that each time it happened he would laugh out loud on stage.

Offstage, Maley was critical. "So it's funny, but don't ruin the number with *your* laughter." Hope agreed. And yet it happened again. This time Maley barked, "If you don't stop that guffawing, Hope, you're out of the show." Hard as it was, Hope stopped.[7]

Despite occasional chances to do comedy, it seemed Hope and Byrne were fated to be just dancers. They continued that way into 1926, appearing in two scripted tabs, "The Moonlight Cabaret," in which they were given fourth billing, and later in "The Mix-Up," in which they got their first top-billing.

Between tabs, for a week or two at the most, the team would roost in Cleveland where they hung out at the Hopes', and where Mahm fattened them up on her lemon meringue pie. They would rehearse in the living room, using the upright piano and big mirror that hung over the fireplace. As soon as he could, Les would find Mildred.

"How's Kathleen?" she asked once.

"Kathleen who?" he said.

"The one in Morgantown," she said in a tone that cooled his ardor.[8] It didn't take long for Les to catch on. When he was gone for so long, Mildred would spend time at the Hopes' visiting with Mahm. George, his youngest brother, was a big blabber; he would tell Mildred all he remembered from Les's letters home about his beautiful Irish doll. But Mildred could be pacified on the dance floor, and afterwards they would do some "front porch lovemaking." When he went away again Mildred was just as undecided, and so was Les.

By early 1926 Kathleen had left the show. She had always wanted to open a dress shop in Morgantown, and with money she had saved and with more from Les, she swung the deal. Whenever Les got to New York, in later years, he would haunt the Seventh Avenue showrooms and sample shops to pick up stylish things cheap for Kathleen's boutique.

Day and night Hope and Byrne plotted ways to improve their act, mostly by injecting more comedy. Hope would usually play the straight part while Byrne was the zany who triggers the laugh, like:

> Byrne walks across the stage with a suitcase, sets it down, then steps over it. Hope says: "How are you?" Byrne says: "Fine. Just getting over the grippe."
>
> Byrne walks across again with a woman's dress on a hanger, and Hope says: "Where are you going?" Byrne says: "Down to get this filled."

The reality was that if they had aspirations for more than specialty dancing in a tab show they had to get out. So, in the spring of 1926 they quit. As Hope later said: "There's no possible way to measure the value of those Hurley years, the poise and seasoning they gave me. I remember when I landed the part of Huck Haines in *Roberta* and played it without falling apart on the first night the producers didn't know how many openings I'd been through."[10]

They had an introduction from one of the Hurley gang to a Detroit agent named Ted Snow. Armed with a fistful of reviews from the *Parkersburg Sentinel* and the *Norfolk Ledger,* which had adjectives like "novel" and "clever" and "wonderful" and "nifty" and "phenom," and bolstered by Hope's brashly naive version of sophistication, they got themselves booked into Detroit's State Theater. Snow got them $175 a week, which was $75 more than they made with Hurley, and two days later was able to book them into a nightclub spot at the Oriole Terrace for another $75. They were elated.

They opened April 25 at the State and played four shows, then jumped on a streetcar and went out to Oriole Terrace for their late night spot, and then back downtown to do a little gambling at Reilly's, a place they had heard about from one of the State stagehands. It would have been better for Les had it been three-pocket billiards. As it was, they gambled away their first week's salaries that first night and as everyone who knows vaudeville can tell you, you don't get paid until the end of the engagement.

But they clicked with audiences and therefore with Snow. The M.C. at the State was Fred Stitt and Hope watched him carefully more because of his material than his style. Though Stitt sang a lot in his act, his comedy was patter based on "the latest happenings in the daily news." That intrigued Hope.

After the second week, the *Detroit Free Press* review of May 10, 1926, was saying "the very clever soft-shoe dancers" and "Hope and Byrne, two young men in grotesque costume with their eccentric dancing, won the big applause Sunday." Snow managed to book them at several other smaller theaters around Detroit and then "by demand" returned them to the State. That second time around their names moved up in the newspaper ads and were set in larger type: HOPE AND BYRNE—DANCING DEMONS.

Ted Snow asked Harrisburg agent Ed Fishman to book the boys into the Stanley Theater in Pittsburgh. But before going to Pittsburgh, they hopped over to Chicago because Hope insisted they get the Tiffany of publicity photos by Maurice Seymour. Les was beginning to sense the importance of packaging, the power of promotion and publicity. They bought new costumes: Eton jackets and big white collars and high-waisted pants and white spats. They wore high hats and carried black canes with white tips. They posed and mugged for the camera. Then they went out and bought a new theatrical trunk; their old one, not untypically, was being held together with a hunk of rope. They went for the top of the H.M. line, which only the class acts could afford.

The Pittsburgh date was a good one but was merely a stop "on the way," a rehearsal for big time which was, of course, New York. Knowing they couldn't hit New York without a fresh act they worked out the following routines:

Our act opened with a soft-shoe dance. We wore the high hats and spats and carried canes for this. Then we changed into a fireman's outfit by taking off our high hats and putting on small papier-mâché fireman hats. George had a hatchet and I had a length of hose with a water bulb in it. We danced real fast to "If You Knew Susie," and a rapid ta-da-da-da-dah tempo, while the drummer rang a fire bell. At the end of this routine I squirted water from the concealed bulb at the brass section of the orchestra in the pit. It not only made an attractive finish but it had the added advantage of drowning a few musicians.[11]

Understandably, that pair of beanpole-thin vaudevillians who came out of Pennsylvania Station on that autumn morning in 1926, and stood staring at Manhattan for the first time, believed themselves to be two of the freshest, most original entertainers of the decade. They found a room at the Lincoln Hotel and went to find the B.F. Keith office where they flashed their photographs and asked for bookings. What they got were several audition bookings, which were tryouts in second, third and fourth-line vaudeville houses where the salary was minimum while agents looked you over.

Meanwhile, Abe Lastfogel of William Morris called them back solely on the strength of the photographs they had left with the agency and booked them as the "deuce" spot in a Morris package for the Keith circuit. It turned out to be one of vaudeville's current success attractions, eighteen-year-old Siamese twins named Daisy and Violet Hilton. These British-born oddities, orphaned just after birth, were raised in San Antonio, Texas, by foster parents who encouraged their music and dance training and then exploited them as a freak-show-type attraction. In their act they talked about their unusual life, they sang, played saxophone and clarinet solos and duets, and danced. Then they were joined by Hope and Byrne for a more elaborate routine where they danced back to back. They were a well-produced curiosity that packed people in for sometimes as many as four strenuous shows a day, each requiring Hope and Byrne to do their own act in the second spot, and then a vigorous finale with the Hiltons. For six months the show played Philadelphia, Washington, Baltimore, Reading, Youngstown, Pittsburgh, York, and Providence, Rhode Island.

In May 1927 when the show had reached Reading, Hope and Byrne began to believe their press notices and they became restless. They called themselves "Dancemedians" and the local critic raved:

Hope and Byrne have untamed feet. They just behave as if they have no control whatsoever, but of course their control is perfect. The boys are versatile dancers with humor crowded into every step.[12]

When the boys got to Providence they faced the producers with a showdown. For the hours they were putting in they wanted more money. They were told "no deal," so the boys packed their trunk after the last show and waved the Hilton troupe off to Boston.

Back in New York in early summer 1927, Hope and Byrne put up in the Somerset, a theatrical hotel just off Broadway. The Somerset was right next to the Palace stage door and especially popular with vaudevillians because

the management would carry you if you found yourself "between engagements." But the pair still had money from their Keith tour thanks to the
modicum of wisdom they had gleaned from their Detroit fleecing at Reilly's.
Word of mouth provided them some nightclub dancing dates, but by day
they made the rounds and auditioned for every musical production and revue
that was casting. In August they unexpectedly hit—and hit high.

They received a call from choreographer Earl Lindsey to audition for
Sidewalks of New York. They were signed for specialty dancing and small
speaking parts. It was a Charles Dillingham production of a show with words
and music by Eddie Dowling and Jimmy Hanley. The show starred Dowling's wife Ray Dooley, fresh from her *Ziegfeld Follies* triumph of the year
before, and featured a group of celebrated vaudevillians including Smith and
Dale, monologist-composer James Thornton, the old minstrel Barney Fagan,
and Josephine Sabel of "Hot Time in the Old Town Tonight" fame. The
plot centered on the vicissitudes of an obstreperous young convent-raised
child (played by Ray Dooley) trying to find love and happiness on the
streets of New York. In the cast as a tap dancer, and bringing the rehearsals of the show much publicity because of her romance with Al Jolson, was
Ruby Keeler.

At the first reading at the Knickerbocker, Hope and Byrne found their
parts were small indeed, brief specialty dance bits in the show's opening
scene, and they shared that assignment with another pair of young vaudeville
hoofers (Charles) Gale and (Alan) Calm. It was disappointing but at least
the four became good friends. In later years Alan Calm became Hope's
stand-in and dialogue coach for movies and television.[13]

It wasn't all bad. Rehearsals were endlessly fascinating to Hope who loved
to watch the big-timers work. And being a Broadway chorus boy had its
benefits, such as being able to charm an aspiring young actress named Barbara Sykes who lived at the Princeton, another theatrical hotel. Hope still
treasured his boyish crush on Mildred, and still combed Seventh Avenue
dress showrooms for samples to send to Morgantown, but for fascinating
Barbara he would move over to the Princeton.

Sidewalks opened at the Garrick Theater in Philadelphia September 5.
Hope, Byrne and Calm found rooms at the Maidstone Apartments near
Walnut and Tenth; Gale and his wife were nearby. The show got good
notices, but as the unavoidable doctoring and tightening took place, director
Edgar MacGregor decided the show needed an uplifting dance number and
asked Hanley to write a new scene utilizing his tune "We've Been Thrown
Out of Better Places Before" featuring Keeler and putting Hope, Byrne,
Calm and Gale to better use. Hanley went to work. Meanwhile the boys did
their tiny bit and watched from the wings.

Hope was lonely for Barbara during the Philly tryout. His roommates
suggested he invite her to come and keep house for them and comfort Lester.
Hope wired her and she wired back: WILL BE ON THE SIX O'CLOCK. Les was
ecstatic. He would have time to meet her, take her to the apartment and get
to the Garrick by seven-thirty. When he walked into the dressing room that
night his face was serious. No Barbara. He wired again and got the same
response: WILL BE ON THE SIX O'CLOCK. But no Barbara. This went on for several days and finally she arrived on Friday's six o'clock.

In her honor Byrne and Calm planned a party at the Maidstone. They invited the entire *Sidewalks* cast of 110 and figured half would come. Half did and brought their fair share of bathtub gin and rotgut whiskey. The party was going fine when Billy O'Rourke, one of the chorus boys, knocked on the door. He was in drag and asked if he could bring some of his friends to join the party. The noise level went up at this point and the manager came to calm things down. When he spotted the male dancers in drag he called the police. In the meantime the O'Rourke party decided to leave, and as they headed for the third floor stairway, the manager caught up with them. A Mack Sennett comedy followed: a massive chase along corridors, up to the next floor, downstairs, up again and down again, with police joining in and with screams and pratfalls.

Hope and Barbara, Calm and Byrne laughed until they were weak, then fell into bed—Les and Barbara in the double bed behind the sliding French doors off the sitting room. The lovers talked for hours. In the morning Barbara came out, all dressed, with suitcase in hand and Les behind her. They went to the railway station. It seems that after Les left New York she had fallen in love with a piano player who lived at the Princeton, which explained why she kept missing the six o'clock.

After four weeks in Philadelphia and a week in Atlantic City, *Sidewalks* opened in New York at the Knickerbocker Theater on Monday, October 3, 1927. That was a magnificent season: 53 musicals and 217 plays on Broadway. Besides *Good News, Rosalie* and *A Connecticut Yankee*, there was Cantor in the *Follies*, Cohan in *The Merry Malones*, and the artistic and commercial success of that season, *Show Boat*. Cornell was playing in *The Letter*, Max Reinhardt was unveiling his *Midsummer Night's Dream*, and the Lunts were starring in *The Doctor's Dilemma*.

Sidewalks was a hit, which was probably why the new Hanley production number never materialized. Keeler's specialty dance, "The Goldfish Glide," was tremendously popular with audiences. MacGregor decided the show had enough dancing; and since all Hope and Bryne were doing for their featured performer pay was the short opening bit, he gave them two weeks' notice. They managed to stretch that to a month, and then were back on the street.

Someone introduced them to an agent named Milt Lewis who found them a second billing spot on an eight-act vaudeville bill at the B.S. Moss Franklin, a big showcase theater. Cockier than ever, with a Broadway show to their credit, they decided to pad their spoken comedy and deemphasize their dancing. They knew their humor had to be more sophisticated than the bill's headliners, a classic slapstick team who knew every trick in existence for milking applause. But what they came up with were chestnuts like:

HOPE: Where do bugs go in the wintertime?
BYRNE: Search me.[14]

After their first show at the Franklin, they knew they were not second-spot material. Hope talked to Al Lloyd at the Morris office who was interested enough to try to fix their act and to look for bookings elsewhere. Lloyd also talked to senior agent Johnny Hyde who had been promising to look them over, but Hyde wouldn't go to the Franklin.

"Why not?" begged Hope.

"Because I heard about it," Hyde said coldly.

"You did?" Hope asked, his stomach sliding.

"You ought to go West, change your act, start over," advised Hyde.[15]

The team had hit bottom—out of *Sidewalks*, a flop with the comedy stuff, almost broke and psychologically damaged. Hope argued loudly that the answer was Chicago, second biggest vaudeville town—"that's where the money is."

They were broke enough to realize they could use some bookings on the way back to Ohio, so they called Mike Shea in Cleveland and he put them on the bill in New Castle, Pennsylvania, after playing a few days at the Metropolitan Theater in Morgantown first.

In New Castle, they were third on a three-act bill. That was a lot to swallow and so was the pay, $50 each for three days. The manager asked Hope as a favor to come out after the last act and do a solo billboard spot announcing the coming attraction. So Hope obliged; he came back out and said, "Ladies and gentlemen, there's going to be a *good* show here next week." Some laughter. "Marshall Walker will be here with his Whiz Bang Revue." Hope knew the act. It was another Gus Sun attraction. Walker was a rube comic who traded on barnyard and tight-fisted farmer jokes. "Marshall is a Scotsman. I know him. He got married in the backyard so the chickens could get the rice."[16]

The audience roared. The orchestra in the pit below loved it, too. At the next show Hope added another "Scotch" joke, about the Scotsman who sat up all night and watched his wife's vanishing cream. That also got a roar. At the next show he added two more of the same kind and got twice as much laughter. There was so much laughter that it was clear something unusual was happening.

One of the pit musicians took Les aside. "You had that audience right where you wanted it. That's what you ought to be doing. Emcees are hard to find. Good ones can take over and make a place hot. Your double act with that dancing and those corny jokes, that's nothing. Listen to me."

Les walked away and did some hard thinking. He didn't agree that their dancing and joking were that bad. Yet he had always secretly toyed with the idea of going it alone. But one of the toughest things to do is to break up an act, especially when two people have shared so many hard and good times together. Whatever George's flaws, Hope *liked* him.

Byrne noticed that Les was troubled, and he knew why. "I think I know what you're going through, Les. You want to try a single. After what happened here I don't blame you. I'll go back to Columbus and take it easy for a while, maybe start a dancing school."

Hope said, "Let me try it alone for a couple of weeks—if it works we'll break up the trunk."

Next day Hope and Byrne grabbed the same bus for Columbus, and then Les took the train for Cleveland. He tried calling Mildred right away but she was out of town. He went home and Mahm opened the door.

"What's happened?" she asked.

"It's Christmas," Les said.

"That's weeks away," she said, pouring him coffee. "Where's George? Something's wrong, isn't it?"

"I'm going to try it on my own. George likes the idea." Les looked at his mother and watched her face relax.[17]

"Now, then—" she said, and Les sat there listening while his mother filled him in on all the family doings. Ivor (married twelve years) was having his troubles with Gertrude but his business was doing well. Jim was away working in Pittsburgh. Fred's marriage to LaRue Gibbons was a big success and so was his provisions business. Jack was still at Chandler and married again. Sid was in auto mechanics. George was in his last year of high school and taking dancing lessons, hoping that one day Les would put him in his act.

"Where's Dad?" asked Les.

"He keeps busy. He's out back right now—I think he's carving me a bird bath. Les, why don't you talk to him about your decision?" Avis always insisted that Harry was the head of the family.

"I will," Les said. "But Mahm, what do *you* think?"

"I think you're every bit as good as that Frank Fay any day."

One of the things I learned at the Stratford was to have enough courage to wait. I'd stand there waiting for them to get it for a long time. Longer than any other comedian had the guts to wait. My idea was to let them know who was running things.[1]

5. Stratford to Proctor's 86th

The morning of Cleveland's first snowfall of 1927, Les took the streetcar downtown to the Erie Building to call on Mike Shea. Shea listened to Hope's fast talk, refused the offer to read through his newspaper clips and asked him what he wanted.

Hope said fearlessly that he could do a single act. "You know, singing, dancing, talking—working in blackface." It was desperation, and luck, that forced him to mention blackface. Shea booked a rotary unit—a different theater each night—in and around Cleveland, and he put Hope in the show.

Grateful and cocksure, Hope danced out of Shea's tiny office and down to the street level.

I went out, bought a big red bow tie, white cotton gloves like Jolson's, a cigar and a small bowler which jiggled up and down when I bounced onstage. I'd picked up some new material here and there, plus a few things I'd thought up for myself. For an encore I did a song and dance. I scored well even if I was scoring in a Lilliputian world.[2]

He lived at home, ate well and could take the streetcar to whatever theater the unit was playing. The fourth night, however, Hope missed his trolley. By the time he got to the theater it was nearly time to go on, so he didn't try to apply his burnt cork. He just grabbed his bowler, stuck a cigar in the corner of his mouth and sailed out through the wings. Somehow he scored even larger than he had in blackface. Shea told him, "Leave the cork off. Your face is funny the way it is."

Funny would not have been Hope's description. He thought himself handsome, sexy. All the next day he stared at himself in his chifforobe mirror, and he discovered that the way he tilted his chin or darted his eyes back and forth could be amusing. But it was the audience's reaction to his corkless face that convinced him.

After the New Year, Hope had regained his confidence and decided to go to Chicago to get a fresh start. He dropped George Byrne a note and told him what he planned, packed his trunk and hopped the train for Chicago. He began haunting agents' offices, but he couldn't make a dent. He had no contacts, and it didn't seem to matter that he had worked a lot, even on Broadway. But he had never worked as a single. He found a coffee shop that had a waitress who thought he was cute so he got credit.

Chicago, like the rest of the nation, was riding high in the spring of 1928. Chicago was the biggest entertainment center west of the Hudson and, like New York, was riding the crest of a motion picture wave. Most of the theaters in town had converted to a policy of feature films and vaudeville, which usually meant this format: a screen feature, rotating acts booked by RKO (the Radio–Keith–Orpheum organization that by this time ruled the vaudeville booking business), a house orchestra and frequently a house master of ceremonies who stayed for weeks, sometimes months. It was a busy town; it was a tough town.

And it was late May when Hope decided he was ready to admit failure. He owed for food, for clothes, for musical arrangements; he was starving, and he couldn't pay his rent.

He was leaning his skinny frame against a newspaper hutch on the sidewalk in front of Woods Theater Building, working up his nerve to show the Clara Bowish receptionist at the Marcus Loew Agency his sexiest grin, when he was overjoyed to see his old pal, Charlie Cooley, now a successful vaudevillian, going in. Hope admitted to Cooley how bad things had become. It touched Cooley to see the self-confident hustler this far down.

"Come with me," Cooley said. They went into the Woods Building and upstairs to a small office that had CHARLES HOGAN—NATIONAL PLAY HOUSES, INC. in gold leaf on a glass-paneled door. Behind the door was a five-foot-four Irishman with sandy hair and green eyes peering through silver-rimmed glasses. He talked tough but had a soft heart. Cooley knew Hogan well, well enough so that if he said, "Can you give this guy a job?" then nothing else needed to be said.[3]

It happened that Hogan had to fill a master of ceremonies spot at the West Englewood Theater for three shows on Decoration Day. "It pays—" but Hope didn't even hear. He almost wept. The pay was $25.

After the second show, the manager at West Englewood said to Les, "You're going to play the Stratford next Sunday."

"How do you know?" asked Hope.

"Hogan called to find out how you were doing and I told him. Now he's putting you in for three days out there as master of ceremonies."

The Stratford was a well-attended neighborhood vaudeville theater, actually a converted movie house. They had built an apron out from the regular small stage so that the house could accommodate both a band and dance acts. The Stratford audience consisted mainly of loyal neighborhood people, so their likes and dislikes were registered in bloc form. If a performer clicked, "they let him live" and their noisy reception meant that a particular acrobatic dance team, singer, baggy-pants comic or whatever had found a home. It was the same—perhaps even more so—with the M.C. The Stratford had had the same M.C., Ted Emery, for two years and he would still probably own that stage except that he had become "difficult" to work with and had to be replaced. The theater tried a succession of comedians after Emery but no one clicked, and Hope was just another tryout.

On the same bill with him was a likable little fellow named Barney Dean doing a rather tired single act. Although he wasn't much onstage, Dean was endowed with an unusual sense of humor. He had an uncanny ability to gauge the "rightness" of a piece of material and could transform a faltering bit of comedy.

Hogan was a sucker for Dean's act and booked him when and where he could. Charlie called up the Stratford manager to check on Hope and liked what he heard. Then he asked to talk to Barney Dean. "We're doing fine," Dean said.[4]

Hogan said, "I know how *you* did. *You* laid an egg. How is Hope doing?"

"Hope did real good. You'll be hearing about him," Barney said. And Hogan trusted Dean's judgment. He struck a deal with the Stratford to extend Hope's stay to two weeks. Whenever Hogan went out to watch the show, he realized more and more he had a "find" in this master of ceremonies whose rapid patter of introduction was frequently far better than the acts themselves. At the end of two weeks the contract was stretched to four weeks at a salary of $200.

In these initial days of his new career track Hope decided to change his name from Lester to Bob because he figured Bob sounded "chummier" and looked better on the marquee. Hogan and Dean approved. Hope found himself leaning on his new friends for support, and they and Cooley formed the nucleus of an "in" group that would remain intimate with Hope for forty years.

Hope now recognized that comic patter was his real meal ticket, and singing was sometimes a good way of getting closer to his audience. It was a folksy, family audience at the Stratford, composed of people who would return maybe twice a week. They expected to hear some of the same jokes, but they liked a change of material. Hope had to scramble to stay alive and he got jokes however and wherever he could.

He poured through James Madison's *Budget,* an annual paperbound assortment of gags, sketches and parodies that cost a dollar. Sometimes he cribbed from *College Humor,* or begged the other acts that played through the Stratford to give him jokes. Buying comedy from good comedy writers (if you could find them) was much too expensive for Hope.

Hope was a gag scribbler. His pockets were crammed with bits of paper with joke cues scrawled in the margins of letters.

He also dreamed up gag situations. One of his most successful began with an offstage crash "that sounded like someone dropping a trunkful of glass." Hope would walk onstage dusting off his hands and adjusting his tie as if he had just taken part in a terrific fight. Then he would look back into the wings and say, "Lie there and bleed."

What the Stratford provided for Hope was the loamy soil for producing the hallmarks of a personal style. He both needed and got the experience of handling jokes of different types.

> I'd lead off with a subtle joke, and after telling it, I'd say to the audience, "Go ahead, figure it out." Then I'd wait until they got it. One of the things I learned at the Stratford was to have enough courage to wait. I'd stand there waiting for them to get it for a long time. Longer than any other comedian had the guts to wait. My idea was to let them know who was running things.[5]

Because the four-week extension eventually became a six-month stay at the Stratford, Hope had to come up with a fresh series of gags every week. That meant he had to try out a lot of bad jokes. And that is where speed and timing became important. If he told a bad joke fast enough it didn't matter much, it was all in the timing.

Hope was experiencing the heady sensation of being in control, of manipulating his audience. He learned the discipline of always being "up" for an audience, whether 2 or 20 or 200 people, and keeping up a nonstop pace whatever the audience's response.

He also had the freedom to experiment, and although he was attracted to subtle material, he knew that the audiences he played to were not capable of too much subtlety. "There's a line between smart and too smart. They liked a simple kind of humor but also I could get them to work on a gag they thought was more subtle than it really was. But it made them feel good they'd won a contest."[6]

Stratford's regular paychecks were doing wonders for the total Hope person. The kind of act he had adopted—bowler and cigar and more than a touch of brash—was helping to build his reputation of being a "new boy" in town. He stood six feet tall, with a lithe, athletic body. He had sandy hair and sexy eyes that could flicker with interest when he listened or conversed, and could quickly change to a sensual stare. Eating regularly had filled out his frame just enough. Employment gave a boost to his sex life, too. He had a small, cozy apartment and he had Louise Troxell.

Louise was a local product, daughter of hardworking Roman Catholic parents. Louise had some office skills and planned to be a secretary, but she also had one eye on the stage. With her doll-like face, stylishly marcelled hair and fashion-model body, Louise was as classy as anyone Hope had encountered the day she sauntered into one of the hangouts near the Stratford. They met and soon fell in love. And in October of 1928, when Hogan offered Hope a change of pace from the Stratford, suggesting he hit the road for a while, the comedian decided to take Louise along and put her in the act as his foil, his Gracie Allen.

He would be working on stage and in the middle of his patter, she would appear. Hope says:

> All she had to do was walk on and stand there looking beautiful while I told a story, then feed me lines. She'd come out holding a little bag in her hand and say, "How do you do." I'd say, "What have you got in your little bag?" and she'd say, "Mustard." And

I'd say, "What's the idea?" And she'd say, "You can never tell when you're going to meet a ham."[7]

Sometimes Hope would ignore her presence for quite a while before turning toward her. Then:

LOUISE: I just came back from the doctor.
BOB: That's nice.
LOUISE: Well, the doctor said I'd have to go to the mountains for my kidneys.
BOB: That's too bad.
LOUISE: Yes, I didn't even know they were up there.[8]

The first punchline got a laugh because it put Hope down, the second because it was so unexpected. And when Hope grimaced with pain from being stuck with such a cute dumbbell, it engaged audience sympathy.

Wichita and Kansas City audiences and media loved the act. Goodman Ace, in those days a reporter for the *Kansas City Star,* wrote: "Hope's gags are new and the wristwatch thing is a wow." Hope describes it:

I'd begin to sing a song and as I sang I looked at my wristwatch every few bars. Finally I took a bottle of medicine from my pocket, said, "Pardon me," took two spoonfuls of the stuff, and finished my song. Then I'd shake my whole body and say, "I forgot to shake the bottle."[9]

They played a few other dates on Keith's Western Circuit, including South Bend, where Hope sensed the importance of topicality and of situational acuity:

I was still wearing the brown derby, and I had a big cigar stuck in my kisser. When I walked out on stage in South Bend, there was a roar of applause. When I told my first joke they screamed. I couldn't figure it out. Finally I got it. I had a Notre Dame audience; Al Smith was running for President. A brown derby and cigar were his trademarks.[10]

Just before 1928 became 1929, Hope went to Chicago and signed a contract on New Year's Eve with Charlie Hogan to appear for four weeks, with an option for six months, back "home" at the Stratford. Before the end of the run Hope was making $300 a week.

This time at the Stratford, Hope was confident of technique, but desperate about material. He was using up too fast whatever he found and always needed more. He lifted routines from other comics and adapted as he saw fit. Not that this was so rare a practice. W.C. Fields was notorious for lifting lines, and Fred Allen was irked for years by an episode arising from Jolson's theft of material from him. Bert Lahr accused Joe E. Brown of stealing his comedy character, and Hope himself, when accused of adopting J.C. Flippen's brown derby and cigar-twirling mannerisms, said: "That's not true. You notice how Flippen rotates that cigar from right to left—well, I do it from left to right."

Hope was always prowling for walk-on gags, especially necessary for an

emcee's frequent appearances and disappearances. One of his most successful was a routine using the orchestra leader as the foil, which he lifted from
Frank Tinney's act.

HOPE: Charlie—would you mind helping me with a joke? I'll
come out and say, "I went to the dentist this morning
but I only had a dollar" and you say "What happened?" Then I'll tell the funny answer which will convulse the audience and they'll roll in the aisles. Then
we'll have the audience put back in their seats and
everyone will be real happy and—ha-ha-ha—here we
go. (*Hope walks off*)

HOPE: (*Bouncing on stage*) Hello Charlie!
O.L.: Hello Bob.
HOPE: I went to the dentist this morning.
O.L.: You did?
HOPE: Yes—and I only had a dollar.
O.L.: Where did you get the dollar? (*Audience laughs*)
HOPE: Wait a minute! You're not supposed to say that! If you
don't mind, let me get the laughs. I'm the comedian
around here. Just ask: "What happened?" and I'll tell
the joke. After all they're paying me to be funny. You
just wave your stick, Charlie. Understand? (*Hope
walks offstage*)

HOPE: (*Announcing from the wings*) Here we go Charlie!
HOPE: (*Bouncing onstage*) Hello Charlie!
O.L.: Hello Bob.
HOPE: I went to the dentist this morning. I only had a dol-
lar.
O.L.: What happened?
HOPE: I had to get buck teeth![11]

They laughed every time. Hope would use it again and again. But stealing,
borrowing, rearranging, patching, eternally searching for fresh material to
keep Stratford audiences contented and returning was hard work. Hope
finally decided he would be better off as a moving target than as a fixture in
a small-time house.

Hope dipped into his stockpile of material and put together an act he
called "Keep Smiling," with Louise, of course. They played dates for the
small-time Western Vaudeville Managers Association in Sioux City, Peoria
and Bloomington and then he got a wire from Hogan telling them to go
immediately to Oklahoma City where "Smiling Eyes" was to become the
featured comedy spot on a four-act vaudeville bill touring what was known
as Interstate Time.

For the first time in his life Hope had the star spot on the bill. His pay
began at $300 and soon moved to $325 a week. He could afford to give
Louise some spending money, send Avis $50 or so, and after Hogan had
taken his, there was still a bit for tucking into the shoe.

The other acts were about average small-time vaudeville. Third billing went to a mediocre dancing act performed by the Cirillo Brothers, four zesty Italians from Springfield, Massachusetts. Hope thought they were wonderful. In fact, twenty years later they showed up with regularity doing bits on his television show in the 1950s and 1960s. They were about five feet six, hot-tempered and lusty bachelors all. They traveled in their own Ford touring car with its super-chrome fittings, running boards and a rumble seat that saw its share of sexual conquests in country lanes just outside town.

After Oklahoma City, where audiences were fairly responsive, the troupe moved to Fort Worth for a two-week stay. At the first show, as soon as the Cirillos came offstage, Hope swung out through the wings and launched into his snappy opening material, but there wasn't much reaction. The Louise spot worked, and after that he worked even harder—he played even cockier, faster, more flippant. It wasn't working. He says:

> I had killed 'em with this stuff at the Stratford, and hadn't done that bad in Oklahoma City, and it was the same act. Here I was laying the biggest egg in my life so far. I really died! I didn't know what to make of it.[12]

When he came offstage, there was no loud applause dragging him back for a bow or an encore. In a foul temper, he threw his derby on the floor and said furiously that he was quitting the show. "Get me a ticket to *my* country!" Hope, known to the troupe as mild-mannered and friendly—a bit conceited, perhaps, fresh, yes, audacious and flirty, sometimes—had never been known to be mean or loud or foul-mouthed. The unit manager quietly told someone to go and find Bob O'Donnell.

Angry and disappointed as he was, Hope was persuaded by Louise to go back out for the afterpiece, that final segment of a vaudeville bill where the acts return for the closing production number.[13]

Afterpiece over, Hope went grim-faced to his dressing room and slammed the door. A short silence and then a person Hope had never seen before opened his dressing room door and stepped inside. Hope faced his dressing table, still wearing his white flannel trousers and dark serge coat.

"What's *with* you, fancy pants?" O'Donnell asked.

"Who are you?" Hope asked, turning away from his mirror, ready to order the intruder out. No reply. Hope turned back and looked at himself in the mirror and then looked at the stranger's mirror image. Then he removed his coat and started to take off his makeup. "I'll tell you something. I don't get this audience," Hope said, turning around. "I'm not for these people. That's the matter."

"Why don't you relax?" O'Donnell said, still standing. "You've got plenty of time. Why not slow down and give the audience a chance? These people are Texans and they like things a little slower, but they're nice people. They came inside to be happy. It's summer and it's hot. This is Texas. Let them understand you. Why make it a contest to keep up with your material?" He moved toward the door and said, "Relax and I guarantee you'll be all right."

"Thanks so much," Hope said sarcastically. O'Donnell walked out and the unit manager stepped in. Hope demanded to know who the man was. When he learned that O'Donnell was the manager of the Interstate Vaudeville Circuit, Hope said, "I don't care who he is—how much nerve can one man have?"

But Hope gradually cooled down and decided the advice might be worth taking. O'Donnell was out there for the next show and then came backstage. Hope had worked less abrasively. He says, "That was a turning point for me." O'Donnell worked with the comedian for the remainder of his Fort Worth engagement. "He changed my tempo and made me wait for laughs from *all* my material," said Hope, "and I had no trouble getting through to the audience after that."

From Fort Worth the troupe moved to Dallas. Hope had learned an important lesson—the need to be sensitive to geographical and cultural differences in audiences. The only problem Hope had with any Dallas audience was getting them to concentrate on his gags while a loud backstage fight was going on among the Cirillos.

During the supper show of their first day in Dallas, just as the Cirillos were finishing their act, Tony accidentally—well, probably accidentally—bumped his brother Charlie and threw him off balance, spoiling the precision of the routine. And the Cirillos were famous for their precision. At the next show Charlie managed to return Tony's bump, and at the next show Tony got bumped by Andy. It became a chain reaction until the pushing turned to shoving and when, by the second show of their second day in Dallas, they came off stage, they started a fist fight in the wings.

Hope was in the middle of his opening routine when he realized the distraction was too great, so he excused himself and went to the wings. "Simmer down," he hissed at them. "I'm trying to work. In fact I was just telling this nice audience," Hope was backing slowly out onstage again, "what an attractive, lovable quartet you boys are." They untangled for a moment, Hope smiled and went on with his act. But the fighting began again, even louder this time with excited screams and thumps. The audience laughed, thinking it was part of Hope's act. It had been funny, at first, but it was hard to go on working against that noise. By the time Hope finished, the police arrived and tried to arrest the Cirillos. Angry as Bob was, he defended them saying it was part of his act. The police believed him.[14]

The troupe pushed on through August of 1929 and in Charleston, Hope received a telegram from someone named Lee Stewart in the B.F. Keith office in New York. This confused Hope. For months he had been corresponding with a pair of agents named Morris (not William) and Feil, and Hope felt that if anyone should be contacting him it would be them. With the kind of encouraging and flattering mail they had been sending him, he figured them for a cinch deal at the Palace or perhaps an audition for the Shuberts.

Hope did not know that his new mentor, Bob O'Donnell, had been so impressed with his talent and headliner potential that he had wired the Keith office urging them to sign Hope for the Orpheum circuit. In his wire to Hope, Lee Stewart suggested that he leave the company and come to New York immediately. Bob and Louise drove triumphantly northward in the secondhand Packard that Hope was forced to describe as "a shiny monster that ate gas and oil like a dragon eats people."

In New York they checked into the Lincoln Hotel, and as early as he dared the next morning he went to see the agents from whom he had received the encouraging mail, Morris and Feil. He breezed into their office, what there was of it.

"Here I am," he said confidently.

"Who are you?" asked Feil.

"Bob Hope. I'm the fellow you've been writing to."

"What do you do?" asked Morris.

Hope looked disdainfully at Morris. "You mean after all our correspondence, you don't even know what I do? Okay, just give me my photos."[15]

He called Lee Stewart and went to meet him at the Keith office. Stewart seemed intelligent and straight. He said, "Keith wants you to show us your act. Bob O'Donnell says you're good."[16]

"Where does Keith want me to show?" Hope asked shrewdly. He had already had some experience with New York houses and the rest was vaudeville lore—the ones to play, the ones to avoid if you could.

"At the Jefferson," Stewart said. The Jefferson was on Fourteenth Street and well known for being a tough place to show; audiences there were rowdy.

"I can't show there," Hope said flatly. "I'll show uptown at the Hamilton, or Riverside, or the Coliseum." Then something perverse in him forced him to add, "And if you want me you'd better hurry. Don't fool around."

"You sure you won't play the Jefferson?" Lee pressed.

"No Jefferson," Hope snapped and he was downstairs and out on Broadway walking under the Palace marquee with his nose and chin high.

Back at the Lincoln, he called the William Morris office and tried to get some interest going based on his Interstate Time. Then he called a spotter he had heard about at the Publix Circuit and took some photos there.

It was several days of waiting before Stewart called to tell Hope he had an uptown theater for him to show in. It was Proctor's 86th Street. He would play four days.

"Who's on ahead of me?" Hope asked.

"Leatrice Joy from the movies," Lee said.

"Okay," agreed Hope.

"It's not much money," said Stewart.

"I don't care about the money," Hope announced.

"Are you nuts?"

"I just want them to see the act. Publix is after me but I'm willing to let Keith's see the act, too. If they don't like me, okay. But I don't need money."

Hope was bluffing and probably Stewart knew it. Lee said, "Okay, okay. But a word to the wise, kid. Publix is no Keith's and William Morris isn't going to put you on the Orpheum time and they sure as hell aren't going to put you in the Palace." It was Stewart's way of reminding Hope of the subtleties and politics of the booking business, and particularly that it was Keith, not Morris, who booked the Palace.

After Hope hung up from his conversation with Stewart, he called Charlie Yates, an agent who had once bailed Hope and Byrne out when they were starving, to see if Yates could find him a little showcase in the area where he could break in some new comedy ideas.

Yates found him three days, four shows a day, at the Dyker in Brooklyn for $75. But he didn't go over well there. The Dyker attracted a raucous neighborhood crowd who liked raucous comedy. They applauded and fell into the aisles over physical stuff and Hope's subtleties, peppered at high speed in a small Brooklyn house, got not much farther than the boys in the band.

Stewart came out to Brooklyn for Hope's last performance, and on the way back to Manhattan that night on the IRT, the two men engaged in some plain talk while Louise snoozed on Hope's shoulder. Lee reminded him that Proctor's 86th was a big barn, and he was worried about Hope's ability to project to the top balcony. But Hope wasn't worried about projecting. If he had anything it was a big strong voice that carried and could be heard in the last row.

Hope finally turned to Stewart. "Look, Lee, I open there tomorrow, and if I don't score, we don't talk to each other again. Okay?"

Hope arose earlier than usual. Backstage before the midafternoon show, he asked the doorman what the audience was like. "Tough," he said, looking Hope over. "The toughest in New York."

"Tougher than the Palace?" Hope asked.

"Who ever told you the Palace is tough? Critical is the word. That's an audience of 'pros,' and if you're good enough to be booked there, the audience knows that, respects that, and they're on your side. Here is different. Here they dare you to be good. This is a show house—but I don't have to tell you that. Who are you showing for—Keith's?"

Hope nodded. Not normally given to jitters or nerves, he was suddenly terrified. He went outside into the alley and walked back and forth. He walked over to Madison and then around the block, twice. Back in the theater he stood in the wings watching the other acts, chewing his prop cigar. Louise stood a few feet away watching him, leaving him alone, aware that this showing for Hope was his passage to the Palace.

Leatrice Joy went onstage to big applause. Hope was aware that current newspapers were carrying stories and items about her stormy marriage to John Gilbert. He had never forgotten how that audience in South Bend had reacted because they thought he had linked up with the morning headlines. What if—but by the time he was fingering that thought, Leatrice Joy was making her exit. She took her bow and the music changed to an uptempo entrance for Hope. He tilted his derby, wobbled his cigar and strode out to the center of the stage. After the music faded and the audience settled a bit, Hope looked out into the faces and picked out one a few rows back on the isle. "No, lady, this is *not* John Gilbert." It turned out to be the right thing to say. The audience roared.

For the next seventeen minutes he used every good gag he knew, including a few modified Frank Tinney bits that were surefire. He could hear and feel the audience warmth. Just before Louise made her entrance he did the "wristwatch thing" and after Louise he wound up with a song and dance-off. The gags had been fresh enough; his timing impeccable. The audience was asking for more.

For my exit I did two bows; then dropped my left hand as a signal to the electricians and the orchestra leader. I'd arranged that sig-

nal in advance. It meant that the orchestra would stop playing my
bow music while the audience was still at its peak, and the spotlight would go black, leaving the audience with nothing. It worked
out the way I hoped it would. They couldn't switch off their
applause that quickly, so they kept on clamoring. I stood there in
the wings for a full forty seconds and let them applaud.[17]

When the stage manager nervously prodded him to take his final bow, Hope
said, "Relax, brother. I'm the one who's showing." He waited a few more
seconds and then signaled for the spot. He strutted back out to stand in the
light, did an encore dance and walked off.

Lee Stewart wasted no time getting backstage to congratulate him. "I
knew you had it. How about that audience?"

"How about the way I bombed at the Dyker?" Hope mocked, remembering Stewart's fear expressed the night before on the IRT.

"That's no theater," Lee said, smirking.

A few minutes later Johnny Hyde came in and told Hope how much he
liked the act and asked if Hope could accompany him downtown to the
William Morris office after the next show.

Hope refused, insisting the interval was too short between shows.

"How about after the last show tonight?" Hyde asked.

"At *midnight* you'll be there?" Hope asked incredulously.

"We'll be there. We're in the Bond Building," he prompted.

"I know," said Hope.

But after the second show Stewart was prepared to offer Hope a Keith
contract for the Orpheum Circuit—big time—at $400 a week. Hope turned
away from Stewart and said, "Not enough." Lee said Keith wouldn't go
above $450 and Hope said, "Fine." He signed for three years with the vision
of the Palace stamped on his eyeballs.

VAUDEVILLE AND BROADWAY

1929–1937

*I sat there waiting for me to appear on the screen and leave
me speechless with my talent. Then the screening began. I'd
never seen anything so awful. I looked like a cross between a
mongoose and a turtle.*[1]

6. Hollywood, Who Needs It?

The panic that swept through financial offices the morning of October 24,
1929, was only the herald of a terrible wipeout. It was several days before
Sime Silverman would be able to crack his sardonic WALL STREET LAYS AN
EGG, and weeks before the bewildering truth registered generally.

Brokers and investors were said to be jumping from upper Wall Street
windows, but along Broadway B.F. Keith agents were so busy worrying
about what was threatening their 300 vaudeville theaters, they hardly
noticed. They were faced with a panic of newness. It was not only the sudden
success of Warner Brothers talking pictures, but the creeping delirium of
radio and all that free entertainment. The Keith task was to convince the
American public that entertainment was a stage full of girls, comics and
acrobats; that vaudeville was an American institution too essential to fade.

Certainly Bob Hope believed vaudeville was healthy, especially now that
he had become an exclusive Keith property. It was something like being
stamped USDA Choice. Because of this new status he had to bring something special to his premier Orpheum tour across some legendary stages: the
old Palace in Chicago, the Orpheum in St. Paul, his hometown Cleveland
Palace. The tour would take him and Louise north to Winnipeg and Calgary,
west to Vancouver and down the Coast to Seattle, Portland, San Francisco,
Los Angeles and San Diego, then back to New York by way of Salt Lake
City, Denver, Omaha, Kansas City and St. Louis.

Hope was concerned about the quality of his material, and he felt the need
for professional help. He had heard about a gag writer named Al Boasberg
who turned out some funny lines for Benny and Cantor and the popular
"Lamb Chops" routine for Burns and Allen. Hope said later, "Al was a great
joke mechanic. He had a fabulous memory for classic jokes; he could fix
jokes, he could switch them around, he could improvise."[2] Hope cultivated a
friendship with Boasberg. They would meet at a restaurant and sit until
closing, constructing a few gags or a routine. Boasberg was especially clever
with "Dumb Dora" situations, and Bob encouraged this because he instinctively felt that Louise would be important to the tour. Boasberg would invent
this kind of exchange:

LOUISE: I passed your house last night.
BOB: You did? And you didn't come in?
LOUISE: There was too much noise. Bob, what *was* all that
         noise at your house last night?
BOB: Oh, that was my father. He was dragging my pants
         around.

LOUISE: A lot of noise for a pair of pants.

BOB: I know, but I was in them. (*Pause for laugh*) But Lou—you look great!

LOUISE: You look pretty great yourself, Bob.

BOB: Yes, I come from a pretty strong and brave family. Did you know that my brother once slapped a gangster in the face?

LOUISE: Your brother slapped a gangster in the face?

BOB: That's right.

LOUISE: I'd like to shake his hand.

BOB: We're not going to dig him up just for that.[3]

For his first appearance under the new contract, Hope was booked into the Brooklyn Albee. The feel of that first weekly $450 paycheck was delicious. He immediately set aside $50 for Mahm, and he was coerced into raising Louise's salary to $100. But he still had $300.

After the Albee engagement, Hope moved to Proctor's 86th Street. On November 5, 1929, *Variety* noted:

> Hope, assisted by an unbilled girl appearing only in the middle of the act for a gag cross-fire, has an act satisfactory for time it is playing. If some material, especially where old gags are found, could be changed, chances are this would double strength of turn. . . . Strongest is interlude in which Hope feeds for unbilled girl, latter of the sap type and clever at handling comedy lines . . . Next to closing here, and had no trouble.

Louise's hat size seemed to increase as she realized her value to the act. In fact, she threatened to quit if Bob didn't give her her own spot in the show.

Hope bristled at the blackmail and immediately wired Mildred Rosequist to join him for his Orpheum tour set to begin the following week in Cleveland. Hope went a step further. He asked Mildred to marry him.

Mildred wired back that she was engaged to marry someone else and she was sorry.[4] Hope crumpled up the telegram and decided to make up with Louise who was just waiting for him to ask.

Showing in Cleveland would obviously be a special event for a lot of Hopes. For Bob himself it was more than local boy making good. It was coming home for the first time since he had heard from Jim that Mahm might have to have treatments for a tumor that could be cancer of the cervix. Mahm would not let a doctor examine her. She would not discuss it. Mahm was thrilled to think of her son standing on a stage built on a sandlot corner where her kids had played in 1910.

The more she thought about it, the more apprehensive she became about his appearance. Harry couldn't go to the opening because he was in one of his completely sober periods and was doing the ornamental stonework on a courthouse out of town. Mahm thought it out carefully and decided she would not add to Les's nervousness by his having *her* out front being nervous too.

That first matinee Bob searched the audience for Avis. He didn't believe

he wouldn't come. He had brought her a hat from New York with lilies of
the valley on the brim and he would have spotted her at once. The family was
well represented. But no Mahm.

The next day, after the *Cleveland Press* raved about the performance,
Avis told Jim she would go with him to the matinee. They arrived during
Harry Webb's zany comedy orchestra act. Jim Hope described what hap-
pened:

> From the moment she took her seat, she trembled from head to
> toe. Tears ran down her cheeks and her fingernails were cutting
> my hand. I was afraid she would faint.
>
> And when Les made his appearance, her entire body stiffened.
> When she heard the reception by the audience, acknowledging
> him as a neighborhood boy, she relaxed. She listened to every
> syllable, nodding her head as though approving every word.
>
> Toward the end of the act, I handed her my handkerchief think-
> ing she'd use it to wipe the other hand. Instead she patted her
> forehead. Whether it was the fluttering of the handkerchief that
> caught Les's eye or what, but just as he was taking his last bow,
> he spotted us and proudly he said, "There she is, folks! That's
> Mahm! The one with the lillies of the valley on her hat. There she
> is. Way back there. Stand up and let these folks see you,
> Mahm!"
>
> She didn't really need to. The expression on her face was
> enough.[5]

The party later that night at 2029 Euclid was festive. There was in the air
a decidedly new note of respect for brother Les. They all agreed he had
arrived. And they got to meet Louise, but there were nine different opinions
of her.

The older brothers impressed Bob with their business skills—Ivor doing
well in metal products, Fred doing even better in provisions, and Jim cock of
the road as a traveling supervisor for the power company. Talk inevitably
entered on the market's crash of a few weeks before, and the unbelievable
awareness that billions of dollars of corporate profits, both on and off paper,
had vanished.

Bob listened to their talk, feeling instinctively that the vaudeville theaters
and movie houses would not go dark, and that he, strange as it sounded,
might have to bail everybody out. As he looked around the house, at the
familiar and shabby furniture and surroundings, as he looked at Mahm and
Harry, he became convinced that during the remainder of his stay in Cleve-
and he and his brothers should put their parents in a new home.

Real estate values were dropping all over the city, including exclusive
Cleveland Heights, and this is where Bob decided to look. After a day or two
he found a house at 3323 Yorkshire Road but kept the fact from his parents.
Then just before he left town he announced to Avis that he was throwing out
all her old furniture.

"Why ever for?" she said defensively. "It's old, but it's seen us through.
We don't need new furniture."

"It goes—and so do you."

"You're talking nonsense, Les."

"Seriously, Mahm." Bob picked Avis up off the floor and whirled her around. "Let's take a ride, Fred."

Bob carried her outside and put her down in the passenger side of the front seat and got in the back. Fred got behind the wheel and they drove toward Cleveland Heights. Fred stopped the car. Bob got out and opened the door for Avis. They walked her to the door and told her she was home. She cried. She told them they were crazy. She cried some more but she moved. And the only old things her sons allowed her to take to the new house were her beloved sewing machine and her piano.[6]

Bob and Louise went on to Chicago to play the Palace. Boasberg had wired Hope some material, including a new routine for the Louise spot. She was to stroll out and say:

LOUISE: My mother just got one of those new washing machines.

BOB: She did? Well—how does it work?

LOUISE: Not so good. Every time she gets into it she's black and blue all over.[7]

The gag scored a fair laugh, and a few seconds later they were finishing their exchange when Hope altered the final joke:

BOB: My brother slapped Al Capone once.

LOUISE: (*Really surprised*) He did? Why, he's the bravest man I ever heard of. I'd like to shake his hand.

BOB: We're not going to dig him up just for that.[8]

The joke got a huge laugh. After the show, Frank Smith, the Palace manager, told Hope that the Capone joke was in doubtful, perhaps dangerous taste. He went further. "You ought to drop it."

"I can't, Frank," said Hope, "not with that size laugh."

"Laugh or no laugh, if you're smart you'll dump it. The boys from Cicero, sometimes even Big Al, come down here on Saturday nights. I wouldn't care to be you if they don't like it."

"I'm going to keep it in," said Hope, and he did. On Sunday morning his telephone at the Bismarck rang. The caller asked for Ben Hoke.

"Who's this?"

"Never mind who. You the comedian doing the Al Capone joke?"

"Who are you?"

"Do yourself a favor. Take the joke out of your act. We'll be around to show our appreciation."

The call persuaded Hope to drop the gag from the remaining Chicago performances. He fully expected to encounter some sinister characters whenever he and Louise emerged to walk along the dark stage alley, but no one ever showed up.[9]

After playing some smaller houses in Illinois and Michigan, they moved on to the Twin Cities for a split week at the St. Paul Orpheum, and then on to the Orpheum in Winnipeg. Up to this point they had been traveling in winter wind and snow but by the time they reached Calgary, the weather was springlike. Hope was restless for some physical activity, and he began talking bout learning to play golf. Actually it was a matter of renewed interest. In *Golf Digest* of January 1979 Hope was quoted:

> I had tried to play in Cleveland during the early 1920's but I just had no feel for the game. I had never taken lessons and I was terrible.
>
> But during the spring of 1930 on the Orpheum circuit, I'd be waiting around the hotel lobby in late morning when the Diamond Brothers, another act, would come down with their golf clubs. They played every day. One day, I said, "Well, hell—I'll go out there with you." I hit a bag of practice balls and played a few holes. It was fun.

Before that 1930 tour was over, Hope had played a number of full rounds and started a lifetime love affair.

Vancouver was next and then Seattle. Hope was receiving regular communications from Al Boasberg, wires, letters or phone calls with gag ideas. During one of the Portland calls, Boasberg offered to set up a screen test for Hope in Hollywood. One of Al's friends, Bill Perlberg, was a successful agent and had some strong studio contacts. Hope liked the idea.

After their week in San Francisco, Bob and Louise hit Los Angeles and checked into the Hollywood Hotel. Perlberg called Hope at the hotel, and Hope played coy.

"My friend Al Boasberg thinks you're worth taking a look at for pictures," said Perlberg. "He says you've got style."

"Boasberg drinks," said Hope expecting a laugh. No laugh.

"How would you like to make a test?"

"Well, I think I can squeeze it in before we go to San Diego."

"Thursday you get yourself out to the Pathé lot in Culver City."

"What will I be doing? I mean, isn't there a script?"

"You'll do your regular act," Perlberg said. "I hear you have a dame with you. Bring her along."

"How big an audience?" asked Hope.

"No audience."

On Thursday morning Bob and Louise took a cab out to Culver City. When the technicians were ready to roll, Hope launched into his act and a few people on the set—stagehands and assorted bystanders—laughed loudly here and there. The act didn't work quite the same without a real audience, yet Hope felt cocky about the test. He said: "I was so sure I clicked that even though I dropped a bundle in a gambling joint in Agua Caliente that first weekend in San Diego, I was oblivious—I could see movie offers pouring in."

Hope left his whereabouts in San Diego with Perlberg's office and all week he fully expected a telephone call. But none came. Puzzled and offended he called Perlberg on Monday morning when they got back to Los Angeles.

"How about the test?" Hope asked.

"Yeah?" said Perlberg.

"Well—when do I see it?"

"You want to?"

"Sure I do."

"Pathé will be happy to show it to you."

"Okay. How do *you* like it?"

"Go and see it," replied Perlberg.

Hope went out to Culver City alone. He was told to go to Projection Room 3–H but no one offered to take him. He sat in the darkened cubicle alone. He later said:

> I thought it was strange that nobody else was there until I looked around and saw that even the projectionists were wearing gas masks. My nose hit the screen ten minutes before the rest of me. I always knew my body had angles but didn't realize how much they stuck out. It was awful. I felt I was watching a stranger I didn't want to know. Of course there was no audience and no laughter, but even so I couldn't believe how bad I was. When the lights came up I wanted to get out fast.[10]

Hope was hurt by the rejection, so he immediately adopted the attitude that he was too good for Hollywood. Louise agreed with him. And as they made their way to Salt Lake City, and to Denver, and Omaha, Kansas City and St. Louis, it was the New York Palace and only the Palace that pulled them like a magnet. "Who needs Hollywood, anyway?" They actually convinced themselves they had just had a very close call.

I was eating in the restaurant next door and when I got up to the cashier I discovered I didn't have any money. So I told her, "I left my money in my dressing room and I'll pay you next time I come in." She says, "That's all right, we'll just write your name on the wall until you come in again." I say, "Wait a minute, I don't want my name on the wall where everyone can see it." She says, "Don't worry, your coat will be hanging over it."[1]

7. Heaven on 47th Street

Hope's inaugural Orpheum tour ended in 1930 and Lee Stewart applauded the results. Despite the worsening economy, box office receipts stayed healthy for vaudeville. Stewart assured Hope that he should be going out on a second tour in a couple of months. In the meantime Hope decided to drop off in Cleveland to see Mahm, while Louise went to Chicago to see her dad.

Actually there was more to the Cleveland visit. Bob had received a letter from Avis while on the road. It was about George, her last and, in many ways, the son she fretted over. Since his graduation from high school he had flitted restlessly from job to job. He had shown signs in school of being interested in "theatrical things," wrote Avis. She thought maybe Les could talk to him, help him.

"Can't he help you somehow, Les?" asked Avis. "Maybe he could watch and listen and learn for a time. It would do him good to get away from here."

"Let's see you dance, George," Bob said. "Go ahead, Mahm—play a little 'Tea For Two.' George—try a soft shoe."

"I can't, Les. Not well enough. I've tried. But I'll get it—I really will. I promise. I'll do anything you ask me to do. I want to go with you."

"Okay." Bob noticed Avis was smiling. "Okay. I've been thinking of putting together my own little unit. I've got a lot of ideas for doing some crazy—some very different kinds of things. I could use you as a stooge."

"A what?" George asked.

"I'll put you in the audience. When I'm up there doing my monologue, or whatever's going on, you'll start heckling me. I've been thinking of asking Toots Murdock—a pal from Toledo—to do that also. The two of you arguing and making smartass comments from the audience would be all part of the act."

George was barely twenty, but he was eager and Bob was willing to take a chance with him. Besides, he could save a little money on George, in view of the payroll he was contemplating. He envisioned having his own touring company.

During those notorious Wednesday afternoon executive sessions in the conference room of the Palace Theater Building on Broadway, Lee Stewart kept pushing his favorite client. Those were tough meetings, attended by two dozen Keith managers and bookers, meetings that determined the fate of the country's vaudeville performers. So powerful was Keith's control of the business that two words from the mouth of one of these managers—"no interest"—could ruin a career. Hope wanted a chance to qualify for the New York Palace, and Stewart was persistent on his behalf, working him as much as possible in the New York area.

At the Coliseum, a prestigious Manhattan showcase, Hope found himself sharing the bill with the most talked-about picture of the year, the Academy Award-winning *All Quiet on the Western Front*. An uncompromising anti-war film, it was directed by Lewis Milestone and starred Lew Ayres as a sensitive young German soldier who generates exceptional audience sympathy throughout the film. In a powerful closing scene, Ayres is killed by a single sniper bullet while reaching for a butterfly that has landed on a barbed-wire fence. As comedy emcee for a split-week engagement, Hope was to bounce on stage immediately following the film. Pit orchestra leader Sid Fabello arranged a special musical bridge between movie fadeout and the vaudeville portions.

At the first matinee, when the screen rumbled upward, the spotlight caught Hope stage left, hat moving, eyes sparkling, firing off his first line of paradiddle; he was as welcome as plague. Wet eyes had not yet dried and some people walked slowly toward the lobby. Later Hope would reflect:

> I should have known it couldn't possibly work. The audience was still in shock. The mistake was putting a film like that with vaudeville. And if I had been smart I would have leveled with the audience—you know—go out there and lay it on the line. I would have said, "Hey, my part of the show has to go on sometime. They

say I'm funny—at least that's what they're paying me for." But what I *did* was get mad![2]

Hope came offstage and indulged in one of his infrequent tantrums. He demanded to know how the management expected him to get laughs after such a dramatic film. Somehow he managed to endure three more agonizing days, sighing with relief when he was able to move over to Proctor's 58th Street for the second half of the split. Proctor's 58th was known for taking vaudeville seriously and would never fall into the same trap as the Coliseum. But when Hope looked at the newspaper Wednesday morning he saw *All Quiet on the Western Front* playing at Proctor's 58th Street also.

He picked up the phone and dialed the Keith office. Lee Stewart was sympathetic to a point.

"Fun's fun," said Hope, "but this is ridiculous. I quit."

"What about the contract?"

"The hell with it!"

"Bob?"

"What?"

"Do it!"

Hope did it. He knew he had to comply because Keith held the keys to the dressing room doors at the Palace. And needing to play the Palace was eating Hope alive, despite the inescapable knowledge that this consummate showcase of vaudeville was losing its luster.

Two years earlier, Silverman had moved the vaudeville section further back in *Variety* to expand the motion picture news and advertising. In 1929 *Variety* announced solemnly that "the fate of vaudeville as a business" would certainly be decided that year, or the next. In panic the New York Palace changed its policy of two-a-day in favor of the poisonous five-a-day, and despite that change the theater was losing an average of $4,000 a week.

Yet Bob Hope still viewed the Palace as the mark of achievement, and he trusted Lee's promise of a showing there soon.

Meanwhile, Stewart set him up once more for the Orpheum Circuit in the fall of 1930. But Hope would not go out without a new concept. His obsession was to build an act strong enough to match the talkies. He and Boasberg constructed a kind of mini-revue that would allow Hope to work in one as well as work with Louise. He also could do bits with stooges; there would be a fairly substantial afterpiece. Boasberg called the whole thing *Antics of 1930* and it had a flavor of what Olsen and Johnson did in *Hellzapoppin* some years later.

They incorporated ideas Bob had been waiting to try, like using George and Toots as audience hecklers. Hope and Boasberg primed and pruned *Antics* right up to the day Boasberg left for Hollywood to work for Eddie Cantor and also write a movie script. And as the Orpheum tour began *Antics* had a certain freshness. It opened with an actor named Johnny Peters who looked amazingly like Rudy Vallee, seated alone onstage playing a saxophone. Hope walked out and introduced Peters who stood up and began singing "My time is your time" into a megaphone. Hope picked up a baton and started conducting Peters. Then from one of the side boxes of the theater:

TOOTS: Pssssst! George! How do you like it?

GEORGE: Sounds just as bad over here.

HOPE: Now, just a minute! Don't you know you can be arrested for annoying an audience?

TOOTS AND GEORGE: You ought to know!

After more heckling from the stooges, Hope would go into his monologue which might include his recently acquired hotel routine:

> . . . it's very exciting at my hotel . . . the other day a lady guest came down to the lobby and demanded to see the manager. She said, "This is terrible—there's a bat in my room" . . . and the desk clerk said, "Now, don't get excited, lady, we'll send up a ball." . . . and another guest walked into the lobby and said, "Is there a Katz registered here?" . . . and the clerk said, "No, there's no Katz here," and the guest said, "Well, if one comes in send him up, the mice are eating my shoes." . . .[4]

Following the monologue Hope would introduce other acts and eventually Louise would wander out on stage and they would engage in several routines including this new one by Boasberg:

BOB: What are you crying for?

LOUISE: Mother just threw father out of the house.

BOB: What for?

LOUISE: Something about saying Grace.

BOB: Ah—you mean saying Grace before meals?

LOUISE: No, saying Grace in his sleep. My mother's name is Mary.[5]

Some of Hope's material for *Antics* was in clear violation of vaudeville's classic taboos. Although Keith's hard-line policies had liberalized regarding the use of blatant political allusion and sex, there were still certain theater managers who were old-fashioned. Hope's material was borderline and his swiftest material combined both politics and bathroom humor:

> . . . isn't this some theater! . . . I was just standing out in front watching the other acts when a lady rushed up to me and said, "Pardon me, young man, can you help me find the rest room?" . . . and I said, "Yes m'am, it's just around the corner" . . . and she said, "Don't give me any of that Hoover talk."[6]

As President Hoover's attempts to reassure Americans that business and industry would recover became futile, and his oftquoted "Prosperity is just around the corner" more and more a national joke, that particular gag became increasingly successful for Hope.

During the late winter of 1931, with the Depression haunting towns and cities that could hardly believe their own bread lines and soup kitchens, Hope and his *Antics* company were luckier than many of their jobless colleagues. Unemployment had more than doubled from 1930 figures. Some 28,000 businesses had closed and 2,300 banks had failed. The corporations that survived announced 10 percent wage reductions, and some would go higher.

Logically, radio was the popular entertainment because it was so accessible. Movie houses enticed patrons with cheap seats, bank nights, free dishes, food baskets and double bills. Luckily for Hope, Keith bookings were dependable. *Antics* in 1931 went all the way to Vancouver, Oakland and Los Angeles, then came back to the East Coast by way of St. Louis, Chicago, Milwaukee, Grand Rapids, Decatur, Detroit and Cleveland—this time the Cleveland Palace. It was a raw, cold mid-February.

Bob was always happy to see Mahm, though this time she seemed smaller and thinner and more fragile than he had ever remembered. But she and Harry seemed settled in their new "mansion."

Bob did not see Mildred this time but brother George did. George stubbornly clung to a childhood hope that his older brother would one day realize his love for Mildred. George confided in Mildred how much he hated Louise. He said Louise went around acting as if she was already Mrs. Bob Hope. But Mildred really couldn't help George with that problem.

The Cleveland engagement had further significance. Tuesday afternoon Hope's dressing room door opened, and in walked Lee Stewart. Hope was dressing. He looked up.

"Bob, have I got a—"

"*Palace!*" Hope yelped, jumping up and turning to grab Stewart.

"You got it!"

"When?" Hope's eyes glistened.

"Monday," Lee said, thinking that this was probably the most emotional he had ever seen Hope. Reflecting on that time, Stewart told *Silver Screen* for their March 1942 issue:

> . . . he almost kissed me. I never saw such a happy and excited guy in my life. And it's natural. Every actor looked forward to the time when he would play the New York Palace. And thousands of them went through their whole careers dreaming of that and never realizing it. It gave nine out of ten players the heebee-jeebies. I've seen old timers nervous at the thought. And Bob—he was excited, enthused, nervous—and plain scared. Before the close of his Cleveland week he was on the edge of a nervous breakdown. Yet in spite of his nervousness his brain was clicking. He knew he was going into fast company—that he was following the best in the business.

Between shows Hope agonized. "I gotta get a gag," Hope said, looking at himself in the mirror.

"What do you mean?" Lee asked.

"I've got to have something special to carry me. I've got to find something good."

Toward the end of the week in Cleveland, after Lee had returned to New York, Hope turned to Louise and said, "Listen to this. I'll get Milt Lewis to find me five or six guys to carry signs in front of the Palace—yeah—they'll carry signs that say I'm unfair to my stooges. That ought to get attention."

This would be, of course, in addition to a large cut-out sign that he had agreed to underwrite for the Palace outer lobby with the banner: BOB HOPE, THE COMIC FIND OF THE WEST.

As Hope predicted, the stunt attracted crowds on Monday morning.[7] Six sandwich-sign men walked back and forth advertising: BOB HOPE IS UNFAIR TO STOOGES, LOCAL 711 and BOB HOPE IS UNFAIR TO DISORGANIZED STOOGES and still another, REFUSES TO PAY FOR THEIR LUMPS, BUMPS, DOCTORS AND HOSPITAL BILLS. The gag was working just as Hope wished, but not as Palace manager Elmer Rogers wished.

"For God's sake, Hope, get those sandwich men out of there! The crowd is taking that picketing gag seriously and won't come inside."

Fortunately, Palace advertising and publicity man Arnold Van Leer loved what he saw. Bob Hope was clearly *his* kind of entertainer, someone who understood publicity and promotion. Van Leer got on the telephone to all of the New York media to make sure they appreciated Hope's gag. Most of the newspapers printed something about the gag and it fanned business.

Bea Lillie was the headliner and Hope was billed in second spot.[8] Also on the bill was Vivienne Segal, fresh from Hollywood, Harry Hershfield, the humorist and decidedly offbeat vaudevillian, as well as Noble Sissle and Harry Delmar's Revue. It was actually a second, holdover week for Lillie and consequently the critics didn't pay much attention to the new acts that joined the lineup. There were a few lukewarm phrases but it was Jerry Wald's review in the *Graphic* that sizzled Hope. Wald wrote: "They say that Bob Hope is the sensation of the Midwest. If that's so, why doesn't he go back there."

Hope was bitterly disappointed. Hershfield, however, recognized Hope's talent and sympathetically tried to bolster his wounded feelings. It helped, but Hope was still anxious, especially about the big Sunday night show.

Sunday nights were Celebrity Nights at the Palace. They helped to draw customers to average bills, and sell-out social events when the headliner was someone like Sophie Tucker or Eddie Cantor.

Rogers had asked Hope to emcee the Sunday show and the prospect made him jittery. He would be expected to introduce celebrities in the audience (if there were any) and hope they would agree to come up on stage and entertain. Al Jolson, it is said, made his only Palace appearance as a Sunday night celebrity guest.

That night Hope was doing a rather poor job and he knew it. But luckily Ted Healy—who, after seeing Hope on the Albee stage one time, said, "Brother, you've got it"—was seated in the first row. Seated a few rows behind Healy was Ken Murray. Hope felt those two might save the night.

Hope introduced Murray first. Murray stood up in place and waved his arms to audience applause. Then he sat down while the audience continued applauding. Hope watched and waited. Then Murray stood up and made his way to the aisle and then down to the orchestra pit, climbed down inside and then using a trombonist's knee and shoulder, climbed up onto the stage. There was continued laughter and applause.

Murray bowed to the audience and said, "I'm going to tell a joke!" At that moment Ted Healy stood up in the front row and hollered, "I've heard it!" The audience howled, and as more and more people recognized Healy the applause grew. Whatever awkwardness had existed was disappearing and the three comedians bantered through a lively exchange.[9]

Theater histories could hardly record that Hope's arrival at the Palace was notable. His debut occurred at a time when the theater's management was struggling to maintain its preeminence as the nation's premier vaudeville showcase. Later that same year, with the record-breaking nine-week marathon run of Cantor and Jessel, and still later with the return of Sophie Tucker, the Palace shone as brightly as ever. But, sadly, it was in its last great years.

It all seemed so strange, talking into a microphone in a studio instead of playing in front of a real audience. I was nervous on those first radio shows and the Vallee engineers couldn't figure why they heard a thumping noise when I did my routines until they found out I was kicking the mike after each joke.[1]

8. Benefits, Benchmarks and Ballyhoo

In 1932, a year that William Manchester has called "The Cruelest Year" of the Great Depression, 15 million men and women were out hunting for jobs that didn't exist. Those white- and blue-collar workers who were lucky enough to get a paycheck took home only about $50 a week, or $75 every two weeks, and considered themselves fortunate.

Bob Hope had just played the Palace, and because of that distinction he could be merchandised more effectively on the RKO circuits. He was not only regularly employed, but for a full week of work he took home close to $1,000. But this did not make him complacent. There is consensus among those who knew Hope at this period that after the Palace he was striving for refinement of style. Some saw in him a new "drive," some saw a new "sense of professionalism," and others a desire "to be the best." This review in the *Chicago Sun* on September 4, 1931 suggests an emerging stage presence:

Equipped with the sort of engaging personality that will put over any material, Hope has the practiced trouper's idea of timing his humorous sallies, emphasizing them with mugging and pauses so that they never miss.

It was also clear to those around him that if anything might come close to defeating him it would be poor material. Hope had been fortunate in his association with Al Boasberg, but Boasberg had now moved permanently to the West Coast to write for Cantor. However, in 1931 Hope met Richy Craig, Jr., a young vaudevillian who had, Bob and many others thought, "an original turn of wit."

Variety's review of Hope's act on March 5, 1932, undoubtedly reflected Hope's growth and his association with Craig:

> Just a so-so lineup on tap here this week, with Bob Hope playing the role of lifesaver. It took this funster to finally wake them up to a degree. After he got under way he had them howling at his comedic actions and great comedy material. . . . Hope is a pippin performer and his ad-libbing helps tremendously to get many extra laughs from his supporting company and the musicians in the pit, as well as the audience.

Hope's ability to make a scripted piece of comedy seem spontaneous was invaluable and, with his "go to hell" kind of emceeing, was chiefly responsible for putting him into his first significant Broadway assignment.

Lew Gensler had seen Hope at the Palace and liked him but wanted a second opinion to cinch his idea that this newcomer would be right for a revue called *Ballyhoo of 1932* that he and Norman Anthony were producing. The musical would be virtually an "in the flesh" version of a six-months-old popular magazine of slightly risqué, barbed humor called *Ballyhoo* and edited by Anthony.

Hope liked the idea, and Keith was delighted to give Hope leave from his three-year contract because his marquee value would increase with a stage success.

He joined an impressive cast that included Willie and Eugene Howard, Jeanne Aubert, Lulu McConnell, Vera Marsh, and Paul and Grace Hartman. The sketches, directed by the producers, were irreverent spoofs of Greta Garbo's mannerisms, of Columbus Circle revolutionaries (Hope was in this one singing "Rewolt! Rewolt!"), nudists, Southern evangelists, and the evening's high point came when the Howards were joined by two buxom female singers for a burlesque version of the *Rigoletto* Quartet.

Hope enjoyed the summer rehearsals because his pal Richy was featured in a Broadway revue called *Hey Nonny Nonny* which he had helped create along with E.B. White and Ogden Nash. The revue closed early, which saddened Richy. But worse news followed. Richy was told he had an advanced condition of tuberculosis. Hope was devastated; the memory of Lloyd Durbin's death had always stayed with him. Despondent but feigning high spirits, Hope put Richy on a train for Saranac in July. He wished Godspeed and a quick recovery.

Ballyhoo was a shambles when it opened at the Nixon Theater on the Atlantic City pier. Recalled Lee Stewart, "There were so many scenes that the lights became fouled up—actually it was rather frightening. There was a blazing short circuit and the theater went dark. The management feared the audience was ready to panic and rush the doors." Lee Shubert, one of the backers, was standing backstage and asked if someone would go out front and calm the audience.

"I will," said Hope, his hands shaking. "At least, I'll try. How long before the lights—"

"Go!" said Shubert.

Hope stepped out into an almost pitch-black theater and started his vaudeville act. Part of the audience thought this was the way *Ballyhoo* was supposed to open and the rest settled back, reassured by Hope's gags. As soon as he heard laughter he relaxed and kept working until the lights went on in the pit.[2]

The same kind of scene was repeated two weeks later when the show moved to Newark. But on this night the delay in the curtain was caused by confusion over eleventh-hour changes and a new opening dance number by Bobby Connelly. Shubert again ordered Hope to go out and pacify the audience. Hope protested that what worked in Atlantic City to quiet a frightened audience wasn't going to work for a savvy show-business crowd, but Shubert insisted.

Hope glared at him and then strolled out as nonchalantly as he could, saying, "Ladies and gentlemen, this is the first time I've ever been on before the acrobats." Laughter. He was right—this crowd knew all about vaudeville.

". . . but we're doing a new number for you tonight, and we had a little late rehearsal, and things aren't quite set up back there yet—and—this is a new show—and—hello, Sam!" Hope looked up toward the balcony, shaded his eyes to see better, then looked back at the audience, "That's one of our backers up there." Laughter. "He says he's not nervous, but I notice that he's buckled his safety belt."

By then the audience was with him. Hope continued until he got the signal to get off. Backstage, Shubert, Gensler, Anthony and Patterson congratulated him, and somebody said, "God, we ought to leave that bit in the show. It's a different way to open."

Hope chalked that up to gratitude, but the next day he was approached by Gensler. Hope replied, "I like it, Lew—but to repeat what happened last night is a phony premise. Let me find something like that but more honest and more flexible. I'll tell ya—I'll open up a complaint department."

And that night, just before curtain time, Hope slipped into one of the side boxes (they were always slow sellers) and instead of a spotlight on the conductor for the overture, the spot focused on Hope.

"Good evening, ladies and gentlemen. Tonight we're introducing something rather novel. It's called the Complaint Department. That's me." Laughter.

"No, that's right. If there's anything about our show you don't like just come to me. Maybe you've got some funny ideas of your own. We can use 'em."

Hope continued in that vein for a while longer. "Well, the management just wanted you to know how much it cares about your opinions. Now, for the show! Okay, Mr. Conductor, the overture! Max? That's Max Meth, folks, our conductor!" The conductor didn't move. Hope clapped his hands together twice. Nothing.

From the orchestra pit came sounds of snoring. "Hey, fellas, wake up! Let's go! Time to make music! Boys??? Fellas???" More snores.

Hope took out a pistol and shot it in the air. The snores became louder.

Hope turned and lifted a small cash register from below, set it on the box railing, pushed a lever and made the bell ring. The orchestra men jumped to their positions, Max raised his baton and the overture began. Hope picked up his cash register, bowed and vanished. The audience was with him all the way.

Critics were more enthusiastic about the Gensler–Harburg songs than they were about the Anthony sketches or the antics of the Howards or Hope. During *Ballyhoo*'s 16-week run, however, there were some interesting portents of things to come in Hope's career. For example, Willie Howard, Lulu McConnell and Hope were asked to take part in one of the experimental television galas on CBS station W2XAB, which had gone on the air locally in 1931. The three of them worked in front of a single camera, totally bleached out by a barrage of mega-strength light. The signals transmitted were fuzzy, flickering images, hard to distinguish. When Howard and Hope left the studio in the early afternoon Willie said, "Television's a turkey." And Hope agreed.

Another novelty for Hope during the *Ballyhoo* run was radio. Besides a brief appearance on Keith's *R.K.O. Theater*, Hope made several appearances on Rudy Vallee's Fleischmann show, an extraordinarily popular hour that had about 24 million people listening, the third highest rating in radio. Vallee varied his programming from low comedy to serious dramatic sketches, and his guests ranged from Olsen and Johnson to John Barrymore. It was an important showcase for any performer, and despite the fact that Vallee's show did not have a live studio audience, Hope's fairly sophisticated comedy spots there helped to build his reputation as a versatile professional. Hope says, "It all seemed so strange, talking into a microphone in a studio instead of playing in front of a real audience. I was nervous on those first radio shows and the Vallee engineers couldn't figure why they heard a thumping noise when I did my routines until they found out I was kicking the mike after each joke."[3]

One of Hope's happiest times during the *Ballyhoo* run came when Richy Craig returned from Saranac. Richy looked healthier but he complained of being not quite recovered and he lacked his old confidence. He was apprehensive because he had been out of circulation for nearly five months. As it happened, Hope was scheduled to do a benefit in Poughkeepsie on Thanksgiving Eve and asked Richy to join him.

"We ought to have some special material," Richy said thoughtfully. "I've got some new stuff for myself that I worked up over the past few months. That's important because I understand Berle's been doing *me* since I've been gone."

Hope laughed.

"No, I'm serious, Bob."

"Miltie only steals bad gags, Richy. Your stuff doesn't suit him."

"You're probably right, but it gives me an idea for a bit we can do together. Let's do a parody on Berle's gag stealing." Hope liked the idea.

Hope opened the benefit, and after Vera Marsh sang, Richy came on. Hope, listening to his friend offstage, thought Richy was back in stride. Then he heard a heckler trying to ruin Richy's act. Hope worried that his pal's physical and mental rehabilitation might not withstand the attack. But without faltering, Richy said:

They took a fellow to the hospital in Poughkeepsie just last week . . . he had to have a brain operation. So they took out his brain and examined it . . . and while his brain was out, he got up off the operating table . . . and jumped out the window. But they found him . . . he was sitting in a theater heckling the actors . . . [4]

When he finished, to generous applause, Hope went back out and they worked their way around to the subject of Berle.

> He steals everybody's act,
> Comics say that that's a fact.
> What's to do about it?
> Let's put out the lights and murder Berle.[5]

It worked well with this audience, but then almost anything worked at benefits. Spirits were generally high, people were in a devil-may-care mood and knew that the entertainers were working free.

Hope did benefits for several reasons. They gave him the opportunity to try out new material and gave him valuable audience exposure; they sometimes were very well publicized and good for his image. Doing benefits also afforded him incomparable chances to meet and work with other name performers and to mingle with the affluent. Lastly, and important, too, Hope was generous with his time, and, at heart, he cared. And he knew Mahm would like it.

Tamara led into it by saying, "There's an old Russian proverb: When your heart's on fire smoke gets in your eyes." And I wanted to say, "We have a proverb in America, too: Love is like hash. You have to have confidence in it to enjoy it."[1]

9. *Gowns by Roberta*

Even before the *Ballyhoo of 1932* company could adjust to the chilling fact they would be closed down on November 30, Hope had booked himself into the Capitol Theater for two weeks beginning December 2. His name would be paired on the theater marquee with that of Bing Crosby, who was making his first personal appearance in New York since his splashy motion picture success in Paramount's *The Big Broadcast*.

The two men had met casually several weeks earlier near the Friars Club on Forty-eighth Street. Bob was in *Ballyhoo*, Bing had hit town to star in the Cremo radio program and neither of them had a notion they would be headlining a bill together in a few weeks.

From the start they liked each other. More significant, they watched each other work. As Bing watched Hope, he envisioned the possibility of some banter between them. So on Sunday, Bing came to the theater earlier than usual.

"How do you feel about working in a couple of jokes?"

"What kind?" asked Hope.

"Well—something along the 'Who was that lady?' line, I suppose. What do you think?"

"Why not let me come out and say 'Hey, Bing. Do you think we ought to do some of our impressions for this crowd?' And then you say, 'Do you think it's the right crowd?' And I say, 'I don't know. Maybe we should risk it.' That kind of thing. Then we'd do some of those really old solid routines—like the two farmers meeting on the street."

Crosby liked it. They worked out a routine of two businessmen meeting midstage and reaching into each other's pockets. Then they would walk back to their own side and come back as two orchestra leaders meeting on the street. When they met each pulled out a baton and conducted the other as they conversed. Then they would walk back to their own sides of the stage.

Hope recalled: "The gags weren't very funny, I guess, but the audience laughed because we were having such a good time—and I guess it was clear that we liked each other. We would laugh insanely at what we dreamed up."

Hope cannot recall whether "ski-nose" and "butter belly" were born during this engagement or not, but the camaraderie that later spawned such sobriquets *was* formed at the Capitol. Improvisations during their "impressions" on stage broke each other up and almost every show was a challenge. But, as Barry Ulanov has observed:

> They never did settle upon which was the straight man and which the comic. It's that moot point which has served so well for so many years as the base of the Hope-Crosby comedy—a suggestion of rivalry, an intimation of swords-point differences always successful as a pattern of comedy, particularly meaningful in the United States where feigned anger, vigorous physical attack, and vituperative verbal abuse so often veil attachments between friends, especially when the friends are men and don't want to be mistaken for anything else.[2]

During the Capitol engagement, Hope faced the news that his mother's cancer was incurable, that it was a question of time—months, a year perhaps. She was now mostly confined to her bedroom. Bob paid for a new telephone line installed by her bed so they could talk frequently. He also wrote her letters filled with anecdotes and cheerful news about his on and offstage activities, sometimes including a joke. Avis kept them all within reach for reading and rereading. Harry shuffled aimlessly around the rooms and grounds of their new Cleveland Heights house, somewhat lost and helpless.

Another problem was Louise. She had been a part of his stage act for five years, and for whatever she had contributed to his success he was grateful. She wanted more. She wanted to marry him. In fact, they had gone so far as to take out a marriage license in January 1932. But Louise was simply not in Hope's future plans.

His perennial professional problem, his hunger for new comedy material, sent him into a huddle with his pal, Richy Craig. One stinging line from the *Herald Tribune* review of his previous Capitol appearance still haunted him:

"Bob Hope . . . . acted as master of ceremonies using material that was not new but effective." To change that, he obviously needed jokes written exclusively for him, in the most up-to-date comedy tone.

Occasionally, Hope's judgment about material failed, as in the case of his routine based on a popular song titled "My Mom." Hope would say, "Ladies and gentlemen, I don't sing serious songs often but here's a song about a little lady I know is dear to all of us."

> My Mom, I love her,
> My Mom, you'd love her,
> Who wouldn't love her, my Mom.
> That sweet somebody,
> Thinks I'm somebody,
> I love her, I love her, my Mom.

Out from the wings toward center stage came a little old lady. She trudged up to the microphone and tugged on Hope's sleeve.

Hope would stop the orchestra. "How many times have I told you not to bother me here."

"Son—" she would say, "gimme a little money to have my teeth fixed."

"What did you do with the two dollars I gave you last month?" asked Hope.

"Please, son, I haven't eaten for days."

"If you aren't eating what do you need teeth for?"

"Please, son—"

"Mom, how'd you get over the wall? I thought you were happy there. I sent you that shawl—"

At this point Hope would signal for two stagehands to escort the unwilling woman offstage. Hope would continue his song, ending with, "She's my madonna, my Mom."

Hope thought it was a smart routine, fresh and satiric.

Immediately after the second show, Louis Sidney sent for Hope. Behind his big desk Sidney's eyes were magnified through thick glasses and his voice was fatherly stern. "Bob, take that 'My Mom' number out of the show."

"How come?"

"You're upsetting people. You should know this audience. We get plenty of old ladies and they're complaining about the way you treat that woman on stage."

"They must know it's satire."

"Please take it out."

Hope could not agree. He liked the number. Besides people had laughed at both performances. After the third show, Major Bowes, host of the *Capitol Family Hour* radio show, called backstage. "Bob, you're going to take that Mom bit out, aren't you?"

"What is this? Major, it's a funny bit. I have a mother too, you know—" Hope stopped. Was that Avis trudging out to center stage? "Yeah. You're right. Thanks."[3]

This lapse of taste was most surprising in view of his deep love and concern for his own mother. It was the concept of the gag which he had liked so much, its sharp poke at traditional values. But he'd have to use the concept another way.

After the Capitol, Hope got another crack at the Palace. But it was a sad time for the house once known as "Heaven on 47th Street." It was no longer able to attract the biggest names, no longer able to compete financially with the Capitol or the Paramount. By September 1935, its economic disease would prove fatal.

However, it was during the Palace's last stand as a vaudeville showcase in 1933 that Max Gordon saw Hope there and decided to sign him for a leading role in his production of the Kern-Harbach musical comedy *Gowns by Roberta*. The show was about an American college fullback who inherits his aging aunt's fashionable dress salon in Paris. When he takes over the business he falls in love with the chief designer who, in musical comedy fashion, turns out to be a Russian princess. The fullback's best pal is a fast-talking orchestra leader named Huckleberry Haines. The show's conflict, mild as it is, centers on the question: Will the fullback get the Russian princess or his college sweetheart?

Gordon went to Kern and told him he believed their search for a Huckleberry Haines had ended.

"What are you trying to do, palm off one of your old vaudevillians on me?" Kern asked tartly.

"Okay, okay," countered Gordon, "we don't have anyone for the part. Let's go over there this afternoon and you decide."

Gordon and Kern sat in the back of the Palace watching Hope work, and then went around backstage. Gordon let Kern ask Hope if he would accept the part, and Hope didn't hesitate.[4]

Hope enjoyed the elegant company. Legendary British star Fay Templeton was coaxed from retirement to play the aging Madame Roberta. Tamara, highly publicized after being discovered entertaining in a tiny Russian cafe on Fourteenth Street, was hired to play the dress designer. She was given the showstopping "Smoke Gets in Your Eyes." George Murphy, who had scored in Heywood Broun's *Shoot the Works*, was hired to play the fullback but early in rehearsals was replaced by juvenile Ray Middleton, who had a better physique. Murphy took the smaller part of Haines's manager. In other small parts were the suave Sydney Greenstreet, handsome Fred MacMurray and rubber-faced Imogene Coca. And in the pit orchestra, well hidden from view, was drummer Gene Krupa who was getting nightly lessons in reading music from a trombonist named Glenn Miller.

From the earliest rehearsals Hope thought the book too melodramatic for musical comedy. Because it lacked any true humorous situations, any laughs must emanate from individual gags. Hope tried wherever he could to hone a ragged comedy line to a sharper edge, clearing every change through Otto Harbach. Hope recalls:

> There was one line I really wanted to insert that everybody thought was too much . . . in fact, so much so we shouldn't even discuss it with Otto. You see, the big moment in the show was when Tamara sang "Smoke Gets in Your Eyes" to me. I'm sitting there . . . I light a cigarette and watch her . . . I'm listening.

At that point she's telling me that she loved Ray Middleton but it wasn't going anywhere. Tamara led into it by saying, "There's an old Russian proverb: *When your heart's on fire smoke gets in your eyes.*" And I wanted to say, "We have a proverb in America, too: *Love is like hash. You have to have confidence in it to enjoy it.*"[5]

Harbach didn't like the line, feeling it would disrupt the beautiful ballad coming up. So Hope reluctantly dropped the idea.

The musical was expensive with costs running around $115,000. Though it was decorative, Gordon felt it was not impressive enough. However, Kern was overall supervisor of the show and he was calling the shots. He had mounted many lavish numbers, yet when the show tried out in Philadelphia, it looked patchy. Opening night reviews were bad enough to convince Kern that they needed an overhaul.

Max called Hassard Short in New York, and Short agreed to do the necessary rewriting and redirecting, under the condition that Kern and Harbach stay out of his way.

Short arrived the next morning with a mink-lined coat thrown over his shoulders and said he was ready. Almost at once he redesigned the sets and ordered new costumes. He speeded up the action and advised Hope to "do whatever you can think of to get laughs. It's deadly."

Hope, encouraged by Short's directive, acted on his conviction that adding a joke to his scene with Tamara would score. One night in Philadelphia, Hope talked about the joke to Kern and said he would like to try it. Harbach was not there and Kern said, "Why not?"

So I put it in . . . and I was right, because it pulled one of the biggest laughs . . . no, it was the biggest laugh in the show. It served as a release in a dramatic scene. Pretty soon Otto heard about it . . . and he was nice enough to say the joke was successful . . . and that he was wrong.[6]

In all, Short's reconstruction work was miraculous. Gerald Boardman writes, ". . . [Short] created a mounting of such visual beauty that many of the libretto's languors were handsomely glossed over."

By this time Hope knew that Mahm was dying. He managed to telephone her several times a week, and every third week he would make a trip to her bedside. He drove his shiny new Pierce-Arrow all night to arrive Sunday morning before noon, spend a few hours talking with her and his dad and brothers. Then he would drive back, rehearsing lines, singing songs, whatever it took to keep himself awake.

Roberta, the new title for the show, opened at New York's Amsterdam Theater on Saturday night, November 18. It was definitely not a smash hit. Most reviews were divided between "nice" and "forget it!" and the influential Benchley damned it with faint praise. Despite the reviews the show had a steady cumulative growth and finally became the second longest-running production of the year.

One night Richy Craig appeared backstage, ashen-faced and a bit shaky.

"Are you okay, Richy?" Hope asked.

"I'm fine. Really I'm fine. I need your help."

"Anything. What is it?"

"It's Berle."

"Berle?"

"Yes, Berle. You know how I feel about him stealing gags. Well, I think I found a way to cure him. Next Sunday night there are four benefits—big ones—here in town and I want you to do them with me."

"Four? Richy—even I—Bobby the benefit nut—try to draw the line at three."

"I've seen you do five. Now, listen—don't ask how I did it but I have in my possession just about all of Berle's current act. Berle is scheduled to do these same benefits Sunday night and I know the order in which he plans to do them. I want us to get on the bill early enough at each one and "do" Berle's act before he gets there and when he follows us, he'll die."

Hope fell down laughing at the idea and agreed, although the more he looked at Richy, the more he worried.

That Sunday night Hope and Craig got an early spot on the Level Club benefit, did Berle's jokes, and grabbed a cab for the Waldorf-Astoria to do the second benefit. Berle arrived at the Level Club, got his cue to go on, did his jokes and bombed. Berle was stunned.

At the Waldorf, Berle came in and stood around for a few minutes and then the stage manager told him to go on. The same thing happened. When he came offstage, he said to the stage manager, "I don't get this at all. Something stinks and I don't think it's me." One of Berle's pals came up to him. "Hope and Craig were here ahead of you doing your stuff and then said to the audience, 'Don't tell Berle we were here. Let him bomb!' and they ran out."

Berle then switched his schedule for the next two benefits. He took a fast cab uptown to the Nordacs Club for the retarded children's benefit and did his act plus all that he could remember from both Hope's and Craig's material. Then he tipped off the audience to what he and they had going.

When Hope and Craig arrived at the Nordacs, they did their act and bombed. They were still pitching when Berle walked out on stage and said, "I finally caught you—you sons of bitches." Before they all left the stage Jack Osterman came up from the audience and added a few more jokes, one of which was a put-down of Craig. He said, "What did you do before you died?" It brought a big laugh.[7]

A few weeks later, Richy could no longer hide the fact that his tuberculosis had returned. But this time he wouldn't give in. One night after his fourth show at the Palace, he sat in his dressing room coughing blood. Berle came in and found him. While Richy was rushed to the hospital, Berle went out on the Palace stage and did Richy's act. Craig died three days later.

A few weeks later Berle and Hope organized a benefit in Craig's memory for his widow, and Hope was overwhelmed when Richy's wife handed him her husband's old joke books. He later said, "That was a night. We got everybody who was in town to appear. It was really something—Eddie Cantor, Ted Lewis, Pat Rooney, the Ritz Brothers, Martha Raye—forty acts. Richy would have loved it."[8]

*From then on I was at the Vogue every night, waiting to take
her home. I must have given the doorman at her apartment
hundreds of dollars in tips to let me park in front of the joint
and sit there with her. I sent the chauffeur home and we
talked. It was our Inspiration Point, our Flirtation Walk
. . . there in front of the Delmonico on Ninth Avenue.*[1]

10. Why Erie?

There was probably no period in Hope's life more filled with emotional highs
and lows than the last months of 1933 and the first months of 1934. For
openers, he had *Roberta*. He was working with giants in a show that was
tuneful and attractive if not the dazzling hit the critics had expected of Kern.
And even though the show's first weeks in New York were shaky (Max
Gordon had asked the cast twice to take salary cuts), Bob was making more
money than ever before.

He could even afford to hire a chauffeur for his Pierce-Arrow. He bought
a Scottie dog and named him Huck. He reveled in the fact that he was
occupying Marilyn Miller's old dressing room at the New Amsterdam. He
reveled more in the number of showgirls that Huck, his Pierce-Arrow, and
his unfailing seduction approach could deliver to his Central Park West
apartment.

Still, there was a feeling of sadness that he wasn't fully able to handle.
Sometimes when he watched happy couples like George and Julie Murphy
he felt lonesome, as he did the night that George, Julie, and their friend,
Bobby Maxwell, invited him to join them for an after-show drink at the
Vogue Club on Fifty-seventh Street. The Vogue had been put on the map by
Bea Lillie, and on this particular night, December 21, a singer named
Dolores Reade was appearing there.

Dolores Reade had a Libby Holman-Marian Harris type of voice, low and
husky. When they walked into the club she was singing "It's Only a Paper
Moon." Hope liked what he saw immediately. She was tall and graceful with
the studied poise of a fashion model. He learned she had been dating Bobby
Maxwell on and off. She ended the set with "Did You Ever See a Dream
Walking?" and came over to their table.

Up close she was livelier than she had been in stage light, and Bob was
intrigued. They all agreed to go dancing at the Haw Haw Club. When they
got there George and Julie danced. Bobby Maxwell disappeared completely.
Dolores and Bob made very small talk. In *Modern Screen* for November
1943 Dolores recalled:

> I hadn't caught his name and wasn't the least inter-
> ested . . . but just to make conversation I asked him if he
> wanted to dance. "No," he said, "I don't like to dance." I thought
> that was odd—especially because I figured he was a pal of
> Murph's and was in his show, and probably was a chorus boy. But
> when he said he didn't want to dance that was all right with me,
> too.

Just then George and Julie came back to the table and George asked me to dance. We had danced around the room just once when Bob cut in saying, "I've changed my mind." I was so astonished that for the first time I took a good look at him. I saw a very young, and at that moment, a very serious fellow—but then and there, I knew I liked him.

They ended up at Reuben's for a sandwich about two o'clock. By this time Bob was aware that Dolores was something different. He knew he wanted to see her again and he asked her to come to *Roberta*. She picked Wednesday matinee, December 27.

Bob went to Cleveland for Christmas. The Hopes felt it might be the last for Avis, whose condition had deteriorated in the past few months. Bob knew that Dolores had made an impression on him when he found himself describing her in response to questions about his marital status. These kinds of questions coming from his brothers were natural, since Ivor, Jim and Jack were all already working on second or third marriages.

When Bob rushed back to New York after Christmas in Cleveland, he was thinking about Dolores. Intentionally he had failed to describe his role in *Roberta* because he wanted her to be surprised. Dolores said later:

When I got home that morning after spending those first few hours with Bob, I told my mother that I had met my future husband. Being accustomed to my crazy outbursts, she casually asked me who he was. I turned to her and confessed I didn't really—probably just a chorus boy.[2]

Dolores came to *Roberta* with a friend, and when it was over Dolores declined to go backstage. Bob was mystified. Two days later he couldn't bear not knowing so he went to the Vogue Club.

"What happened?"

"I didn't come back—because I wasn't aware you had such a big part in the show—I mean, I ought to have known. I thought you were in the chorus," she said sheepishly. "I'm embarrassed."

Bob waited for her to finish and they went out for a drink. "What are you doing New Year's Eve?"

"Working," she replied. "You?"

"Same. How about after?"

She nodded and smiled. They sat outside the Delmonico on Ninth Avenue where Dolores lived with her mother in an apartment short on privacy. Besides, Dolores' mother, Theresa Kelly Difina, had vowed she would bring her two daughters up in a careful Irish Catholic fashion, and live to see them married to good Irish Catholic men. Dolores and her sister Mildred seldom brought home men who were good enough. This "chorus boy" was no exception.

It was, therefore, with pleasure that Theresa accompanied Dolores to Florida on January 14 for her engagement at Miami's Embassy Club. Her daughter needed time and distance between herself and Hope.

Dolores and Bob talked to each other for hours by long-distance telephone, and during one of these calls confessed their love for each other. During another of their calls Bob mentioned marriage and Dolores offered to break her Embassy Club contract.

But before that could be decided, Avis died on Sunday, January 22, 1934, and Bob went to Cleveland. Her death was both a blow and a relief. He had watched her waste away, and near the end he knew it could be only a continuous series of hypos and pills to deaden the pain. She had shrunk to seventy-five pounds. In her helplessness she no longer represented the indomitable Mahm he knew, his best girl, his biggest booster.

It was Avis who had stood up for him against his dad or his brothers when he quit well-paying jobs because they interfered with his plans for a show business career. It was Avis who wrote letters of encouragement when he was starving in Chicago. He was glad she would not be in pain any longer.

After the funeral Bob returned to New York, lonely and drained of energy. When he called Dolores in Miami, she told him she had already notified the Embassy Club to forget the option for the second month. She expected to take the sleeper on February 13.

Theresa waged an unrelenting campaign against the idea of their marriage. The gossip columnists were busy, too. One item pointed out that Bob's heart belonged to "someone else" (presumably Louise), and that he had promised to marry her. Dolores raised this issue about the "someone else" over long-distance phone lines. Bob sputtered and said it was nonsense, that he hadn't seen the girl in question in months.

Dolores was mollified and, for a reason known only to Bob and Dolores at the time, decided on Erie, Pennsylvania, for their vows. Hope says, "I don't know why—she had me in such a thick, pink fog."[3] It was a fast trip. Bob's understudy had to appear only twice. They were married on February 19 and two days later Bob was back on the New Amsterdam stage.

Dolores set out at once to make their three-room furnished apartment more homey. And she took a serious interest in Bob's professional life, too. She encouraged him in his search for a top-flight agent and was pleased when he hooked up with Louis Shurr, whose clients included Bert Lahr, Victor Moore, Lou Holtz, William Gaxton, Ken Murray and a variety of newcomers including George Murphy. Shurr was one of New York's colorful figures, a shortish (five-foot-five), beak-nosed go-getter who drove around in a chauffeured limousine usually accompanied by one or another supertall showgirl who would be wearing a mink coat that Louis loaned all his girls.

Shurr was dubbed "Doc" by his Times Square clients and friends because he had been successful in salvaging a few troubled Broadway shows during their out-of-town tryouts. Shurr had noticed Hope in *Ballyhoo*, had caught his act at both the Palace and the Capitol and was, of course, familiar with *Roberta*. He was vigorously touting Murphy for a film contract and he had the conviction that Hope, too, would ultimately make it in the movies.

Hope, however, besides sharing the general Broadway snobbery toward Hollywood, still tasted gall over his 1930 screen test for Pathé. And he didn't need Hollywood's money. Between his *Roberta* salary and his radio guest spots he was able to save $500 a week. So he was lukewarm when Doc Shurr said he was trying to land Hope the part of Huckleberry Haines in the already announced film version of *Roberta*. While Bob was rejected for that part, Louis did manage to get an RKO offer for a featured role in a Jack Oakie picture. They demanded a screen test and Bob reluctantly agreed, partly because it was shot in New York. When Dolores came out of the screening room she said she thought Bob looked like a turtle.

In March 1934 Hope agreed to an offer from Educational Pictures in Astoria, Long Island, to make a musical short with Leah Ray called *Jumping Beans*. The deal would enlarge to include five more pictures if the first one clicked.

Hope was stricken when he saw himself in *Jumping Beans* at the Rialto on Broadway. He was appalled at the way he and Leah cavorted about the set after consuming Mexican beans. Slinking out of the theater, Hope bumped into Walter Winchell, who asked how he liked his film debut. Hope cracked, "When they catch Dillinger, they're going to make him sit through it twice."

Winchell, whose daily column was an assembly line of gags and one-liners, used Hope's wisecrack the next day. Jack Skirball of Educational phoned Doc Shurr, screaming, "We're having enough trouble selling that guy without him knocking the picture. He's fired!" Shurr phoned Hope and scolded him. Hope, in turn, called Winchell, begging for a retraction but Winchell refused.[4]

A short time later Shurr had another screen offer for Hope, this time from Warner Brothers who wanted Hope to appear with Dorothy Stone in a shortened version of Cole Porter's 1929 Broadway musical *Fifty Million Frenchmen*. It was to be called *Paree, Paree* and would be shot entirely at Warners' Eastern Studio on Avenue M in Brooklyn. Hope managed to keep his mouth shut when they screened it, and Warners were pleased enough to pick up his option for five more Vitaphone Comedy shorts to be made at Eastern during the next two years.

In June 1934, Hope made another guest appearance for Rudy Vallee's Fleischmann-sponsored radio show. On June 5, *Variety* covered the event:

> His easy-going, underplayed style is as likeable on the air as upon the rostrum of a variety or legit house. His jokes are aged, but his delivery and general approach to humor is modern.
>
> Seems no reason why Hope could not do well on a regular commercial assignment. Perhaps it may be argued he has no catch phrases or distinctive identification, and this may be valid cause for caution up to a point.
>
> But he wears well, his knack of self-joshing and unabashed realization of his own daring is calculated to please where more perspiring methods of getting laughs exhaust and enervate.

was an astute assessment of the power of Hope's persona in overcoming male material.

Hope was beginning to appreciate the power of radio and film. He was frustrated watching two of his fellow players in *Roberta* packed off to the West Coast with movie contracts. The first was amiable Fred MacMurray who borrowed Hope's black silk topper to go with his rented tuxedo for a Paramount screen test in New York. Weeks later MacMurray was in Hollywood.

~~Hope was trading stories with some other actors in Doc Shurr's Times~~
Square office the day Louis told George Murphy to start packing so he could pick up a Columbia Pictures contract in Hollywood. Hope looked enviously at Murph and then rather pleadingly at Shurr, "Murph, if it can happen to you maybe it can happen to me."[5]

I stroked her arm . . . Then I nibbled it gently . . . Then I hugged her . . . She did another half-chorus and I lay down on my back and looked at her adoringly. If it hadn't been so obvious to the onlookers that we were really in love, the act would have fallen flat.[1]

11. *Say When*

Hope's *Roberta* contract expired in June, and to avoid having to go on the road with the show he decided not to sign another agreement. As it turned out, the show lasted only another two months and closed in New York. But it had been a milestone in Hope's career. He was now a genuine Broadway headliner—without an immediate offer to be sure—but with talents that Louis Shurr believed highly marketable.

Assured that by late summer there could be another Broadway show in his life, Bob asked the Loew booking office to set up an eastern cities vaudeville tour for himself and Dolores. He then set out to create an entirely new comedy act. His old one had been given to a young, struggling comic named Lew Parker, and Parker was doing well with it. In gratitude, Parker introduced Hope to a pair of young gagsters, fresh from writing variety shows at NYU. Their names were Lester White and Fred Molina. Hope liked their bright, contemporary college humor and asked them to write him a touring vehicle.

But Hope himself created his bride's material. After Bob finished his monologue, he would introduce Dolores and she would come onstage and sing one song. During the applause for her number, Hope would wander back on, letting her begin her second song. Then he moved closer and looked her over appreciatively. He would look at the audience and let them feel his lovesick pleasure. While Dolores continued, still relatively unshaken, Bob would stroke her arm and examine it lustfully. He would even bite her playfully, inviting audience giggles. Then he would hug her and this would break her up. Hope would say, resting his head on her shoulder, "Don't let me bother you. Just keep right on."

Dolores would restore her dignity and begin again, but this time Hope would lie down on the stage in front of her, relishing every movement she made. By then the audience was enjoying it as much as Hope but, as he points out, only because the clowning was done in the spirit of two people in love. In the *Woman's Home Companion* of November 1953 Dolores recalled:

That was an exciting and challenging experience. What he expected was perfection. He never let down for a moment on stage and heaven help me if I did! I simply had to go out there every show and pitch. Hard. We did six and seven shows a day. Sometimes my mind would wander and that was fatal. Bob would get very angry and right there on stage in the middle of the act, he'd crack, "What's the matter with you, tired?"

That particular Loew tour lasted about ten weeks and went as far south as Washington, then hit Baltimore, Wilmington and Philadelphia before going into New Jersey, Connecticut and finally Boston. The freshness and the satiric bite of the material White and Molina had turned out for Hope was not lost on critics, audiences or other comedians for that matter. Doc Shurr telephoned Hope in Hartford to tell him that Harry Richman wanted him for his new Broadway musical.

In August Dolores and Bob came home to their 65 Central Park West apartment and Hope began his huddles with librettist Jack McGowan and composer Ray Henderson for their Richman vehicle called *Say When*. This *Say When* bore no resemblance to the 1928 revue of the same name; it was about two radio entertainers (Richman and Hope) who meet a rich banker's two daughters (Betty Dell and Linda Hopkins) on a transatlantic liner and fall in love. The rich banker objects to the prospect of having show-business sons-in-law until the entertainers find a stray blonde in the banker's life.

Richman, a true superstar of the 1930s, was responsible for picking Hope as his costar and putting $50,000 in the show himself on the condition that Hope appear in it. Richman's faith in Hope never faltered even when he realized that Hope had most of the best lines. The songs, too, were not quite right. Richman lamented:

The book was very good but the music was only mediocre. When I tried to get it changed, I discovered to my surprise that I couldn't change a note without the author's consent, and he wouldn't give it.[2]

Actually, Richman seemed to be the only one suffering. Henderson and McGowan were enthusiastic and confident of their star's performance. They even had a notorious backer who attended rehearsals faithfully and seemed content with the progress of his investment. His omnipresence intrigued Hope until one day he asked Richman who the man was. "He's Lucky Luciano, that's who he is," said Richman.

With tryouts set for Boston, Dolores was asked if she would like to do a single at Boston's Loew's State during the *Say When* run there. She hesitated. A nightclub single was one thing, but doing a proscenium stage act without Bob scared her. But she put together a few songs, took what she trusted were the right clothes and prayed.

Bob spent most of those first Boston days ironing out wrinkles in his part and sleeping late mornings, including the day Dolores did her first show. In fact, he was still asleep when his bedside phone rang. It was Dolores. "Come over here," she said, half-crying. "This is a mess. It didn't work. They didn't like me. The band was too loud and the lights were awful. It was *all* wrong."

Hope dressed and raced to Loew's State in time for her second show. She was right. The best part was her voice and that was partially drowned by a loud band. Hope played tough manager, demanding a magenta spot for her dress, a pin spot for her face, a mute for the orchestra and suggested some simple staging. Dolores took notes. This mustn't happen again.[3]

Things at *Say When* were also smoothing out except in Richman's head. He knew he was supposed to be the show's strongest element and was aware it wasn't working out that way. When the show left Boston for the New York opening, Richman was still scrapping with Henderson and McGowan about writing him a hit song. On the train that November 7 afternoon, Richman asked Hope to share a bottle of champagne with him in his drawing room. Hope believed Richman intended to suggest a switch that would beef up his own part and weaken Hope's. But instead the veteran showman praised Hope's singing voice and timing, apologizing for his own inability to generate excitement. "I'm the star of this thing, Bob, but if I'm weak, it won't help any of us."

Yet opening night reviews were the sort box-office managers fall on their knees for. Atkinson in the *Times* said the offering at the Imperial was a "lively show made to order for the itinerant trade of the Great White Way." Anderson called it "a daffy and hilarious show." Benchley called it "a real musical comedy," and Winchell put the cherry on top with "merriest laugh song and girl show in town."[4]

But Richman, despite such rave reviews, still wanted to improve his part. Henderson and McGowan were now convinced that the show needed only a cooperative star. From the producer's point of view the show was a critical hit and even the least savant of theater touts would bet that *Say When* would be in black figures in three months.

Finally Richman gave up trying to doctor the score. He reasoned with Hope that "if I can't be happy this show is doomed." The producers were in a squeeze. Richman had the controlling share of money behind the show. Plus on November 21 a musical opened down the street at the Alvin that boasted a marquee of Gaxton, Merman and Moore, a tuneful score by Cole Porter, glowing reviews and audience excitement that it was not only the hit of the season but the fourth biggest show of the decade. It was *Anything Goes*. Now that there wasn't room for more than one smash musical on the boards. But *Say When*'s star fire had gone out and the cast knew it. Richman pulled rank and posted two weeks' notice.

This move did not catch Hope off guard, as Richman had kept his costar informed of his every intention. So Hope urged Shurr to find him a big Christmas present to make him forget the demise of *Say When*. Shurr responded almost immediately with a radio audition for a series spot as emcee of Bromo-Seltzer's *Intimate Revue*, which starred Jane Froman, James Melton and Al Goodman's band. Hope panicked because he needed a fresh monologue for the audition. Once again it was Richman who stepped in. He invited Hope to his famous Beechhurst estate, opened the elegant bookcase coverings on his extensive joke files, including innumerable radio scripts, and told him to take his pick of material. Hope took about a dozen or so scripts and was quoted for years afterwards as saying, "Harry Richman was the guy responsible for my success in radio." As for Harry, he decided to

;o to Florida to begin a new phase of his career. He did return to Broadway a decade later in *New Priorities of 1943*, a vaudeville mélange that closed after 54 showings.

Hope's audition for Bromo-Seltzer was December 21 and it was clear to the sponsors that the audience liked Hope. The laugh arrow kept kicking at the right side of the meter. He was signed and his first regular show was January 4 although *Variety* didn't review until January 15, 1935:

> Hope is intermittently very funny. At other times either his material falters or his delivery is a bit too lackadaisical. In general Hope should avoid too much nonchalance. It's a luxury not allowed by radio. He must work to put himself and his stuff over, as the poker face mugging that means something on the rostrum doesn't percolate through the cosmos.
>
> Hope is easy to take, but hard to remember. His problem then is one of emphasis. A good central idea rather than reliance on kidding the announcer and the patter of bright persiflage would hold more weight.

Hope dreamed up a faster, hard-hitting comedy idea when he parodied a society editor with a Winchellesque approach:

> FLASH! . . . Newport, Rhode Island . . . box of matches goes off in Reginald Depeyster's hip pocket . . . no permanent damage . . . just a flash in the pants. . . .
>
> SPLASH! . . . Miami Beach . . . young Puffy Welling- ton . . . missing three days . . . now located . . . had lost his trunks while bathing . . . and was forced to keep running in and out with the tide. . . .[5]

Hope was not entirely comfortable about what he was doing in the early Bromo-Seltzer shows. But there was an idea growing in his mind that he hoped would add variety to his radio personality. Hope decided he needed another foil, a Louise for radio. Dolores was not suited for the role, and besides she didn't want to do it. At Doc Shurr's office one day Hope met a winsome young Southern girl named Patricia Wilder from Macon, Georgia. She was a perky blonde with a quick, natural wit and Hope thought she would be perfect.

She was nicknamed "Honey Chile," largely because of her accent which Hope described as "thick spoonbread." Shurr had set up a Capitol Theater engagement for Bob after *Say When* closed, and this proved an ideal time to give Honey Chile an audition before a theater audience:

> I took her on for a couple of tryout shows. I was worried about the possibility of her having stage fright—until she walked out in front of her first Capitol audience and said, 'Pahdon me, Mistah Hope. Does the Greyhound bus stop heah?" and instead of look- ing at me, she looked at the audience and smiled. I knew then that Honey Chile was born unembarrassed."[6]

She was written into the *Intimate Revue* scripts and almost immediately the

new character was well received. The routines were simple but Hope discov
ered that regardless of what she said it was much more *how* she said it:

HOPE: . . . you know, Honey Chile, there's a lot of comedians on the air, why did you pick me out as your
partner?

HONEY: 'Cause I had a fight with my folks and I want to do
something to disgrace 'em. . . .

HOPE: Uh-uh, you probably picked the right party. . . .

HONEY: You know, Mr. Hope, I've got two brothers home that
I'm sure would be a big hit on the radio. . . .

HOPE: What can they do?

HONEY: The same as you, they just act crazy.

HOPE: Aha . . . what's their names?

HONEY: The oldest is Ed.

HOPE: What's the young'uns name?

HONEY: Ed . . .

HOPE: Two boys in one family by the name of Ed?

HONEY: Yes, Father always said that two Eds was better than
one.

HOPE: Your father said that? What's keeping him off the
air?

In spite of newspaper publicity, critical response and enthusiastic mail from
listeners, the Hope-Honey Chile exchanges were added too late to boost the
Hooper rating of a doomed show. The last broadcast of the series was April
5, 1935.

*When I began to warble this ditty to Eve, she walked away
from me and I followed her, sang another eight bars, leaned
over her shoulder and breathed deeply with unrequited passion. When I looked into Eve's eyes and sang, "I can't get
started," the people didn't believe it. The first four rows
could hear my motor running.*[1]

12. *Ziegfeld Follies of 1935*

In late spring of 1935, Hope took Dolores and Honey Chile on the road to
play a few of the big Loew movie houses, and at a time in entertainment
history when stage presentation was scratching and clawing for survival
they were held over in Chicago!

Their return to New York was Hope's first opportunity to respond to
Warners' urgent reminder that he owed them a second Vitaphone Comedy
Short. And that early morning when Hope reported in front of Eastern Stu
dios on Brooklyn's Avenue M, he was gritting his teeth. By 1935, Hope had

established a pattern difficult to break: He was a night person. He liked staying up until two or three in the morning and then being able to sleep until noon. Unfortunately, film companies traditionally rolled their cameras by the light of day and they started at dawn.

Working for studio boss Sam Sax also wasn't easy. Sax paid his stars high salaries but worked them unmercifully so that he could complete a two-reeler in three days. The first film Hope did for Warners was called *The Old Grey Mayor*, a farce about the undoing of an eloping couple. Hope managed to make two more Vitaphone Shorts in 1935. One was *Watch the Birdie*, in which he played a wisecracking, practical-joking lover. In *Double Exposure*, he played a wisecracking, practical-joking sidewalk photographer.

In between and after the Vitaphone shorts, Hope continued to work the Loew chain with Dolores and Honey Chile. In late summer, Louis Shurr negotiated with J.J. Shubert for Hope to have the leading male comedy spot in a new edition of the *Ziegfeld Follies*, which was being coproduced by the Shuberts and Ziegfeld's widow, Billie Burke. The undisputed draw for this edition would be Fanny Brice with John Murray Anderson directing. Anderson hoped to have it ready for Broadway by mid or late fall, but casting difficulties, illnesses and production snags for a show touted as "the most fabulous *Follies* of them all" delayed the schedule by two months. Rehearsals got under way in October, with out-of-town tryouts set for November, but it was not until Christmas night 1935 that the highly publicized show opened at Boston's Opera House.[2]

The rest of the cast was strong: Ken Murray, Gertrude Niesen, Josephine Baker, Eve Arden, Judy Canova, Edgar Bergen and Charlie McCarthy, Cherry and June Preisser, Hugh O'Connell, the Nicholas Brothers and Stan Kavanagh.

Vincente Minelli designed what was universally regarded as a tastefully sumptuous production and George Balanchine was making an auspicious debut as choreographer. The show had Vernon Duke's music, Ira Gershwin's lyrics with added special material by Ogden Nash, Dave Freedman and Billy Rose. The brothers Shubert beamed with pride and wielded their power throughout the entire affair.

As the show unfolded in Boston, it clearly needed pruning. Anderson saw that it was too long on male comedy and too short on good material for Fanny. Hope's comedy was thoroughly integrated throughout the evening, first with Brice, then with Niesen and then with Arden, and he had the show's hit tune, "I Can't Get Started With You." Murray, on the other hand, had two solo monologues and if anyone could be eliminated it was he.

Lee Shubert drove to Boston for the tryout, and when the curtain fell he went backstage to see Murray. He told Ken that his act was "dirty" and asked him to change it. Murray was offended. He eventually walked but not for that reason. From the start he had been angry about his billing. He claimed he was hired by Lee Shubert as the lead comic. His agent, Louis Shurr, had set the deal. But, interestingly enough, Hope had been hired also as lead comic and his agent was Louis Shurr. Shurr's explanation to each of his clients must have been classic.

The *Follies* began to shape beautifully. Hope could not have been more

content with the month in Boston. He had two important scenes with Fanny
one in which they parodied the British rich in "Fawncy, Fawncy," and
another where he played the director of her *enfant terrible* Baby Snooks
sketch. But Bob's standout scene came with tall, statuesque, redheaded
beauty Eve Arden (veteran of an earlier *Follies*) to whom he fervently sang
"I Can't Get Started With You."

In this scene, set on a street corner, Arden was in a stunning evening gown
and Hope in evening clothes. He was trying to seduce her, but without suc
cess. As he tried to persuade her, she was hailing a cab. Undaunted he sang
about his accomplishments as a hero in the Spanish Civil War, as a globe
trotting pilot, as a North Pole explorer, as a consultant to Roosevelt, even as
God in *Green Pastures*. Arden remained unmoved. Then Hope desperately
grabbed her, embraced her passionately, and slowly she melted. With this
Hope straightened up, adjusted his cuffs, exulting in a conquest, and said
"That's all I wanted to know. Well, good night!"

Hope had other reasons for jubilation at this time. During rehearsals for
Follies in November, he had signed on as comedy star of a radio series
known as the *Atlantic White Flash Program*. Part of his charm for the spon
sors was that he was a *Follies* star, and another part of his charm was that he
had a talked-about foil named Honey Chile. The sponsors were so enthusias
tic that they arranged to send Honey Chile to Boston, so that during the
month of January Hope's comedy segments could be inserted into the show
from a radio studio there.

Hope's Christmas present from Honey Chile was, however, bittersweet
She told him she had been signed to an exclusive RKO contract and would
be leaving for Hollywood in February. Hope immediately wired Louis Shurr
and had him begin a search for a new Honey Chile.

Meanwhile, Hope, whose memory has always been unusually accurate
about names, places and faces, remembered a young blonde who had audi
tioned for the Honey Chile role a year before. She was pretty green-eyed
Margaret Johnson, a well-educated Dallas girl whose aspirations had
included teaching after she earned her Masters Degree from Baylor. But she
was also photogenic and, it turned out, ambitious.

She was no Patricia Wilder, but she was suitably fey in her reading of the
part and her drawl was genuine, and when the changeover took place in late
January the transition was smooth.

The saddest part of Boston was seeing Edgar Bergen and Charlie leave the
show. Hope and Bergen had become good friends and Hope respected Berg
en's extraordinary presence with his dummy. Anderson, however, had to cut
a vaudeville specialty and Bergen's act was getting less applause than Stan
Kavanaugh's juggling.

The *Ziegfeld Follies* (1936 Edition) opened January 30 at the Winter
Garden. It was a costly show to produce and the critics, not surprisingly
cheered Fanny Brice, Gertrude Niesen, Bob Hope and Eve Arden. They
were less enthusiastic about Josephine Baker, too chic and French for New
Yorkers. Reviewers said that this *Follies* was better than the previous Shu
bert revival. Minelli and Balanchine and Anderson had given the *Follies*
back its grandeur and its elegance.

Arden wanted very much to be Fanny's understudy, but the Shubert claimed it was impossible to understudy a unique performer, one who never missed a show. Eve, however, had learned the Brice sketches and was a capable comedienne. One night, Fanny was too ill to go on and the Shuberts wanted to close down, but Eve argued her case and won.

Then she was frightened. She said to Bob, "The only place where I'll worry is the 'Baby Snooks' sketch. What if I blow it?"

"We'll do what Fanny and I do. When she has any line trouble I just grab her and we tussle for a few moments, just long enough for me to feed her a cue and she's fine. So will you be."[3]

Hope's reaction to Fanny Brice was predictable. He found her unquestionably magical as an entertainer and troubled as a woman. Despite a reportedly happy marriage to Billy Rose, she seemed lonely, and sadness crept into her joking whenever Bob and Dolores shared a late supper with her.

Brice was plagued by painful arthritis; she also had trouble with her teeth. Her doctor had prescribed analgesics, but one night in Philadelphia before curtain time she apparently had mistaken her sleeping pills for her pain killers. Hope remembers sadly:

> In the last act of the show she had a specialty and in the middle of it she couldn't remember where she was and would start the number over again. We were all in the wings watching her, and dying for her, because she was such a marvelous woman and still such a great star. I'm sure each of us was trying to figure out how we could miraculously save her from this. John McManus conducting in the pit tried to get her out of it musically but she was dazed. Freddy de Cordova, our stage manager, finally had to bring down the curtain. He brought her off quietly and she didn't come back for the finale. I'll never forget seeing her—*her* floundering and confused—[4]

Fanny, like Hope, kept up a killing schedule, and it was increasingly evident that her health was a problem. She was in rare form the May night that New York's richest, most celebrated, turned out to mark the thirty-fifth anniversary of the Shuberts' theatrical life. The gala evening saw Al Jolson, Lou Holtz, the Howard brothers, Sophie Tucker, Jack Benny, Bert Lahr, Ethel Barrymore, Helen Hayes, Katharine Cornell and so many others perform. Hope was one of the emcees. Yet scarcely a week later the *Ziegfeld Follies* announced it was closing for a vacation, promising to reopen when its star attraction regained her health.

But Hope didn't mind. His radio status was improving steadily, mostly because he took his job of providing weekly comedy on the *Atlantic Family* (the new name for his show) seriously. One reporter who observed Hope's mode of operation wrote:

> Bob has three writers (Lester White, Fred Molina, Bud Pearson) who work for him. Early on Monday mornings they bring the prepared script to his apartment and the four of them go over it together. Sometimes it's swell and sometimes it isn't, and when it isn't they often stay up all night Monday and Tuesday trying to re-write it. They dig into Hope's collection of eighty thousand

jokes for ideas, they try to rehash old material, to think up new stuff. By Wednesday morning the sponsor must have a copy of the script. By Wednesday night he OK's it or doesn't OK it. If he doesn't Bob and his writers have got to work all day and night Thursday re-writing it again. Friday it's rehearsed and changed and shaped up. Saturday it's rehearsed some more. Saturday night it goes on the air, and Monday the whole procedure starts over again![5]

But meticulous concern over the script wasn't the whole of it. Hope's wisdom in featuring the Honey Chile character so prominently, and a barrage of publicity by both a private press agent named Jimmy Davis and N.W. Ayer's publicity staff, were equally important. By the end of April, what had originally been thought of in the trade as the Frank Parker show was slowly being known as the Frank Parker–Bob Hope Saturday night show, with some columnists reversing the billing, and some omitting Parker's name altogether.

When Louis Shurr asked him if he wanted to exercise his option to rejoin the *Follies* when Fanny returned late in the summer, Hope said no. He did exercise his option to make two more Vitaphone Comedy Shorts for Warners in Brooklyn, *Calling All Tars* and *Shop Talk*, probably his best two-reeler.

If working that hard wasn't enough, Hope managed to fill some of his late week nights, and almost all of his Sunday nights, with benefits. It didn't matter how many, if he was needed he went. In *Billboard* of May 30, 1936, Alan Corelli of Theater Authority said, "In looking over the 200 benefits of the past season, Willie and Eugene Howard, Harry Hershfield, Rudy Vallee, Bob Hope and Pat Rooney appeared in the greatest number."

During the first week of June it was announced that Frank Parker would desert the *Atlantic* show for Paul Whiteman's radio program, leaving Hope virtually in charge of the store, and when Atlantic asked if he would continue through the summer—a time most radio personalities took time off for a Hollywood film commitment, or to do the state fair route or just to rest—Hope eagerly said yes.

Even with a new visibility as the absolute star of the show, Hope was still plagued with personal criticism about the quality of his material. With the large number of comedians working in radio at the time, all depending on a limited number of gag writers and using them at high speed, mediocre material and gag larceny were not uncommon. The show had a low rating but Hope was gaining valuable experience for what was coming.

I'm afraid I used to go a little too far clowning with her and kidding with her in the show. I used a lot of ad libs and tomfoolery not in the script. Every three or four days the stage manager came to me and said, "Mr. Hope, I wish you'd used more discretion. . . ."[1]

13. *Red, Hot and Blue!*

It is probably safe to say that in many minds in 1936 Bob Hope was like the American economy—coming right along. The fact that he was being evaluated so carefully and critically by the media was promising. His radio show ratings were not very high, but they were higher than *Fibber McGee* or Jimmy Durante. Because he had scored so well in *Say When* and the *Follies*, he was an obvious contender for Broadway roles.

On the homefront, things were blissful. Bob and Dolores were very much in love, and they enjoyed midtown Manhattan living in their spacious Central Park West apartment with its enormously long green and white living room, its spectacular view of the park and Fifth Avenue buildings beyond and their two Scottie dogs.

Both Bob and Dolores seemed to crave activity. Bob's day was broken up into hours for writing, rehearsing and performing, eating, playing golf in the summer, and working out at Harold Reilly's gym in the winter. On weekends they played 72 holes of golf and Bob, especially, was becoming remarkably skilled in the sport. He could never get enough of it. Since he first sampled the game in 1930 he had played on more than 100 courses around the United States, not to mention Bermuda.

Dolores loved entertaining, playing bridge and playing golf with and without Bob. One reporter wrote in the *New York Journal* on March 6, 1936:

> She's becoming one of the most popular hostesses among the air crowd; if you're invited to one of the famous Saturday night parties she gives for her bridge-fiend hubby, you've received as coveted an invitation as there is to be had in radio.

She supervised the Hopes' domestic and social lives as much as Bob allowed, did some charitable work in her Catholic parish, and as often as invited, sat in on Bob's writing and rehearsal sessions. Bob would ask her to read a line aloud sometimes. Although he would frown when she offered suggestions, more often than not he followed her advice.

Late in the spring of 1936, even before *Follies* shut down due to Fanny's illness, Louis Shurr was busily selling Hope to Vinton Freedley for a musical comedy which bore the title *But Millions!* Already signed for it was Ethel Merman. This show had been expected to be a regathering of the talent responsible for the enormously successful *Anything Goes* (420 performances)—Merman, William Gaxton, Victor Moore, Cole Porter, Howard Lindsay, Russell Crouse, and Freedley as producer. Lindsay, of course, would direct.[2]

Broadway soothsayers and oracles worked long hours trying to predict who actually would be signed for the show. Despite rumors about Gaxton and Moore, there were also hints that both Jack Haley and Jack Benny were being considered for the suave comic role. Merman recalls that the producing triad wooed Gaxton by promising him *the* fat part, but did not anticipate his arrival at a meeting among themselves and Merman when they were telling her how big *her* part would be. Gaxton listened while Lindsay and Crouse double-talked, then walked out and never came back. As it happened, he had already received a better offer of a bigger part in *White Horse Inn*.

Early in June, Freedley and Shurr arrived at terms that gave Hope star billing in what would have been the Bill Gaxton role. But the producers were still searching for a low-comedy star. Victor Moore was not being sought, but Jimmy Durante *was*. However, Durante was currently resting at Capri. Freedley attempted several unsatisfactory transatlantic telephone conversations with Jimmy, sent telegrams and received cryptic replies. Finally Lou Clayton signed for Durante. Now all that remained as a stumbling block was an unsatisfactory book, which now carried the title *Wait for Baby*.

Lindsay and Crouse had rewritten *Anything Goes* but this would be their first original script together. They did a lot of staring at each other and some staring away from each other. Finally, fellow-writer Frank Sullivan begged them to get out of steamy, sticky Manhattan and take up residence at Saratoga Springs. There they wrote a first act. Inspired, they booked passage on a steamer for Ireland and in the clear air of shipboard life, they tore up what they had written as trashy. Back in New York City they started again, and came up with an incredible script called *Red, Hot and Blue!* The plot almost defies description but one observer attempted to characterize it this way:

> Former manicurist, now a millionairess, 'Nails' O'Reilly Duquesne (Merman), hires happy ex-con 'Policy' Pinkle (Durante) to help her conduct a lottery for charity which she decides to 'throw' in favor of her boyfriend, Bob Hale (Hope), who is in love with the memory of a lost childhood sweetheart who branded herself by sitting on a hot waffle iron. (Not your simple little boy-meets-girl plot this!) In the end, 'Nails' and her lawyer find true love but not before plenty of burlesque situation and jokes.

Despite the delays in what was still a cumbersome book, Cole Porter completed his score and began publicly to extol its virtues. He was particularly pleased with one number called "It's De-lovely," which he had planned for the MGM film *Born to Dance* but never used. Porter said the song was inspired during a 1935 trip around the world when at the sight of Rio harbor at dawn he was impelled to say, "It's delightful!" In one interview, Cole told the reporter that his wife Linda was with him and she had responded with "It's delicious!" In still another interview Porter told what was actually the case, that it was his dear friend Moss Hart who said, "It's delicious." In both versions of the story Porter said it was Monty Woolley standing nearby on deck who said, "It's de-lovely!"

Delightful to Hope was the idea of singing it with Merman, and the prospect of working on the same stage with the incomparable Durante and a few other friends like Lew Parker, Grace and Paul Hartman and the very funny Vivian Vance.

Rehearsals were hilarious, according to Hope. And he could only be an amused bystander to the almost disastrous billing battle which concerned the positioning of star names above the title. Merman had been promised left-hand position, but so had Durante. Hope hadn't been promised anything other than star billing, so the standoff was between the steel-throated Ethel and whiskey-voiced Jimmy, or, rather, their agents. Finally Cole Porter suggested a criss-cross billing, which was alternated every other week.

VINTON FREEDLEY
Presents

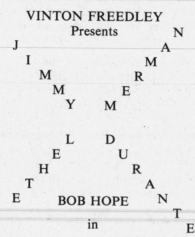

in

RED, HOT, AND BLUE!

What unnerved Hope during rehearsals was the way the book kept changing. When the show moved to Boston, their notices were barely kind, the chief complaint being that there was too much libretto. The show lasted three and a half hours, two and a half of which were first act.

Freedley pressed for a tighter show and asked Porter to write a new Merman song to substitute for one that wasn't working. Cole obliged with "Down in the Depths on the 90th Floor." But when Robert Russell Bennett urged Cole to improve one of the composer's favorite numbers, "Ridin' High," Porter not only resisted haughtily but walked out. He took the train to New York with only a farewell to Merman.

Freedley was livid. He implored Porter to return. The cast, struggling with daily book changes and seeing Porter's defection, sniffed disaster. But when the show reached New Haven for an additional tryout, and the critics blamed the score for some of the show's unevenness, Porter relented and returned to work.

Through it all, Hope sensed the need to guard his own visibility in the show and resist being squeezed out in the battle of the bigger stars. When it appeared he was being axed from the first act finale, for example, he sent Louis Shurr to argue with Lindsay and Crouse about reinstating him so the audience would not forget he was also one of the principals. And besides, from time to time he would toss out an ad lib that the producers asked be left in.

Nonetheless, Hope was unashamedly awed by the outstanding talent he worked with in *Red, Hot and Blue!* Especially, he recognized in Durante a highly skilled artist who took very seriously the business of being an "irresistible vulgarian." Hope recalls a missed cue in Boston:

> He walked to the edge of the orchestra pit, said, "Ha-cha-cha" to the orchestra . . . then he came back to me, gave me a frustrated look and slapped his hips. Next he walked over to the wings and said in a loud voice, "Trow me da book." No one can blow lines louder and funnier than Jimmy and it broke up the audience. Later I realized that this forgetfulness on Jimmy's part was framed. He'd worked it out down to the last frustrated motion. . . .[3]

If Lindsay and Crouse and Freedley were alert to Jimmy's cutting up and his word-torturing, they were also wary of Hope's ad-libbing. They admired the way he could work in a topical reference, and the way he would punch up a flabby line. But they suspected he might damage the show if he was given free rein.

Merman had some of those same fears. "Hope would almost rather kid me and break me up and get the chorus girls—or anyone else on the stage—to laughing than he would to make the audience laugh." Hope is quick to admit that where Merman was concerned he may have gone too far. "I probably kidded around with her too much. I was using ad libs and tomfoolery not in the script."

Merman has been quoted as saying she specifically objected to the way Hope lounged at her feet during their second duet in that show, a love ballad called "You've Got Something." Hope says, "I read that and it simply isn't true. Merman was a great audience—the greatest audience. It was the number—a bad song—it needed some help. It wasn't Merman who got upset, it was Porter. He told the stage manager to tell me to quit clowning and sing it straight."

Red, Hot and Blue! opened at the Alvin Theater on October 29 and it was a gala occasion. Everything about it added up to success, its stars, producers, writers, the music. The advance sale alone guaranteed it to be a hit. Cole Porter arrived for the opening with Mary Pickford on one arm and Merle Oberon on the other, and as was his custom at all first nights of his musicals, he laughed heartily at each bright spot as if he were hearing and seeing it for the first time.

Howard Lindsay remained at home in New Jersey taking telephone reports from his wife, Dorothy Stickney, at the Alvin. Russell Crouse paced the lobby. The critics were generous, agreeing it was no reprise of *Anything Goes* but simply a nonsense vehicle for its clowns. So the book was dismissed, and even Porter's music, except for "It's De-Lovely," was judged second-rate. Merman and Durante were seen as the show's energy and several critics boldly called it Durante's triumph. Hope was not ignored. Winchell wrote: "Hope is a clever comedian when the material is better than it is at the Alvin," but John Mason Brown wrote, "Hope as a comedian is a cultivated taste that I must admit I have never been able to cultivate." The *Evening Journal*'s John Anderson wrote: "Mr. Hope is, as usual, urbane, sleek and nimble of accent. He knows a poor joke when he hides it and he can out-stare more of them."[5]

Raves or pans, what mattered most was that Hope was back on Broadway in an important showcase. He was back in New York where motion picture and radio deals were set by Hollywood "scouts" and visibility was the key. Hope had all but dropped his pretense of total contempt for Hollywood.

So this was to be a crucial regrouping period in his career. He felt constant pressure to locate the right radio format, something different and ear-catching and a packaging that would deliver big-star prominence. He had a fair name already, but he was best known on the radio for dizzy dialogues with Honey Chile, and on the screen for "selected short subjects." His best work to date had been his standup comedy for Orpheum and Loew audiences, and his suave comic portrayals on Broadway stages. There was hardly a home in the nation without a radio set, and he longed to be invited into every living room in America.

As 1936 faded into 1937, *Red, Hot and Blue!* was still doing brisk business. Hope was drawing a four-figure salary, but for the first time in several years his name was less visible on the entertainment pages. He certainly hadn't slowed his pace, especially in benefits. Of the 125 major benefits that the New York Theater Authority reported for the 1936–1937 theatrical season, Hope had contributed to over half of them either as emcee or as performer.

Being associated with Durante meant there was abundant opportunity for benefits. Jimmy was a pushover for any touch. One night some "boys" in Hackensack asked Durante to come across the river and do a few jokes for them at their annual banquet, and Jimmy asked Hope if he'd like to go along. Hope agreed, although Jimmy was not clear—which was characteristically Durante—about who would benefit from their performance.

All the way uptown to the George Washington Bridge, and from Fort Lee down along the Palisades, Jimmy was saying encouraging things about the people they were going to entertain.

In front of a nondescript hotel, they piled out and went upstairs and down a long carpeted hallway to a banquet room. The roar of JIMMMMMMM-EEEE and a few calls of SCHNOZZOLA went up, then Durante went to the platform, which held a three-piece band, and launched into his trademark routine, "Who Will Be With You When You're Far Away," which was always laced with pauses for funny lines. Then he did "Inka Dinka Do," got a big hand and stopped.

"Hey," he said, "I want you to meet a guy who's in the show with me—Bob Hope. He's a good friend and I know you're going to like him. Bob—"

Hope jumped up at his name. In the short time he was waiting for Jimmy to finish he had found out these tough-faced men were beer salesmen. And they were not laughing at his sophisticated standup material with its double meanings. Hope said later:

> I went over with a hush and I thought *I've done my part.* So I looked around and said, "Hey, let's bring our friend Jimmy back." Everybody applauded but Jimmy wasn't there. I looked toward the door. The doorman shrugged and said, "He went that way." I said, "Well, get him, will you?" and to kill time plunged into a golf routine for four or five minutes. "Now, here's Durante!" The hard-faced citizens out front applauded again. I

looked at the door and the guy there said, "I told ya. He went
down the hall." I said, "Fellas, it's been wonderful. . . ."[6]

Hope waved and went for the door. Out in the hall he looked for Durante
thinking he might have had an emergency call to the men's room. Then he
went to the hotel desk and there was told that Jimmy had left some time
ago.

On the street Hope found Durante sitting with Harry Donnelley in their
big car. They were laughing. "How'd it go up there?"

"I thought this was *your* night. What kind of thing was that—leaving me
hanging out like that?"

Durante was nearly choking with laughter. "I didn't figure you'd talk all
night." Jimmy enjoyed his joke. It may have been his way of letting Hope
know who was the star, or dulling some of Hope's brass.

Hope didn't appreciate the gag at that time. But when *Red, Hot and Blue!*
had ceased to play to capacity crowds at the Alvin, Paramount persuaded
Freedley to close on Broadway and move to Chicago. Except for a gigantic
opening night snafu over scenery, the musical was acclaimed by the critics
and settled down for what appeared to be a long run.

One night the first week Durante asked Hope to do a benefit with him at
the Lake Shore Athletic Club. After the curtain calls they changed and
drove over to the club about midnight. Everyone in the room sounded drunk.
There were shouts of "Hey, Jimmy" and "Hey Schnozz" and Durante sat
down at the piano and did his showstopper in *Red, Hot and Blue!* and a joke
or two, then called for his costar Bob Hope. Bob came out, sized up the
crowd which was fast nearing a boisterous state, did some snappy lines and
got a good reception. But suddenly it was déjà vu. At one point he looked
over and saw Jimmy heading for the door, so in a loud voice he said,
"Thanks, folks. I've enjoyed this. But I've been on long enough. Let's bring
back Jimmy Durante."

The audience reacted raucously. They applauded and cheered. Durante
turned around just as he was signing an autograph and someone told him
he'd just been reintroduced. He stood there bowing and blowing kisses.

Hope was still praising him, however. "We can't let him get away without
your favorite number." Now the crowd was on its feet. "How about it, Jimmy?"

Jimmy started back toward the stage. "Jimmy Durante, right here, ladies
and gentlemen!" Hope was applauding as Jimmy came toward him. "Hackensack, you son of a bitch!"

Hope went outside and took a cab back to his hotel. The next day Durante
scrawled YOU ARE A LOUSE on Hope's dressing room mirror and scattered
powder around.

But the two men had tremendous respect for each other, and for roughly
forty years they enjoyed any opportunity to clown together.

While I was on the Woodbury Show . . . Paramount realized I was very stubborn and that I was going to stay in show business, regardless of my talents. So they decided to give me a chance to play opposite Shirley Ross . . . and she requested I play as far opposite as possible. . . .[1]

14. Hollywood, Take Two

The closing of *Red, Hot and Blue!* at Chicago's Civic Opera House on May 3, 1937, only two weeks after its warm critical reception, dismayed its producer but not its stars. Merman, Durante and Hope had other fish to fry.

Ethel went off to make the film *Happy Landing* with Sonja Henie and Don Ameche, Jimmy stayed in Chicago to fill a nightclub engagement before doing some radio guest shots. And Hope hurried back to New York to write a comedy script because he was auditioning for the Lennen and Mitchell ad agency to be the master of ceremonies for the Jergens-Woodbury–sponsored *Rippling Rhythm Revue*. This radio show had originally been conceived as a musical variety format to air over NBC at nine on Sunday nights. But this season, Sunday night had become the arena for comedians, and Lennen and Mitchell wanted to get into the ring.

Hope had listened to as much radio comedy as he could in an effort to know what other comedians were doing. The question was: How different could he be? After Louis Shurr's call to him in Chicago, Hope had only five days to create a fresh format. Feeling that his vaudeville background was his strongest asset, he decided to borrow a few components from his stage act.

At the top of the show he wanted to use the stooge idea, so he devised the following opening: A newsboy calls "Extra! Extra! Read all about it! Hope goes on the Woodbury Program—Extra! Extra!" Next the announcer, Ben Grauer, was to say: "It's the talk of the town! Bob Hope joins Woodbury's *Rippling Rhythm* tonight. Everyone—everywhere—is talking about it—on the streets!"

(Traffic)

1ST MAN:	Hey, Sam—what's your hurry?
2ND MAN:	(*Breathless*) Didn't you hear? Bob Hope's goin' on the Woodbury program tonight. So long!
1ST MAN:	What you doin'—rushing home to your radio?
2ND MAN:	No—I'm goin' to the movies.
	(*Drum and Cymbal*)
GRAUER:	In the homes!
WOMAN:	John, what are you doing?
MAN:	Haven't you heard? Bob Hope goes on the Woodbury program tonight.
	(*Crash*)
WOMAN:	Why, John—you broke the radio!
MAN:	You're telling me!
	(*Drum and Cymbal*)

GRAUER: ~~At the Medical Center!~~

NURSE: Doctor! Doctor! We're all out of ether—How can
            we operate? How are we going to put the patient to
            sleep?

DOCTOR: Turn on the radio—Bob Hope's on the Woodbury
            program.[2]

After a suitable straight program opening and commercial message, Hope
would be introduced:

GRAUER: And now ladies and gentlemen, we give you Wood-
            bury's new comedian, who will keep you lathered
            with laughs, bubbling with joy, and clean with his
            new brand of humor. That young comedy star, Bob
            Hope.
            (*Applause*)

HOPE: Thank you, ladies and gentlemen, and thank you,
            Ben—that introduction really got me—bubbling
            with joy, lathered with laughs—you've got me all
            washed up already.

What Hope was doing was different from anyone else. Other Sunday-night
comedians had the advantage, or disadvantage, of their well-entrenched per-
sonae or of the situation in which they played their lines. Hope was out there
doing monologue.

Later in the show he worked with a new Honey Chile, Clare Hazel, a
pretty young actress from Bennettsville, South Carolina. Two reasons were
given for the disappearance of Margaret Johnson: one, her voice was too
similar to that of Judy Canova, the star of an NBC radio program immediately preceding the *Rippling Rhythm Revue*; two, she had an offer from
Columbia Pictures.

Some reviewers found Hope labored. But *Variety*, the source most actors
believe, said on May 12, 1937:

Bob Hope's addition to *Rippling Rhythm Revue* as m.c. and fun-
ster appears just what the doctor ordered. Certainly his presence
patches those lulls that have been bobbing up of late. Fashion in
which Hope maneuvers the program, glibly filling in gaps and
introducing numbers, definitely sets him up. Result was one of the
swiftest moving *Rippling* stanzas in many weeks. Hope added
enough fresh chatter and gags to give entire broadcast a
lift. . . .

When it was announced a few weeks later that the Woodbury program
had been picked up for another thirteen weeks, Hope's spirits soared. Radio
thought he, was the route to popular success and exactly where he wanted to
be. But he realized he needed an expert to guide him through the fast
growing complexities of this big-business medium. "I met a young agent
named Jimmy Saphier. I not only got to know him, I liked him. I found him
shrewd boy who knew the business, and my kind of guy." Hope felt Saphier
to be creative and courageous. He was right. Saphier, in later years, said:

I had watched Hope at the Capitol and had seen him in a Broadway musical before I heard him on the radio and I felt it was a shame the home listeners weren't getting the best of him. Radio simply wasn't using his talents properly. I knew this and I sensed Bob knew it but didn't yet know how to overcome it. His work with a foil was funny, but his strength seemed to me and also to him—eventually—to be centered in what he did best—the monologue.[3]

Hope and Saphier signed an agreement for a one-year period. They never signed another, and their profitable association lasted nearly 40 years until Saphier's death in 1974.

The other area Hope felt deficient in was his public relations. He had noticed how network radio publicity could result in phenomenal national exposure with a single item. And one unfortunate experience taught him the value of a press agent in softening a negative story. The incident revolved around Hope's role as first baseman on a softball team that was made up of radio actors and musicians who played exhibition games for charity in Central Park on Sunday afternoons. The games attracted attention and were generously publicized, especially now that the team was winning.

One Sunday in June, two days after Hope signed a contract with Paramount Pictures for his first Hollywood feature, *The Big Broadcast of 1938* (a fact that got less attention than it should), he was feeling good and "cutting up." According to an Associated Press wire story on June 23, 1937:

> Those baseball games are still going on in Central Park. Frank Parker, who started them, hasn't turned up in the last few Sundays, but he has sent his substitute, Bob Hope, to play first base. Personally we don't think there is much hope for Hope—as a first baseman. The guy is always clowning. Last Sunday there was quite a turnout of spectators. Honey Chile, Bob's stooge, was on the sidelines heckling as Hope let the ball go by him. She brought three very charming ladies along, and Bob put on a show for them.
>
> Radio celebrity or not, it didn't make much difference to the rest of the gang who take their baseball seriously. A press agent playing shortstop almost took a poke at Hope for missing a beautiful throw to his position. "Keep your mind off the girls, you lug," he yelled at Bob. "This is a ball game." Hope quieted down.

After that, Hope became increasingly convinced that a story like that could have been minimized if he had a reliable press agent, one who could get Bob's Paramount movie deal and his new Honey Chile the attention they deserved.

The publicist Hope admired most was Mack Millar, who was handling press for Shep Fields among others. Mack was acquainted with most of the reporters and columnists who mattered, plus several Hearst executives. He was a tough-talking, soft-hearted guy who gave as good as he got from Winchell, Sullivan and the influential Runyon. Hope knew it would be difficult to entice Mack away from New York but approached him anyway.

"Shep has also been signed for *The Big Broadcast*, Bob," said Mack. "So I'll be out there for a few weeks and if there's anything I can do, I will. In fact, if there's anything I can do for you while you're still in town, let me know."

Not long after that, Hope asked Mack if he could help with an effort to publicize his prediction that "the monologue shows promise of being a new major radio trend." A few days later, Mack called and told Hope he would be talking to Sam Kaufman of the *New York Sun*. Kaufman was a crack entertainment columnist whose policy was well known among publicists: Sam Kaufman does his interviews without press agents in the room. This interview, which appeared on August 5, 1937, in the *New York Sun*, was a remarkably self-fulfilling prophecy.

"I'm curious about your monologue prediction, Bob—er, do you object to people calling you Bob right away?"

"No—no, that's fine. Well, it won't be a new thing by a long shot because Will Rogers certainly clicked with it on the air many years ago. But the monologue is now showing definite signs of being a main comedy trend. The stunt is a takeoff on the old vaudeville days and that, perhaps, is why former stars of variety shows—like myself—can spot early signs of its big radio future."

"Tell me more about a monologue."

"Well, my solo bits are patterned after my stage style. True to vaudeville formula, I attempt to make my topics newsy and seasonal. But I also find that the microphone has certain limitations that are absent on the stage, and I can't, for example, make humorous references to such headline events as child marriages and coronations."

"Why not? Too timely—too touchy?"

"Frankly—yes."

"Okay. Do you want to say more on that?"

"Frankly—no."

"Oh—well—uh—what else can't you do in radio?"

"I've always approached it like I would the stage. And you can't. Like all beginners, when I auditioned I was ghastly. I went too fast. And the lines that used to snap like a whip on stage became just a blurr through the microphone. So I consciously had to slow down and—"

"Didn't Winchell tag you for your mannerisms?"

"Yeah—Winchell said that he would tell me to stop that God-awful 'hmmm-ha-ha-hmmm' noise that I made at the end of each joke—it may be funny on the stage but on the air it sounds as if I'd eaten too many green apples. Do you believe that? So I've cut out the moans, coughs and grunts and all the ways that I was trying to convey grimaces—and then the press and audiences seemed to love it."

"What about all this controversy about live studio audiences?"

"Well, I've had some doubts. You know *Radio Daily* quoted my question about whether the people at home were getting as much kick out of the program as the people in the studio. It's not difficult to get laughs from your studio audience because you can influence them by your physical personality—but I'm not at all sure the listener is having the same hilarious time, and after all, it's the listener who pays for the performance."

"Do you need an audience?"

"Sure I do. But I worry about the listener. I work best with an audience. I can feel out a response. Now, maybe an audience wouldn't be right or necessary for some of the situation comedies. But I have to say that comedy and laughs go together."

"He who laughs alone laughs least?" Kaufman prompted.

"Exactly. Studio laughter can be just as important to the faraway listener as it is to the comedian. A very funny joke uttered in an empty studio could fall flat over the air with all that mass laughter missing. The home listener gets a far greater kick out of a joke when he has company, and he gets the point quicker when he hears the studio audience reaction. Let's face it, the program can seem funnier than it actually is with studio laughter."

"Then it's good for everybody?" Sam asked.

"Not really. The critics object—they say we clown around for the studio audience and try to break them up and the home audience is missing the gag."

"Don't you think that's a fair criticism?"

"Probably—but let me tell you from an entertainer's viewpoint, it's important to get the feel of audience response while on the air. This is especially true of monologues. The only way you can time a piece of material right is with an audience. Counting their laughs and observing their expressions are both vital to a successful comedy program. I've counted twenty laughs in an average monologue bit. This is important from a production point of view because it allows us to accurately time the show. I know where to pause to let a joke strike home. If I fail to hesitate at just the right moment, the point of a joke might slip by."

"Do all comedians analyze their style and their comedy production this carefully?"

"I don't know about the rest—but I would bet a guy like Benny—in fact I *know*—he simply has to consciously make these judgments. He has such fabulous timing. His whole act is timing. And he needs a studio audience as well. He gives 'em that look. It's all a matter of eye appeal."

"Explain that."

"Eye appeal may sound silly for a radio show but not really. Take Honey Chile. I've had three of them since the *Intimate Revue*—Patricia Wilder, who got a movie contract out of it—Margaret Johnson, who is also headed for Hollywood—and now Clare Hazel who does legit stage work all week— she's touring in *Brother Rat*—and then flies in here to do our program on Sundays. Each one was picked for looks as much as for voice."

"You find looks that important?"

"Yes, and for two reasons. First, a beautiful girl adds a decorative touch to the studio setting and as I already said I believe in catering to studio audiences. Second, when it comes to publicity and photographs, the program gets a much better break with a pretty girl as a subject."

"One more question. What got you into radio in the first place?"

"Well, as you know I was doing a Broadway show and vaudeville in between. I saw radio as promotion—as pure publicity to build audiences for my stage work. But then the more I got into it I saw the way it was going and it's the hot thing of the future—and—I really liked the money."

"One more?"

"Sure. We've got a few more minutes."

"You're going to Hollywood?"

"Yeah. I'm doing it. All my friends tell me it's not going to be as bad as I think."

The door opened and Dolores stepped in. "Is it okay? Are you through?"

"Not quite. Dolores, this is Sam Kaufman of the *Sun*. My wife Dolores, Sam. She knows how I feel about moving to the Coast. We've always hated the idea of leaving New York. And this may not be permanent—probably won't be. I've only signed for the one picture—with options if that one works. Sounds good, though—Shirley Ross, Dorothy Lamour, W.C. Fields, and our radio band, Shep Fields, too. Remember Lamour when she used to sing at Number One Fifth? Beautiful girl."

"And Jack Benny?"

"No. Benny's out—that's how I got the part."

"Oh," said Kaufman. He looked at Hope. "What about radio? Your thirteen-week contract with Woodbury?"

"My boy Jimmy Saphier has been talking to them. They've been thinking about switching the show to Hollywood anyway. And even if they don't, we feel we can work it out so I can continue to do my part long distance—from the NBC studios in Hollywood. It's been done before."

Kaufman stood up to leave. "Still playing first base in Central Park?"

"You heard about that, huh?"

"I heard you nearly decked some press agent."

"It was the other way around. I could have flattened him——. But it's a celebrity charity game. What do you want? People come out there *expecting* some high jinks. We're not baseball players, for God's sake—we're entertainers. What's wrong with getting a few laughs?"

HOLLYWOOD
1938–1941

When I stepped off the train in Pasadena, there was no block-long limousine waiting to whisk Dolores and me to a mansion in Bel Air. No dancing starlets with baskets of grapefruit. Not even a redcap with wilted gladiolas.[1]

15. New Boy in Town

For many years Hope has joked about what didn't happen when he, Dolores and Doc Shurr got off the Super Chief that Thursday, September 9, 1937, in Pasadena. To hear him tell it, their arrival went unnoticed. Not quite. A Paramount publicity man and a photographer from the *Los Angeles Morning News* were there. Dolores picked up their Scottie, Suds, for a pose with Bob and the photog snapped a standard publicity shot of two stylish visitors from the East.

On page 13 of Friday's *Morning News*, a small photo was headlined: A COMEDIAN AND HIS WIFE. It captioned Hope as "never appeared in a major screen feature."

Hope admits he was still nursing a "log-sized chip" on his shoulder from the 1930 screen-test rebuff. He tartly reminded Shurr that their "seven-year Paramount contract with options" worked both ways: What they really had was a one-picture deal with no promises either way.

The Hopes checked into the Beverly-Wilshire, and although the film was not scheduled to roll until the following Monday, Bob went to the studio that same day to meet producer Harlan Thompson and some others on his staff. Assistant producer Billy Selwyn wanted Hope to hear the duet he and Shirley Ross would be singing in the picture. As they walked over to the music department, Selwyn praised the bouncy melody and the lyric that Leo Robin and Ralph Rainger had written and described the urbane setting. Hope nodded. He had already read the script.

The plot of *The Big Broadcast of 1938* was standard silly, involving a transatlantic race between two ultramodern ocean liners, the S.S. *Gigantic* and the S.S. *Colossal*. The drawling W.C. Fields would play the skipper of the *Gigantic* with Hope cast as a radio announcer who is emcee for the musical variety shows that take place in the ship's lounge. Hope's job was to introduce Tito Guizar and Kirsten Flagstad, among others. Hope's was a stereotype of the ego-ridden entertainer on the make. He has three failed marriages, one of these to Shirley Ross. In their bittersweet duet, "Thanks for the Memory," Bob and Shirley engage in a sophisticated exchange about their past life together.

Hope liked the song at once and asked if he could borrow a transcription so Dolores could hear the song. When he got back to the hotel, Dolores was upset.

"I don't think I like this town," she said.

"Why? You'll get used to it."

"I went to the beauty parlor today—it's the one where everyone goes. The manicurist asked how I happened to be here and I told her you were in show business and that you were here for *The Big Broadcast.* Then she asked me my name. I told her and she didn't even look up. I said I'm Mrs. Bob Hope and she said she never heard of you. I said you were one of Broadway's biggest stars and a radio name as well. I told her to listen Sunday night—"[2]

"That reminds me, did Wilkie Mahoney call?" interrupted Bob.

"Bob, don't you care?"

"Sure I care, Dolores, but wait until you hear the song they've given me in the picture. I brought it home for you to hear."

From the massive Capehart phonograph an untempo melody was tinkled out by a studio pianist. "What do you think?"

"This is your solo?"

"No—I only have a duet with Shirley Ross. It's called 'Thanks for the Memory' and there's a whole scene built around it."

"I don't think it's much."

"I think it's terrific myself," Bob said defensively.

"You know what I'd like?" Dolores asked.

"What?"

"To have a good cry,"

"Go ahead," Bob said.

Bob spent Saturday rewriting and timing the *Rippling Rhythm Revue* monologue with Wilkie Mahoney. Hope would be delivering it at approximately 6:15 on Sunday in an NBC studio in Hollywood for inclusion in the New York-based show.

The next afternoon, he and Dolores went to the studio so that Bob could work with the engineer, timing the monologue to fit the five-minute spot. The NBC executive assigned to help him showed up, and Hope asked what time the audience would be admitted.

"What audience?"

"For my monologue."

"There isn't going to be an audience."

"*What*? I have to have an audience to bounce my comedy off of, or I'm dead. What shows are here today?"

"Bergen's next door."

"What time?"

"Five-thirty to six."

"Perfect."

Hope went next door where Bergen was rehearsing and when Edgar was free Bob asked if he could steal his audience. The ventriloquist, once bounced from the *Ziegfeld Follies*, now had *the* top-rated radio program on Sunday night radio. He liked Hope and agreed to help. Together they instructed the NBC audience page-ushers to set up a rope path for the audience leaving the Bergen studio so that, like cattle, they would be prodded blindly into Hope's adjacent studio.

Once there, the audience was bewildered. Some refused to stay. A few recognized Hope but most were uneasy. Hope stood on the stage saying, "Come on in, folks, and sit down. I'm Bob Hope and I'm going to do a show for New York in a minute or two. It's a very funny show and I think you'll enjoy it." The following two weeks, until the Woodbury series ended, NBC printed tickets and Hope had his own laughers.

Early Monday morning September 15, Hope reported to Paramount for makeup. After introductions, makeup artist Wally Westmore invited Hope to sit in the chair and then, like an artist or photographer, studied Hope's nose from every possible angle.

"I can shadow this for you now but if you're smart you ought to think about some surgery."

"What?" Hope flared, "I've been doing pretty well with this nose up to now."

"All I can tell you is that the camera is going to get a lot closer to you than any audience has so far."

"You never played vaudeville," cracked Hope.

At home that night Dolores reacted violently. "No! They're not going to talk you into it. I love your face the way it is."

"But it might make a difference when it comes time to offer me a better contract."

"Bob, your whole personality is in your face. They want to turn you into just another leading man. No—please don't."

Nevertheless the idea was kept alive at Paramount by executives who couldn't make up their minds and by Westmore in the makeup chair each morning.[3]

Another problem was Hope's vaudeville delivery. After each comedy line, he would pause for a laugh. Hope observed, "I was merely obeying the old theatrical impulse to wait for laughs. I felt that I could shake the habit but it might take time." After a few days, Hope's remarkable self-discipline took over and the pauses disappeared.

More serious was Hope's inability to sense the important role of the eyes in creating a credible film performance. Leisen finally decided he should counsel the newcomer.

"You know that Harlan and I saw you in the *Follies* and *Red, Hot and Blue!* and we liked the way you work. When Benny dropped out on us we thought you were the only one," Leisen said.

"Thanks, Mitch. I appreciate that. But I must be doing something wrong."

"Not wrong. I want to give you some advice and I hope you remember it. Try to think through your eyes. When you're thinking about what you're going to say, you will alter the muscles of your eyes. All the great movie actors deliver the line with their eyes before they say it with their mouths. Remember that—think the emotion and it will register in your eyes."

These wise words preceded the shooting session in which Hope and Shirley Ross were to sing "Thanks for the Memory." Leisen wanted to try something unusual. Normally, Bob and Shirley would have prerecorded the song and then synchronized their lips to the soundtrack. This time, Leisen ordered the Paramount orchestra moved on to the set and, against Robin's and Rainger's wishes, he slowed the tempo.

When Hope and Ross finished the scene, both Robin and Rainger were in tears. One of them said, "We didn't know the song was that good." The crew applauded.

Hope later learned that Dorothy Lamour had been offered the song. She had realized it could result in Hope's making an impression, and generously insisted he and Shirley do it together.

Hope was grateful that he got on so well with his director, unlike Bill
Fields, who refused to take direction from anyone. He would rewrite his lines
and then proceed to do the scene in his own style, which infuriated Leis-
en.

Fields, particular about the company he kept, seemed to like Hope and
sometimes invited him to share a drink in his dressing room. Hope says:

> . . . he didn't like too many people. He didn't want people
> around. But he liked me, and I got to know him. He was marvel-
> ous. All he ever really wanted to do in the movies was to rework
> his vaudeville material and make it fit in whatever picture he was
> making. He'd read a script and tell the producer he could fix it up
> for $50,000. What he would do was put in business from his
> vaudeville act—like the golf game which he put into *The Big
> Broadcast*.[4]

At that time Paramount had under contract a powerhouse of comedy tal-
ent, and for Hope to be in their company was both unnerving and challeng-
ing. Besides Fields, there were people like Gracie Allen, Benny Baker, Jack
Benny, Ben Blue, Bob Burns, Charles Butterworth, Bill Frawley, Russell
Hayden, Roscoe Karns, Bea Lillie, Harold Lloyd, Martha Raye, Charlie
Ruggles and Mae West. On the dramatic side were box office leaders like
Edward Arnold, Lew Ayres, Charles Bickford, William Boyd, Gary Cooper,
Bing Crosby, Robert Cummings, Marlene Dietrich, Frances Farmer, Gabby
Hayes, Marsha Hunt, Dorothy Lamour, Carole Lombard, Ida Lupino, Fred
MacMurray, Ray Milland, Lloyd Nolan, Anthony Quinn, George Raft,
Shirley Ross and Randolph Scott.

Being part of such a film factory and only a beginner, so to speak—
pending contract renewal—compelled Hope to step up his publicity operation. One day on the *Broadcast* set, Hope saw Mack Millar, out from New
York, talking to his client Shep Fields. Hope waited until he was finished.

"What's your opinion of Paramount's publicity set-up, Mack?"

"Tops."

"They'll treat me right?"

"That depends. No studio publicity department no matter how big and
how good can do a job for all its stars. They do the best job on stills. They
shoot up a storm, they'll send out as much as you're willing to pose for. The
news and feature side is tougher."

"I'd like to hire you—but you're too far away. I can't afford you."

Mack took a long, long look at Hope. "Yes, you can. My wife Rita—lovely
gal—wants to move to California. I've been thinking of opening up out here.
If you'll be my first client, I think I can swing it. I'll need $200 a week."
Millar looked at Hope searchingly.

"One fifty—with promises," countered Hope.

"Deal."

There was no formal contract, no terms, no guarantees, but their relationship lasted until Millar's death in *1962*.[5]

Millar's immediate strategy was to augment every news story or puff item
the studio office issued, and to make up a few of his own. In early November
there were several items of news that Mack could thump his tub about. One
Paramount liked the rushes of *The Big Broadcast* well enough to pick up

Hope's option. Two, Hope had been handed an important role in *College Swing*, a part originally announced for Jack Oakie.

Hope's landing an A picture like *College Swing* was a career break. Oakie's publicity reason for exiting the film was "interfering schedules" at RKO, but *Daily Variety*'s version suggested that Oakie felt he might get lost amid the likes of Burns and Allen, Martha Raye, Edward Everett Horton, Ben Blue, Betty Grable, Jackie Coogan, the Slate Brothers, Charlie Butterworth, Skinnay Ennis, Nell Kelly, John Payne and popular radio soprano Florence George in her screen debut.

Oakie's defection caused Hope to ask questions. After reading the script, he had little doubt that the insignificant part would bury him. Hope discovered the producer was Lew Gensler, his old friend from *Ballyhoo of 1932*. Figuring that Gensler owed him a little something from *Ballyhoo* (if only a little unpaid salary), he persuaded Lew to fatten the part.

The plot of this picture was even sillier than his first, but he was lucky in having scenes with zany Martha Raye, and Mack Millar predicted that their novelty duet "How'dja Like to Love Me?" by Frank Loesser and Burton Lane would be as big a hit as "Thanks for the Memory." It wasn't.

Off the set, Hope welcomed the chance to make new friends like trombonist Jerry Colonna and singer Skinnay Ennis, and renew some old friendships as well. Inevitably, his reunion with fellow Paramount player Bing Crosby was most exploited by Paramount's public relations department. The reunion was, in fact, associated with a publicity stunt on the golf course, only the first of many. On October 15, 1937 the United Press sent out this item:

> On Sunday, Crosby and Bob Hope, who just arrived from Broadway to work in pictures, will play for the dubious title of "Golf Champion of the Entertainment World." The loser will work for one day as extra in the other's current picture.

It made good publicity sense to put syndicated columnist Ed Sullivan in the match as Bing's partner because there would doubtless be mentions in several columns. Hope, who shot an 84, lost to Crosby with a 72, and there were suitably chagrined looks on Hope's face in press photographs over the prospect of working as an extra in Crosby's film *Doctor Rhythm*.

But publicity stunts, column items and a yet unreleased movie were the extent of Hope's credentials in a tough and snobbish town where an entertainer was chiefly recognized by his box office charisma. Hope was concerned about his stalled radio career and badgered Jimmy Saphier continuously to find him a series. Unfortunately, no sponsor thought Hope was quite ready.

Meanwhile, all Hope could do was to keep himself visible through publicity appearances and as many benefits as he could find to do. Both Bob and Dolores were depressed and Dolores was ready to pack up and return to Manhattan.

Hope's most cheering gift that first Christmas in California came from Saphier, whose negotiations with Albert Lasker of the Lord and Thomas ad agency netted Hope a guest spot on the Lucky Strike-sponsored *Your Hollywood Parade*. The best part of the deal was Lasker's guarantee of a permanent spot on the show if Hope clicked in one or two guest appearances.

Dick Powell was the show's headliner, Rosemary Lane the girl singer and music was by Al Goodman's orchestra. The theme of the hour-long program was Hollywood—its films, its people, its music and its glamour, with movie personalities appearing for interviews with Powell, or in scenes from current Hollywood films, or in original short dramas by Arch Oboler.

Hope's initial guesting was scheduled for December 29 and because *College Swing* was still shooting, he and Wilkie Mahoney would sit up for hours (sometimes they'd work the night through) preparing two five-minute monologue segments. The first segment featured gags about Christmas, self-effacing remarks about his own tentative movie career, followed by a dialogue with Powell that further publicized the recent golf match with Bing Crosby.

In his second monologue segment the subject was Santa Anita and horses and more about Hollywood stars:

> . . . My grandfather, Colonel Hospitality Julip Hope, A.B. . . . Always Broke . . . was interested in horses ever since he was old enough to steal them . . . Grandad's racing colors were beautiful . . . black and white stripes . . . he had his winter quarters at San Quentin. . . . He would have enjoyed Santa Anita, especially on opening day . . . with all the movie stars and the fashion show . . . what a day for the stars to dress . . . Paulette Goddard came in with a silver fox cape around her neck which later turned out to be Charlie Chaplin . . . Barbara Stanwyck took no chances . . . she had her tailor with her. . . .[6]

Hope's material was not hilarious, yet his timing must have worked especially well because the trade press and the daily radio columnists praised his debut.

Lasker informed Saphier that Lucky Strike owner George Washington Hill liked Hope. Hill was, as radio sponsors go, a kibitzer and an omnipresent force in all three of his radio programs. He objected to Powell as an emcee but liked his singing, and said he would prefer to have Hope running *Your Hollywood Parade*. But the best Hope was offered was a regular featured comedy spot on the show for the remainder of its run, which unfortunately ended March 23, 1938.

Before that date, Bob Hope was "discovered" by Hollywood and by many of the nation's most influential columnists and motion picture critics. On March 8, *The Big Broadcast of 1938* was previewed by most of the major news outlets and the scene between Hope and Shirley Ross singing "Thanks for the Memory" was noted as a standout. Hope was personally singled out by Walter Winchell, Nick Kenny, Ed Sullivan, Hedda Hopper and Louella Parsons as a candidate for film stardom. Damon Runyon in his March 13 column was so impressed that he wrote the first half of his syndicated column celebrating the emotional impact that the Hope–Ross scene had on him.

Hope was also beginning to reap personal affection and respect because of his M.C. chores at several important industry benefits, including the Film Welfare League, the glittering Temple Israel benefit and the all-star tribute to the memory of Ted Healy. At the Ted Healy affair, Dolores took the stage

'or three ballads, and during the third song Bob repeated his vaudeville trick
of lounging at his wife's feet. The inordinate applause helped Dolores feel she
belonged in her new surroundings.

As Hope was handed his third film assignment at Paramount, *Give Me A
Sailor*—a second-rate potboiler with Martha Raye—other demands on his
time were increasing, especially for studio promotions, publicity and benefits. Capable as he was, he ran out of time and needed a buffer, a road
manager, someone he could trust who would help him to keep things straight
and to say no, a hard thing for him to do.

Bob instinctively thought of his brother Jack, the older brother, an aspiring songwriter who was keeping himself alive by supervising two meat markets in Akron, Ohio. He was sensitive, intelligent and a fan of Bob's. He was
also between marriages. So Bob picked up the phone one day.

"How's it going, Jack?"

"Lovely, Les. Say—I've got a song that would be just the—"

"Forget the song, Jack. How would you like to drop what you're doing and
come out and help me? I need someone to take care of my business."

Jack was stunned, then shouted. "Of course I will. I'll leave right
away."

Jack quit his job, packed his bags, got into his 1937 Pontiac and drove
nonstop to Los Angeles. Having no idea where to find the house that Bob and
Dolores had leased from Rhea Gable, he drove straight to the Paramount lot.
Exhausted and grubby, he pulled up at the De Mille Gate in his dusty road-
ster and asked if he could talk to Bob Hope.

"Who shall I say is calling?" asked the guard.

"His brother!" With blond hair, blue eyes and thin face, Jack in no way
resembled Bob. "I'm his brother. *I really am!*"

The standoff between the gateman and Jack lasted until Bob was finally
reached by phone. Jack arrived on a bright day for his brother. Louella
Parsons, the Hearst soothsayer whose words were gospel to some and a
scourge to others, had noted in her October 10, 1938 column:

> . . . Bob Hope, scoring both on radio and in 'Big Broadcast',
> has been given a star dressing room at Paramount. . . .

*I believe I was the first of the comedians to hire several
writers at a time. I think I was also the first to admit openly
that I employed writers. In the early days of radio, comedians fostered the illusion that all of those funny sayings came
right out of their own skulls.*[1]

16. This Is Bob (Pepsodent) Hope

Even before *Your Hollywood Parade* was canceled, talks between Albert
Lasker in Chicago and Jimmy Saphier in New York had begun, and the
transcontinental conversations between Saphier's office and Hope's new star
dressing room at the studio became longer and more frequent. The subject of

all these negotiations was a very big prize—a long-term radio contract. Lord and Thomas had reached the decision that after nine years the *Amos 'n' Andy* sales pitch for Pepsodent toothpaste was losing its power. Now the agency boys were searching for a new comedy sound to sell their product, and they liked the breezy, topical monologues they heard from Hope on their own Dick Powell show.

Hope, of course, wanted top money, but even more than that, he wanted creative control. Saphier wrote Bob a letter outlining the details of a proposed six-year contract, to begin in September 1938 at $3,000 a show and progress to $5,000 for each program in 1944. It guaranteed Hope full production control. But Saphier also warned that Pepsodent's head man, Eddie Lasker, Albert's brother, had not signed on the dotted line because of Hope's tendency toward risqué material, and because Hope was considered by some industry people to be too brash. Saphier wrote:

> If there ever is the slightest question raised about the good taste of any joke, he (Lasker) thinks that the mere fact that anyone questioned it should be sufficient reason to take that joke out. I quite agree with him in this respect . . . One off-color gag in an otherwise socko routine can easily nullify all the good efforts of your work.
>
> The other point is also one we have discussed before, and that is the care we should take to prevent your being a smart alec . . . on this show let's try to build a lot of sympathy for your character, and have the rest of the cast bounce their jokes off you. This, too, is very important, as only sympathetic comedians have a chance for long life on the air.[2]

Saphier's perceptions were sharp, and Hope was pleased.

However, Hope was troubled about the direction of his movie career. It was option time again but Paramount was being cagey. *Give Me a Sailor* was finished but not ready for release. *College Swing* was playing in theaters but Hope's performance hadn't thrilled the critics. And although *The Big Broadcast* was no longer before the public, the hit tune "Thanks for the Memory" *was*. Mack Millar made certain that studio boss Y. Frank Freeman's polished oak desk—and all the rest of Paramount's executive oak desks—were piled high with copies of Damon Runyon's glowing review of Hope's performance in that film, and any other pro-Hope clippings he could find. Still no contract.

But Hope kept busy. He grabbed Edwin Lester's offer to re-create his role of Huckleberry Haines in the Los Angeles Light Opera's West Coast premiere of *Roberta*. Hope was delighted to be back onstage and show Los Angeles what he could do with an audience. The show was scheduled to run from June 6 to June 21 at Philharmonic Auditorium downtown. Tamara and Ray Middleton returned to their original roles, and young screen actress Carole Landis played Sophie. The opening was glittering. Kern was on hand to acknowledge the new songs he had written for this revival. Hollywood loved *Roberta*.

The day the show opened, amid a flurry of high-strung publicity, Y. Frank Freeman called Shurr and said the studio was picking up Hope's contract. Further, they said they planned to rematch Hope and Shirley Ross immedi ately in a film tailored especially for them entitled *Thanks for the Memory* (actually it was a dusted-off shelf property formerly called *Up Pops the Devil*).

Shurr reminded Paramount that there would have to be a slight delay in plans because, while the studio vacillated, Hope had signed himself to a summer vaudeville tour on the Loew circuit. The day after *Roberta* closed, Hope took Dolores as his girl singer and Jackie Coogan as a clowning partner and flew to New York. They opened June 23 at Loew's State and Bob was happy to be back on Broadway. Once in New York, he found himself describing, and defending, life in Hollywood.

"What's the essential difference between your work in films and your work on the stage?" a *New York World-Telegram* reporter asked.

"This!" Hope jutted out his chin, raised one eyebrow and fixed his eyes in a silly stare. "That's for the screen. That—and a close up, and you've got what the camera needs." Then he reassembled his features and made a different kind of body movement. He hunched forward and raised his neck like a giraffe. "Now, this is what you have to do here so they can see you all the way to the back row."

"Do you like it out there?"

"Why not? They're giving me better parts. And I can play golf with Dad—Crosby, that is—all year round, and go to quiet parties."

"Quiet parties?" the reporter asked incredulously.

"Most of the movie fellows don't drink. You can't drink and get up at five o'clock. So you can go into a party and when the waiter says 'What's yours?'—you can say, 'A glass of water' and nobody notices."

Hope's comment seemed to be flying in the face of stereotype and the reporter just stared at him, puzzled.[3]

On July 17, Bob and Dolores went back to Los Angeles. And this time their arrival was marked by a move toward permanence, a new rented house with their own furniture on Navajo Street in the Toluca Lake section of North Hollywood. They were just a short walk from Hope's favorite golf course, Lakeside. It was also just a short walk to Warner Brothers, to Universal, or to Columbia's ranch. Crosby was a neighbor, and so was W.C. Fields, Mary Astor, George Brent, Ruby Keeler, Jimmy Cagney, Humphrey Bogart, Ozzie and Harriet Nelson, Slim Summerville, Brod Crawford and a number of directors, writers and producers. It was convenient to almost anyplace in the city and yet it had the privacy film stars claimed they craved. There was a modest, man-made lake around which were several waterfront estates and hideaway homes with views of the golf course.

The Hopes were glad to be reunited with their own furniture and they soon settled into a social life revolving chiefly around golf, events at the Lakeside clubhouse and their Toluca Lake neighbors. Dolores was grateful for the early and close relationship they developed with Charles and Mildred MacArthur who lived nearby. He was one of the film colony's best talent agents, and she was a Yorba, a sixth-generation Californian and a Lakeside and Pebble Beach golf champion. And Dolores, for the first time in California, felt her homemaking instincts ripen. It had become evident to Bob and Dolores that if they wanted children they would have to adopt them, and Dolores was ready to start a family.[4]

The publicity for Bob's new radio series was released in mid-August but nothing changed at Paramount. The studio seemed to have low-budget pictures in mind for him. So Hope returned to work to make *Thanks for the Memory* with a resigned attitude. He told Hedda Hopper, who had a featured role in the film and who also was a *Los Angeles Times* gossip columnist, that he refused to get into a battle with Paramount for putting him in B pictures. "I'd rather make a good B than an epic that people take instead of sleeping pills."[5]

Besides he had plenty on his mind. He was now a radio producer, when he wasn't acting on a soundstage. His dressing room, which had always been a turmoil of wardrobe and dialogue conferences and an endless chain of meetings with talent agents and publicity people, was now also the scene of interviews with gag writers and meetings with NBC officials and advertising agency executives about format and procedures.

Amazingly, in the midst of the babble of many voices and a scene that resembled total pandemonium, Hope remained calm and professional, ready in his makeup, in his wardrobe, and always line perfect.

Shirley Ross was impressed with Hope's editorial skills, his ability to improve a line or fix a comedy scene. She told a writer, "He's shrewd. I don't think there's anyone in Hollywood his equal at weighing the possibilities of a joke. And I don't know anyone with such a terrific capacity for work and play at the same time. No matter how hard we're working, nothing interferes with his love of fun."[6]

Hope liked to work to an audience and he used his stage crew to test jokes both behind and before the camera. He gagged his way through rehearsals and frequently director George Archinbaud was not amused. A case in point was the chewing gum episode.

Both Hope and Ross chewed gum for relaxation and to keep their breath fresh. They chewed through rehearsals, which irritated Archinbaud who could not get his cameras focused "as long as those two wagged their jaws." There was a standoff, and word spread that there was trouble on Stage 8.

The showdown came the day that Bob and Shirley were scheduled to sing the film's love ballad "Two Sleepy People." Rumors spread throughout Paramount that they were planning to sing and chew gum at the same time. The day of filming, office workers and assorted technicians from other film units sneaked onto the Archinbaud set to watch Hope and Ross work—or more precisely, to watch them chew. Archinbaud's temper rose, and the more he fumed the more obstinately the stars chewed. Then Archinbaud's attitude shifted. He remained patient while his stars sang in rehearsal, "Here we are—out of cigarettes—holding hands at midnight—chewing wads of gum—" Archinbaud announced a take and just as he was asking for the camera to roll, Hope and Ross on cue removed their gum and stuck it under the arms of their chairs. A ripple of giggles ran across the set behind the crew. As the prerecorded music started, Hope said sotto voce, "I thought we'd draw a better house than this—most of these are in on passes."

It was fortunate for everyone at Paramount that Hope was easygoing, but probably most fortunate for Hope himself. Otherwise he would never have been able to make movies and put together his radio show simultaneously. But put together a show he did.

His biggest dilemma was format. How innovative could he afford to be?

As Hope looked over the winners—Benny, a fall guy whose show revolved around a clearly defined stingy character, and Bergen, a self-effacing ventriloquist with an impudent brat—he was confident that what he contemplated was different enough to catch on. He believed that what his sponsors liked about him was the snappy monolgue. Most half-hour comedy formats were in two parts: First was a star-and-cast spot, and after the middle commercial came the main sketch, or development of the running situation. Hope saw his show in three or four distinct segments. After the monologue would come the continuing cast spot, then a guest star exchange with Hope, and finally a song sketch that might include everyone. The song sketch had worked well on the Woodbury show and he felt it was worth repeating. Hope was depending on his fast-paced rhythm to sustain the twenty-nine-minute show.

He needed the best new writers he could find, and ferreted out a group of gag writers that soon were to be known as Hope's Army: Al and Sherwood Schwartz, Milt Josefsberg, Jack Douglas, René Duplessis, Norman Sullivan, Norman Panama, Melvin Frank and Dr. Sam Kurtzman. It was going to take an army of funny minds to think up a first-class monologue plus sketch material every week, and Hope liked the idea of hiring a lot of young, ambitious guys all on the make and all in competition with each other. He wasn't paying them very much, so he could afford a lot of them. He planned to order from each writer a full show and he would take the best from each for a final script.[7]

Instead of his usual beautiful-girl foil, Hope hit upon the idea of using Jerry Colonna. Colonna had impressed Hope during the filming of *College Swing*, but it wasn't until Hope had worked several of Bing Crosby's Del Mar Turf Club parties that he realized Jerry was a versatile, zany entertainer, with his bulging round eyes, walrus moustache and piercing voice.

All the successful radio half-hours had personality announcers, and so Hope selected Bill Goodwin because he was especially clever with comedy lines. For the customary funny orchestra leader, Hope chose his golfing pal Skinnay Ennis who had put together his own band a few months earlier. If anyone on the show could act the foil, it would be the lean Ennis, whom Hope would soon call "spaghetti in search of a meatball." Rounding out the weekly musical chores plus handling musical commercials would be a group called Six Hits and a Miss who were Marvin Bailey, Pauline Byrnes (the Miss), Vin Degan, Howard Hudson, Mack McLean, Jerry Preshaw and Bill Seckler.

Ten days before the September 27 debut of the show, Hope called together his army for a story conference. He told them the guest star would be sophisticated screen actress Constance Bennett.

At their next meeting, the writers read their material, and Hope selected the best jokes and routines for an extra-long, sixty-to-ninety-minute script.

The following day, the cast did a preview of the longer-than-needed script before an audience at NBC's Sunset and Vine studios. During that Sunday night preview show, the program was transcribed so that on Monday Hope could listen and decide what material played best and how much of which routine should be cut. The best of the material was selected for the thirty-minute Tuesday night air show.

Hope saw these Sunday night run-throughs as a free-for-all vaudeville show for the audience as well as valuable research for the production staff. He made love to the crowd. The *Milwaukee Journal* of December 22, 1938, reported:

> If a joke died, Bob would be the first one to acknowledge the fact. He would bow low to the audience and intone: "Move over and let me in on the wake." Then he ripped out the wilted gag from the script page before the eyes of the audience who are delighted at being "in" on the creation of a big time radio show.

Hope's musical theme for the Pepsodent show was to be Gershwin's rollicking tune "Wintergreen for President" from the Broadway musical *Of Thee I Sing*. The new words were "Here's Bob Hope for Pepsodent" and it would cost the program $250 for each weekly use. Hope balked at this, especially since he had already begun to use "Thanks for the Memory" as his walk-on music for personal appearances and benefits. Lord and Thomas agreed to drop the Gershwin tune in favor of an opening up-tempo and a closing sentimental version of "Thanks."

On that first Tuesday, Hope spent the day as usual at Paramount, and then drove the few blocks from Melrose to the Vine Street parking lot. At six o'clock (PST), Hope went onstage:

> . . . How do you do, ladies and gentlemen . . . this is Bob Hope . . . (*single laugh from the audience*) . . . Not yet, Charlie. But don't leave! . . . Well, here we are with a brand new sponsor . . . a brand new program . . . a brand new cast . . . and ready to tell some . . . jokes. I'm very happy to be back on the air again. I've been very busy all summer working on a few projects . . . what do they want all those ditches for, anyway? But I'm happy. We have a nice cast on the show, ladies and gentlemen, that consists of. . . .

Bill Goodwin broke in on cue to say: "Connie Bennett, Jerry Colonna, Skinnay Ennis and his orchestra and Six Hits and a Miss." Then Hope continued.

> Thank you, Bill. That's our announcer, ladies and gentlemen, known to his inmates as Bill "Teeth" Goodwin. Show them your teeth, Bill. That's enough. Two more payments and they're his. My uncle just left town . . . he was here with the American Legion Convention. . . . It was a nice, quiet convention. The second night the boys at the hotel gave the house detective twenty-four hours to get out of town. But I want to thank the American Legion for getting me a half day off, last week at Paramount. They came over to the set I was working on and took the camera with them as a souvenir. Paramount didn't mind that so much, but they'd be very thankful if the fellow from Texas would please bring back Dorothy Lamour. And the parades were wonderful . . . One thing I noticed the women *look* different this year. You know, up on top of the head like. . . . Gee, I never knew they had ears. . . . My girl had her hair up so high she had to

Above left, Harry and Avis Hope, just after their marriage at Cardiff, Wales, April 25, 1891. (*Bob Hope family photo album*); *Right,* five-year-old Leslie, at left, with brothers Fred, Jack and Sid on the street walk near their Bristol, England, home in 1908 just before coming to America. (*Bob Hope family photo album*)

Below, this 1924 snapshot taken in front of their house on 105th Street near Euclid in Cleveland shows the entire Hope family: (standing, left to right) Fred, Jim, Jack, Harry, Avis, Leslie (Bob), Ivor, and (sitting, left to right) Sid and George.

In 1924, Bob and his sweetheart Mildred Rose-quist dreamed of being the Vernon and Irene Castle of 105th and Euclid Avenue. (*Bob Hope personal file*)

Les Hope and Lefty Durbin at the time they formed an act and worked with Fatty Arbuckle at Cleveland's Bandbox Theater in 1924. (*Bob Hope personal file*)

In 1925 Hope and his partner, George Byrne, toured the Gus Sun Vaudeville circuit in a Tab show called "Smiling Eyes." Here is the cast in front of the New Orpheum Theater in Lima, Ohio. (*Bob Hope personal file.*)

Hope, Ray Middleton, Lyda Roberti and Sidney Greenstreet in a scene from *Roberta* (1933). (*Bob Hope personal file*)

In 1934, while he was appearing in Jerome Kern's *Roberta* on Broadway, Hope met a married fashion model and nightclub singer Dolores Reade. (*Photo: Maurice Seymour*)

Fanny Brice (standing) and three of her co-stars in *Ziegfeld Follies of 1935,* (left to right) Harriet Hoctor, Bob Hope and Gertrude Neisen. (*Bob Hope personal file*)

Jimmy Durante, Ethel Merman and Hope were the stars of the Cole Porter-Howard Lindsay-Russell Crouse musical *Red, Hot and Blue!* during the 1937 Broadway season. (*Photo: Van Damm*)

Above left, Hope's first feature film—*The Big Broadcast of 1938*—with co-stars W. C. Fields and Shirley Ross. (*Paramount Pictures Corporation, courtesy Universal Pictures*); *Right*, Hope, Dorothy Lamour and Bing Crosby in their first collaboration, *Road to Singapore*, in 1939. (*Copyright 1940 Paramount Pictures Corporation, courtesy Universal Pictures*)

Below, Judy Garland joined Hope's Pepsodent radio cast as a regular in September, 1939. (*NBC Radio photo*)

Above left, Hope and his 96-year-old grandfather, James Hope, are surrounded by Hitchin townfolk during the comedian's first return visit to England in September, 1939. (*Bob Hope personal file*); *Right*, Hope's tireless entertainment of GIs in the European Theater of Operation in 1943 inspired war correspondent John Steinbeck to write, "There is a man!" (*Bob Hope personal file*)

Below, Hope and his fearless gypsies—(left to right) Jerry Colonna, Tony Romano, Barney Dean, Patty Thomas and Frances Langford—man an "ack-ack" gun for shooting photographers aboard a naval vessel in the South Pacific during July, 1944. (*Bob Hope personal file*)

Above, the legendary Babe Ruth and Bob Hope clown on the green during one of their many wartime fund raising golf tournaments in the early 1940s. (*NBC photo: Elmer Holloway*); *Right*, Hope and Crosby are off on the "Roads" to *Singapore* (1939), *Zanzibar* (1941), *Utopia* (1944), *Rio* (1947), *Bali* (1952), *Hong Kong* (1962), plus dozens of radio and television shows and golf matches. (*Copyright 1945 Paramount Pictures Inc., courtesy Universal Pictures*)

have the perfume sprayed on by a tree surgeon. I worked on that
gag all summer, too, but I didn't get it finished . . . I saw a sign
on a beauty parlor today . . . Marcel and your ears pinned back
for a dollar. Really . . . my girl friend had her ears pinned back
so far that when she's on the telephone she can listen with both
ears at the same time. She's sort of a Dracula with freck-
les. . . . You'd like her. . . .
(*Looks at the band*)
fellows? . . . No, huh? . . . And now, ladies and gentlemen, I
want you to meet our band—Skinnay Ennis and the boys. Are
you ready Skinnay? Okay, One—two—(*band laughs*). No, no,
boys—not the laugh—I mean your side line. You know—the
music? Take it, Skinnay. (*audience applause*)[8]

The monologue, which lasted seven minutes and contained 23 tightly com-
pressed jokes delivered at top speed, is a model of some 400 such radio
monologues Hope was to present between 1938 and 1952. His character is
alternately self-confident, self-effacing, impertinent and ingratiating. There
is a careful balance between subtle jokes and buffoonery, and a wide range of
joke types that would become an integral part of Hope's versatile style.

After the monologue Skinnay's band played "Change Partners," and
Goodwin did the first commercial. Next came the Bennett-Hope intimate
spot, filled with casual banter and that faded into a sketch about a girl's
baseball team:

	(*Cheers . . . crowd noise up and down*)
HOPE:	What a crowd here! Who's playing tonight, Con-nie?
CONNIE:	The Brooklyn Debutantes versus the Dead End Girlies. Listen to the cheers!
CHORUS:	We are the Brooklyn Debbies, A roaring, fighting team, And if we do not win the game
MEL:	I think we'll simply sca-reem!
CONNIE:	Isn't that wonderful—let's sit here next to the hairdressers' union.
GOODWIN:	No, I don't like the bleachers.
HOPE:	You died with that. . . . Say, there's something wrong with the looks of that baseball diamond—
CONNIE:	Yes, the girls changed it to a square cut—it's more stylish.
GOODWIN:	Look at that woman going around and around without stopping at home! Who is that?
HOPE:	Oh, that's Mrs. Roosevelt.

Next came the Six Hits and a Miss singing "My Walking Stick" from the
current Fox film *Alexander's Ragtime Band*. Then Hope introduced for
"lovers of classical music" Señor Jeray Colonna:

	(Applause)
ORCHESTRA:	(*Music up "Ah sweet Mystereeeeeeee" Colon-na sings . . . Interrupted by Hope*)

HOPE:	Just a second. I know I have a lot of enemies, but who sent *you* up here?
COLONNA:	Silence, rogue! Do you realize that you've interrupted the Great Colonna when the mood for song was beginning to creep upon him . . . creep . . . creep . . . creep . . .
HOPE:	I wish you'd creep out of this studio.
COLONNA:	But I am not *finished*!
HOPE:	What's your opinion against millions of others. . . . Is there anything else you can do, Señor, while we're waiting for the wagon?
COLONNA:	Oooooh, yes . . . a dash of drama. Never will I forget the time I played *Romeo and Juliet*. In the first act Juliet tossed me a rose—tenderly—from between her teeth.
HOPE:	What happened in the second act?
COLONNA:	Very tenderly—I tossed back her teeth.
HOPE:	Ladies and gentlemen, at this point I'd like to announce that any similarity between Señor Colonna and a human being, living or dead, is purely coincidental. . . . Check.

Goodwin's second commercial followed Colonna's singing of "Mandalay."
The final sketch, with its foreshadowings of *Dragnet* speech patterns, was a
fast-paced satire of radio sleuths. In fact, the entire program moved swiftly
and the show was evenly paced between comedy and music. Hope closed
with what became his lifelong signature:

ORCHESTRA & HOPE: "Thanks for the Memory"

HOPE:
(*talking*)

1.
Thanks for the memory
Of this our opening spot
Oh! I practically forgot—
You'll *love* the show next Tuesday—
There's a scene where I get shot. . . .
You'll like that so much.

2.
Thanks for the memory,
And Connie, I feel blue
To think that we are through—
Just drop in any Tuesday when
You've nothing else to boo,
And thank you so much.

3.
And though now we are sorry to leave you,
It's just for a week we'll be missin'—
To show Pepsodent that you listen,
Mail in the doors
From four drug stores. . .

HOPE:
(*talking*)   Say, Bill. . . .
GOODWIN: Yes, Bob.
HOPE: What goes for next week?
GOODWIN: Well, our special guest is Miss Olivia de
                        Havilland. Skinnay Ennis and the band will
                        be back; Jerry Colonna; our Swingsters, Six
                        Hits and a Miss; and of course . . . you.
HOPE: And you. (*singing*) Thank you so much.
(*ORCHESTRA:*   *Music up*) (*Applause*)

Variety's review on October 5, 1938, warmed Hope's heart:

That small speck going over the center field fence is the four-bagger Bob Hope whammed out his first time at bat for Pepsodent. If he can keep up the pace he'll get as much word of mouth for 1938–39 as Edgar Bergen got for 1937–38. He sounded like success all the way.

Hope must be trying because the script showed plenty of thought. But it's his particular gift not to seem to be trying. And that's a great psychological aid. It suggests wearing qualities.

Or, maybe, we're neglecting the writers. However he or them is/are, house rules allow an extra bow.

Pleased as he was at the show's initial reception, Hope was still not satisfied. He thought the show too disconnected and too reliant on jokes rather than character. So in the weeks to follow, with a variety of guest stars, among them Madeleine Carroll, Shirley Ross, Groucho Marx, Joan Bennett, Pat O'Brien, Rosalind Russell, Paulette Goddard and Judy Garland, Hope tried to establish himself as more of a type; he carefully selected gags that either accentuated the dumb wise guy or the bragging coward character.

Besides leaning heavily on comic sidekicks Colonna and Goodwin, Hope began giving more funny lines to Skinnay Ennis. Then he added other characters, some played by Mel Blanc, others by Elvia Allman and Blanche Stewart. Hope invited Patricia Wilder, his first Honey Chile, to do a few shows, and after she left, he hired comedienne Patsy Kelly as a full-time regular.

Besides its flexible format, the key to the show's success was its tight, unhackneyed writing and Hope's skillful editing. The comedian's rat-ta-tat delivery, his infectious traveling salesman manner which seemed so right for its time in American social life, his average good looks which his films and still photographs established for the public—all this was building an audience.

Jerry Colonna had become one of the show's most popular attractions because of his nonsensical phrases like "Greetings, Gate, let's operate" and "Who's Yuhudi?", which were fast becoming street parlance.

By the end of December, it was clear to Lord and Thomas, to the rating services like Hooper, to the radio critics and columnists and to the general public that Hope's show was a hit. The annual *Radio Daily* poll of newspaper critics showed Hope in fourth place behind Jack Benny, Fred Allen and Edgar Bergen.

True to his word, Bob told Dolores to proceed with the adoption plans. They decided on a boy, and took the advice of George and Gracie Burns to apply at what was perhaps the country's most distinguished foundling home, The Cradle at Evanston, Illinois. Opening negotiations with the Cradle's director Mrs. Florence Walrath, they discovered, to their disappointment, that there would be a long waiting period.

With the Pepsodent show grooving into a workable routine, Hope turned to his limping film career. He agreed to do a Preston Sturges script Paramount had sent him that would costar him once again with Martha Raye. Yet another B effort called *Never Say Die*, Hope and Raye made it a romp and its dismissal by critics as a failure is somewhat unfair.

When Paramount analyzed the reviews of their new film *Thanks for the Memory*, they realized that "Two Sleepy People" would probably become a hit parade item. Quickly they hired Lew Foster and Wilkie Mahoney to rewrite for Hope and Ross a Ben Hecht–Gene Fowler play called *The Green Magoo*, renamed *Some Like It Hot*. Despite some potential, including another hit parade song titled "The Lady's in Love With You," the picture never really sparkled.

In February Hope was asked by the studio to be a presenter at the Academy Award ceremonies held at the Biltmore Hotel in downtown Los Angeles. Hope's growing reputation as *the* master of ceremonies in town was probably responsible for the choice. It was the beginning of a long association.

In March two noteworthy events occurred. The first was an awakening by Paramount executives to Hope's talents. They had noticed his audience appeal at the Academy Awards but were extremely impressed by his accelerating radio career and general public appeal. They decided to cast him in a picture called *The Cat and the Canary* costarring one of Hollywood's most publicized actresses, Paulette Goddard. After reading the script, Hope knew the chance he had.

The second event was a chance of a different sort. Bob accidentally opened a letter postmarked England that lay in a pile on his desk. After reading it, he was tempted to call Dolores immediately but decided to wait until dinner to speak about it.

"How would you like to take a trip?"

"You heard from The Cradle," Dolores said eagerly.

"No. Where would you most like to go?"

"Evanston."

"I know how much having a son means to you, Dolores," Bob said, looking at her across the table, "but I'm talking vacation."

"You're what? You—a vacation?" Dolores couldn't believe her ears. "Bob, you're joking."

"No. Now, where have you always wanted to go?"

"Paris."

"Okay, you got it."

"When? I don't believe you."

"I got a letter today from my Aunt Lucy in England asking for an autographed picture. She said she'd been getting mail recently from relatives all over Britain asking if I was Harry's boy who'd made good. She lives in Hitchin with my grandpop and she asked if I'd like to come over and visit and stay with them. Grandpop is ninety-six and still rides his bicycle every day."

"What has that got to do with Paris?"

"We'll do both. I finish *The Cat and the Canary* in the middle of May and our last Pepsodent show is June 20. We can play a couple of vaudeville dates they want me for on the way to New York."

"Will we play Chicago?"

"We can."

"Bob, will you—?"

"I'll call Florence Walrath tomorrow."[9]

Of course, my steward told me when I got on board, "If anything happens, it's women and children first, but the Captain said in your case you can have first choice." [1]

17. Family, Family Everywhere

It really was like old times, being back at the Orpheum in Minneapolis and taking in that special backstage smell. Bob thought the familiar odor especially heady that steamy June 26 afternoon when he, Dolores, Jerry Colonna, his brother Jack and Jack's new wife, an actress named Marion Bailer, began their first week on the road.

Next week they would play Chicago and, after a stopover in Cleveland to pick up Uncle Frank, they would slide into Atlantic City for a two-day appearance on the pier, and then into New York for ten days at the Paramount. After that it would be an honest-to-goodness vacation—the *Normandie*, a Hope family reunion in England and a European holiday.

The 65-minute show they unveiled at the Orpheum was the product of Hope's new radio writers and his own voluminous gag files. *Variety* of June 28, 1939, called it "loaded with good material," and Hope was tagged as "flip and fresh, yet friendly and intimate." This engagement was special because it marked the start of a lifelong stage association between Hope and Colonna, one that went beyond the weekly radio stints to include countless American cities and military bases the world over, and symbolized by Colonna's hollering from the wings, "Hey, Hope! Your laundry's back!" Bob would holler back amiably, "Thanks, Jer!" Then Colonna got an audience scream with "They refused it!"

In Minneapolis, Dolores was high-strung. Before leaving Los Angeles, they had scheduled their screening interview at The Cradle for their last day in Chicago. Florence Walrath had told Dolores that The Cradle had "passed" the prospective parents in a "preliminary examination stage." She explained, however, that a microscopic investigation of the Hopes was still in progress.

The interview went well. Mrs. Walrath dealt directly with what she termed the sensitive problem of children brought up in the glare of publicity in celebrity households. She had numerous examples in her files of entertainment children whose role models were less than exemplary. She added, however, that she was encouraged by respected character witnesses in Los Angeles that the Hopes were "conservative," "sober," and "loving." As Bob and Dolores were leaving, Mrs. Walrath invited them to stop at The Cradle on their return from Europe because she believed she "just might have the right child for you."

"A boy," injected Bob emphatically.

"We'll have to wait and see, Mr. Hope," she said.

That evening, Bob and Dolores were invited to a dinner party aboard the yacht of Pepsodent's boss Ray Smith. At seven-thirty Albert Lasker stopped at the Drake Hotel to pick up the Hopes and drive them to a Lake Michigan pier where a launch was waiting. As the tender plowed through choppy water, Lasker raised his arm and pointed off toward the impressive silhouette of the boat they were approaching. He put his other hand on Bob's shoulder and said, "I want you to remember one thing: Amos and Andy built that boat."[2]

Hope's usually mobile face froze. Dolores saw an expression she had rarely seen but she knew it meant that Bob was capable of saying just about anything. She held her breath.

"When I finish with Pepsodent—our Mr. Smith will be using that yacht for a dinghy," Bob said with only his eyes smiling.

The remainder of the evening was pleasant. Smith toasted Bob's first successful season. Then, as they walked slowly to the gangway, Smith reached into his inside jacket pocket and produced a fat legal-sized envelope. "I hear that you are taking a vacation in Europe. Here's something that may come in handy on the trip." Bob thanked him and slipped the envelope into his pocket. They said goodnight.

Back in the hotel room, as he was removing his dinner jacket, he ripped open the envelope. Inside were round-trip tickets (deluxe suites both ways) for outbound travel on the *Normandie* and return travel on the *Queen Mary*. There was also a $2,500 letter of credit on a London bank.[3]

"Dolores," Bob said, waving the tickets and the letter of credit, "start brushing four times a day."

The Hope clan—Fred and LaRue, Sid and Dorothy, Ivor and Gertrude, and Bob and Dolores—held an informal reunion the following week around a large table in the dining room of the Hotel Cleveland. Sid, a mechanic and a farmer, was living quietly at Ridgefield Corners, Ohio, about 40 miles southwest of Toledo, and so his presence there was a special treat. Ivor and Bob discussed arrangements for opening their jointly held company, Hope Metal Products. Everyone was very pleased that Bob had gotten kid brother George a writing job in Hollywood. Jim, too, was missing from this group, but no one was surprised. He had gone to the West Coast even before Bob and had tried to get into show business. He had failed and was reportedly envious of Bob's success.

The remainder of the tour went by swiftly. After Atlantic City, they opened in New York and during their twelve days at the Paramount, they managed to see the World's Fair, but only because Mack Millar had been able to get Grover Whalen to declare a "Bob Hope Day at the Fair," and Bob and Dolores rode in an open car through the fairgrounds with colorful Fiorello LaGuardia.

Bob and Dolores had an inkling of the celebrity-filled passenger list for their Wednesday's sailing. But they were not at all prepared for the dockside confusion of what the press described as "an army of 500 autograph seekers staging wild scenes." Screaming fans encircled Charles Boyer and his wife Pat, Norma Shearer, Madeleine Carroll, George Raft, Edward G. Robinson and his son Eddie, Jr., Roland Young, Ben and Bebe Lyon. It was a media feast. Besides the film stars, the press was pursuing best-selling author Marjorie Hillis, Irish prime minister John Cudahy, and former president of the Dominican Republic Rafael Trujillo. As Dolores and Bob headed for their gangway, they were trailed by newsmen asking for details of their family reunion in England and their first European holiday. They were asked if they feared the war clouds hanging over the Continent and Hitler's threats. "There won't be a war," said Hope confidently.[4]

Before Hope could expound further, the newsmen thronged to an official limousine that had just pulled up. Eleanor Roosevelt stepped out, surrounded by Secret Service men. She had come to say both official and personal good-byes to her uncle David Gray, who was accompanying Treasury Secretary Henry Morganthau on what was mostly a vacation in Scandinavia.

Looking at this carefree throng in such a holiday mood, it was unthinkable that there could be a world conflict coming. Not one of Hope's monologues for Pepsodent during the past season suggested world or national upset. In fact, the nation's recovery from a deep recession to a mood of prosperity had never seemed so complete.

With all the friends and celebrities on board, the voyage was much more of a social whirlwind than Dolores and Bob had anticipated. Everyone, including Uncle Frank, had a wonderful time. When the *Normandie* docked at Southampton, Uncle Frank went straight to Hitchin in Hertfordshire. The other Hopes took the boat train to London.

During their first week there the Hopes began to unwind. They hardly missed a day of playing golf, and each night they saw a play or a musical. One day they drove out to see Bob's birthplace at 44 Craighton Road, Eltham.

The second week, they went up to Hitchin to spend a day or two with the Hope patriarch, Grandfather James, who at ninety-six still ruled the family. Bob and Dolores took a room at the Hitchin Inn and threw a big family party at one of the locals. Uncle Frank had already had his own homecoming party, so this one was really for the purpose of letting some forty British Hopes gather to bask in the pride of having a famous film star relative in their midst. Hardly any of them had seen one of Bob's movies, but they knew he was a celebrity in the States.

After dinner, the guests awaited living proof of their American cousin's fame. Bob got up and told a few jokes, which got a rather cool reception. His grandfather, unsmiling, just stared at Bob, who finally said, "Hey, let's bring Uncle Jack up here. I understand he's a pretty good whistler."

Then the patriarch stood up. "You're doing this thing all wrong," he said. "You don't know these people. You're a tourist. Let me do the introducing."

For the next twenty minutes Grandpop introduced the entire Hope clan and even danced a little dance step to prove what a ninety-six-year-old could still do.[5]

Paramount's London office had a photographer sent up to Hitchin, and Bob and Dolores posed for pictures with the aunts and uncles, and with the remarkable James Hope. Then, after a round of farewells, Bob and Dolores returned to London. A few days later they headed for Dover and the boat train to Paris.

Sadly, they were never really able to explore the enchantment of Paris. Americans were beginning to sense what seemed so clear to international observers, including so unlikely a voice as gossipy Louella Parsons in Hollywood, that Hitler's troops were poised to march. Bob spent most of one night on the transatlantic telephone with Paramount executives and NBC radio brass who wanted the Hopes to return to Los Angeles as quickly as possible. The lead item of Parsons' Friday, August 25, 1939, column revealed:

> With war imminent, Hollywood yesterday realized how many of its important stars are still in Europe. Tyrone Power and Annabella . . . Charles Boyer . . . Robert Montgomery . . . Maureen O'Sullivan . . . Bob Hope, who planned a European holiday, is cutting his visit short to hurry home.[6]

Bob and Dolores had deluxe suite accommodations for the mid-September sailing of the *Queen Mary* from Southampton. Now it was rumored that the August 30 sailing might be her final civilian crossing. First-class space was finally located on what later would be described as a "woefully overcrowded ship." Even for seasoned vaudevillians, this frantic flight to cross the English Channel and make Southampton in time for the *Queen Mary* sailing was a chilling experience. There were hundreds of frightened Americans and Europeans who were hell-bent on making that crossing.

In spite of so much evidence, Hope refused to believe war was that close. How he could have misread Hitler's invasion of Poland as anything but an invitation to massive conflict is puzzling.

On Saturday, September 3, both England and France declared war on Germany. Early the next morning, the passengers got the news. Dolores was coming back to the cabin from Mass and woke Bob.

"You were wrong," she said, holding the bulletin in her hand.

"What happened?" he asked sleepily.

" 'German troops in 'blitzkrieg' action have reduced Polish towns and villages to rubble,' " Dolores read to him. "It says here that Russian troops have entered Poland from the East and that the Poles are trying to save themselves. It's awful. The British Dominions have called emergency parliament sessions for the purposes of declaring war. If Canada goes—surely we will, too."

"Now, Dolores—"

"Bob, you ought to see what's going on up in the salon. People are sobbing. One woman stopped me and said that there are German submarines waiting for orders to sink this boat. They've issued blackout instructions and people are crying—and scared—"

"There's nothing to be frightened about."

"I'm thinking that if the Nazis blow up this ship we'll never see our baby
oy."
"Stop that. I've got to get up and see the captain. We're supposed to do a
hip's concert tonight but I don't know if we should."
The captain thought comedy was exactly what the *Queen Mary* passen-
ers needed at this time, so Hope spent the rest of the afternoon putting
ogether a routine and writing special lyrics for his theme song.
When he went on stage that night and looked around the room, he decided
o begin by telling the truth. He admitted that he told the captain he didn't
hink doing a ship's concert was appropriate. He said he still wasn't sure, but
hat the captain and a few others had prevailed. "Maybe—just maybe
hey're right. It might help if all of us here try for a few minutes to forget the
ragedy that faces the world and have some fun."
Probably Hope's comedy character of the brave coward was never more
ratefully received than it was that night when he cracked, "Of course, my
teward told me when I got on board, 'If anything happens it's women and
hildren first, but the Captain said in your case you can have your choice.' "
Ie did his regular vaudeville act for an hour and finally did the parody he
ad written that afternoon:

> Thanks for the memory
> Of this great ocean trip
> On England's finest ship.
> Tho' they packed them to the rafters
> They never made a slip.
> Ah! Thank you so much.
>
> Thanks for the memory
> Some folks slept on the floor,
> Some in the corridor;
> But I was more exclusive,
> My room had "Gentlemen" above the door,
> Ah! Thank you so much.

he crowded-to-capacity salon roared when Hope finished his song. The
aptain asked him for a copy of the parody for the ship's log, and sent a copy
o the ship's printing shop. When the ship docked at the Cunard Line pier
ach departing passenger received a copy. Mack Millar ran a copy of it over
o *Variety* where it was used as a boxed item in Wednesday's roundup of
eturning show-business figures from abroad.[7]
The Hopes rushed to Mrs. Walrath's office in Evanston. She told them
hey had passed final inspection, and that they could have a baby girl about
ght weeks old. Dolores melted when they went to the showing room. She
idn't want to leave the baby when Mrs. Walrath asked if they might go
ack to her office to talk. She asked the Hopes how they felt.
"She's beautiful," said Dolores.
"She's all right," said Bob.
"Perhaps you ought to wait—" Mrs. Walrath said.
"No, we want her," said Dolores.
But Mrs. Walrath had the feeling Bob was uncertain about adoption.

Dolores assured her that Bob was only disappointed because he had his hear
set on a boy, and that her husband often used flippant remarks to mask hi
emotion.

Nevertheless, Mrs. Walrath made them wait. Bob and Dolores went on t
California while some legal papers filed with the State of Illinois cleared
Finally, one morning the following week, Dolores answered the telephone t
hear the news that she could come back to The Cradle for their new daugh
ter. Dolores went alone and brought home what Bob had called "that littl
puzzlehead" whom they agreed to call Linda Theresa.

> Crosby: *"As I live—Ski-snoot!"*
> Hope: *"Mattress hip!"*
> Crosby: *"Shovel head!"*
> Hope: *"Blubber!"*
> Crosby: *"Scoop nose!"*
> Hope: *"Lard!"*
> Crosby: *"Yes, Dad!"*[1]

18. Three for the *Road*

NBC ordered star treatment for Hope when he began his second season o
broadcasts. They even tossed a party to launch the freshly decorated Bo
Hope Studio in their blocklong pale green building at the corner of Sunse
and Vine. But the other cause for rejoicing, as Hope returned to the air, wa
that Judy Garland had joined his cast as a regular, to sing and do comed
with Bob. The chemistry created between Hope and Garland when sh
guest-starred the season before generated enough audience response to con
vince Pepsodent that Judy's price, recently boosted by her recognition as
major talent, was worth paying. Judy's initial dialogue with Hope went thi
way:

HOPE: Ladies and gentlemen, one of my most pleasant duties in
        returning to the air this week is to present a new addi-
        tion to our cast . . . Metro-Goldwyn-Mayer's young
        singing star of *The Wizard of Oz* whom you will soon
        see with Mickey Rooney in *Babes in Toyland* . . .
        Miss Judy Garland!

JUDY: Thank you very much. Hello, Mr. Hope.

HOPE: Hello, Judy . . . you know the last time you were here
        you were just a guest . . . now that you're a permanent
        member of our cast, how do you feel about it?

JUDY: Oh, I'm really happy to be here, Mr. Hope. You know,
        my schoolteacher's happy I'm on the program too. She
        says I ought to be glad to take anything to get started.

HOPE: But Judy . . . are you sure you'll feel at home on this
        program?

JUDY: Oh, yes, Mr. Hope . . . you should have seen the
        strange creatures I worked with on *The Wizard of Oz.*
HOPE: Judy Garland, is that the way to talk to me . . . after
        I've been so nice to you . . . why only yesterday I
        bought you an ice cream soda—with two balls of ice
        cream, too!
JUDY: Yeah . . . and with two straws, too!
HOPE: Well, I gave you a head start, didn't I?[2]

Hope's writers traded on Judy's "little-girl-next-door" image at the start,
but by the close of the radio season they had brought her up to her actual
age—eighteen—and there was more sting in her voice when she deflated
Hope's ego and dampened his fumbling romantic attentions.

Another innovation of the 1939–40 Pepsodent season was in the already
familiar character voices of Elvia Allman and Blanche Stewart. In a sketch
on October 24, the ladies were cast as a couple of ugly coeds that bandleader
Skinnay Ennis "dug up" as dates for Hope and Goodwin. The idea caught
fire.

BLANCHE: Say, we'd better finish dressing right away, Cobi-
           na . . . what are you gonna wear . . . your or-
           gandy Creep de Shiney . . . or your LIVER
           PILL SCHLEMIEL?
ELVIA: Oh, I dunno . . . I wanna look good . . . but I
           wanna be ready to defend myself at the same
           time . . . Say, Brenda, have you seen my bottle
           of bay rum?
BLANCHE: Don't you remember? We used it last
           night . . . in the Martinis! . . . Well, whaddye
           know, Cobina! I can't find my false eyelashes!
ELVIA: I got them . . . I'm brushing off my coat!
BLANCHE: I wonder if they're too long? Should I cut them
           down to three inches?
ELVIA: I don't know . . . but every time you wink your
           eye, you flag down the Super Chief. . . .[3]

Both preview audience and regular show audience reaction proved so enthusiastic for these new characters (who were, essentially, satiric jabs at society
debutantes Brenda Frazier and Cobina Wright, Jr.), that Hope made the
shrill, frustrated old maids a continuing feature. Some weeks, their banter
approached the outer limits:

ELVIA: I've been in the sun an hour Brenda . . . is my
           face red?
BLANCHE: I can't tell, Cobina . . . I'll have to wait till you
           comb your eyebrows back!
ELVIA: Gee, Brenda, isn't it wonderful when fellers try to
           kiss under water?
BLANCHE: I'll say . . . but we haven't had much luck since
           we drowned them last two.
ELVIA: Come on . . . let's dive down and *look at them
           again!*

All in all, Hope's show was better than before. Tightly written, sometimes
outrageous, always topical, the *Pepsodent Show* had risen in popularity to
become the third most-listened radio program in the nation, just behind Jack
Benny and Edgar Bergen.

One of its dominant themes, sometimes as much as 50 percent of the program's total content, was Hope's exaggerated view of life as a Hollywood
personality. In the satire, the comedian managed to fit more and more com-
fortably into his role as quavering braggart and lovable fall guy.

This characterization was also working well for Hope on the screen. His
newest film, *The Cat and the Canary*, opened in November to spectacular
critical notices. Respected critic Howard Barnes said in the *New York Herald Tribune* on November 23, 1939, "Mr. Hope is a pillar of strength in
holding the film to its particular mood of satirical melodrama." Hope's particular favorite among the reviews appeared in the *Motion Picture Herald*:

> Paramount here has solved neatly for itself, exhibitors and cus-
> tomers, the heretofore perplexing problem of what to do with Bob
> Hope, admittedly one of the funniest comedians who ever faced a
> camera, yet never until now the surefire laugh-getter on the
> screen that his following knew him to be in fact.[4]

In addition to developing a character on which so many of his future film
assignments would be based, *The Cat and the Canary* gave him the first
opportunity to wisecrack in a manner that seemed entirely spontaneous and
was as unexpected by the movie audience as the stage ad lib.

Credit must go to producer Arthur Hornblow, Jr., who lectured Hope
sternly on the importance of taking direction, and to stage-wise Elliot
Nugent for his patient and intelligent handling of the comedian both before
and behind the camera. It was a happy marriage of stars, script and production. Hope called his leading lady, Paulette Goddard, "beautiful and talented." And it didn't hurt the picture that Paulette was both protégée and
wife of the world's most famous clown, Charlie Chaplin.

At one of the celebrity events at Santa Anita racetrack one Saturday during the filming, Hope spotted Paulette on Chaplin's arm and went over to say
hello.

"You know Charles, don't you?" she said.

Hope had always admired Chaplin, had won a prize or two in Chaplin
lookalike contests at Luna Park. A few years before, Hope had waited on a
New York City street for an hour and a half because a friend had told him
that Chaplin was inside the restaurant. He would have liked to tell him all
that, but such blatant idolatry wasn't good form. Instead he told him how
much he had admired *Modern Times* and what a treat it was working with
Paulette.

"Young man," Chaplin said, "I've been watching the rushes of *The Cat
and the Canary* every night. I want you to know that you are one of the best
timers of comedy I have ever seen."[5]

Nugent understood Hope's absolute dependence on the wisecrack as the
supreme technical device. He had the sensitivity to recognize that in the role
of Wally Hampton the comedian's screen persona was coming into bloom
and insisted that the topical gag be fired off in the most spine-tingling
moments of the picture.

Some of the most quotable jokes from the film came in moments of Wally's terror. Once when he was forced to sleep in a spooky mansion, Nydia Westman asks, "Don't big empty houses scare you?" "Not me," says Wally, "I used to be in vaudeville." And, "Even my goosepimples have goosepimples."

There was even a foretaste of Hope's lechery lines: "My mother brought me up never to be caught twice in the same lady's bedroom."

The only classic Hope gag not used in this film was the Crosby assassination joke. The "feud" between them was well entrenched by then, at least as far as golf tournaments and their respective radio programs were concerned. Bing, on the air for Kraft Foods since 1935, had started using Hope putdown jokes during the spring of 1938 when Hope was a guest on his show.

Hope retaliated by telling jokes about Crosby's reluctant racehorses. "Let me tell you about those streamlined trains. They go right by Crosby's stables, and every morning Bing goes out and lines up the horses. 'See,' he tells them as the trains whiz by, 'that's what I mean.' "[6]

Before long they had worked out a series of epithets for each other that if and when they were strung together sounded like this:

BING: "As I live—ski-snoot!"
BOB: "Mattress hip!"
BING: "Shovel head!"
BOB: "Blubber!"
BING: "Scoop nose!"
BOB: "Lard!"
BING: "Yes, Dad!"

That kind of word-slinging plus their Saturday night clowning at Bing's Del Mar Turf Club were noted by Paramount's production chief Bill LeBaron. The studio owned a property called *The Road to Mandalay* that scriptwriters Frank Butler and Don Hartman had adapted from a South Sea tale entitled *Beach of Dreams*. LeBaron had first thought of casting Fred MacMurray and Jack Oakie as a couple of vagabond entertainers on the lam in the tropics. Both stars turned him down. Next LeBaron's thoughts turned to the combination of Burns and Allen with Crosby, but George and Gracie couldn't fit it in.

What about Lamour in a sarong with Crosby and Bob Hope? The idea, first suggested lightly, became a hot business proposition and Butler and Hartman went to work retailoring their script. Bing said, "I was intrigued with the idea of working with Bob and Dottie because it seemed to me it would be a winning combination—a foreign land—natives—music—Dottie in a sarong—Bob being a clown—me singing the ballads."[7]

Paramount put Victor Schertzinger in to direct the script which now had the title *The Road to Singapore*. Schertzinger's background was in musicals. He directed his pictures in a leisurely and dignified fashion. Crosby recalled, "His awakening was rude. For a couple of days when Hope and I tore freewheeling into a scene, ad-libbing and violating all of the acceptable rules of movie-making, Schertzinger stole bewildered looks at his script, then leafed rapidly through it, searching for the lines we were saying."[8]

Lamour, who prided herself on the accuracy of her lines, was also bewildered because she failed to recognize her cues.

Enter two angry writers, Butler and Hartman. They resented all the tampering with their words. To rub even more sand into their wounds, Hope called out, "Hey, Don, if you recognize any of yours, yell 'Bingo!' "[9] At which point, an enraged Hartman left the stage to complain to LeBaron.

Schertzinger told someone, "You know, I really shouldn't take any money for this job. All I do is say Stop and Go." But the director soon realized that the kind of movie emerging each day was fresh and spontaneous; furthermore, the front office was delighted.[10]

Bob and Bing were reassured as well. One day they slipped unnoticed into back seats of the darkened projection room during the eleven o'clock "rushes," and heard one or another of the production staff and studio brass howling with laughter.

The plot line for *The Road to Singapore* was simple and accidental. Josh Mallon, played by Crosby, and Ace Lannigan, played by Hope, run off to the South Seas to avoid unwanted weddings. They land on the island of Kaigood where romance beckons in the form of sexy Mima, played by Lamour, and danger threatens from Mima's dancing partner, Caesar, played by a menacing Anthony Quinn. The one-line plot for this *Road*, as well as for the sequels, was always this: The boys are in a jam, or as many jams as possible, and they have to clown their way out.

Crosby has said, "The jams are plotted in the script and although they're bogus situations and on the incredible side, they are important because they hold the story together and provide a framework for our monkeyshines. Gags can't be played against gags; they have to be played against something serious even though the serious stuff is melodramatic. Hope and I invent many of these gags from predicaments as we go along."[11]

There were times during the filming that Hope and Crosby got so carried away with their adlibs that they forgot about Lamour and she would yell, "Please, fellas, when can I get my line in?"[12] Bob has said, "We used to rib her mercilessly. It used to get so crazy that it was like a tennis game with Dottie in the middle watching. Fortunately, she had a great sense of humor. Most dames would have walked off the set in a huff. Bing would say, 'If you find an opening, Dottie, just throw something in.' "

Lamour said, "After the first few days, I decided it was ridiculous to waste time learning the script. I would read over the next day's work to get an idea of what was happening. What I really needed was a good night's sleep to be in shape for the next morning's adlibs. This method provided some very interesting results on the screen."

Singapore did much to foster the Hope-Crosby friendship. It was a symbiosis that suited each admirably and apparently was a response to a need in both men. Bing, for example, frequently appeared to associates as cold and unresponsive. He was puzzled about his own success and once called himself a freak in the business. He had actually considered retirement in 1937, and many people, including Barry Ulanov, believe Hope gave Bing a "shot of adrenalin; he made Bing's work a pleasure; he helped squash Bing's tentative plans to retire to his ranch, or sail around the world, or breed horses for a living."

And the move toward intimacy was significant for Hope as well. He had been close to Whitey Jennings as a youth, and Richy Craig on Broadway, and there would be a handful of reasonably close men friends during his career, largely fostered on the golf course. But his closest male attachments were his brothers, and those relationships were the result of his highly personal view of family.

Ulanov, in his portrait of Bing, observed: "They played games with each other, and for each other, like little boys, never ceasing to find delight in each other's company, wondering constantly that this sort of game could and would continue to be a job of work."[13]

Perhaps symbolic of that childlike approach to their work was the pat-a-cake sequence they performed in each *Road* picture. The Boys got themselves trapped, usually menaced by burly thugs, and to get themselves out they faced each other, raised their palms and played pat-a-cake for a few moments and then, in a surprising switch, smashed their opponents in the jaws.

It was to their credit that their taste dictated the limits of their insouciant behavior. There was, for example, just the right amount of abandon in the scene in *Singapore* when Hope and Crosby don sarongs and cavort to their own ocarina accompaniment.

True, they may have gone too far the day of the soapsuds fight that left a foamy trail from Stage 5 to the Paramount Commissary. Bob, Dottie and Bing began spraying each other with cans of special effects soapsuds on the soundstage and chased each other down studio streets and around lunch tables. A mostly amused audience of film workers applauded, but Paramount brass bemoaned the delays in repairing hair, makeup and costumes. Yet it was the unexpected, the circus atmosphere, that prompted hairdressers, cameramen and grips to literally fight for an assignment to a *Road* picture.

Needless to add, there was a pall around the lot when *Singapore* was wrapped up. But Paramount brass rejoiced. All those Hope–Crosby highjinks were expensive. Besides Arthur Hornblow was biting his nails waiting to reteam Hope and Paulette Goddard in *The Ghost Breakers*, a sequel to the box-office winner *The Cat and the Canary*. In the plot, Hope is innocently embroiled in a murder and Goddard conceals him in her steamer trunk as they head for her haunted castle on an eerie island off the coast of Cuba.

During the filming, Hope was tapped to be the single master of ceremonies of the twelfth annual Oscar awards dinner held February 29 in the Ambassador Hotel's Cocoanut Grove. The year 1939 had been an especially auspicious one for Hollywood. Its combined skills had turned out more critically acclaimed motion pictures than any previous year in the colony's history, including Selznick's monumental four-hour *Gone With the Wind*, MGM's beguiling *The Wizard of Oz*, John Ford's stark and classic *Stagecoach*, MGM's touching *Goodbye Mr. Chips*, Goldwyn's romantic *Wuthering Heights*, Warner's emotional *Dark Victory*, as well as the tough *Of Mice and Men* and the politically disturbing *Mr. Smith Goes to Washington*.

Those ceremonies marked the last time that the winners were given to the press in advance of the actual presentation. The *Los Angeles Times* released the names in its early bird edition and destroyed the suspense. The following year, the Academy brought in the firm of Price Waterhouse to control the results.

The night belonged to *Gone With the Wind* and Hope cracked, "What a

wonderful thing, this benefit for David O. Selznick."[14] Eight Oscars were
given out for the Civil War spectacular, including the prestigious Thalberg
prize to Selznick personally. Hope was particularly proud that his Pepsodent
songbird Judy Garland won a special statuette "for her outstanding performance as a screen juvenile during the past year."

When *Singapore* was sneak-previewed in Hollywood in late February,
Hope devoted a segment of his Pepsodent show to a sketch based on the film
and, when it was released in March, he did another sketch about it, and still
another in April. Fortunately the movie received glowing reviews and proved
a box-office winner. Paramount quickly sent Hartman and Butler to the attic
to dust off another unused script. Hartman said once, "You take a piece of
used chewing gum and flip it at a map. Wherever it lands you can lay a *Road*
picture so long as there are jokers who cook and eat strangers. If they're
nasty and menacing, it'll be a good picture. The key is menace offsetting the
humor."[15] They found a Cy Bartlett script called *Find Colonel Fawcett*, a
quasi-serious Stanley-in-search-of-Livingstone theme, and Butler and Hartman turned it into *The Road to Zanzibar*. Paramount invited Hope, Crosby
and Lamour to travel again.

Hope, however, had already arranged to take his radio show on the road
for the last five weeks of the Pepsodent season and at the same time do
personal appearances in Joliet, Chicago, Detroit, Cleveland and New York.
It was vaudeville time again and to Hope there was nothing more exciting.
Moreover, now he had two sizable film successes behind him and was still
working for the same money; maybe they'd appreciate him more when they
knew he was building a bigger radio audience.

Even Hope did not know how big that audience had become. When the
Pepsodent gang (plus Dolores) opened in Joliet they were asked to add an
extra show because of the crowds trying to get in. But Chicago crowds were
something else again. Hope had contracted for five shows a day at the Chicago Theater, but the lines circling the entire city block were such that the
management realized that even the five shows could not accommodate everyone.

"Let's cut the movie entirely," suggested Hope.

"Can't do it," said the manager, although his face showed he was thinking
about it.[16]

The financial agreement for this tour was a $12,500 weekly guarantee and
50 percent of everything over a $50,000 gate. The house attendance record
was being broken daily. The theater was taking in $73,000 a week and Hope
saw his personal share reach $20,000.

Hope looked outside again and saw those lines. "Well, at least why don't
we cut out the news and previews at all performances and see if we can
squeeze in one more show."

They did better than that. They shaved enough to do seven stage shows.
The crowd didn't stop even for rain. Hope called Louis Shurr.

"Doc, I want you to fly to Chicago."

"Why?"

"I want you to see something."

"I really can't leave town right now."

"What's more important than me?"

"Well—"

"You don't happen to have Abe Lastfogel's number handy do you?" Lastfogel was, by then, near the top of the William Morris hierarchy and Morris had always wanted to tie up Hope for all media. Shurr found the fastest way to Chicago and made his way backstage.

"Come here," Hope said, and walked the little man over to a peephole in the Lake Street door of the theater. "That's important. How often do you see crowds that big? That is a $50,000-a-picture crowd and I want you to go and see the boys at Paramount and tell 'em that's what my price is going to be."

Doc, however, had another plan. He had already talked to Y. Frank Freeman who insisted that Hope fulfill his current option price. But Shurr also knew that Sam Goldwyn wanted Hope for a picture. Goldwyn had just loaned Gary Cooper to Paramount and felt he deserved to have the favor returned.

Shurr went to Freeman and asked if Hope could be loaned out to Goldwyn. Freeman agreed, providing Hope completed his current schedule of four films. Then Doc and his partner, a tough bargainer named Al Melnick, went to see Goldwyn.

"I knew you would work it out for me, Louie," Goldwyn said. "I'm going to make a very funny picture with this Hope."

"For what kind of money, Sam?" asked Doc.

"What does he want?"

"A hundred thousand," said Melnick bluntly.

Goldwyn sputtered and told them to forget it. Meanwhile Hope's public appearance tour, with its record-breaking crowds, was a topic of all the syndicated columns. Offers and counteroffers continued. Hope was willing to stake everything on the figure Melnick proposed to Goldwyn. Unless he could establish his worth away from Paramount, he would be another victim of the big studio practice of working actors at originally-agreed-upon contracts long after the actor had begun to reap big profits for the studio.

Goldwyn, on the other hand, figured Hope would capitulate sooner or later. Then, in a fortuitous turn of events, Paramount asked Hope to emcee the premiere of *The Westerner*, the film Cooper had made as a loan-out from Goldwyn. The premiere was to be staged in Dallas and Fort Worth simultaneously, or nearly so, with eight stage appearances scheduled in a single day. Hope was anxious to do it because he wanted Goldwyn to be grateful to him, and he knew that Goldwyn would be there as one of the celebrities from Hollywood. He let it be known how inconvenient this act of goodwill was for him since his Pepsodent radio series was having its seasonal premiere the same week.

The last show of the day in Ft. Worth was held at the Will Rogers Coliseum. Just before going on stage Hope said to Goldwyn that he certainly hoped they would be able to get the deal set for their picture together.

"Later, Bob," said Sam, "we'll talk later." He was smiling.

Hope was smiling, too. He had an idea. Part of the prearranged stage business for the film premiere was to have all of the Hollywood celebrities— including Cooper, Edward Arnold, Charlie Ruggles, Lillian Bond, Bruce Cabot and Goldwyn—troop across the stage single file behind him, unannounced and without even a glance toward Hope and the audience. Hope would look fleetingly over his shoulder and turn back to the audience to say, "Oh, that's the new unit breaking in for next week." Sam loved being part of a shtick like that.

Then Hope said, "And now may I present one of the really great men in our business, Mr. Sam Goldwyn."

Goldwyn came out beaming to big applause. He bowed and when it was quiet looked at Hope. "I haven't made a comedy since Eddie Cantor left me. I never found a comedian who I thought could do as well—until now. I finally found one in Bob Hope."

Applause. Hope took the mike firmly in his grip. "That's awful nice, Sam. Now let's talk about money."

"Later," Sam whispered. "We'll talk later."

"No, let's talk about it here. These people won't mind. Let's get really comfortable. Why don't we just lie down and talk things over?"

Hope got down on the stage floor and brought the mike along with him. The audience roared. Hope waited and finally Goldwyn, caught up in the spirit, got down on the floor with Hope. "Now, Sam, about my salary." Goldwyn reached for the mike but Bob pulled it away. "What did you say, Sam?" Then Bob whispered something in Goldwyn's ear and they both got up. "It's going to be a great pleasure to make a picture with Mr. Goldwyn." The audience was howling and the media people all took notes.[17]

Hope returned to Paramount to make *The Road to Zanzibar* with Crosby and Lamour as well as with Una Merkel and Eric Blore. Victor Schertzinger was directing once again and he had learned some things about the Hope–Crosby chemistry since *Singapore*. He felt Crosby was funniest when he was the schemer and Hope was much funnier as the victim. It was much better when it was understood that Crosby would be the lover who wins and Hope would be the aptly dubbed "junior" who is all false confidence, nervous laughs and who loses.

Clowning on the set was standard procedure even though the frequent comic disruptions and the flow of traffic caused by casual visitors and invited guests frustrated producer Paul Jones's efforts to bring *Zanzibar* in on budget. The gags, however, were not necessarily limited to those that Hope laid on Crosby or vice versa. One day, during a rehearsal with Lamour, Hope and Crosby were exchanging one of their rapid-fire routines designed to upset Dorothy. When they finished they turned to her and said, "How about it, Dottie?" Lamour smiled demurely, and as her smile widened she exposed to the camera and the crew—and her costars—that her makeup man had blacked out her front teeth. Bob and Bing fell down laughing.

Meanwhile the Pepsodent season was prospering despite the loss of Judy Garland. The show returned to a guest star policy with strong cast spots featuring Brenda and Cobina and the antics of Colonna and Ennis. Ben Gage had replaced Bill Goodwin. The show had gained so much in popularity that not far into the season the Hooper rating was 28.2, just a few points behind Bergen. Jack Benny still held the commanding lead at 36.2, but *Radio Daily* named Hope as the "top comedian of the nation," based on a poll of radio critics.

On the home front Dolores was trying to adjust to the shrinking slice of the total Bob Hope time allotted to her and to baby Linda. With a five-day shooting schedule at the studio and a weekend schedule of rehearsal and show preview, it was catch as catch can. She was thrilled when the call came from Florence Walrath in Evanston that the baby boy they had asked for was finally available, and Bob asked if he could do the honors alone at The Cradle this time. He had learned his lesson about how to behave with Mrs. Walrath. But later he reported to his friends, "The attendants stuffed me into one of these rear-entrance zoot suits and a surgical Santa Claus beard. Then they marched me into a glass cage and exhibited me to a series of little characters who went wild about me. At least they clawed the air and screamed."[18]

Humor aside, what took place when a tiny male child was held up for his inspection was unexpected. The child turned his face and showed a profile that caused a nurse to say, "He looks just *like* you." Bob thought so, too. When they walked away from the window, he said: "That little character with the ski-slide nose—that's for me."

Bob called Dolores and she went to Chicago to pick up Anthony—little Tony—and fly back home with him.

> *. . . I'm happy to be here again, ladies and gentlemen, for my annual insult . . . (he pats Oscar on the head) . . . Remember me, shorty? . . . Snob! . . . I don't mind not winning but the Oscars look at me as if I was an agent . . . the only thing I ever got from the Academy is saddle blisters. . . .*[1]

19. *They Got Me Covered*

The strong, aristocratic timbre of Franklin Roosevelt's voice broke the tension of 1,400 film makers meeting at the Los Angeles Biltmore for the thirteenth annual Academy Awards banquet on February 21, 1941. Roosevelt, just reelected for a third term, had asked the Academy for six minutes of ceremony agenda to praise the movie industry for its contribution to national defense and for boosting American patriotism and morale. The President's aides could hardly ignore the statistic that in the year 1940 motion picture admissions exceeded $735 million, and industry predictions indicated that the figure would rise to a billion in 1941.

Roosevelt lauded the film personalities who were making fund-raising appeals in motion picture theaters aross the nation. Hope, for one, had spurred national campaigns during the past two months for the Red Cross, the Greek War Relief, Franco–British War Relief and Roosevelt's own beloved cause, the March of Dimes.

Hope was the emcee for this Oscar ceremony and in his usual playful vein. Looking longingly at the long row of gleaming golden statuettes, he said, "I see David Selznick brought them back!" referring to the unprecedented *Gone With the Wind* sweep the year before.

Hope glanced accusingly at his own studio's banquet table. "They've just

loaned me to Samuel Goldwyn for one picture—a sort of lend-louse bill."
The audience roared. "I see Paramount has a table, Metro-Goldwyn-Mayer
has a table, Warners has a table and Twentieth Century-Fox has a table.
Monogram has a stool."

Because it was the Academy's first awards using sealed envelopes, Hope
had just cracked that the banquet was "six courses of nervous indigestion,"
when Walter Wanger stepped to the microphone:

> Ladies and gentlemen, I would like us to pay tribute tonight to a
> man who has devoted his time and energy to many causes. His
> unselfishness in playing countless benefits has earned him a
> unique position in a hectic community where his untiring efforts
> are deeply, profoundly appreciated. Ladies and gentlemen, the
> Academy this year presents a special award for "Achievements in
> Humanities"—for his unselfish services to the motion picture
> industry—this silver plaque to—Bob Hope![2]

Hope was stunned. "I don't feel a bit funny," he said, holding up the plaque
and kissing it. "How am I going to get this thing in my scrapbook? I'll have
to build a whole new room for it."

When Hope sauntered into his Paramount soundstage the next day he was
applauded by his coworkers. The movie was *Caught in the Draft*, probably
Hollywood's first comedy about the rather serious subject of conscription.
Hope was cast as Don Bolton, a movie star who enlists in the Army, after
resisting the draft, to win the Colonel's daughter, played by Dorothy
Lamour. It was produced by Paramount's new production chief, Buddy
DeSylva, and directed by David Butler.

Butler, dubbed by Hope "Old Blubber Butt," provided the cast with extra
laughs the first day of shooting. Hope describes it:

> I think it was Dave's first picture on the lot and he wanted to
> make a strong impression upstairs. So he gave us a big, booming
> 'All right, now, let's get going. Lots of pepper now,' and we
> launched into the first scene which involved No Man's Land,
> trenches and a lot of big mud holes. I love that guy. Dave weighed
> about three hundred, but nevertheless he was running here, and
> yelling directions about how we must run to dodge the explosions,
> and suddenly he vanished into one of those mud holes and sank up
> to his neck. When he came up sputtering the rest of us almost fell
> into deep mud holes laughing. I'm afraid we had to leave him
> there while we sent for a derrick to haul him up.[3]

The film then ran into weather problems and attempts to shoot some
essential scenes on location were repeatedly thwarted. Finally the weather
cleared, and because they were already way over budget, Butler was trying
to get his last two important location setups in a single day. He had two
locations, both about twenty miles away from Paramount and six miles from
each other.

Butler completed the first set-up in early afternoon and asked Hope to
meet him for the second at Paramount's ranch in Malibu Canyon, which
happened to be an area Hope knew had some especially good real estate

opportunities. He piled makeup man Harry Ray in his car and they drove off to look at the property. Hope lingered too long and the daylight began to fade. Realizing this, he raced to the ranch just as Butler was exploding. The studio quickly brought in a truckload of extra lights to augment the fading sunlight. Paramount was angry with Hope, but Hope bought the land that today is worth millions.

The thoughtlessness and self-indulgence revealed in this episode came to the surface a number of times during Hope's first flush-of-success period in Hollywood.

His platoon of writers, who spent more time with him than his family, saw a man the public didn't. It was they who daily fed the showman's ego and did what they could to feed his hunger for approval (though only an audience could really satisfy that appetite). They saw that beyond the normal drives of an entertainer, Hope craved the material rewards of success to make up for all he didn't have as a child, for those years of struggle as a hoofer.

When his writers called him Scrooge, it was less for his penuriousness than for his running roughshod over the sensibilities of others. They tell how Hope on one payday stood up on a chair and made airplanes of their checks, floating them down to waiting hands. It was a gag, of course, but it was also a clear message of his status—and of theirs.

At writing conferences there evolved a ritual of Hope sending out for his prime passion, ice cream. It was the youngest or newest writer who must go for it, and invariably Hope would order less than his writers could eat. Bob would take his share, and the others scraped up what was left.

The writers worked on holidays, were summoned from a dinner table and ferreted out of town on a moment's notice at Hope's whim. And frequently their caviling was only an excuse for a gag at Hope's expense. One of the best examples of this comes from senior gagsmith Norman Sullivan who says that Hope hired some young "relief writers" for the summer months and that one of these part-timers asked him, "What does Bob do about summer?" Sullivan replied tartly, "He lets it come."

Actually, those same writers expected to be awakened in the middle of the night by Hope, they sweated for him, they got ulcers for him, they waited for Christmas presents from him, they idolized him. In those days there was always about an even dozen gag writers but not always the same dozen. They were replaced when they lost their freshness. Mort Lachman said, "There were 9,000 guys waiting to write for Hope."[4] There was excitement writing for him. He was on his way up. He was hot and getting hotter.

In March 1941 his movie career was blooming. The New York critics said, "*Road to Zanzibar* is mostly nonsense but it is nonsense of the most delightful sort." He had started filming the spy-spoof *Nothing but the Truth* with Paulette Goddard and there was success written all over that picture.

Hope was pleased with this radio season, too. One Saturday afternoon after Hope had finished a script session at NBC in Hollywood and was leaving the parking lot, producer Al Capstaff hailed his car to a stop. "How would you like to do the show for the Air Corps at Riverside—one of our Sunday night previews, or maybe the real thing—out at March Field?"

"Why not invite the fellas to the studio?" Hope countered. His routine, a grind to any other performer, was demanding but comfortable; it was nicely

geared to his golf game and he didn't have to drive more than fifteen minutes
to either studio.

"Too many guys."

"How many?"

"A thousand—maybe two."

Hope's eyes blinked. He turned his head away and thought about that size
crowd fanned out in front of him. He could hear the sound that 2,000 joke-
hungry servicemen could make, all laughing and applauding.

"Get more details. I like it." He drove away.[5]

The arguments in favor of doing an origination from a military base were
hard to beat. It would be an innovative radio idea. It would provide Hope
with responsive, enthusiastic audiences. It would provide Hope with a body
of engaging topical subject matter that was tailor-made for his persona. Last
but certainly not least, it would be a humdinger of a promotion for his soon-
to-be-released *Caught in the Draft*.

His first GI broadcast was on May 6, 1941. The program was produced in
his established radio format, with opening monologue, cast-member comedy,
music, a guest star sketch, and the usual commercials. The important difference was the total adaptation of the comedy to a military context. These
excerpts from the initial monologue are indicative:

> How do you do ladies and gentlemen, this is Bob (Army Camp)
> Hope . . . telling all soldiers they may have to shoot in the
> swamp or march in the brush, but if they use Pepsodent no one
> will ever have to drill in their mush. . . . Well, here we are,
> ladies and gentlemen, at March Field, one of the Army's great
> flying fields, located near Riverside, California . . . and I want
> to tell you that I'm thrilled being here . . . and what a wonder-
> ful welcome they gave me . . . as soon as I got in the camp I
> received a ten-gun salute . . . they told me on the operating
> table . . . I watched them putting gas in one of the big bomb-
> ers . . . and boy what a big tank . . . just two pints short of
> W.C. Fields . . . but all these fellows were glad to see
> me . . . one rookie came running up to me, very excited, and
> said: "Are you really Bob Hope?" I said: "Yes" . . . but they
> grabbed his rifle away just in time . . . another soldier had in big
> figures on his back . . . one thousand three hundred and twen-
> ty-nine . . . I said: "Draft number?" . . . and he said: "No,
> that's when I get to the bathtub." . . .[6]

The opening "This is Bob [wherever he was] Hope" not only bracketed the
context within the personality, but also telegraphed the significance of the
context. Further, his use of "Well, here we are at . . ." immediately fixed a
geographic location, establishing Hope as a traveler, a fast mover. "I'm
thrilled being here," for all of its surface enthusiasm and ingratiation,
implied the incongruity of Hope being "thrilled" to be entertaining at some
remote military installation under the circumstances of national mobiliza-
tion. Hope and his writers elicited both soldier and civilian laughter from
instances of simple, harebrained foolishness, reluctant heroism, and even
blatant cowardice set against a climate of high seriousness, a stern military

regime where ordinary men were being prepared for war. Hope's exploitation of the soldier's resentments, hardships and habits permitted the soldier to laugh at his environment and at himself as a victim of that environment, while arousing sympathy in the general audience.

It took several days to assess the impact of the March Field experiment and consequently the following week's show originated from Vine Street. But on May 20 Hope took guest star Priscilla Lane and his regular cast to the San Diego Naval Station. The show's third GI trip, the next week, was for Marines at San Luis Obispo, and on June 10 Hope took Mary Martin and director David Butler to the Army's Camp Callan where he also previewed, to a wildly enthusiastic crowd, his latest film effort, *Caught in the Draft*.

The new movie was from the moment of its release a runaway box office success; it became the biggest moneymaker Paramount had that year. On July 7, 1941, *Time* magazine reviewed the film favorably, and then followed with ten paragraphs of personality profile concentrating on Hope's business acumen:

> Bob Hope has made twelve pictures to date (three of them this year), has five more lined up and waiting. He is on the NBC air every week for Pepsodent. If people grow weary of Hope's stylized impudence, it will be largely due to the star's appealing avarice.
>
> Physically, Bob Hope's biggest asset is his chin, a granitic abutment fit to warm the heart of any quarry-bound sculptor. However, he rarely leads with it. Around the Paramount lot he is known as a "hard man with a dollar."

Crosby fired off a letter to *Time* that said, "My friend Bob Hope is anything but cheap. He does an average of two benefits a week. His price for a personal appearance would be about $10,000, so he gives away $20,000 every week of his life. Is that cheap?"[7]

The magazine rebutted, "*Time* agrees with Bing; however, Bob from time to time has been known to put undue pressure on a nickel."

The one uncontrovertible statement by *Time* was that Hope had a sharp business sense. His instinct for marketing and promotion was acute, and Pepsodent was anxious to involve him in a national promotion stunt that could put their toothpaste into the top sales bracket. They were searching for something that gave them a closer identification with Hope. Along the way, Hope had an idea.

As soon as his last Pepsodent show was aired and the final scenes for *Nothing but the Truth* were dubbed, Hope took a plane for New York. Pepsodent's marketing genius Vic Hunter and Lord and Thomas' John McPherrin sat down with Hope in the comedian's St. Regis suite. Hope suggested, "Instead of running a contest or giving away a lifelong dental policy or whatever—how would you like to give away a book that I would write—a comic autobiography—you know, one where I could really rib myself like I do on the air. I've got a dozen clever elves on the Coast to help me. Do you have any idea how much fan mail we've been getting, and how much of it asks for pictures and biographical stuff? There's another angle to this. I've got a picture that will be released in the fall, just about the time you're ready to drop this stunt. It's called *Nothing but the Truth*. I think we can tie the two together in some way—maybe use that as the title. Why don't you talk to the boys at Paramount?"[8]

Lord and Thomas was thrilled to have so much of its creative work already done, and Paramount saw the potential of a national promotion for one of its stars. Pepsodent agreed to pay for the printing; Paramount agreed to help promote it. Their plan was to photograph every major Hollywood star reading a copy of the book. Lord and Thomas planned a mock "literary tea" at Billingsley's Stork Club for press and celebrities. All this for a book that would cost ten cents and a boxtop from a tube of Pepsodent. Hope retained the ownership rights.

Elated by the prospects of adding "author" to his accomplishments, Hope left New York for Cleveland to talk with Ivor about Hope Metal Products (their jointly held company) picking up some defense contracts, and to see the rest of his family there. He shared with them his most recent letter from Granddad in Hitchin who, nearly ninety-eight, was "busy dousing incendiary bombs" and serving as self-styled air raid warden.

Hope then went back to Hollywood to begin *Louisiana Purchase*, the screen version of Irving Berlin's long-running Broadway original. Paramount's script was a toothless satire of fiery Louisiana politics and the corruption surrounding the Huey Long family.

It was fortunate that the Hope writers weren't overtaxed trying to punch up the *Louisiana Purchase* script that summer, because their backs were bent over their typewriters pecking out pages of one-liners suitable for inclusion in the comic reconstruction of the comedian's thirty-seven-year life. In late night hours, and in scattered periods on weekends, Hope dictated bits and pieces of ideas he wanted included in the book and gags that he thought should be developed. Neither he nor the writers cared about biographical accuracy. The thrust of the humor was deflating the Hope success story, satirizing elements of the American Dream.

Taken as a whole, *They Got Me Covered* (as the volume was finally called) was a 95-page paperback giveaway distributed in the hundreds of thousands as a souvenir program for Tuesday night's broadcast. The first half, with its struggles for fame, was Horatio Alger peppered with folk wit; and the second half, with its put-down of the glamour life in Hollywood, was almost a predecessor of *Mad Magazine*. The principal running gag, as expected, was Hope's adolescent lechery for the likes of Hedy Lamarr and Madeleine Carroll. Not surprisingly, one quarter of the book was devoted to a smart-alecky behind-the-scenes look at his own Pepsodent show, including a burlesque scene showing a dozen gag writers at work.

The pages seemed to be meant for reading aloud. It was a long monologue without the dots and dashes of Hope's delivery. Alva Johnson, commenting on the book in *Life* magazine, was the first critical observer to apply the word "humorist" to Bob Hope, and also the first to suggest his resemblance to Josh Billings, Bill Nye, Petroleum V. Nasby and others allied to the popular oracle tradition in American humor.

The strength of the book rests in a simple, graceful quality that Woody Allen, among others, has cited as the epitome of Hope's style. Much of the book is still funny today, particularly the sequence that covered his prize-fighting career:

I was very popular because I had a peculiar weaving, bobbing style the crowd loved to watch. I used to weave and bob around the ring for ten minutes after the other guy had won and gone home. I'll never forget my first fight. When the bell rang I danced to the center of the ring—then they carried me to the corner. Then the bell rang again and I danced to the center of the ring— then they carried me to my corner.[9]

While *They Got Me Covered* was rolling off the presses and waiting to be ordered by Pepsodent users, Hope took his radio gang to Chicago for the program's 1941–42 seasonal premiere on September 23. Hope proudly introduced Frances Langford as his newest cast regular, aware that her popularity as a movie and recording personality would be an immediate asset to the show's ratings. And to fire up the book promotion, Hope's longest comedy sketch that night was all about the publishing business.

The next day Hope went on to New York for the Stork Club literary reception promoting the book. Then followed in quick succession radio remotes in Washington and Cleveland, interrupted by a show for a veteran's hospital and the Philadelphia premiere of *Nothing but the Truth*, where the veterans presented Hope with a citation for humanitarianism. Then it was back to California.

When his radio broadcasts resumed from NBC's Hollywood studios on October 14, there were few changes. In addition to lush-voiced Langford, there was Ben Gage as announcer-stooge, replacing Bill Goodwin. Brenda and Cobina were off on an extended vaudeville tour. But Hope, Colonna and Ennis worked together as usual, and a guest star policy was reestablished. Paulette Goddard was up first and naturally she and Hope plugged *Nothing but the Truth*. Several of the comedy sketches during the fall season were serializations of Hope's tongue-in-cheek autobiography. These constant reminders to the 23 million weekly listeners speeded up the mail-ins for the two million copies Pepsodent had printed as a first edition.

Also this same fall, Hope was finally making a movie with Paramount's beautiful English-born star Madeleine Carroll. For the two previous radio seasons Hope had been praising her looks and joking about making a film with her. Hope learned that it was Carroll herself who had suggested they be teamed for a film. Bob asked his two young writers Norman Panama and Mel Frank to write a screenplay for them. It was called *Snowball in Hell* and it involved a second-rate vaudevillian with a penguin act who becomes unwittingly involved with a beautiful British secret agent who is trying to keep Nazi spies from stealing the plans of a new fighter plane. Hope told his radio listeners:

. . . she's a spy . . . and she keeps chasing me. . . . That's right, Madeleine Carroll keeps chasing me. . . . And you think Walt Disney makes fantasy pictures! Yes sir, I guess I'm the only man in this country right now who wants longer working hours. . . . This morning the producer asked me to study my lines . . . I'm working on a picture with Madeleine Carroll and he wants me to study *my* lines! . . .[10]

On Saturday, December 6, Hope had agreed to ride a horse in the annual

Santa Claus Lane parade sponsored by the Hollywood Chamber of Commerce. Hope said he would ride providing they gave him a wornout delivery wagon plug, and as he plodded along, he would be preceded by a huge placard reading BING CROSBY'S FASTEST RACEHORSE. Hope was warmly applauded by the huge turnout of fans and Christmas shoppers who lined both sides of Hollywood Boulevard that Saturday afternoon.

Hope slept late on Sunday morning. It was eleven when Dolores came in with his coffee and the newspapers. As she walked toward her dressing room she told him about the photos of the Santa Claus Lane parade in the rotogravure section of the *Daily News*, and about a rather extensive feature piece on *Louisiana Purchase* in the *This Week Magazine* supplement of the *Los Angeles Times* of December 7, 1941. When his eyes began to focus Bob scanned the *Los Angeles Times* article.

One paragraph in the story disturbed him, because it revealed fairly accurately his income. There were all kinds of nuts running around, and he had two little children who could be kidnapped. The story said:

> The comedian's gross income during 1940, from radio, movies and personal appearances totaled $464,161.78. Even after business deductions, Bob paid, for 1940, federal and state income taxes totaling $142,047.66. His 1941 gross income will probably rise to $575,000, but considering the defense rates Congress has approved, he may remind himself of his favorite joke about Crosby: "Bing doesn't pay a regular income tax. He just calls up Secretary Morganthau each year and asks, 'How much do you boys need?'"

It was eleven-twenty. He was listening with one ear to the pro football game coming from New York's Polo Grounds and musing about the article. Dolores had gone downstairs to supervise the children's lunch and had come back up to her sitting room next to their bedroom. She had snapped on her radio to listen to the New York Philharmonic concert because Artur Rubinstein, whom she had recently met, was going to play a Brahms concerto.

Then Bob heard words he couldn't quite believe and yet he knew he had heard them. He sat up straight, yelling, "Dolores!"

She came quickly to the door. "What happened?"

"The Japs bombed Pearl Harbor," he said savagely.

"Are you sure? There's nothing on CBS but music." She went back to her own radio. "Oh, my God," she said returning with the front page of the *Los Angeles Times* in her hand. "Bob, do you realize that Japanese envoys were meeting with Hull today—"

"Those bastards. They've stabbed us," he said, getting out of bed. "Dolores, why don't you drive with Jack and me to Long Beach tonight? We're doing a preview of our show for the Navy. It ought to be some kind of show."

On Tuesday evening Pepsodent relinquished its air time to President Roosevelt, who had asked for the most-listened-to time slot on radio for his second declaration of war speech to the American people.

Bob's public and private reaction to the nation's crisis was reflected by his opening speech on the December 16 broadcast. With no signature theme song, he began:

Good evening ladies and gentlemen . . . this is Bob Hope, and I just want to take a moment to say that last Tuesday night at this time I was sitting out there with you listening to our president as he asked all Americans to stand together in this emergency. We feel that in times like these—more than ever before, we need a moment of relaxation. All of us on the Pepsodent show will do our best to bring it to you. We think this is not a question of keeping up morale . . . to most Americans, morale is taken for granted. There is no need to tell a nation to keep smiling when it's never stopped. It's that ability to laugh that makes us the great people that we are . . . Americans! All of us in this studio feel that if we can bring into your homes a little of this laughter each Tuesday night we are helping to do our part. Thank you. . . .[11]

THE WAR YEARS
1942–1945

I don't know if you've ever been kissed by a camel, but I've got to tell you it's not like being kissed by Raquel Welch. This particular camel may have been listening to my radio show because after he kissed me he spat right in my face.[1]

20. Victory Caravan

It was New Year's Day 1942 and Hope was lying in bed listening to the Rose Bowl game. Ordinarily he would be in Pasadena watching the game. But this year, for precautionary reasons—what had been described as "sensitive wartime restrictions"—the game was moved to Durham, North Carolina, where Oregon State had gone to play, and to win.

As had been the custom for the past three years, the Hopes would hold open house in Toluca Lake for the Crosbys, the Colonnas, the Malatestas (Dolores' sister and brother-in-law), the MacArthurs—maybe Jack Hope and his new wife, Lee—and George Hope. Also David Butler, Louis Shurr and the Jimmy Saphiers.

Instead of the trip to the Rose Bowl, there would be a punch bowl, a buffet and perhaps a screening of *Louisiana Purchase* or Bing's latest, *Holiday Inn*. Hope was stretched out on his oversized bed and, while he listened to the game, scribbling down some parodied lyrics to his theme song which he might sing, if asked, later in the day.

This had been an extraordinary year for him with some very thankful memories. Both the press and his film colleagues had boosted his stock.

Besides his Special Oscar, Hope had received many awards. On December 9 the nation's radio critics voted Hope not only the "Leading Entertainer" and the "Leading Comedian" in America, but also voted him their most prestigious commendation as "Champion of Champions." The Hollywood Press Photographers also gave him their highest award. Perhaps closest to his heart, *Motion Picture Herald* on December 26 announced that Hope had joined the inner circle of top moneymaking film stars for the enormous box office returns from *Caught in the Draft*.

And speaking of *Caught in the Draft*, Granddad's most recent letter described the long queues outside London's Odeon Theatre where the picture was playing. James Hope wrote that the film was playing continuously night and day, and asked Bob to come to Britain as soon as possible to entertain his "countrymen" and to make them forget their troubles. Hope said he was going to do just that.

In fact, 1942 was, despite several warnings from his doctor Tom Hearn to slow down, a cyclonic year. There was an exhibition golf tour with Bing Crosby for the Red Cross and other war relief causes in February. There was the filming of *Road to Morocco* (probably the funniest *Road* picture); after that, the Hollywood Victory Caravan of twenty-one major film stars touring the country for the Army and Navy Relief Fund; then back to Hollywood to film Goldwyn's *They Got Me Covered*; then off to Alaska for his first overseas USO tour, interlaced with at least fifty benefit appearances, and, of

course, his regular schedule of weekly radio shows, most of which originated
from military bases. And since it was Hope's custom to preview a radio show
at one base and do it live from another, he ended up with two GI entertainments a week.

As soon as Hope completed *My Favorite Blonde* in January, he and Crosby sat down with Fred Corcoran of the Professional Golfers Association to
discuss the exhibition matches they would play in February. Bob and Bing
decided they could begin at the Western Open Golf Tournament at Phoenix
and then swing into Texas for matches at Houston, Dallas, Fort Worth,
Corpus Christi and San Antonio. In San Antonio, the highjinks on the golf
course got so frenzied that Hope did a striptease down to his shorts as a
bonus prize for the highest single donation to war relief.

After the Red Cross Benefit Match in Sacramento (which made extra
headlines because Bob, with all his pranks and banter, won), and after each
had performed his weekly radio chore, Bing and Bob met at Paramount to
prepare for the *Road to Morocco*. For some, this film typifies what is meant
by a Hope–Crosby collaboration. Director David Butler had learned to cap-
italize on his stars' improvisations. A serious, meticulous craftsman, his early
schooling in the Mack Sennett rough-and-tumble silents enabled him t
anticipate and deal with the unexpected.

The one thing all three men knew with certainty was that a *Road* picture
meant spontaneity, and that too many rehearsals deadened the fun.

Butler said later, "If anything happened that was out of the ordinary, I'
always let the camera run—and we got some of our funniest stuff after th
scene was over. I'd even let the camera roll until they got off the set, o
walked out, or whatever happened."[2]

The *Morocco* script, once again from the imagination of Frank Butler and
Don Hartman, was ideal wartime escapism. Crosby as Jeff Peters and Hope
as Turkey Jackson are shipwrecked and washed up onto the Moroccan
shores. Crosby sells Hope into slavery to pay their dinner check, and Hope
becomes the captive of the beautiful Princess Shalimar, played by Dorothy
Lamour. Eventually Crosby arrives to save Hope from the vengeance of the
sheik, played by Anthony Quinn, and Crosby wins Lamour—naturally.

One of the film's funniest sequences typifies the Butler approach. At th
opening of the movie, Bob and Bing do a scene with a trained camel whose
assignment was to sneak up behind them and lick first Bob and then Bing o
the cheek. The gag in the film was that each man thought the other was
doing the kissing. Hope said some years later, "I don't know if you've ever
been kissed by a camel, but I've got to tell you that it's not like being kissed
by Raquel Welch. This particular camel may have been listening to my radio
show because after he kissed me he spat right in my face."[3]

Hope staggered backwards, shocked by the unexpectedness of the spit and
repulsed by the vile stench of the spittle. Crosby doubled up with laughter as
did most of the crew. Butler kept the camera rolling.

"Great scene," Butler said finally. And when someone remarked what a
lucky break they got with the camel, Butler said, "Lucky my foot. I worked
with that beast for weeks!"

Morocco had its perilous moments as well. Butler took the cast over to the

Twentieth Century-Fox backlot to shoot a scene in which Bob and Bing were being chased down a narrow alley by a band of wild horses. Hope and Crosby took their places and on signal began to walk down the alley. They were supposed to reach the halfway point when the horses were cued to move. But when Butler yelled for a camera roll, the assistant director had already cued the horses and they were soon bearing down on Bob and Bing. The two turned and saw they could be trampled to death before they reached the other end. Bing saw a hole in the pavement and dropped, while Bob flattened himself against a shallow doorway until the horses got past.

They angrily made their way back to Butler. A former stuntman himself, Butler had not seen any danger in asking Hope and Crosby to work with the horses.

"What in hell was that?" screamed Hope.

"You nearly lost your stars, Dave," said Crosby, nursing bruises from his tumble.

Butler's hulking frame was shaking and between laughs he said, "Yeah— how about that? We got a great shot."[4]

Just as the filming of *Morocco* ended, Paramount released *My Favorite Blonde*, and Hope arranged to premiere the picture at military bases in connection with his Pepsodent show originations. At his radio show on April 7 he played host to hundreds of young air cadets in Hollywood. The next week he introduced Rita Hayworth to airmen at Santa Ana and to sailors at San Pedro, and in both halls the noise almost lifted the roof.

On April 29, Hope, Frances Langford and Jerry Colonna flew to Washington, D.C., to catch up with the Hollywood Victory Caravan. A special train carrying some of the nation's most popular entertainers had crossed the country, rehearsing as they went, and were all set to kick off a two-week whistle-stop tour for Army and Navy Relief funds in the nation's capital. The stars were Desi Arnaz, Joan Bennett, Joan Blondell, Charles Boyer, James Cagney, Claudette Colbert, Bing Crosby, Olivia de Havilland, Cary Grant, Charlotte Greenwood, Bert Lahr, Laurel and Hardy, Groucho Marx, Frank McHugh, Ray Middleton, Merle Oberon, Pat O'Brien, Eleanor Powell, Risë Stevens and Spencer Tracy—plus, of course, Frances and Jerry.

A three-hour variety package of popular songs, dances, comedy sketches, dramatic scenes and readings, even operatic arias, had been created by producer-director Mark Sandrich and musical director Alfred Newman. The special material was written by such heavyweights as Lindsay and Crouse, Moss Hart, George Kaufman and Jerome Chodorov with original music added by Jerome Kern, Johnny Mercer, Frank Loesser and Arthur Schwartz. Hope, as master of ceremonies, was faced with the responsibility of keeping it moving, holding it together by introducing acts, joking between acts, as well as acting in scenes with Claudette Colbert, Spencer Tracy, Crosby and Colonna.

Hope arrived in Washington barely in time to join the others at a White House lawn party given by Eleanor Roosevelt. Later they all converged on Constitution Hall for a rehearsal which lasted all night. From the start of the tour Hope was the subject of admiration for his high energy level and his unerring ability to thread the ragged parts of the show together. He was also the target of some playful barbs because he was trying, as usual, to sandwich in his radio show, golf exhibition matches with Crosby, and whatever other business he could accomplish in cities they were visiting.

Before they opened that night, Groucho Marx dropped an acerbic comment as he fretted about his own role in the show. "It's all right for guys like Hope. He has seventeen guys writing his jokes for him. But I've got to do the worrying about my own material."[5] Sandrich told Groucho that Hope had only six writers along and their job was to write his radio show for the next two weeks. Groucho snapped, "Only six? For Hope that's practically ad-libbing."

Herb Golden, reporting the event in *Daily Variety*, April 30, 1942, applauded the "pluck and all-out patriotism of top-flight stars who rehearsed all night." He went on to label the effort "Bob Hope's Victory Caravan" because he felt:

> . . . it was only those performers, and fortunately there were a lot of them, who had the benefit of gagging with the Pepsodent peddler who came out completely satisfactory on the comedy end. As long as Hope was on stage the show had zest and lift. With his departure it dropped to various levels of mediocrity.

Hope spent much of his time on the train to Boston in his compartment, huddling with his writers over a script, so he missed out on the barber shop harmonizing in the club car among Lahr, Marx, McHugh, O'Brien and Cagney.

There were thousands of people waiting at South Station when the train pulled in, thousands more lining the streets leading to the Statler Hotel. Hope had made prior arrangements to meet PGA head Fred Cocoran for dinner at the Union Oyster House and confessed he would not be riding in the motorcade to the Boston Garden. The news irritated both the Boston and the Caravan officials, but producer Sandrich said, "What the hell! Who's going to know?"

With difficulty, Hope and Cocoran managed to push their way through huge street mobs to the Oyster House where they sat in an obscure corner and ate shrimp and soft-shell crabs. Cocoran described to Hope the exhibition matches that would be sandwiched between the Caravan shows and Hope's radio show the following week when a man from a nearby table interrupted. "I want you to know that your appearance here has been a life saver for me, Mr. Hope. My wife has been giving me holy hell because I forgot her opera glasses, and she was saying the evening would be ruined unless she could get a close-up view of Bob Hope—just as you walked by our table. Thanks. It saves me a lot of grief."

Hope smiled. "Nice I could help." Then he stood. "Hey, what time is it?" As usual he was without a timepiece. "We've got to get to that parade."[6]

Corcoran threw a wad of bills at the waiter and they ran for the door. The streets outside were jammed. Haymarket Square was impossible to penetrate. They started to walk toward North Station. People were facing the street and cheering. Bob muscled his way through the line and tried to see the motorcade. "Isn't this silly," he said. "All these people standing on the street trying to get a peek at a homely guy like Hope. What's he got I haven't got?"

"Ahhhh—shut up!" the man beside him said.

Corcoran stifled a laugh and suggested to Bob that what the other stars had, and what he didn't have, was a ride to the Boston Garden. A few minutes later they managed to find a taxi and the driver ingeniously carried them to about 500 yards from their destination. Hope jumped out, pushed through a line of spectators, leaped over a saw-horse barrier, ran and climbed on the running board of one of the moving convertibles. Once in, Hope started waving at the crowd. A scream went up, "There's Bob Hope!" He was told later that there were many such screams all along the parade route—all mistaken identifications—because in twilight the stars were not easy to distinguish, flanked as they were between military escorts.

The Boston show went better than Washington's, and Philadelphia's the next day was better than Boston. The train pushed on toward Cleveland, Detroit, Chicago and St. Louis, St. Paul, Minneapolis, Des Moines, Houston and Dallas. Hope's chores were so well grooved that he could actually enjoy his departures from the tour to do his radio show and golf benefits. And though he seemed to be looping in and out of the Caravan life, Bob's value to the tour was unquestioned. His nightly high spirits, his good-natured wisecracks about a band of Hollywood gypsies kept the stars laughing both on and off stage. One of Hope's most engaging routines on stage each night was his sly revelation to each audience of the secrets of backstage life and what was really going on between whistle-stops. Sadly, Hope was missing most of that camaraderie himself.

But Hope was always a part of the marvelous before-show dressing room tableau. John Lahr described a nightly ritual of that tour presided over by the beloved Stan Laurel and "Babe" Hardy, who always managed to be first to arrive backstage at any theater:

> Their make-up would be set out neatly in front of them, with a clean towel folded carefully over it. Between them each day was an opened bottle of whiskey.
>
> Laurel and Hardy waited quietly as the actors came in. Gradually everyone moved down toward their corner, sharing a drink and theater talk.[7]

Groucho, at first reluctant to enjoy the Caravan, later confessed how much he enjoyed taking part in quartet contests from midnight till daybreak, and said how amused he was by a "million-dollar crooner straining his voice to top the sound of the train and trying hard to outdo an obscure baritone who insisted he was Bob Hope." Marx caught himself before he became maudlin about the tour, adding "it isn't safe for a comic to get too sentimental." Bert Lahr had no compunction about sentimentality. He called the wartime fund-raiser a "caravan of love."

Perhaps the best reflection of the stars' attitudes was witnessed the final night in Houston. A capacity crowd of 12,000 in the Houston Coliseum cheered and stomped unaware that there were that night actually two shows going on simultaneously. Because it was Tuesday night, Hope's Pepsodent show was being broadcast from an adjacent theater filled with hundreds of airmen from Ellington Field. Hope, Langford, and Colonna dashed back and forth between theaters doing their Caravan solos and sketches in addition to their thirty-minute broadcast. Cary Grant shared the M.C. chores with Hope that night for the victory show. When the broadcast was finished, travel-weary stars from the Caravan began showing up at the second theater to perform for the spellbound GIs. The show for the airmen lasted two hours and it was one o'clock before the applause ended.

After the Houston show, the Caravan stars dispersed. They were all very, very tired. But Hope, to everyone's disbelief, was starting out with Langford and Colonna for four more weeks of entertaining GIs, scheduled to do 65 shows at a variety of military bases and hospitals including Pepsodent radio shows at New Orleans; Atlanta; Quantico, Virginia; and Mitchell Field, Long Island.

The Victory Caravan was merely a vanguard of the movie industry's war effort. Through the War Activities Committee, Hollywood raised nearly a million dollars for the USO, over a million for the war bond drive, more than two million for Army and Navy relief societies, distributed films to camps and bases, and set and kept a long-range goal to raise a billion dollars in war bonds by sending seven troupes of film stars to appearances in 5,000 theaters located in 300 cities of the nation.

While many stars were doing camp shows and selling bonds, Hope's GI entertaining would become legendary. This 65-show tour was merely a rehearsal of what was in store for him during the next three years, during which he would become remarkably adept in becoming a part of his audience, in speaking the GI language, in ribbing their gripes. His many walks through hospital wards to cheer the sick and dying were never easy experiences, but he knew instinctively that the only way he could get through an intensive care or burn ward was with gags. Yet one of his earliest incursions into this sensitive area made a deep impression on him. He shared some of these feelings with Al Sharp, a reporter from an Atlanta newspaper, when he arrived at that city's Biltmore Terrace hotel three days later.

"Come on in here," said Hope in a tired voice. He drew the reporter away from the crowd in his suite to another room, closed the door and dropped down to a couch. Hope had a day's stubble of beard. "Phew—boy, am I tired—I mean really tired. We did three shows last night down in Louisiana and then flew in here a little while ago in an Army transport." Hope yawned. But he wanted to talk.

"We've been on the road for two weeks. And what do you know? Our baggage is lost. Just like vaudeville. They tell me it'll be here tomorrow morning. I hope so because I've got a few more weeks of this to go. But I'm kidding. I love it. And I get a kick out of flying in those planes—we do quite a bit of it—going to and from Army camps and Navy bases. You see a lot—and it's interesting—and it's tough.

"The other day in New Orleans," Hope continued, "the Merchant Marine hospital staff heard we were in town and asked us to come out and cheer up some survivors from a tanker torpedoed near there a few days before. I was a bit upset about trying to cheer the boys up. We knew some of them were burned so badly they would die. But they wanted the gags, so we went."

Hope stood up. "After seeing those fellows all burned, I thought as I came
out of the hospital, that's what Lew Ayres meant when he refused to kill
folks." (Ayres had made national headlines with his announcement of being
a conscientious objector.) "Of course we've got to kill people—because we've
got an aggressor creeping up on us to stab us in the back. But I admire Ayres
for his stand. It took courage to do that. It's against his religion to kill folks.
He's volunteered for the Medical Corps—and it takes courage to go into the
front lines and care for people." Silence.[8]

> *We were trying to get back to Anchorage from Cordova
> when the sleet and hail hit us. It got worse and worse and
> then over Anchorage our radio went out. Dubowsky, the
> crew chief, handed us Mae Wests and gave us instructions:
> "If we have to abandon ship, pull this! If you land in water,
> pull this!"*[1]

21. Frozen Follies

Hope spent the summer of 1942 working for Sam Goldwyn: that is, during
the week he worked for Goldwyn and on weekends he worked for another
Sam, doing camp shows and PGA-arranged war-relief golf benefits with
Crosby.

He settled into Goldwyn's Santa Monica Boulevard studios in mid-July
with costar Dorothy Lamour and director David Butler to do the picture he
had wrestled over with Sam on that Dallas stage. Doc Shurr's partner, Al
Melnick, had carved an extraordinary money deal that guaranteed Hope
$100,000 and a percentage for his work, a deal particularly remarkable at a
time when studios had agreed to curb salary increases for the war effort.

Hope used to say laughingly he shamed Goldwyn into his salary demand.
Goldwyn may have been eccentric, but he was a good businessman, and even
without his glasses he could read box office figures, and he was impressed, as
most producers would be, that the New York Paramount in January had
taken in the unheard-of figure of $24,000 for a single day's admissions to
Louisiana Purchase, grossing a mammoth $92,000 for the week. Since that
time, for its four-week run in May, *My Favorite Blonde* smashed all the
previous attendance records at the Paramount. Hope was clearly one of the
hottest properties in films and worth Sam's investment.

When Sam learned that Hope's comic autobiography had sold 3 million
copies, he changed the script's title to *They Got Me Covered*. Hope was cast
as a clumsy foreign correspondent recalled by his Washington office for having missed the story of the Nazi invasion of Russia. He and his fiancée,
played by Lamour, expose Axis saboteurs and he gets his job back.

One day Hope's former stand-in Lyle Morain visited the set in his sergeant's uniform. He asked Bob to consider making an entertainment tour of
those desolate Alaskan bases where some of his buddies were stationed. Al

Jolson had recently returned from doing shows in Alaska. Comedian Joe E. Brown had taken a load of athletic equipment up there and traveled for 33 days from base to base by plane and dogsled. Hope also spoke with Edgar Bergen, who told him he "relished 13 shows a day, done in gun emplacements, on the sides of hills, the backs of trucks, on barges and landing wharves." Hope asked brother Jack to find out if an Alaskan tour could be arranged.

Hope called newlywed Frances Langford, who was interested but said she doubted her husband, Jon Hall, would let her go. Hope called Hall and convinced him that Frances would be in safe hands. Next, Hope called Colonna who was ready to go but had a practical concern: "How can we get to Alaska in September and still do our first Pepsodent show?"

Hope had an answer, though he was talking off the top of his head. "I'm nearly finished with this picture for Samuel the Golden, and barring trouble we should be doing the final shots on Saturday, September fifth. If we could fly out on Tuesday the eighth, we'd be up in the north country for a good ten days. We could get back to Seattle on the twenty-second for the radio show, fly around Washington and Oregon to camps and bases there, then back to Seattle for our second radio show on the twenty-ninth. Easy. We'll need a musician. Any ideas?"

"Get Tony Romano. Best guitar in the business."

Early the morning of September 5, Jack Hope came into his brother's dressing room.

"Bad news, Bob," Jack said into the mirror. "General Buckner, the commander up in Alaska, can't guarantee you'd be able to get back to Seattle in time for the radio show; weather's too variable. They've got unflyable conditions everywhere—thick fog-heavy rain—"

"Is that final?"

"It's fair warning, I guess."

"Send him a wire—say—"

Jack interrupted, "His message came by way of the Victory Committee in Washington—"

"I don't care where it came from. Send Buckner this wire direct from me—from us—right now. Say 'Four disappointed thespians with songs and witty sayings are anxious to tour your territory. Please give us your consent and let us take our chances with the weather.' Sign it Bob Hope, Frances Langford, Jerry Colonna and Tony Romano. Do it now."

Bob and Dolores went up to Pebble Beach to play some golf and to wait for Buckner's response. On Sunday, Jack reached them with a terse message from Alaska: YOU LEAVE TUESDAY. It was signed Major General Simon Buckner.[2]

The troupe flew to Seattle and then north along the Canadian and lower Alaskan coastline, over the almost unspeakable beauty of white-crusted mountains, endless forest and wild waterways, past Juneau and Whitehorse to Fairbanks. When they stepped off the plane they were disappointed to see that the airport looked pretty much like Lockheed's in Burbank.

Almost immediately, they met Special Services Captain Don Adler and their pilots, Captains Marvin Seltzer and Bob Gates. Over dinner at the local officers club that night they learned they would be hopping from outpost to outpost in the Army's stripped-down version of the DC–3. They were advised to enjoy these few comfortable hours in "The Country Club of Alaska" because everything beyond Fairbanks was rugged.

On their way back to the VIP billets, Hope bought a hundred postcards which he planned to write as they flew around the country. They headed for Nome in the morning and stopped once, at Galena, for refueling. While they waited, GIs seemed to materialize from nowhere, and when a crowd had gathered it seemed a good time to break in their act and so they joked a bit and sang some songs from the back of a truck. Then they flew on to Nome and the Bering Strait, an area the GIs had tagged "Devil's Island." Hope later wrote:

> We went right to work doing shows for small groups in one Quon-
> set hut after another. They were a tough audience, those guys in
> Nome. They'd been there so long they didn't want to thaw out. It
> wasn't their kind of country in the first place. Most of them were
> from Alabama . . . but when those kinds did finally warm up, it
> was terrific. We came out of one hut and there were about six
> hundred standing in the rain. We tried to do a show but if Tony
> had gotten out his guitar it would have shrunk . . . so we packed
> the whole six hundred guys in one Quonset hut that normally
> holds three hundred. Now I really know how it feels to play a
> packed house. We were working on the stove.[3]

After an entire day of hut shows, the local commander collected the overflow of servicemen, including some Russians, into a big hall in downtown Nome and that show lasted all evening.

The little band of entertainers, military escorts and pilots was fast becoming Hope's "family." They shared the same goals and the same hardships. Langford was called "Mother," Captain Setzer was "Junior" because he was the youngest, and Hope was their "Dad."

At Fort Richardson in Anchorage, Buckner and his aides welcomed them. Over a Ping-Pong game, the General told them what good things he had heard about their tour so far. "What we're suffering most up here, Bob, is cabin fever. Some of these boys have been stuck out in a God-forsaken outpost for more than a year—with old books, old newspapers, old movies and stale relationships. I don't think you have any idea what you're doing for them."

After a big show at Fort Richardson, they hopped over to Annette, Canada, to do a show for the Royal Canadian Air Force. In that audience were about thirteen hundred U.S. Army construction engineers and workers building the new Alcan Highway. They had come to the show in bulldozers, jeeps, trucks, anything that moved. They were a highly vocal audience of rough, tough but friendly men.

One joke that everyone loved was one that Hope had been telling since Nome:

> You heard about the airman who was making his first parachute
> drop? Well, his First Lieutenant told him which cord to pull, and
> told him that when he hit ground there would be a station wagon

waiting to drive him back to the base. So the airman jumped out of the plane and when he pulled the cord nothing happened, and he said, "And I bet the station wagon won't be there either."[4]

They got as far as Cordova on their way back to Anchorage when their pilots decided to set the plane down and spend the night.

"Ahh, come on, Junior," coaxed Frances. "The General's invited us to a big block dance in Anchorage tonight. Let's go on."

"Can't risk it, Mother," said Setzer. "We got strict orders not to fly you at night. It's our ass if we do."

"If the weather's good, I'll take the responsibility," said Bob. "You can blame me."

They took off and were barely into the air when they began to get some sleet and hail. The pilots ploughed on, and though it is not a long ride from Cordova to Anchorage, it seemed endless in weather that got even worse.

It became clear to the passengers in the main cabin that there was trouble. They could hear Setzer and Gates shouting at each other just before Corporal Dubowsky, the cabin steward, closed the cockpit door. Hope looked at Colonna, who was slowly stroking his moustache and looking at Hope with those huge brown eyes.

The call light flashed in the cabin and Dubowsky went into the cockpit. When he came out he sat down next to Langford. He reached under her seat and took out a parachute and a Mae West. "You'd better put these on. We may have to ditch. If we should have to abandon ship, pull this. If you should land in water, pull this one."

"Water?" Frances asked.

"I think we're lost," said Dubowsky who moved over to show Hope, Colonna and Romano how the parachute worked and how to activate the Mae West in the water.

"How bad is it?" Hope asked. "I mean, really."

"They're having trouble with the radio."

Just then the plane felt like it had been smacked by something hard. "What was that?"

"Felt like prop wash from another plane—and, man—that was close."

"This kind of thing isn't very good for my guitar," said Romano, who had turned chalk white.

"Remind me to tell you something when we're all landed safe and sound," said Langford smiling.

Hope stared at her incredulously.

"I bet the station wagon won't be there either," said Colonna expressionlessly.

After an eternity of circling and waiting to see if anything would clear, they saw a jab of light and the plane dipped and started downward. The plane came out of the soup in a blaze of searchlights. The propwash they had felt was from a United Airlines ferry-service plane that had radioed the report of a backwash. Buckner ordered every available searchlight trained on the sky. When Setzer and Gates saw a finger of light pierce through the fog, they took a chance that it might be the field.

Hope, with his steel-trap memory, asked Langford what she had meant on the plane.

"I have always wanted to make a parachute jump. I was really half-hoping we'd have to."

The weather didn't clear for two days. Hope learned that producer Bill Lawrence had arranged for Edgar Bergen and Kay Kyser to substitute in the opening show. But on Monday the weather broke and they flew down to Seattle in time to rehearse and do the show. The next morning, Hope said to the other three, "Let's go back."

So instead of playing for Army and Navy personnel in Washington and Oregon, they flew back to Alaska and spent the next five days in the Aleutians, landing first in Anchorage to meet Setzer and Gates and a new plane.

Their first stop was Maknek on Kichak Bay near the Katmai Volcano, at the headlands of the Alaskan Penninsula. Then they went further out to Unimak Island. The troops were fanned out in front of them, seated on the cold, wet ground. Told that there was a lot of guard duty there, Hope asked a kid sitting at his feet if he had to walk much. There was sprinkled laughter at the question, but when the kid replied, "I don't know—but when I enlisted I had feet!" Hope roared, and so did the rest of the audience. The comedian was learning what the GIs wanted most, liked best—needed—was humor turned on themselves, a chance to ventilate their hardships, their fear, their loneliness.

Frances was the first woman to set foot on Unimak Island, and later that same day at Fort Glenn, while she was singing "You Made Me Love You," tears started streaming down the cheeks of a young soldier in the front row. Hope said later:

> I saw it—and pretended not to, but one of the officers standing with me nudged my arm and said: "Get the kid." I felt a silly trickle running down the side of my sharp smeller so I tried not to look at the Commanding Officer, but out of the corner of my eye I could see him about to leak out of the corner of his eye. And then we both looked at each other and—well, we both darn near bawled.[5]

Hope watched as the GI's buddy put his arm around his pal's shoulder and as Frances was finishing it started to rain. The schedule called for them to play their last two days at Dutch Harbor and Attu but the weather out there was too foul. They turned back and did their last show at Kodiak.

Bob, Frances, Jerry and Tony flew back to Seattle to do the season's second Pepsodent show. Next day they were back in Hollywood.

For a time, Alaska was foremost on Hope's mind. He talked about the trip to everyone who would listen, urged other performers to go there. He said publicly that he had asked Paramount to delay *Let's Face It*, his next major film role, until he could do another tour of Alaska. But he was also talking about wanting to entertain GIs in England, North Africa and the Pacific.

The delay in starting *Let's Face It* had other components, however.

Let's Face It was a Herbert and Dorothy Fields–Cole Porter musical that had run for a year on Broadway starring Danny Kaye and Eve Arden. Shurr and Melnick were trying to convince Paramount executives that Hope should now be paid the same kind of money Sam Goldwyn had thought he was worth.

In the meantime, Hope was doing camp shows. *Road to Morocco* was now in release, and *The New York Times* applauded the film for its lampooning of exotic romance pictures.

Also on the edge of release was *Star Spangled Rhythm*, a prime example of a film genre that flourished during the war. Designed to utilize all of the studio's stars in a single, patriotic variety format, *Star Spangled Rhythm* was an extravaganza built around a serviceman storyline. It featured Bing Crosby, Ray Milland, Vera Zorina, Victor Moore, Mary Martin, Veronica Lake, Fred MacMurray, Dorothy Lamour, Dick Powell, Alan Ladd, Franchot Tone and Paulette Goddard—all doing songs and sketches that were at odds with their screen images. Hope played master of ceremonies and acted in several sketches.

In November and December Hope took advantage of the delay in starting *Let's Face It* to take his radio show east of the Rockies for camp show originations in Colorado, Oklahoma, Missouri, Iowa, Ohio and Indiana. When he returned, the *Let's Face It* deal was set; Hope would receive his $100,000. Harry Tugend wrote the screenplay and although some of the good Porter music was retained, the film was retailored to fit Hope. There was no attempt to use the Danny Kaye tongue-twisting patter songs or to duplicate Kaye's acting style. It was, rather, a surefire formula for success, casting Hope as another GI in a musical farce loaded with topical gags about rationing and shortages, Veronica Lake's peekaboo hair, Willkie's defeat and Hitler. Hope's costars were Eve Arden, Betty Hutton and Zasu Pitts.

In February, during the filming, Hope and Lamour were invited to make impressions of their hands and feet in wet cement on the Grauman Chinese Theater forecourt. A large crowd watched Bob and Dottie hug and clown a bit, then Hope dipped his nose in the cement. "This isn't quicksand, is it?" Laughter from the crowd. "If this hardens I won't be able to blow for months."

On March 4, 1943, at the Ambassador Hotel's Cocoanut Grove, Hope appeared once again as master of ceremonies for the annual Academy Award Ceremonies. Plaster statuettes (replaced by gold ones after the war) were handed to Greer Garson for her courageous *Mrs. Miniver* and to Jimmy Cagney for his energetic *Yankee Doodle Dandy*. "White Christmas" was the best song and the entire evening had a warm sentimental feeling about it. It was also characterized by military ceremony and uniforms throughout the audience. Marine Private Tyrone Power and Air Corps Private Alan Ladd unfurled a huge industry flag that carried the names of 27,677 film workers who were in uniform.

The subject of who was and who was not in uniform ultimately became a sensitive topic in Hollywood. Specifically, the subject of whether or not actors should be drafted was being aired by syndicated columnists, fan magazine writers and editorial pundits. Hope once discussed this question with columnist Ed Sullivan.

"Some night I'll be out there telling my jokes," said Hope, "and some big guy will stand up in the front row and he'll give me a Bronx cheer and yell 'Whyinhell aren't you in service, Hope?' And that is the $64 question won't be able to answer."[6]

Sullivan reasoned with Hope that in or out of uniform he would undoubtedly be doing the same kind of job, boosting morale. So why not continue to do the camp shows as a civilian? Yet obviously Hope was troubled.

Sullivan took the issue to his readers, and a week or so later he wrote in his *New York Daily News* column, "Here's something interesting—and it indicates how smart is John Q. Public: Nearly everyone says that Bob Hope, married and father of two adopted children, should be deferred."

Another of Hope's journalist friends, a McNaught Syndicate columnist named Henry McLemore, was in London as a correspondent. He wrote an open letter to Hope on April 24, 1943, urging the comedian to go to Britain to entertain. Hope asked brother Jack to work with the United Service Organization (USO), through its camp show division, to see how long a tour he could make and whether or not he could broadcast his radio show from overseas. Pepsodent was enthusiastic but Paramount was not. Hope owed them movies. Hope learned that a summer tour was preferred by the USO, which meant the radio season would be finished before he left.

Hope astonished everyone with his decision to hit the road in April as soon as *Let's Face It* was completed, to do a ten-week camp show tour through Arizona, Texas, Louisiana, Florida, Georgia, South Carolina, Virginia and Ohio. If the USO European tour began in June, Hope would be on the move continuously for five months. From his friends and associates came concerns for his health. Dolores had never stopped worrying about Bob's health or his workload or the constant traveling, but she had grown less edgy since she had begun her own American Women's Voluntary Services job. She wished that Linda and Tony saw more of him, but she had made a kind of peace with herself about his absences. "He's done this all his life," she would say, "and he's always traveled. I think he really loves that life. He's a rover by nature. The first year we were married I saw so little of Bob that I wasn't sure we'd make a go of it. Now, of course, I've gotten accustomed to his being away, and I couldn't imagine life being any different."[7]

Brother Jack tried to dispel fears that Bob couldn't stand the pace. "Our grandfather's still riding his bicycle to the pub at ninety-nine. Aunt Polly lived to be a hundred and three. We're sturdy stock."[8]

Bob took Barney Dean along with him on the camp tour. As part valet, stooge, companion and jester, Dean's pixie appearance and wild sense of humor lightened the load during that grueling grind through the Southern camps. Barney told Crosby, "I don't mind telling you it was a great experience and a mad one. In the first place, there were never less than three telephones in our rooms, and all of them rang at the same time every second of the day and night. And people, people, people. It was maddening. But Bob didn't seem to mind. In the second place, he thinks he's Superman. He does practically all the work himself. He's so healthy he never gets tired. He made me weak just watching him."[9]

Barney was never able to forget what happened the night they arrived in Atlanta, grimy and exhausted and ready for a rest before the next day's Pepsodent show. Frances and Jerry had collapsed in their rooms. Everyone else was looking forward to a bath and relaxation and a change of pace. When the telephone rang in their hotel suite Barney grabbed for it. Bob was stretched out on his bed. The voice at the other end belonged to one of Paramount's wardrobe boys who had been drafted and was now stationed near Savannah.

Bob reached over to his bed table and grabbed his extension. "Mike!

—How about that!—You like it, huh? Where?—Albany? Where's Albany?—Barney?—Hundred miles? That's nothing—Sure we can—We'll be
there—What do *you* think?—Why shouldn't I come?—You get the guys
lined up—We'll be there—we're leaving now—"

Hope called some of the others and, understandably, they begged off. But
Hope went. He took Barney with him and he did a show for the stunned
wardrobe boy and his Army buddies. Just like those vaudeville days, Hope
would do anything, go anywhere to get on.

> **Well, I'm very happy to be here . . . (boos from the**
> **audience) . . . of course, I'm leaving as soon as I finish this**
> **show . . . but this is a great country. Africa . . . this is**
> **Texas with Arabs . . . I was on the "Road to Morocco"**
> **once, but this time I'm doin' it the hard way.**[1]

22. I Never Left Home

One of Hope's major disappointments in those final weeks before his European USO tour was that Colonna could not go. Jerry's commitments for film
and personal appearances were too binding and too important to his
income.

In his place Hope decided to try Jack Pepper, a song-and-dance man he
had known in vaudeville and had met unexpectedly during his Southern
camp tour. At Loew Field in Texas, Private Pepper broke through a crowd
barrier and ran to shake Hope's hand. Now Hope was calling Pepper's commanding officer and asking to borrow the chubby performer for a few weeks.
As for the others, Langford had gotten reluctant permission from her actor
husband Jon Hall to be missing for another two months, and Tony Romano
was luckily available to be their "orchestra."

A gala homecoming party thrown by the city of Cleveland, and his final
Pepsodent show of the season from nearby Camp Perry on Lake Erie, were
the final events on Hope's spring schedule. On Sunday there was a huge
parade. Riding in open convertibles down Euclid Avenue smiling and waving
were Bob, Dolores, Frances, Jerry, Tony, Vera Vague and even Private Pepper as the thousands waved flags and cheered. That night they did a preview
of the Tuesday broadcast at the Cleveland Stage Door Canteen. The next
day Bob and Jerry appeared at the "Ernie Pyle–Cigarettes for Yanks" fund-
raising benefit.

When Bob and Dolores arrived in New York on June 16 and checked into
the Waldorf-Astoria to await his flying orders, the comedian felt ill. The day
before at Camp Perry he had received his first typhoid and typhus shots and
now he wanted to crawl into bed. But when he was on his feet again, he was
told that the USO wanted him to be photographed and briefed and given a
special passport. He was also told that there would likely be a delay in their
departure. The USO did not want news of the Pan Am Clipper's departure

leaked. There was a gentleman's agreement at the start of the war that no unarmed clippers would be attacked but, as Hope commented to Dolores, "everyone knows the agreement isn't worth the gentleman it was written by."

Finally they were told to be at Pan Am's La Guardia Marine Terminal at one o'clock in the morning on June 25. After customs and ticket processing, they waited in their small family groups for the famous Clipper bell to ring. When it clanged, Bob and Dolores still lingered by the gate.

Bob kissed her. "Well—" he said.

"Well–" Dolores looked at him. In this half-light he still seemed too tired to be starting out on such a trip. "Take care of yourself."

"You know I will."

Dolores hugged him close. "Please be careful."

"I told you I would."

"Well, do," she emphasized.

"I will." When the "all aboard" was yelled, Hope looked once again at his wife and started toward the plane. He said, "I wish you were going," but he wasn't sure she heard that.

Finally, after delays for bad weather and refueling, the Hope entourage arrived at Foynes, Eire, where they transferred to another plane for a ride to Bristol where they would board a train for London. In London, they were booked into Claridge's, and were surprised to find that the hotel, despite shortages and depleted staff, managed to be proud and poised. Londoners in general accepted bomb disfigurements, tight rations and their daily fear of attack with extraordinary good nature.

The troupe was taken in tow by Bill Dover, USO chief in England, who found them a bar of soap which they shared and nursed for weeks. Next day they endured still more shots and fingerprinting. They were assigned APO numbers so they could receive mail. They met Captain Eddie Dowling whom Hope had not seen since *Sidewalks of New York*. Eddie, a special services officer, arranged for newsreel coverage "to let the men know you're in the neighborhood."

That afternoon Dover found Hope a driver and a Signal Corps photographer and they drove to Hitchin to see his granddad. He spent about three hours with the old man talking family. James Hope said bluntly that his grandson wasn't spending enough time with his family and understood only too well Hope's poignant story about how four-year-old Linda had said "Goodbye, Bob Hope" instead of "Goodbye, Daddy" when he left California. Next morning they were introduced to their drivers, all from the English Women's Corps—Zena Groves, Eve Luff and Marie Stewart—and their transportation, two 1938 Hudsons and a 1938 Ford painted countryside brown. On that morning they began a remarkable five-week odyssey through thousands of miles of unmarked lanes and roads (intentionally unmarked to confuse potential invaders), entertaining at three and sometimes four installations a day, some huge bomber aerodromes, smaller fighter bases, supply depots and many hospitals, doing jokes, singing songs, free-wheeling their performances as the situation required.

Their first full show was at a bomber base called Eye Aerodrome, and they arrived just before a mission was to fly out. On stage a few minutes later, Hope said:

I've just arrived from the States. You know . . . that's where
Churchill lives . . . he doesn't exactly live there . . . he just
goes back to deliver Mrs. Roosevelt's laundry. . . . You know,
they're drafting all the leading men in Hollywood. But Crosby is
still there. If they keep it up, most of the romantic heroes will be
on the adrenalin side. . . . Can you imagine Lana Turner waiting to be kissed by Lewis Stone while he looks for a place to plug
in his heating pad . . . ?[2]

Hope later said, "We soon discovered you had to be pretty lousy to flop in
front of these guys—they yelled and screamed and whistled at everything."
From the bomber base they drove to a nearby fighter base and Hope tried
out his draft routine:

. . . take Pepper, for instance, his draft classification was
2F2F . . . Too Fat to Fight. . . . They don't even ask your age
anymore. They just hand you a copy of *Esquire* and watch what
page you turn to. . . . I asked them what my classification was
and they said 7L . . . coward. . . . [3]

The Hope troupe quickly caught the spirit of their mission and after that
there was no limit to their energies. Their third show was at a supply depot,
and their fourth and final show of that first day was performed at a large
hospital, actually a series of eight-to-ten-minute shows in a number of different wards. During the walk-through, Hope would go to each bed and say
something like "Did you see our show—or were you sick before?" or his
celebrated "All right, fellas, don't get up." At one point he decided to give
them a little soft-shoe dance between two beds and the floor happened to be
highly polished. Hope slipped and fell on his left wrist. They took him to
X-ray and there was no serious damage, but it bothered him now and again
during the next five weeks.

However, no injury or discomfort, no weariness, no personal concern of
any kind seemed to impair Hope or his company during those weeks of crisscrossing Britain, at least according to those who witnessed this marathon of
GI entertaining. Burgess Meredith wrote to Paulette Goddard:

The most wonderful thing about England right now is Bob Hope.
The boys in camp stand in rain, they crowd into halls so close you
can't breathe, just to see him. He is tireless and funny, and full of
responsibility, too, although he carries it lightly and gaily. There
isn't a hospital ward that he hasn't dropped into and given a show;
there isn't a small unit anywhere that isn't either talking about his
jokes or anticipating them. What a gift laughter is! Hope proves
it.[4]

Hope and his troupe moved to the west of England, to Wales and then back
to London.

When they went north to Colchester in Hertfordshire, not far from Hitchin, Bob arranged for his granddad to see the show. In fact, Hope went to
Frank Symons' house where James was living and found he had gotten out of
a sickbed and was dressed in morning attire, wing collar and all. Bob brought

his grandfather up on stage and joked with him and they posed for many pictures. Later, Hope had reason to worry that he had done the wrong thing. The following week, on July 22 when Hope was playing Yorkshire bases, he got word that James was dying. By the time Hope got to Hitchin the old man was gone, but Bob was there to see the streets lined with townspeople paying their respects.

From Hitchin, Hope flew over to Belfast for three days of shows in Northern Ireland. They flew there in a Flying Fortress and the Army gave the Hope Gypsies several forms to fill out, one of which asked for the person to notify in case of death. Hope impishly scribbled: "Louella Parsons, *Los Angeles Examiner*."[5] OWI gag writer Hal Block, sitting next to Hope, howled. Hope said, "I promised Lolly first crack. I hate to do it because if we go down, Hedda will never speak to me again."

Two events marked the final days of the five-week invasion by Hope. The first was a big farewell variety show at the Odeon Theater exclusively for servicemen, produced by Eddie Dowling and featuring, besides the Hope troupe, Adolph Menjou, Hal LeRoy, Hank Ladd, Stubby Kaye, Brucetta, Grace Drysdale, the Blossom Sisters and several other performers from USO units. King George and Queen Elizabeth were reported to have come in after the show began and sat quietly in a darkened box without fanfare.

Vogue's London correspondent Lesley Branch asked Dowling if she could watch Hope prepare for the show because her magazine wanted a picture of him at work and "rehearsals show you both actor and man." What impressed her was the man in motion, his unflagging pace. As she watched what could only be described as the pandemonium of a big complex variety show in rehearsal, she discovered the other facet of his effectiveness—his concentration. In her September 1943 feature for *Vogue* she wrote:

> He was there, in the middle of it all, keeping right on rehearsing various acts impervious to the uproar, as concentrated as a Yogi. . . .

The second event began at a cocktail party the day of the Odeon show, given at the Dorchester in honor of a group of "inspecting" U.S. senators. Attending the party were Averell Harriman, Anthony Drexel Biddle, Ambassador John Winant and a host of generals and admirals. The only reason Hope went was that he believed Winston Churchill would be there, but the Prime Minister couldn't attend. Hope revealed his disappointment to one senator he knew, Happy Chandler, and the Texas politician said he could fix that.

The following day, Chandler called Claridge's and asked Hope to accompany him to the House of Commons. Hope was picked up in Chandler's Rolls-Royce and in a few minutes the car stopped in front of 10 Downing Street. Hope looked wonderingly at the senator and asked, "Here?" Chandler nodded.

A group of senators were standing in Churchill's study waiting for him to come in when Chandler and Hope joined them. Almost simultaneously Churchill walked in from another door. The receiving line moved quickly and suddenly Hope was standing in front of Churchill. The prime minister looked—and looked again—and smiled. Hope shook Churchill's hand and

told him what a pleasure this was. Hope had been told Churchill laughed
heartily over *They Got Me Covered*. But before words could be exchanged,
Churchill and the senators stepped out to a small garden for a conference.
Ambassador Winant moved quickly to Hope's side and suggested he wait for
Chandler in Churchill's study. Hope said he would leave as soon as he got
Churchill's autograph on his "short-snorter" (an England five-pound note
that represented his "pass" for crossing the Atlantic). While Hope waited,
Winant obliged, taking the bill out to the garden, and when he returned
Hope left, but not before being asked to sign the official guest book.[6]

That same day, July 31, a remarkable newspaper column, "There Is a
Man" by John Steinbeck, appeared in London's *Daily Express*. Steinbeck
had filed it July 20, 1943, to New York's *Herald Tribune* and it had been
picked up by countless papers around the world. Steinbeck saw Hope as a
clown-hero to the GI:

> When the time for recognition of service to the nation in war-
> time comes to be considered, Bob Hope should be high on the
> list. . . .
> He has caught the soldier's imagination. He gets laughter
> wherever he goes from men who need laughter. . . .
> It is hard to overestimate the importance of this thing and the
> responsibility involved. The battalion of men who are moving
> half-tracks from one place to another doing a job that gets no
> headlines, no public notice and yet must be done if there is to be a
> victory, are forgotten, and they feel forgotten. But Hope is in the
> country. Will he come to them or won't he? And then one day
> they get the notice that he is coming. Then they feel remem-
> bered.
> This man in some way has become that kind of a bridge. It goes
> beyond how funny he can be or how well Frances Langford sings.
> It is interesting to see how he has become a symbol.

Bob Hope could not help but be moved by the implications of Steinbeck's
commentary, coming as it had from one of America's most sensitive and
careful observers.

The next day Hope and company were flown to Prestwick, Scotland, to
await their transfer to North Africa. While they waited, Hope was asked to
perform in a staging area for newly arrived GIs. Not unexpectedly, Hope led
a rousing chorus of "We're Off on the Road to Morocco" as their plane took
off from Prestwick and headed south for Marrakech. Their arrival in Morocco, however, had been set for two days earlier by the USO, and so their
military escorts had flown back to Tunis. Fortunately, General Jimmy Doolittle had insisted that a B–17 stand by in Marrakech just in case. So after a
quick look around the town, they took off for Algiers, where they were met
by Captain Mike Cullen of Special Services and three other officers who
would be their hosts for the next month. One of those officers, Colonel Bill
David, insisted that Hope accept a green linen suit of his own to replace the
warm clothes Hope had been wearing throughout Britain. That green suit
was all Hope wore for the next four weeks through North Africa and Sicily.

When it was safe to fly, they took off for Tunis where they were warmly welcomed by Jimmy Doolittle. They immediately went to work, first at the Red Cross Club for two shows back to back, and then for three days they alternated between bomber and fighter groups. Hope's opening phrase, in itself, became one of the tour's biggest laughs:

> Hiya, fellow tourists! . . . Well, I'm very happy to be here . . . (*boos from the audience*) . . . of course *I'm* leaving as soon as I finish this show. . . . But this is a great country, Africa . . . this is Texas with Arabs . . . I was on the *Road to Morocco* once . . . this time I'm doing it the hard way . . . and I tried to find a few Lamours over here, but they all wear their sarongs a little higher . . . under their eyes.[7]

As the Hope troupe worked its way through these audiences of combat-hardened desert troops and fighter pilots, the media people were becoming more and more curious about the rapport set up between comic and audience. When they asked if it was "foxhole humor," he said that his jokes were not that different from those he would tell at Camp Callen in California. But he touched their particular reality, spoke their language, with lines like, "It's so hot around here I took one look at a pup tent and it was panting," or, "Those guys out there are really tough! They don't bother manicuring their nails . . . they just stick their hands under a rock and let the cobras bite off the cuticle."[8]

Frequently it was the GI himself who provided big laughs at a Hope show. Hope described one very visual gag:

> Just as I stepped up to the microphone to start the show, a light tank came shoving through the crowd like a fat woman making for a seat in a crowded subway car. People gave way in all directions. A tank commands plenty of respect. I thought it was out of control. It looked as if the thing was going to mow us right down, and I was getting ready to jump off the platform when suddenly, right in front of me, it stopped.
>
> The top flew open and a guy crawled out wearing a tanker's crash helmet and enough grease on his face to sing "Mammy." He was dragging a folding chair which he set up on top of the tank. He sat down, crossed his legs, smiled, waved at me, and said, "Start the show."[9]

Beyond the laughs there was always the danger. They endured several terrifying air raids, with tracer bullets as well as bombs flying around them. Ernie Pyle in one dispatch, "Bob Hope Visit Tonic for Troops," which appeared in the *New York World-Telegram* on September 16, 1943, described the Hope troupe under enemy attack:

> I was in two different cities with them during these raids and I will testify they were horrifying raids. It isn't often that a bomb falls so close that you can hear it whistle. But when you can hear a whole stack of them whistle at once, then it's time to get weak all over and start sweating. The Hope troupe can now describe that ghastly sound.

The invasion of Sicily on August 18 paved the way for the Army's reluctant decision to let the Hope group fly to Palermo three days later. It was the closest to the ground fighting they had been or would get; the smell of battle was still in the air.

Sunday night at the Excelsior Hotel in Palermo would stay with Hope for a lifetime. He had gone to bed at eleven-thirty after a tiring day of entertaining and sat up with a start a few minutes later. He talked about it afterward:

> All of a sudden there was a distant voom! and I saw a tracer bullet go scooting across the sky. When I heard the drone of JU-88s, I knew we were in for it. The docks, which were naturally the target for the raid, were only about two blocks away. . . . They say when you're drowning your whole life flashes before your eyes. I don't know about you, but with me it's the same way with bombing. I thought of my first professional tour in vaudeville. . . . I thought of what I didn't say to Dolores as we stood by the Clipper dock. . . . I thought of doing everything in the world but going to the bomb shelter in the basement. I began to talk to myself. . . . The delightful dialogue was interrupted when a great big hunk of red-hot flak sailed past my window and the Heinies started dive-bombing. One Nazi, obviously aiming for my room, also let go with all his machine guns on his way down. Between the strafing and the screeching of the Stukas as they dived, you've got a noise that I'd trade any day for a record of you know who. And the Germans weren't making it all themselves. We were throwing plenty of stuff at them, too. I joined in. I threw up my dinner. After you've listened to a raid for a little while you begin to be afraid that just the noise will kill you; then after you've listened to it a little while longer you begin to be afraid it won't. You want to curl up in a ball . . . you want the ball to be batted out of the park. You want a home run! You want! There must have been a hundred Junkers in that raid with fighter escort. That was the most frightening experience of my life. . . . [10]

Hope was still in bed shaking when Captain Cullen came into his room to tell him Frances was safe although there was plaster all over her bed and floor. Tony had been with the chef in the kitchen and Pepper had been in the shelter.

Next day they crossed Sicily to do several shows, including one for the 9th Division and another for the 1st Infantry, both between Palma and Licata. From Licata they were flown back to Bone, Tunisia, where they appeared for a big audience of soldiers, sailors, WACS, WRENS and Red Cross personnel in a staging area for more of the Italian invasion. Hope, nearly numb with fatigue, limped out on stage still in his rumpled green linen suit. He hollered "Hiya tourists!" and it was during this show that someone way back in the crowd called out, "Draft dodger! Why aren't you in uniform?" Hope figured that whoever said that must either be too blind to see what he'd been through, or too embittered to care, or it was his version of a gag. Hope yelled back, "Don't you know there's a war on? A guy could get hurt!"

From Bone they flew to Kairouan to do two shows for the 82nd Airborne troops. They remained overnight to have breakfast with the men and then headed to Algiers, where they were treated to clean laundry and Hope got rid of his green linen suit. Following an afternoon show, Hope huddled with Hal Block on a script for a radio show that the troupe was to broadcast by transcription from Algiers to the States.

In the midst of rehearsals, Captain Cullen interrupted them to say that General Eisenhower would like them to come to his headquarters. For Hope this was probably the greatest thrill of his tour:

> Meeting General Eisenhower in the midst of that deadly muddle was like a breath of fresh air in a lethal chamber. It quieted us all, brought us all back to our senses, and in every way paid us off for the whole trip.[11]

Eisenhower told them how much their work was appreciated, and consented to autograph pictures for them. He said, before they departed: "I understand you've had some excitement on your trip. Well, you're perfectly safe here in Algiers. We haven't had a bombing in three months. We're too strong for 'em here. They can't get in."

That night after the broadcast Hope went back to the Aletti Hotel. He ran into a number of foreign correspondents who were anxious to talk about his tour. At about three in the morning Hope went to bed, and an hour later he was roused by instructions to go to the bomb shelter. For the next hour and a half there was one of the worst bombing raids Algiers had suffered. Wave after wave of Junkers hit the Allied flak and some bulldozed through. Even the normally cool and unflappable Frances cried and trembled through that one. It was a nerveracking finish to their tour. They missed their eight o'clock Plane for Prestwick, but their escorts pulled some strings in high places, and that same evening they were on their way back to Britain.

From London they flew to Iceland, their first stop on the return trip home. No sooner had they landed when they were told that bad weather over the Atlantic would hold them for a day's delay. So they agreed to do two shows and ended up doing a third, aware of how hungry the GIs were for any touch of home. Finally they were on their way home.

By any measurable criteria, the 20,000-mile trip was dazzling. *Time* was impressed enough to put Hope's picture on its September 20, 1943, cover (his first), and inside the magazine in an article titled "Hope for Humanity," the comedian was elevated above the dozen or so major entertainers trouping the war zones. He was labeled as a legend, one that sprang up "swiftly, telepathically" and "traveling faster than Hope himself." *Time* said that throughout this "tearing trip" of 250 shows in eleven weeks, Hope represented "measurable qualities in a mystical blend," calling him funny, friendly, indefatigable and figurative. Hope had developed, to the delight of millions of people—and especially to hundreds of thousands of American GIs—into an American folk figure.

> . . . thanks to his vibrant averageness, Hope is any healthy, cocky, capering American. He is the guy who livens up the summer hotel, makes things hum at the corset salesman's convention,

keeps a coachful of passengers laughing for an hour when the
train is stalled. With his ski-slide nose and matching chin, he
looks a little funny but he also looks normal, even personable,
seems part of the landscape rather than the limelight.

And though he hugs the limelight with a showman's depthless
ego, in Hope himself is a hunger, or perhaps a final vanity, to
reach people as a human being. For a performer who scarcely
takes time out to live, perhaps it is the only way of being one.

He was greeted everywhere as a hero—at Lakeside, at NBC, at Paramount,
at the driving range he owned across from Warner Brothers studios and at
home. Dog-tired, he answered the many queries by telling anecdotes and
ended by saying, "But wait till you read the book." There was growing opinion, derived from those who traveled with him, those who met him at home,
friends and acquaintances—Dolores, especially—that he was a sobered Bob
Hope.

Braven Dyer heard him telling some locker-room buddies at Lakeside that
it was "the most wonderful experience of my life—I wouldn't trade it for my
entire career. Until you've actually seen them in action, you have no conception of their courage. And that noise—that terrifying noise of battle—is
awful. I don't know how those kids stand it day after day, but they do." Dyer
said the sincerity, coming from the normally flip and unsentimental Hope,
moistened several pairs of eyes.

Dolores felt Bob had developed a deeper love and respect for people. She
would hear Bob on the telephone for weeks after his return talking both long
and short distance to parents, sweethearts and sometimes children of the GIs
he had encountered on the trip. Hope had come home with his pockets full of
little slips of paper with scrawled names and addresses and wisps of messages
to be delivered. What *Time* had called "the straight link with home" was
being lived out in fact.

I think I should apologize to our President for some of the
things I've said on radio. Especially about Mrs. Roosevelt.
Like when Churchill and Roosevelt were discussing cam-
paign strategy, they talked about when to attack the enemy
and how to keep Eleanor out of the crossfire. . . . [1]

23. Good Evening, Mr. President

Hope felt that the war correspondents who had covered his foxhole tour—
Ernie Pyle, Bob Considine, John Steinbeck, Quentin Reynolds, Mos Miller,
Bill Lang—had written vividly but only scratched the surface. As a matter of
fact, an idea for writing some kind of detailed eyewitness account, presumably humorous, played around in his mind for much of that eleven-week
tour. Now that he was home, the national magazines and Sunday supple-
ments were calling Mack Millar demanding byline stories or routines of his

gags and anecdotes about the trip. Evidently there was quite a market for his thoughts about GI Joe and his experiences at the war fronts. Several nights he worked very late at his desk reconstructing events, sorting out faces and places and conversations. Fortunately, he had an excellent memory and could separate events by geography and by the sound and texture of an audience. But after a few nights it became clear to him that he needed help.

He had known a writer named Carroll Carroll, one of the J. Walter Thompson agency's best men, for many years. Originally from New York, Carroll had come to California to work with Bing on his Kraft Music Hall show and had also made some valuable contributions of gag ideas for several Crosby films and the *Road* pictures. More important, Carroll was doing some work for the OWI and understood military lingo and what was going on in the war. Bob called him for a lunch date.

Over lunch, Hope told Carroll that Simon and Schuster wanted an immediate manuscript and that he needed someone to help him.

"I've never written a book," said Carroll. "What's wrong with your own writers?"

"I don't want them. Have you ever tried?" Hope took some sheets of paper from a big brown envelope and handed them across the table. "This is what I've been working on but the publisher says it isn't a book—yet. Fool around with it and do a beginning. If we like it and Jack Goodman of Simon likes it we'll go. You ought to know *this*, though; all *your* money is up front. The royalties go to the National War Fund."

Carroll took the brown envelope and tipped it over. Out fell scraps of paper, a couple of matchbook covers, several Claridge envelopes scribbled on, dog-eared pages of monologue, some business cards and an assortment of ragged pieces of paper. "What do you want to call the book?"

"*I Never Left Home.*"

"Why?"

"Because everywhere I went I met people from places I knew or had played vaudeville or had lived. I kept running into people I knew."

"And they knew you. I understand what you mean. It's a great title. I'll work out something from this material and let you see it soon."[2]

Carroll went back to his office and tried to work on current assignments, but he kept returning to Hope's material. He read it through. It was the week of the *Time* cover story. He leafed through his copy. It was soon clear to him that the compassion Hope displayed overseas was missing in what he had written. Carroll decided that if Hope was to be perceived as "the clear link with home," those same home folks must see through Hope's eyes the courage of their fighting men, and the GI reading this book must sense the country's gratitude for his sacrifice. Carroll grabbed a piece of typing paper and stuck it in the machine. He wrote what he believed to be a moving preface and also arranged some of the early material into a scenario that was both lively and suspenseful. He sent it to Bob.

Hope read it at once. Four days later, he called Carroll and told him he had read the preface to his editor and they both loved it. Together they rewrote the opening words and it became the most compelling and motivating writing in the entire memoir:

I saw your sons and your husbands, your brothers and your
sweethearts. I saw how they worked, played, fought and lived. I
saw some of them die. I saw more courage, more good humor in
the face of discomfort, more love in an era of hate, and more
devotion to duty than could exist under tyranny.

I saw American minds, American skill, and American strength
breaking the backbone of evil. . . .

And I came back to find people exulting over the thousand-
plane raids over Germany . . . and saying how wonderful they
are! Those people never watched the face of a pilot as he read a
bulletin board and saw his buddy marked up missing. . . .

I didn't see very much. And God knows I didn't do any fighting.
But I had a worm's eye view of what war is.

Dying is sometimes easier than living through it . . . .

But this is not a book about the serious side of the war. That
isn't my field. All I want you to know is that I did see your sons
and daughters in the uniforms of the United States of America . . . fighting for the United States of America.

I could ask for no more.[3]

They met every Wednesday evening with a secretary named Jane Brown
in the Hopes' living room on Moorpark Street. Every word spoken was taken
down in shorthand and transcribed. On the following Wednesday Hope
would read a chapter and make changes.

"It was a hard grind," Carroll recalls. "I was still doing my regular job at
J. Walter, and writing for the OWI. Hope edited each chapter as it was
finished, made notes for me, and gave copies to his team of gagmen to punch
up with fresh material. Then I went over the whole thing again, took the best
of the new stuff from his gagmen, and dovetailed it into the appropriate
places."

They worked that way for ten weeks and by December it was ready for the
publisher. Simon and Schuster sent it to artist Carl Rose who drew a series of
witty illustrations. It was slotted for spring publication.

Meanwhile, Hope's sixth season for Pepsodent had begun, and predictably
the Hope show became the most-listened-to radio program in the nation. The
Pepsodent show was originating from a different camp or base, and the guest
stars were entertainers like Marlene Dietrich and Jimmy Durante. His cast
regulars were Frances Langford, Jerry Colonna and Vera Vague, but his
bandleader was Stan Kenton because Skinnay Ennis had joined the Army.

At Paramount there was consternation over the start of the much-antici-
pated next Road picture. Getting Bob, Bing and Dorothy together was difficult. While this effort went on, Bob found himself doing two or three benefit appearances a week. He appeared on numerous transcribed radio shows
for servicemen, kicked off the Motion Picture War Chest Campaign, and
found time to head up a fund-raising drive to help the YMCA keep the
children of war-working parents off the city streets.

When Road to Utopia finally rolled in November, there was some discord
between the famous threesome who had traveled those other sucessful roads
together. This was the first Road script not written by Hartman and Butler

Hope's two young writers, Panama and Frank, had dreamed up a Gold Rush cliffhanger about two vaudevillian/con artists who find a stolen map that rightfully belongs to the beautiful Sal, played by Lamour. The film contained some of the wildest stunts of all the *Roads* and ended with a sequence that raised some eyebrows.

Melvin Frank recalls that when he and Norman Panama finished their script, then came the ordeal of selling the idea to each principal individually. "In those days," says Mel, "they were *enormous* stars. It's impossible to imagine the prestige of those three people. You really had to have their okay on the script, even though they were under contract and could be forced to do what you wanted. So we sat down with Crosby and explained our ideas and we would make it sound like it was going to be *his* picture. Then we'd tell Hope the story and make it attractive from his point of view. Then we'd tell it to Lamour though she knew we had already run it by the other two."[4]

It was particularly tricky to convince actors to do complicated or potentially dangerous stage business, like the scene in *Utopia* involving a trained bear. In that scene, Bob and Bing crawled under a rug in a mountain cabin to hide when a grizzly bear came in looking for them. The bear was supposed to walk over the lump in the rug. The trainer warned Bob and Bing not to move when the scene was over until he had reclaimed the bear and chained him securely off camera. It all worked well in rehearsal, but for the actual take, when the boys scrambled for the rug and the bear wandered in growling, he stood on top of them and menaced them dangerously. Hope and Crosby were terrified while the trainer struggled to take control of his animal. After some sharp words to the director, the boys went to their dressing rooms and refused to continue to work with the bear. The following day that same bear tore the arm off his trainer.

Aside from such near-misses, the two men maintained a casual approach to movie-making that was occasionally accompanied by thoughtlessness. "We had a ball," said Bing. "We had directors who let us suit our own schedules. If we had a golf game or wanted to hit the track for a big race at Santa Anita, I'd say, 'Can't you do something with Hope or Lamour today?' and we'd work it out."[5]

One of those days both Bob and Bing wanted to play in a charity match and were oblivious, or pretended to be, to the fact that they were scheduled to shoot a musical scene with Lamour. It was a scene, incidentally, that was being rescheduled from a previous Hope–Crosby truancy. That day Lamour got into her tight corset and long black evening gown after her six o'clock makeup session and got to the soundstage about nine o'clock. No Hope and Crosby. She and the rest of the players, the extras and the crew waited. Most of that time she had to lean on a slant board provided for actresses with wardrobe too tight for sitting. At the lunch break she got out of the gown and, though she objected loudly, agreed to get back into it for the presumed afternoon shooting.

About four o'clock, Gary Cooper wandered onto the stage and heard a furious Lamour sputtering about two inconsiderate actors. "Dottie," Cooper said, "if I were you, I wouldn't take it. Go back to your dressing room, out of your dress and get the hell out!"

Lamour left in a rage. No sooner had she gotten into her street clothes when the boys arrived. De Sylva's office called to find out why she wasn't on the set. She told the Paramount brass how she felt and, although both Hope and Crosby guiltily teased her about being temperamental, and in their own ways both apologized, "they never pulled another stunt like that on me."[6]

Utopia provided Bob and Bing with their most-repeated duet, "Put It There, Pal," and it also provided Hope with his most quoted joke from any of his collaborations with Crosby. In the picture, the boys courageously saunter into a rough Yukon bar, and when Hope is gruffly asked what he wants, he says, "Lemonade." But when he sees the expressions on Crosby's and the bartender's faces, he adds, "In a dirty glass." The film also provided the censors with a dilemma. In previous *Roads*, Bing had always gotten Lamour at the finish, but in this one, a crack in the ice pack separates Bing on one side from Bob and Dorothy on the other. Many years later, an aging Crosby pays a call on the long-married Hope and Lamour, and when the couple's son is introduced he is the image of Crosby. It was a racy touch for its day but the censors eventually passed it.

When *Utopia* finished shooting, Hope was left with a bad head and chest cold, presumably caused by fluctuating soundstage temperatures. The cold had also settled in Hope's left ear and was exceedingly painful. His doctor, Tom Hearn, advised him to stay in bed. Although he refused that advice, he did listen to Dolores' protests when he wanted to leave with the Pepsodent cast for a month-long camp tour of the South. So they flew without him to Brookley Field, Alabama, and that next Tuesday night, February 29, Hope did the monologue from his Hollywood studio.

A few days later, somewhat recovered, Hope flew to Florida in time for the March 7 show at an officers training school. Almost nothing in this world could have kept him from getting back on his feet because he knew he had to be up to speed for a singular honor being accorded him the following Saturday, March 11. This year it was NBC's turn to provide entertainment for the Gridiron Dinner in Washington, the annual roast of Washington politics and politicians by the press corps. President Roosevelt was scheduled as the honored guest and Hope, who had been waiting for such an opportunity to do an in-person show for the President, was excited.

On Saturday Hope flew to Brookley Field to play golf with General Mollison, but the weather turned so stormy that their game was rained out. There were fears that no planes would be flying, and NBC was pulling strings. Mollison got a teletype from General "Hap" Arnold that said: HAVE PLANE COMING NORTH TONIGHT. MAKE SURE HOPE IS ON IT.

Even so, Hope was an hour late arriving at the dinner and comedian Ed (*Duffy's Tavern*) Gardner had replaced him as the M.C. Fritz Kreisler had already played, Gracie Fields had sung and Elsie Janis had entertained, followed by a trained seal. When Hope arrived, Fred Waring and his Pennsylvanians were in full swing. Hope was the tag end and he knew, after this long show, that he had to be fresh. The head table would be to his left, and the audience had turned their chairs away from their banquet tables to face a small stage. Hope bounced out:

> Good evening, Mr. President, distinguished guests . . . I was
> late getting here because we flew through mud all the
> way . . . and then coming in from the airport I was on the bot-

tom layer of the taxi . . . but I'm delighted to be here . . . I've
always wanted to be invited to one of these dinners . . . and my
invitation was a long time coming. . . . I thought it had been
vetoed by Barkley . . . (*big laughter*) . . . Perhaps I shouldn't
mention Alben here . . . it's too much like talking about Frank
Sinatra to Bing Crosby. . . . [7]

The first political wisecrack, jabbing at Roosevelt's problems with Congress,
was an instant hit. Hope noticed how the audience looked sideways at the
head table to see how the President was reacting. Hope pressed on:

Trying to find a room in Washington is like trying to find "My
Day" in the *Chicago Tribune* . . . (*loud roar of laughter*) . . .
and did you know . . . (*continued laughter*) . . . speaking of
the *Chicago Tribune* that Fala is the only dog ever housebroken
on that paper . . . (*more laughter*). . . . [8]

Hope looked to his left and Roosevelt's head was tilted back and he was
laughing. Those references to Eleanor's daily newspaper column and to the
President's feud with the *Chicago Tribune* were front-page items.

Hope probably couldn't have scored in front of a more receptive audience,
or one that would send more glowing accounts to the corners of the nation
and around the world. Several members of the fourth estate, as syndicated
columnist Richard Wilson did in the *Des Moines Register* on March 12,
1944, made this comparison:

The gap left by the death of Will Rogers, as a comedian whose
barbs at politics and politicians were particularly appreciated in
Washington, has been filled.
Bob Hope has stepped into the shoes of Will Rogers in this
respect, and from now on he will be sought in Washington, to
provide that extra touch at the capital's lavish public functions.

The next day Hope returned to Florida to rejoin his radio cast for more
camp shows, and once again, he began to feel ill. It was the same cold that
had never really left his system but he decided to continue despite it. As soon
as the March 28 show ended, Hope took the troupe for six days of entertaining camps and bases in the Caribbean.

On April 4, he was back to do a camp show at the Arizona–California
border, and when Dolores took a look at him she drove him to Palm Springs
to rest.

Five days later he checked into Goldwyn Studios for his second feature for
Sam. The script, *Sylvester the Great*, was a period piece, a comedy swashbuckler about a hapless actor protecting a princess from pirates. Hope's
leading lady was Virginia Mayo, and his costars in the film—Walter Brennan, Victor McLaglen and Walter Slezak—were particularly effective. The
release title of the picture was *The Princess and the Pirate*, and it turned out
to be the last film Hope would make for a full year.

The reason for this year-long hiatus in Hope's movie-making was an
impasse that developed between himself and Paramount. Hope said, "I
asked my lawyer, Martin Gang, how I could hold on to some of the money I
was earning instead of seeing it all going to finance those B–17s and battle-

ships. He told me the only way was to form my own production company and make movies in partnership with Paramount."[9] This notion was, of course, not popular. Hope braced himself for a fight, possibly a long and bloody one.

Hope and Y. Frank Freeman went to lunch at Perino's and after a few amenities, Hope dropped his bomb. "Frank, I'm going to form my own production company."

Freeman looked stunned. "Why do you want to do that?"

"Money—so I can hang on to more of it."

"It won't work, Bob. We couldn't allow it. I'd like to talk to you about the movie we want you to do called *Duffy's Tavern*. Now what's bothering you about it?"

"Frank, I'm telling you I'm going to make pictures for my own company. I'd like to have more say in what I make and how I make them."

"I don't see how we can let you do that, Bob. If you insist we'll have to suspend you."

"Okay, I guess you'll have to suspend me."

About a month before the Goldwyn film finished shooting, the USO and Hope jointly announced that the comedian would take Frances, Jerry and Tony to the South Pacific war zones during July and August 1944. At the same time, the *New York Herald Tribune*'s Sunday supplement published a Hope-authored piece called "Sure Fire Gags for the Foxhole." The announcement and both stories were intended to fit into a larger publicity and promotional campaign to herald the publication of *I Never Left Home*. Simon and Schuster launched a barrage of newspaper copy, taking full-page ads that made full use of the Carl Rose illustrations as well as comic photographs of Hope. Hope made several suggestions that were adopted, including advertisements that poked fun at him and the book.

One advertisement showed Hope in a photograph that likened him to a most-wanted criminal. The copy below read: "This man is Bob Hope. He has written a book. Worse still, he has managed to get it published."

The first edition of 100,000 copies appeared in an eight-ounce paperbound format suitable for mailing to servicemen and women overseas. It sold for one dollar. Almost immediately a hardcover edition of another 100,000 copies appeared in the bookstores to sell for two dollars. By September a half-million copies were sold. By the following year a million and a half would be sold.

Columnists like Walter Winchell, Leonard Lyons, Erskine Johnson and Hedda Hopper gave it their rapturous blessing, as did critics like Bennett Cerf, and Tom O'Reilly of *The New York Times*.

A highly dramatic testimonial of Hope's identification with the GI came on Tuesday, June 6, which was both Hope's final Pepsodent broadcast of the season and, of course, D–Day on the shores of Normandy. That night Hope abandoned his prepared jokes and together with his writers wrote a speech containing this moving passage:

> You sat there and dawn began to sneak in, and you thought of the hundreds of thousands of kids you'd seen in camps the past two or three years . . . the kids who scream and whistle when they hear a gag and a song. And now you could see all of them

again . . . in four thousand ships on the English Channel, tumbling out of thousands of planes over Normandy and the occupied Coast . . . in countless landing barges crashing the Nazi gate and going on through to do a job that's the job of all of us. The sun came up and you sat there looking at that huge black headline, that one great bright word with the exclamation point, "Invasion!" The one word that the whole world has waited for, that all of us have worked for. We knew we'd wake up one morning and have to meet it face to face, the word in which America has invested everything these thirty long months . . . the effort of millions of Americans building planes and weapons . . . the shipyards and the men who took the stuff across . . . little kids buying War Stamps, and housewives straining bacon grease . . . farmers working round the clock . . . millions of young men sweating it out in camps, and fighting the battles that paved the way for this morning. Now the investment must pay— for this generation and all generations to come.[10]

Hope's voice was heard by an audience estimated to be 35 million people, as many or more than would listen to one of the President's fireside chats. The text was widely reprinted.

On June 22, Bob, Frances, Jerry, Tony and a vivacious young dancer named Patty Thomas and durable gagster Barney Dean took off in a C-54 litter plane which was enroute to Saipan to pick up wounded. More than a few people both in Washington and in Hollywood thought the Japanese-infested islands of the Southwest Pacific no safe place for entertainers. Their first drop was safe enough, the Hawaiian Islands.

From Hawaii, they flew in General MacArthur's personal plane, a big Liberator called Seventh Heaven piloted by Captain Frank Orme, to the desolate atoll called Christmas Island. Hope said later:

The only entertainment they'd had there till we arrived was the Gary Cooper troupe the year before. This is a place with flying cockroaches, blister bugs, land crabs and other crawly things, enough to make you cringe. And no fresh water.[11]

The next day they were glad to be headed for fresh-water Canton Island, but it wasn't much different.

They stopped at Tarawa, and then at Kwajalein in the Marshall Islands, where Hope commented on the makeshift windmills that operated the island's laundry and told his audience that he heard a voice with an Alabama accent say, "We'll sure enough be clean with Hope on the island. He'll keep those windmills goin'."

From Kwajalein they hopped to Saipan, to Majuro and then to Bougainville. Exhaustion was beginning to show on everyone. And by the time they had played Munda and Tulagi, they agreed to take the Australian rest cure.

They hitched a ride over to Brisbane where Lieutenant Frank Ferguson— who incidentally lived in North Hollywood near the Hopes—was to fly them in a big PBY, a Catalina Flying Boat, to Sydney. The prospect of clean laundry and sleep made the all-day plane ride bearable and they were in high

spirits. Ferguson let Hope take over the controls and fly the Catalina. He was
standing behind Hope when the right motor conked out and the plane started
to dip. Ferguson shoved Hope from the seat and ordered them to jettison
everything that was loose. They obeyed, throwing their luggage, souvenirs,
cases of Scotch and the plane's tools overboard. Ferguson was trying to find
water for his ship's pontoons because they were flying over land at the time.
His finger found the Camden Haven River on the navigational map and he
lowered the plane toward it. There wasn't much water in the river but he
believed he saw enough to make a landing. They braced themselves for
impact and when the aircraft hit the water, it bounced, landed, bounced
again and came to a stop on a sandspit. While it was bouncing, Ferguson
yelled for them to jump out as soon as they were able, because the exhaust
fumes might blow the plane sky high. Soon afterwards, local residents who
had seen the plane come down arrived and found enough small boats to bring
the entertainers to shore. Next, they located several vehicles to drive them to
the nearest little village of Laurieton, where almost the entire population of
six hundred turned out on the streets to register disbelief, then joy, at having
Bob Hope in their midst.

Hope and company decided to show their appreciation by performing for
their rescuers, and the postmistress declared it "the greatest day in the history of Laurieton." By noon, nine Australian and American military staff
cars arrived to pick them up for the hundred-mile drive to Newcastle where
they boarded a plane for Sydney. Newspaper headlines in the Sydney *Daily
Telegraph* on August 15, 1944—BOB HOPE'S PLANE IN FORCED LANDING; STARS
DOWN ON NORTH COAST—stirred the citizens of Sydney into a frenzied airport
welcome, and thousands of cheering people filled the streets to watch them
arrive at the Australia Hotel. Three squealing young women threw themselves on the ground in front of Hope as he stepped from his car; and one
woman, in the excitement of the moment, threw her handbag at Hope's
head; Hope chewed gum rapidly and looked apprehensively around until he
was rescued by military police.

It wasn't all rest and relaxation in Sydney. The Hope troupe performed at
two hospitals, at a benefit for dependents of service personnel, and in a
motion picture studio where their show was filmed for distribution to GIs in
remote areas of Australia and New Zealand. Hope also did some writing.
The interest in this South Pacific tour had grown so intense back in the
United States that King Features Syndicate was soliciting a series of humorous byline articles from Hope. Hope was so willing that he agreed to do a
daily column. But there were some problems, not the least being Hope's
ability to get the column transmitted from some of the remote locations on
the tour. Also, the military did not want the whereabouts of the troupe
known until after they had departed the combat zone. Hope decided to write
his impressions out of sequence. He began with the dramatic ditching of
their Catalina at Laurieton and the second column would be about their lay-
over on Christmas Island. The columns were scheduled to start in American
newspapers on August 28, 1944.

After four days among the adoring Australians, the troupe went back to
the shooting war. These excerpts from Hope's daily column, which appeared
in American newspapers as "Bob Hope's Communiqué," provide some high-

lights of the final days of the tour. These final columns were not printed until after Hope arrived home on September 10:

SOMEWHERE IN THE SOUTHWEST PACIFIC—Sept. 13 . . . I hardly believe it myself but the other day when we were giving a show on Noemfoor Island they shot a Jap 1200 yards from the stage. I don't know whether he was coming or going to the show, but if I had known about it I would have been 1200 miles away from the island. Not that I am nervous, but lately we have been playing so close to some of these surrounded Japs I swear the last two rows have been wearing kimonos. . . .

SOMEWHERE IN THE SOUTHWEST PACIFIC—Sept. 14 . . . We did a show at Wake the other day . . . They had a stage set up right near the runway so we could escape if we laid an egg, I guess . . . and the show was almost ruined by the planes taking off. . . . Every time you read a straight line you have to wait until the plane takes off before delivering the punch line . . . it plays havoc with one's timing . . . Frank Robertson, International News Service war correspondent, has been helping gather this trivia . . . It's nice to have someone to share the blame . . . We've typed this stuff in planes, on tree stumps and any place we could set a typewriter up. . . . [12]

When the cast stepped out of their military transport at Burbank's Lockheed airstrip, Hope told reporters that they had traveled a total of 30,000 miles and had performed 150 times. Their last leg from New Guinea took them 50 hours.

At home the comedian showed off his souvenirs. He was particularly proud of his Japanese pistol and gave his children a lecture on the use of firearms. "You've got to be very sure they're empty before you pull the trigger," he said. As he demonstrated the gun discharged and a bullet ripped through the door of his wardrobe closet. Dolores screamed. Bob apologized.

Two days later Hope was doing his radio show at the Marine Air Station in Mojave, California. He would continue to do the Pepsodent program from camps and bases across the nation throughout the fall and through the following spring.

Hope did not show up at Paramount for the shooting of the studio's star-filled movie *Duffy's Tavern*, as he had told Freeman months before, and would not enter the Paramount lot until mid-September 1945.

The media was quick to question Hope. "We've both said our little sarcastic things," he said. "But I really suspended the studio. I'm not on salary. My contract calls for straight picture deals. The time out will be added on to my contract. And if someone will suspend the war I'll be happy to start another picture. As it is I'm booked with GI Joe, and besides, I'll give the country a nice rest. How often can people stand to look at my kisser?"[13]

When I walked into USO headquarters in Chatou, it looked
as if Central Casting had opened an overseas branch. I ran
into Alfred Lunt and Lynn Fontanne, Bea Lillie, Reginald
Gardiner. . . . Really, a lot of stars like Cagney, Cooper,
Annie Sheridan and Paulette Goddard made offshore trips
for GIs and never said a word about it. So different from
YOU-KNOW-WHO. . . .[1]

24. Back for More

Nineteen forty-five was a year when everything came together for Hope. Not that there was ever much doubt about his continuing appeal or the value of his accomplishments. But the events of this year were of the sort that sealed his destiny.

In January his radio program became, for the first time, the undisputed national pastime, having outdistanced its closest rival, *Fibber McGee*, by six rating points on the Hooper. Consequently, Pepsodent and Hope negotiated a new ten-year contract and although neither Lever Brothers nor Hope would reveal the exact figures, Jack Hope said there was a million dollars in the contract for every year it ran.

And, as Will Rogers had done years earlier and Eleanor Roosevelt more recently, Hope had joined the Fourth Estate. His daily humor column, now called "It Says Here," was a staple item in all the Hearst newspapers and a fairly well-publicized feature in other large and small dailies nationwide. Hope supervised; that is, he generally chose the topic and edited what his writers submitted. As a satiric commentary on selected phenomena of the 1940s scene, the column allowed Hope to use more colorful language than he could use in his radio monologues. Furthermore, in print he discovered other things besides Hollywood to joke about, and as he broadened his purview, and as his interest in the humor of politics gradually increased, so did references to him as a latter-day Will Rogers.

It was a year of much travel: After two strenuous national camp show tours, the comedian turned around and took a USO troupe to Europe for his last of six wartime tours overseas. He spent three months in England, France, Germany, Austria and Czechoslovakia.

And 1945 was the year that Harry Truman invited him to entertain the "first family" at the White House. It was also the year that Hope, once again in charge of the Oscar ceremonies, gritted his teeth as his pal Crosby stepped up on the stage of Grauman's Chinese Theater to accept a statuette for his acting role as a priest in *Going My Way*. But the Oscarless Hope could point with pride to his own unique statue-honor, a bust sculpted by Max Kalish to be placed in the Smithsonian Institute's gallery of noted Americans.

More significant, perhaps, was Hope's victory over Paramount in his fight to become an independent producer. He formed Hope Enterprises and won the right to a voice in his own films.

But it wouldn't have been much of a year without an award or two. In fact, the year started out that way. Hope was on a national camp tour in January and arranged to have his radio show performed for the Signal Corps at Fort Monmouth, New Jersey, so he could go into Philadelphia to be honored. It was "Bob Hope Day" there, complete with a tickertape parade. The Poor Richard Club, proper and prestigious, had voted him their gold medal for "outstanding contribution to the nation," the second entertainer in their forty-year history to be so honored. The first was Will Rogers.

From Philadelphia, Hope took his radio cast to Quonset Point, Rhode Island, for a Naval Air Station show, and the next day into Boston for a huge war-wounded benefit at the Boston Garden. Then they headed south to Florida and Tennessee for more camp shows and worked their way back across the country.

Hope made it back to Hollywood just in time for his role in the most ambitious "Command Performances" radio program attempted by the Armed Forces Radio Services during the war. *Life* reported on March 12, 1945, that besides Hope, there was Bing Crosby, Frank Sinatra, Jimmy Durante, Judy Garland, Dinah Shore, the Andrews Sisters, Jerry Colonna, Cass Daley and Harry Von Zell in a musical comedy based on Chester Gould's popular comic strip *Dick Tracy*. The show was called "Dick Tracy in B Flat or For Goodness Sake Isn't He Ever Going to Marry Tess Trueheart?" It was an assemblage of stars that no commercial radio program could have afforded to put together, and free admission tickets were fiercely fought over by its audience of mixed-branch servicemen and women. They cheered Durante as The Mole in his version of "The Music Goes Round and Round," and whistled when Judy Garland as Snowflake said to Flattop, "I appeal to you on bended knee," and Hope leeringly quipped, "Kid, you appeal to me in any position."

After that broadcast, Hope went down to Palm Springs to rest. His doctor warned him that he had slightly high blood pressure. He was told to rest between radio broadcasts. One of the columns suggested he was ill; another report from the mid-West had him dead. Mack Millar says that about once a week his office would receive an inquiry concerning Hope's death.

Hope was quite alive the night he presided over the Motion Picture Academy's seventeenth annual awards ceremony. Hope took over when the show went live on network radio that evening, and before he had a chance to do any monologue, Walter Wanger handed him a lifetime membership in the Academy. Hope cracked, "Every year they give me a consolation prize. A life pass. . . . Hmmmm . . . now I know how Roosevelt feels!"[2]

When Gary Cooper announced that Bing Crosby had won the Oscar for his role in *Going My Way*, Bing came up to the stage, bald-headed and somewhat shy. When Cooper handed him the statuette, he looked as if he might not say anything, and Hope snapped, "You'd *better* say something."

Crosby said, "It just goes to show you what a great and democratic world we live in, when a broken-down crooner like myself can win this Academy crockery. If Leo McCarey can lead me through a picture like this one—now if he can find me a horse to win the Kentucky Derby."

And Hope leaned into the microphone, "Now I know how Dewey felt! . . . No, I think it's just great! Really! . . ."

Ingrid Bergman won a statuette for her performance in *Gaslight* and, during a mix-up in the presentation of the gold figurines, Hope said, "Wouldn't it be wonderful if there was one left over?"

Less than a month later, on April 12, 1945, the world was jolted by the death of Franklin Roosevelt from a cerebral hemorrhage. FDR had gone to Warm Springs to prepare for the inauguration of the United Nations at San Francisco at the end of April.

When the President died, Hope wanted to reflect his and the nation's grief in his daily column but chose an oblique approach. On April 21, 1945, he wrote:

Dear Fala,
   You probably don't remember me. But I knew you back in our kennel days when we were a couple of young pups—in fact we chewed our first bone together, remember? In writing you this letter, I'm speaking for dogs throughout the world. For we are all deeply grieved to hear of the death of your master. Your personal loss is felt by all of us. You know as well as I do that leading a dog's life is no bed of roses. But a dog's life is for dogs. Human beings shouldn't horn in on our territory. But lately a lot of men and women and kids have been leading a dog's life, and your master was one of the humans who didn't like to see that sort of thing happening. That's why we respected him—he wanted to keep human beings in their right place. And he did something about it. He made plans, and people had confidence in his plans because his integrity and sincerity were felt the world over. In other words, he made a lot of people see the light, or as we'd put it, he put them on the right scent. Let's hope they can keep their noses to the ground and work it out for themselves, even though his personal guidance has been taken away from them.

                                              With deepest sympathy,
                                                             Fido

   As Hope devoted eight of his daily columns to an event like the United Nations Conference at San Francisco, it is surprising that there is no mention in any of his May columns of the cessation of war in Europe. On the other hand, it is not surprising that Hope was saying nothing in print about his sticky contract squabble with Paramount. He didn't have to, really, because the syndicated columnists were doing the job for him. Sob sister Florabel Muir summed up the situation as a "Mexican stand-off" and laid the problem at the feet of Paramount's new ruling executive Henry Ginsberg who had jockeyed the corporation through their recent $16-million winning streak. In the *New York Daily Mirror* on April 22, 1945, Florabel wrote:

Henry would like to give Bob Hope what he wants but he feels that if he does he will establish a dangerous precedent. . . .
   When a star of Hope's stature announces he doesn't want to work for nothing, who can blame him? Which is why we are going to see more and more top stars going as independent as they can.

Florabel's column preceded by only a short time the succinct announcement by Paramount on May 6, 1945, that Henry Ginsberg had signed a new seven-year exclusive contract with Hope which allowed the comedian to make one picture a year for himself, and work in partnership with Paramount on other pictures. The battle was won and its decision was a benchmark for Hollywood filmmakers. It opened the floodgates for independent movie deals and tolled the knell of big studio autonomy.

On May 12, Hope took his Pepsodent cast to Washington for a three-hour show, which included his radio broadcast, to kick off the Seventh War Loan Drive. Sixty-five hundred people pledged $2.5 million in bonds to see the show, and one of the rewards for Hope was an invitation by Harry Truman to stage a show in the Gold Room of the White House. He took Frances, Jerry, Vera, Tony and Skinnay Ennis (back from the war) to entertain the Truman family. There were about 35 or 40 people in all. As they walked in, Hope said, "Man, this looks like Missouri already." The President laughed.

Truman asked to see the same show Hope had been performing at U.S. camps and overseas. Afterwards there were lemonade and cookies and a tour of the White House personally conducted by Harry, Bess and Margaret. When the house tour was finished, they stood in the portico where two months ago the Vice President had become President, and from somewhere nearby a cannon fired two shells. Margaret said excitedly, "What was that, Dad?" And before Harry could respond, Hope said, "Nothing, my dear. Just my hotel's auditing machine figuring up my bill."[3]

With praise from the nation's new President still ringing in his ears, Hope moved from the White House to the Smithsonian for the unveiling of his statue in the "living hall of fame." It was announced that 8 million GIs had voted him this honor in a polling of U.S. and overseas troops.

Hope continued the Seventh War Loan Drive in Chicago where he and Crosby did a very successful charity golf match at the Tam O'Shanter course, and 50,000 bond buyers jammed Notre Dame Stadium at South Bend on May 28 to watch the Pepsodent players romp through their specialties.

The Crosby–Hope golf matches for wartime causes continued, as did Hope's camp and hospital tour. After appearances in Sedalia, Missouri, and Salt Lake City, Hope went back home to rest for a few days. Then he and Dolores flew to New York so she could wave him off on the *Queen Mary* for his two-and-a-half-month journey for American occupation forces in Europe. The USO had sent an impassioned call to entertainers not to abandon the GI now that the shooting had ended. Hope was among the first to say yes, and although he could not take Langford—she had signed a contract to do a summer radio show—he collared Colonna, and Patty Thomas, plus singer Gale Robbins, pianist June Bruner, accordianist Ruth Denas and comedians Roger Price and Jack Pepper.

The Hope troupe opened at London's Albert Hall on the Fourth of July for 10,000 GIs and then they moved over to Paris, where they met up with Alfred Lunt and Lynne Fontanne, Bea Lillie, Reginald Gardiner, Clifton Fadiman, John Kieran and Franklin P. Adams, the stars of radio's *Information, Please!*

From Paris they were driven to Amiens to entertain some troops who were first ashore at Normandy, and from there south to Marseilles where they performed in front of 150,000 Pacific-bound soldiers who were waiting around in dusty, barren staging areas. There, Hope ran into more stars: Sonja Henie, Mickey Rooney, Bobby Breen and opera's glamorous Grace Moore.

A soccer field at Nice was the site of one of Hope's last shows in France. During the evening Hope learned that Maurice Chevalier was sitting out front. Chevalier had become a controversial figure during the war, accused of collaboration with the Nazis. Hope had known him at Paramount and respected him. One of the American officers objected when Hope asked to have Chevalier brought to him.

"Don't introduce him. He's suspected of being a traitor."

Hope looked at the officer. "I don't know anything about that. I'm not a judge and jury. I'm just an emcee and this guy is one hell of an entertainer."

Chevalier came backstage smiling, but looking a bit uncertain. He was wearing a white turtleneck sweater and red trousers and it was clear that he had hoped to make an appearance.

He sang "Louise" and several other Chevalier standards and the audience gave him a standing ovation. That night, sipping brandy at the château where the Hope troupe was staying, Chevalier said, "I will never forget what you have done for me in that ball park in Nice."[4]

In Germany they played for the 29th Division at Bremen, for Airborne troops in Berlin, for the Air Force at Bad Kissingen, the Army at Heidelberg, more Air Force at Furstenfeldbruck, and the armored personnel at Fritzlar. The Navy called him back to Monte Carlo to play for the destroyer U.S.S. *Gridley* and then right back to Kassel, Munich and Nuremberg for the GI Olympics. It was while they were sitting in the old Nuremberg Stadium, renamed Soldiers Field, that the announcement was made over the sound system that Japan was offering to surrender. It had begun to rain but even so, the cheering lasted for thirty minutes. "Even C. B. De Mille couldn't improve on the noise those Yanks made," said Hope.

At Mannheim Hope picked up prizefighter Billy Conn as a replacement for Patty Thomas who became ill and was hospitalized for a few days. They finished the tour in Austria and Czechoslovakia. The talk everywhere was when would V–J Day happen? What would happen to Bob Hope after V–J Day? How would he reconvert from war to peace? At one point he said, "In common with the GIs, I kept thinking of a nice long rest. The only difference was that the GIs really wanted one and I was afraid I'd be given one."

It didn't take long for the newspapers' entertainment columnists to begin speculating about Hope's reconversion to civilian radio. The sponsor was getting letters, too. People asked, "Why isn't Hope doing shows for *us* now?"

Hope believed that his answer to reporter Jack Holland ought to suffice: "As long as there are fellows—and girls—still in the service, they get the first call. They need entertainment now as much as ever—if not more. The days they spend waiting to get home or the hours they lie in hospital beds are plenty tough—and a laugh won't hurt them."[5]

But the critics didn't go away.

THE TRUMAN YEARS

1946–1952

*. . . on the second anniversary of D-Day, we established a
small beachhead at Spokane, Washington, and started crisscrossing the country . . . double-crossing the audiences
. . . the guys showed up just the way they did when they
were in the Army. Only this time they had to pay.*[1]

25. *So This is Peace*

When World War II was over, the world view of the average American,
civilian or ex-GI, had shrunk. The forced altruism of the past five years had
switched suddenly to self-centered survival. Reconversion was the word for
how to beat the shortages and unemployment. The diplomats and the politicians would have to find out how much validity there was in Wendell Will-
kie's dream; the guy with the lunch pail was trying to figure how long before
his wife could have her new washing machine. Peace promised a payoff, and
people were trying to collect.

In much the same frame of mind, Bob Hope came home to Hollywood
from five years of giving away his time, energy and talent, and decided it was
time to play catch-up. He had to refire the burners under his flagging movie
career. His last film, *Road to Utopia*, was both a critical success and a gold
mine, but that was months ago. Normally, Paramount would have at least
one Hope film in reserve, waiting for release, but now the cupboard was
bare.

To make matters worse, Hope came home to squabbling. While he was
still in Europe, Paramount hustled to find a suitable vehicle for his triumphant return to the lot, finally settling on a comic version of the 1924
Rudolph Valentino swashbuckler *Monsieur Beaucaire*. Everyone agreed
that Hope's reluctant hero persona in powdered wig and satin breeches was
funny, and light centuries removed from khaki and parade drills.

Panama and Frank labored over the script and had completed most of it
when Henry Ginsberg assigned Paul Jones as producer. Jones was dissatis-
fied with the script and assigned a new writer. Angrily Panama and Frank
complained to the Writers Guild, who supported their claim. So the project
was hung up. But Hope pressured Ginsberg to back down, and forced Jones
to accept the Panama–Frank script which Hope and director George Marshall found hilarious.

The movie had a strong cast. The women—Joan Caulfield, Marjorie Reynolds and Hillary Brooke—were attractive, and character parts—played by
Joseph Schildkraut, Constance Collier, Douglas Dumbrille, Patric Knowles,
Cecil Kellaway and Reginald Owen—were exceptionally effective. Yet it
was a taxing experience even for the energetic Hope. Each day he was faced
with elaborate sight gags and gimmicks, pratfalls or water dunkings, and
always strenuous dueling scenes with the skilled fencer Schildkraut. Hope
became uncharacteristically impatient.

After all, he had a new stake in the outcome. When the picture was previewed in nearby Alhambra, both Paramount executives and their new part-

ner Hope felt it looked "too straight," and perhaps too subtle. So comedy writer Frank Tashlin was hired to heighten the slapstick, and after some reshooting, the film was previewed again. This time audiences loved it. It belongs in the golden dozen of Hope's best movies.

Almost at once Hope began another film, *Where There's Life*, in which he played a bumbling disc jockey who discovers he is heir to the throne of a mythical kingdom.

The film was nothing exceptional. It simply provided Hope with a fairly predictable life-style for a few months. In fact, between this film and the one before it Hope was reasonably sedentary for almost a year, which was unique in his career. It gave him more time to be with Dolores, Linda and Tony. Forced to rise early (something he abhorred) when he worked in films, he could have breakfast with them. If he had a late studio call, he would play games with them. He grabbed his movie camera and shot hundreds of feet of them playing with Suds (the Scottie) or Red Sun (the Great Dane) in the ten acres of backyard that now comprised his Toluca Lake property.

During this period Bob got close to another member of his family, his mother-in-law, Theresa DeFina. She sold furs at Franklin Simon's department store in New York, but she liked California and would come for a month or so in the spring. Considering her hostile reaction to Bob when he married Dolores, the unexpected had occurred. Bob and Theresa developed a joking relationship based on genuine respect. There was a toughness in Theresa that reminded Hope of Mahm. Theresa recognized Bob's need for family love and support; she considered him shrewd, clever and protective of things both he and she valued, and frequently found herself at odds with Dolores over decisions he made or intended to make. Theresa encouraged Bob and Dolores to adopt more children; she volunteered to go to The Cradle with them, or for them, if Florence Walrath could find another baby.

Another member of his family Hope got to know better, but unfortunately lost in 1946, was Uncle Frank. Frank, his dad's older brother, had moved from Cleveland to El Segundo, California, in the 1920s and was a frequent visitor to Moorpark Street. Still a clear-thinking eighty-one, Frank, who had been a hard-working tradesman all his life, brought Bob and Dolores his common sense philosophy, his attitudes about human dignity and thrift. "Such a beautiful man, in looks, in thoughts," Bob said. "Dolores and I were completely in love with him. He was a great stabilizer. He taught me moderation."[2]

Hope's feelings for family were genuinely strong. In addition to his immediate family, he had become the "big daddy" to many of his relatives, some in Ohio, some nearer Toluca Lake. These family ties deepened his concerns about his own future and the empire he was building.

In an article entitled "Hope Springs Financial," *Newsweek* reported on May 6, 1946, that Hope's current annual earnings were impressive. He would probably gross around $1.25 million from movies and radio shows in 1946. In addition he was getting another $30,000 a year from his newspaper column. Trusted advisers like insurance man Al Lloyd and his accountant Arthur Nadel had steered him into annuities, blue chip investments, government bonds. His part-ownership of Hope Metal Products, under Ivor's direction, was netting about $100,000 a year.

Legal wizard Martin Gang responded to Hope's need to protect his income by creating a new corporation just to handle personal appearances; Bob had decided it was time to stop doing them all for charity. Gang also suggested Hope form still another corporation to cover those activities that fell into categories other than films or personal appearances. Hope planned to write another book with Carroll Carroll, this one relating his USO experiences in the South Pacific and more recently in Europe. Also, he had been approached by Capitol Records to release a dramatized version of *I Never Left Home.*

In spite of all his holdings, Bob had a rude awakening. He found himself cash-poor. When he opened his income tax bill and saw the figure $62,000, he almost fainted. Fortunately, he and Nadel persuaded the Treasury Department to grant him an extension based on two things: Hope's promise to pay as soon as he started his next movie, and Hope's reminder to his government of the number of successful War Bond drives he had kicked off during the past five years.

Hope had a second rude awakening. For the first time in several years he had slipped to a decimal point behind *Fibber McGee.* The advertising agency and the network told him why: He had neglected to alter his format; he had insisted on continuing to play for military audiences, which had alienated his civilian home listener; and that listener, they said, was now more tuned to situation comedy and wanted to forget the recent war.

Hope was so used to praise from critics for his wartime shows that he was baffled by their current "picking" on him. He was discussing this with the *Milwaukee Journal*'s entertainment writer J.D. Spiro on the set of *Where There's Life.* "They're undoubtedly right when they say my radio show hasn't been all it could be. I know it needs some reconversion, but it takes time to reconvert, and we haven't had it. After four years of playing to thousands of GIs all over the globe, you just can't come down instantly to playing to 300 people out in front. Besides—you can see what I'm doing— my schedule—look here—just this week I'm doing the United Jewish Appeal show, a guest shot for Tony Martin, and another for Bob Crosby—a transcription for Armed Forces Radio."

"Will you change your show, Bob?"

"Yeah—somewhat—for the fall. We'll probably go more toward situation but you know my style is topical stuff. Anyway, we'll have Vera Vague back—and Jerry. Langford's gone but we'll have some big guest singers."[3]

Despite his assurance to his media critics or his sponsor that he would make changes in his show, there were no perceptible differences during that season, and when the Hooper and Crossley ratings came out in late spring, Hope was the leader. This intensified his feeling that it didn't matter so much what he was doing because the people out there liked him.

Knowing they liked him and feeling that a personal appearance tour for the money was a sure way of getting enough cash to pay his taxes, Hope asked Louis Shurr to book a national tour of twenty-nine cities in thirty-one days. On short notice he couldn't sign his resident touring company, but he booked young Paramount newcomer Olga San Juan as his sexy singer, a chorus line of starlets and some back-up variety acts. Hope asked Mack

Millar to line up several publicists who could begin thumping through cities
like Seattle, Spokane, Denver, St. Louis, Oklahoma City, Chicago, Houston,
New Orleans, Birmingham, Atlanta, and Norfolk. Ultimately, it was Jack
Hope, Rufus Blair of Paramount publicity, Louis Weiner, who was Crosby's
press agent, and Mack who hit the road to circulate the posters and broad-
sides, releases and banners that said:

BOB HOPE

IN PERSON

IN A BIG TWO HOUR

HOLLYWOOD LAUGH SHOW

GALS! GAGS! FUN! COMEDY! LAUGHS!

45—RADIO—STAGE—SCREEN—STARS—45

DON'T MISS IT! ONE PERFORMANCE ONLY

HERE HE COMES, FOLKS

BOB HOPE

IN PERSON![4]

There was nothing new, after all, in show business promotion since P.T.
Barnum. After break-in performances at Glendale, San Diego and Fresno,
two chartered Transair DC–3s took off for Spokane. Not only would there be
a two-hour stage show in the city's Gonzaga Stadium, but an exhibition golf
game with the city's most famous citizen, Bing Crosby.

Rain threatened to cancel the Hope–Crosby match but it took place anyway in foul weather, and Seattle's *Post-Intelligencer* sent one of its reporters
to cover it. The story that resulted may well be the first major newspaper
piece whose theme was an attempt to put the mythic and symbolic elements
of Hope's image in perspective. To the reporter, Douglass Welch, the news of
Hope's recently formed corporations, coming as they did on the heels of his
stunning wartime philanthropy, seemed like the seed of a good feature story.
As Welch said to Doc Shurr, "Bob Hope is big business and we want to write
him up as we would any successful corporation."

Welch pressed Shurr for information on Hope's finances, income taxes
and Hope Enterprises. Shurr refused to answer, snapping, "There are too
many people already thinking about Hope's income and tax and we don't
want anymore. No, forget it. Why don't you write something people will
want to read," he railed, "like, for instance that we have 40 people in the
troupe, that we have some very beautiful girls, that the show is colossal and
straight from Hollywood." As Shurr scuttled off, he added, "What kind of
questions are these?"

Welch never got to interview Hope but his story, which appeared in the
Post-Intelligencer on June 6, 1946, could have been tougher. Calling him a
corporation, Welch wrote:

> Wherever he goes, the whole board of directors ambles right
> along with him. They not only do all the things that the directors
> of any company normally do, but in addition they have been
> trained to laugh in the right places. "Oh, that Hope! He kills us,"

the directors say in chorus, laughing fit to kill and slapping their thighs. "That's our boy over there making funnies. Yes, it is! That's our boy!" In public, Hope looks like a parade. Even when he goes to the gentlemen's retiring room he looks like a platoon. He is constantly surrounded with busy, worried and preoccupied people, with briefcases, papers and knitted brows.

Spokane was also the setting for a curious non-encounter between Bob and his older brother Jim. Jim was the one family member who was not able to accept Bob's phenomenal success gracefully.

He had come to California where he sold real estate and found some extra work in movies. Following one disastrous relationship, Jim met and married pretty Wyn Swanson, young, talented and ambitious to be in show business. She looked good on stage and had an appealing singing style, she could write in a variety of forms, including comedy, and she composed songs. Together, Wyn and Jim created a vaudeville act and were booked by the Levey office primarily because of the Hope name. They were shipped out to the sticks and were currently playing a circuit of towns and cities in the Northwest where stage shows with movies could still attract a fair crowd.

Unknown to Jim and Wyn, but certainly not unknown to the Levey office, they were booked into the Post Street Theater in Spokane during the week that brother Bob and his extravaganza would be playing in Gonzaga Stadium.

On Bob's first morning in the city, Don Halladay of the *Daily Chronicle* was ushered into Hope's suite at the Davenport Hotel for an interview. "How do you feel?" asked Halladay.

"Look at these blisters," Hope said, pointing at his feet. "We finished a picture by working half the nights, and on Memorial Day, too, to make this date." He yawned. "I didn't get to bed until nearly three. I was directing traffic all night. I thought the cabs were coming in the window. I had a nice carbon monoxide snooze."

"How does it feel with two Hope shows playing the same town?"

"What?" Hope asked, looking at Mack. "What d'ya mean?"

"Your brother Jim," said Mack. "Jim and Wyn are playing a vaudeville date around the corner at the Post Theater."

"You got to be kidding," Hope said. Then to Millar, "How come nobody told me?"

"Nobody knew until this morning."

Halladay's eyes went from Hope to Millar and back. Mack said quickly, "They ought to do pretty fair business considering everything—"

"That," Hope broke in, "is unfair competition. You know I've got six brothers—each playing a town."

Later that afternoon, a nameless reporter from the *Daily Chronicle* called Jim Hope at his hotel, asking him if he and Wyn would be available for a news photo with his brother. Jim was told he would be alerted as to the exact time and place after the details were cleared with Bob. Wyn was thrilled. She and Jim rifled through their wardrobe trunk for the best of their street clothes and got more excited when still another reporter called from the city newsroom to tell them to stand by.

They stood by for several hours, but no further call. Jim was too proud to telephone Bob or the newspaper. They were told Bob turned down the suggestion of a press photo or a joint news interview. In fact, Jim learned that his brother was emphatic in refusing to see him. However, Jim found out that Bob had asked Louis Shurr to "slip over to the Post and catch Jim's act."

Later that same night, Jim and Wyn had a late after-show supper at the Davenport, and heard people excitedly saying that the Hope troupe had come back from the Gonzaga and were upstairs getting ready to go to the airport. The couple stood unobserved in the lobby crowd as Bob left the hotel. Nor did anyone recognize them as they walked arm in arm back to their hotel. Wyn Hope has since said, "Somehow I feel that if Bob had read a review of our act before he was asked to meet Jim, it would have worked out. Believe me, Jim Hope and Wyn Swanson were no threat to Bob's career and fame. In fact, we were helping to bury vaudeville."[5]

Hope and company flew out of Spokane, moved from city to city until they had pretty much covered the nation, and started back toward California. Their last two shows were in Topeka and Kansas City, and during the very last performance, Fred Hope called the theater to tell Bob that Sid's cancer, which had been checked for a time, was spreading.

Sid Hope knew he was dying, which is why he needed to see Bob. For the past seventeen years he had lived quietly as a machinist and farmer in the little village of Ridgeville Corners, Ohio. Sid never craved the business or entertainment worlds that attracted his brothers; he preferred the country life with Dorothy, his wife, and their five children. Sid was too young to die. He was forty-one, two years younger than Bob.

When Bob got the call from Fred, one of his backstage guests was Secretary of War Harry Goodring who immediately arranged for a Navy plane to fly Bob to Columbus to pick up Fred and then go on to Toledo. The brothers would drive the rest of the way from Toledo. The Navy plane would then fly to the airport at Defiance, Ohio, wait for Hope, and take him back to Kansas City where the Transair DC–3 would be waiting.

At Ridgefield Corners, a sleepy landscape of scattered farms, very few people would ever know that Bob Hope, the famous comedian, was visiting his brother. They were the lookalike brothers, Bob and Sid. That's what Dorothy was saying as they sat out on lawn chairs in the shade. Sid was amused when his kids tried to climb up into Bob's lap. Fred came out and Bob joked about his crop of wavy hair. "If Paramount saw that they'd cancel my contract." Bob amused everyone by telling them about filming the bear scene in *Road to Utopia*.

Sid, reluctant to have his brother leave him, told Bob that the nearby Archbold Airport had a 2,800-foot runway and the CAA supervised twenty-four hours. Bob asked Fred to call Defiance and find out if the Navy pilots could pick him up in Archbold. They could, and they did.

Before Bob left he said, "Sid, you're going to get well."

"Don't lie to me, Les. I know I'm dying. I have cancer. I just want to ask you one favor—take care of my kids."

In August, not quite halfway through the shooting of *My Favorite Brunette*, Sid died, and Bob chartered a plane to take the California Hopes to Ohio. Every living offspring of Harry and Avis Hope gathered at Ridgeville Corners' St. Peter's Lutheran Church.[6]

Hope stepped back into his life of making movies and preparing for his fall radio season in his usual driven fashion. *Brunette* was a frenetic, fast-paced spy comedy in the tradition of the successful *My Favorite Blonde*, with Hope and Lamour on the run from Peter Lorre, Lon Chaney, Jr., Charles Dingle and John Hoyt. It was Hope's first independent film production and he did not spare the cost. He paid Bing Crosby $25,000 for a cameo appearance in the movie's surprise ending.

If he was being meticulously careful to make an appealing film comedy, he was just as neglectful in making the changes he had vowed to make in his radio program. So the morning after the September 26 Pepsodent premiere, Hope should have been prepared for the critical response. From the *Chicago Daily News*, the headline: TOOTHPASTE BUT NO NEW TEETH IN BOB HOPE'S OPENING SHOW. The dean of radio critics, Jack Gould of *The New York Times*, on October 1, 1946, put it in even harsher terms:

> Bob Hope opened his ninth season on the air last Tuesday evening in the noble tradition of Jake Shubert's "The Student Prince."
>
> You could enjoy it if you had not heard it the first, second, third, fourth, fifth, sixth, seventh and eighth times.
>
> It was all there in this order: (1) Irium (2) Pallid Patter (3) Irium (4) Joke about Bing Crosby (5) Jerry Colonna Arrives (6) Hope Insults Colonna (7) Colonna Screams (8) Irium (9) Vera Vague Arrives (9) Hope Insults Vera (11) Vera Shrieks (12) Irium.

On the other hand, Hope's ratings were good enough news to Lever Brothers' Charles Luckman, who agreed to raise Hope's weekly take by $2,500. And Hope had to believe it was his tireless "machine-gun sputtering" of gags that earned him the American Legion's highest award, their Distinguished Service Medal, in San Francisco on October 1. He stood on the stage with FBI chief J. Edgar Hoover, Secretary of State Cordell Hull, and draft administrator Hershey to receive his honor. Hope had the audience on its feet when he said, "Until every hospitalized kid is on his feet again, this job isn't finished."[7]

Two weeks later he was able to top himself. He was summoned to Washington where, before 40 top military men, the chiefs of staff and top congressional leaders, General Dwight Eisenhower—Hope's personal hero—presented him with the nation's highest civilian award, the Medal of Merit, for his wartime entertaining. As the press photographers and newsreel cameras clicked and turned, Hope said to the group, chewing gum vigorously, "A little more respect, please, fellows!"[8] And after the ceremony, he sat with Eisenhower in his Pentagon office where they reminisced about their meeting in North Africa and Hope reminded him of the blitzing air raid in Algiers. Hope polished the medal with his sleeve and Ike laughed when he heard, "Boy, wait till Bing hears about this!"

All Bing had to do to hear about the medal was turn on the radio or look in the afternoon paper because the story blanketed the nation's front pages.

Hope went from the Pentagon to the White House for a meeting with Harry Truman. It was a short meeting and a private one. Hope said, "I had to thank him—after all, he had to put his okay on it." He told friends afterwards he was shocked by Truman's drawn, tense face, so different from two years before.

On the heels of this, Dolores called him to announce she was meeting him in Chicago. Florence Walrath had another baby waiting for them at The Cradle.

They went to Evanston to pick up a two-month-old girl and as soon as Bob saw her he said, "What a doll!" Dolores smiled, and didn't seem to hear the words Mrs. Walrath was speaking. "I have a surprise for you. There's a baby boy, too."

"You mean—" Dolores watched while the nurse came with another baby, this one three months old. "Oh, I don't think—"

Bob left her in the viewing room and walked back to Mrs. Walrath's office to discuss the legal details with a lawyer. Dolores joined them and wanted to draw Bob away so she could discuss with him the idea of taking two babies.

"Dolores—I've already signed—for both."

"Whatever made you do that?" Dolores asked when they were leaving.

"I couldn't bear to think of leaving him behind," he said.

A few days later there was a double baptism at St. Charles Borromeo in North Hollywood. When it was over, Bob stayed behind for a moment talking to the priest in the vestry. Suddenly he turned and found a man standing next to him with a baby in his arms.

"Take him out to the car," Hope ordered.

"Oh no you don't," said the stranger. "This one happens to be mine."

The King watched us leafing through the book of autographed pictures and then slipped me the royal needle. "Look at him," he said, "he's hurrying to get to his own picture." "Why not?" I asked. "It's the prettiest."[1]

26. King's Jester

At the close of 1945, Americans were reading novels by Marquand and Caldwell and nonfiction like *Peace of Mind* by Joshua Liebman, *The Egg and I* by Betty MacDonald and Bob Hope's third book, *So This Is Peace*, which had jumped in a few weeks from sixteenth to fifth place on the best seller lists.

Hope had once again asked Carroll Carroll to organize his personal notes, his newspaper columns, monologues, press clippings and create a pastiche covering his South Pacific and European USO entertainments, as well as his most recent month-long tour of one-night stands through postwar America.

Carroll attempted to make something meaningful out of the ironies in the word "peace," and the opening lines were especially deft:

We're at peace. We're not enjoying it, but we're at it. And it's sensational what can happen in just one year of it.

We have famine in the midst of plenty and plenty in the midst of famine. The United Naitons held meetings. But the meeting nations were never united. Great Britain's lion turned on Russia. The Russian Bear tried everything but Unguentine on Byrnes. And the whole UN setup got a cut out of Connecticut.

But we're doing all right. As soon as the war ended, we located the one spot on earth that hadn't been touched and blew it to hell.[2]

The rest of the book, however, was a succession of gags in the typical Hope radio technique, his "Commando Method": Strike hard and fast and get away in a hurry. All in all, the book was uneven; but the promotional campaign was stunning, making use again of the irreverent full-page ads that insulted Hope:

WE ARE FORCED BY A CONTRACT TO ANNOUNCE THAT, OVER THE PRO-
TESTS OF HIS TAX MAN, HIS PUBLIC AND OURSELVES, THIS MAN HAS WRIT-
TEN ANOTHER BOOK. PIQUED BY THE SMALL SALE OF *I NEVER LEFT HOME*
(1,620,000 copies mostly to relatives) MR. HOPE HAS GRITTED HIS
TOOTH AND HAS SAT DOWN TO (some perspective advance readers
say "sat down on") HIS TYPEWRITER TO PRODUCE THIS MINIM OPUS. IT
DEALS, OFF THE BOTTOM OF THE DECK, WITH RECONVERSION. IT IS NO
FUNNIER THAN *I NEVER LEFT HOME* BECAUSE, HOPE SAYS, IT COULDN'T
BE.[3]

Just before Christmas the book passed the quarter-million sales mark.

On New Year's Day, 1.5 million people lined Colorado Street in Pasadena to watch Dolores and Grand Marshal Bob Hope waving from a rose-colored float in the 58th Annual Tournament of Roses Parade. Early the next day, Hope reported at Paramount to begin work on his fifth collaboration with Crosby and Lamour, this one called *The Road to Rio*. On this trip, Bob and Bing each owned a third of the picture. Crosby had formed Rainbow Productions about the same time Hope Enterprises was born, and Bing's deal with the studio was similar to Hope's.

Rio changed their attitudes about picture making, because as part-owners they were concerned about costs for the first time. Hope said, "Bing and I hardly left the set, except to go to the men's room."

Rio's plot was familiar. Scat Sweeney, played by Crosby, and Hot Lips Barton, played by Hope, are on the lam and stow away on a liner bound for Rio de Janeiro. They meet the beautiful Lucia Maria de Andrade, played by Lamour, and naturally become embroiled in a sinister plot. One of the songs, "But Beautiful," climbed to the top of the sheet music sales.

During the filming of *Rio*, Paramount Pictures launched the first commercial television station west of Chicago. The studio had been experimenting since 1939 with the new medium, and beaming to a few home receivers from a tiny station called W6XYZ headquartered on the studio lot at Melrose and Bronson. On January 22, 1947, that station became KTLA and inaugurated service, to probably no more than 350 sets, with a special telecast. Bob Hope was M.C. and he introduced producer Cecil B. De Mille, Dorothy Lamour, Jerry Colonna, William Bendix, Ann Rutherford, William Demarest, Peter Lind Hayes, the Rythmaires, and the DeCastro Sisters. Hope said that he and his cohorts were not happy about the glaring lights that made them wringing wet after a few minutes on the set. "I don't know where you're going to find performers who will undergo this heat."[4]

Of course, it was still a year or two before many performers would have to care. Radio was still the chief free entertainment in the nation, and Bob Hope was still the undisputed comedy king. As long as this was true, complaints from the sponsor could be largely ignored.

However, in April the "king" was censored by NBC and a barrage of criticism arose from the fourth estate about the network's foolishness. It all started with Fred Allen who on his Sunday night program told a joke about a mythical NBC vice president and was cut off the air for about ten seconds. Hope was incensed about NBC's thin skin and arrogance. "If Allen's gag had been in poor taste or blue, I could see it." Hope started to refer to Allen's trouble with NBC in his Tuesday night show and was blanked out for six seconds. Hope was saying: "You know Las Vegas . . . that's the place where you can get tanned and faded at the same time. . . . Of course, Fred Allen can get faded any time. . . ."[5] That same evening Red Skelton referred to Allen and was also cut off.

Two weeks later, NBC cut Hope off the air because he told his guest star Frank Sinatra that he would be joining him tomorrow night on his show. At rehearsals he had said "CBS" but had decided not to use it on the air. Nevertheless, the trigger-happy engineers cut Hope off. Bob was tempted to get into a blistering fight with the network, but luckily NBC's president, Niles Trammell, issued a statement saying that Allen should never have been faded, and furthermore suggested that Allen, Hope and Skelton be made honorary vice presidents of NBC. The publicity lasted for almost a month, and Hope ended his season with his all-time highest listening audience.

As that season ended, Hope gave in to Dolores' insistence on a vacation. They chose South America and took Linda and Tony along. Bob also took along his masseur from Lakeside Country Club, Frederico Miron, known as "Doctor" Freddy Miron. Freddy was a Cuban and so he could interpret for the Hopes, and also babysit Linda and Tony when needed. They played golf in Rio de Janeiro at the LaGavia Country Club, which had been cut out of a jungle. On the fifteenth hole Bob stooped to pick up his ball and didn't notice at first that there were red ants crawling around the bottom of it. The ants spread to Hope's hand and he was bitten several times before he got rid of them.

At the Montevideo airport, the Paramount field man met them and whisked them off to the elegant summer home of the wealthy Argentinian Albert Cernadas. Cernadas was the husband of Hope's former radio stooge, Patricia (Honey Chile) Wilder, and the Hopes had the estate all to themselves. It was winter in South America and Cernadas had taken Honey Chile to Europe for the summer sun.

The rest of the vacation was spent in Buenos Aires, Santiago, Lima, Balboa, and finally Cartagena, where the Hopes boarded the Grace Line's newest luxury ship *Santa Rosa* for the cruise back to New York. Bob returned with a badly sunburned face, which delayed for a week the start of his new movie *The Paleface* with Jane Russell.

The Paleface turned out to be Hope's biggest box-office film. His role as Painless Potter, a correspondence-school dentist, was typical, a cowardly

braggart, the unwilling hero and unlikely husband of hyper-mammary Jane
Russell, who plays Calamity Jane. Part of the film's success has to be at-
tributed to the song "Buttons and Bows" written for Bob by the team of
Livingston and Evans, whose first collaboration for Hope had been *Monsieur
Beaucaire*. "Buttons and Bows" was a superb saddle-jogging song that
everyone knew would be a hit. When the time came to record it commercial-
ly, the industry was facing a strike. The day the musicians were to walk out,
Dinah Shore recorded the song with eight impatient musicians in a crouch,
ready to run for the door. Her version of the tune sold in the millions and
"Buttons and Bows" went on to win an Oscar for the best movie song the
following year.

While all this was happening at Paramount, there was trouble brewing in
Hope's radio paradise. Pepsodent, which had dumped *Amos 'n' Andy* at its
height, was getting tired of *The Bob Hope Show*. It was costing them more
money than a radio show ought to, partly because it traveled and traveling
shows were expensive to produce, and partly because of Hope's $10,000-
a-week salary. But there were other complaints: Hope's reluctance to reconvert more swiftly to peacetime radio, his occasional lapses in taste, his frenetic life that allowed him to dole out only a fraction of the time necessary to
produce an effective comedy product.

Insiders were not surprised to see the fight brought out into the open. Hope
announced that after the El Capitan studio premiere, he would take the
radio show on the road. On October 1, 1947, *Variety* blasted his first
show:

> Here's the epitome of radio's "sad saga of sameness." Apparently
> it's just too much to expect that Hope would veer an inch from his
> time-tested routine. His answer, it goes without saying, is: Why
> get out of the rut as long as there's pay dirt in it? And top pay dirt
> at that! By Hooper's count, too, Hope seems to be justified. His
> routine is apparently one of the things we fought the war for, like
> Ma's apple pie. Question simply is: Who's going to outlive the
> other, Hope or the listening public?

Hope had no time to heed this warning because he was, as usual, moving
fast. Professionally, he could smile at it when he landed on top of the ratings
in late October. And, personally, he was rewarded November 2 at a Friars
Club roasting in Los Angeles where Jack Benny, George Jessel, Al Jolson,
George Burns and a host of other peers paid tribute to him in their usual
outrageous manner.

On November 4, Hope took his radio show to Claremore, Oklahoma, to
observe what would have been Will Rogers' sixty-eighth birthday. Hope's
broadcast was remarkable, for his closing, to the amazement of his writing
staff and the ad agency people, was a sermonette on Hollywood politics.
Hope's weekly policy was to close his broadcast with a fervent plea to his
listeners to support some charity. During the war he had pitched war bonds
and patriotism, and in peacetime it was philanthropy. This night he tackled
the "red-baiting" of filmmakers:

> The only sad thing about coming to Claremore is that Will Rog-
> ers isn't here to say a few words about our troubled times with the

tolerance and humor that made him an all-time great. "I see by the papers," he might have said, "they've uncovered a few Reds out in Hollywood. Personally I've never preferred my politics in technicolor, and when boy meets girl in the movies, I like to have them riding on the Freedom Train."[6]

This is the longest public mention of the Hollywood Communist investigation Hope made, and there is reason to suspect that he would not have done this on the air without the protection of Rogers' image. As Hope had said more than once:

> . . . I'm usually selling a product everybody buys and I don't want to alienate my audience. It's pretty hard to do a comedy show and stay in the middle and please everybody when you're kicking current subjects around all the time. Will Rogers used to get away with it. But he was supposed to be a crackerbarrel type. I've got a lot of crackers in my barrel but there was only one Will Rogers.[7]

What brought the sponsor fight to media attention, however, was not this speech, but Hope's decision to accept the invitation from Buckingham Palace to attend the wedding of Princess Elizabeth to Philip Mountbatten and to headline a giant Command Performance gala at London's Odeon Theater. He found out he could transcribe parts of his radio program in advance— Bing Crosby was prerecording his Kraft show every week—and do the monologue portion of his show direct from overseas. Pepsodent bellowed its objections, asking Hope to cancel his plans. Hope refused. Pepsodent issued an ultimatum stating that unless he did so, the firm would "deprive him of his regular Tuesday night facilities on the National Broadcasting Company." The real issue, of course, was this: Hope wanted to continue crisscrossing the nation with his radio cast, doing personal appearances and radio broadcasts in front of big audiences rather than being limited to a Hollywood studio.

Jimmy Saphier hastily went to New York and the rumor mill began churning. The most persistent story had Hope leaving Pepsodent and NBC, joining the American Broadcasting Company, and, under Kraft Foods sponsorship, being slotted in a time period back to back with Bing Crosby. It was an ad-man's dream and it apparently worried Lever Brothers.

Meanwhile Bob and Dolores went off to their royal wedding and Command Performance. They threw a large party in their *Queen Mary* suite the day they sailed from New York. At one point Hope turned to Saphier and said, "Forget Luckman, Pepsodent and Lever Brothers. Make the best deal you can with anyone!" Then he turned back to the party.

This London jaunt was a high point in Hope's comedic life, partly because his ad libs with the King made world headlines. Hope's staff for the trip were Norman Siegel of Paramount publicity and Fred Williams, probably his all-time favorite gag writer.

At the Command Performance following the royal wedding, Hope charmed the audience that included King George and Queen Elizabeth, Princess Margaret, Denmark's Queen Ingrid and Roumania's King Michael. Princess Elizabeth and her Philip were honeymooning at Romsey in Southern England. The evening was a benefit for the Cinematograph Trade Benevolent (which corresponds to the Hollywood Motion Picture Relief Fund). Hope had brought with him, as a gift to the royal newlyweds from Hollywood's film colony, a richly embossed album whose pages contained stamps bearing likenesses of past and present movie stars, and the stars' autographs.

The Associated Press reported that the royal box shook with laughter over Hope's routine about how difficult it was for him to get tickets for the royal nuptials and how far away he had to stand to watch "four white mice pulling a gold-covered snuff box."

All afternoon at rehearsal Hope and Sir Laurence Olivier had been joking about nervousness and the protocol required for introductions to the King and Queen. Just as the King was approaching the Hopes that night, Bob looked across at Olivier whose eyes darted frantically down toward his crotch and back up again. Clearly Olivier was trying to alert Hope that his fly was open. Bob, half-suspecting a trick but still not entirely certain, broke his formalized receiving line smile and looked down at his fly. At which point Olivier stifled a triumphant smirk.

After the receiving line, Hope was scheduled to deliver the stamp album to Princess Margaret. Siegel handed it to Bob who opened it for Princess Margaret to see. As he was thumbing through the pages, the King looked over Margaret's shoulder.

"Look at him," the monarch said, "he's hurrying to get to his own picture."

"Why not? It's the prettiest," Hope replied.

"Is Bing's autograph there, too?" the King asked.

"Yes," said Hope. "But he doesn't write—he just makes three X's."

"Why three?" the King asked.

"He has a middle name, of course," reminded Hope.

The King laughed and handed the album to the Queen who said, "Elizabeth would never forgive me if we left this behind."

The following day newspapers in London, New York, and the world over, carried front-page items with headlines like KING MAKES "STRAIGHT MAN" OUT OF BOB HOPE. Even the stern-voiced Edward R. Murrow couldn't resist including the story in his communiqué from London.[8] That day Hope announced to a London press conference that he was flying to Germany to entertain American occupation forces.

Laudable as Hope's gesture was, Dolores felt her husband was pushing too hard. How close to actual physical collapse he was cannot now be judged, but those around him saw a man who should be in bed. However, at an Embassy party Hope had talked with Secretary of State George Marshall, whose remarks about the "forgotten" occupation forces in Europe affected Hope. In spite of his exhaustion, Hope did whirlwind shows in Frankfurt and Bremerhaven. He didn't stint with a voice that was tired and a throat that was irritated and slightly infected. Near the end of the Bremerhaven show his voice literally gave out and he couldn't talk. The audience recognized a much-too-tired trouper who could not go on and they stood up and cheered him.

Hope had to forgo his last two shows at Munich and Garmisch. He flew back to London and got ready for his Tuesday night radio broadcast with

British comedian Sid Fields. The next day Hope decided not to return on the steamship *America* with Dolores, but to fly back to New York for talks with Luckman.

The two men met over lunch at the Waldorf and temporarily settled the matter. Hope would not leave Lever Brothers, but as to his association with Pepsodent, that was another matter. Hope would travel with the radio show to a few college campuses, balanced with other shows from the El Capitan in Hollywood. Hope would probably have a new product to flog in the coming year, and he promised to overhaul the show.

Two days later, Hope surprised Dolores by meeting her ship's early-morning arrival. They stayed in New York long enough to see the highly touted Joe Louis–Joe Walcott prizefight at Madison Square Garden, and then returned to the Coast.

Before going to Palm Springs for a rest, Hope had a physical examination. Tom Hearn, Hope's personal physician and close friend, told him it was imperative that he restrict his activity to his radio program. The comedian, however, could not resist one more crack at the media. Twenty-five top press and syndicate representatives gathered at Paramount to hear him talk about his recent trip to England and Germany, to hear his opinions about America's posture in the world and to get advance news about his next picture. Hope's serious tone—on the heels of joking about King George joining him for the next *Road* picture—surprised almost everyone.

"The most important thing for us in America today is to maintain our friendship with the people of Europe. We must support the Marshall Plan. This is a wonderful Shangri-La we're living in over here and we should share it with the Europeans before other forces move in and make them our enemies."[9]

A reporter asked, "What's next on your schedule, Bob?"

"Rest," he said.

"What about the benefits you're announced to do—that war fund for Occidental College, the Shrine charity show, the boys home in Pomona—Mack was telling us—"

"Well, you know how it is—you can't let the kids down."

"If you're booked through Christmas and touring hospitals in January when will you rest?"

"I sneak a nap between three and six."

"Weren't we supposed to talk about your next picture?"

"Yeah. It's called *Sorrowful Jones* and it's a remake of *Little Miss Marker*, that starred Shirley Temple a few years back. Damon Runyon wrote it and Bob Welch is going to produce it. We've got Lucille Ball and we're looking for a little girl to play Martha Jane."

"We hear you're going serious in this one."

"Who snitched? Mack tell you? Well—why not? It's about time I did something a little different. It's still a comedy but I get to do some straight scenes for a change. Listen—if Dad can do it—"

If any doubt existed about Hope's value as a news source, it was dispelled at that press conference. The next day the media carried hard news stories describing Hope's world view rather than his plans for a new movie.

What had created Bob Hope as an authority on foreign policy? It was no sudden phenomenon, but rather a gradual awareness on the part of the media that Hope was a jester in high places, that he had access to important politicians, business leaders and the military. Although it cannot be said that in 1948 Hope had the ear of such important people, he was often in their company and was a sounding board for their philosophic views. Furthermore, no one—newsmaker or media—could overlook the power of a comedian who reached more than 30 million people every week.

This certainly has been an unusual experience flying into Berlin. It's the first time I was ever in a corridor and didn't have to worry about house detectives. . . .[1]

27. Christmas in Berlin

As the forties began to fade, television was like an underworld mobster trying to muscle in on showbusiness. Movie moguls and radio producers helplessly watched the little round picture tube gathering strength. Radio as the core of family entertainment was beginning to decay. *The New York Times* critic Jack Gould wasn't concerned that television would kill radio; he believed radio might kill itself. On September 19, 1948, he wrote:

> Can it overcome its repetition? Can it meet the incessant cries of its professional critics that it must develop "something new" and "something different" or, like vaudeville, slowly perish from familiarity?
> Mr. Hope, this season, has dispensed with the talents of Vera Vague and Jerry Colonna and is trying a less brash and more humble routine. . . .

To quicken audience interest, Hope hired Doris Day, whose recordings and Warner Brothers movies had swiftly lifted this former Les Brown vocalist to stardom. Bob had come close to hiring Doris the year before when he was auditioning bands. His brother Jack had brought him a recording of Les Brown's group playing "Sentimental Journey" with a vocal by Day. He ended up hiring Les, and as Brown explains it, "It wasn't that he didn't like Doris' singing; it was a question of Hope's loyalty to Langford, who had a drinking problem, and Hope, who is one of the few truly compassionate people in our business, didn't want to compound Langford's problems by firing her."[2]

Hope also hired comedienne Irene Ryan and a fresh young singer, Billy Farrell. Les, of course, handled the music and Hy Averback was his comedy announcer.

What Jack Gould termed Hope's "less brash and more humble routine" was a revamped monologue format billed as "Bob Hope's Swan's Eye View of the News," a sort of comedy Walter Winchell. The season premiere show of September 14 went like this:

Monologue

HY:	Denver, Colorado. The Western phase of the election campaigns will begin in Denver next week. President Truman will speak one night and will be followed two nights later by Governor Dewey.
HOPE:	Well, this campaign promises to be a hot battle . . . Truman has announced he's not going to leave the White House, and Dewey says he's moving in. That'll be a nice situation . . . I can just see the towels in the White House bathroom . . . marked "His" and "His." . . .
HY:	Berlin, Germany. Big four talks over removal of Soviet fuel and food blockade were on the verge of collapse as President Truman announced today that the American air-lift will continue to bring supplies into Berlin at all costs.
HOPE:	From what I hear . . . everybody over there blames the situation on the way the Russians have policed the city . . . You see, Berlin is divided into three zones . . . British, American and "Wait till it gets dark, Fritz, and we'll make a dash for it." . . . When the Americans do something, they do it thoroughly . . . Yesterday a B-29 flew in a hundred tons of chewing gum . . . and right behind it was a plane with a load of theater seats to stick it under. . . .[3]

Clearly, this new format traded heavily on Hope's increasing dependence on political humor. That does not mean, however, that politics dominated Hope's monologues or his sketches. First always in quantity among Hope gags was the self-deflating joke. Running second was the joke centered on the entertainment world. Politics ran third.

That was an all-important third in the fall of 1948. When Truman defeated Dewey, after every major newspaper and pollster in the nation predicted a Republican landslide, Hope sent a one-word telegram to the White House that said "Unpack." It was highly publicized and Hope was flattered to learn that Harry placed it under the glass top of his Oval Office desk. In his monologue Tuesday, Hope said:

> . . . Yessir, the Democrats did so well in that election, they're even coming out with a few new products named after the President . . . they've got a thing called the "Harry Truman Popsicle" . . . It's a frozen Republican on a stick. . . .[4]

Truman proved to be ideal humor material. In contrast to the patrician Roosevelt, Harry's "hellcat" image made him human, and Hope's Washington cronies informed him that Harry chuckled over the comedian's mild attacks on Truman's fights with his Republican Congress, his White House piano playing, and his squabbles with Washington media over Margaret's unfulfilled musical aspirations.

All these political gags pleased the radio critics, who liked the new "feel" of Hope's radio show. Hope's rating was a respectable 23.3, a notch or two behind Benny and *McGee*.

Interestingly enough, the same night of Hope's seasonal premiere, Tuesday, September 14, Milton Berle walked out on the stage of a New York television studio as master of ceremonies of the first *Texaco Star Theater*. And although there were only 47 television stations in the nation, and scarcely one million sets in use—mostly in the East—"Uncle Miltie" captured considerable media attention. The fact that it was Tuesday night—which to years of radio listeners was "Comedy Night" and to many people "Hope Night,"—and that Berle chose to lead off the program with a bullet-like monologue of one-line topical gags so akin to the Hope style fascinated many observers.

One of those curious observers was Associated Press reporter Bob Thomas who visited Hope at Toluca Lake. "What about television?" Thomas asked Hope.

"As a matter of fact," Hope said almost confidentially, "Hope Enterprises is already working on a few video ideas, along novelty lines, including a show for me."

"Weekly show?"

"No, that's too much. People could get tired of you that often. I'd like to do occasional shows, full hour shows. Imagine—imagine what you can do on television! Radio—people complain if you try to milk an audience with sight stuff. But with video everything is sight. You know how I sometimes throw the script during my radio show? Well, I could throw it at the audience and they could throw it back."

"You seem a bit cagey about television, Bob," Thomas said.

"I guess I'm still waiting to see how it goes."

"What do you think about Berle?"

"I think my material sounds pretty good in video," Hope cracked. "Seriously, I don't think I would work that hard. He's doing both a radio show and the Tuesday night television show for Texaco. And I understand he took a sizable cut in pay to do television. He must be nuts. If I could do both the radio—and television—at the same time—maybe—they tell me that Berle's entire budget for the Texaco show is $15,000. Is he working free?"

"I hear that General Motors wants to get you into television."

Hope looked steadily at Thomas and didn't answer. Then he said, "That's right."

"So—?"

"I don't have any time," he said.

"Are you being hassled by Paramount, or NBC, or Lever Brothers?"

"Uh—" said Hope, "not at all. I'm free to do anything I want. Listen, when they can pay me—"[5]

A few weeks later, Hope decided to take Dolores, Linda and Tony to Tahoe for Christmas. But a telephone call from Washington changed all that. Stuart Symington, Secretary of the Air Force and one of Hope's golf partners at Burning Tree, suggested strongly that President Truman would be grateful if Bob would headline a troupe of entertainers who would give up their holidays at home to go over to Germany and cheer up the GIs involved in Operation Vittles. Symington graphically described the cadre of Air Force pilots who were going without sleep to shuttle back and forth, every few minutes, from Wiesbaden to Templehof Airport bags of coal, sacks of flour and cans of food through a thin and perilous air corridor.

"I'll do it, Stu, but I'd like to do my radio show from Berlin. What do you think?"

The very next day doors began to open. Both NBC and Lever Brothers blessed the venture; the White House gave Hope a starter set for his guest star list, Vice President Alben Barkley and General Jimmy Doolittle. On his own, Hope enlisted Irving Berlin, newsman Elmer Davis, the beautiful Jinx Falkenburg with her husband Tex McCrary, a dozen Radio City Music Hall Rockettes and, of course, his own Swan radio gang minus Doris Day, who had a film commitment. In her place, Hope invited Jane Harvey and took Tony Romano to play accompaniments for her and for Dolores, who would also be there. Linda and Tony would have to stay home.

They traveled in Symington's Constellation and the spirit generated among the troupe en route to Berlin was extraordinary; Symington had given Hope the support he needed and was along on the trip himself, as were the omnipresent confidant Charley Cooley, Jimmy Saphier, radio producer Al Capstaff, and three writers, Mort Lachman, Si Rose and Larry Gelbart. They would be using an Air Force band for musical accompaniments in Berlin.

Their first stop, for refueling only, was Burtonwood, a British air base where the shuttle planes were flown back for rehabilitation, repair and rest, after ther nonstop runs over Germany. It wasn't more than a few minutes before they discovered how serious the morale problem was there. These GIs were the heroes behind the scene in this highly publicized mercy airlift, and they were suffering from intense British resentment locally. Several officers asked Hope to do an impromptu show. Hope couldn't turn them down, and besides, the rehearsal time was useful.

At Wiesbaden, the GIs had been waiting in a big, drafty hall for several hours and let out an earsplitting war whoop when the Rockettes tap-tapped out onto the stage in their abbreviated tights.

After shows at Nuremburg and Frankfort, there was a Christmas Eve party hosted by General Lucius Clay who informed Hope, sadly, that decreasing visibility and heavy snows might prohibit the entire troupe from reaching Berlin in time for the radio show the next day. So Bob hugged Dolores and got into an airlift plane with Al Capstaff, Hy Averback and crates of canned milk and corn, to fly the two-hour ground-hugging, wing-scraping corridor route to Templehof in the heart of West Berlin.

Early Christmas morning, the rest of the cast managed to hitchhike down the Corridor, and that afternoon, one of the cruelest days of that winter, they entertained at the Tatania Palast Theater, an old vaudeville house. Hope opened with a joke that referred to the local black market and it produced an almost deafening roar:

How do you do, everybody. This is Bob (here in Berlin to entertain the men in the airlift) Hope saying I'm here with Swan Soap in lots . . . meet me tonight in Potsdamer Platz . . .

As we arrived over Berlin several Soviet planes started to buzz us, but the first Russian pilot took one look at me and said, "They're okay, look at the hammer head—and sickle" . . .

And the people here really know me. Whenever I walk down the streets of Berlin, everybody follows me yelling and cheering. Any of you fellows know what *Schweinehund* means?[6]

Before the show ended, Staff Sergeant Robert Kelso of Armed Forces Radio rushed up to Hope and begged him to come to his radio station after the show and talk to all the GIs who couldn't see him in person. Hope, preoccupied, brushed Kelso aside with, "Yeah—yeah—I'll try to do that."

That night the Clays gave a party in their West Berlin quarters for the Hopes, the Irving Berlins, Symington and Secretary of War Kenneth Royall, and U.S. ambassador to the Soviet Union Walter Bedell Smith and his wife.

That party broke up after midnight and, heading back to their hotel, Bob reached into his pocket and produced a business card that Sergeant Kelso had thrust at him backstage at the Tatania Palast. "Where is this?" he asked his GI driver.

"Not too far, sir."

"Wanna try it?"

"At this hour, Bob?" asked Dolores.

"Go," he said, and they drove off. Twenty minutes later, on an unlighted street, the staff car chugged to a stop, out of fuel. They trudged the last few blocks on foot, through snow-covered passageways, some still littered with rubble, helped along by the driver's flashlight. Finally they arrived at the address and inside Kelso sat hunched over a control panel and turntable playing records and talking. He turned around and almost fell out of his chair. "Oh no—no—" he said, "I don't believe this one." Then he turned back to the mike and faded down the recording. "Hey, guys! Have I got news for you! It's Bob Hope. I'm turning the mike over to him!"

Hope started talking. Kelso poured Dolores some coffee and slipped away. The staff car driver vanished, too, to find another car. The Hopes were absolutely alone. Bob kept his monologue going, gesturing all the while to Dolores to find out what was happening, but she couldn't find anyone anywhere. Twenty minutes went by and finally Kelso returned. "Nice of you to come back," cracked Hope. Kelso had run off to wake up the other disc jockeys at Armed Forces Radio because "Who would believe me if I told them Bob Hope dropped in on me at two-thirty in the morning the day after Christmas?"[7]

28. "We'll Move Your Pin on the Map"

Four thousand miles west of Berlin, people lined up in the glitter of Times Square to see Bob Hope's latest movie, *The Paleface*. It had opened a few days before Christmas and Howard Barnes wrote, "Rarely has he been so funny." Bosley Crowther was less enchanted, calling it "just another amusing runthrough of well-worn slapstick routines by a boy who has bunions on his bunions from the number of times he's run the course."[2]

The film, however, would become Hope's biggest movie moneymaker, grossing about $7 million and entrenching his popularity as one of the nation's most watched entertainers.

Aside from its Hit Parade ballad, "Buttons and Bows," this technicolor film caught Hope at the peak of his form as a visual comic. It was probably Hope's most accomplished "reluctant hero" performance, his braggadocio set against a classic Western format with gunfights, screaming Indians, hair-raising chases and tough-talking outlaws; Hope's appealing slapstick as he bumbled through this sacred American genre was exactly right for the public at that particular time. Lucky for Hope, too, because what he was currently giving his radio public was becoming less and less appealing. His Hooper and Crossley ratings at midseason showed that he was trailing *Fibber McGee,* Bergen, Benny and Allen.

That rating gap was one reason Bob was anxious to take his radio cast out to the American people in another whirlwind cross-country tour. With hardly time to catch his breath from the Berlin airlift junket, he started out again.

He nearly lost the tour's important "added attraction," Doris Day. She didn't like the money she was offered, and only when Hope agreed to pay her $2,500 above her regular radio salary did she agree to join Irene Ryan, Bill Farrell, Hy Averback and Les Brown.

The thirty-six-city marathon began in Texas, made a big Southern city sweep, traveled north as far as Boston, then back across the country ending in Oakland, California. True, Hope wanted to get closer to the people, but he also needed cash. He had to cover his taxes and put up his share of his next movie project, *Where Men Are Men* (the fourth remake of Harry Leon Wilson's novel *Ruggles of Red Gap*).

Surprising no one, the tour was an enormous success. In terms of revenue it netted Hope $700,000, which meant that his personal daily share was about $11,000. He was enjoying himself, and his appreciation of Doris grew. He would later say:

> I used to call her "Jut-Butt"—I'd say, "You know, J.B., we could play a nice game of bridge on your ass." A truly great body and

she was wonderful about taking my kidding. I always called her "J.B." on the radio show but only the band knew what the initials stood for.[3]

Hope said that Doris, like Judy Garland, had "natural talent." He lauded her comedy timing, the way she handled a ballad, and especially her smile. "She has that rare quality of making people feel good by just walking on—whatever she radiates lifts them." Hope was shocked when Les Brown musicians told him Doris was a nervous wreck most of the time.

The weekly broadcasts from Hollywood's El Capitan theater made Doris excessively nervous. She later wrote in her book *Doris Day: Her Own Story*,

> My overriding memory of these shows was how much time I spent in the toilet. I had by then developed a real aversion to live radio, and before every performance one end of me or the other would erupt. Bob would be out on the stage warming up the audience and I would be flat out in my dressing room, moaning to my agent and the producer that I couldn't go on, that I had to be taken off the show, that I couldn't do it, that I couldn't go out there and face all those people—and sing! . . .[4]

Doris had mixed feelings about the Hope whistle-stop tours, calling them "frightening, educational, exhausting, enjoyable, depressing" experiences.

During that six-week swing, they hit a different city every day and on some days, when a matinee was included, they might hit two. It was winter and Doris wrote in her book, "We often flew through storms and turbulence that had me praying more than once. I developed a chronic fear of flying that haunts me to this day."

But Doris learned a great deal from Hope about timing and delivery. Hope was, to her, "a joyous man to be with. There's something quite pixie about him, his mischievous face, the way his teeth take over his face when he smiles. And the way he swaggers across the stage, kind of sideways, beaming at the audience." Doris found him naturally funny, "in fact, funnier than when he's restricted to his writers' material."

When that tour ended in early February, the script for *Where Men Are Men*, now titled *Fancy Pants*, was still not ready. Hope played golf (naturally), did some radio guest appearances and made an important decision about his career. Saphier had told Bob that CBS wanted him to quit his ten-year association with NBC and join a few other defectors to CBS—Benny, Amos and Andy, Bergen, even Crosby. CBS was expanding, offering better money deals, long-term contracts, better time slots, promises of television shows. But Hope, though concerned about his lag in the ratings and certainly interested in more money, decided not to budge. What he did not announce was that his new exclusive contract with NBC included the network's commitment to bankroll some future projects of Hope Enterprises, and promises to promote all of his efforts for them more intensely. And NBC was talking seven figures in their plan to retain his services for television.

Time and *Newsweek* both had recently labeled Hope a newly arrived millionaire based on his radio and movie incomes alone. Actually, his invest-

ments had left him cash-poor. When he learned *Fancy Pants* couldn't roll
until late spring, Hope told Shurr to book him another series of one-nighters
with Doris, Les and the others in his radio cast. For two grueling weeks in
April, he did a lightning tour of twenty-one cities in fifteen states in sixteen
days, doing straight personal appearance shows, several benefits, a couple of
golf exhibitions and two Swan radio broadcasts. But Uncle Sam got his money on March 15.

Fancy Pants finally came before the cameras in June, directed by the
inventive George Marshall. Bob and his costar, the multitalented and convi-
val Lucy Ball, were the toast of Paramount in those days, because *Sorrowful
Jones* was garnering better than average critical notices nationwide for both.
Unexpectedly, there was critical praise for Hope's sentimental scenes with
little Mary Jane Saunders, the appealing moppet in the film. The Paramount
front-office boys approached Hope with the idea that he recite the Gettys-
burg Address in *Fancy Pants* just the way Charles Laughton had delivered
the speech in his screen version. Hope said, "When I suggested that a few
months ago, they laughed at me. You know what changed their minds?
They've been reading the *Sorrowful Jones* reviews that say Hope can really
act. Do you know how tough it is for me to try being serious? People look at
me and they automatically start to laugh. Working with that kid gave me a
chance to do something serious without being too obvious."

During this time, Bing and Bob got involved in an oil venture. Hope had
met oilman Will Moncrief at a Fort Worth benefit, who invited him to put
up $50,000 to tie up a few thousand acres of oil-speculation property near
North Snyder in Scurry County, West Texas. Hope asked Bing to go along.
Their first drop ended in failure; the drilling brought up salty water. Hope
wanted out, but Bing said he would sink another $50,000 if Hope would. On
August 9, it became for them "the road to oil." Six miles northeast of their
first site, at Huckabee, they hit a gusher capable of producing 100 barrels an
hour and promising the partners close to $3.5 million apiece.[5]

Hope's oil euphoria lasted a few days until he took a fall. The *Fancy Pants*
script called for him as Humphrey, an English actor-turned-butler in the Old
West, to learn to ride a horse. Lucy was to teach Bob how to ride, not a real
horse, but on a wooden barrel contraption rigged to buck and roll. Hope
nervously agreed when he watched a stunt extra test it. He was helped up
onto the wooden horse but when it began to buck, he slipped, pitched sidewards, and fell. He lay on his back with his eyes closed, unable to move.

He was carefully raised onto a stretcher and rushed to nearby Presbyterian
Hospital where the doctors at first believed he might be paralyzed. By the
time Tom Hearn arrived, the shock and spasm had lessened. There were no
broken bones, just badly bruised muscles.

A steady procession of agents, writers, celebrities (a record number)—and
lawyers—trooped to Hope's bedside during his week-long hospital stay. The
most persistent rumor was that the comedian would sue Paramount for some
astronomical amount. Hope was too shrewd a businessman for that, but also
too shrewd a publicist to resist teasing studio boss Henry Ginsberg in a way
that brought Hope, the studio and *Fancy Pants,* thousands of dollars in
media attention—an open letter to Ginsberg explaining his hospital bill:

If your economy-minded production heads had used a real horse instead of putting me over a broken-down barrel, I would not have landed on my back on Stage 17 with an injury which you will see from the bill, was not cheap . . .

When I woke up in the hospital four nurses were standing over me, a doctor as feeling my pulse, and another doctor was busy on the phone checking with the Bank of America on how much we could go for . . .

The X-rays were a little confusing at first. My chest kept showing up the figures 24.2. I had forgotten to tell them I had my last year's Hooper rating tattooed over my heart. The more X-rays they took the more the doctor looked worried. It seems they couldn't find much wrong with me and the doctor had promised his wife a new mink coat. He finally got desperate one day when he thought I was asleep I heard him scream at the X-ray people: "Find something even if it's on another patient."

But I could see that I had them over a barrel at this point—if the word is not too sensitive for you—and with one longing look at my gall bladder, the doctors allowed me to go home.

The remainder of the bill will be self-explanatory, although I imagine the occupational therapy—$1,400—may be a little out of line. You see, Henry, the occupation I picked up was horseplaying, and we both know it's not a poor man's pastime. Please understand that this puts me in a deep debt to you, almost as deep as you are to the doctors.

> Yours in our great work,
> Bob Hope

Hope opened his new radio season that year, his twelfth on the air for Lever Brothers (and his last for that company) in El Segundo, California, on September 21. His monologue addressed the subject of America's fastest growing preoccupation:

. . . But I'm glad to be back on radio. It seems to have so much more to offer than television . . . things like money . . . but I like television . . . I have one of those sets with a screen so small you have to sit right next to it. Last night during dinner Hopalong Cassidy lassoed three of my boiled potatoes . . . and all during dinner I had to keep Milton Berle's hand out of my soup. . . .[7]

More and more Americans were hoisting TV antennae up on their rooftops, or crowding around store windows on Saturday nights to laugh at Sid Caesar and Imogene Coca in Admiral's *Broadway Revue*. This was smart comedy mounted with taste and elegance and Hope believed for the first time that this medium could be his "room," too.

He was interested enough to tell Saphier to reopen discussions with General Motors. His timing, as usual, was impeccable. Dr. George Gallup, head of the Institute of Public Opinion, had just released results of a poll taken to find out who and what made the nation laugh. Three thousand personal interviews took a cross section of men and women over twenty-one, asking rich, poor, young and old the question: Of all the comedians you have heard or seen perform on the stage, on the radio or television, or in the movies—which one do you think is the funniest? The following story was printed from coast to coast:

> Princeton, N.J., Sept. 18. All America loves a laugh, and almost every American has his own idea as to who is the funniest laugh-maker ever in the business.
>
> But the reigning comedian, in the public's mind, is Bob Hope.
>
> He outdistances his closest rivals in the American Institute of Public Opinion's first "comedy star derby"—with stage, screen, radio or television stars all included—by a commanding ratio of almost 2½ to 1. Next come Milton Berle, Jack Benny, Red Skelton and Fibber McGee and Molly—all close on the heels of each other. . . .[8]

Milton Berle's sudden rise in popularity was starting its second season, for which the critics had dubbed him "Mr. Television." Add to this Hope's less than commanding supremacy in those parts of the nation where television viewing was densest—the Northeast and Middle Atlantic states—and the message became clearer about the power of the video image.

Hope could not help but be impressed with the dramatic leap in stations—127—now beaming signals, or the fact that programs could now be seen coast to coast. Saphier told him that the latest Commerce Department figures showed over 2 million sets now in use.

But Hope was also concerned about his movie career. It was clear to him that some motion picture houses, in spite of having tried Screeno, giveaways, twofers and triple bills to lure customers, would begin going dark. It was also clear that fewer movies would be made, that the big investment would be in epics and super-ballyhooed spectaculars with special effects that might draw people away from the tube. Hope feared that his December release, *The Great Lover,* might suffer from this spreading apathy. His fears were reduced when *Motion Picture Daily* announced he was reigning king of the box office. He liked the feeling of being the number one guy in pictures, and people reacted wildly when he and Dolores stepped out of their limousine in front of the Pantages Theater the night of the *Twelve O'Clock High* premiere on December 20.

Hope, who hated premieres, was there because it was the dramatization of Brigadier General Frank Armstrong's real-life efforts to shape heroes out of his 8th Air Force wing during World War II in England. Hope admired Armstrong when they met in England in 1943 and knew Armstrong would be at the premiere, as would General Curtis LeMay and Hope's pal Stu Symington, who was en route to Alaska.

At the after-premiere supper party at Romanoff's, Hope sat next to Armstrong who talked about his Alaskan Command and said impulsively, "Why don't you fly with me tomorrow and say Merry Christmas to the boys up there?"

"Not this year, Frank. I left my kids last year and I can't do it again."

The next day Symington telephoned Hope's office. "Stuart my boy," said Hope, "I thought you'd be on your way up north by now."

"I had some last-minute things here in Los Angeles." There was a pause. "Bob, how about saying yes to that invitation from Frank."

"I don't want to leave the kids. You grabbed me last year, remember?"

"Why not take the kids?"

From a distant part of the house, Hope could hear a voice screaming, "Yes, Daddy, yes!" and he knew Linda was listening in on the line again.

He yelled, "Dolores!" and she suddenly appeared in the doorway of his dressing room with Linda and Tony jumping up and down. "Tell him it'll be thrilling," she said.[9]

Hope told Symington he would bring Linda and Tony, but Nora and Kelly were not ready for that yet. Symington slyly told Hope that Armstrong had not left for Alaska either and was prepared to fly them in his own B–17. A few moments later Armstrong called and said, "I'll meet you at four o'clock at the Hughes Aircraft runway."

It was noon and Hope realized that he had less than four hours to organize an entertainment unit. Cowboy singer Jimmy Wakely agreed to go. So did Patty Thomas and Les Brown piano player Geoff Clarkson. Bob asked Dolores if she would sing for her trip. She said yes, but what would she wear?

Next he called senior writer Norman Sullivan and said, "Norm, you're going to have to put next Tuesday's show together without me. I'm going to Alaska."

There was a pause, and then Sullivan said, "Very well, we'll move your pin on the map."

Hope laughed and said, "I'll call you tonight from Seattle for some deep-freeze jokes."

At three-fifteen Hope was packed and standing in the downstairs entry-way waiting for Dolores. Mildred MacArthur had come over to help Dolores get everyone organized and packed.

"Dolores!" Bob yelled. "We're leaving."

Mildred came to the top of the curving stairway and looked helpless. Bob knew from that look Dolores wasn't anywhere near ready.

"Dolores! Get down here—now! There's a B–17 parked on a runway wait-ing for us and we're going to be on it. I mean right now!"

Mildred MacArthur said that in all the years she knew the Hopes, Bob was never madder than he was at that moment. As he headed for the driver's side of the car, Dolores dashed out, pushed her luggage into the back seat and the car sped off.

Armstrong's B–17 dropped the Hopes off in Seattle and Symington's Con-stellation picked them up the next morning for the trip to Anchorage. It was twenty-eight below and they had to make an instrument landing in dense fog. But after their planeside welcome and the Hope children had been taken to the Armstrongs', the troupe went to the base hospital for their first show. They did 12 shows in three days, and ate five or six Christmas dinners.

Hope never failed to convulse his audience of "crease-faced, red-eyed, purple-nosed" GIs when he grabbed the mike and jutted his chin: "Be happy, you guys, be proud—brace up—you know who you are, don't you? God's Frozen People!"

At one of the last stops, Eielson Air Base, the little troupe sat down for their third Christmas meal of the day and Bob noticed quite a few uniformed men standing against the messhall walls staring at them.

"What's with these guys?" Hope asked an officer. "Don't they get to eat?"

"They've eaten, Bob. The men up here drew lots to get into the recreation hall to see you and they lost—but they get to watch you eat."

"Hell, that's no good," Hope said. "Have you got a good electrician on the base?" When the electrician arrived, Hope showed him how to turn the telephone instrument on the wall into a public address unit. In a short time he was doing a monologue.

Between that impromptu show and the last one for the Navy at Kodiak, Hope developed a bad cold and lost his voice. Even with a whisper mike he could hardly be heard. That night, when he climbed aboard the Symington plane to go home, he said to the steward, "Just find me some soup and some sleeping pills."

I want to thank the thousands who wrote letters about the first show . . . also the three who mailed them . . . No . . . I did get about five thousand letters, the FBI's going over them now. . . .[1]

29. Easter Sunday

The second half of the twentieth century was barely three days old when Southern California was gripped by subfreezing temperatures. Hope was still trying to shake the cold he had picked up in Alaska, so after meeting with his writers to set material for the next radio show, he headed for Palm Springs to recuperate in the sun. No matter what happened, he intended to play in the Crosby tournament the following week.

But it wasn't any warmer in the desert. In fact, fruit growers were smudging their groves night and day hoping to salvage part of their crop.

Elsewhere in the nation, and in the world, things were equally chilly. A cold chill was spreading from Europe to the whole world because of a confirmed report that the Soviets had tested a second A-bomb in Siberia.

On a more personal front, Lever Brothers was starting to act cool toward Hope and his show, partly because of his plunge in the ratings to 13.9, which was half of what Benny was getting. More distressing, *Fibber McGee* (who followed Hope on Tuesdays) had a higher rating. Finally, Lever Brothers still rankled at Hope's originations from colleges and military bases, which they felt were unnecessary and too costly.

Saphier saw the end coming and began casting his net for new sponsor ids. But a more pressing matter was television. So while Hope was trying to ouch up his game before going up to Pebble Beach, and cursing the chilly ain that kept him from the golf course, Saphier brought Hugh Davis to see im. Davis, executive VP of Foote, Cone and Belding in Chicago, and a ongtime friend of Hope and Saphier in New York, had a new offer from the Frigidaire Division of General Motors. When Hugh thought Hope was in a mellow mood, he said, "What about television, Bob?"

"Naw, I don't think so," said Bob. "I'm busy enough. Besides, I don't know much about that medium."

"What would it take to change your mind?"

"You can't pay me enough."

"What do you want?"

"Fifty thousand," Hope said coolly, knowing the figure was beyond any being contemplated, let alone paid to any performer in TV. Davis nod-ed.[2]

The next day one of Hope's favorite gag writers, Fred Williams, came down and the four of them played golf before it rained. After Saphier and Davis left, Bob and Fred worked on the retakes of *Fancy Pants*.

At about eight-fifteen, Bob and Fred decided to drive up to Los Angeles. They got into the Cadillac feeling mellow. Hope was at the wheel.

At Beaumont, Hope turned onto Highway 60 toward Riverside and, as usual, pushed the gas pedal to the floor. The big car raced ahead at 75 miles in hour, all alone on an asphalt pavement slick from rain and greasy in patches where the growers were smudging the orange trees.

Hope does not recall whether or not he jerked the wheel, but the car swerved suddenly, slid sideward, hit a ditch, and rolled over like a stunt car before slamming into a tree. Both doors opened on impact and the men were hurled out in opposite directions into ankle-deep mud. Hope said later:

> I remember seeing little sparks. I remember how my neck jerked and how I thought, "This is it. I'm going to die." I remember everything that happened til I got hit on the head and blanked out.

Fred never lost consciousness. He felt a sharp pain in his left leg but realized he had to get Bob and put distance between them and the Cadillac in case it caught fire.

As Fred limped toward Bob and saw that the comedian, having regained consciousness, was trying to get up, he went to the side of the road and flagged down an approaching car. Tires screeched and the car stopped. Sam Crother, the driver, murmured, "Holy shit!" when he sighted the muddied Williams, and laughed when he saw the equally muddy Bob Hope trying out his golf swing.

Crother drove them to Riverside Community Hospital. Fred's injury was only a bad bruise and he stood ghoulishly over Hope while he was being examined.

When the doctor came back with the developed X-rays he said, "You're a lucky man. By rights you should be dead. Anyway you have a fractured clavicle and you won't be playing golf for a while."

A *Riverside Press and Enterprise* reporter stuck his head around the corner. "It *is* you. What happened?"

Hope described the accident, concluding with "It's all right though. The thing I hate is that I'll have to miss the Crosby. That's what I went down to the Springs for," he said wistfully. "I went to practice up on my golf. I was just in my prime, too."[3]

The accident altered more than Hope's golf plans. Since he would have to be in a cast for several weeks and strapped up for a month after that, he could not make a movie; but he could still stand on a stage and tell jokes. He asked Shurr to book him on an Eastern public appearance tour with the radio gang, and Lever Brothers went along, vowing this was the last time they would pick up such a tab.

A few days after the accident, Hope got a call from Hugh Davis in Chicago. "Would you consider doing one television show for $40,000?" asked Davis.

"For myself?"

"Yes."

"You mean they'll supply the guest stars and the rest of the production?"

"Yes."

"You got it. I'll have Jimmy call you right back." Jimmy worked out a package deal of four additional shows for a total $150,000. Frigidaire had an existing agreement with CBS that could present a problem because of Hope's existing contracts, but that was smoothed out and Hope's TV debut was set on NBC for Easter Sunday.

Meanwhile, sandwiched in between his usual heavy personal appearance schedule and his regular radio show schedule was an extraordinary return to vaudeville. He signed a contract for $50,000 a week to appear at the Paramount Theater as the stage attraction with a movie called *Captain China*. Aware that the motion picture business had taken a nose dive, Hope was determined this engagement would not be ordinary. To insure that, he hired Jane Russell and the Les Brown band.

To sell this important date, Hope summoned the full phalanx of press agents and publicity support. Hope relied on publicity people the same way he did on gag writers; he hired as many as he needed for the job, and he knew them by their strengths. Mack Millar was the mainstay, a crusty, unrelenting pro who blustered his way from coast to coast, extracting pro-Hope stories and items from reporters who respected Millar because he always delivered his client and because he knew the territory. Then there was Fran Liberman, young but extremely intelligent, tasteful, witty and discreet. His specialties were the wire services, the entertainment trade papers and the tricky job of working with columnists like Hedda and Louella. Both Rufus Blair and Norm Siegel of Paramount's publicity staff were superb writers and Hope trusted NBC's highly regarded publicity chief Syd Eiges to cover him with his top writers and photographers. Then, too, Hope had special people all over the country, like Arnold Van Leer in Boston and Bob Bixler in Dallas, who could do a publicity job for a day, a week or a month.

But Hope himself was the master publicist. He never refused a request for an interview, talked on the telephone for hours with columnists in distant cities and had almost daily conversations with people like *Variety*'s Army Archerd and *Chicago Sun*'s Irv Kupcinet. And it paid off.

Mack outdid himself publicizing the Paramount show. Besides his usual blanket of handouts (column items, feature stories, jokes and photographs of Hope and Russell), he dreamed up a promotional tie-in with the Hearst-owned *New York Journal-American* (which carried Hope's daily column). The paper agreed to sponsor "The Laugh A Day Contest" in which the public would submit favorite jokes, gag lines or funny twists to topical events and they all would be judged by Hope, Russell and Arthur Godfrey. Godfrey, who had become a buddy of Hope's, agreed to plug the contest and announce the winners on his daily radio program.

En route to New York, Hope had two things to do in Washington. One was to receive from his pal Stuart Symington the Air Force's highest commendation. The other was to emcee his favorite dinner, the White House Correspondents' annual banquet toasting and roasting the President. That got better than average press coverage, not only for what he said to and about Truman, but for what he said in his own behalf. One of the guests at that banquet was Charles Luckman, whose sudden departure from Lever Brothers had caused speculation in top business circles. Hope hardly ever allowed himself feelings of animosity, but on this occasion, Hope grinned and said to his black-tie audience: "I hear Lever Brothers are behind a Broadway show called *Where's Charley?* Luckman did not laugh. After dinner, Hope told those around him, "I was only kidding." But he wasn't.

In New York, Paramount Theater's manager Bob Weitman told Hope that business in Times Square was rotten, so Bob shouldn't think any less of himself for not being able to fill that cavernous movie house. This was like dropping the gauntlet at the comedian's feet. He *had* to show Lever, Paramount, NBC—and General Motors—he was still the undisputed "star of stars."

What no one could understand was why Bob Hope would be willing to subject himself to six shows a day for two weeks. That meant he would be on stage for 45 minutes each time for a total of 84 shows. One person who sought the answer was *Herald-Tribune* critic Otis Guernsey, Jr. When Guernsey was escorted backstage at four-thirty the first day, Hope had already done three shows. He was sprawled on a cot in his dressing room "like a king at a levee, in the attitude of self-satisfied exhaustion." George Raft, who had just executed a soft-shoe dance with Hope onstage, and one-time screen idol Jack LaRue were sitting nearby talking to the comedian, along with half a dozen others. It was hard to distinguish who was talking.

"There was a line outside at four A.M., I hear."

"I don't believe that, but the house was jammed shortly after eight when we opened the doors," said Weitman. "We're already 2,000 ahead of *Samson and Delilah*."

"We keep this up we may knock this building over," said Hope.

Guernsey waited, anxious to ask Hope some questions. Finally he had his chance. "I've been figuring out that you'll be on stage here at the Paramount 56 times as long as you are for your radio show in the same two-week period. Why? It can't be for mere cash."

"You're right. Matter of fact, I'll work harder in one day here at the Paramount than a whole week of one-night stands when I leave here. And I'll make a lot more money on the road."

"Then why?"

"First of all, I love it. Or I wouldn't do it. You have to understand the full benefit of these two weeks won't be apparent until it's over. See, I started in this sort of racket, and I feel that you've always gotta go back to where you came from, every so often, to sharpen up."

"You? Need to sharpen up?"

"Sure. I haven't done a regular stretch before a paying audience in eleven years. This audience—it varies from show to show—there's a lot of ribbing at the first ones but it begins to soften up as the day goes on. At the end of my run I should have improved my comedy timing and everything else about the act under all kinds of conditions. You know, Otis, there is nothing quite as stimulating as the atmosphere of a stage job."[4]

Another of Broadway's observers, Alton Cook, covered the Paramount opening:

> Bob has mellowed considerably in the decade he has been away from Broadway stages. He no longer is so strenuously eager to please. His charm has increased with his new casual air.
>
> The test is that he stays on the stage without much assistance for 40 whole minutes, a very long time for anyone to remain the life of the party and get away with it.[5]

What was most significant to Hope was that he broke the theater's box-office record with receipts of $141,000 the first week.

By the second week, Hope was flying high. His mood prompted Leonard Goldenson, then head of United Paramount Theaters, and Bob Weitman to ask Hope if he would spearhead the national fund drive for Cerebral Palsy.

"There are a half-million kids and adults afflicted with this thing, Bob," said Weitman, trailing Hope who walked toward his bathroom.

"I don't see how I can give it the time it deserves," said Hope.

"If you would see those kids," pleaded Leonard. "They need us—need you—need hope, if you'll pardon the pun, and we'll collect the money. Your drive and exposure would give us a boost."

"Okay. What do you want me to do?"

"You can start by going with me to P.S. 135 over on Fifty-first Street tomorrow for some publicity. They've got special classes for palsied kids there. Bob, to say I'm grateful—no, to say I'm blessed is more like it."

Hope at first resented this bulldozer approach. But next day when he went to the school for publicity pictures, and four-year-old Alice White dragged her heavy braces over to his side, and five-year-old Terry Wetzelberg climbed up on his lap, he was hooked. So much so that he ordered Mack Millar to include Cerebral Palsy appearances throughout the remainder of the spring tour. He did CP shows at Rochester, New York; Cincinnati, Ohio; Owensboro, Kentucky, and in three different Kansas cities. For these shows he was joined by Marilyn Maxwell (replacing Jane Russell, who had movie commitments). He also hired a young singer named Antonio Benedetti whom he had heard singing in a nightclub, and that was the beginning of Tony Bennett's career.[6]

After resting at home for a few days following the tour, Hope flew back to New York to rehearse for his long-awaited television debut. The cast, assembled at NBC's refurbished-for-television New Amsterdam Roof, included Bea Lillie, Douglas Fairbanks, Jr., Dinah Shore, dancer Hal LeRoy, novelty pianist Maurice Rocco, singer Bill Hayes and the Mexico City Boys Choir. Max Liebman, who had created the successful Sid Caesar–Imogene Coca series, was producer, and Hal Keith the director of what was being called a *Star Spangled Revue*.

It would be a 90-minute program, telecast live to 27 stations of the NBC network and kinescoped for rebroadcast a week later to 18 other NBC affiliated stations west of the Rockies. Frigidaire had arranged with its dealerships in 18 top markets to take two and three newspaper ads in the Easter Sunday papers. NBC alone had spent $25,000 on publicity and promotion and were confidently expecting to draw the largest viewing audience in TV history.

Of the many "opening nights" in Hope's career to date, this was the rough one. "I couldn't believe how nervous and jumpy I was. You'd have thought I was some green kid the way I reacted. I worried about my material and especially the pacing of it. I knew this was a quite different medium from either radio or film but I hadn't figured it out yet."[7] He was jittery enough to think he could use an extra bit of luck, so he telephoned Miss Hughes at his Toluca Lake office and asked her to send him by the next airplane the black silk topper he had worn in *Roberta*. In the opening sequence of the telecast he would appear in white tie and tails.

Hope's opening monologue, if not the snappy stuff that tickled Paramount audiences a few weeks before, provided a foretaste of the commercial drum-beating that would permeate his broadcast comedy for the next decade:

> What a fine looking audience . . . (*looks audience over and counts with his fingers*) . . . Oh, excuse me . . . I thought I was still at the Paramount working on a percentage . . . Now ladies and gentlemen, doing this big special Easter show on television is a high point for me . . . for years I've been on radio . . . you remember radio . . . blind television . . . but I want to tell you that Frigidaire has been a brick about the whole thing . . . especially, where the money is concerned . . . ah, the money . . . are you listening, Washington? . . . Yes, Frigidaire has been very generous with me . . . they told me I could have my salary any way I wanted it . . . big or little cubes. . . .[8]

Hope's new top-hat image, the presence of top show business names in an expensive, classy format, and the choice of Easter Sunday for broadcasting all had a cumulative effect on Hope's debut. It wasn't the material as much as the personality of the star, the publicity buildup, the showcase and a general realization on the part of everyone involved that television had broken out of its shell. The single show cost four times the figure set for the entire production budget of Milton Berle's top-rated weekly show.

When the 90-minute show went off the air and the critics hit their type-writers, opinions were divided. Without exception, Hope's $40,000 salary and the cost of the production were mitigating criteria for the judgments.

John Crosby, in the *New York Herald Tribune* on April 11, 1950, called Hope's "invasion" of television "historic," because most stars, he said, were staying away from "the dreadful thing." He wrote that in the light of the unprecedented production costs, the debut "fell rather seriously short of expectations," but he conceded it was "a pretty good show." Crosby's major criticism was as follows:

> Throughout the show, Hope appeared to be trying to find some middle ground between movie technique and radio, to discover, in short, what television consisted of exactly.
> He never quite succeeded. . . .

The *Journal-American*'s John Lester found Hope "petrified with fear," while Ben Gross in the widely read *Daily News* called Hope "telegenic, easy-going and graceful, his personality, somewhat subdued yesterday, is much better suited to TV than to radio." *Variety* was generally disappointed both in the comedy and Frigidaire's commercials. Harriet Van Horne in the *World-Telegram and Sun* praised Hope's "showmanship" and felt the success of the show rested in his personality.[9]

A week later, on April 16, 1950, *New York Times* critic Jack Gould wrote a rhapsodic review, which NBC immediately used in full-page ads in the media. Everyone came off looking good, especially Hope:

> What the viewer saw was the true Hope of the old "Roberta" and Palace days, the master of ceremonies who was relaxed and leisurely and never in a hurry. Here was the polished clown in the tradition. His impishness had the light touch, and his gags were sent across the footlights with the deftness of deliveries. To the audience at home he communicated that priceless feeling that they, too, were conspirators in the make-believe while to his supporting company he conveyed that esprit and cohesion which is the trade-mark of the born showman.

Hope himself considered his debut and the show something of a disaster. He had been nervous and jumpy before the cameras, and it showed. He returned to the West Coast to prepare for his next film, *The Lemon Drop Kid,* and to polish up the script for his second television show for Frigidaire. Hope was irked by criticism from fellow performers that his TV salary made it difficult for "less reckless sponsors" to put the talents of Bing Crosby, Al Jolson, Frank Sinatra or Danny Kaye into the new medium. To prove how wrong this was, Hope hired Sinatra to make his TV debut on his Mother's Day Frigidaire show. He also hired Peggy Lee and ballet stars Michael Kidd and Janet Reed. He brought back Bea Lillie and used comedian Arnold Stang and singer Bill Hayes.

Hope and Sinatra arrived in New York with plenty of extra rehearsals scheduled; this time Hope was determined to win over the critics as well as the home viewers. He made fun of his spotty debut and kidded about his salary:

How do you do, ladies and gentlemen . . . I'm very happy to be
here again on television. This is my second show for the Frigidaire
people. I'm surprised, too . . . I saw the kinescope of my last
show on the Coast. It's convenient . . . I can lay 'em here and
hatch 'em a week later . . . I want to thank the thousand who
wrote letters about the first show . . . Also the three who mailed
them. . . . No. I did get about five thousand letters . . . The
FBI's going over them now . . . Radio was a wonderful medium
for a while but now Arthur Godfrey makes everyone else sound
like a spot announcement . . . he gets five thousand fan letters a
week . . . one from each sponsor . . . He's on eighteen hours a
day and now they've got a new program from midnight to six
A.M. . . . "Arthur Godfrey Snores." . . .[10]

The show went far more smoothly than its predecessor and was warmly
received by the critics. Hope confessed that part of his nervousness had been
adjusting to the moving cameras and gesturing technicians. "It was like trying to do a nightclub act with three waiters with trays walking in front of you
every time you reached the punchline." He decided to take control of the
situation. "I tied down the cameras, and gave orders that no one moves while
the show is on—the only way not to get killed on television is to set it up the
way *you* want it, not the way *they* want it."[11]

Hope was back in California after his second television show, when the
stalemate between himself and Lever Brothers became a parting of the ways.
After 12 years of being consistently in the golden circle of radio giants (and
for several seasons being in first place), Hope was being dropped because of
unreconcilable differences.

Those differences had by now gone beyond the objections to his traveling
the radio show, or even to his slump in the ratings. It centered on Hope's
demand that he be allowed to prerecord his radio show on tape as Crosby was
already doing. His contract with Lever Brothers specifically limited his services to "live broadcasts." Hope took the matter as high as Superior Court,
which ruled against the comedian. Defiant, Hope announced he would pretape his show as required, and Lever Brothers pulled the plug.

Saphier had been, in the meantime, working up a deal with NBC, and
almost simultaneously with the Lever decision the network announced it was
signing Hope to an exclusive long-term agreement for both radio and television which, Hope confided (publicly), would net him close to a million dollars annually. His final Lever contract had been raised to $22,500 for each
broadcast, which netted him something like $875,000 for the season. Now
with an exclusive NBC contract and what he might make from a new sponsorship deal, he would be doubling his income for the same effort. At the
moment, however, he had no sponsor, though Saphier was talking to Chesterfield Cigarettes and to Buick Motors. Luckily, his NBC contract guaranteed him air time even without a sponsor.[12]

Meanwhile, Hope checked into Paramount to begin work on his second
Damon Runyon characterization, *The Lemon Drop Kid*. From the start, it
had been plagued with script and casting snags. Hope had wanted Jan Sterling, a striking blonde from Broadway, as his leading lady but she could not

wait out the picture's delays. So Hope decided to take a chance with former band-singer-turned-actress Marilyn Maxwell, with whom he had just toured. He liked the way she handled a comedy line, he liked her not-so-dumb blonde sexiness and he figured her career might take off the same way Marilyn Monroe's had.

The Lemon Drop Kid was a blatant attempt to recapture the blend of cynicism and sentiment that had made *Sorrowful Jones* so appealing.

Both the studio bosses and Hope believed there was big money in this one if properly done. Same producer, same director but somehow this film was expected to succeed on standard sight gimmicks. The day they filmed Hope as a little old lady, furiously peddling a bicycle down a city street, Bing Crosby was on the sidelines watching and called out, "What's matter, kid? Did the front office preview your last picture?" Hope almost ruined the shot laughing, but that would have been the least of the problems facing this picture before it was finished.

I really didn't intend to perform so far north but the 1st Cavalry went through and the suction pulled me with them . . . And some of these towns are changing hands so fast one soldier bought a lamp with three thousand wan and got his change in rubles. . . .[1]

30. On the Beach at Wonsan

A few days before Hope started *The Lemon Drop Kid*, North Korean troops burst across the 38th parallel, swept south and surrounded Seoul. On their first day of shooting the picture, Douglas MacArthur assumed command of United Nations Forces for an unconventional police action that would become known as the Korean War.

The initial counteroffensive of that conflict began in mid-September, but even before that a plan was building in Hope's mind for taking a USO unit to the fighting front. He shrewdly calculated that at the same time he could make several personal appearances in Japan, where *The Paleface* was doing good business and could run much longer if Hope showed up. Hope got things moving by calling one of his golfing buddies, World War II flying ace Rosy O'Donnell, now the general in charge of all the Far East bomber squadrons. Several days later, new Air Secretary Thomas K. Finletter offered Hope the use of two C–54s which would allow him room for a troupe of 50 entertainers. That meant he could take the entire Les Brown band along, as well as his radio show technicians. It could be the largest GI overseas entertainment ever attempted. Hope grabbed at the opportunity and agreed to an early October departure, just as soon as *The Lemon Drop Kid* could be dubbed and his third *Star Spangled Revue* for Frigidaire telecast from New York.

Hope's new radio sponsor, Liggett and Meyer, was enthusiastic about his plan to transcribe his 30-minute show from various locations during the four-week tour. For his glamour girl, Hope picked Jane Russell. He signed country singer Jimmy Wakely, dancer Judy Kelly, the singing Taylor Maids, specialty dancers the High Hatters, and Les and the boys. He also planned to take Charlie Cooley, a masseur, Hy Averback, producer Al Capstaff and his NBC soundman extraordinaire, Johnny Pawlek.

In the midst of planning the Korean junket, he was also producing a Cerebral Palsy benefit in Hollywood Bowl with Jane Russell, Danny Thomas, Dinah Shore, Gene Tierney, Gordon MacRae, Eddie Bracken, Mel Tormé, Marge and Gower Champion and a number of big bands. He was hustling to finish *The Lemon Drop Kid*, and each noon he and his writers huddled in his dressing room to plan the September television show.

Hope was disappointed in the rough cut of *The Lemon Drop Kid*, finding it lacked in that Runyonesque sentiment he had gotten out of *Sorrowful Jones*. Paramount studio boss Barney Balaban was happy with it and wanted it readied for a final cut. "Let's get it out for the holiday trade," he argued. "I don't think so," said Hope, reminding Balaban of his partnership interest and pointing out the film's flaws, not the least of which was the picture's biggest scene, the Christmas sequence for which Livingston and Evans had written a marvelously lilting tune, "Silver Bells." Hope suggested the studio hire Frank Tashlin to do some rewrite. Tashlin agreed but only if he could direct the retakes. Paramount howled, but finally relented. Unfortunately, by the time the differences were resolved, retakes couldn't be scheduled until November when Hope would be back from Korea and Maxwell from her Eastern cities tour with Martin and Lewis.[2]

In late September Hope flew back to New York for his third Frigidaire special, this time costarring Lucille Ball, Bob Crosby and Dinah Shore, with help from the Jack Cole dancers and Al Goodman's orchestra. Hope was beginning to get the feel of what he should be doing in this medium, as Terence O'Flaherty's review in the *San Francisco Chronicle* on September 26, 1950, affirms:

> I love you, Bob Hope. Last night the cinema kid with the ski-shoot nose gave a little peek of what television is going to be when the big entertainers move in and take over. For the first time "The Star Spangled Revue" turned out to be something approximating the grandiose title of the show. Hope himself had good material to work with and he looked happy about it. . . . All in all it was "one fine, fat show," as my neighbor, Mrs. Pellachotti, expressed it, and she is a very particular woman.

Hope came home from New York with hardly enough time for a restful turnaround before preparing for another departure, this time for Hawaii, first stop on the Far East tour. At the last moment Jane Russell canceled because her film *Macao* was not quite finished. Hope tracked down Maxwell in Pittsburgh, where she agreed excitedly, but said she'd have to catch up with them in a few days. Bob booked Gloria DeHaven for the Hawaiian shows and the first radio broadcast.

That first chunk of the Asian tour was a series of puddle jumps around Pacific islands. The early shows were at Hickham Field, Pearl Harbor, and hospitals like Tripler on Oahu; then they moved to the Johnson Island, Kwajalein, Guam and eventually Okinawa. Maxwell had caught up with them, and DeHaven had gone home. The unit was well broken-in, spirits were soaring, and the Les Brown band was trying to live up to Hope's humor about them: "The band loves flying—sometimes they even come inside the plane."

Hope was lucky to have that band. Les provided a high quality sound, a consistent source of comedy, and, above all, loyalty. His band was one of the hottest moneymakers in the nation at a time when big bands were going out of style. Yet Les would invariably juggle or cancel dates to arrange his schedule around Hope.

On their arrival at Haneda Air Base, Hope received a formal invitation from General MacArthur to lunch with him at the American Embassy the following Tuesday. The message invited Hope to bring 20 members of his troupe. Hope's problem was how to choose the 20. The stars were automatically included, as was brother Jack and producer Al Capstaff. Hope decided to fill the remaining eight spots by a lottery open to everyone except the musicians. Of the four writers who were on that trip—Chet Casteloff, Larry Gelbart, Charlie Lee and Fred Williams—only two won the lottery, Gelbart and Williams. Typically, Charlie Lee was unruffled, but Chet was bitterly disappointed and begged to be included.

"Would you like to take my place?" Hope asked sarcastically.

"Hey—would you?" Chet said. "No, I suppose not. But there must be a way—"

"Chet—they only have room for 20 of us. We can't embarrass them—besides, you lost fair and square."

Late Tuesday morning Embassy staff cars picked up the 20 and took them to the reception. The other guests were members of the general's staff and some top diplomats. When MacArthur himself arrived, they were ushered into a big dining room. Each guest was seated at the long formal dining table by a white-gloved Marine. Hope noticed out of the corner of his eye that one guest still stood, looking bewildered, and Hope suspected the worst. He looked around and spotted Casteloff sitting immediately to the right of the general. Hope was flabbergasted. Before he could try to correct the situation, Mrs. MacArthur had already called for another chair and table setting, and everyone squeezed together to make room. No one at the luncheon had a better time than Chet, applauding the general's welcoming remarks, feeding him jokes.[3]

Later that day Hope did his monologue and a comedy dialogue scene with Maxwell for his radio show before an audience of 3,000 GIs and command VIPs in the Ernie Pyle Theater. That night, a slightly longer version of the show was performed for 10,000 GIs at a huge municipal hall. Hope came on grinning: This was strictly comedy for American consumption, urbanized foxhole humor. It was important for Hope to appear as the clear link with home, reflecting the attitudes of the average American toward its former enemy.

Yet it was quite different when Hope was not facing GI audiences. Marilyn Maxwell told some friends later, "In Tokyo, when people recognized him they yelled, 'Oooooo, Bobba Hopa!' and one time when we were going someplace in a convoy, a really old American-built sedan absolutely crammed with Japanese just barged into our procession and serenaded him with 'Buttons and Bows.' " The comedian halted the convoy and shook each Japanese hand that was extended out of the car.[4]

The most grueling and exciting moments of that tour took place in Korea. Their destination was Seoul, but they had to be diverted from landing at Kimpo Air Base because it was sneak-bombed a few hours before their scheduled arrival. The troupe, bundled in GI winter clothes, huddled together in the backs of trucks which took them over shell-cratered back roads to a stadium in the capital city. Thousands of GIs had been sitting there for more than an hour in bitter cold and biting wind, some in icy mud, and most carrying sidearms, some with rifles resting on their knees. Hope, his face reddened with cold, delivered a particularly sharp monologue reflecting the mercurial nature of the Korean War, whose battle lines were almost impossible to follow:

> . . . I really didn't intend to perform so far north but the 1st Cavalry went through and the suction pulled me with them . . . And some of these towns are changing hands so fast one soldier bought a lamp with three thousand wan and got his change in rubles . . . Seoul has changed hands so many times the towels in the hotel are marked "His," "Hers," and "Who's sorry now?" . . . But the way the war's going doesn't bother the Russians. They just run the newsreels backward and it looks like the North Koreans are advancing. . . .[5]

From Seoul, the troupe moved on to Taegu, then Taejon, where Hope said to Colonel Leyden, "You know, I promised to do a show for the First Marines. Do you know where they are?"

"Sure," said Leyden, "they're at Wonsan."

"Can we go?"

"We just took it. No sweat."

Their planes flew eastward, circling the Sea of Japan before making a big sweeping approach to the Wonsan airstrip. Maxwell later said, "When we looked out the plane windows, we saw a most startling thing. Below us was what looked like the entire Seventh Fleet forcing a huge beachhead landing. We even thought we saw one ship hit a mine."

When the two C–54s came to a halt on the airstrip at Wonsan, there was no sign of human activity. The buildings seemed deserted; there was a feeling of sudden abandonment about the scene.

Part of the crew, with weapons drawn, advanced to a nearby hangar which was empty. Finally they all got out of the planes and were wondering what to do next when several jeeps came speeding across the runway. Out of one stepped General Edward Almond, and out of another stepped Vice Admiral Arthur Struble, both looking bewildered. "How long have you been here?" they asked.

"Twenty minutes or so," said Hope. "What kept you?"

"Twenty minutes? You beat us to the beach."

"You're kidding," said Hope. "How could we beat *you* to the beach?"

"We just landed. Didn't you see us landing?"

"We thought it was our audience coming to see the show," cracked Hope.[6]

Almond and Struble were six days late taking Wonsan because, as official dispatches described, "bad weather and one of the densest mine fields in history delayed the landing." In the meantime, South Korean troops had done their part in flushing out the enemy and driving them north toward the Chosin reservoir. There were wire service stories in United States newspapers about Hope beating the Marines to the beach.

After the two-hour show, Struble invited Hope to spend the night on his ship, the *Missouri*. Hope, exhausted, agreed gratefully. When Struble and Hope stepped out of the Navy chopper onto the flight deck, there were hundreds of sailors standing at attention in two long lines. The two men walked in a kind of review between those lines and Hope heard muffled greetings here and there like, "Hey Bob," and "Ski Snoot," and way off in the distance someone shouted, "Old Niblick Nose!" After a stiff drink and a good dinner, Hope felt so relaxed that he did a solo concert in the fantail for a bunch of the crew.

Next day the remainder of the troupe was choppered out to the *Missouri* for a two-hour show, and that afternoon the troupe was transferred over to the *Valley Forge* for a show on its flight deck.

The final show in Korea was to be performed in the yard of the former Communist headquarters at Pyongyang to what remained of the divisions who had just fought to defend the battle line drawn at the Yalu River. The troupe was driven from airstrip to show site in personnel carriers, and as they bumped along they could not avoid seeing the body of a twelve-year-old boy who had just been shot, and several more bodies hastily covered with straw.

From things that General Almond and Admiral Struble had said, Bob got the feeling that this strange confusing war was not the simple matter that several officers at the MacArthur luncheon had guaranteed it would be.

As he waved goodbye to the GIs who swarmed around their planes just before takeoff, Hope caught the eye of one soldier who hollered to him, "How about your parka?" Hope took his off and threw it to the young man. Les Brown was standing next to Hope and another GI begged for his. Les threw it to the kid. In minutes, the rest of the troupe had shed the thick jackets and thrown them to guys who needed them.

The troupe returned to Tokyo where Bob recorded a tribute to Al Jolson who had just died. Jolson, in failing health, had come to Korea in September and had tirelessly sung songs and talked with combat groups wherever they could land a helicopter, and it was believed that the strenuousness of the trip had hastened his death.

The final leg of the tour took place in what the GIs called the "Icebox Circuit"—the Aleutians and Alaskan mainland. Hope and the group landed at Shemya where 400 entertainment-starved men were waiting, and again at Adak and at Amchitka. They went on to Anchorage and then to Fairbanks where Hope did his fourth radio show of the tour. As it came to a close, Hope in a voice resonant with emotion, paid tribute to the many people who helped make the Korean tour possible, to the GIs, and to the United Nations forces he had entertained. Once again, Hope was most eloquent when defending the courage and the mission of the military:

It's a long way from the conference rooms of Lake Success to the marshaling yards outside Pusan, Korea, but when he saw the grouping of French, Turks, Filipino, Australian, British, and South Koreans in one composite army while a Swedish group was setting up a field hospital for the wounded, we knew and we're sure Joe knows by now that the United Nations is far past the blueprint stage. It's in the bazooka, bomber and battleship stage, and the men fighting alongside each other may not understand each other's language, but they understand each other's ideals. . . .[7]

Besides the four network radio broadcasts that originated from staging areas and actual battlefield locations, Hope wanted to re-create for television viewers what the shows had been like. For his fourth Frigidaire special he introduced Marilyn Maxwell, Jimmy Wakely, Judy Kelly, the Taylor Maids, the High Hatters and the Les Brown band. A typical review was Bill Irvin's in the *Chicago Sun-Times* of November 27, 1950:

It is little wonder that Hope and company wowed 'em in Wonsan and toppled them in Tokyo . . . Hope's Sunday night show didn't measure up to some of his previous TV appearances but it packed the quota of laughs needed by GI's in Korea, and that's the important thing.

Hope was unerring in his perception of public sentiment which, at that moment, focused on American boys fighting and dying in Korea. The comedian's dramatization on television screens of his clown-hero adventures at the fighting front was a new way of reinforcing that figurative image recorded by foreign correspondents, in two Hope wartime memoirs, in newspaper columns and on radio.

Almost immediately after returning from Korea, Hope went to Paramount for the retakes of *The Lemon Drop Kid*. He was pleased with Tashlin's rewriting and restaging of "Silver Bells." The picture came together and "Silver Bells," with its remarkable 1,643,687 copies of sheet music and 31,800,000 recordings sold, could be called a golden hit. Bob and Marilyn got together to record the song but Bing beat them to it, and his version got most of the play.

As the year 1950 ended—a year in which Hope had a brush with death, made his television debut, closed an era with Lever Brothers, signed a multimillion-dollar contract with NBC, set the Paramount theater box-office record and took the most ambitious show ever attempted to an overseas GI audience—Hope was still maintaining a murderous pace.

Inevitably someone had to ask the question: "Is Bob Hope killing himself?" There was a certain déja vu in the rash of stories that appeared with a common theme, and this one, from *Modern Screen*, July 1950, will do:

Practically everyone who has worked with Hope during the past two years had made a similar observation. It is impossible to watch the unrelenting way he drives himself without nervously wondering when the breaking point will come.

Jack Hope suggested his brother may never have lost his adolescent fear that

"this might be his last week's work, that if he isn't good, people may not ask
him back again." Some columnists noted that Dolores was spending more
time in the company of Roman Catholic churchmen, and suggested that her
husband's long absences had driven her to seek counsel from prominent the
ologians. It was also suggested that Bob's being so frequently in the company
of Marilyn Maxwell was evidence that the two were having a serious love
affair, although Hedda and Louella both ran items in their columns advising
that the comedian's marriage was as solid as ever.

Perhaps most poignant was a press photograph taken in his Toluca Lake
yard, standing next to a five-foot-square greeting card, with Nora and Kelly
standing by him. The words, supposedly written by the children, but showing
Dolores' fine hand as well, read:

> WE ARE SO HAPPY YOU ARE HOME,
> NOW PROMISE US YOU WON'T ROAM
> AWAY BEFORE WE'VE KISSED YOUR CHEEK,
> AT LEAST UNTIL SOMETIME NEXT WEEK.
> FOR DADDYS COME AND DADDYS GO
> BUT YOU'RE A SPECIAL KIND YOU KNOW.
> NOW PROMISE US THAT YOU WON'T ROAM
> WE ARE SO HAPPY YOU ARE HOME
> (UNTIL AT LEAST SOMETIME NEXT WEEK)[8]

It is much easier to see the explanation for Hope's vagabond obsession in
his consistent striving for more money and more laughs. Hope cites a night in
Oakland, California, when he came offstage dripping with perspiration and
he held up a check for $19,000 for one night's work. "Gee, look at that
Charley. Remember when we used to get $5 a day for hoofing in Cleve
land?"

As for the other motivating force, he says, "There's nothing in the world
like hearing people laugh. It's the greatest noise there is. . . . Without live
audiences to play to, I'd be cutting out doilies in no time."

It was the laughs probably even more than the $25,000 weekly salary that
motivated him to move his Chesterfield radio show from one military base to
another during the Korean conflict. Liggett and Meyer were perfectly con
tent with this because the GI format suited the "Sound Off! One! Two!"
theme of their advertising campaign.

Hope picked West Coast camps and bases to broadcast from in those early
spring months of 1951 so he could make a comic intrigue film, *My Favorite
Spy*, with beautiful Hedy Lamarr at Paramount during the week. This time
he played a burlesque headliner who happens to be a perfect double for
notorious undercover agent.

During the final days of shooting in early April, Hope was increasingly
looking forward to his spring tour. He had asked Lew Grade, his agent for
Britain and Europe, to book him for a two-week swing through the music
halls of England and Scotland. He would pretape a show at a few military
bases, before the tour culminated in a week's booking at the famed Palla
dium, the last bastion of continuous week-to-week vaudeville in the world.
The New York Palace only opened its doors these days for big single acts
like the current comeback being staged by Judy Garland. In addition, Hope

was to compete in Britain's Amateur Golf Championship to be held at Porth-cawl, Glamorgan, in Wales.

Jane Russell was otherwise booked, so once again Maxwell got her chance. Hope's final domestic show was taped in Durham, North Carolina, on April 13 and the next day Bob and Marilyn were aboard the *Queen Mary.*

To appreciate better this episode in Hope's life, we must turn back a few months to the filming of *The Lemon Drop Kid.* One day during shooting, Hope was introduced to a little man with a stiff white collar, an Anglican priest from England named Butterworth, who was touring the United States drumming up contributions for his version of Nebraska's Boys Town. But-terworth had a rehabilitation center called Clubland in London's East End, which had been badly bombed during the war and faced extinction without financial help.

Hope listened to the kind-faced vicar, and said, "Listen, I may be in Lon-don next spring, and if I am I'll do a benefit for you."

Butterworth beamed; but he was also cautious. When Hope went back into a shot, Butterworth asked Cooley, "Does he mean it?" And both Cooley and Monty Brice chorused, "When Hope says he'll do something he'll do it."

Just before leaving for England Hope heard from Grade that the Palla-dium had booked Judy Garland for the time period Hope had specified, and the alternate dates the Palladium offered did not fit the comedian's schedule. Grade, however, countered with a two-week booking at the Prince of Wales Theatre and Hope agreed. Then he thought of Clubland. He made sure that the money he was getting for his British tour was big enough, and called Grade in London. "Lew, have them make the contract between Reverend James Butterworth and the theater. I'll play two weeks for twenty-five grand a week, but only if the club gets the dough."

Butterworth was summoned to Grade's office and when he was told of Hope's generosity, he cried. When Hope and Maxwell walked down the gangplank at Southampton, Butterworth was waiting on the dock.[9]

In every English and Scottish appearance, Hope was a sellout. He was literally mobbed by fans and autograph seekers when he tried to get through the alley to the stage door and had to have help getting to his dressing room. He stayed onstage for 80 minutes, the longest stage show he had ever given. When he got offstage he hollered: "Where's Jimmy? Where's Jimmy But-terworth?"

"He's just leaving. He said he didn't want to be in the way."

"Bring him back," said Hope, "I want to talk to him. Bring him to the party."

So the minister went to Ciro's with Hope, Maxwell, Mrs. Sid Fields and Jerry Desmonde, and kept saying, "I can't believe all this money is ours." Every night for two weeks Hope had the same kind of enthusiastic crowd, and each night he could look down at the first row and see the adoring face of "the little Rev" aimed up at him. Afterwards, Butterworth would come backstage and coax Hope to visit Clubland. Finally, on the Friday of the second week, Hope went to the boys' school with a check for 20,000 pounds sterling. The minister took him on a tour through the carpentry shop, the gymnasium, the table tennis alcove, the works. Finally, Butterworth shoved a little boy named Michael forward to accept the check from Hope while press photographers clicked away. Many years later, at a film festival in Acapulco, Mexico, actor Michael Caine said: "Bob, I've waited years for the opportunity to tell you in person that I was the shy urchin who took that check from you at Clubland."

Sandwiched in among all the other events of that tour were some GI shows, one at Burtonwood, England, and several in Germany, including one in West Berlin. And Hope did get to play the Palladium, at a Sunday night charity gala to benefit Britain's equivalent of Actors Equity. Hope and Maxwell had the headliner spot and were joined by comedienne Beryl Reid, harmonica virtuoso Larry Adler, actor Peter Sellers and singer Petula Clark.

Hope and Maxwell had a few days of relaxation in Ireland before arriving at Porthcawl for the British Amateur tourney.

In the two rounds of the tournament, Hope lost to a spectacled, pipe-smoking Yorkshireman named Chris Fox. As one newspaper account described the close of the match:

> Munching a slice of home-made cake given him by a woman spectator, and with his free hand around his stage partner Marilyn Maxwell, Bob Hope walked down the 17th fairway here beaten but happy.[10]

When Hope got back to California a few days later he wrapped up the Chesterfield radio series for the season and went to Washington, D.C., where Harry Truman presented him with the USO's highest honor, on the anniversary of his first GI show at March Field in 1941. The citation read simply "To the GI's Guy."

THE EISENHOWER YEARS
1952–1959

*I'm really on the spot when I do political jokes. I'm usually
selling a product everybody buys and I don't want to alienate
part of my audience. . . .*[1]

31. Liking Ike

The politicization of Bob Hope was gradual, somewhat random. If he
appeared to blow with the wind, it was because on Tuesday nights he was a
door-to-door salesman and he couldn't offend his customers. One could confidently say that his personal interest in politics followed his fame and financial security.

Current public opinion blamed Truman for "handing" China to the Communists, for "losing" the Korean War, for "harboring Reds" in the government. Knowing Hope's Horatio Alger views of the American system, and his
intimacy with the GI and with generals, it is likely that he applauded Truman's policies of economic reconstruction, his Berlin airlift, his tough stand
on Korea, and even his consistent support of the UN.

But it is also likely that Hope, along with so many Americans, welcomed
Republican promises of prosperity and their pledge of routing the Reds from
high places and maintaining a posture of world supremacy.

Hope and the American public both encouraged a somewhat reluctant
candidate, approaching slowly on a white charger, whose courage had won
his nation a stunning victory in 1945, and whose charisma landed him the
presidency of Columbia University. Hope and the nation—most of the
world—liked Ike.

In one of Hope's Chesterfield monologues of that period, delivered just
after Princess Elizabeth and Prince Philip had visited Washington, there is a
rather backhanded reference to Truman's uphill struggle for popular
appeal:

> . . . Then Elizabeth asked Margaret what a Republican
> was . . . and Margaret said, "I don't know, every time the sub-
> ject comes up, they made me leave the room." . . . But they had
> a nice visit, and when the princess left the White House, she said,
> "I hope to be back next year, Mr. President" . . . and President
> Truman said, "Me, too!"[2]

It became increasingly clear that Ike was more than just a national hero to
Hope; he was someone the comedian felt close to because of their meeting,
however brief, during his North African GI tour of 1945 and because Ike
had pinned one of the Nation's highest honors, the Medal of Merit, on his
lapel.

In the spring of 1952, Truman declared he was not a presidential candidate and, despite the election year accusations of "scandalous administration," Hope did not join the media rancor. "I would never do a joke to hurt a
campaign or any party. I can't afford to go out and start knocking Demo-

crats and knocking Republicans, because I'm usually selling a product everybody buys and I don't want to alienate part of my audience."[3]

In the public media, Hope favored a subtle dismissal of the First Family.
The bit in this 1952 monologue comes from Hope's pointed reference to
Fulbright's investigation of steel industry tax fraud, which haunted Tru-
man's final Washington days:

> . . . They finally finished remodeling the White House and it's
> open to tourists . . . President Truman isn't too happy about it.
> He's annoyed at the Republican visitors. They keep bringing their
> suitcases . . . I don't know whether the Democrats expect to
> win the election or not but the whole second floor is done in coon-
> skin . . . They had to build the whole White House out of
> wood . . . the President is allergic to steel . . . The Trumans
> haven't decided on their future plans yet . . . Margaret wants to
> continue her concert work, but Harry keeps looking at the piano
> and singing, "There's a Hock Shop On a Corner in Pittsburgh,
> Pennsylvania . . ."[4]

The way Hope approached this particular election year is indicative of his
growing interest in public affairs generally during this important expansion-
ist decade of his life. For example, in June 1952 he enthusiastically endorsed
NBC's suggestion that he serve as one of the radio/television news commen-
tators at both the Republican and Democratic conventions in Chicago. But
before going to Chicago, Hope took on a much-applauded chore: hosting
with Bing Crosby a unique 14½-hour telethon to raise a million dollars to
assure the 333-member U.S. Olympic team's trip to Helsinki.

Inspiration for this endurance TV fund-raiser came from Hearst's syndicated sports writer Vince Flaherty, a two-fisted drinking buddy of Hope and
Crosby. Flaherty, with the blessing of Olympic chief Avery Brundage, got
promises of solid publicity and financial backing from Hearst's domestic and
foreign operations to help sponsor the telecast.[5]

Nothing like this had ever been attempted. In addition, this was to be Bing
Crosby's television debut, and Dorothy Lamour was co-host. Who was not
going to tune in with the promise of Frank Sinatra, Burns and Allen, Uncle
Miltie, Martin and Lewis, Peggy Lee, Frankie Laine, Donald O'Connor,
Eddie Cantor, Georgie Jessel, the Ritz Brothers, Abbott and Costello, Fred
MacMurray, famous sports figures, a host of kiddy favorites and a strong
representation of jazz musicians and big bands?

Most of it would take place on Hope's home stage, the El Capitan,
although there would be cut-ins from CBS studios in New York where most
of the athletes would appear. Most historic of all, both NBC and CBS would
carry it to their hundreds of stations.

The long day of preparation leading up to the broadcast, was spent
between the Hope house and the Tudor-style eight-room office across the
driveway, where Hope's staff was coordinating the telethon. Writers, technicians, cue-card printers, musicians, agents, messengers came and went, and
there was heavy traffic on that special staircase leading from the Hope main
hallway to Bob's bedroom antechamber.

The unflappable Marjorie Hughes supervised construction of the long script. She and Hope had culled through thousands of gags in his now-famous joke vault in categories like sports, sports figures, Crosby, Lamour, *Road* pictures, elections, conventions, and, of course, Olympics.

Hope's writers had been working almost constantly for days and were to stand by all through the telethon as well. Hope attended to each detail meticulously, personally making sure that both networks were providing fresh studio audiences for each hour of the long broadcast to keep the enthusiasm high for the rotating performers.

By midafternoon he was sitting downstairs behind his massive oak desk talking over three telephone lines to stars, agents, producers, press agents, arrangers and conductors in a fascinating display of show-business flattering, cajoling, encouraging, promising, commiserating and pressuring.

Inside the main house, Dolores and Mildred MacArthur helped the cook and two maids prepare dinner for 15; when dinner was announced, Hope came to the table with a sheaf of monologue jokes, anxious to try out on his captives (something he frequently did), but he was defeated by the sounds of earnest eating, the exulting cries over the roast beef, Yorkshire pudding, five vegetables, two salads and the strawberry shortcake. Hope finally gave up. "Dolores," he snapped, "how do you expect me to compete with this kind of food?" He dropped his napkin and jumped up hurriedly.

Less than an hour later, Dolores, Mildred, the children and some close friends in the neighborhood gathered around the oval picture tube. The household help came in from the kitchen and stood watching and laughing at Hope's monologue before they served drinks and coffee. As the hours went by, the children nodded and dozed one by one, then each was sent to bed. Soon the only ones left were Dolores and Mildred, who decided to stretch out on Bob's oversized bed to watch the rest of the show.

At six-thirty little Nora, in pajamas and barefoot, leaped up on the bed between Dolores and Mildred. Behind her came a second little girl, shy and tentative, the three-year-old daughter of one of the maids.

Linda, still in pajamas, came in whispering, "Is Daddy still on?" She sat on her father's short divan with her arms locked around her knees. Kelly came in next and crawled up next to Nora. Finally Tony and Pat Wayne came into the room in pajamas with their six-guns strapped around their waists and tried their best to seem nonchalant. They dropped to sitting positions at the foot of the bed.

"Did he get the million?" asked Tony.

"Not yet, dear," said Mildred, "but he will."

Two hours later the million figure did pop up on the studio tote board and everyone in the studio and in the Hope house let out a holler. (Of course, a month later the Olympic Committee was still trying to collect on some of those pledges.)

Hope brought Doc Shurr home for breakfast at about eleven o'clock; then he crawled into bed.

A few days later, Hope took Dolores, Linda and Tony with him to Chicago for the Republican Convention. Hope did a short monologue each evening as part of the network's total coverages:

> Show business could take a lesson here at the Republican Con-
> vention on how to put over a personality. Flying in here I passed
> four pigeons wearing Taft buttons . . . The way Taft and Eisen-
> hower campaign managers are ballyhooing their respective candi-
> dates, you'd think they had a transfusion from Cecil B. De-
> Mille. . . .[6]

Hope was no longer writing his daily newspaper column. After Willia
Randolph Hearst's death that year, Hope's column had ceased to interest tl
Hearst editors, but King Features had asked him to resume the chore for or
week in Chicago, and some of his humor had a Will Rogers ring: "This tow
was known as the Windy City even before the politicians arrived," or "Tl
hotels are jammed . . . hot and cold running rumors on every floor."[7]

A few weeks later at the Democratic Convention the idea of political co
ventions was getting stale. The biggest media excitement was over Nixon
criticism of Adlai Stevenson's humor.

This was a presidential year for Hope, as well. He decided that it would b
good for publicity and his ego to run for office in the show business aren
Chicago columnist Nate Gross was the first to tip the story, in the *Chicag
Herald-American* on June 20, 1952:

BOB HOPE SEEKING AGVA PRESIDENCY

> TOWN TATTLER: Bob Hope is running for president, but this
> is no mock campaign like that being conducted by my tongue-
> in-cheek pal, Jimmy Durante, or my perennial presidential favor-
> ite, Sophie Tucker. . . .
>
> Bob's candidacy is for presidency of the American Guild of
> Variety Artists. . . . To Bob it would mean the attainment of a
> boyhood dream. At long last everyone would address him as "Mr.
> President."

Needless to say, Hope won a landslide victory and went off quite content o
his summer holiday with Dolores, Linda and Tony to Vermont, after whic
he took a business trip to London and other European cities to plug h
newest film, *Son of Paleface*. He was followed by the media wherever h
went and his actions were described in exacting detail.

Hope flew to Stockholm, then to London for some appearances in conne
tion with the film, and then to Cannes to meet Princess Honey Chile an
Prince Alec Hohenlohe. Then to Helsinki for two days at the Olympics.

When he got back to London it was time for his long-awaited commerci
debut at the fabled Palladium. On stage he said:

> I came over on the *United States*. It's a wonderful ship. It cost us
> ninety million. That's money we had left over after Churchill's
> last visit . . . You have to hand it to Churchill . . . If you
> don't he comes and gets it from us anyway. . . .[8]

Hope's Palladium monologue was partly written by London-based comedia
Denis Goodwin, so its topicality was deft and tasteful. One of London's mo
respected critics, Peter Forster, reviewed:

A brilliant Palladium bill is headed by Bob Hope, surely the most endearing of the American comedians. His very entrance is a joy as he ambles on, jaw jutting, eyes roving, abounding in that old, indefinable, heart-warming quality of your true star comedian.

Mr. Hope is funny to look at, funny to hear, funny without effort and without flagging. What matter how many joke writers assist? Today's comic with radio, film, and TV markets, must use material in a month that would have lasted an old timer a decade. Nobody could provide Mr. Hope's impeccable timing or the charm that robs personal comment of any offense.[9]

Hope's shadow during those two weeks at the Palladium was the lovable Butterworth, who finally convinced the comedian to visit the refurbished boys' hospice to see what had been done with his money. Butterworth posed for pictures with Bob in the main vestibule next to a stone marker that proclaimed Hope's beneficence. Hope's plaque was adjacent to one placed there in honor of the dowager Queen Mary, who was the school's patroness. Hope was so touched by Butterworth's devotion to rebuilding these boys' lives that he volunteered to do another benefit.

He telephoned Lew Grade to help him book the Stoll Theatre and to find a few acts to support him. Hope wasn't anxious to book a big show because he had an ace up his sleeve, a somewhat chancy card, but well worth playing if he could. He had heard that Crosby was arriving in England for a day or two, en route to a movie location near Paris. Bing had never before appeared on a London stage and if he would show for this benefit it would be a sensation. Bing's reaction to Bob's invitation, however, was negative. He was cordial but said an appearance was out of the question. Bob thanked him and said he hoped he would change his mind. Meanwhile, Hope dropped hints with some media contacts that Crosby might, just might, decide to make his London debut at the Clubland benefit, and then left the decision up to Bing.

At showtime there was no Crosby. Yet Hope clung to the notion that Bing would try to surprise him. Jack Buchanan had agreed to compere the first half of the show. Bob was backstage with his London gag writer Denis Goodwin going over some new material for his second-half monologue when a stagehand sidled over to Hope and told him confidentially that Crosby had been spotted at a pub "over the road." Hope told Denis to stand by while he and the stagehand took off to locate Bing. When they walked into the pub, Bing was relishing his drink and conversation with some of the locals. He invited Bob to join him and had no apparent plan to get into makeup, or put on his toupee, or sing, or joke or do anything but enjoy his drink.

"Come on, Bob—join me," he said, "or don't join me as the case may be."

"There are a lot of folks over the road, and it's for a good cause."

Bing took a last puff on his pipe, swallowed his drink and said, "What are we waiting for?"

Hope took Crosby up to a rehearsal hall where pianist Pat Dodd had been waiting in case Crosby showed and wanted to rehearse. But some over-zealous agent had steered about two dozen journalists and photographers up to the rehearsal hall and there was no time for a run-through.

Hope went down to open the second half and in his act did his usual gags about "Dad," and someone hollered, "Where is he?"

"It's pretty late for that old gentleman to be out. He's probably in bed sipping his hot milk." The audience moaned, then the spotlight moved across the stage and there was Bing, with his pipe, leaning against the proscenium arch. Donald Peers, also on that bill, told what happened:

> The applause was like something you never heard. It was just fantastic. He did some songs and there were lots of titles shouted at him from the audience. He would start one or two, but not having rehearsed them he would get so far and then say, "Well, that's enough" or "I can't remember the rest of the words. . . ."[10]

By the time Hope got back to Hollywood, rehearsals began for his first *Colgate Comedy Hour* of the new NBC–TV season. It was less than a month to election day and Hope, quite uncharacteristically, devoted his full monologue to politics. Hope said:

> Thank you . . . I'm happy to be back on the Colgate Hour and, by the way, I want to thank all the candidates for giving up this time to make room for *another* comedian . . . I'm so confused I don't know whether to join the Democrats who are voting for Eisenhower, or the Republicans who are voting for Stevenson. Or Crosby who's still voting for John Quincy Adams . . . This election will really make history. It'll be the first time the General waits while the troops \make the decision . . . But the Gallup Poll is very positive this time. They've come up with a statement that there *will be* a President elected . . . My Aunt Gladys heard Nixon's speech on television but she got the whole thing confused. She said, "I feel sorry for Mrs. Nixon . . . Imagine having to wear a cloth coat with a cocker spaniel collar!" . . . And both parties are after the farm votes. They've made so many speeches, the farmers expect the biggest crops of their lives . . . Eisenhower paid us a visit this week and tied up traffic. Naturally, everybody was excited. The Republicans out here claim he can walk on orange juice. . . . One Democrat wandered into the Eisenhower rally by mistake. I saw him this morning. It's a beautiful embalming job . . . I'm happy to be back for the campaign excitement. I was in Europe. I bring you regards from your money. . . .[11]

The monologue's total concern with politics makes it a rare phenomenon among the hundreds of radio and television monologues in Hope's career.

But the humor is essentially harmless, though expertly crafted. Charlie Lee, in *The New York Times Magazine* of October 4, 1970, said: "His stuff seems braver than it is. When you examine one of his jokes it's never lethal. We never do anything about a politician that really hurts—it's always their golf shots or their noses or their money—never their policies, never what they're doing."

Hope's valedictory to Truman's administration came at the close of the comedian's November 1952 television monologue. He had just described the Republicans' jubilation over Eisenhower's plurality. In the style of the crackerbarrel humorists, it was a mock farewell note from one leader to another.

> Dear Ike . . . have found it necessary to leave town. Sorry I can't be here to meet you. You'll find sandwiches in the icebox, cigars in the humidor, and Landon in the deep-freeze. However, I don't suppose you'll be eating the sandwiches inasmuch as you just cooked Stevenson's goose . . . In the Blue Room you'll find a large picture of Taft, send it back to him . . . please erase the mustache first. My future plans are still indefinite. I've been thinking of writing a book, but I'm having trouble getting a typewriter from General MacArthur. I've even thought of staying on in Washington . . . but Bess wants me to get into something with a future. I must say it's pretty dull in Washington these days. I'd like to play a little poker . . . but where can you find three other Democrats now? There's a rumor going round that you have an important job for me in your new Cabinet. Do you really think we need an ambassador to Abyssinia? Signed, Anxious . . .[12]

One of Hope's most difficult decisions was the one in 1952 to lampoon one of the most controversial and volatile, if not the more odious, subjects of the decade—Senator Joseph McCarthy.

Mort Lachman says Hope's hesitancy about ridiculing McCarthy was founded on the fear of misreading public sentiment. Many in the Hollywood community were pro-McCarthy; Ronald Reagan, for example. Still, a full 18 months before McCarthy was finally discredited, Hope decided it was a joking topic. On his heavily viewed December 1952 telecast, the comedian told his audience he had a letter from Santa Claus:

> Dear Robert . . . Thank you for your nice letter . . . and the beautiful new brown suit you sent me . . . But tell Senator McCarthy I'm going to wear my old red one, anyway . . . I had it first. . . .[13]

In May 1953, referring to a golf game in Washington with Eisenhower and some of his cabinet, Hope cracked:

> I had to be cleared by the FBI. . . . the Secret Service . . . the Army and the Navy . . . and *they* all had to be cleared by Senator McCarthy. . . .[14]

Hope started to get letters from disturbed Americans who branded the comedian as a Communist. But he continued to use jokes involving the color red throughout 1953 and by early 1954 he was using jokes that suggested the Senator's creeping paranoia:

> Senator McCarthy was out here for a visit, but he rushed back to the nation's capital. He's been gone almost a week and he doesn't even trust the Republicans with Washington that long . . . He

almost missed speaking here . . . He got off the train and spent
two days at Union Station investigating red caps. . . .[15]

When the hearings began, Hope's humor reached its sharpest cutting edge:

> Senator McCarthy is on a new type of television show. It's sort of
> a soap opera where everything comes out tattle-tale
> gray . . . But I have it on good authority that McCarthy is
> going to disclose the names of two million Communists . . . he's
> just got his hands on the Moscow telephone directory . . . Even
> President Eisenhower is careful what he says on the air these days
> because McCarthy may demand equal time in the White
> House.[16]

That hardly constitutes a stinging denouncement but, considering Hope's
15-year avoidance of such controversial material, it was significant. Hope
knew that he was solidly in step with Eisenhower's contempt for McCarthy,
and that even Republican congressmen were ready to smash the Wisconsin
lawmaker. Still, for once Hope found himself ahead of public sentiment. It
would take months and a bizarre display of the Senator's arrogance and
recklessness through protracted televised hearings to convince the broad
electorate of McCarthy's demagoguery.

Hope's reaction to McCarthy only strengthened both his joking relationship and his growing personal closeness with Ike. Of all the Presidents Hope
joked with or about, whom he joined on the golf course or chatted with in the
Oval Office or on his bedside telephone, Eisenhower was the true hero, as
well as friend. That helps explain the two dominant humor themes that persisted: the President as warrior and as golfer.

Even when Ike was campaigning for the presidency in civilian clothes, as a
politician and peacemaker—and after his election—Hope saw Eisenhower's
military image as his most figurative aspect.

> . . . the election has created a new slogan . . . It's now, "Join
> the Army and see the White House" . . . Now that he's Presi-
> dent, Ike is Commander-in-Chief of all the armed forces. The
> poor guy . . . he just can't get his discharge papers . . . Hav-
> ing a general for President is gonna be something . . . I can't
> wait till he puts Congress on KP. . . .[17]

But it was the golf course that supplied the bond to their closeness. It
began in April 1953 when Hope reacted to media coverage of the President's
golfing jaunt to Augusta, Georgia. The comedian shared his unrestrained
enthusiasm with his television audience:

> Did you see him arrive in Georgia with his golf shoes under his
> arm? I think he's working too hard . . . I always wear mine on
> my feet . . . But no matter what jokes we make about our Pres-
> ident's golf, we feel as the rest of the people in this country
> do . . . This is what I mean:
>
> (Hope sings)
> You're free to go where you go

Do what you do
Just follow through
And we'll be happy.

The White House lawn is all yorn
Who cares if it's torn
Just follow through
And we'll be happy.

Since you made August Georgia
So very pop-u-lar
Those Dixie Dem-o-crats
Are wearing black homburg hats.

As long as you've got that drive
We'll all survive
Just follow through
And we'll be happy.[18]

Hope appears to have assumed the mantle of presidential apologist. Within a week of that telecast, Hope received a call from his old pal, Stuart Symington, now Senator Symington (D–Missouri), inviting him to play a round at Burning Tree with himself and Ike. Hope recalls:

> Of the memorable things which have happened to me on a golf course, the round I played with Ike Eisenhower in 1953 is the topper . . . The President, Senator Bush of Connecticut, Stu and I made up a foursome. Ike and I were partners . . . I asked, "What do you want to bet?" "I usually play for a dollar, dollar, dollar," he said. This means that a dollar is wagered on the first nine, another on the second nine and another on all eighteen. "Funny thing," Ike went on, "I've just lent a million and a half dollars to Bolivia, and here I am playing for a dollar, dollar, dollar."[19]

The following night, at the White House Correspondents' Association annual banquet, where Ike was a willing target, Hope quipped:

> . . . I knew the President when he was still a general and really had power . . . I played golf with him yesterday . . . It's hard to beat a guy who rattles his medals while you're putting . . . Ike uses a short Democrat for a tee . . . He was hitting the ball much further than I . . . He had Senator McCarthy's picture painted on the ball. . . .[20]

And on his next telecast, Hope told his audience:

> . . . I had the pleasure of playing a round of golf with the President the other day . . . and I'd like to go on record right now by saying that if he slices the budget like he slices a ball, the Nation has nothing to worry about. . . .[21]

As might be expected, Hope did not deal directly with the subject of Eisenhower's serious heart attack of 1955, but during his recovery in the first term, and well into the second term, the comedian found the President's time away from the White House a rich source of comedy:

> . . . Of course he paints a lot now instead of playing golf. It's fewer strokes . . . As a painter he's ahead of his time . . . we won't have apples that shape for a hundred years, at least. . . .[22]

Other than his ridicule of McCarthyism, Hope confined his Eisenhower administration satire to nonsubstantive issues, like America's lag in the missile contest with the Soviets. Hope said:

> Ike visited Cape Canaveral the other day. He felt right at home there with those big divots . . . One rocket's been in Florida so long, it has a tan. . . .[23]

When Hope did refer to Ike, near the close of his second term, it was to endorse the President's several goodwill tours:

> Ike left today on a good will tour . . . that means, "How much and for how long?" Nixon briefed him on South America . . . but he's going anyway . . . Ike's not afraid. He's been through two wars and Ladies Day at the Gettysburg Country Club . . . It's a good thing we're paying Ike a salary. Think where we'd be if we were paying him by the mile . . . No, our President really travels. It's getting so he just goes to the airport and says to the pilot, "Anywhere, we got trouble all over." . . .[24]

Hope's affectionate goodbye to Ike, when he stepped down as chief executive, provided a succinct summation of the comedian's joking relationship with a President and a friend:

> You remember Ike . . . he was the pro in the White House . . . He'll have a lot of time to play golf . . . The unemployment office doesn't have many jobs in his category . . . But I hope he enjoys himself. . . .[25]

. . . it's starting out to be a busy year for me. With my television show, my daytime and nighttime radio shows, pictures, personal appearances . . . I'm also working on a plan where when you close your eyelids, I appear on the insides of your eyeballs. . . .[1]

32. *Have Tux, Will Travel*

Probably the most persistent cliché in the media's coverage of Hope, particularly in the early fifties, was that of his unrelenting life-style. It was one thing for him to demonstrate during World War II that he could drive himself to exhaustion making GIs laugh, but in the ten years that followed, he stayed on the merry-go-round, loving every turn, and for him there never seemed to be enough brass rings.

Astonishment bordered on disbelief in 1952 when Jimmy Saphier completed negotiations with General Foods for an unprecedented $2-million radio deal that would deliver Hope to American homes daily, five times a week, beginning in November.[2] General Foods also agreed to sponsor his nighttime radio show beginning January 1953. This omnipresence was a gamble for Hope's seventeenth consecutive season on NBC, but Hope pointed out that CBS had Arthur Godfrey on the air, radio and television, almost around the clock, and it hadn't affected *his* popularity.

This experiment was, as several tagged it, "Hope for the housewives"—15 minutes of comedy patter, a bit of music, and casual chat with guest stars and ad libs with the audience at 11:45 in the morning when the ladies at home were getting ready for lunch. On his very first broadcast November 10 Hope only appeared for about ten seconds because the remainder of the show was devoted to taped messages of insult and sarcastic good wishes from cronies like Benny and Crosby who, as *Variety* put it, were "kidding on the square" about the whopping salary he was getting for this daily grind.

Next day, however, Hope poked fun at himself and his assignment:

> How do you do, ladies and gentlemen. This is Bob "Jello to make you mello" Hope . . . Yessir, I'm back at home at work and guess what? . . . This season I'll be broadcasting Monday through Friday. Mmmmmmmm . . . Hope will be on the air five days a week. Isn't that wonderful? This new arrangement should make me very popular. When I did my show just once a week people used to say, "Wasn't Hope lousy last Tuesday?" Now they can say, "If you think he was lousy on Tuesday you should have heard him on Wednesday. I hear he was almost as bad Wednesday as he was Friday when I tuned him out because he made me so sick on Thursday" . . . Well, of course . . . (*applause*) Thank you. . . .[3]

The critical consensus was that Hope's live stage presence came across especially well in his exchanges with the studio audience. Hope later said: "Most people asked how old I was and all that stuff, which is fun because I have stock lines for a lot of it. But one day this guy got up and waved his hand and he said, 'Which way does a pig's tail turn, clockwise or counterclockwise?' It was such a wild question that the audience laughed like hell, and when they finished laughing I said, 'We'll find out when you leave.' The theater rocked, it just rocked. It was so good that after that, I put a plant in the audience in some of those shows to get that laugh again."

Although the new Hope format didn't exactly steal the market, his Nielsen rating of between 3 and 4 million listeners a day was considered an achievement. General Foods felt more comfortable about their investment, which also included a new edition of the comedian's nighttime radio show.

After 16 years of being heard on Tuesday nights—it used to be called Bob Hope Night—the new show would be heard on Wednesdays. Also sponsored by Jell-O, it was produced by Jack Hope, announced by Bill Goodwin, with music by Les Brown, and jokes written by writers like Larry Marks and

Norm Sullivan. On the kick-off show Hope's guest was the man who had sold Jell-O many years himself:

Sound:	*Door open:*
JACK:	Hello, Bob!
HOPE:	Jack Benny!
	(*Applause*)
HOPE:	Gee, this is great, Jack.
JACK:	Don't mention it. I figure the least a person can do to honor an old friend is to drop in and pay his respects.
HOPE:	I'm still warm, you know . . . feel . . . (*extends wrist*) . . . You sound like the advance man for Forest Lawn.
JACK:	I'm sorry, Bob . . . I didn't mean that the way it sounded.
HOPE:	Forget it. I really appreciate your coming over here . . . as busy as you are with radio, television, counting. . . .
JACK:	(*ad libbing*) I'm a guest and I haven't had a joke yet . . . oh, it's nothing.
HOPE:	You can kid about it if you like, but this is a very generous thing you're doing, Jack . . . dropping in to wish me luck on my opening show.
JACK:	Bob . . . (*long Benny pause*) . . . I'm not here just to wish you good luck. There's a slight misunderstanding.
HOPE:	Misunderstanding?
JACK	Yes . . . I not here entirely on my own . . . You see, Mr. Cleaves, the head of the Jell-O Company, sent me over here to supervise your opening show.
HOPE:	(*indignant*) You? Supervise *my* opening show?
JACK:	Now Bob, don't get all worked up . . . look at it this way. I've had a long and very pleasant relationship with the Jell-O Company, and you've just joined up. In a manner of speaking, I was here before you.
HOPE:	You were here before anybody.[4]

And so it went. Right down to the tribute with which Hope always closed his nighttime programs, radio or television. This particular tribute ought to be noted because it reflected a dominant theme in the comedian's personal philosophy:

Ladies and gentlemen, the noisemakers and the paper hats have been put away, and 1953 is getting down to the business of being a New Year . . . and this promises to be a big one . . . a year in which the attainment of peace and security will be everybody's job . . . the men at the top . . . the kids at Korea . . . and those here at home. The best way to start this job, ladies and gentlemen, is with optimism and faith . . . faith in the things that have made us strong and free. Always remember . . . de-

featism only leads one way . . . down. So let's start 1953 with
the firm belief that things can be better if we work making them
that way. So, from all of us to all of you everywhere . . . the best
of everything in 1953.[5]

o a nation which had just elected Eisenhower this could hardly fail to be
oving. On January 14, 1953, *Variety* had a short but enthusiastic
view:

After many years of bigtime radio, it's virtually impossible to associate Bob Hope with any other format than that which he's been
using. His return to nighttime radio on behalf of Jell-O offers the
same fast-gagging, informal and always likeable comic.

ariety was wrong. Its show business sages simply could not divine the
merican public's infatuation with television as that season rolled on. Com-
ly and variety programming in nighttime radio was sounding the death
ttle; of the eleven shows that aired during the 1952–53 season, only four
rvived into the following year: Hope, Crosby, Benny and Bergen. Sponsors
ere simply not interested in reaching so few listeners.
So it is significant that at a time when entertainment tastes were changing,
ope was still enjoying success in all media. He had been particularly active
Paramount during the year. First there was *Off Limits,* a picture that
ixed military policemen and prizefighters, and costarred him with Mickey
ooney and Marilyn Maxwell. Then came another wacky excursion with
rosby and Lamour, their first in five years and their first in technicolor,
he Road to Bali. Finally there was a frothy thing called *Here Come the
irls,* probably the closest Hope ever came to being in a typical Hollywood
m musical, with Rosemary Clooney, Arlene Dahl and Tony Martin.
NBC was not unhappy about the size of Hope's viewing audiences for his
ce-a-month *Colgate Comedy Hour.* General Foods was pleased enough
ith Hope's sales pitch for them to sign him to another exclusive television
ntract for the next three years. Then, of course, there were always personal
pearances for money, and others for charity, many of those involving his
ssionate avocation, golf. Not to mention the ongoing concerns of being
GVA president, of being honorary chairman of the Cerebral Palsy fund-
ising nationwide, and time devoted to the Damon Runyon Cancer Fund
d the Boy Scouts. His tolerance for work was incredible, suggesting an
traordinary range of interest and perhaps the fear of having an empty
oment in his life.
The Friars Club testimonial dinner for Hope on February 27, 1953,
serves special mention, not so much because the standup performers of
merica were honoring one of their own kind. They had done that twice
fore on a large scale; in 1951 they applauded Joe E. Lewis and in 1952
ey gathered for Jack Benny. This time it was interesting because of the
liber and nature of the roasters and toasters who made up the head table
d the fact that it was being broadcast over NBC radio. When the Friars
nored Lewis and Benny, the dais held all the big comedians—pros like
ssel, Berle, Burns and Allen. For Hope there was Fred Allen, Berle and
ssel plus an eclectic group that included newspaper editor Louis Seltzer of
he Cleveland Press; Senator Stuart Symington; two city mayors, Cleve-

land's Tom Burke and New York's Vincent Impelliteri; America's eldes
statesman, Bernard Baruch; colorful former Vice President Alben Barkley;
military hero, General Rosy O'Donnell; movie czar Eric Johnston; and thre
of Hope's "bosses"—RCA chief Frank Folsom, NBC top man Frank White
and the octogenarian chairman of Paramount Pictures, Adolph Zukor.

Hope had agreed to the testimonial, providing it was a fund-raiser for
few of his personal charities, the USO, Cerebral Palsy, Boy Scouts and, o
course, the Friars Relief Fund. He wanted a minimum of awarding, an
finally agreed on one statuette to be presented by the Boy Scouts, out of th
12 that were offered. The other 11 awards were later mailed to his office.

Fifteen hundred people came to see Hope roasted—people like Toots Shor
Ed Sullivan, Bob Considine, and Bob O'Donnell.

Fred Allen was in good form, with lines like "I feel there is *nothing* any o
us can say about Mr. Hope that he has not already said about himself."

Dinner chairman Jesse Block referred to Hope as "your average America
who makes three million a year." Berle called him "America's secon
greatest comedian." The elderly Baruch, who had gotten out of a sickbed t
attend the dinner, said, "May the Lord take a liking to you but not too soon,
and then was escorted back to bed. And there were the expected accolade
describing what Hope has meant to the GIs, to show business and to charity
not to mention Paramount Pictures, the National Broadcasting Compan
and, as several pointed out, the U.S. Treasury.[6]

Hope stood when he was presented the Boy Scout statuette, as did every
body else. Then he waited for the room to settle.

> No man can be this great . . . but you've finally convinced
> me . . . I never felt so humble or so deductible . . . I really
> don't know what to say . . . Everything's already been
> said . . . And, of course, I love Milton . . . I love to sit home
> and watch him on TV and see how my jokes are doing. . . .

He introduced Mack Millar, and asked his brothers George, Fred and Ivo
to take a bow. Then he asked Dolores to stand. She took a rather short bo
and Hope said, "Is that all you're going to show of that fashion investment?
Then he added, "I suppose this is the first time Dolores knows what I do for
living. She probably thought I was a test pilot for United Airlines."

Hope missed two of his favorite Friars that night, Benny and Crosby. Jac
was in Cedars of Lebanon Hospital in L.A. because of abdominal pain.
turned out not to be serious and he sent a telegram of regret. Bing's attitud
was clear on such matters: "I never go to those things."

It was a good night for charity. The roast netted $20,000 which was spl
four ways. Joey Adams, the Friars historian, says that Hope thanked every
one except the men's room attendant that night and seemed genuinely move
by the expressions of love that poured out to him from the four corners of th
room. Before he sat down, Hope said, "This could happen to a guy like m
only in show business. This has to be one of my finer moments."[7]

In the months that followed, there were other "finer moments" for Hop
Before he left New York, Hope assisted in the kick-off of the 1953 Red Cro
Drive and emceed a banquet honoring his movie boss Adolph Zukor. Bac
home, between tapings of his Jell-O show, he accepted life membership i

he Hollywood Women's Press Club, and presided over the premiere of his
ewest film, *Here Come the Girls.* He also emceed the Academy Awards
how, and received the first annual Al Jolson Memorial Medal from the
'eterans of Foreign Wars.

He flew up to Denver for his first board meeting as part-owner of radio
tation KOA. He came home to do another *Colgate Comedy Hour,* went to
Vashington to play golf with Eisenhower, judged a dance contest with the
)uke and Duchess of Windsor at the Greenbriar Hotel in White Sulphur
prings, went back to New York to emcee the Damon Runyon Cancer Fund
enefit, back to Los Angeles to do the annual Police Show, then to Chicago
·here he did the Cerebral Palsy telethon, played in a charity golf match, did
 Colgate Comedy taping, and finally flew back home to celebrate his fif-
ieth birthday.

Shortly afterward, Hope checked into Paramount to start his forty-ninth
lm since stepping before cameras at the Warner Brothers studio in Brook-
yn in 1933. This latest would be called *Casanova's Big Night,* his thirty-
ixth starring role in Hollywood. A costume farce reminiscent of *Monsieur
·eaucaire,* it costarred Joan Fontaine and Basil Rathbone, under the skillful
irection of Norman McLeod.

Making *Casanova* anchored Hope in one place long enough for him to
pend some hours with free-lancer William Thornton Martin, professionally
nown as Pete Martin. Martin was a prolific writer who had just collabo-
ated with Crosby on a lighthearted autobiography titled *Call Me Lucky.*
Iope decided that he needed an autobiography too. The deal with Simon
nd Schuster called for a pre-publication series of episodes from Hope's life
) run in the *Saturday Evening Post* for nine weeks under the title *This Is On
1e.*

When the hardcover version of this same material appeared later in 1954,
he episodes were rearranged and there were some new passages, as well. The
ew title was *Have Tux, Will Travel, Bob Hope's Own Story, as told to Pete
1artin.* Hope announced that any profits derived would be channeled into
he Bob and Dolores Hope Foundation, created to handle the hundreds of
equests his office received for handouts, and into the Cerebral Palsy
'und.

From Philippe Halsman's rather prosaic photograph of Hope on the front
ust jacket to the occasional inclusion of dates to attempt historical accura-
y, the book avoids the monologue sound of the previous literary efforts.
1artin made some effort to find the Hope personality both in and out of his
potlight, but the private man seems fairly public. Up till the early 1940s,
1artin follows Hope chronologically. From the early 1940s to the early
950s, however, the book deals in themes like his GI entertaining, near-miss
ccidents, golf, his attitudes about other comedians and comedy, his relation-
hips with his family, his coworkers, and the unmistakable drive that had
rought him to this success story.

Hope's boyhood is presented in a series of idealized tableaux, and the
omedian's deeper relationships are not shared with the reader at all. Hope
oes not emerge as an unfeeling man but as one who has difficulty in
xpressing his emotions.

This superficial kind of autobiography was very much in vogue in the fifties. For *Saturday Evening Post* readers one needed a certain candor, but the chief requirement for a success story was an uplifting message. Fortunately, Hope fitted the prescription admirably. His life was so public, and publicly lived, that there was little room for scandal or what Hope called "negative stuff."

However, there were events in Hope's life that could have helped to flesh out parts of the Hope personality. Indeed, *Have Tux* is more noteworthy for what it leaves out than what it includes. But it is not surprising that Hope omitted the widely publicized court battle involving himself, his brother Jim and the woman Jim lived with, Marie Mali, who claimed to be Jim's wife. At Jim's request in 1939, when Hope was tasting his first big successes in radio and films, Hope hired Marie on a part-time basis to assist his regular secretary Annabelle Pickett. Actually, Marie already had a full-time job as a secretary with Texaco, but she was so impressed by her "brother-in-law's success" that she wanted to be part of it.

Marie assisted in the cataloging and indexing of Hope's 60,000 odd jokes, answered fan mail and addressed the 10,000 Christmas cards he sent out each year. Her salary was about $50 a month. She worked a few hours each evening and, at the going clerical rates, she earned about $12.50 a week. But when she and Jim found out just how much Bob was making, she felt underpaid. Bob assured her a bonus. Meanwhile, Bob had loaned Jim $1,400 and expected it to be returned.

Against Jim's strenuous objection, Marie hired a lawyer and brought suit against Hope for two years' back pay at the rate of $50 a week. Hope's lawyers, Sturges and Russell, filed a countersuit against Jim to recover the loan. The case came to Superior Court in January 1943 with considerable local and national coverage.

Marie told the court that when she tried to talk money matters with Bob, "He told me to sit tight—that I'd get a big hunk of bonus. But the bonus wasn't forthcoming." Her attorney told the court that people doing similar jobs in Hollywood were paid between $150 and $200 a week.

Hope countered through his attorneys that he "definitely had not promised her a bonus," and furthermore he objected to letters Marie had sent him criticizing his secretary Annabelle, which "caused an uprising in my organization."

Jim and Marie were crushed when the jury failed to agree on a verdict and Judge Jess Stephens threw the case out of court. Through the long and raucous affair, Jack Hope, representing Bob, and Jim Hope faced each other in court daily and never spoke. Jack was saddened that such an unpleasant matter—and unnecessary, too—caused the first serious rift between Hope brothers.[8]

That business had a positive side, however. It was during this legal fracas that Marjorie Hughes arrived, fresh out of Sawyer's Business School, and was hired by Annbelle. Later she said, "I found out why I was hired—there was no star-struck faltering in my voice, no celestial fire in my eyes." In time, Miss Hughes' orderly mind, her loyalty, her discretion won Hope's respect and the job as his private secretary for 31 years.[9]

Another event that might have added zest to this narrative was the day the police raided his home. It was spring 1946 and Hope had just finished fou lays of preparation as producer-director-emcee of the annual Los Angeles Policemen's Benefit Show at the Shrine Auditorium. The show, on a Saturday night, was a big success and the next day Hope was busy rehearsing and doing the Sunday run-through preview of his Pepsodent show at the El Capitan in Hollywood. At home, Dolores was hosting a huge open-air Roman Catholic benefit. Devout churchwoman that she was, Dolores had thrown open their six-acre side lawn for an old-fashioned country fair and bazaar to raise money for an order of Carmelite nuns. Perhaps it was out of naiveté, and perhaps not, that so many of the attractions at this outdoor party were games of chance, some with dice, some wheels of fortune, some raffles for baked hams and home-baked cakes. About an hour after the crowds had entered the Hope grounds, several North Hollywood police cars roared up and officers swarmed through the fair. "It's a raid," gasped Dolores. A detective said into a bullhorn, "We have a complaint that there is gambling in progress here. We're going to have to ask you to leave." The police broke up the games, closed down the party and Monday morning's newspapers carried bold headlines about the gambling raid at the Hope residence.[10] Hope took it calmly and decided not to make a fuss, despite his associates' sputterings about the ungratefulness of the men in blue. And the next spring Hope emceed the Police Benefit just as he had done the previous six years and would do for twenty more.

Although Hope talked in *Have Tux* about bad-taste gags and jokes that misfired, he failed to mention a $100,000 libel and slander suit brought against him in 1950 by the Forest Hotel on Forty-ninth Street in New York. While Hope was playing the Paramount, he had cracked: "I got into town today and the Mayor gave me the keys to the city, and I checked into the Forest Hotel where they gave me a cell—the maid changes rats every day." The hotel management brought slander charges for the joke itself, and libel charges because they claimed it was scripted. Martin Gang, who by then had become Hope's attorney and has remained his legal advisor, filed an affidavit denying that the comedian used a script for personal appearances, and said "any reference to the hotel was without malice." The words of that joke, according to the lawyer's statement, "in the light of the circumstances surrounding their utterance, could not have been understood by any reasonable person as to have been uttered other than in jest." There was, subsequently, a quiet settlement of court costs.[11]

Another lawsuit Hope omitted from the autobiography was the one he instituted against Time, Incorporated, in late 1950, charging that in the November 6 issue of *Life,* his good name had been maligned by critic John Crosby. In a piece titled "Seven Deadly Sins of the Air," Crosby wrote: "Writers got $2,000 a week in Hollywood for copying down Fred Allen's jokes and putting them on Bob Hope's program." Hope asked the court for damages in the amount of $2,010,000, claiming the article implied he was guilty of plagiarism, exposing him to hatred and ridicule by the public, which tended to discredit his standing in the entertainment business.

But in May 1951 Hope requested the suit be dropped because, after private discussions, he was satisfied that the "offending paragraph had been left in the story inadvertently and there was no intention to harm him." *Life* publisher Andrew Heiskell went public to soften the media coverage, saying his magazine "had been on most friendly terms with Hope for many years and wished to continue."[12]

The year *Have Tux* appeared, 1954, was a benchmark for Hope. A quarter of a century earlier he was a hungry comedian in a Chicago vaudeville house, leering and gagging his way to the top. Now he was there, and he would not know, of course, that there were still to be another 25 plus years of career ahead of him, or just how celebrated he would become.

He was beloved by a large segment of the American public through the force of his personality, his jokes, and because of his screen image that cast him as the perennial juvenile—as Leo Rosten said, "The perfect symbol of the man Fate is determined to make a jerk." Rosten describes Hope's "take-off of the adult wolf with adolescent impulses":

> A tie-fumbler and a neck-stretcher, he ogles the dames and hints at midnight seductions, but you know he'll end up with candied cashew nuts and a uke. He is Penrod playing Don Juan. The minute a babe sails into view, he breaks into a leer, but he breaks into a sweat if the girl so much as flutters her lashes. His leer, indeed, shows the triumph of innocence over intention, his type gets seasick in a boudoir.[13]

This image of Hope was what made it possible for him to ride through, relatively unscathed, the publicity surrounding *Confidential* magazine's account of his alleged affair with one of Hollywood's more sexually active and publicity-seeking blond starlets, Barbara Payton. It was written by Horton Streete from information apparently provided by the actress and some of her friends and presumably verified by *Confidential* attorneys. The relationship was described as beginning in March of 1949 in Texas where Hope was playing in a Dallas charity tournament. Streete says that millionaire Bob Neal had introduced Payton to Hope at a party in his hotel suite. "They hadn't known each other six hours before they knew each other as well as a boy and girl ever can."[14] The story never became any more explicit than that, but continued to characterize the hectic, catch-as-catch-can nature of their meetings in New York, Washington and other cities.

Among Payton's "revelations" were these: that Hope was no "Casanova," that he "was one of the closest guys with a buck she ever knew," that he was vain and "seldom passed a mirror without taking a long look at his own skinose" and that he liked her cooking.

For Bob to admit to his fans in 1954 that he was "no angel" was perhaps enough, because the comedian's sly way of referring to sex both on and off the screen implied much more than it actually said. Nor, for that matter, did he need to say that his "attractiveness to other women," as Dolores referred to it, caused his wife any problems. Dolores has said, "Every woman's husband is attractive to some other woman. I have tried to do the only thing any woman can do—keep busy, try to remain interesting, and cling to my own conceits. When doubt has troubled me, I think, 'But why shouldn't he love me before anyone else?' "

It's very exciting to be here in Moscow with you Demo-crats . . . you must be or you wouldn't be here . . . I hope you'll be cooperative tonight. On my passport I wrote "Comedian" and I'd hate to have the Russians think I lied . . .[1]

33. Hard Road to Russia

On March 19, 1953, an event occurred in Hollywood that many observers believed would never happen: The motion picture business finally recognized television. Motion Picture Academy historian Robert Osborne explained:

> Close to the time for the 1951 Oscar show to take form, several major film companies (Warner Brothers, Columbia, Universal-International and Republic) refused to come up with their usual share of the expenses to help underwrite the ceremony. The timing seemed right. Had NBC–RCA not made a $100,000 bid for radio and television rights at that moment, there would have been no Oscar ceremony that year.[2]

And if there were no ceremony, Bob Hope would not have emceed the awards for the seventh time, nor would a nationwide audience have had the opportunity to witness his third Academy honor (still not for acting), a statuette for "his contribution to the laughter of the world, his service to the motion picture industry, and his devotion to the American premise."[3]

It was quite a night for the movies, being the twenty-fifth Oscar handout; and quite a night for television, too, being the first time viewers had been treated to a horde of big-time film stars on their home screens. This was the year De Mille's *The Greatest Show on Earth* won for best picture, and Hope can always say he acted in an Oscar-winning movie because of his cameo appearance in that film. Shirley Booth almost did a pratfall when she came up on stage to accept her award for *Come Back, Little Sheba.* Gary Cooper drawled his shy "thank you" for *High Noon,* and De Mille received his statuette from the hands of legendary Mary Pickford.

Hope's monologue that night was fittingly pungent, rapping the running battle between the film colony and television:

> . . . Everyone said that television and the movies would finally get together and it finally happened. Tonight, you're watching the wedding. The only thing you couldn't see was the shot-gun . . . What a marriage! Now the question is which one wears the nightgown . . . Paramount doesn't mind my doing television shows . . . In fact, they insist on it. I think it's a pretty sneaky way to cripple a new medium. . . .[4]

Paramount executives were indeed arguing that television would destroy his movie audience; big boss Barney Balaban warned Hope that *Casanova's Big Night* would lose a million dollars because theater owners were becoming angry and spiteful. Although *Casanova* ended up earning more than $3 million at the box office, movie-making was in a troubled metamorphosis. Studios tried lavish spectaculars, three-dimensionals, concentrated on fewer film starts of higher quality—anything and everything that might bring back the departing moviegoer.

Worried by all this as a coproducer, and weary of the brickbats frequently tossed at his film acting, Hope was willing to try something novel, something more challenging. And beneath the gags he was hungry for a real Oscar. Two of his former radio gagmen, Mel Shavelson and Jack Rose, approached him with the concept for a dramatic film biography of Eddie Foy. Foy was one of America's most beloved vaudevillians who happened to be a son of a bitch offstage. He had married a beautiful Italian dancer and was an indifferent husband and irresponsible father to seven children. When Foy's wife died suddenly, he was left with the kids, and in desperation Foy turned them into a successful vaudeville act. It was a strong script, clearly one in which Hope's knowledge of vaudeville would be essential and in which his accustomed screen persona would be out of place.

"I like it," said Hope.

"Then you're in trouble," Shavelson said.

"Why?" asked Hope.

"Because I want to direct it," said Mel.

"That's no big deal. My last three pictures were so bad I can't sink any lower."[5]

After taking a careful look, Hope Enterprises took 44 percent, leaving the rest to Shavelson, Rose and Paramount.

Hope said: "The big challenge about *Foys* was that for the first time I had to play a real-life character and one that the public knew, and having to do some pretty heavy scenes. I wanted to get inside Eddie Foy as much as I could so I read everything I could find and even studied some old silent movies he had made. Fortunately, I had some help from Bryan and Charlie Foy and Eddie, Jr., was technical adviser on the picture."

Hope went into training like an athlete. To match Foy's consummate artistry as a hoofer, Hope hired Nick Castle to help freshen up his footwork. Shavelson and Rose approached Jimmy Cagney to do a cameo part in the film, re-creating his Oscar-winning role as George M. Cohan. And when Hope and Cagney join forces for a challenge dance during a Friars Club banquet scene in the picture, their performances display a virtuosity that is still considered one of the finer moments in film history.

Hope was thrilled that Cagney agreed to do the cameo role, and touched by Cagney's rationale.

"I'll do the bit on one condition," said Cagney.

"What's that?" asked Jack Rose.

"That I don't get paid."

"But why?" asked Shavelson.

"Because when I was breaking in as an actor," said Cagney, "I could always get a square meal and a place to flop at the Foys. This is my way of paying them back."[6]

As a serious actor, Hope was fairly successful in reaching Foy's darker side, the arrogance, the hostility, the self-indulgence, the unpleasant attitude about human relationships, and the self-pity over the death of his beautiful Madeleine. Hope said later:

> The toughest scene for me to do was when I had to plead with a judge for custody of my children who had been taken from me because of child labor laws. It was a long dramatic speech, quite a change of pace for a guy who is accustomed to one-liners. On the night before I had to do the scene, Barney Dean died. Maybe that's how I got through it.[7]

There was added reality in Eddie Foy, Jr.'s, narration.

The total effect was a credible film biography. To some extent the script, and more pointedly, Hope's portrayal, were criticized for lack of warmth, suggesting "the humor lacked the endearing qualities needed to offset the cutting edge of Foy's calculating side."

But on June 1, 1955, the *New York Daily News* critic, in awarding her four stars, reflected the general feeling that this picture was a Hope benchmark:

> . . . (He) doesn't have to take any more insults from Bing Crosby about his acting. Hope can now hold up his head with Hollywood's dramatic thespians as, for the first time in his career, Hope isn't playing Hope on the screen. He's acting and doing a commendable job.

Hope's new fall season of television specials highlighted his unique position as the enduringly popular monologist on the entertainment scene. So many funnymen had turned to situation comedy for survival. *Minneapolis Tribune* critic Will Jones, overjoyed that the comedian was just playing himself, wrote on October 13, 1954:

> It suddenly struck me that it's been a long time since I've heard a comedian do that. The screens have been taken over by a breed of funnymen whom the critics delight in describing variously as imps, pixies, buffoons, clowns, sad sacks, or characters. They're all acting like mad.

Also on October 13, *World-Telegram and Sun* critic Harriet Van Horne gave Hope a mixed review:

> Perhaps Hope is shrewd, rather than reactionary, to cling to these machine gun solos. He does them awfully well. I'm a little disappointed, though, that the level of the humor hasn't been raised over the years. The average Hope joke hasn't even a nodding acquaintance with the epigram. It's college humor most of the time. Other comedians come equipped with wittier jokes and a more satirical outlook. But they don't get the steady unremitting laughs Hope gets.

Hope was bothered by the critics harping on his show's "sameness." In fact, when he received an invitation to emcee a Royal Command Performance in London, he had Saphier tell NBC he intended to cancel his scheduled

November television special and, instead, film an "international review" in Europe with stars like Maurice Chevalier, Orson Welles and Edith Piaf, none of whom had ever appeared on American television. When NBC officials demanded to know how Hope could leave them with an unfilled sixty minutes, costing them $100,000, the comedian explained it was more important for him to do a "first" and to film a show abroad because "TV comedy shows are all full of the same old faces, getting older."[8]

NBC advised Saphier that Hope simply could not treat them that way, and Saphier reasoned back that his client was trying to make TV history. Hope responded with "Let them sue me if they want" and sailed for England.[9] In London he rehearsed the benefit show for Queen Elizabeth, and tried to assemble an interesting cast for his international revue. He flew to Paris and charmed Maurice Chevalier (who said he owed Hope one) into making his American television debut; he cabled Bea Lillie; he heard the 182-voice Cologne Male Choir at a London concert and hired them on the spot; he had seen French ballerina Laine Dayde in Paris and signed her. At the Command Performance he was intrigued by "two noticeable blondes," Moira Lister and Shirley Eaton, and he hired them, too. As a topper, he hired the suave Reginald Gardiner to mouth the General Foods commercials in a haughty British manner.

The Hope retinue that invaded the rented BBC studios for that London filming included Jack Hope (who was producing), director Jim Jordan, Jr., three writers, a production supervisor, an assistant producer, soundman John Pawlek, several representatives from NBC, General Foods and the advertising agency. BBC's Bill Ward, in charge of the local crew, was stupefied as this Hope contingent kept arriving. Used to a modest half-dozen technicians to produce his full-hour show, he gasped: "I don't know what half of them are doing. And I simply haven't any idea how to control them."

When the filming was over, Hope flew to Paris, and sitting in the drawing room of his George V suite, he chatted with Art Buchwald who was then writing his "Europe's Lighter Side" column for the *Herald Tribune*.

"What did you do about commercials?" asked Buchwald, knowing the British didn't use them.

"We had originally planned to use Reggie Gardiner, but ended up with a wonderful British newsman named McDonald Hobley—veddy distinguished voice—a guy who had never done anything like talking about Jell-O or Swansdown or Minute Rice. He said to the audience 'Now, however amusing it may sound to you, don't laugh at the commercials. So while I mention names that you have never heard before—or are likely to hear again—*do* be serious, won't you?' He killed me."

"I hear they almost didn't let you into France."

"This is such a wonderful country. They give you the choice of going to jail or becoming a citizen of Paris. I forgot my passport; I left it in London. And the French authorities threatened to lock me up. Next thing I knew they were kissing me on both cheeks and pinning a medal on me."[10]

Martin Ragaway, one of three writers with Hope on that trip, entered the room. Buchwald asked him if he got to see much of Europe on such a trip. Ragaway said, "He locked us in our hotel room in London for three days, and kept the key. Finally, on the third day, he said, 'Gee, I've been very inconsiderate of you people. You boys probably haven't seen anything of London. No, don't go away.' Then he went downstairs and bought forty picture postcards of London scenes and sent them up to us."

Hope flew back to Los Angeles in time to watch the international show on his own TV set. He thought the show could have been better, and a large number of television reviewers in America agreed. The show had, predictably, a huge audience. Actually the show wasn't so bad. Unfortunately, NBC had fired off a barrage of hyperbole, with press releases raving, "With the simple idea of filing the first truly global television show, Hope made history."[11] Not surprisingly, MacArthur of the *Washington Star* wrote: "If this is history, Arnold Toynbee has been ploughing a long furrow in the wrong field."[12]

Hope fared much better in *That Certain Feeling,* the movie he made for Paramount that same year. It was adapted from the Jean Kerr–Eleanor Brooke comedy success on Broadway, *King of Hearts.* Benefiting from a sophisticated script, nicely adapted by Panama and Frank, with superb direction from Panama, Hope was able to deliver a first-rate performance as a neurotic cartoonist named Francis X. Dingman, who has trouble juggling his work and his wife, played deftly by the 1953 Oscar winner Eva Marie Saint. This is undoubtedly Hope's most sophisticated motion picture.

About this time, Hope dropped a couple of remarks to Hollywood columnists about retiring. His long-standing friend, reporter Bob Thomas, asked, "Do you mean it?"

"I was down in Palm Springs playing golf with Charlie Yates," said Hope, with a frightened look, "when he died right next to me in the golf cart. He just lay back—and went. He was there for 20 minutes before they came for him. You know, he was my first agent in New York. He was a good friend. It happened so fast."

"What were you thinking?" asked Thomas.

"It didn't really affect me for three days. Then the shock set in. I was terribly upset. I began to feel all sorts of pains and things wrong in my body. I thought I was dying. About this time NBC came to me with a new contract to sign and I said nothing doing. I was going to retire."

"Are you serious?"

"Sure I was serious. I was terribly depressed. I went to see Tom Hearn and he gave me a complete physical. He chased me out of his office. In fact, he chased me down the street. He said I was too healthy. And, you know, my spirits changed."

"To what?"

"I signed a five-year deal with NBC to do eight shows a year. I've finished up the movie with Eva Marie Saint and then I plan to do two television shows in Europe because I'm going over to London to do a movie with Katie Hepburn. Taking the whole family with me."[13]

The picture in London with Katharine Hepburn was *Not for Money,* a *Ninotchka*-type story by Ben Hecht. This was an outside film deal with MGM and Hepburn's original leading man was supposed to be Cary Grant. When Grant became unavailable, Hope's name was suggested, and although

everyone had mixed feelings, especially Hecht, the idea seemed a good one
Hope's performance in *The Seven Little Foys* allayed the Hecht–Hepburn
fears.

Things went badly between Hecht and Hope. It had to do, according to
Hope, with the script. When Hope arrived at London's Dorchester Hotel, he
called Hecht, who was staying at the more conservative Connaught Hotel
"Ben, this script isn't finished."

"I know," said Hecht, "but it's coming along."

"Maybe I can help," offered Hope, meaning he would assign a couple of
his writers to punch it up.

About ten minutes later, Hecht and Hepburn and assorted production
people arrived at Hope's suite, prepared to hack out the closing scenes.

"Wait a minute," said Hope, "it's not that large. I just had a couple of
hokey thoughts about the script."[14]

But at that point Hope's "hokey thoughts" were more than Hecht had, so
as the days went along Hope's and his writers' ideas were reluctantly
accepted in the interests of completing the project. Clearly Hecht and Hepburn
were not pleased, nor was Hope.

> But we managed to get through the picture and I must say Katie
> was a gem. She played the Jewish mother on the set, fussing over
> everyone who happened to sneeze.[15]

Hope's writers eventually took over the final script-doctoring and they renamed
the film *The Iron Petticoat*. Hecht took out full-page Hollywood
trade paper ads with his own $75 to tell the industry how he felt:

> My dear Partner Bob Hope:
>   This is to notify you that I have removed my name as author
> from our mutilated venture, *The Iron Petticoat*.
>   Unfortunately, your other partner, Katharine Hepburn, can't
> shy out of the fractured picture with me.
>   Although her magnificent comic performance has been blow-
> torched out of the film, there is enough left of the Hepburn
> footage to identify her for her sharpshooters.
>   I am assured by my hopeful predators that *The Iron Petticoat*
> will go over big with people "who can't get enough of Bob
> Hope."
>   Let us hope this swooning contingent is not confined to yourself
> and your euphoric agent, Louis Shurr.
>
>   (*Signed*) Ben Hecht

Hope replied in kind, advising Hecht that the picture was immeasurably
improved following his departure. Of course this was not the case. The picture,
even with its good moments, was a mistake, and after its initial release
it was retired.

But what rose rather majestically from this sorry venture was a kind of
phoenix. First for publicity purposes, and then later because it was a pioneering
idea and thus a challenge, Hope decided he must film a television show
inside the Soviet Union.

First attempts to get inside Russia were in the hands of Betty Box, producer of *The Iron Petticoat,* who had tried to clear Soviet on-site locations for filming. When those negotiations collapsed, Hope thought, why not try to stage the world premiere of the picture in Moscow? If not that, then why not try to televise an NBC–TV comedy special from Moscow?

But first, he had two movies to make. Shavelson and Rose had pursuaded him to try a second straight dramatic part, showing him Gene Fowler's biography of colorful New York mayor Jimmy Walker. But the cost projection was sobering. To insure accuracy beyond the Fowler text, Shavelson and Rose paid $50,000 in clearances. The producers had to negotiate with Walker's first wife, his sister and two adopted children, Walker's top aide while he was in office, as well as other politicians and associates. Clearance also came from Walker's second wife, actress Betty Compton. Attorneys worked many weeks before production could begin, to reduce fear of any litigation over the interpretation of Walker's personal and political escapades. Costarring with Hope, and adding measurably to the credibility of the biography, were Alexis Smith as his first wife, Vera Miles as Betty Compton, Paul Douglas and Darren McGavin. George Jessel, Jack Benny and Sammy Cahn appeared in cameo roles.

Believable as Hope is in the picture, which holds up well even today, one feels he could have gone a bit further in clarifying the dualities of Walker's personality. Walker was both attractive and unsympathetic, witty but naive, moral and corrupt. Naturally the lighter moments worked particularly well, but Hope is also superb in several dramatic scenes. Hope's portrayal of Walker as the broken man, conning enough money to afford his own exile from the city he has ruled and loved, is one of the comedian's most effective moments on film.

Critics greeted the film, called *Beau James,* graciously but without the consideration many felt it deserved. Most critics have placed Hope's Jimmy Walker role as another milestone in his long movie career for another reason: It was his only tragic role and the last time he attempted anything serious.

In contrast, his next move, *Paris Holiday,* was based on a Hope idea and produced by him at a staggering cost. His costar was Fernandel and neither of the two comedians could adequately speak the other's language. Fernandel smiled a lot, particularly over the $120,000 he got paid. It was filmed in Paris and Hope's jokes about this venture say more than any serious words could do:

> *Paris Holiday* set a new record: three men were killed on the picture. All of them auditors. The cost went a million dollars over budget, but it was all United Artists' fault. Handing me the money to make a movie is like asking Dean Martin to tend your bar.[17]

Hope's critics and his friends said, "Stick to acting."

In November 1957 Hope went to London to tape a television special and to sneak-preview *Paris Holiday.* While he was there the obsession for entertaining inside Russia manifested itself again. He went to the Soviet Consulate at 5 Kensington Palace Gardens and applied for visas to cover himself and a modest technical crew. Next he telephoned his New York press agent

Ursula Halloran and asked her to initiate some action at the Washington end. His plan was to represent one of his own movies in a cultural exchange. He suggested *Paris Holiday.* Then he telephoned NBC's Moscow correspondent Irving R. Levine, asking him for advice and any possible help in facilitating his request. After weeks of waiting, he telephoned Jock Whitney, United States ambassador to England, asking him to help speed up the process. Whitney said he was, in fact, going to a cocktail party where he would undoubtedly run into his Soviet counterpart, Russia's ambassador to Britain, Jacob Malik. Whitney called Hope back in Los Angeles and said that Malik inquired, "What does your Mr. Hope want to do—entertain our troops in Red Square?"

More weeks passed. Ursula Halloran wasn't making much progress in Washington despite Hope's friendship with so many government people. Hope impatiently called Irving Levine again and asked why he couldn't just book himself onto an Aeroflot plane and fly into Moscow. Levine diplomatically explained that impossibility.

All this time the media was covering Hope's efforts meticulously and registering each failed attempt. When he flew back to London for the official world premiere of *Paris Holiday,* he renewed his efforts at the consulate. Silence.

Then, quite unexpectedly, while back in California, Hope got a call from NBC's Washington office. It was Julian Goodman informing him there were six visas waiting for him at the Soviet Embassy. Hope had applied for sixteen. Besides his own visa, there would be one for Ursula, and another for press agent Arthur Jacobs who, representing United Artists, would arrange the Moscow premiere of *Paris Holiday.* After all, this was to be a cultural exchange. There were visas for Hope writers Mort Lachman and Bill Larkin, and the sixth was for Ken Talbot, who was one of Britain's most able lighting–cameramen.

Hope was instructed on the behavior expected of him and his associates inside the Soviet Union; he was cautioned that his visa was limited to Moscow; he was told that the film he shot there would be developed there. Hope agreed, aware that his would be the first United States television show to be entirely produced inside Russia.

A week later, Hope and the reduced television crew flew from New York to Copenhagen, where Hope, Halloran and Jacobs, with the print of *Paris Holiday* in his care, boarded a Russian Aeroflot jet for a direct flight to Moscow. The other three flew to Moscow via Prague.

Hope was greeted at the airport by Irving Levine. Standing nearby to cover this whirlwind seven-day trip were two reporters from *Look* magazine, an INS correspondent, and a Magnum free-lance photographer. Hope was also assigned an interpreter–guide–government representative, all in the person of Larissa Soborova.

Hope was making this trip at a time when American–Soviet relationships were surrounded by mystery, suspicion and, as always, competition. Consequently, in his public statements about this trip, Hope shrewdly played to American taste by exaggerating the cloak-and-dagger aspects:

> Whenever I'd enter my room, I'd pound on the wall and yell, "Testing! Testing! One! Two! Three! Am I coming in loud and

clear?" And whenever we were discussing anything that might in any way be misinterpreted, one of us would look up the ventilator and holler, "Only kidding, Kru!" We were actually half-joking when we did this, but it was a joke only because there was a possibility that the Big Bear was listening.[18]

Arthur Jacobs could not pull off the hoped-for coup, the premiere of *Paris Holiday,* but he did manage to get Hope on a worldwide radio conference circuit with Fernandel in Paris to plug the picture. After that, Jacobs' work was done and he flew back to New York.

With guts, ingenuity and daring, the now-reduced team of five toured Moscow with their watchful hosts, selecting sites, loading film, painting cue cards, pressing wrinkled garments, shooting scenes at carefully approved locations, sneaking forbidden still and motion pictures for later insertion into the TV show, and generally depending on blind luck to prevail.

At Red Square, Talbot shot Hope against the spiky Kremlin towers, walking toward Lenin's tomb with a snakelike line of citizens behind him. Then he walked across the Square to complete an assignment Hope later joked about:

> Jack Benny asked me to bring back a fur hat with a part in it. So I crossed Red Square to visit the GUM department store . . . Don't let anyone tell you that the Russians aren't passionate. At the perfume counter they displayed such sexy sounding scents as "Kremlin" and "Our Moscow." I don't know how they missed "Moonlight on the Collective Farm," "Volga Boatman," and "Essence of Tractor." This one not only smells good, but it's wonderful for lubricating a fan belt. Instead of "My Sin" it's "Where Do I Go to Confess?"[19]

Hope also had help from Soviet cameramen in shooting such events as the Moscow circus and a fashion show at GUM. He was offered and decided to use exclusive film of violinist David Oistrakh, ballerina Galina Ulanova, the celebrated Russian clown Popov, and controversial character comedian Arkadi Raikin. Hope also bought from the ministry footage of the Ukrainian State Dancers.

Ambassador Llewellyn Thompson's office remained in constant touch with Hope and discovered that the Soviets were stalling Hope over the arrangements for a public hall where the comedian could perform his one-man concert for the English-speaking community and other foreign diplomats. Thompson hastily interceded and offered Hope his own official residence, Spasso House. In a matter of two days he had managed to build a camera platform for Talbot and the Russian crew, set up stage facilities in the large reception hall and issue invitations.

Just prior to that show, Hope went back to his hotel room and found his briefcase forced open and his gags spread out all over his bed. There was no effort to hide the perusal of his material, mostly jokes he was using in his monologue, or had considered using. Some of them had made him nervous so he had rejected them, like: "They have a national lottery here. It's called living."[20]

Hope did about an hour's worth of comedy for the select audience at Spasso House, and the parts that were edited into a TV monologue were these.

> It's very exciting to be here in Moscow with you Demo-
> crats . . . you must be Democrats or you wouldn't be
> here . . . I hope you'll be cooperative tonight. On my passport I
> wrote "Comedian" and I'd hate to have the Russians think I
> lied . . . The State Department was glad to let me come here.
> I'm cooperative, I'm personable, I'm charming and expendable.
> But it's really a thrill to be in Russia. I know I'm in Rus-
> sia . . . this morning my stomach got up two hours before I did
> and had a bowl of borscht . . . How about that vodka. Now I
> know why they got their sputnik up first . . . I'm surprised the
> whole country isn't up there with it . . . The Russians are over-
> joyed with their sputnik. It's kind of weird being in a country
> where every ninety minutes there's a national holiday . . . any-
> body without a stiff neck is a traitor . . . it's the big topic of
> conversation everyplace but the dog show . . . It's pretty ner-
> vous staying in a country where the Government owns everything.
> If you steal a towel, it's a federal rap. I've had to unpack three
> times . . . But it's amazing the way people can get the wrong
> impression. One Russian official showed me a picture of the
> starving people in America. People without shoes and nothing to
> eat, absolutely desperate. And I couldn't argue with him . . . it
> was a picture of the bus station at Las Vegas. . . .[21]

Because of Russian help in photographing the monologue, the film was processed in a Soviet film laboratory, and the gags were studied carefully by Rachuck and two other authorities, Michael Radeyev, Deputy of Film Export, and Alexander Davydov, head of Soviet Export Film. At a cocktail party given by the Ministry of Culture on Hope's final evening in Moscow, the three men took him into a small office.

"Mr. Hope, the monologue which we have in our lab is magnificent," said Davydov, "but there are just a few jokes which might better be left out."

"Which ones?" said Hope nicely.

"*The Russians are overjoyed with their Sputnik. It's kind of weird being in a country where every ninety-two minutes there's a national holiday. Anybody without a stiff neck is a traitor. It's a big topic of conversation everyplace but the dog show,*" recited Davydov from prepared notes. "Trai-tor is a very serious charge in Russia."

"We are not implying Russians are traitors," argued Hope. "What we are trying to do is state in a humorous way how proud the people are of their Sputnik. Exaggeration is one of the basic forms of comedy."

Davydov thought about this and then said: "Perhaps you could eliminate all reference to the Sputnik. It is not really a subject for comedy."

"We are anxious to cooperate but we must be reasonable," Hope said. "Satellites and missles are a big topic in Russia just as they are in America. We both lose if we treat you any differently than any other country in the world. Listen, here are the jokes I told on my last television show—"I guess you heard the big news from Cape Canaveral. Our government has launched another submarine. . . . Actually the test firing of missiles is going very well. They hit the target every time. As a matter of fact, there's hardly anything left of Bermuda. . . ."

The three Russians laughed. Hope beamed, figuring he had won the round. Then Davydov said that he would submit a list of jokes that he would appreciate being cut out and Hope agreed to accept the list. Next, Davydov smiled as he handed Hope a bill for $1,200 for lab fees and other crew expenses. He said he would be glad to release the film with Hope's assurance of paying.[22]

After Hope's departure the next day, Lachman and Larkin collected the film and rushed it back to Hollywood for editing. It was broadcast on April 5, 1958, with Hope narrating in a humorous commentary. Though not one of Hope's most widely watched programs, Nielsen audience ratings show nearly 25 million people, or more than one third of the available viewers, were tuned to the Moscow broadcast. NBC scheduled a repeat showing following the announcement that the program had been awarded two of the television industry's most pretigious honors, the Peabody and the Sylvania merit awards for 1958.

For the closing sequence, showing Hope walking through the streets of Moscow, the comedian chose this simple powerful statement:

> For five days and nights I have stared and walked and wondered. It's a strange city. I missed the street signs, the hubbub of traffic, the colorful clothing, the billboards, and the neon gleaming in the night. Yet there is much that is the same: people trying to make a living, people trying to keep their families together. And kids, wonderful kids with great faces. It would be wonderful if someday their kids and our kids could grow up into a world that spoke the same language and respected the same things. Right now the world is busy building a bomb for every letter in the alphabet. That cannot be the answer. But there must be one. We must find some plan for peaceful co-existence, so that human beings don't become obsolete.[23]

I put in a call to Marilyn (that's Hollywood talk for I had my agent call her agent) and as it happened Marilyn really wanted to come, but couldn't because of studio commitments (that's Hollywood talk for we'll never know whether she wanted to or not).[1]

34. The Eye

Of all the sex goddesses and superstars who invaded Hollywood, there was only one that Hope wanted for his radio and television shows and couldn't get—Marilyn Monroe. The closest he came was Christmas 1954 when Air Secretary Harold Talbott asked Hope to put together an entertainment package for the hardship base GIs stuck in the remote ice-bound terrain of Thule, Greenland. The cold war with Russia was at its ripest; Thule was both an early warning station and a Strategic Air Command base with severe morale problems. And, very important, Bob's closest military pal, Rosy O'Donnell, was in command there.

Talbott pitched hard to Hope to bring Marilyn. Presumably she was the Air Secretary's personal choice, she was certainly the hands-down favorite of the Thule GIs. When Hope agreed to make the trip, he exacted a promise from the Air Force to give him, beyond the usual transportation, some technical assistance so he could film the shows for a television special. This would be the first of the celebrated overseas "Christmas Shows." Hope wanted Marilyn but he couldn't get her, despite the fact that she had once told him she would go with him whenever he asked. Hope was positive she was being over-managed and that his request never got to her.

He was fortunate in signing a major male film star, Bill Holden, who was bringing his beautiful wife, Brenda Marshall. But Hope still wanted a sex queen. He later said:

> I just had about given up when, a few nights before we were set to leave for Greenland, I emceed a Big Ten Conference football banquet, and among the guests was a beauty contest winner, Miss UCLA. She was wearing a sweater with team letters and the U and the L were outstanding. Although she was a virtual unknown at the time, this doll was strikingly beautiful and unbelievably stacked. Obeying an impulse I invited her to come along to Thule.[2]

Her name was Anita Ekberg. Hope also had invited Margaret Whiting, Jerry Colonna, Patty Thomas, Peter Leeds, Robert Strauss, Charley Cooley, and columnist Hedda Hopper. The Les Brown band was along, too, despite the fact that the 100-member Air Force Band had been booked for Thule long before Hope agreed to go.

There were five or six thousand men stationed there; two hundred of them had worked steadily around the clock for two days prior to Hope's arrival erecting a temporary stage, laying cables, setting up lights and chairs, connecting microphones. The Hope plane landed in sub-zero weather. Worse, because it was so close to the North Pole, it was dark twenty-four hours a day at this time of the year. Hope's monologue fitted the formula for foxhole humor:

> I'm very happy to be here in Thule. The temperature is thirty-six below. Only . . . we don't know below what . . . the thermometer went AWOL . . . The guys get pretty lonesome up here. When a wolf howls he starts a community sing . . . It's so lonely here one guy is going steady with his tattoo . . . and his friends keep asking him if she's got a sister . . . You're not even allowed to think about girls up here. At night a sergeant walks through the barracks and wakes up anybody with a smile on his face. . . .[3]

Hope's sketch for the troops was about GIs in Greenland who write back to the States for a mail-order bride. Anita Ekberg played the girl, and when she entered in a fur coat the capacity audience of 3,000 men stood up and cheered and stomped and whistled. "She took off the coat and stood there in a low-cut gown that showed cleavage that made the Grand Canyon look trivial. It was bedlam."

Hope's second show and second filming of that 1954 trip took place at Goose Bay, Labrador, on New Year's Eve. By this time the whole cast was well-grooved into their lines and the tempo of the show was exactly right. At the show's end, the cast sang "Auld Lang Syne" and Hope hollered out "Happy New Year and God bless you!" and there followed madness.

> . . . five thousand people in that tightly packed gym were yelling and screaming, laughing and crying. People were blowing horns, throwing confetti. The stage was overrun. The orchestra was blasting. Everyone was hugging everybody. The din was overwhelming. It was a moment of sheer animal hysteria that I can still hear and see vividly.[4]

Nine days later a documentary of this tour was presented as a *Colgate Comedy Hour*, and that showing handed Hope his highest television viewing audience to date, and one of the biggest audiences drawn by any commercial program up to that time—a 60 percent share of the available sets in use.

The following Christmas, Hope was in London shooting *The Iron Petticoat* and still the USO found him. They asked him to do some holiday entertaining for GIs, but the shooting schedule couldn't be bent sufficiently, particularly since the Hecht–Hepburn difficulties were still raw to the touch. But he was committed to filming a television show in London which had a December 27 broadcast date. So he decided to take some entertainers to do a show at an American base at Keflavík, Iceland.

During auditions for the London television show, Hope was struck by the good looks and unusual physical attributes of a tall, shapely blonde named Joan Rhodes. A former fashion model, she was then making her living doing a strongwoman act in European music halls. She could break eight-inch nails, rip telephone books, bend steel and lift heavy men up over her head. Hope decided she would be a treat for the GIs in Iceland.

Together they worked out a funny routine. Hope would be singing "Embraceable You" alone on stage when Joan would walk out seductively, and without notice lift Hope up into her arms and cuddle him while he was still singing. The sight of this appealing woman lifting Hope as if she were King Kong got so many big laughs at rehearsal that the comedian decided to take the bit one step further. For the TV cameras in Iceland, Hope suggested that she lift him up over her head. He recalls:

> When the big moment came, she hoisted me up and I stood on her hands. There I was high over Iceland. Then she began to totter backward. I thought she was ad-libbing that totter. Well, she wasn't. I went over her head onto the floor. The floor was cement. The audience roared when I hit. They thought it was part of the act. The TV cameras that were filming the show were still going, and while I was flat on the floor I yelled "Cut!"[5]

Hope's nose was bleeding but otherwise he didn't seem to be badly hurt. He was shaken up and bruised, but he managed to finish the show.

In November 1956 Air Secretary Talbott again asked Hope to go to Alaska, which resulted in a particularly delightful overseas Christmas show, and a huge viewing audience for a new commercial sponsor, Chevrolet. Hope's costars on that six-day tour of three Air Force bases and the Alaskan Command headquarters in below-zero weather were Ginger Rogers and Mickey Mantle. Ginger was vivacious and glamorous, but most of the attention on that trip was focused on the young center fielder who had just been named "outstanding athlete of the year," besides leading his league in home runs during 1955 and 1956, and also being "most valuable player" for those years. Mickey was a national hero and a natural comedian. Hope's gag writers produced one of their cleverest sketches for Mantle and Hope, a satire on the modern Army draftee, played by Mantle, who arrives at boot camp and is met by a tough first sergeant, played by Hope.

In another sketch, Hope played the boob to Ginger's Klondike Lil, and near the end of the sketch, she had to zap Hope with a prop breakaway bottle. But in the hangar at Fairbands the prop bottle had frozen, and when Ginger smashed it against Bob's head it didn't break. It merely stunned Hope into momentary unconsciousness. Ginger, keeping the comedy moving, tapped him again with it and Hope slumped to the floor. Ginger ad-libbed, believing Hope was faking. When he came to, he stood up and was more concerned about maintaining continuity while the cameras rolled than making a fuss.

During the summer of 1957, when Hope was winding up *Paris Holiday* with Fernandel, he had to find an audience who understood English to appreciate a European-filmed television special he was committed to. His writers suggested he find some GIs, so he chose Nouasser Air Base, twenty miles outside Casablanca in Morocco. Three Air Force C–54s were supplied to pick up a troupe of 70 in California—entertainers, technicians, the Les Brown band, costumes, scenery, all manner of equipment—for the flight to Morocco. There were some newspeople, too, including Art Buchwald whom Hope brought along from Paris. The cast included Marie "The Body" MacDonald, the actress who had held the nation spellbound by her bogus kidnapping charge; Eddie Fisher; Ann Miller; and Bing's eldest son, Gary Crosby.

Hope by now had considerable experience piecing together these shows on foreign soil, but Buchwald was fascinated with "how much blood, sweat and tears, and an occasional laugh, went into the making of the production." Clearly Buchwald had not guessed how essential Hope's leadership was and kidded about it engagingly:

> Mr. Hope, who oversees every part of his production, is an exacting boss. Five times a day everyone in his troupe had to kneel down and facing the direction of NBC, chant: "There is only one Hope and Timex is his sponsor."
>
> Anyone caught sleeping during the three days we were in Morocco had his option dropped. Rehearsals, which started in Paris three days before the trip and continued right through the weekend, ran until 2:30 in the morning. At dawn, while a man stood on

a minaret overlooking Casablanca calling faithful Moslems to prayer, Hope stood on the roof of the El Mansour Hotel calling his people to rehearsal.[6]

The Christmas tour of that same year, 1957, was the most ambitious Yule offering Hope had attempted to date, and it became the prototype for all successive overseas trips that he made for GIs during the next 15 years. There was nothing impromptu about it; Hope set aside two full weeks for a backbreaking itinerary that included shows in Hawaii, Wake Island, Okinawa, Japan, South Korea, Guam and Kwajalein before the plane would touch down finally in Los Angeles on December 30.

Hope took along the full Les Brown band and one of Hollywood's glossier sex symbols, Jayne Mansfield, who was incomparable in attracting attention to her bright straw-colored hair and her mammiferous body—like appearing for photos in a pink furry bikini. Jayne's husband, weight lifter and wrestler Mickey Hargitay was also on hand, as was singer Erin O'Brien, columnist Hedda Hopper, and three or four other fourth estaters like Mike Connolly of the *Hollywood Reporter*, Terrence O'Flaherty of the *San Francisco Chronicle* and Irv Kupcinet of the *Chicago Sun Times*, all of whom were pressed into acting chores from time to time during the trip.

On Christmas morning in Seoul, Korea, Hope was invited to breakfast at Major General Thomas J. Sands' headquarters, and there the comedian met for the first time Francis Joseph Spellman, the American cardinal who had become as famous as Hope for his Christmas tours of GI bases overseas. Hope was not prepared for the whimsical side of this man. He said, "Cardinal, it's amazing how far we two have had to travel before we finally met."

"Yes," Spellman said, "and I'm glad we're not competing for audiences either—though I understand we're playing some of the same spots."

Hope laughed, "I play 'em first, then you come along and give 'em absolution."

Al Scharper of *Variety* was at that breakfast, and when Hope introduced him as editor of *the* show business daily, the Cardinal didn't miss a beat with "I'm pleased to meet you. I work for the other Bible."[7]

The most moving moments of that tour took place along Korea's 38th parallel at two extreme hardship bases. At noon, the troupe performed at Bayonet Bowl for the 7th Infantry whose men were "perched on a hillside crouched in the snow." Pot-bellied stoves backstage kept the entertainers from freezing while they waited to go on. The musicians took turns leaving the windy stage to get their fingers thawed. Hope hollered into the wind:

> Here we are in Korea, the Miami Beach of the Far East . . . (*big roar*) . . . And how about this weather . . . All day long my undies have been creeping up on me looking for a place to hide . . . And if they find one, I'm going to crawl in, too. . . .[8]

Hedda Hopper wore three layers of clothes to do her sketch with Hope, and while Erin O'Brien sang "I'm Dreaming of a White Christmas," her dream came true all around her.

When the technicians had wrapped up that location and moved on to the next, the troupe prepared to play for the 1st Cavalry Division at Wallenstein

Bowl further along the perimeter. By then the light was just beginning to go;
a fog began to roll up one of the valleys, chill and damp. It was about five
below during the show and the helicopter pilots who had brought them in
warned Hope he had better cut his show short. But Hope was reluctant:

> I was held back by the eyes of the men out front following the
> members of our cast as one by one they were hustled off to the
> waiting choppers. It was like the look on the faces of people at
> airports seeing other people off, or on the faces of your kids when
> you tell them you're going out for the evening. I'd start another
> routine, then another. I couldn't help it. The shadows were getting
> longer and darker. The crew of the last chopper felt their way
> through the cabin counting noses. One that should have been easy
> to find was missing—mine. They figured it was the ham in me
> that wouldn't let me offstage, so finally they came up and
> grabbed me firmly, leading me away shouting a last punch-
> line . . .[9]

It was precisely that kind of attitude that extended Hope's "soldier in greasepaint" image year after year, and fixed his identification with the GI more
securely than even the servicemen could imagine. For Hope, that sound, that
din of whistles, that rise and fall of laughter, that truly enthusiastic applause,
that massed sound of "Silent Night" was intoxicating. When the results
appeared on film; the expressions on so many close-up faces, those portraits
of ecstasy, wonder and the sadness of separation from home, made the
Christmas Shows unique among entertainment offerings, either on the spot
or later on television.

By the next December it was an established custom: Hope would fly some-
where with a big show for North Africa, Spain, Germany, Italy and Iceland.
(And there would be unscheduled shows in the Azores going over and at
Prestwick, Scotland, coming back.)

Hope could not find an available glamour star for the trip, so he was forced
to leave McGuire Air Force base in New Jersey headed for Europe with only
Jimmy Saphier's promise that he would locate a Brigitte Bardot or a Sophia
Loren who would be willing to join the tour for at least a few shows. The core
of the cast included folk singer Randy Sparks, dancer Elaine Dunn, country
singer Molly Bee, Hedda Hopper, Jerry Colonna and Les Brown.

But this tour had trouble branded on it from its impromptu show at the
Azores on. There were peculiar time constraints imposed by project officers,
expectations by commanding officers and other hosting dignitaries, the dis-
tances between shows, the amenities—particularly the shows in Morocco—
all these taken together conspired to drag Hope down. During the tour's first
76 hours, Hope managed to sleep only seven.

A few minutes after landing at Morón, Spain, they sloshed through rain to
the mess hall for a quick meal. The post commanding officer, Colonel Ernest
Nance, was there to greet them, and as he stepped forward to take the comedian's hand, Hope felt something snap inside his head. He sagged sidewards
and sat down on a bench. He later said:

> I saw his welcoming smile through a haze. The walls of the room

closed in on me. . . . I shook my head to clear away the mental fog, but it was still there. . . . I was supposed to put on a show at Morón for several thousand Air Force men and their families. Instead I ended up at the base hospital stretched out on an examining table. My face had turned a ghastly white. . . .[10]

Hope looked up at the two young Air Force doctors examining him and said he was feeling better, but they had already given him something to make him sleep. When he awoke he was allowed to go over to the show site and make a brief appearance.

Next day the troupe flew on to Madrid for a bigger show at Torrejon Air Base. Saphier had cabled that Gina Lollobrigida was working in Spain on a movie, *David and Bathsheba*, and could be reasoned with to make a guest shot for the right financial consideration. Jack Hope called Gina's manager and he informed Jack that Gina might be induced to appear at Torrejon for $10,000 in cash and in advance. Nobody on the Hope trip had that much cash with them, so the money had to be wired from Los Angeles to a local bank. Jack Hope picked it up and went to Gina's hotel room. While she watched, he counted out the bills.

Gina sang "Non Dimenticar" and did a sketch with Bob, who had made a remarkable recovery overnight. Before she walked out on stage, Gina insisted that Hope's cameraman, Allan Stensvold, and his soundman, Dave Forrest, promise that evening in an aircraft hangar that she would come across on film like a glamour queen.

They flew on to Naples for a show on the flight deck of the U.S.S. *Forrestal* but, as their luck was pursuing them, a gale wind came up which toppled some of the scenery overboard into the bay. Hope called off the show long enough to transfer everything below deck.

On Christmas Day they arrived at Rhine-Main Air Base near Frankfurt, and did a show followed by a big holiday party thrown by the commanding general. During the cocktail reception that preceded the dinner, Hope was suddenly overcome by the mysterious ailment again. By this time the local press, the wire service reporters, not to mention Hedda, had a story too big to leave alone. Hope had collapsed and apparently there was something seriously wrong with him. Dolores called him in a frantic state. He told her it was nothing, and nothing showed up in medical examinations except exhaustion.

The next day he walked onstage at Hanau, Germany, to a tremendous ovation as if he was perfectly fine, and from there they flew on into West Berlin for an all-service show at Fleugelhorst gymnasium. Hope kept up the pretense that his dizzy spells were, in fact, due to the speed of the trip and his lack of sleep. But at Keflavík, Iceland, the last stop of the tour, after his dance routine with Elaine Dunn, Hope felt dizzy again and this time he was almost certain it had something to do with his eyes. He wondered, too, if the fall he had taken on his head here at Keflavík in December 1955 might have done more damage that he thought.

When he arrived home in North Hollywood, Dolores had already set up an appointment for him to be examined by Tom Hearn. It was New Year's and, as Hope later said:

We had about 200 people out at the house for a party New Year's
night after the Rose Bowl game. I found myself sticking close to
the door and poking my head out for some fresh air. That funny
dizzy feeling, you know? I just couldn't get enough fresh air.[11]

Next day he went back to see Hearn and found his blood pressure was up to
165. But he insisted on going to General Laboratories where the overseas
tour film was being processed and screened because he felt sole responsibility
for selecting each frame of his Christmas show. One afternoon after the
screening he stopped by Lakeside for a hole or two of golf and "everything
seemed out of focus for a bit" and then it cleared up.

On January 8, Hope drove down to Palm Springs to play golf with Jimmy
Demaret. "I found myself stumbling a bit. I played three holes and was
suddenly tired. I turned to my caddy and said, "Let's quit." When I got back
to the locker room I looked up at the wall and the pictures hanging there
started dancing around. That's when I got scared."[12]

Hope returned to Los Angeles and went to see eye specialist Maurice
Beigelman in Beverly Hills, who diagnosed a blood clot in the vein of Hope's
left cornea. He warned Hope about overwork and stress of any kind lest the
clot move and destroy his vision totally.

At a rehearsal for his television show at NBC one night he became too
dizzy to continue and Mort Lachman brought him home. Two other eye
specialists were called in. But in a day or so of rest Hope felt much stronger.

Then, at a rehearsal for his March TV show, his vision fogged up so badly
he called Beigelman, and Beigelman made a long-distance call to one of the
nation's outstanding eye specialists, Algernon Reese at New York's Columbia Presbyterian Medical Center. The following day Bob and Dolores were
on a plane heading east.

Hope's New York press agent, Ursula Halloran, summoned the media out
in force, and perhaps it was her zeal or lack of precise information that
resulted in the overwrought newspaper headlines that day: BOB HOPE SERI-
OUSLY ILL—FLYING HERE TO SAVE EYE or BOB HOPE IN WEAK CONDITION—SUFFERS
HEART AND EYE TROUBLES.[13]

At Columbia Presbyterian, Hope was subjected to a thorough testing and
examination by Reese and his associates and finally, after several days, one
of those colleagues, Dr. Stuart Cosgriff, came into Hope's room at the hospital. "Bob, you must slow down. You've been moving too fast."

"I know, but I love it. I love those laughs."

"Sure, only your blood vessels can't hear them."

"What have I got, doctor?" asked Hope.

"You're suffering from a circulatory problem. It's a vascular thing."

"You can operate?"

"No need. This is something we can take care of with tranquilizers and
cortisone. Nature's been kind to you. It's given you a warning. Sometimes it
doesn't, it just strikes. With rest and proper care you'll get the other half of
your sight back."

When Bob and Dolores arrived back in North Hollywood a few days later,
there were many messages, including offers of eye transplants. Hope told
Marjorie Hughes to tear up his personal appearance schedule and to help

him cancel everything in his next few months except his television commitments.

It was probably the most difficult thing I've ever had to do. I
almost drove Dolores crazy. I had to learn how to rest. I had to
learn how to conserve my strength. Like sitting down during TV
rehearsals, and letting my stand-in substitute for me . . . Dolores has been a great help. She screens my calls, makes sure I get
at least eight hours of sleep at night and has cut our social engagements to a minimum. At the slightest hint that I'm tired she
insists that we go home. In fact, my illness has brought us closer
together. Last year she sent me a telegram on my birthday that
said, "Congratulations wherever you are!" We hardly ever spent
an evening at home together. Now we do, and it's wonderful.[14]

THE KENNEDY YEARS
1960–1963

And I think President Kennedy has picked some pretty good
help . . . Harvard is emptier than our Treasury. It's quite
a thing. There's so many professors in the Cabinet, you can't
leave the White House without raising your hand. . . .[1]

35. Facts of Life

For a number of years before the the problem flared, in fact, ever since
television began dramatizing more forcefully Hope's image as "the GI's
guy," Mack Millar complained that the government had never gone far
enough in expressing its gratitude.

"He hasn't done too badly," replied Jimmy Saphier. "He's been honored
by three Presidents in one way or another. He has a stack of awards and
medals from every branch of the military. What more could he want?"

"What Congress did for George M. Cohan and Irving Berlin," answered
Millar.

"But would they do it for Hope?"[2]

That question triggered an unflagging five-year campaign. Millar spoke to
his other comedian client, Eddie Cantor, who began an exploratory maneu-
ver with California congressman Bill Knowland. In the spring of 1958, Cantor sent this message to Saphier:

> For more than a year I have tried to have Senator Knowland get
> to the White House so they might have Congress strike off a
> medal for Bob Hope. It would be good not only for Bob, for no
> man deserves the honor more, but it would be good for all of show
> business. . . .
>
> Warmest regards,
> Eddie[3]

Knowland's final correspondence with Cantor included a copy of a letter
from Wilton Persons, deputy assistant to Eisenhower, stating that Hope had
already received the highest honors available to American entertainers,
and

> . . . further recognition, at least at this time, would not be advis-
> able in view of the fact that several thousand entertainers have
> participated in the troop entertainment program and over-empha-
> sis on the contributions of any one person might adversely affect
> the entire program.[4]

Mack was undaunted, saying, "if they don't go for the Congressional
Medal, I'll try for the Nobel Peace Prize." Millar found plenty of sympathy
from Hope's friends in high places.

However, nothing could be more influential than Hope's own behavior.
Despite stern warnings from his eye specialists, and a blunt order from Tom
Hearn to behave, the comedian proceeded to make arrangements for a USO
Christmas tour in 1959. Dolores opposed it, but Bob assured her that he

~~knew how to handle his illness; besides, he felt stronger. In honesty, he was~~ not thrilled that the Defense Department was asking him to entertain in the frozen wilds of Alaska. But he was soon dreaming up ways of dramatizing and glamorizing the sub-zero tour for maximum publicity.[5]

First thing he did was to sign Jayne Mansfield, the buxom actress who had developed into a publicist's dream, second only to Marilyn Monroe. Hope also signed a fast-rising young television Western star named Steve McQueen and invited McQueen's beautiful wife, Neile Adams, along to sing and dance. Hope figured he would cinch the appeal of this trip and boost its promotional value by bringing back together his World War II cast. He coaxed Frances Langford out of retirement (she was now Mrs. Ralph Evinrude), found both Patty Thomas and Tony Romano available, and his trusty sidekick Colonna was always ready. Les Brown was unavailable, so Hope put the final touch of nostalgia on this tour by hiring Skinnay Ennis' band.

On that long haul from Los Angeles to Anchorage, they stopped at McChord Air Force Base to refuel. Mansfield spent most of her time in a public telephone booth, and when the troupe deplaned at Elmendorf Air Base, there was an Alaskan animal trainer waiting for Jayne. He had a baby lion with him, and when she cuddled it, a barrage of media and GI photographers went crazy; they went crazier still when she insisted on putting the beast into the dogsled with herself and Mickey Hargitay as they were taken to their quarters. The lion cub was tame, but its teeth were still sharp and the playful nipping at rehearsals was more than the cast could handle. But Bob understood Jayne's publicity needs. She once told Flaherty, "I will never permit anything to stand between me and 170 million people—we were meant for each other."[6]

Still, Jayne could go too far; her enthusiasm for titillating both her GI audiences and the press was boundless. For instance, on Christmas Day at King Salmon, their northernmost stop and a hardship post where troops had to be rotated frequently, Jayne decided to give the boys a "special thrill." The show took place in a reverberant, Quonset-type hangar whose stage was improvised out of two flatbed trucks hauled together. The troops sitting on the bare cement floor were high-spirited, sex-hungry.

For their intimate comedy spot, Bob and Jayne were to come onstage from opposite sides, with Hope going out first to bring her on. As he climbed up to the flatbed and started toward the front of the stage, he looked across to where Hargitay was helping Jayne up the narrow steps on her side in a sheer, very low-cut pink gown—so low-cut that Jayne's nipples were showing. From the GIs crowded close to the stage, angling for photographs, this brought war whoops, whistles, shouts that shattered the eardrums. Hope turned back and leaned down toward his brother. "Jack, I don't believe her. She can't do *that*! We're filming."

Jack turned Bob around and headed him back toward center stage. "You're the only one who can handle this!"

And Jack was right. When Bob reached center stage he hollered, "We've got a gal here—I think you're going to like. It's Mr. and Mrs. Mansfield's favorite child, Jayne—right here!"

Jayne came out all smiles, eyes and teeth flashing, her breasts jiggling like molds of Jell-O in pink containers. As she got closer she could not avoid the insistent bobbing of Hope's eyes downward, and by the time she got to his side, she had managed to pull her dress up.

Through the noise and flashes, Hope said, "I think they like you, darlin'." Before she could respond, one out-of-control GI threw himself on the floor prostrate in front of the stage and yelled, "Just let her breathe!"

That night at a cast party, Hope asked her to sing "White Christmas" and she did it with considerable warmth and simplicity. He said, "Somewhere beneath that blond hair and that plastic make-up was a lovely young woman singing softly, and meaning every word of it." Hope used Jayne time and again on his show; in fact, he used her on a show just before her fatal auto accident. "She had joy, that girl. She had bounce. She was an upper all the way. She had fantastic style. I could never figure her out. One minute she was the most naive little girl in the world and the next minute you had the feeling she was putting the whole world on. She had a pool that was pink and heart-shaped—and that was Jayne—pink and heart-shaped. I really miss her."[7]

During that Alaskan USO trip, Hope had a brief flare-up of his eye trouble but was careful to deny it. He was convinced that although the nation could be sympathetic with his misfortune, nobody really likes a sick person. Most of all, no entertainment corporation wants to put their money on a poor risk. He became annoyed, in fact, that the NBC publicist on that trip reported some moments of Hope dizziness at the Fairbanks show to an Associated Press stringer. Alarmed, Dolores telephoned from Toluca Lake, but Bob dismissed the story as the work of an overzealous press agent.

During the year that followed that Christmas trip, Eisenhower was easing himself out of public life and making way for his young successor, Jack Kennedy. Hope's approach to Kennedy was extremely interesting because of all Hope's joking relationships with Presidents, this one came closest to fitting the classic role of court jester. Hope's Kennedy humor sprang initially from the superficial aspects of the Massachusetts politician's life, and gradually became more concerned with presidential decision-making and issues arising from the new regime.

Hope first noticed Kennedy when he showed popular strength as a candidate in the spring of 1960:

> I must say the Senator's victory in Wisconsin was a triumph for democracy. It proves that a millionaire has just as good a chance as anybody else.[8]

In February 1961, Hope was asked to share the dais with Kennedy at the annual convocation of the exclusive and politically irreverent Alfalfa Club in Washington. By this time, his jabs were less superficial. Before his audience of cabinet members, congressmen, top military men and judges, Hope said slyly:

> And I think President Kennedy has picked some pretty good help . . . Harvard is emptier than our Treasury . . . It's quite a thing. There's so many professors in the Cabinet, you can't leave the White House without raising your hand . . . The Secretary of Defense was twenty minutes late for a meeting this

morning and he had to bring a note from his mother . . . they're
doing great . . . but one little thing worries me . . . What if a
war starts during recess??? . . .[9]

Hope admits that it was not his own humor that night but one of Kennedy's quips that produced the loudest laughter. The President feigned surprise that anyone could possibly object to his nominating his brother as attorney general, adding, "What's wrong with his getting a little legal experience before he goes into business for himself?"

In mid-April, Hope made sly reference to Kennedy's rocking chair, and then said:

And have you heard about President Kennedy's new youth peace corps to help foreign countries? It's sort of "Exodus" with fraternity pins . . . Did you read where President Kennedy's press conferences were being beamed to Russia? . . . the Russians love the show . . . they've . . . added a laugh track . . . And did you read where President Kennedy's asking for two and a half billion more for the budget? Kennedy hasn't thrown out Ike's old budget . . . he's using it for petty cash . . . And our national sport is back on the scene this week . . . with the crack of the bat . . . the old squeeze play . . . the crowds screaming . . . yes, it's income tax time again . . . That's "The Price is Right" with Democrats. . . .[10]

Hope's humor here is wittier, more sarcastic, more skeptical, more probing than most of his monologues in the past. Camelot seems to have brought out the best in Hope and his writers.

The state of Hope's art during this high-quality period is probably not better displayed than in the monologue of his closing show of the 1960–61 season.

There's trouble in Cuba . . . Laos . . . Vietnam . . . along about now, Mr. Nixon must get the feeling he won . . . Things are so bad that last week Huntley tried to jump off Brinkley . . . Even Norman Vincent Peale said a discouraging word . . . Laos . . . Vietnam . . . Cuba . . . The Congo . . . I think we're getting out of the world just in time . . . We knew something had gone wrong with our foreign policy. We sent care packages to Laos . . . and the Thank-You cards came back written in Russian. . . .[11]

Not only Hope's humor was maturing during this period. He was not yet fifty-seven years old, but by no means an old man despite the graying in his sideburns. His body was still firm and athletic from his long nightly walks and his daily golf. The eyes were very alive, which seemed to deny the trouble that lay behind the left one.

Hope knew his life-style had to change. "I had two choices, keep up the pace of the past 20 years and find myself doing monologues from a wheelchair, or slow down and live with my illness until I had it licked."[12]

Restricted now from his former wild schedule of whistle-stop traveling, he was forced back to the more sedentary medium of movie-making. And the first picture he chose turned out to be one of his very best. *"The Facts of Life* was a daring picture for me. It was the story of two handicapped people who fall in love. Their handicaps were his wife and her husband."

When he first read the script, Hope thought it too straight, unsuitable for him; but Panama pointed out that the humor was derived from the bitter-sweet dialogue and situation, rather than from broader gags.

When Lucille Ball read it, she cried. "It's beautiful. Who do you see playing the man?"

"Hope," said Mel Frank.

"Okay," Lucy said, "If you can get him, I'll do it. But just one thing—"

"What?"

"I don't want it to be 'The Road to Infidelity.' "

Hope and Ball agreed they must submerge their own personalities and they dug into their parts. Almost without exception the critics found the picture "a cut above" what either of the two comedians had been doing lately and it was a box-office winner, too.[13]

Hope's next movie, *Bachelor in Paradise*, was another domestic comedy but without much dimension. Its theme was America's great move to sub-urbia and the sexual attitudes of housewives, but Hope's costar Lana Turner didn't seem to fit. Hope said he had to sit through it once on a commercial flight and "The stewardess handed out programs—and containers. At least nobody walked out."

Hope's third picture during the eye-recovery period was filmed on location in England. His rediscovered domestic life must have been infectious, because he took the family with him for the four months of filming the seventh and final Hope–Crosby collaboration, *Road to Hong Kong*. For both Hope and Crosby, living at the Dorchester in Mayfair and driving out to Shepperton studios every day was a nuisance, so Dolores and Kathryn started looking for houses in the country closer to the studio. But it was Mel Frank who found Cranbourne Court. Mel showed it to Dolores. She worried about the $1,000 a week rental but loved the butler and the furnishings. She pulled Bob and Bing off the golf course to go look at it, and it was Bing who suggested they both rent it. Mel Frank says, "They were like two little boys going to school every morning."[14]

The big flap during the filming concerned their leading lady. Producers Panama and Frank thought Lamour was no longer the alluring "girl in the middle " she had been ten years earlier and were talking abut Brigitte Bardot, Sophia Loren and Gina Lollobrigida. Bing favored Bardot: "Mind you, I think she might be a little on the young side for Hope." But Bob held out for Lamour and was not happy that she had been offered only a small part, just to maintain the Hope–Crosby–Lamour tradition. In fact, the Panama–Frank agreement with United Artists included a stipulation that the picture could not be made without her. However, they hired Joan Collins for the love interest.

Dorothy was living in semiretirement in Baltimore as the wife of Bill Howard and raising two sons, Ridge and Tommy. At first she was thrilled to be included, but after hearing from Louis Shurr and Panama that it was a small part, and that Collins had the better role, she was humiliated. The six pre-

vious *Roads* were built upon a triad, and besides, she was younger—10 year
younger—than Bing and Bob. Right up to the time the picture started, she
read in gossip columns: Bing didn't want her—Bob was fighting for her—
Bing would take her in a small role. She asked for more lines and more
money and the telephoning between London and Baltimore was frequent. In
desperation, Hope begged her to come over and do a song and a comedy
scene playing herself. She finally relented, and felt much better when the
British press gave her a huge personal reception and took her side in the
question of a fatter tole. She did her little part, sang "Softer Than a Whisper," and went home to Baltimore.[15]

When Lamour came out to Hollywood at Hope's request to help promote
the picture on his TV show, she heard that Bing planned to plug the movie on
his own TV special. She called Bing, suggesting she be included, and he told
her that it was too late to write her in. Dorothy says, "When Bill and I saw
Bing's special we were shocked to see them using big blow-ups of me, and
they kept referring to me all through the show. I couldn't understand what
had happened to Bing. Sometimes he could be sweet as ever, and then an
aloofness set in that never had been there before."

Road to Hong Kong was the weakest of the seven adventures. Try as they
did, the old Hope–Crosby zest had pretty much evaporated. It did have one
of their great songs, "Teamwork," and guest appearances by Dean Martin
Frank Sinatra, David Niven, Zsa Zsa Gabor and Peter Sellers. Sellers was
particularly hilarious as a doctor from India who is trying to cure Hope's
illness. He takes out an eye chart of Hindu letters and asks Hope to read it
Hope says he can't and Sellers picks up an Indian reed instrument and starts
playing, using the eye chart as music. A snake appears and Sellers charms it
When the snake subsides, Hope asks, "What would you do if it bit you?"

"Very simple," said Sellers, "I'd cut the wound and suck out the poison."

"But what if it's in a place where you can't reach with your mouth?" ask
Hope.

"That," Peter said, "is when you find out who your friends are."

Soon after that, Hope started using a variation on that joke. He would say
that he and Bing were on a camping trip and that he, Hope, was bitten by a
poisonous snake on his posterior and that Bing rushed off to the nearest
doctor for help. When Bing got to town, the doctor said, "You'll have to suck
out that poison or Hope'll die." Bob said to his audience, "So Bing walked
back, and when he got there, I said, 'Where's the doctor? What did he say?'
And Bing said, 'You're going to die.' "

The only other large-scale operation of Hope's eye-recovery period was the
GI tour, which he simply could not give up. The 1961 tour to Newfoundland
Labrador and Greenland was no exception. He brought Mansfield, Anita
Bryant, newcomer Dorothy Provine, and the current Miss World from Brit-
ain, Rosemarie Frankland.

As Hope sailed further into 1962, it became clear to himself and to his
audiences that he was back in stride. He was still spending more time at
home but he was also becoming more visible in different parts of the country
In March, after receiving the Milestone Award from the Screen Producer
Guild, he flew to Miami for his annual Parkinson's Disease benefit and then

up to Palm Beach for a Project Hope golf benefit. A few days later, back in Hollywood, he went to the Palladium for a Screen Writers Dinner, and during the evening when the emcee suggested that there might be a few of Hope's writers in the room, 30 or 40 people stood up.

Most of Hope's earlier writers had gone on to bigger things, but the current list was probably as good a group as he had ever had: there was the clever and reclusive 25-year veteran Norm Sullivan; Lester White, who had written for him in vaudeville; Johnny Rapp, from a distinguished comedy-writing family; Mort Lachman, his head writer, whom he called the Owl; and Bill Larkin, who had accompanied him to Moscow. Subtlest and perhaps the one who came closest to receiving Hope's highest praise was British-born Charlie Lee.

Hope was then spending $500,000 a year for gags from that group. "Our meetings," said Rapp, "can take place anywhere—at Bob's house, in the office, at bus depots, at the airport, sometimes in men's rooms."[16] Their combined talents were responsible for keeping him charged. As *Life* observed in mid-1962, "Any other comedian would long ago have died trying to keep up Hope's kind of humor." They went on to describe Hope's appearance at Oklahoma State University, where his crisp, witty monologue showed beyond question that the champion of comedy was still going strong:

> New York has always been the melting pot but this last session of the United Nations nearly melted the pot . . . Actually it seems silly . . . The UN invites people like Khrushchev, Nasser and Castro to discuss how the world can get rid of people like Khrushchev, Nasser and Castro . . . The President's been plugging milk. I don't think he owns a dairy. I think he's really sincere . . . I hear he plans to split Massachusetts in half—High Mass and Low Mass . . . No, but I like to see politicians with religion—it keeps their hands out where we can see them . . . Hollywood Catholics are different. They're the only Catholics who give up matzoh balls for Lent . . . Have you seen those society ladies doing the twist? They're using parts they haven't used in 50 years . . . Some night the music will stop and they'll all be arrested . . . Jack Benny played golf until last year. He quit because he lost his ball—the string broke . . . I used to be quite an athlete—big chest, hard stomach. But that's all behind me now . . .[17]

Thank you for this great honor, Mr. President. I feel very humble but I think I have the strength of character to fight it. . . . There is one sobering thought . . . I received this medal for going out of the country. I think they're trying to tell me something. . . .[1]

36. The Rose Garden

June 4, 1962, found Bob Hope and his number one son, Tony, together a Georgetown University for an unusual academic procession. With Dolore and Linda and a big audience watching them, Tony marched in to pick up his earned liberal arts bachelors degree, and Bob stepped forward to accep his first honorary doctorate in humane letters, for "unstinting generosit with his gift of laughter."

"How does it really feel, Bob?" one newsman asked.

"Some educators in Cleveland are going to be surprised to see this gown. went out of eleventh grade into dancing school, that's how it feels."[2]

The Hopes injected a somewhat casual note into what was ordinarily a dignified occasion. But the playfulness began to spread when Hope was con ducted to his place in the block-long processional to the platform. Jesui theologian Gustave Weigel, commencement speaker, walked over an pinned his Phi Beta Kappa key on Hope's gown to the delight of the othe Jesuits.

When the Very Reverend Edward Bunn, president of the university, con ferred Hope's degree, he said to the 3,000 graduates, parents and friend that it was unprecedented for such a recipient to respond publicly, and afte a pause said, "But I know you would never forgive me if I didn't ask Mr Hope to give some kind of response."

When the enthusiastic applause faded, Hope with his impeccable timin said, "I wouldn't forgive you either." Holding up his degree inscribed i Latin, he said, "I can't wait until I get home and have my son read this t me." Probably the strongest laugh came from his closing admonishment:

> My advice to young people going out into the world: don't go. I was out there last week and the stock market was down so far I came right back in. . . . I put a dime in a telephone this morn- ing and a voice said: "God bless you."[3]

Meanwhile, up on Capitol Hill, the House was getting ready to discuss a measure, already passed through the Senate, for authorizing the Treasury t cast a $2,500 gold medal for Hope; the highest recognition that could ever b offered a civilian. Even getting this far offered testimony to support fron fellow entertainers like Eddie Cantor, genuinely devoted admirers like Sy mington, and many others, but no one worked harder than Mack Millar.

Mack in his dogged pursuit of this medal was playing his role in the Hop concept of total salesmanship, marketing and product identification. Fo Hope, the mere fact of his comedy was not sufficient. He felt that no matte how clever the comic, in order to maintain or enlarge his fame the fickl

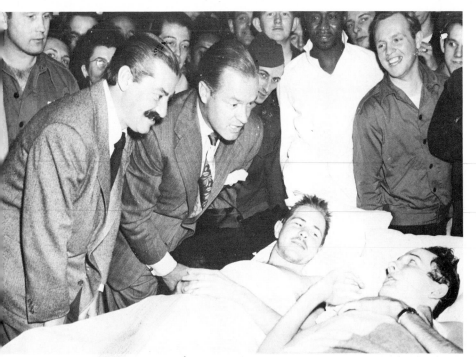

Above, Hope with sidekick Jerry Colonna, cracks, "Don't get up for us, boys!" to Pvt. Charles Brown (center) and Pfc. Ben Collina, on a visit to Walter Reed Hospital during their marathon entertainment of military bases and hospitals in the '40s. (*Public Information Office, Army Medical Center, Walter Reed Hospital*); *Below left*, following Hope's first Royal Command Performance at London's Odeon Theatre in November, 1947, Bob and Dolores meet Their Majesties, King George (in background) with Loretta Young, while Queen Elizabeth chats with the Hopes. (*Bob Hope personal file*); *Right*, Ike's favorite jester and one of Hope's favorite presidents. (*Bob Hope Desert Classic*)

The Bob Hope Family at home in Palm Springs (mid-'50s). Standing (left to right) Linda, Tony and Kelly; seated are Dolores, Bob (holding dog, Recession) and Nora. (*NBC photo*)

Left, at Wallenstein Bowl, Korea, with the late afternoon fog beginning to roll in, Hope is reluctant to leave the men of the 1st Cavalry Division during his USO tour of the Far East in 1957. (*NBC-Burbank photo*)

Below left, at a 1960 dinner honoring Eleanor Roosevelt, Hope jokes with President-elect John Kennedy and Vice President-elect Lyndon Johnson. (*Photo: Mike Zwerling*)

Below right, like father, like son—Dolores Hope receives an academic kiss from Tony and Bob. Bob received an honorary doctorate in humane letters at Tony's graduation from Georgetown University, June, 1962. (*Bob Hope personal file*)

Hope couldn't resist a joke even when Kennedy handed him the Congressional Gold Medal. Stuart Symington in background. (*White House photo*)

The outstretched hands that brought Hope back to Vietnam for nine Christmas shows from 1964 to 1972, the year that U.S. troops were withdrawn. (*NBC photo: Frank Carroll*)

...ght, Jack Benny was one of Hope's very special ...ends. (*NBC photo: Gary Null*)

...low, to open his 1966 television season, Hope ...vited nine of his motion picture leading ladies to ...are the billing. Front row, left to right: Lucille ...ll, Joan Fontaine, Hedy Lamarr, Signe Hasso; ...ck row: Joan Collins, Dorothy Lamour, Hope, ...rginia Mayo, Vera Miles and Janis Paige. (*NBC ...oto: Gerald Smith*)

Left, Hope rehearsed strenuously with Jimm[y] Cagney in 1955 for the challenge danc[e] sequence in *The Seven Little Foys*. (*NBC pho[-]to: Paul Bailey*)

Above, while filming *Fancy Pants*, Hope r[e-]ceives a visit from another Paramount sta[r] Fred Astaire. (*Copyright 1950 by Paramou[nt] Pictures Corporation, courtesy Universal Pi[c-]tures*)

Left, for his 1979 television show filmed in th[e] People's Republic of China, Hope rehearses [a] soft-shoe routine with ballet superstar Mikha[il] Baryshnikov. (*NBC photo: Ron Tom*)

rea during the 1964 Christmas USO
he author with Hope and an MP named
(*NBC photo: Paul Bailey*)

g a round of the Bob Hope Classic char-
f tournament in Palm Desert, California,
nedian greets the crowd from a golf cart
like his famous profile. (*NBC-Burbank*

on the campaign trail for Presidential
Ronald Reagan. With Hope and Rea-
rally in Peoria, Illinois (November,
are President Gerald R. Ford and
Bush. (*Photo: Tom Carter, Peoria*
l Star)

"Pops" with granddaughter Miranda. (*NBC-Burbank photo*)

public had to be constantly reminded. No one in modern show business was more skilled in the manipulation of an image.

Along with such image-building went the recognition that Hope would always be a news event, even in his sadness. Hope had been booked for one of the biggest personal appearance assignments since his illness, the Seattle Aqua Festival in July, for $100,000. Afterward, he, Dolores, Nora and Kelly took their annual vacation on a yacht in Alaskan waters. Ship-to-shore radio notified Hope one morning that his brother Jack had been removed suddenly to the Leahy Clinic for acute hepatitis. He was operated on near the end of July and went into a coma. Dolores flew east on July 31 and remained with Lee at the hospital around the clock. Jack came out of the coma, and Bob arrived on August 3. He stayed, except for a few hours, at Jack's bedside until he died in the afternoon of August 6.[4]

Coincidentally, not far from Jack's hotel room a set of galleys sat on a desk in the Boston firm of Bruce Humphries Publishers. It was the soon-to-be-published book by his brother Jim entitled *Mother Had Hopes*. Jim had been boasting for years that he knew more about the Hope family than anyone else and one day he would tell all, including a generous hunk of material about Bob. Jim claimed he had kept notes from midnight conversations with Mahm, talks with his father, his aunts and uncles, the other brothers.

Wyn had urged her husband to actually write it after so many years of talking about it, and only she and Humphries knew about the manuscript. Before publication, Humphries advised Jim they wanted a foreword written by Bob. Jim was irate. Humphries said, "No foreword, no book," and Jim angrily replied, "You can go to hell! It's my book and I don't want my brother to have any part of it." The galleys went into the trash. There were, however, two remaining copies of the manuscript. Wyn Hope delivered one to Bob at the time of Jim's death, and Bob locked it up in his joke vault.[5]

Because of Jack's illness that year, Bob had learned to depend more on Mort Lachman for help in his movie and television production decisions. And it was Mort who got the call from producer Harry Saltzman in London (he had been involved with Betty Box on *The Iron Petticoat*) asking if there was any chance Hope would consider making a film at the Mount Kenya Safari Club in Africa. After the story was punched up to resemble some of Hope's classic spy adventures of the past, the notion of an African location plus a leading lady of Anita Ekberg's description became more attractive. The picture had to be made in October and November, which meant Hope had to tape his two fall television shows before he went (minus the monologues, of course, which were always taped at the last minute).

As Hope's luck of late would have it, internal strife in Kenya canceled the location. But Hope had gone too far with his preparations to turn back, so with United Artists' blessing, they decided to use a man-made jungle at Pinewood Studios in England.

The months before he sailed on the *Queen Elizabeth*, Hope planned to wrap up another unfinished project, a continuation of his mid-fifties autobiography. Bob had decided the focus of the book was to be his trip to Russia, with a few movie experiences and overseas GI entertainment tours thrown in.

After discussion with Ferris Mack at Doubleday, Hope chose for his book title *I Owe Russia $1,200*, based on the bill he received from the Soviet Ministry of Culture for film clips never delivered. Hope and golf-playing writers Mort, Bill, Les and Johnny took off for several long weekends to write the book; they drove up to the Montecito Hotel in Santa Barbara, then down to the Kona-Ki Club in San Diego, then up to Harrah's Club at Tahoe, and finally Mort went up to Seattle with Bob while he played in a benefit tournament at the Broadmoor. But the book got finished, full of glib, mon-ologue-type prose that was frequently funny, frequently heartwarming, and it was dedicated: In the memory of Jack Hope, my brother, my producer, my friend.

The picture he was making at England's Pinewood Studios was *Call Me Bwana* in which Hope played an inept explorer hired by the U.S. government to locate, in densest Africa, an American moon-probe missile that landed there in error. Along the way he meets beautiful enemy spy Anita Ekberg, and, inexplicably, champion golfer Arnold Palmer.

And there was more sadness. Monty Brice, successor to Barney Dean as the omnipresent gag writer on Hope movies, suffered a heart attack on the set November 8 and died almost immediately. That same night, when Hope got back to his Dorchester suite, there was a message waiting for him that Mack Millar had died of a heart attack in his Coldwater Canyon home in Beverly Hills. Mack was only fifty-seven; Monty was seventy-one. At the time of his death, Mack was aglow over his success in pursuing the Congres-sional Medal, and had just added one final *coup de maître:* He had nego-tiated something quite unprecedented in the history of the Hearst Publishing Company. They had agreed to devote an entire issue of their Sunday supple-ment, *The American Weekly*, to a 15-page photo essay on the comedian to be called "Bob Hope, Favorite Jester of the Western World." It was timed to precede the big award.

While Hope was in London he did his fourth Command Performance for British royalty, this one for Queen Elizabeth and Prince Philip. Transatlan-tic telephone lines were active in late November and early December as Mort and Bob discussed the USO Christmas tour to the Far East, which was scheduled to begin December 19 and take them to Japan, Korea, Okinawa, Taiwan, the Philippines and Guam. Hope also spoke almost daily with the two men on his Hope Show staff at NBC who literally engineered these annual trips: Sil Caranchini, who supervised staging and production detail at each location; and John Pawlek, who engineered the sound. Hope's cast for this trip finally included Lana Turner (in her first such live road show engagement), Janis Paige, Anita Bryant and Amecee Chabot, the United States entry in the Miss World competition, as well as the indispensables, Jerry Colonna and Les Brown. The top-secret part of this particular trip was that, quietly and "conditionally," Hope had argued the Defense Department into letting him go into South Vietnam to entertain the Marines and the "advisors" stationed there.

Not more than two hours after the giant military transport lifted off the runway at Los Angeles International Airport, the Defense Department radioed Hope's escort officer on the plane that the stop in Vietnam must be canceled. They feared that the combat situation there created an "unneces-

sary risk." Hope was disappointed; he had received many letters from
Marines begging him to come. But what made the cancellation particularly
difficult to accept was the scene that unfolded in his tent-dressing room at
Iwakuni Air Base in Japan on December 22. When he stepped offstage near
the end of the show and went into his tent, he happened to be alone. In the
half-light, off to the side of his makeup table, stood a tall figure wearing a
beret and an unusual uniform.

"Mr. Hope, may I speak with you?"

"Who are you?"

"I'm from Nam. I hitchhiked here to see you. I won the toss. I've got a
scroll here with a hell of a lot of names on it. We don't get many entertainment breaks over there, and I want you to know how much good you could do
for us."

The soldier stepped aside and began to roll out the scroll, and it would have
stretched beyond the edge of the tent. Hope hollered for Mort and said, "Do
you believe this? Look at all those names. They're from Vietnam. We gotta
do something." Hope had to go back onstage but he asked Larry Glaab, the
project officer, to call his Defense Department superiors and hold the phone
for when he came back offstage.

In a few minutes they had a priority line and were talking to the Pentagon.
It was another polite but very firm turndown. All this time, the young man in
the red beret stood in half-shadow listening, but when it came time for Hope
to relay the disappointing news to his young visitor, the kid was gone. He had
slipped out of the tent. Janis Paige was standing in Bob's tent; she grabbed
his arm as he went by her and all he said was that he was AWOL and wanted
to remain anonymous to avoid disciplinary action later.[6]

But this trip, without Vietnam, turned out to be extraordinarily rich and
varied. Lana Turner proved to be a genuine show business trouper. Even
when she developed laryngitis, she insisted on doing all of her routines with a
whisper mike.

Then there were the heartwarming scenes of the Hope troupe singing
Christmas carols around a controversial tree erected and decorated in the
demilitarized zone at Panmunjom; and colorful scenes like Hope being carried aloft by pygmies at a Negrito Village near Manila, and another time,
being serenaded by bright kimono-clad children at Okinawa. For his monologues, the Kennedy family was once again a target:

> . . . It's been a slow year back home . . . only one Kennedy got
> elected . . . The Kennedys had a nice Christmas . . . Jackie
> got a new pair of water skis, the President got a pair of hair clip-
> pers, and Ted got a nice present . . . Massachusetts . . . I'm
> only kidding. There was a wonderful Christmas spirit in Wash-
> ington this year. The Kennedys held a drive to raise money to buy
> toys for needy Republicans. . . .[7]

It is not surprising that the documentation of this tour on television in late
January was nominated for a 1963 Emmy Award, that it won the Golden
Globe Award from the International Press of Hollywood, and won a TV
Guide Award.

Unquestionably, that show pleased the Chrysler Corporation with whom

Jimmy Saphier was negotiating a most lucrative television deal. Hope ultimately signed a long-term, multimillion-dollar package to be Chrysler's principal spokesman as well as producer-performer of one of his most ambitious undertakings ever: a full-hour (occasionally 90-minute) weekly series of drama, comedy-drama, and variety shows called "Bob Hope Presents the Chrysler Theater."

Hope would be paid $500,000 each time he starred in a production, and $25,000 each time he filmed an introduction to the weekly dramas.

Those dramas, produced by Dick Berg at Universal Studios, were the focus of much attention in the entertainment world. Berg had persuaded playwright William Inge to write his first TV drama and had signed other writers like Budd Shulberg, Don Mankiewicz and Rod Serling, plus award-winning directors and actors. Performances by Anne Bancroft, Jason Robards, Shelley Winters and Piper Laurie were highly praised; there were several Emmy awards for the series. But like other costly, high-quality dramatic productions on television, there was limited popular interest, so Chrysler opted to dump the dramas after the third year and continue as sponsor of Hope's highly rated comedy specials. This Hope–Chrysler relationship was to last ten years, rivaling the comedian's long association with Lever Brothers on radio.

Another Saphier task at this time was to help Hope shore up his sagging public relations operation. Bob had always believed that Millar was the best around. Now he was gone. Saphier, however, had long felt that Millar was old-hat, that he was uncomfortable with the new, more intellectual class of journalists who resented hard-sell publicists and press agents.

Jimmy had also been disappointed in Bob's personal choice of Ursula Halloran to handle the television shows from New York. Since 1960 she had been racked with personal problems; she did not seem to be able to cope with the pressures of high-level public relations work. Reluctantly Bob agreed she had to be fired.

In her place came Allan Kalmus, one of the brightest young public relations men in New York, and a veteran of NBC's publicity staff. He was clever in television promotion, had strong media contacts, and, importantly, knew his way around NBC's executive floor. Allan had what Mack could never have or understand, the Harvard background, the Madison Avenue look that was part of the Camelot atmosphere of the present administration.

Kalmus was particularly effective with the media when the National Association of Broadcasters decided to break tradition and present their 1963 Distinguished Service Award to the entertainer.

In September, Kalmus had his first opportunity to operate in the big leagues, when it came time for the gold medal to be presented. There had been some uncertainty about the actual date of the ceremony so Hope had taken Linda, Nora, Kelly and Freddy Miron with him for some fishing and relaxing not far from Vancouver. They were cruising through the San Juan Islands when Stuart Symington reached them by ship-to-shore phone with news that the medal was ready for presentation on September 11. Dolores and Tony had flown to Washington from Los Angeles.

On September 11, the family was escorted into the oval office, and then

Kennedy and Hope strolled out to the rose garden. Seated in rows of chairs on the South Lawn were about 100 congressmen, including Stuart Symington, Democratic Senators Frank Lausche and Stephen Young of Ohio, and Republican majority leader Frank Halleck of Indiana. Also present was Rita Millar, Mack's widow, who was later introduced to Kennedy as "the lady whose husband thought this up."

When Kennedy handed Hope the medal on behalf of himself and the Congress, he said it showed "the great affection all of us hold for you, and most especially, the great appreciation we have for you for so many years going so many places to entertain the sons, daughters, brothers and sisters of Americans, who were very far from home." He motioned to anyone who might want to come and get a closer look at the medal. "This is the only bill we've gotten by, lately, so we want you up here."

"Thank you for this great honor, Mr. President. I feel very humble, but I think I have the strength of character to fight it." He paused to let the laughter die. "This is a great thing. There is only one sobering thought: I received this for going out of the country. I think they are trying to tell me something." Big laughter.

Kennedy took the medal in his hand and turned it over. "Presented to Bob Hope by President Kennedy in recognition of his having rendered outstanding service to the cause of democracy throughout the world. By the act of Congress June 8, 1962."[8]

Inside, Kennedy gave the Hopes a personalized tour, introducing them to his staff and security officers as they went. One officer, Robert Suggs, bore a remarkable resemblance to Hope and Kennedy asked press photographers to shoot the two men in profile with himself in between. That photo became a worldwide wire release.

As the Hopes were leaving, more of the press corps gathered around Hope for his reaction, and he told them what tough competition the President was in the wisecracking department. Just then Kalmus noticed that comedian Milton Berle had entered the White House lobby. Berle kissed Dolores and then moved in close to Bob.

"What are you doing here?" asked Hope.

"Lunch," said Miltie. "I wonder if it's free." The press corps laughed. "Where's your medal?"

Hope held it up for Berle to examine. Berle snatched it out of Hope's hand and put it in his pocket.

"Oh, you want that, too," cracked Hope. With bulbs flashing and reporters straining to catch every nuance, Hope reached into Berle's pocket and retrieved the prize. "Berle can look at it when it's in the shrine."

"Shrine?" several people asked at once.

"Oh, yes," said Bob. "There'll be a special little place, with a turnstile attached. Don't you think we ought to make a little laundry money?"

This was the first public mention of an idea Hope had toyed with for some time, the establishment of a Bob Hope Museum which would house the thousands of mementos, souvenirs of war, gifts from grateful people, plaques, citations, trophies, scrapbooks, wardrobe from his films, and props from films and television. It was one of Hope's plans for immortality.

Another plan in the same vein was unveiled less than a month later. Hope flew into Dallas Love Field on Friday, October 4, and as he stepped out of the plane, there were thousands of students from Southern Methodist University on hand to cheer him. The screaming students were voicing their gratitude to Hope for his beneficence; the Dallas media had been fanning the publicity for his Coliseum show the next day with the news that he had made an outright gift of $302,000 for the establishment of a Bob Hope Theater in the new six-building, $8-million Owen Art Center on the SMU campus.

For the month that followed Hope behaved like the new Chrysler star-producer-commercial spokesman he had become. He rehearsed his comedy special, taped it, filmed introductions to the dramatic series, filmed commercials, and if he had extra time, he did book-autographing parties, the Baseball Writers Luncheon, a personal appearance in Indianapolis and a tribute to Cecil B. De Mille.

He paid heavily for that indulgence. On October 25, while playing golf in Palm Springs, he was overcome by dizziness and knew the hemorrhaging had started again behind his eye. Dr. Beigelman advised complete immobility, and Hope complied for three agonizing weeks of stillness, much of it in darkened rooms. On November 12, Allan Kalmus called from New York to tell Bob that Ursula Halloran had been found dead in her apartment from an apparent overdose of barbiturates and liquor. Hope told Kalmus he would fly to New York the next day because he wanted to see Algernon Reese at Columbia Presbyterian, and that he would attend Ursula's funeral in Pittsburgh.

Reese told Hope that his eye problem could not be corrected by surgery then or ever, and that his hope for recovery might rest in a new photocoagulation process developed by a Swiss surgeon named Dr. Dohrmann Pischel. Hope flew home on November 18, frightened by the prospect that the situation might be beyond help. He was in this frame of mind the morning of November 22 when John Kennedy's skull was ripped open by sniper bullets in the Dallas motorcade.

Hope's eye condition worsened during the next few days, while the nation mourned, and on the day of Kennedy's burial, Hope and Dolores were on a plane to San Francisco to be examined by Dr. Pischel at Children's Hospital. The verdict was that Hope's eye was not then in a condition to accept the treatment. By December 1, Hope felt his condition intolerable. He called Beigelman, who called Pischel, and on December 6 Dolores took Bob, now wearing dark glasses, back to Children's Hospital for the delicate treatment.

Hope was placed on an operating table, his head held rigidly in a vice-like contraption, the photocoagulation gun positioned above him, and the beam directed through the cornea to coagulate the hemorrhaging cells behind the eye. The first treatment was not sufficient. On December 10 he had a second and then he was given special dark glasses with tiny pinholes for openings, so that his eyes would focus in a straight path.[9]

Meanwhile, the 1963 Bob Hope USO Christmas tour of Europe, less than a week away from takeoff, had to be put on "possible cancel." Caranchini and Pawlek were somewhere in Turkey setting up stages, having already prepared the bases in Italy, North Africa and Greece. Mort Lachman was trying to find them to bring them home when Hope telephoned from San

Francisco that he planned to make the trip. "Pischel wants me to take it easy for a couple of weeks. I'm going to slide down to Palm and lay real low. If all goes well, I'll meet you in Turkey."

Pischel thought Hope insane, but nevertheless released him to Dolores' care, and Hope remained in his darkened room wearing those special glasses, while his troupe—including Tuesday Weld, Anita Bryant, the Earl Twins, beauty contest winner Michele Metrinko, the legendary vaudevillian John Bubbles, Jerry Colonna and Les Brown—took off for Istanbul.

The troupe rehearsed at the Hilton Hotel there for two days and then did several shows at nearby air bases with Colonna as emcee. On December 22, Dolores put Bob on a TWA flight to New York where he boarded a Lufthansa flight to Frankfurt, where a U.S. fighter jet picked him up and took him to Ankara. When Caranchini and Pawlek met Hope at the airstrip and saw the comedian's drawn expression and black pinhole glasses, they couldn't believe he would ever step on stage. Hope, however, knew differently. The Defense Department had assigned one of their best young medical men to this tour to watch over Hope, and Freddy Miron was along to keep the comedian relaxed. After the Ankara show had been on for 20 minutes, Hope got up from his nap and he strolled out on stage to the kind of ovation that stars dream about. Later, commenting on this experience, Hope would say:

> I thought that all I'd do was come on and tell a few jokes, then get off and go back to bed. But the electric current that sparked between me and the crowd had to be the world's greatest therapy. It sure was for me, anyway. I stood there, feeling stronger and stronger with every laugh.[10]

With each successive show, Hope got braver and, although he sometimes felt a little woozy onstage, he would say:

> I'm very thrilled that you could make it . . . I'm very proud to be here . . . I just thought you'd like to see a new kind of Turkey. . . . It's wonderful working at bases with exotic names like Karamursel, Eskisehir, Incirlik and Diyarbakir. In case of war, I hope we don't have a phone operator that stutters. . . .[11]

By the time the troupe reached Naples, ten days later, Hope had become irrepressible. For that last show, Hope wanted to do the challenge dance, originally planned for himself and Bubbles, that Lachman had scrapped because he thought it too dangerous for Hope to attempt. There were audible gasps when the crew heard Hope say, "Put on your dancing shoes, John, we're going to fly tonight."

"Beautiful, baby, but what are we going to do?"

"We're going to ad-lib."

He and Bubbles did some steps that both had forgotten they ever knew, and when they came offstage, Hope was like an excited kid.

For Hope this had been the most important "comeback" in his life.

THE VIETNAM YEARS
1964–1972

. . . Hello, advisors . . . here I am in Bien Hoa. That's Vietnamese for "Duck!" . . . Nice to be here in sniper valley. . . .[1]

37. Operation Big Cheer

When the January 15, 1964, issue of *TV Guide* hit the newsstands of America, on its cover was a Ronald Searle caricature of Hope, dressed in a dark suit, white shirt, American flaggish necktie, with his raised left hand holding the Statue of Liberty torch. The cover caption read: BOB HOPE, AN AMERICAN INSTITUTION.

Inside, Dwight Whitney's story was significant because it was the first time a popular magazine (one whose circulation was reputed to be the nation's largest) carried an article about Hope that contained material the comedian considered "negative stuff." Times had changed since the days when Hope could amend or kill an unfavorable story.

Whitney looked carefully at Hope's stature, his accomplishments, his pleasures, his world view, and wrote what he felt:

> . . . Hope has long since ceased to be a mere jokesmith, quipster and all-around funny fellow—or even father. He is more a sociopolitical force. As such he belongs to no one not even himself. It has been estimated that in the 25 years since old Ski-Nose first rose to fame on the coattails of Bing Crosby during the "me and Bing era" he has raised close to a quarter of a million dollars for worthy causes. He has traveled to almost every country in the world, often to entertain troops at Christmas, a time when any sensible father of four contrives to stay home. His stature as the world's foremost funny humanitarian has put in his pocket more brass hats, politicos, industrial wheel horses and Russian generals than any comedian since Will Rogers, and has widened his sphere of influence-without-portfolio to the point where he is sometimes called upon to facilitate matters which have baffled the State Department.

None of that was objectionable. What outraged Hope were suggestions that there was unrest or division in Hope's Camelot—particularly in regard to Dolores:

> The wonder is that Mrs. Hope has managed to preserve her own individuality, and by doing so has freed him to live the sort of life he wants, a nuance by no means lost on him. She is the rock, the mother of their four adopted children, the presider over the home he needs to come back to. They are separate but equal. He fills the house with his golfing pals; she invites men of the cloth. Bob has long since become inured to arriving at his Palm Springs house late at night, to find a strange priest walking the grounds.

The two men introduce themselves, pass the time of day, and go to bed.

Quite probably, it was essentially the unrest of the times that created both the tone of the story and Hope's reaction to it. The early 1960s was the setting for altered perceptions, just one of which was the removal of the lacquered gloss over the entertainment world, that fairy-tale treatment of show business lives and of the end product. Even an "institution" like Hope could now expect to have his life closely inspected by a new breed of reporters whose attitudes tended to be more liberal, whose regard for press agentry more suspicious.

Hope was by no means detached from this changing society. His youngest children, Nora and Kelly, were constantly reminding him of the "hair" scene by their own entertainment preferences. In addition, perhaps as a challenge, he had urged his young booking agent Mark Anthony to increase his number of personal appearances at colleges and universities. Since 1960 Hope had performed to enthusiastic crowds at some twenty campuses like Ohio State, the University of Indiana, Duke, Tulane, and the Universities of Oklahoma, Maryland and Texas.

While he was interested in performing for youth, and maintaining his appeal, Hope's comic persona was undergoing a gradual change. The drugstore lecher, the flip-and-brash smart aleck, was beginning to seem a little like an elder statesman. Even his movie roles were changing.

Hope's only film role of 1964 was that of a widower with mixed feelings about sexual morality, in a weak script called *I'll Take Sweden*. Hope was cast as a worried father trying to wean his teenaged daughter, Tuesday Weld, away from her motorcycle-riding boyfriend, Frankie Avalon. Hope takes Tuesday Weld to Sweden where he himself falls into a casual affair with Dina Merrill. It's a youth-oriented film with forced situations, and Hope seemed uncomfortable in it.

If Hope's mastery of comedy seemed slightly dented by some bad decision-making in his film career, there was no question about his appeal when he took a USO troupe to the battleground of South Vietnam during the Christmas season of 1964. Such a gesture in itself was hardly novel; this was Hope's twenty-first year of entertaining GIs. But this was such a highly publicized and treacherous war, a war that intruded painfully, grimly into American consciousness every day on television news.

Hope learned in October he had been cleared to go to Vietnam but was asked by the Defense Department to keep it quiet for security reasons, to safeguard the GIs who obviously became a better target gathered into a large audience than scattered through the jungles. Hope tried to honor his promise but word kept slipping out. He confessed to reporters he was eager to go. Why not? Like mainstream America, Hope trusted that with this necessary police action, commitments made by Eisenhower in 1955 and later by Kennedy in 1961, we would push back the Commies with our expertise, our awesome war machinery, our millions of dollars. Public opinion polls of 1964 upheld the justice of our presence in Southeast Asia.

For this tour, Hope's mainstay performers were Jerry Colonna and five women: Anita Bryant, Janis Paige, rising young actress Jill St. John, singer

Anna Maria Alberghetti and the beautiful Ann Sydney of Australia, the 1964 Miss World. Tony Hope, on Christmas vacation from his law studies at Harvard, was also invited to go along.

The tour opened with several shows in bitter cold and snow flurries in Korea and then headed south to Thailand with one in-between show at Okinawa. The first day in Bangkok was a rest-break for the 75-member troupe. Next day the troupe flew up-country in Thailand for a show at Korat Air Base and returned in time for a cocktail party thrown by the Foreign Press Correspondents' Association. Back at the Erawan Hotel, the 75 tired but excited troupers had a protocol briefing, got bathed and in their best clothes, to be driven in a fleet of Mercedes-Benz limousines to a sit-down dinner at the Grand Palace (formerly the eighteenth-century walled royal town) with the King and Queen of Thailand in a setting De Mille could never have duplicated.

The invitation had come about this way: When Hope and Lucy Ball were making *Facts of Life* at Desilu Studios in June 1960, the Thai King Phumiphol and his beautiful wife Queen Sirikit were guests on the set to watch the filming. As they were leaving, the King extended an invitation to Hope to visit his country and to bring with him Les Brown so that he would have someone to play duets with on his saxophone.

It was a magical experience, eating exotic food from golden plates and dinnerware, watching an impromptu show performed on a specially built teakwood stage in a courtyard surrounded by a collection of spiked towers, all flood-lit white with gleaming gold. The King, thrilled at being invited to play with Les Brown's band, was tireless.

Next day, Christmas Eve, following a show at Ta Khli Air Base, the troupe boarded their C–141 Lockheed Starlifter, cheering when the wheels lifted off the runway to take them south around the tip of Cambodia, across the lacy Mekong Delta to Saigon. As the plane entered the war zone, apprehension registered on many faces. Some felt more secure when they looked out through the tiny portholes to see a fighter escort assigned to guide them to the airstrip.

The first show in Vietnam was at Bien Hoa Air Base, a few miles from Saigon. Because of possible enemy ground fire, the tower advised the pilot to make a steep landing, which alarmed the troupe. They understood the reason when they looked at the shell-pocked airstrip and saw the few destroyed aircraft not yet hauled away.

The security measures enforced for Operation Big Cheer, the code name for the show, were remarkable. The project officer at Bien Hoa told director Jack Shea that there were as many troops guarding the perimeter of the base as there were watching the show, and every enlisted man and officer in sight either carried a rifle or a sidearm.

> . . . Hello, advisors . . . here I am at Bien Hoa. That's Vietnamese for—Duck!—Nice to be here in sniper valley . . . you remember Vietnam . . . it's the place Huntley and Brinkley are always talking about. We're going to Saigon and I hope we do as well here as Henry Cabot Lodge . . . he got out . . . I understand the enemy is very close. But with my act, they always

are . . . This is terrible country for a coward. Can you imagine not knowing which way to run? You've heard of the NBC peacock . . . this is the Far Eastern Chicken. . . .

There is a new subtlety in Hope's humor, illustrated here by his easy reference to Lodge, his consciousness of media's role in the war, and the shared awareness with his audience that "advisors" were technically noncombatants in a deadly shooting war.

Bien Hoa had never been intended as one of the major shows but it ended up lasting two hours because the audience was so enthusiastic. There was a fast hospital ward walk-through and a quick drink at the officers club and then to the buses for a short ride to Saigon. But suddenly those plans got changed. Reports of lively sniper activity on the road between Bien Hoa and Saigon suggested that it would be better to fly into the capital's Tan Son Nhut Airport.

At Tan Son Nhut were General Ben Sternberg and his aides who had raced out from Saigon and were standing in the tropical sun as an improvised welcoming party. The troupe was loaded into a convoy of sedans driven by armed MPs. Each sedan was preceded and followed by a jeep loaded with machine-gun–ready policemen.

At one point on a narrow, heavily congested one-way street, the convoy halted. An MP with a two-way radio told them he understood a fire had broken out in a hotel across the street from the Caravelle where Hope and the cast were staying, but things were under control.

A moment later the convoy moved forward and the driver's window was shattered by something hurled at it. Soon the convoy turned into a sweeping boulevard lined with once-elegant French-style townhouses and it was easy to see why this city had been known as the Paris of the Orient. On every side of the convoy, hundreds of Vietnamese couples rode on motorbikes through the dense Christmas Eve traffic.

When the convoy finally reached the Caravelle, blue smoke layered with brown dust hung everywhere, sirens wailed, people were running in several directions, and rubble and piles of broken glass lay everywhere. The atmosphere was tense.

Surrounded by MPs, the troupe was herded into the lobby, whose carpet was also littered with fragments of glass from its shattered windows. Bit by bit the information came through that only minutes before the Hope group arrived, the Brinks Hotel, an officers billet across from the Caravelle, exploded. Earlier that afternoon, a 1956 Dodge station wagon loaded with TNT and dynamite was driven into the courtyard of Brinks while most of its residents were celebrating or preparing to celebrate Christmas Eve. The driver set a timing device and ran. The blast gutted the billet, killing a number of officers, wounding many and causing considerable damage to buildings in every direction.

While the troupe was being assigned rooms, General Sternberg and some of the Operation Big Cheer personnel went up to Hope's suite for some serious talk. They argued that it might be too dangerous for Hope to remain in the city. But when the MPs said they could handle the security, Hope said he would stay for the two scheduled nights in Saigon.

The sole activity scheduled that night was for cast members only, a reception at Ambassador Maxwell Taylor's residence. All the female entertainers were too shaken to want to go so Hope took Les and Jerry with him, and it was here that Hope made his formal stand about not leaving Saigon—or leaving Vietnam, for that matter—despite the demoralizing effect of the explosion and the possibility of further incidents. Taylor told Hope that 8 men had been killed in the blast and that 75 wounded had been taken to a Naval hospital. As he spoke, Garrick Utley of NBC News arrived at the Ambassador's front door inquiring if Hope planned to visit the wounded.

A few minutes later, Hope, Brown and Colonna were making the rounds with doctors and nurses in the wards of this Naval Medical Corps facility. Only Hope was allowed into the burn ward where surgeons were removing the pieces of glass from burned bodies. Hope recalls:

> Burn wards are the toughest of all. And when it's a combination of burn and splintered glass—well, you wonder if your stomach will let you continue. But somehow I managed. I went around grabbing all the hands that could be raised to shake and I touched those who were smiling at me. One kid was lying on his stomach and they were taking slivers out of his butt with tweezers and others were waiting for that operation, with nurses dabbing them with some kind of topical anesthetic. One kid was bent over while a doctor was working on his head and when he heard someone say "Bob Hope," he jerked his head away from the doctor and looked up at me, his face covered with blood. He said "Merry Christmas" as if he really meant it and I don't suppose I will ever forget the way he said it. It still chills me.[2]

Back at the Caravelle, Hope noticed it was a quarter to twelve and he had promised Dolores to attend Mass. He called Colonna, Jack Shea and Barney McNulty and started out of the hotel. The cathedral was off limits because of a recent assassination attempt, so they walked, escorted by two Marines, to the Rex Hotel across the square where Mass was being said in an upper room.

At a quarter to one, they began walking back toward the Caravelle along streets that were sandbagged and bunkered. The early Christmas morning had an eerie rather than a joyous feel. Suddenly, from nowhere, stepped a figure into their path and there was a flash of light. Someone screamed, someone else said, "Jesus Christ!" and Hope turned ashen. It was a GI who had apparently been following them and had taken a flash picture. Hope convinced the Marines not to arrest the soldier.

According to the so-called top-secret plans for Hope's itinerary while in Vietnam, there were always two possible locations for each show, and the one actually selected would be notified only two hours before showtime. This meant that for the six shows Hope performed, twelve stages had to be built and six potential audiences disappointed. And the irony of it all was that Hanoi Hannah seemed to know which of the two show sites had been selected even before the Operation Big Cheer personnel did. She announced it each day on her broadcast.

Christmas morning, the nod went to Vinh Long, a small base with three hundred GIs in the Mekong Delta. Hope took a stripped-down version of the show: Jill, Janis, Anna Maria and Miss World, plus Colonna and a single musician, guitarist Bobby Gibbons. The show took place on a truck bed in the middle of the compound and Hope's biggest laugh came from this joke "A funny thing happened to me on the way to my hotel from the airport. I met a hotel going the other way."[3] What amazed Hope, in this most bizarre of wars, was the lightning speed of news which allowed him to be as topical as he wished.

Later that day, Hope led his group to Ton San Nhut Air Base for what turned out to be the biggest audience in Vietnam, probably ten thousand or more, with special guests General Westmoreland and his wife Kitsie. Afterwards there was a hospital ward walk-through and then the cast went to the Westmorelands for dinner.

The day after Christmas, Hope's Big Cheer players flew north to a remote base called Camp Halloway at Pleiku, deep in Montagnard country and not far from the Ho Chi Minh Trail. It was unquestionably the most dangerous location the Hope troupe played because Cong raids were frequent.

From Pleiku, they took off for Nhatrang, the headquarters for the Green Berets. In peacetime, Nhatrang was the country's most popular seaside resort, the site of Madame Nhu's summer home. Even now it was the first choice as a rest and rehabilitation center for all three participants in this war, the Americans, the South Vietnamese and the Vietcong.

And all three moved about in relative freedom both day and night. Nevertheless, the Hope show was performed in the middle of the Special Forces camp to what may well have been the most appreciative audience of the whole tour. Later that night there were a dozen informal parties thrown for the Hope troupe in a dozen different hooches.

The troupe was bedded down in two rather faded resort hotels. Early next morning, one of the cameramen woke and began screaming. The lower half of his body was black with ants. He leaped up and ran down the hallway to the common bath facilities, but there was no running water. Anita Bryant and her husband Bob Green (who always accompanied her) heard the screams and came to help. Anita produced some bottles of Coca-Cola to wash down his thighs and legs.

Final stop in Vietnam was Da Nang or "Dog Patch" as the GIs called it. Because of Vietcong activity nearby, armed guards were everywhere and the troupe's nerves were beginning to show. As soon as "Silent Night" had been sung and the equipment packed, the troupe was driven in a maximum security bus (heavy bars over the windows) to the airstrip where the Lockheed Starlifter was waiting. When the C–141 lifted up and headed out over the China Sea, there was loud applause, partly self-congratulatory but mostly relief. The tour's final shows, at Clark Field in the Philippines and on Guam, were to big enthusiastic audiences; then it was homeward bound.

Hope was extraordinarily keyed up about this trip and especially about the dramatic film footage the camera crews had caught from this 23,000-mile adventure. The camera showed a Hope who didn't mind showing some graying at the temples, a sunburned face, a slight paunch; a Hope who sauntered out with a golf club a little less bumptiously but just as impudently, a wisecracker. And loved, too. Loved for his jokes, for bringing sex objects for them to fantasize about, for taking their minds off ugliness for a few hours, for squeezing a wounded GI's hand or signing his plaster cast or introducing a Jill St. John to a ward full of wide-eyed wounded. Except for the passing of time, there was no perceptible difference between the mission of 1943 and that of 1964.

When the hard news about Hope's Christmas tour died down, the publicity about his up-coming Chrysler-sponsored television special began. And it was a barrage. Hope spent his days either at the studio screening footage for the 90-minute telecast or talking to local editors, wire service reporters, and entertainment writers in distant cities. All the while his publicity staff ground out reams of copy, hundreds of black-and-white and color photographs.

The program itself was lovingly edited. Part documentary, part travelogue, part pure entertainment, it unashamedly focused on the GIs. Hundreds of feet of film were devoted to shots of soldiers sitting in the mud, hanging from trees and power poles and silhouetted as they stood on trucktops and rooftops to watch the show. Most powerful effect came from the close-up faces, laughing, cheering, crying, singing "Silent Night."

According to Nielsen figures, the telecast was viewed in 24.5 million homes, or by more than half of all Americans watching television that night. It was the largest single audience Hope had ever drawn for one of his shows.

Even before Hope's name ceased to crowd the television news pages with his Vietnam telecast, the sports pages began touting a new golf tournament that bore his name. Well, it wasn't really that new. Since 1960, during February, Hope had shown up as a celebrity amateur in a PGA event known as the Palm Springs Classic. Invented by Milt Hicks and Ben Shearer to benefit Coachella Valley charities, the tournament was a fair success but Hicks thought it would fare better if Hope ran it. Bob had long dreamed of emulating the success and prestige of the one up north called the Crosby at Pebble Beach, but he also knew the amount of time and responsibility involved and repeatedly turned down Hicks' offer.

But in 1964, Saphier and Hope thought of involving Chrysler in the deal. Chrysler's Lynn Townsend liked the idea, but only if Hope's name was on it. Hicks proposed that the Palm Springs Classic be renamed The Bob Hope Desert Classic and Hope was elected its president. To cinch its drawing power, he leaned on all the professional golfers he knew so well—Arnold Palmer (who had won the tournament twice), fellow Ohioan Jack Nicklaus, Billy Casper, Gary Player, Doug Sanders, Jimmy Demaret and celebrities like Desi Arnaz, Danny Thomas, Rowan and Martin, Andy Williams, Robert Stack, Lawrence Welk and Frank Sinatra—to help draw a gallery. Hope decided to make it the glossiest pro–am event on the tour. By its second season, the Bob Hope Classic had become not only the largest charity event in the desert but the biggest golf tournament anywhere, with 128 professionals and 384 amateurs playing for a purse totaling $110,000. It was also considered the top social event of the Palm Springs winter season and Chrysler executives didn't mind mingling with the likes of Leonard Firestone, or Dwight Eisenhower, or Walter Annenberg.

However, some Chrysler executives registered alarm in February, after the Classic, when they discovered that Hope had decided to present a sequel to his Christmas-in-Vietnam special as his March 24 program. Hope said, "Look at the ratings we got," and pointed to the thousands of feet of film that were never shown. Chrysler was sympathetic and eager for high ratings but also concerned about changing public attitudes toward the war in Vietnam, as evidenced by draft card burning on college campuses.

Moreover, they were sponsoring Hope in a comedy-variety format, and some of the items planned for this follow-up telecast were hardly comedy. For example, there was a highly charged interview between Hope and cartoonist Bill Mauldin, who had visited his son Bruce three weeks after the Hope Christmas visit. Mauldin described in chilling detail awaking in the night and finding himself in the midst of a Vietcong attack:

> I was awakened by machine gun fire about two in the morning. The first round hit our hooch, killing two men and badly wounding a third. The kid was sort of holding himself together with two hands. He was in bad shape and I tried to get him to go down in a bunker with me but he wouldn't move. He figured he was going to die, and the thought of going down into a hole didn't appeal to him. . . .[4]

Three days before the telecast, Bob Thomas of the Associated Press drove out to Toluca Lake for a late breakfast to talk with Bob about his reasons for the Vietnam sequel. He found a serious, reflective man.

"We shot 30,000 feet of film on that trip and only got to use a small part of it. You see, we played 18 different spots and we had to show all of them because if we hadn't, the folks back home would have been upset. There was so much of Vietnam we didn't get a chance to show, Bob. And that footage is so timely, provocative and interesting, it'll be wasted if we don't get it out right away."

"I've heard you're using newsreel, too."

"We've added some new film. We've found footage of the same troops we entertained in the Philippines now landing at Da Nang. And we see the same helicopter we rode in, reduced to ashes during the raid on Pleiku. And wait till you see the North Vietnam propaganda films NBC picked up in Japan."

"This is important to you, isn't it?" asked Thomas.

"This is important to the world, Bob. Listen—if the Commies ever thought we weren't going to protect the Vietnamese, there would be Vietnams all over. That would be a lot worse than what we are facing now. Like it or not, we've fallen heir to the job of Big Daddy in the free world."

That spring when Hope was resting for a few days in Palm Springs, he played golf with Dwight Eisenhower at the Eldorado Country Club. They talked about the Christmas trip and the war. Hope and Ike agreed that when U.S. troops joined the offensive, there was no other course of action but to win.

The two men also discussed another matter close to their hearts. Hope explained to the former President the status of his tribute to Eisenhower: the construction of an Eisenhower Medical Center for the study and treatment of respiratory and heart diseases, on a choice parcel of land in Rancho Mirage which he had donated for the project. Ike was flattered and touched. Hope also assured Ike that he would be on hand in September at Seneca Falls, New York, for the ground-breaking of Eisenhower College.

Before that September dedication, and in addition to his benefits, appearances and regular Chrysler shows, Hope appeared at:

—The Oscars, for his thirteenth night of being master of ceremonies, although it was almost canceled because of a labor dispute.

—Southern Methodist University on April 30, to hand over his personal check for $302,000 as down payment toward the Bob Hope Theater.

—Cincinnati, Ohio, on May 5 for an exhibition golf match with champion Jack Nicklaus to benefit a halfway house for delinquent boys named The Bob Hope House. It was conceived in 1963 by a Hamilton County Juvenile Division judge named Benjamin Schwartz, whose fervent wish was that Hope be the house's benefactor. Hope promised Schwartz that each year he would come to Cincinnati and create some kind of fund-raising event to keep the home solvent.

—His son Kelly's high school graduation from St. John Vianney in Los Angeles on June 3, and delivered the commencement address to 87 graduates and their parents, friends and teachers, who were jammed into the Wilshire Ebell Theater. In his serious remarks, Hope said:

> . . . You can't read the morning papers without being a little worried about the current college craze of sit-ins and demonstrations. I think it's great that our young men and women are concerned about people's rights because that's the American way . . . that's why the world looks to us for help. . . .
>
> Americans need the new ideas of its young people . . . it needs their idealism, and I only hope they aren't all hoarse when it's their time to be heard from.[5]

(The truth Hope was missing here was that his idealistic youth *were* being heard from.)

—The commencement exercises of Monmouth College in West Long Branch, New Jersey, on June 5 to pick up his fourth honorary doctorate.

—Still another graduation ceremony, this one at Whittier College where he joined Maine Senator Margaret Chase Smith and native son, former Vice President Richard Nixon, to receive another Honorary Doctor of Humane Letters Degree on June 12.

—The Dominican Republic on July 13 with Tuesday Weld, Joey Heatherton, Jerry Colonna and Tony Romano to entertain for the 28,000 U.S. Marines that Lyndon Johnson sent to avert a Communist takeover of that troubled nation.

—Producers' Studio in Hollywood to make his fifty-first motion picture, *Boy, Did I Get a Wrong Number!* with Elke Sommer and Phyllis Diller, directed by his old pal, George Marshall.

—The Screen Actors Guild awards luncheon at the Hollywood Palladium on November 14 to accept their first annual SAG Award "for outstanding achievement in fostering the finest ideals of the acting profession."

—Finally, in the year in which he received the Splendid American Award

from the Tom Dooley Foundation and the first NBC–TV affiliates award 1
any performer, Hope seemed most affected by students of Shell Bank Junie
High School in Brooklyn, New York, who presented him with their Eleano
Roosevelt Memorial Award "for his high ideals, self-sacrifice and goc
will."

During a United Press International interview, published November 3(
1935, the retirement question came up again, to which Hope replied:

"If I retired, I'd be surrounded by about nine psychiatrists. I'm not reti:
ing until they carry me away—and I'll have a few routines on the way to th
big divot."

*I might as well admit it, I have no politics where the boys are
concerned. I only know they're over there doing a job that
has to be done, and whatever is best for them is best for
me.*[1]

38. Hope for President

Mort Lachman was beginning to think the 1965 Christmas tour—singing
dancing and joking its way through the sweltering winter humidity of South
east Asia—should be subtitled "Hope's Hard Luck Follies." After doin
shows for fighter squadrons at Udon and Ta Khli in Thailand, several Le
Brown musicians became so badly sunburned that medics had to treat ther
for sun poisoning. On top of that, Joey Heatherton had developed blister
from rehearsing and dancing her frenetic and sexy Watusi.

Then, at the matinee performance at Khorat for combined USARTHA
troops (a mixed American service crowd plus a big turnout of Thai militar
and government officials) and some Peace Corps volunteers, Hope was jos
tled backstage, lost his balance, and fell five feet into the arms of a surprise
security officer named Robert Raft. Hope was shaken but able to go on wit
the show. Afterwards he felt a sharp pain and allowed himself to be taken t
a medical aid station near Bangkok. It turned out he had in fact pulle
several ligaments in his left ankle.

Despite all that trouble, Hope, Les Brown's musicians and Joey manage
to put on quite a show for King Phumiphol and Queen Sirikit that night a
still another of the many royal residences in the Thai capital.

Next day, they flew into Saigon where the stars were assigned rooms at th
Caravelle and everyone else, about 65, were housed at a newly constructe
8-story military hotel called the Meyercord. It was labeled "maximum secu
rity" which meant it was fenced off from the street and had machine-gu
emplacements on balconies, every other floor. Mary Martin's *Hello Doll*
troupe had christened this place a month before.

That night the troupe was invited by the command escorts to a Christma
party on the Meyercord roof. At almost five o'clock in the morning, tw
hours before their scheduled wake-up call, came a deafening explosion. Th

hotel shook, there was screaming, and terrified people ran along the hallways lining the open courtyard in various stages of undress. It seemed the clean-up crew had been lowering empty bottles and dirty dishes from the rooftop party when the ropes snapped, sending the heavy load crashing to the cavernous courtyard below. Only a few managed to get back to sleep.

Hope's opening monologue at Ton San Nhut Air Base established a new range of perspectives on the war, including in Hope's own language a warning to his audience about American factions back home who anguished over Vietnam:

> . . . No, I just want to say that here I am . . . the longest delivery that "Chicken Delight" ever made . . . I'm happy to be here. I understand everything's great, the situation's improved, in fact, things couldn't be better . . . Well? . . . who am I gonna believe? . . . You, or Huntley and Brinkley? . . . No, we've had all kinds of demonstrations back in the states . . . "Get out of Vietnam," "Don't get out of Vietnam," "Why don't you go back where you came from?" and "I came from Vietnam, that's why!" . . .[2]

The most perilous show of the tour was probably the one at Di An on Christmas noon. Despite the declared 24-hour holiday truce, the show site hacked out of the jungle the day before was an inviting target for Vietcong rockets. When Hope went to the latrine, there was a guard with a machine gun standing outside the door. From inside, Hope said, "Afraid it will blow away?"

"No, sir. It ain't nothing to joke about, Mr. Hope. We draw a lot of sniper fire here, twenty-four hours a day. We're not only surrounded by Charleys, there may even be some in your audience."[3]

When Hope got back to the staging area, he watched a gruff-voiced sergeant major barking orders at the already seated audience. "Now—I want you men to keep the aisle clear on both sides of this stage in case of a mortar attack. The left side will move off to the left, the right side to the right, and you in the center section will move off to the rear. The cast of the Bob Hope Show will take cover in those cozy foxholes next to the stage."

Lachman once attempted to articulate the mystique of a Hope Christmas show: "The servicemen feel so abandoned," he said, "they're so hungry, so desperate for a touch of home, a familiar face, that when they see Bob, a roar goes up, a surge of humanity moves forward, a mass of men cry out in love and friendship. There is something hysterical, religious, fanatical, and overwhelming about their fervor. It happens at every outpost, every camp, every station. And it inspires Bob and the troupe to perform almost beyond endurance. The trips are hell, but every year the same crew of technicians volunteer. They come back battered and beaten, but strangely uplifted. Bob, as you know, is not a religious man. But there is a spiritual, missionary quality to these Christmas trips which is strangely contagious. It has gotten to all the members of his family, and everyone who's worked with him, which is why we have so many repeaters."

Those nine traumatic Vietnam shows produced film footage more spectacular than the previous year. The troop strength in Southeast Asia had been

raised; there were more faces to film, louder laughs to record. Hope had
picked up casual footage of another USO troupe headed by Martha Raye,
Johnny Grant, Eddie Fisher and John Bubbles, a charming interlude with
Cardinal Spellman, and footage of General Westmoreland. As in the past,
Hope spent two arduous weeks of film editing, script polishing and media
interviews prior to unveiling the documentary on January 19, 1966. It
attracted an impressive 55 percent of the total viewing audience for its time
period.

Hope may have provided viewers with heartwarming entertainment, but
he had also raised the consciousness of America concerning the depth of the
nation's commitment to Vietnam. It was one thing to see groups of 25 or 50
GIs flushing out the enemy during a jungle patrol on the nightly news, but to
see thousands and thousands of soldiers and sailors in Hope's audiences
made the war seem much bigger.

And if Hope's efforts to lighten the grimness of the war was not sufficiently applauded by TV critics, or viewers, or the wives, mothers and sweethearts
of the GI, he was warmly applauded from the White House. Hope was
invited to attend the USO's Silver Anniversary celebration in Washington on
March 31 and, as guest of honor, to accept that organization's highest award
from Lyndon Johnson. A day before the dinner, Hope was told the disappointing news that a pressing State matter forced the President to cancel his
appearance.

So it was a pleasurable shock when word rippled along the head table, as
toastmaster John Daly was about to begin the program, that Johnson's
motorcade had pulled up to the side door of the Washington Hilton. Hope
shuffled through his jokes wondering if there were any he ought to omit, just
as the President slipped through a velvet drapery at the far end of the head
table and the orchestra played "Hail to the Chief." Daly said: "Ladies and
gentlemen, the President of the United States."

Johnson paused while the ballroom full of cabinet members, congressmen,
judges, military people, industry executives, actors and agents, and media
stood and applauded him. When the noise abated and people sat down,
Johnson put on his glasses and said:

> Mr. Chairman . . . Mr. Hope . . . ladies and gentlemen
> . . . I have come here today to honor a man with two very
> unusual traits. He is an actor who is not, so far as I know, running
> for public office . . .

The audience loved Johnson's allusion to Ronald Reagan. He went on:

> And he is a frequent visitor to Vietnam who has never been asked
> to testify before the Senate Foreign Relations Commit-
> tee . . . at least, not yet. . . .

Much laughter. Clearly, Johnson would have been happier without the Senate's investigation of the Nation's involvement in Vietnam. He continued:

> . . . I understand he was planning to testify until he discovered
> there was live coverage on only one network . . . and it wasn't
> the friendly network. . . . It isn't that he wanted the additional

exposure . . . it was just that he refused to go up against "I Love Lucy's" rating without some help. . . .

The audience was reacting to the President as if he were one of the nation's top comics.

> . . . it may come as a surprise to some people with short memories that Bob Hope is more than a comedian. The book about his travels to entertain our troops during the Second World War led the best-seller list back in 1944. It was called *I Never Left Home*. Since then he has spent so much time with our troops overseas that there are those who now say he ought to write a sequel. He should call this one *I Never Came Back*. . . .[4]

As the President handed him a silver medal, the audience stood.

Johnson took his seat to the left of the dais, and Hope waited for the room to quiet. "Thank you very much, Mr. President." He looked to his left. "Pretty crazy drop-in, isn't he?" The audience roared. Hope was off and running:

> . . . It's nice to be back here in Washington . . . or as the Republicans call it . . . Camp Runamuck . . . No, but it's nice . . . to be back in Birdland. . . .[5]

Johnson stared up at Hope. Hope stared back, trying to read the President's face. Then in a lowered voice, yet still audible, Hope apologized, "I have to do it, sir . . . it's written here on this paper. . . ." Both Johnson and the audience laughed. And from that moment on Johnson seemed to relish his straight man role, first staring up at Hope, then out to the audience, milking the applause and the laughter.

Hope lauded other veteran USO entertainers like Martha Raye and Johnny Grant, and acknowledged his supporters Stuart Symington and Rosy O'Donnell. Then he looked sidewards, down the full length of the head table to where the glamorous Joan Crawford was sitting, and introduced her. Crawford, now a Pepsi-Cola executive's widow and a board member of the USO, looked stunning in her Balmain gown, sipping from a glass that contained pure vodka.

When the President departed, the banquet was over and Hope invited many of the important guests to his suite upstairs for a late night party. Guests included the Firestones, the Symingtons, Rosy O'Donnell, John Daly, Abe Lastfogel, Anita Bryant and Bob Green, Joey Heatherton, Jerry Colonna, Les Brown, and a crowd of congressmen and bureaucrats known to Hope. As everyone mingled, Hope said to Freddy Miron, "Where's Crawford? Get her in here!"

Freddy, who had been Crawford's masseur long before he met Hope, went into his bedroom of the suite, consulted a scrap of paper on his bedside table and dialed. Crawford answered.

"It's me, Joan—it's Freddy. Bob wants you to come to the party."

"Tell him I'm naked," said Joan.

"Good," said Freddy, "he'll be glad you can make it."

"FRED-DY!!" screamed Crawford, "I said I'm NA-KED!"

"I'm glad you can make it, Joan. Hurry."

Fred hung up and went back into the living room and told Hope that
Crawford was on her way. A few minutes later someone opened the door of
Hope's suite and there framed in the doorway was Crawford, luminous in her
silver lamé Balmain gown, holding a glass of vodka in her hand. She came in,
as only Crawford could, through the crowd to where Hope stood talking to
Symington. She said, "You know something? I haven't got a stitch on under
this thing—and I don't give a good—" She looked around. "Where's that
Cuban?"[6]

In April, the Hopes were in Palm Springs frequently because construction
was starting on the Eisenhower Medical Center. Dolores was particularly
busy because she was to serve as president of the hospital's board.

At the end of that month, Bob received the Silver Lady Award from the
Banshees, a blue ribbon group of communications executives and media
people representing virtually the total press systems of the United States and
Canada.

The overwhelming popularity of his Vietnam television special, the
endorsements of the current and past Presidents of the United States, and
recognition paid him by the Fourth Estate, gave Hope the indisputable message that his mercy missions for the GI were appreciated. Most of America
still approved the country's conduct in the undeclared war. Hope was mystified by growing pockets of dissent over that involvement. The draft card
burnings on college campuses dismayed him, so much so that he asked his
writers to help him put together an article for the widely circulated Hearst-
owned Sunday supplement *Family Weekly*. In it he said:

> Can you imagine returning from a combat patrol in a steaming,
> disease-infested jungle, tired, hungry, scared and sick, and read-
> ing that people in America are demonstrating against your being
> there? That people in America are burning their draft cards to
> show their opposition and that some of them are actually rooting
> for your defeat?[7]

To Hope it was inconceivable that his arguments in behalf of the GI
fighting Communism would not be shared by every patriotic American. It
was how the Hearst papers felt. But to the growing tide of media voices who
questioned the legitimacy of the war, such a position rendered Hope hawkish
at worst and naive at best.

When Hope flew into New York for media exposure in connection with
the opening of his latest movie (a slight comedy called *Boy, Did I Get a
Wrong Number!* with Elke Sommer and Phyllis Diller), he discovered the
media were more interested in his world view than in his acting. Allan Kalmus brought Bruce Porter of the *New York Post* to Hope's Hampshire
House suite, and the subject turned quickly to the Vietnam tours and the
objections that Hope was using his Christmas special for propaganda.

"I don't think that program reflected my political views at all," Hope said
edgily. "But I'll tell you the things I said about our mission in Vietnam was
what I truly believe—and I'm not ashamed to say them."

"You're not against dissent?"

"Listen—one group is fighting for their country and one group is fighting against their country. They're giving aid and comfort to the enemy. You'd call these same people traitors if we declared war. And I'll tell you something else—it's time for Americans to do some right thinking and some smart thinking about their country. I don't know if these fellows have relatives who are fighting over there, or they'd have some compassion for the prob-lems."

"If we left there," Hope said, "the propaganda value to the Communists would be devastating as far as I'm concerned. That's what the whole thing is built on. If we didn't walk out of there with honor, we'd pay for it. The whole country would pay for it."

Porter changed the subject.

"What about actors in politics, Bob—Reagan and Murphy?"

"Well, Ronnie's got a great personality, and show business is not far removed from politics. Reagan has such a great appearance. I don't agree with all he says, but he can sure talk. And he *goes*. Reagan is well, well liked."

"What about Murphy?"

"George? He introduced me to my wife, but I still voted for him." Porter and Kalmus laughed.[8]

After Porter had left, Kalmus asked, "Have you ever thought about get-ting into politics?"

"Why do you ask?"

"A hunch."

"Jack Warner in 1964 asked me to run for state senator on the Republican ticket. I told him it wasn't my bag. But very recently—and I don't want you to use this, at least right now—a couple of the Washington boys came out to Palm Springs to play some golf and afterwards we were sitting around. I said to—ah, to one of them, 'Come on, now, you didn't come out here just to be whipped by me. What gives?' And after a few looks back and forth at each other, one of the biggest lawmakers in the country—"

"Who?" asked Kalmus.

"Never mind. He said to me, 'Bob, we want you to run for President. We think you could win.' And before I could throw up or anything, he said, 'We've already run a few opinion polls on our own and they show you'd get the popular vote.' I was speechless."

"I believe it," said Kalmus. "Weren't you tempted?"

"I'd never been asked to run for President before. I told the senators that being born in England would disqualify me even though I got citizenship through my dad. They told me they planned to introduce a Private Members Bill to nullify the native-born rule."[9]

Actually, at roughly that same time, a letter to the editor of the Louisville, Kentucky, *Courier Journal and Times* on May 10, 1966, suggested the name of Bob Hope be put in nomination for the Presidency on the Demo-cratic ticket. Part of the reasoning was:

> Imagine, if you can, the inimitable character of his State-of-
> the-Union messages? Also, his press conferences would be both
> interesting and witty. . . .
> And there is sound historical precedent for choosing a comedi-

an to guide our destinies in these crucial times. After all, America
has been run by jokers through much of its history.

Kidding on the square? Perhaps. But in Seattle in early summer 1966, radio
disc jockey Jack Morton of station KVI conducted a listener survey asking
this question: "If Bob Hope were to run for the office of President of the
United States today would you vote for him?" Men responded they would
vote for Hope 63 percent to 37 percent; women said they would vote for the
comedian 62 percent to 38 percent. From Hope came an emphatic "Thanks,
but no thanks."[10]

Such popularity suggested that the people agreed with Hope about the
nation's commitment. And Hope, the follower of public opinion, had to
believe that he was thinking like the majority of citizens. That belief must
have been behind his decision to share his feelings about the war in another
channel. He sat down for sessions with Mort, Bill Larkin, Les White, Charley Lee, Johnny Rapp and Gig Henry to fashion from his monologues, production diaries, trip logs, and the personal reminiscences of about two dozen
staffers, a book about the 1964 and 1965 tours of Southeast Asia. It was
called *Five Women I Love: Bob Hope's Vietnam Story*, and though it could
in no way touch the gallantry or popularity of a work like *I Never Left
Home*, it was nevertheless funny and touching.

The book was all about Vietnam, about the laughs and the girls Hope
"packed to take along," and about the horrors of war and the courage of the
GI. After talking with some of the front-line troops, he said: "Not knowing
where the enemy is or who's firing at you can be unnerving. Not knowing
where your friends, or the people back home, stand can be shattering." In the
final pages of the book Hope summarized his views:

> I might as well admit it, I have no politics where the boys are
> concerned. I only know they're over there doing a job that has to
> be done, and whatever is best for them is best for me. I bow to no
> man in my love for my country, and if my zeal for backing these
> kids to the hilt means offending a few part-time citizens and
> thereby losing a few points in the Nielsen, so be it . . . And the
> thing that never stops amazing me is the good grace with which
> they accept their impossible roles. A soldier stands in the twilight
> between his civilization and the raw savagery of war . . . These
> kids seem to be a lot more optimistic about this commitment than
> a lot of our citizens here at home. In their everyday job of fighting
> this treacherous war they know there's no alternative.
> . . . They're not about to give up—because they know if they
> walked out of this bamboo obstacle course, it would be like saying
> to the Commies—"Come and get it."[11]

Hope's compassion for the GI was honest, and so was his belief in the
Yankee tradition of fighting for freedom, and his hatred of Communism, and
his conviction that you fight a war to win. All this anchored him on one side
of the mounting worldwide controversy over Vietnam.

Also in the fall of 1966, Hope met an enterprising young recording producer named Dick LaPalm who convinced the comedian to release a long-

playing disc of his USO shows in Vietnam. Hope gave LaPalm the sound-tracks for his 1964 shows in Korea, Thailand, Vietnam, the Philippines and Guam, agreeing that there ought to be people out there interested in having this recording as a piece of history.

Hope and the other stars on the record agreed to assign their profits to the USO, but unfortunately there weren't many profits to turn over despite the fact the disc was marketed in time for Christmas sales. The recording com-pany was a small one with limited distribution, and there was something vaguely distasteful about the title, *On the Road to Vietnam*, which several critics cited as "opportunistic." Nevertheless, the recording is a valuable document, and convincing aural proof of Hope's glib explanation of why he did the tours: "I looked at them, they laughed at me, and it was love at first sight."

For the Christmas 1966 GI tour, once again backed by the Defense Department and the USO, Hope headed for Vietnam and nearby Southeast Asian points. For the first time in several years, Dolores went along, as did the two youngest Hopes, Nora and Kelly. Hope was pleased that Rosy O'Donnell, now retired from the military and new president of the USO, would be along. Another temporary drop-in was Stuart Symington; and Hope was also grateful for the presence of Colonel Bob Gates, his pilot for that harrowing Alaska flight in 1942.

There was something noticeably missing from this trip. Jerry Colonna had suffered a stroke one evening when he got home from taping one of Hope's specials at NBC. He had become paralyzed through most of one half of his body and his speech was impaired. With therapy and almost daily encour-agement from Hope, either by telephone or in person, Colonna was making a slow recovery at the Motion Picture Hospital and Home in Woodland Hills. But that special whimsical madness he brought to so many overseas trips would be missed.

Hope never produced a less than professional show overseas, but his 1966 edition had particular distinction. He brought funny lady Phyllis Diller instead of a sex star, yet the troops greeted Diller with the kind of reception they gave to Raquel Welch. Vic Damone was a crowd pleaser, and, as usual, Joey Heatherton and Anita Bryant stopped the show.

But the unexpected emotional highs came from Dolores. At first Bob just asked her to "take a bow," but the audiences stood and cheered her, and Bob invited her up on stage. He said, "Sing 'White Christmas.' " She turned to Les Brown and said "I'm not sure I remember all the lyrics," and Bob said, "Go ahead, I'll feed it to you." She handled it beautifully, with a mixture of worldliness and motherliness that had a lot of people out in front and back-stage crying. She got another standing ovation.[12]

For the record, it was the first time Hope allowed himself a public identity in the "face off" which seemed to demand that people take a stand on the Vietnam issue. Hope had reached a personal decision that he wanted to see this war ended. After his initial show in Pleiku, Vietnam, Hope was jeeped over to a news conference in a nearby building. Midway in the proceedings a reporter from *The New York Times* asked the comedian bluntly if he con-sidered himself a hawk or a dove. "You can call me a hawk," Hope said, "if it means that I want to see this thing brought to an early end."[13]

Rosy O'Donnell felt that Hope got added input on that 1966 trip from "insider" talks with Westmoreland. O'Donnell said:

> Bob and Westy would sit up talking a lot that trip. They'd talk about the war, what was happening at home, what it all meant. And that reinforced what Bob was seeing in hospitals. He was terribly torn up by those wards, trying to be gay with a guy whose guts are coming out. He'd put on a bold front, but when he got into the back room with his drink . . . he'd ask why we subject our boys to this, to get killed and maimed for what—to fight but not to win?[14]

In spite of what sounded like sabre-rattling, Hope's televised documentary of that Christmas 1966 tour was restrained. This telecast, more popular than the previous year's, was watched by nearly 56 percent of the total available audience.

Hope's heroic image was probably never more sharply defined than in March 1967 when it was publicly revealed that during his Christmas Eve arrival in Saigon in 1964 he was the unmistakable target of Vietcong terrorism, and that he and his USO troupe narrowly missed assassination. While troops of the 2nd Field Force were flushing out Vietcong sappers operating in a network of underground tunnels, they seized a number of official VC papers, including one that uncovered the plot. Hope received a note from Lieutenant General Jonathan Seaman which said, in part:

> A few minutes ago I read a translation of a document we captured a few days ago in which the VC were pointing out their weaknesses in conducting successful terrorist activites in cities. This quote should interest you: "Attack on Brinks BOQ missed Bob Hope by ten minutes due to faulty timing devices."[15] I'm *not* kidding. . . .

Naturally the news moved swiftly through the Hope organization, was passed on to Vernon Scott of UPI who did some checking with his Saigon bureau and verified that the bombing was meant to include Hope.

In the meantime, a populist movement against American presence in Vietnam was building. On October 21, 1967, over 50,000 people paraded through Washington streets calling for peace. Still his popularity as a "soldier in grease paint" remained high, at least as perceived by *Time* magazine, whose Christmas 1967 cover carried a characteristic likeness of Hope. Inside, a five-page intimate profile called "The Comedian as Hero" retold for a new generation the history of Hope's three-war GI entertaining, the details of his long career, called him "the Will Rogers of the age," commended his durability as the result of good taste, and captioned the major photograph of the piece with "Bob Hope wasn't born—he was woven by Betsy Ross."

Meanwhile, a world away in South Vietnam, Hope was on a stage telling marines at Da Nang:

> . . . Men, I bring you great news from the land of liberty . . . it's still there . . . you may have to cross a picket line to

see it, but it's there . . . But don't worry about those riots you
hear about in the States . . . you'll be sent to survival school
before they send you back there . . . And do you get the college
scores over here? You've heard the results of the big
game . . . UCLA 21 . . . Dow Chemical 12 . . . Dow
Chemical just got even with the students. They came out with
asbestos draft card . . . can you imagine . . . Hey, can you
imagine those peace-niks back home burning their draft cards?
Why don't they come over here and Charlie will burn 'em for
them.[16]

Just a week after Hope's annual January television special of highlights
from his just-completed GI tour—this one dominated by the personalities of
Hope, Raquel Welch, Barbara McNair, and columnist Earl Wilson—came
the 77-day Tet offensive in Vietnam. Shortly after that, Lyndon Johnson
announced he would not seek reelection, and he announced a unilateral
bombing halt in the war. On May 13 the Paris Peace talks began.

On that very same day in May, Hope went to West Point to accept its
Sylvanus Thayer Award, which Hope prizes as second most distinguished
honor of his life, and the comedian seems to have accepted an alternate
position to a clear military win. According to the *The New York Times* of
May 14, 1967:

"I'm a hawkish dove," he said. "It's nothing like a pigeon, but if I
have to lay an egg for my country I'll do it."

One of Hope's jokes at West Point brought a howl of laughter. "I've had a
very busy schedule entertaining our fighting men in our universities . . . I
had an offer to speak at Columbia, but my insurance company canceled it."
And he was applauded loudly after. "We may be fighting an unpopular war,
but we have five or six hundred thousand of the most popular Americans I
know fighting like crazy to preserve our way of life."

Hope's tone of breezy assurance, when he took dynamic Ann-Margret,
football's giant Rosey Grier and television's Golddiggers to Vietnam the next
Christmas, was no doubt occasioned by the prospect of a change of administration in Washington:

Everything's fine back home. Nixon captured Washington and
Jackie Kennedy got Greece. So everything's in good
shape . . . Actually, I'd planned to spend Christmas in the
States, but I can't stand violence . . . Besides it was the perfect
time to come to Vietnam . . . the war was moved to Paris. . . .[17]

39. Father of the Brides

The *Milwaukee Journal* stated flatly on July 13, 1969, that Bob Hope had "undoubtedly been the source of more news, and newspaper feature stories than any other entertainer in modern history." They pointed out that the Hope file of 10 envelopes containing 500 news or feature stories is "solemn testimony that judicious editors and three decades of newsmen have considered him of value. A man may be fairly estimated by the number of clippings in his file. Bob Hope, no mere comic, is a man of stature and of news."

Hope's credibility as a newsmaker seemed to derive from three sources: his perceived wisdom, because he satirized social and political events; his ubiquity, that he had the ear of people in the highest and lowest of places (and seemed to travel with the speed of sound); and his humanity, because he responded quickly and effectively to human need. Hope was dynamic, charismatic, powerful.

That he had news value was perhaps never more vividly demonstrated than in 1969. It all started early in the morning of New Year's Day when Bob and Dolores rode down Pasadena's Colorado Boulevard, as they had done once before in 1947, as Grand and Mrs. Grand Marshal of the annual Rose Parade. One and a half million spectators along the route and an estimated 98 million televiewers around the world watched the Hopes waving from a special Imperial, outfitted by his Chrysler sponsor with TV set and radio transmitter/receiver so Bob could talk to both NBC and CBS video and audio equipment as he passed the reviewing stand.

All went smoothly until Holliston Avenue when suddenly the Imperial's motor went dead. Nothing could start it. The big Chrysler was going to be removed from the parade when five barefoot, long-haired teenagers stepped from the sidelines and volunteered to push the car. Hope accepted and during the rest of the parade milked laughter from the sidelines by pretending to whip the pushers with a golf club, or by getting out of the car himself and helping to push. At the end of the route he handed over to the five boys his and Dolores' tickets and three more for the Rose Bowl Game.

On January 11, both local and national news focused on Linda's spectacular wedding to Nathaniel Greenblatt Lande. A monsignor heard their vows and a rabbi blessed the marriage, while an augmented chancel choir sang sixteenth-century motets during an ecumenical ceremony at St. Charles Borromeo Church in North Hollywood. Afterward, on the rolling back lawns of the Hope estate, 1,000 guests were treated to an extravagant reception under a billowing white silk circus tent.[2]

The company lived up to the Moët et Chandon and cracked crab: Vice President-elect Spiro Agnew (standing in for Richard Nixon) with his wife Judy, Governor Ronald Reagan and Nancy, Ohio's governor Jim Rhodes former California governor Goodwin Knight, and Senator George Murphy.

Also under the big white tent strolled people like generals Jimmy Doolittle and Omar Bradley, clerics like Cardinal McIntyre, tycoons like MCA's Jules Stein, and entertainers like Danny Kaye, Gregory Peck, Jack and Mary Benny, Danny Thomas, Loretta Young and Irene Dunne. On hand as well were the Hopes' brand-new around-the-corner neighbors Dottie (Lamour) and Bill Howard, and Bing and Kathryn Crosby. There was a whopping list of media people, including Bob Considine, Ed Sullivan and Earl Wilson.

You could look at Linda's wedding gifts inside the house, accompanied by a string ensemble, or dance to one of two rotating bands on a dance floor built over the swimming pool. At the height of the festivities, the bride's father made a speech.

When he had his guests' attention, he turned to Linda and Nat and said: "When she was young I traveled so much she rarely saw me. When she did, she thought I was the gas meter man trying to get fresh with her mother."

He turned to Nora, standing arm-in-arm with her fiancé, Sam McCullagh, and ad-libbed, "Why don't you two get married right away before we have to strike the set?"

Gesturing toward his friend Agnew, Hope said, "Ah, Spiro—there's the kind of golfer I go for—not a very good one."

The Hope–Agnew friendship was less than a year old. About eight months earlier the comedian had flown east to receive an honorary doctorate from Brown University, and then swung down to Baltimore to receive a Humanitarian Award from Variety Clubs International. Agnew, then Maryland's governor, was a banquet speaker and he traded jokes with Hope. They got on especially well that night.

Hope sent Agnew this telegram when he was nominated for the vice presidency in Miami two months later: SEE WHAT HAVING DINNER WITH ME WILL DO?[3] Hope also offered the use of his gag writers to give Agnew's image a boost during the Republican campaign.

Over Labor Day weekend, while Hope was playing his annual three-day engagement at the Ohio State Fair, he fixed up a golf date with Agnew, Jim Rhodes and Pennsylvania's Governor Shafer. From Labor Day weekend on, the two men communicated regularly, and Hope added Spiro to his network of intimates who share the latest jokes.

Now, as Linda and Nat's wedding reception drew to a close, Bob put his suitcase into the trunk of Agnew's limousine, got in next to Spiro and Judy, and they headed for Burbank airport. They would take the Veepee's private jet to Miami to watch the Super Bowl the next day.

On January 16, NBC presented Hope's fifth Vietnam Christmas special, and the ratings were slightly higher than the previous year. That put Hope in high spirits, but not for long. The old eye problem, controlled for several years through a combination of medication and sheer luck, flared up again on the night that he flew up to Oakland to appear with astronaut Walt Cunningham at a "Youth of America" show.

He knew the hemorrhaging had started again and so he called his specialists. They ordered him to check in immediately at the Jules Stein Eye Clinic at UCLA for observation and treatment. Dolores moved into an adjoining room at the clinic and, after three days, was able to take him home. The treatment worked but during the following month he canceled everything on his schedule except those events he did annually—the Parkinson's Foundation benefit in Miami, the Orange Show in San Bernardino, the Police Show in Palm Springs, the Fighter Pilots Association banquet in Houston. He cheated by doing two college shows, one at Oklahoma State and the other at the University of New Mexico, and he couldn't resist the invitation from Stuart Symington to play a round of golf at Burning Tree in Bethesda, Maryland. During that trip Hope went to Walter Reed Hospital to see Ike because Mamie told him it might be the last time.

And it was. On March 30, Bob and Dolores sadly flew to Washington to attend funeral services for Eisenhower, and had to return to California immediately because George Hope had been stricken with severe stomach pain and operated on for a peritoneum condition. Bob went straight to the hospital after his midnight arrival and found George out of danger. He drove on to Palm Springs because Nora's formal engagement party was being held there the next day.

On April 11, after taping his television show, Hope felt especially weary but instead of going down to Palm Springs that night to rest, he stayed in the city for a very special party for a cherished member of his staff, his assistant producer Joan Maas. Mort Lachman, Joan's lover for some time, had asked Bob to help them get through a difficult adjustment: the knowledge that Joan had a fast-spreading cancer that doctors agreed would probably kill her in a few months. The next morning Bob drove himself to the desert to be there during Dolores' installation as honorary mayor of Palm Springs. The pace was beginning to build up again.

Three days later he went back up to Los Angeles to present the Jean Hersholt Award to his lifetime friend Martha Raye at the Academy Awards ceremony. And it was sheer vanity that kept him from turning down still another honorary degree, this one from Miami University in Oxford, Ohio, on April 27. But it was there that he felt dizzy again and knew what he must do.

Two days later he was lying on his back on an operating table at New York's Eye Infirmary with Dr. Algernon Reese in charge of the delicate photocoagulation operation. When it was over, Reese told him that was the last time; there was nothing left to work with but scar tissue. Dolores came to New York to be with Bob at the hospital and took him home five days later.

Hope was sufficiently frightened by this most recent bout, and by Reese's warning, to take a month's hiatus and do nothing but play golf. He and Dolores went to Aruba, then to San Juan, then to the Bahamas.

Feeling better after his rest, Hope was able to honor a commitment he had made to the senior class of West Point to entertain at their graduation eve banquet. He felt well enough to appear for Nelson Rockefeller at a Madison Square Garden Republican fund-raiser on June 5. Next day he flew out to Columbus, Ohio, where he was joined by Dolores and his brothers Fred and

Ivor (who was not looking at all well) for a commencement eve banquet at Ohio State.

Next morning close to nine o'clock, while Bob and Dolores were being driven to the football stadium for the commencement, the overhead rotor rasp and chug of Air Force helicopters heralded the arrival of Vice President Agnew. Bob and Spiro were to receive honorary doctorates before a capacity crowd of 35,000. Agnew delivered the main speech and received a standing ovation. Hope had them standing, too, and his reception was louder and longer.

Looking over at Agnew, Hope said, "I'm especially happy this fellow could be here today—and that you recognized him," referring to Agnew's identity problem during the campaign. "Can you imagine—the Democrats charged recently that the Agnew library burned—both books—and one of them hadn't even been colored in yet."[4]

Three days later Hope showed up in Portland, Oregon, in a paid personal appearance as part of the city's Rose Festival, and left the next midday to appear in Chicago for the premiere of his latest movie, *How to Commit Marriage* with Jane Wyman and Jackie Gleason. This picture was a generation-gap comedy focusing on changing perspectives of morality in general and sex in particular. It traded heavily on the Hope–Gleason golf rivalry and insult humor for laughs. Of all the late Hope film efforts, this one has the most polish, due chiefly to Norman Panama's rewriting and direction, but it suffered unfairly from critics' comparisons with more modish comedies being turned out by Mel Brooks and Woody Allen.

From Chicago, Hope made his way to Bowling Green University in Ohio to receive his thirteenth honorary degree. University officials wisely let the ceremony finish before telling Hope that his brother Ivor had suffered another heart attack and had died. As far back as Bob could remember Ivor had been a surrogate father, breadwinner, and for thirty years his partner in the metal products business. Two days later, at the funeral in Gates Mills, Ohio, only Bob and Fred of the original seven brothers were standing there to mourn the family loss. Neither Jim (suffering from emphysema) nor George (recovering from his operation) could come from California.[5]

When Bob and Dolores arrived back in Palm Springs they learned from Mary Hope that George's condition was grave. George at age fifty-eight was losing his battle against throat cancer. His body, destroyed from years of alcoholism, could not fight the spread of this new disease. George had never found the fulfillment he sought in life—not as a stooge in Bob's early vaudeville act, as star of his own vaudeville act, as a screenwriter, as Bob's script reader, or as production coordinator of Bob's television shows. George had grown up being Bob Hope's younger brother, full of dreams and expectations, and they had been his nemesis.

Hope's only paid personal appearance in June was a four-day engagement at the Pike's Peak Festival in Colorado Springs from June 21 to June 25. He had little enthusiasm for this commitment, especially when he discovered ticket sales were soft. The Air Force flew him to Colorado Springs, and he did that first show as if he was auditioning because he felt word of mouth would build business for the rest of the week. During that first show, George died.[6]

Two brothers, the oldest and youngest, dead in one week. Hope felt vulnerable and decided not to continue at Pike's Peak. The promoters challenged him, but Hope had already telephoned Martin Gang for legal advice, then telephoned Danny Thomas who agreed to fill in the remaining shows. Bob spent two solitary days in the desert house before he came back to the city for George's burial at Forest Lawn on June 24. When it was over he drove back to the desert and stayed there.

During the month of July, Hope was subdued. He rested and told Miss Hughes to cancel several engagements. He played golf as much as he could, including a round with Spiro Agnew at a nearby Virginia course when he flew into Washington for preliminary Pentagon talks about his 1969 overseas Christmas tour.

In mid-August Nora Hope married Sam McCullagh, a young administrator at San Francisco University. It was, at Nora's request, smaller, simpler and, for reasons Bob and Nora understood, more gentle than Linda's wedding.[7]

Earlier that day, as Bob was waiting to take Nora to St. Charles Borromeo Church, the two of them were alone in the house. Bob stood at the bottom of the curving stairway of the front hall waiting for his "little girl," and when he looked up she was leaning over the rail above him. She saw him and started down the stairs slowly so he could admire her dress. She stopped when she saw that her father's eyes were glistening.

"I've always been so proud that I had a father everybody loves," she said. "But I love you in a special way I have no words to express. The only tiny cloud on this wonderful day is that I won't be seeing you and mother so often. Goodbye, Daddy!"

Hope's national media index rose in late August when he rearranged his schedule to do a mercy telethon for the victims of Hurricane Camille, which had ripped across Mississippi and Louisiana on August 17 leaving at least 200 persons dead and thousands deprived of their homes and possessions. From a stage in Jackson, Mississippi, Hope did a monologue, and traded one-liners with guests and those who called in with contributions.

In September, Bob, Dolores and their daughter-in-law Judy were among the visiting notables who helped Wapakoneta, Ohio, welcome home their prized native son and world-famous moonwalker Neil Armstrong. And still later that month, Bob had the sad task of trying to speak some comforting words to the family, friends and members of his own television staff who gathered to mourn the untimely death of Joan Maas. All Hope could say was that "someone up there must have needed her badly."

By October it seemed that Hope's energies had returned to their full potential, and he directed them enthusiastically to his return to the musical comedy stage in yet another revival of *Roberta*, this time on the stage of his very own Bob Hope Theater on the campus of Southern Methodist University.

His cast would include Janis Paige and newcomers Michelle Lee and John Davidson. Tickets were being touted among the Texas rich for $500 apiece, but the cause was a good one: the establishment of a Bob Hope Scholarship Fund at SMU.

Roberta became one of the big events that Dallas season. Added media

attention came from the fact that Givenchy of Paris flew its models and fall
fashion line to Dallas as a segment of the musical. Hope made himself available not only for the local media but for a planeload of national TV editors
flown in for the occasion because NBC was taping each performance for
editing down to a shorter two-hour version for television.

On his last night of *Roberta.* during a curtain call speech, Hope said he
had faith in the students of America: "I'm starting out next week on a series
of college shows and I know I will find right-thinking American young
people to want this country to resolve its differences with honor."

Hope showed up the next night at a $100-a-plate dinner for Texas Repub-
licans. He shared the head table with Spiro Agnew, Senator John Tower and
Dallas Times Herald publisher Jim Chambers. Tower, as toastmaster,
seemed to express the feelings of all assembled when he said he felt that the
Vietnam war would determine "whether the United States will survive as the
most powerful nation in the world, and indeed the leader of the Free World.
Ladies and gentlemen, no man has given more heart and more inspiration to
the men who carry your flag than Bob Hope."[8]

*I don't believe in all that sexual permissiveness you hear
about today. Maybe it's because I'm at an age where my bag
is my lunch . . . And all those drugs today, I'd like to see
them smoke the pot I used. . . .*[1]

40. You Can't Walk Away

The buildup of antiwar feeling in America showed unmistakably on October
15, 1969, in a nationwide protest, a moratorium officially backed by university presidents, notable clergy and an impressive group of Democratic lawmakers. This orchestration of feeling was proof that certain vocal elements in
the nation, opinion leaders and activists, from both campus and media, and
even government were serious when they urged: "Let's pull out of Vietnam
at any price."

Nixon opposed this view. So did Hope. Both argued the price was too
much to pay. We would be losing the first war in American history (somehow we had managed to fool ourselves about Korea). Nixon was known to
have said in front of his advisors, "I don't intend to be the first President to
lose a war."[2] Hope was dismayed that his good friend Stuart Symington was
among those Democratic "wise men" who favored a hasty cessation of hos-
tilities.

On October 14, the eve of the moratorium, Bob and Dolores arrived in
Washington for an "Eisenhower Birthday Dinner," a high-powered fund-
raising event to memorialize Ike by dedicating and perpetuating Eisenhower
College. Hope's monologue makes clear that he did not take the moratorium
too seriously:

Good evening Republicans . . . and Democrats. I like to include the help . . . Eisenhower College . . . this may be the first school that will give a degree in golf . . . No, I am delighted to be here for this fine cause . . . I think it's a great idea . . . Our future Republicans have to come from some-place . . . By the way, tomorrow is the moratorium period. A lot of kids will be out of school, and a lot of professors won't be teach-ing. What's new about that? . . . The President would like nothing better than a cease fire, but the Democrats won't stop sniping . . . It isn't the philosophical protest that gets to me . . . what I resent is their moratorium against soap and water . . . I don't know what's happening to the kids in this country. When we went to school we never had a moratorium. We couldn't . . . we didn't know what one was . . . Who's kidding who? If they want to hold a moratorium, fine. But it looks pretty suspicious when it happens on the same day as the world series. . . .[3]

Ten days later, when Hope was starting out on his fall college tour, he seemed steadfast in his refusal to believe that such a groundswell as the Washington march or the flag-burnings on campus could represent a signif-icant voice of disapproval, or that he might be out of touch. When he arrived at the Greenville–Spartanburg airport for his show at Clemson on October 25, the expected exchange with newsmen had a new note in it, a prototype of interviews to come. Predictably, interest moved to Hope's view of the recent protests.

"It didn't help a thing," he said. "To use a worn phrase, the moratorium gave comfort to the enemy. But I've heard about a campus movement getting underway with plans to offset the effect of the moratorium and I can support that."[4]

"Why do you oppose immediate withdrawal, Mr. Hope?" drawled a perky blond campus reporter.

"Because it's not the answer. Sure I want us out of there. I'd rather be playing to troops in Palm Beach, but if we don't settle things honorably, it'll start somewhere else."

"But don't you find more and more students opposing that view?"

"I've found very little sign of unrest. It's those small minorities on campus that make the headlines. The news media are guilty of blowing this kind of disturbance way out of proportion."

Before Hope went on stage that night, he did something unorthodox. After his rehearsal he accepted an invitation from Clemson president Robert Edwards to attend a pre-show reception to meet with wives and widows of fighter pilots who were shot down over North Vietnam and now were either missing or prisoners.

Hope was appalled to hear their stories and said, "I'll talk to the right people the next time I'm in Washington. I promise you I'll do whatever I can do for the POWs."[5]

On Monday evening, November 3, Richard Nixon took his case to the people in a now-famous television speech which included the sentence, "And so, tonight, to you, the great silent majority of Americans, I ask for your support." He was asking public approval of his plan to withdraw troops but without an announced timetable for doing so. It was a tremendous gamble on Nixon's part but he appeared to win it, gaining time to sell Vietnamization, and to negotiate a less shameful exit from Southeast Asia.

The following day, the White House announced that the President had received thousands of telegrams assuring support for his policy. News media were skeptical, suggesting that the flurry of telegrams had been orchestrated by GOP bosses nationwide.

On November 4, Bob and Dolores were guests at Richard and Pat Nixon's White House party for the Duke of Edinburgh who was then on a multi-nation tour on behalf of the World Wildlife Fund. Nixon told Hope about a grassroots movement called "National Unity Week" being sparked by a young orthopedic surgeon, Edmund Dembrowski, of Redlands, California. Dembrowski had come to Washington, set up an office at the Mayflower Hotel and enlisted the backing of top leaders in the American Legion, the Veterans of Foreign Wars, Americans for Responsible Action and similar groups. They chose the week of November 9 through 15 because they hoped to counteract the impact of the next major Washington antiwar demonstration scheduled for November 15. Dembrowski called the White House for help in locating a credible figure to be national chairman, and Nixon asked Hope if he would serve. The comedian agreed.[6] Nixon told him in confidence there were some ultra-high-level negotiations going on that would surely bring the troops home quickly.

On November 7, Hope flew to Peoria, Illinois, for another college show, this time at Bradley University. Like Clemson, the Bradley show was a sellout. As Hope was threading his way through a rather chaotic airport welcome that had gotten out of hand, one startled teenager shouted, "It's Bob Hope!" A cadre of uniformed security policemen moved in immediately and conducted Hope into a lounge filled with reporters.[7]

"What does National Unity Week mean, Bob?"

"It's a way for people all over the country, for the silent majority to speak up."

"Then you would disagree with those critics who are suggesting that Nixon's silent majority speech was intentionally divisive?"

"Divisive?" Hope asked incredulously. He seemed to be weighing the question. "Certainly not. You know there's a lot of brain power being put behind this plan—not the President alone—but all the brain power available, and that's more than these kids who are demonstrating."

Three hours later Hope was brought out to a platform in the center of the Bradley gymnasium by an honor guard of eight pom-pom waving cheerleaders. A blue-gray spotlight followed him out as a band blared his theme song and the crowd rose to its feet and remained there cheering.

And so began his 50-minute solo performance, which had the audience roaring at jokes like:

> . . . I don't believe in all that sexual permissiveness you hear about today. Maybe it's because I'm at the age where my bag is my lunch . . . And all those drugs today. When I was a kid I thought it was daring to take sen-sen . . . and sneak up in the

attic to look at the lingerie ads in the Sears Roebuck catalogue . . . I'd like to see them smoke the pot I used. . . .[8]

Eventually he went offstage, pleased with the audience reception. A
"Thanks for the Memory" played him back on, the audience was standing
He spoke some serious words when the room got quiet. "You know—I've
been—I've had the privilege of entertaining some great Americans in Vietnam. These people who say get out of Vietnam and that's all they know
that's no good. If you get out and walk away, it's like walking away from a
cancer."[9]

The next night Hope stood before an audience of 15,600 students, faculty
and townspeople at the University of Illinois in Champagne–Urbana. His
jokes were the same; the audience reaction strong; and his closing speech just
as fervent, though this time he used the words "silent majority" and spoke of
the threat of a complete Communist takeover of Southeast Asia.

On Wednesday, November 12, Hope ordered his public relations staff to
organize a news conference at his Toluca Lake home. He was afraid that
because the media was focusing so much attention on the upcoming November 15 protest march in Washington, National Unity Week was being forgotten.

During the news conference, Hope said that much media coverage
"doesn't reflect what the country is thinking." He launched into an attack on
NBC News for what he described as "rigged film clips from Vietnam,"
singling out an NBC news feature about how black soldiers in Vietnam were
not receiving the same treatment as whites.

Before the news conference ended one reporter asked how Hope would
classify himself politically. The comedian replied, "I'm like a California
driver—right down the middle. I don't care who's in, I'm with them."[10]

Not coincidentally, on the very next night, November 13, in Des Moines,
Iowa, Spiro Agnew delivered a speech criticizing the media for less than
credible coverage of the Vietnam war. Shortly after NBC and CBS news
broadcasts carried the Agnew charges, both networks received a tide of telegrams from citizens condemning broadcast journalists, and once again newspeople had cause to suspect that this flood of telegrams was carefully choreographed.

On November 15, more than 250,000 people took part in what was probably the largest antiwar demonstration ever held in the nation's capital. The
same day Hope flew to Seattle to do a show at the University of Washington.

Ticket holders to the Bob Hope Show at the Hec Edmundson Pavilion on
the UW campus that night had to cross a picket line to get inside. Seven
hundred war protesters holding lighted candles walked quietly outside in a
vigil for peace. One of the faculty who was in that peace vigil told a *Seattle
Times* reporter, "Bob Hope represents one of the better known hawks in this
country and I think we're all here in response to that. But this vigil stresses
peace domestically as well as on foreign fronts. So it is not so much anti-
Hope as it is pro-peace."[11]

Sitting in his suite at the Olympic Hotel talking to an old friend, reporter
Bob Heilman, he said, "Hell, I'm for peace—but not at all costs. Why don't

they march against the North Vietnamese? Why don't the dissidents march against them? Lots of our kids are being killed. And who's doing the killing? The Communists are the ones who need the demonstrations."[12]

Despite what Hope told a group of reporters in his home November 12, that he was "right down the middle," it was evident to many people that his sympathies were closely allied to current Republican thinking. His friendship with Agnew and the similarity of their views, plus his vocal support of Nixon's policies, regardless of their intent, were perceived as partisan. As he continued the practice of ending his personal appearances with serious speeches and as these tended to be pleas for audience support of the administration, it became obvious that the comedian who had built an entire reputation on neutrality was now going to face charges of political activism, if not bias.

There was nothing new with a popular performer being partisan. America's rich entertainment history has a solid tradition of partisan humor, from Ben Franklin to Will Rogers.

The performer and the partisan fused dramatically in late November, when Hope announced that for his 1969 USO Christmas tour he would entertain Americans in every part of the world and his troupe would, in fact, circle the globe. Moreover, Hope announced, the very first performance, actually a kind of dress rehearsal, would take place in the White House before an audience invited by Pat and Richard Nixon. The first lady invited the entire troupe—performers, production staff, technicians, musicians and assorted others connected with the departure—for a sit-down dinner in the Blue Room prior to the "command performance."[13]

An extraordinary send-off like this one required extraordinary preparations. Howard Miller, west coast director of the USO, who had skillfully arranged the details of each departure for the last ten years, was dispatched to Washington. He immediately began arranging a departure ceremony at Andrews Air Force Base that included Secretary of State William Rogers, Defense Secretary Melvin Laird and Hope's special pals Rosy O'Donnell and "Westy" Westmoreland. He also arranged for hot holiday meals to be put on board, furnished by Willard Marriott's catering organization.

NBC's senior publicist Betty Lanigan, a seasoned newswoman who had been coordinating publicity for the Hope USO trips during recent years, was grounded by lower back surgery, so her boss, former UPI bureau chief Hank Rieger, stepped in. Rieger flew to Washington to work with the Capitol press corps and found in Washington the media were especially cooperative about both Nixon and Hope. Nixon had just announced further Vietnam troop withdrawals and his popularity in the polls had ascended.

That Sunday night, December 14, the troupe had cocktails in the large foyer adjacent to the Blue Room. They went through a reception line to meet Richard and Pat Nixon, and then each took a small piece of paper out of a silver bowl which determined their seat locations for dinner. Dick Nixon sat at the far end of the room with singer Connie Stevens at his right and Pat Nixon sat at the opposite end with Bob Hope at her right.

At the show following the lavish dinner, the Nixons were seated in the front row of chairs set up in the East Room. Next to the Nixons sat Ted and Eleanor Agnew, Melvin Laird, General Westmoreland and Secretary Rog-

ers. In the row behind sat Attorney General John Mitchell and Martha,
Major Charles Robb and Lynda Bird, David and Julie Eisenhower, Henry
and Christina Ford, cartoonist Al Capp, Democratic Congressman Sam
Stratton and a number of other congressmen and military people.

Some of the performers were nervous and there were the usual backstage
problems resulting from improvised dressing rooms and the lack of adequate
rehearsal time. But there was enthusiasm. Hope's jokes: "Mr. Agnew put his
golf ball down and addressed it . . . only the ball looked up and said,
"Who?" . . ." and "Martha Mitchell . . . she's the one who makes Ted
Agnew look like Calvin Coolidge" brought both laughter and applause. Connie Stevens delivered standard ballads, singer Teresa Graves belted out rock
songs, and Suzanne Charney danced so close to Nixon that she stepped on
his foot. Hope cracked afterwards, "We'll have to edit that out, sir."

The plane was scheduled to depart Andrews Air Force Base the following
noon. At eleven o'clock, as requested, Defense Secretary Laird was ready to
make his departure speech. The rest of the troupe was there, and the Lockheed Starlifter was loaded and ready for takeoff. But no Hope. He was, at
eleven o'clock, lying in his bed in a darkened room of the Statler Hilton's
Presidential Suite unwilling to get up. Mort Lachman was in the room with
him, and he had sent for Hank Rieger in case the situation was serious.

"You want us to take off without you, Bob?" asked Mort.

"Yeah. You'd better. I can't make it. I can feel that old pressure behind
my eyes. The thought of the next two weeks is murder."

"I'll call out to Andrews and give 'em the word. You know Melvin Laird is
waiting there for you."

"You're kidding?" said Hope, answering Lachman.

Hank Rieger came into the bedroom. "And Westmoreland, and Rosy
O'Donnell and, I think, Secretary Rogers, but I'm not sure."

Quietly Hope got himself to the edge of the bed and staggered into the
bathroom. Like the vaudevillian he was, he was bathed, shaved, showered,
dressed and packed within minutes. And by noon he was walking into the
hangar and up onto the makeshift stage. Laird was still there. Hope introduced the players and the guests, did some jokes and the plane finally lifted
off the ground at one fifty-five.

The plane took them to Berlin where they did a big show at the Deutsch-
landhalle. Film actress Romy Schneider joined the cast. From Berlin they
flew south to Rome for an overnight rest before they played the aircraft
carrier *Saratoga* which was sitting offshore at Gaeta, Italy. Then on to Ada-
na, Turkey, for a show at Incirlik Air Force Base. By this time Hope was
feeling fine, and he had forgotten everything except the adulation he was
getting from his beloved GIs.

In Bangkok, Hope's 1969 around-the-world tour was virtually guaranteed
a success—if it already hadn't been sealed—by the arrival of moonwalker
Neil Armstrong. And when Hope introduced him there was a four-minute
ovation. Armstrong was best at the question and answer routine which mostly involved how he felt when he stepped out onto the moon's surface. But one
question not unexpectedly brought cheers:

ARMSTRONG: Over here—over here, yes sir?

DUPANG:	Frank Dupang from Honolulu. I want to know why the U.S. is so interested in the moon instead of the conflict here in Vietnam?
	(*Cheers*)
ARMSTRONG:	Well, that's a—that's a great question and one which—ah—which you here may feel there's a good deal of contradiction. We don't feel that that's the case. The American—the nature of the American system is that it works on many levels in many areas to try to build a peace on earth, goodwill to men. And one of the advantages of the space activity is that it has promoted international understanding and enabled cooperative efforts between countries on many levels and will continue to do so in the future.[14]

At still another base a GI asked Neil if he thought that humans would some day live on the moon. Armstrong said he thought they would "but there's a more important question—we have to ask ourselves whether man will be able to live together here on earth." And the applause and cheers went on for several minutes.

Their first show in Vietnam was at Lai Khe for the 1st Infantry. Lai Khe was the core of heavy fighting and just before showtime a Vietcong mortar emplacement had been discovered, aimed at the stage, and defused. International media people from the wire services and news magazines were out in force.

Hope understood what they had been through recently, but he was in no way prepared for the scattered boos that greeted his parenthetical remark that the President had assured him personally that he had a plan for peace. What dismayed some members of the Bob Hope troupe was that when GIs raised their fingers in the peace sign, Hope insisted that they were making the World War II victory sign. Hope's own subsequent explanation of the Lai Khe reception of his Nixon remarks was this:

> Their boos were just a way of answering the President. They were too tired, too worn out, too disillusioned to believe that anyone had a plan to end the war and get them out of that hot, steamy, rotten jungle. They'd heard that song before.[15]

Except for the "booing incident" evidence suggests that audiences appreciated Hope and his show as much as ever. But it was also true that the soldier was not the same GI Hope had met the year before. This was a young soldier, probably a draftee, who could not help but be affected by the fact that 250,000 people, most of them of his own age and culture, had taken part in that "March Against Death" in the capital on November 15.

Nevertheless, Hope's commitment to the GI he knew or didn't know was total. And the idea of a dishonorable ending of America's longest and most frustrating war was unthinkable. Interestingly enough, on the day of the Lai

Xhe incident, in St. Louis, Missouri, the *Globe-Democrat* ran this editorial:

Yes, Virginia, There Is a Bob Hope

We take pleasure in answering at once and thus prominently the communication below, expressing at the same time our great gratification that its faithful author is numbered among the friends of the Globe.

> *"Dear Editor:*
> *I am 8 years old.*
> *Some of my little friends say there is no Bob Hope.*
> *Papa says, 'If you see it in* The Globe *it's so.'*
> *Please tell me the truth, is there a Bob Hope?*
>
> *(Signed) Virginia*

Virginia, your little friends are wrong. They have been affected by the skepticism of a skeptical age. They do not believe except they see.

Yes, Virginia, there is a Bob Hope. He exists as certainly as generosity and devotion exist, and you know that they abound and give to your life its highest beauty and joy.

Alas! How dreary would be the world if there would be no Bob Hope! It would be as dreary as if there were no Virginias.

There would be no GI-like faith then, no humor, no laughs to make tolerable this existence.

Not believe in Bob Hope! You might as well not believe in Santa Claus.

No Bob Hope! Thank God, he lives. A thousand GIs from now, Virginia, nay 10 times ten thousand GIs from now, men will know his name.

Yes, Virginia, there is a Bob Hope. And he has brought hope to countless of your fellow Americans by giving up his own Christmas at home for 19 years.

As long as he lives, Virginia, there is hope he will continue to make glad the hearts of boys away from home.[16]

The postscript on this worldwide tour comes from the American public's reaction to his 90-minute television record of that journey, broadcast on January 15, 1970. The Nielsen Company announced that Hope's USO telecast had the largest single audience for an entertainment (non-motion picture or special event) program in television history. It had been seen by an estimated 64 percent of all available viewers.

You know I have joked about and satirized the foibles of our people and our politics. But there is one subject that doesn't lend itself to jokes, and that is the love I feel so deeply for my adopted country. . . .[1]

41. Some Rain on the Fourth

If the much-quoted *Guinness Book* included records for squeezing the most money out of a charity banquet, or rounding up the biggest crowd that ever watched an indoor variety show, or for bringing together the largest audience to see an outdoor variety show, then Hope's name would be next to each entry. What's more, he set those records in a six-month period.

The charity banquet that raised over $2 million was a fund-raiser for the Eisenhower Medical Center already under construction in the desert near Palm Springs. When the general died in March 1969, both Bob and Dolores seemed consumed by the same passion for a quick completion of the hospital complex, and they assured the board of directors that the two of them would be responsible for locating one-third of the $7 million needed for the first building phase before the end of 1971.

So Hope booked the Grand Ballroom of the Waldorf-Astoria, and agreed to pick up the $70,000 tab for dinner in order that a capacity crowd of 1500 guests, each paying $1,000, could deliver a cool $1.5 million tax-free to the building fund. Hope would arrange the entertainment. More precisely, Chrysler would sponsor a 90-minute TV special documenting this event, calling it "Five Stars for a Five-Star Man" with Bing Crosby, Raquel Welch, Johnny Cash, Ray Bolger and Hope.

By late November, through persistent telephoning and personal visits, Hope had collected nearly half the targeted sum. Besides money raised from fund-raising luncheons, Hope received pledges of $125,000 from Frank Sinatra and Irving Berlin, and Hope's Palm Springs neighbor, *My Fair Lady* composer Fritz Loewe, signed a paper willing to the hospital all royalties from that musical after his death.

The actual dinner on January 27, 1970, was the kind of highly touted event that attracted attention as far away as Paris. The *International Herald Tribune* story of the same date led with news that three presidents—Nixon, Johnson and Truman—were honorary chairmen of a dinner guaranteed to be one of the "biggest money raisers of this or any other social season."

Charlotte Curtis described for *The New York Times* readers on January 28, 1970, the pre-banquet reception that Bob and Dolores hosted in the hotel's Louis XVI Suite as "an all-American blending of bankers, tycoons, astronauts, golfers, admirals, generals and Medal of Honor winners from two wars and Vietnam."

As the guests entered the Grand Ballroom, they passed an eight-foot gold eagle, and at their tables was expensive French wine and table decorations in red, white and blue.

The table assignments had also made Hope nervous. How do you find enough preferred tables for people like Texas industrialist Pollard Simons,

Morgan Guarantee president Jim Hellmuth, Chase Bank president George Champion, oil baron Amon Carter, cosmetic king Charles Revson, and TWA's chairman Charles Tillinghast, to name a few?

Visibly nervous, Hope managed the treacherous job of introducing the three-tiered head table and launched into a monologue that included these wisecracks:

> . . All of the captains of industry are here. Xerox sent a copy of their president . . . And I really didn't expect Nixon to be here . . . He doesn't have a White House in this state . . . I see Spiro's been all over the Far East without starting a war . . . He must be losing his touch . . . And it's so cold here in New York the politicians have their hands in their own pockets. . . .[2]

Hope and Crosby in top hats and tails did a clever song and dance medley from the *Road* pictures. And to Raquel Welch, whose breast-baring gown was a concern to NBC censors, Hope said, "My congratulations to your dress designer and I hope he gets out on bail."[3]

The television version of this gala was aired on NBC February 16 and almost 35 million people watched it. There was some concern, voiced by both television editors and viewers, that not a single black face could be seen in the audience or as a performer on the show.

Hope's letter to columnist Lucius E. Lee of the Columbus, Ohio, *Call & Post* helped to put the matter in clearer perspective:

> Dear Mr. Lee:
> My brother, Fred Hope, who lives there in Columbus sent me your column about our Eisenhower Medical Center dinner and I wanted to write and just explain a couple of things to you.
> As I think he told you, we tried to get Ralph Bunche on the dais that night. He wanted to come but he had his neck in a brace and didn't think it would be too comfortable for that long a time. And he was right because the show did run for almost four and a half hours. . . .
> I also had George Foreman who had just won his fight the night before at Madison Square Garden. He hired a dinner jacket and sat at a table and enjoyed the show immensely. I didn't get a chance to get him on film because when we finally did get the show cut, the first cut was about 29 minutes over. So it was like taking blood out of your arm to get the people on that you wanted the audience to see.[4]

Hope was sensitive to criticism of this nature, and as Mort Lachman said, "You can bet that he was not going to find himself in that position again."

That Eisenhower evening had been so financially successful, however, that Hope planned a similar event for Los Angeles the following April. And if the first one had busted over the 2 million mark, the second one raised nearly that amount with a smaller guest list. Hope was not beginning to kid on the square about his role as a fund-raiser. "People used to walk up to me and say,

How are you, Bob?' Now they take one look at me and say, 'I gave at the office.' "

With these monies, and what Hope had donated from his personal appearance fees, it was possible to finish the hospital portion of the Center and dedicate it in 1971. At that time President Nixon flew into Palm Springs on Air Force One for the ceremonies. Also on hand were Veepee Spiro Agnew, Governor Ronald Reagan and an impressive roster of government officials.

Hope's admiration for astronauts got him involved in producing a benefit in the Houston Astrodome on May 16, 1970, that brought out the largest audience on record for an indoor variety show. Houston civic boosters like Fred Nahas persuaded him to organize a "Texas-sized" benefit to build a youth center as a memorial to Ed White, one of the astronauts who died when their capsule caught fire before an Apollo launch.

The prospect of packing the nation's biggest indoor sports arena (roughly 50,000 seats) intrigued and terrified Hope. Still, he had been pledged the full-time services of an entire Houston public relations firm to work with his own publicists, and whatever promotion NASA might be able to generate. For music, Hope insisted on Les Brown. For stars, Hope got Gregory Peck, who had just completed five months at Cape Kennedy working on the space movie *Marooned,* and Cary Grant, who admitted, "Only Hope could get me to do a show like this one. If it were a job I was being paid for, I wouldn't come. I melt in front of a microphone."[5] Other stars who responded favorably to Hope's personal calls were David Janssen, Dottie Lamour, Joey Heatherton, Glen Campbell and Robert Goulet.

Also appearing that night, but not necessarily through Hope's personal intervention, were Bobby Sherman, Nancy Ames, Frankie Valli and the Four Seasons, the Friends of Distinction, Trini Lopez, John Rowles, the Step Brothers, and football superstar O.J. Simpson.

Billed as "Bob Hope's Extra Special," the show got started extra late because outside the Astrodome traffic that included more than the usual number of Cadillacs, Rolls and Continentals was snarled.

In spite of the delay, the show was a hit, with something for every age group. But it was Hope, Peck, Grant and Janssen's specially written song sketch called "Showmanship" and their funny and sentimental finale tribute to the astronauts, "We Love All Those Wonderful Guys," which captured the audience's full attention; they were aware of the rarity of such an unlikely team engaged in this kind of comedy.

At one point, Hope's face was flashed in lights on the Astrodome scoreboard and the comedian came on to announce that 46,857 people had paid to see the show, a record for the Astrodome and for an indoor variety show in this country. Hope was presented with a life-sized portrait of himself which would hang in the foyer of the Ed White Memorial Center, and as far as the eye could see in the half-light of that huge domed auditorium people were on their feet.

A month and a half later, working on a stage that faced the Washington Monument before an audience reported to be the largest ever assembled outdoors to watch a variety show, Hope had quite different feelings.

It all began on the first of June, when Hope went to Washington to help

Reader's Digest publisher Hobart Lewis, evangelist Billy Graham, and hotel tycoon Willard Marriott plan a patriotic July 4 celebration called Honor America Day. This was an attempt, like the previous Natonal Unity Week, to rally the silent majority and to reunite a Vietnam-polarized society.

The plan was to generate Honor America Day programs all across the nation, with a focus on the big party in the nation's capital that included religious observances in the forenoon at Lincoln Memorial, and a spectacular entertainment package with fireworks on the Mall facing the Washington Monument at dusk. Walt Disney Productions agreed to design and stage the two separate segments of the day.

At a news conference June 4, Hope and Graham announced they had accepted national chairmanships, Hope to put together the Washington Monument variety show, and Graham to do the Lincoln Memorial service.

"It's just going to be an old-fashioned American Fourth of July," said Hope to the assembled media, "a celebration to give Americans a chance to let go—and the country's about ready to let go, believe me. We're downtrodden by the rough news from Vietnam—and countless demonstrations against one aspect or another of American life, but we're trying to keep the war out of this, to make this a celebration instead of a demonstration."[6]

Hope talked about its bipartisan support in terms of congressmen on the committee, backing from labor and the sports world and the space program, and announced that former presidents Truman and Johnson and former First Lady Mamie Eisenhower were honorary chairs. Still on June 9, 1970, the *Washington Post* voiced doubt that this would be just an "old-fashioned Fourth of July":

> The suspicion, as we get it, is that any effort to make something different out of this year's Fourth of July observances is going to take on the trappings of a pro-war rally in support of President Nixon's Vietnam policy, no matter how much the sponsors may wish to avoid it, just by the identity of the principal figures who have so far associated themselves with the idea—that and the electricity in the air. . . . It needs a broader mix, not just of Democrats as well as Republicans but of dissenters as well as supporters. . . . They could make the point a little more explicit by trying to engage the active support of responsible leaders on the other side of the great national debates—of Hubert Humphrey, to take one example, or George McGovern. . . .

By mid-June, the rally had, in fact, engaged Humphrey and McGovern as well as two other administration critics, Senators Muskie and Mansfield, but on June 19 the *Post* persisted: "It's not enough to seek a 'broader mix' and a better balance on the letterhead. The test is in the actuality."

One of the rally's most vociferous critics was one of the Chicago Seven, Rennie Davis, who called a news conference to publicly challenge Hope and Graham about the absence on their already-announced participant lists of any representatives from the political left, particularly those who had been vocal against the administration's Vietnam policy. This, in turn, brought newspaper editorials like this one on June 10, 1970 from Felix McKnight in the *Dallas Times Herald*:

On the Fourth of July, a citizen named Bob Hope will stand alongside the Washington Monument and ask his brothers to cool their differences and act like Americans. It used to be done every Fourth of July—all over the land. Somehow, it went out of style. And we haven't been the same since. But Bob Hope, who has earned his credentials, will use the same hallowed slope that has been available to war dissenters to rally his distressed nation around its flag. . . . It's something another man of 35 years ago might have done. Sadly, very few of the immediate younger generations ever heard of a man named Will Rogers. . . . Will Rogers twitted presidents in homey, spontaneous humor. He could take the heaviest national issues and iron them out in plain language that all could understand. . . . The closest we'll come to a Will Rogers is Bob Hope. He has the national image and respect. He has the same intense love for his country, and he has the guts to stand up to any heckling hippie.

Hope felt that all this charging and countercharging was divisive and he asked Willard Mariott, who was executive chairman of the rally, to call a news conference at the Press Club in Washington June 29.

"We've got Jack Benny—Dinah Shore—Kate Smith—Red Skelton," Hope said, looking very pleased, "and there's Roberta Flack, Dottie Lamour, Pat Boone, Barbara Eden, the New Christy Minstrels, the Golddiggers, Connie Stevens, the Young Americans, Fred Waring. Not a bad list, and there's more. We may be there all night. It takes Jack Benny two hours just to say his own name."

"Some of your critics, Bob, say that young people and dissidents are being excluded."

"That's simply not true" answered Hope. "This is a family affair and we hope everybody comes. For those guys who say we have nobody from talkies, how about Teresa Graves, Glen Campbell, Jeannie C. Riley and B.J. Thomas—"

"What about people like the Smothers?"

"I'm glad you brought that up. I've been trying to get Dick Gregory—he's somewhere in Canada, I'm told—but we may have Tom and Dick. They're thinking about it. I've done 'em a couple of favors in the past," Hope said, winking.

Mariott, after the third time a reporter suggested this celebration was pro-Nixon, said, "It will be absolutely free of politics. It's not to promote anybody's pet ideas. Everybody has been advised to stay away from politics in general and the war in particular. And that includes Bob Hope, right, Bob?"

"Willard, I can't say there won't be any political jokes—that's a matter of editing. As long as we don't get too serious and mess up the show. You know I gotta talk about Agnew's golf game—it's the funniest thing today." Hope was referring to the fact that the Vice President's tee-off shot at a recent tournament hit a gallery spectator.

"The weather forecast is rain, Bob," one reporter said.

"Don't worry. We'll have over 400,000 people out there—the biggest crowd that has gathered for any show."

"Bigger than Woodstock?"

"Yeah—bigger than Woodstock."[7]

Hope flew back to the Coast to confer with several of the stars for this show, and three days later he was back, stepping off the mobile lounge at Dulles Airport with Dinah Shore, Sugar Ray Robinson, Dorothy Lamour, Glen Campbell, Connie Stevens and a dozen other performers tagging behind. Greeting them were a dozen or so photographers, TV newspeople, reporters from the *Star* and *Post,* plus the smiling faces of Jack Benny, Billy Graham and Willard Marriott. Bob pulled Benny and Graham into the group shots for the medial.

"You still expect a big crowd, Bob?"

"Bigger now that CBS and NBC finally decided to televise the show. It ought to give our world a lift. This will be one day we can forget our differences and the next day we can go back to the mat and try again."[8]

Hope set up his operations base at his favorite Washington retreat, a plush, mahogany-rich suite at the slightly removed Shoreham Hotel. Hope rehearsed there with Lamour, Benny and Shore and resisted going over to the stage set up on the Mall because he had gotten eyewitness reports that a sizable crowd—variously described as protesters, demonstrators, hippies and radicals—were wading nude in the reflecting pools, shouting obscenities during the midday services at Lincoln Memorial, smoking pot and being rounded up by policemen on horseback.

A few hours before show time on that Saturday afternoon, Hope remained in his suite, working with Mort Lachman on the evening's monologue and the continuity material with the guests. Bob Jani, Disney's genius of outdoor spectacle, was both producer and director of the three-hour show and fireworks, and he was providing Hope, over the telephone, with a running commentary about the dress rehearsal as it was progressing on the Mall stage.

Finally, Hope's curiosity about the Mall rehearsal got the best of him and he asked a D.C. policeman to drive him over to the show site for a conference with Jani and a short run-through with Les Brown. The rain and the winds that accompanied it had stopped and crews were repairing damage to the red, white and blue bunting of the Disneyesque setting. Off to the side, eyed by security police, were a group of half-naked hippie-types who were drinking Ripple and watching Hope rehearse. At one point he stopped to acknowledge their hollering at him, and he invited them to come see the show that night. Even as he spoke, on the backside of the stage, facing the Lincoln Memorial, a rampaging crowd of protesters attacked an oasis of fast-food vendors, ate the ice cream and hot dogs, drank the pop, and then dragged the pushcarts into the reflecting pools.

That night, before Hope went on stage, an additional contingent of District policemen was called in because a rash of bottle-throwing had started among the hecklers and demonstrators who were fenced off from the main crowd, which National Park figures estimated at above 350,000.

Hope, dressed nattily in dark blue suit, white shirt and striped tie, stepped out onto the stage and looked toward the Washington Monument at the unending mass of people. "Do you believe this? What a crowd! Nixon took one look at it and said, 'My God, what did Agnew say now?' . . . And then Agnew looked out his window at this crowd and said, 'What a great time to say something.' "[9]

The viewers at home got a big talent-filled show, and would not have known anything was amiss in the sidelines if Hope had not said, during one of his introductions, "Where am I? Back in Vietnam?" when some firecrackers exploded at the side of the stage. Even most of that huge assemblage was totally unaware that two canisters of tear gas were hurled by demonstrators into the crowd from behind the storm fence barriers. Only the people sitting closest to the sidelines were treated to obscenities and many did gather up their children and leave.

When Fred Waring's ensemble had finished leading the entire cast in a finale rendition of "Battle Hymn of the Republic," a dazzling display of fireworks burst out over the Mall area, and the massive audience began to move off to their cars and buses. Hope was conducted by policemen from the stage to his car, but not before some of the demonstrators had broken through the police cordon in time to beat their fists against the trunk of the car as it moved away.

Waiting for Hope when he got back to Los Angeles was a letter from comedian Dick Gregory which offered his explanation why he could not accept Hope's invitation to appear in Washington:

> To me the Fourth of July is a time for the most serious kind of national reflection. To me it is a time to analyze the growth of the child, Independence. It is a time to "change the course of human events" and see how America matches up to her most treasured rhetoric. It is time to apply the Declaration of Independence to our national life, rather than revere that document as a quaint expression of Americana.
>
> So, Bob, this Fourth of July, we will both be trying to honor America in our own individual ways. You will be sacrificing your personal holiday, as you have done so many times before, giving your time and talent to bring joy to thousands of Americans. My holiday will be one of serious reflection. I currently am fasting to dramatize the tragedy and hypocrisy of the narcotics problem in America.
>
> I long for the day when Americans can laugh and sing together, can watch Bob Hope and Dick Gregory performing together without considering our political persuasions.[10]

Every place I go I tell what's in my heart and in my head. I don't adjust for the place. I walk in and tell it like I think it is.[1]

42. A Partisan Voice

By the middle of 1970, Hope's political leanings were no longer secret. He still edited his material in favor of neutrality, but even a cursory examination of Hope monologues through two decades suggests more bite to his humor leveled at Democratic administrations than Republican ones. In addition, there were certain activities in the months before and after Honor America Day that suggested where he put his money and how he punched out his ballot in the voting booth.

In the spring Hope helped raise over $350,000 at a political luncheon supporting his friend and former Ohio governor Jim Rhodes for a U.S. Senate seat. (Rhodes was defeated.) He cut television and radio spots in support of his pal George Murphy's successful bid to retain his Republican Senate seat in Washington. He appeared in a film supporting Republican Lenore Romney's campaign in Michigan for a U.S. Senate seat. In addition to campaign contributions to the Ronald Reagan fund, he was also active in fund-raising for the San Jose Republicans, and he and Dolores hosted a reception in their home for Barry Goldwater, Jr.'s, campaign.

In all fairness, the night after the Goldwater party the Hopes flew to St. Louis where Bob appeared at a political banquet supporting Democratic candidate Stuart Symington's bid for Senate reelection.

Whenever Hope was challenged about being partisan he responded by saying that his endorsements were all isolated personal favors. The Murphy and Hope relationship dates back to 1933; both Buckeyes, Rhodes and Hope had been playing golf together for years. Lenore Romney and the comedian met the night she presented Dolores an award at a USO affair. Hope called her "one of the bright gals I've met. I figured if we're going to have women in government, we might as well have *her*."[2] And his love and respect for Symington, despite Stuart's defection from his hawkish Vietnam position, were well known.

Yet Hope stepped firmly into the Republican "big time" in November 1971, agreeing to entertain at a pair of expensive and deftly choreographed "Salute to the President" fund-raising affairs held at Hilton hotels in New York City and Chicago the same night. After Hope and Nixon appeared in New York they flew to Chicago, Hope in a private jet with Nixon's campaign manager Bob Dole, and the President in Air Force One.

The following May, Hope headed a group of Hollywood stars who traveled to Baltimore for a fund-raising "Salute to Ted Agnew." In September, Hope headlined a "Victory '72" dinner for the Republican National Committee in Detroit; the next day he flew back to Los Angeles to appear at a campaign dinner with Nixon. On October 6, Hope emceed a Black Republican dinner; and later that month flew to Boston to share the stage with Pat Nixon at still another last minute fund-raiser.

And in those intervening months, Hope made a number of appearances on talk shows hosted by Phil Donahue, Mike Douglas, Johnny Carson, Irv Kupcinet, during which he left no doubt about his support for the administration.

Why so much fuss? Was it, after all, so important that Americans know precisely how Hope voted? The primary issue was probably a question of power:

> Democratic campaign strategists groan at the thought of Mr. Hope's all-American good guy image being added to the Republican arsenal. In a recent *Reader's Digest* survey of about 250,000 high school students, Mr. Hope was named the outstanding enter-

tainment figure of the 1960s and was second only to the Beatles world-wide.[3]

Hope's potential for influence could not be taken lightly. His media critics were concerned that in his support of the administration he sounded simplistic, and when he said with assurance that today's young people recognize that America had not used its power in Vietnam ("Kids like a show of strength") his critics said he was "out of tune."

Three media stories, breaking in late summer and fall of 1970 and in early 1971, had significant impact on Hope and on the public's perception of him.

First, there was a wire story in August quoting Kenneth D. Smith, entertainment coordinator for Special Services in Europe, who charged that entertainers like Bob Hope and George Jessel could no longer reach today's GI.

Hope, whose eyes and ears could hardly mistake the noisy enthusiasm of his most recent Vietnam tour, fumed at this and asked his friends in the Defense Department and in the USO who Smith was speaking for, and why. Two days later, the Pentagon issued an official disclaimer and a shorter wire story explained that Smith said he was misquoted. However, the idea had been planted and Hope, for one, was impressed enough to add several pot-smoking wisecracks to his Christmas 1970 monologues overseas which brought him applause and cheers, and a refusal by NBC to air them on the network.

Also in August, J. Anthony Lukas, a Pulitzer prizewinning journalist and new staff writer for *The New York Times Magazine,* arrived in Los Angeles to do a story on Hope. Advised by Allan Kalmus that Lukas "was not out there to do a fan magazine story," the West Coast PR staff handled the writer cautiously, monitoring most of the interviews until Lukas complained that the press agents were getting in his way. He insisted thereafter on talking to people like Saphier, Hope's new son-in-law Nat Lande, and the gag writers privately. Even so, he was heard to say, "I have yet to meet someone who will say something unflattering about the man."[4]

But there was sufficient candor to fortify a thesis that Hope of late had vigorously assumed new roles that to Lukas, at least, seemed unbecoming. His story title, "This Is Bob (Politician–Patriot–Publicist) Hope" says it all—that Hope as an enormously popular voice used his undeniably sincere concern for the GI and his conservative theme of Americanism to prolong an increasingly unpopular war, and that his partnership, both silent and active, on the Nixon–Agnew team had created a potent political force.

This was the first major literary effort to understand the "new Hope." Some of the insights that provided this story with its bite came from Hope loyalists who were beginning to feel the pressure of Hope's new political stance. Hope's gag writers, for instance, revealed to Lukas the number of times Hope requested gags from them for Agnew's use in his speeches, particularly the one that attacked the Eastern Establishment Press:

> Newspapers perform a great service. I know at our house we couldn't do without the *Baltimore Sun.* We have two puppies and a parakeet . . . We tried *The New York Times* and it's not

nearly as absorbent . . . I read *The New York Times* every day.
I enjoy good fiction. . . .[5]

Hope's distaste for this article which appeared October 4, 1970, was based on what he saw as gratuitous and offensive "flags" in the story. One was this:

Some members of his staff feel he is growing out of touch even with the troops he visits every year in Vietnam. "He just doesn't understand how the GI of today feels," says one of his writers. "When he sees a V sign in his audience he thinks two guys want to go to the bathroom."[6]

There was also the suggestion that Hope's "greatest single public relations effort has been his entertainment of the military at home and abroad for the past 29 years." The ultimate jab was contained in the suggestion that Hope and his highly motivated PR squad comprised a valuable publicity channel for the Pentagon and particularly the conservative elements. Hope branded the story "irresponsible" and "inaccurate."

The Lukas piece was a prelude to events in November which had far-reaching effects. Mid-month, a few days prior to Hope's trip to London (where he entertained royalty twice and was surprised by "This Is Your Life"), he made a short side trip to Chicago to do a benefit as a favor to his pal Jack Gray, and two paid engagements, one at Flint, Michigan, and the other at South Bend, Indiana, for Notre Dame's homecoming festivities.

Flying from Chicago to Flint in a Beechcraft loaned him by Gerity Broadcasting, Hope was accompanied by *Life* reporter Joan Barthel, a writer who had made a name for herself through several perceptive show business profiles. Hope had agreed with Kalmus that she could be around him for several days to do a kind of "on the road with Hope in the seventies" story. Barthel has said she felt "The private Hope is the same as the public Hope. And his natural habitat is on the road." In the plane Hope responded to her question about the things he currently was saying to audiences:

Every place I go I tell what's in my heart and in my head. I don't adjust for the place. I walk in and tell it like I think it is. Look, you're not going to change certain people's minds. I just think you're going to give people confidence, people who are in doubt about our sanity. I wouldn't play colleges if the people didn't show up, but the audiences get better all the time. I just played Athens, Georgia—11,000 on Friday night—and I played Auburn on Saturday—15,000 more. If they turn out like that it's a sign that they want to see you, they want to hear what you're saying.

Barthel tape-recorded Hope's performance at Flint in its entirety, including his final five minutes of serious talk to the audience. And the next afternoon, Barthel was observing carefully during half-time ceremonies when Notre Dame's athletic director "Moose" Krause led Hope out onto the field for a comic introduction and "Salute to Bob Hope." She was also close by, and tape-recording all Hope said, at his solo concert that night for 12,000 people in the university sports center.

When Barthel's abbreviated excursion with Hope was transformed into *Life*'s cover story for January 29, 1971, there against red, white and blue stripes was Hope's celebrated profile (this was his third *Life* cover) and the headline, BOB HOPE: ON THE ROAD WITH AN AMERICAN INSTITUTION. Inside, however, the story's headline was different: BOB HOPE: THE ROAD GETS ROUGHER. There was a subhead: POLITICS IS PART OF HIS ACT NOW—SOME NEW SOUNDS ARE MIXED IN WITH THE LAUGHTER. That subhead referred to an early reference in Barthel's story that when "Moose" Krause brought Hope out onto the field at South Bend, some students in the upper stands booed the comedian and made thumbs-down gestures. Barthel also reported that in his Flint, Michigan, concert, Hope called the Vietnam war "a beautiful thing—we paid in a lot of gorgeous American lives, but we're not sorry for it."[7]

Reaction to the *Life* story was instantaneous, both from readers and from Hope. He was especially outraged, not by the so-called booing incident (which he maintained from the outset was not directed at him) but at the audacity of saying that he could possibly say or think that war was beautiful. "Moose" Krause wrote a letter for *Life*'s attention explaining that students often make loud "Moo-ing" sounds whenever he appears at Notre Dame. And not a single official connected with the Flint show could recall Hope saying that the Vietnam war was "a beautiful thing." What was universally remembered was that Hope had referred to the men fighting there as beautiful.

Hope was angry enough to call Martin Gang and discuss the advisability of bringing legal action against the magazine. Meanwhile letters decrying his statement began arriving at his Toluca Lake office, and Hope took every public opportunity, in interviews, at personal appearances, on talk shows, in gossip columns, to deny that he could ever think such a thought.

Furthermore, Hope insisted that Kalmus contact *Life* managing editor Ralph Graves and insist that he or his lawyers be allowed to audit the Barthel tape of the Flint performance to determine the accuracy of her quote. But neither Barthel nor Graves would cooperate with Hope.

Then followed a two-month period during which a variety of pro- and anti-Hope feeling was vented in the media. Directly attributable to the *Life* story was a student protest at San Fernando Valley State College over an announcement that Hope was to receive an honorary degree. Students marched across the campus carrying signs that portrayed Hope as a "war-loving hawk." Hope told the Associated Press, "to think they could actually believe I would feel war is good makes me want to vomit."[8]

In mid-March a group of liberal young ministers pressured the New York City Council of Churches to withdraw its earlier designation of Bob Hope as the 1971 recipient of its Family of Man Award. In February, the board of directors of the Council had voted their Gold Medallion to Hope just as they had in previous years to John Kennedy, Dwight Eisenhower, Lyndon Johnson and Richard Nixon. Leader of the dissident clergy, Lutheran pastor Richard Neuhaus, jumped to his feet at the Council's assembly meeting and said he and 20 other young ministers found nothing in Hope's record of public commitment to "the three pressing issues that face the Council—poverty, social justice and peace. On the contrary, Mr. Hope has uncritically supported the military establishment."[9] The dissidents successfully argued that the 1971 medal be awarded posthumously to Whitney Young, Jr., who had died in a swimming accident at Lagos, Nigeria, the week before. The vote was 34 to 22 in favor of Young.

Hope reacted immediately by wiring Dan Potter, executive director of the Council, that he was "delighted the award was going to Young. He was a great American and deserved it, and a lot more than that."[10] But he did that before he learned the full story. Hope's reaction was "If getting hooked on caring about the Americans who have laid down their lives for their country stops me from getting awards, then I'll have to live with it."[11] Council director Potter told the AP that he was "swamped with calls protesting the decision to cancel an award Hope had already agreed to accept. Sixty long-time supporters have written to say they will never attend our dinners again."[12]

Editorials in newspapers and letters to the editors were printed all across the country. Many of these were pro-Hope, like a Bronx resident who on March 21, 1971, wrote New York's *Daily News*, "There's no more hope for the Council of Churches and I think its Faith and Charity are losing ground, too." Television editor Ben Gross said he received a "bundle of mail that was 10 to 1 in favor of Hope." But the anti-Hope mail could not be ignored, either.

Senator Barry Goldwater, one-time Republican candidate for President and a well-known conservative who had battled what he called the "liberal media," asked for space in *The Arizona Republic* to make a statement. It appeared in the June 1, 1971, issue:

> Until Hope made his long-held conservative position completely known in speeches and by backing conservative candidates, he was treated with the greatest respect and honor by the lilywhites of liberalism such as *The New York Times* and the *Washington Post*.
> But the moment he aligned himself with conservatism, and particularly the Republican Party, he became a villain. . . .
> What I am trying to point out is that anyone—and I don't care whether he is the President of the United States, the world's most popular entertainer, or the least known person—who dares to take a stand against the far left is immediately, viciously, libelously and scurrilously branded and it is shameful the way Bob Hope has been treated.

Later that spring, in Oklahoma City, a young television executive named Lee Allen Smith, who had been a Hope fan as long as he could recall, was angry about what he considered unjust criticism of his hero. As head of the Oklahoma City Association of Broadcasters, he was putting together their annual Civic Fourth of July celebration, and Smith had received encouragement from NBC that if he could round up enough big names for the evening's variety show, the network would offer the telecast to its more than 200 stations.

Smith took a chance and called Hope, and it was the kind of platform Hope was looking for. The sponsors of the civic celebration were so grateful they voted to erect a statue honoring Hope in the city's newly dedicated patriotic park.

The significance of this particular event could not be found either in the quality of the show or in the weight of its guest stars, because it was strictly run-of-the-mill variety fare and the performers were people like Anita Bryant, the Golddiggers, the Les Brown Band, celebrity athletes and celebrity astronauts. Its significance was that it would be an old-fashioned Fourth of July address, the kind that Americans for generations expected to hear on this day, written by and spoken by Bob Hope. Hope went to the vault and rifled through several drawers of material, and several nights in late June he worked until the early morning polishing his "remarks" which would be the keystone of the program.

Probably at no other time in his life was it so essential for him to speak to "his" audience, and to speak as unambiguously as possible in order to register his world view. This audience would certainly not be the widely diversified and multi-faceted viewing and listening audience Hope had once commanded. Those who would tune in to Bob Hope in July 1972 were only a part of the audience who would have tuned in to hear a Hope radio show of July 1942. In those intervening decades between the unified forties and the dissenting sixties, the nation was losing its innocence. What once had been such recognizable character types—the average American who always appeared on *The Saturday Evening Post* covers—was all but gone. Hope had risen to fame as one of those Norman Rockwell characters, a bumptious traveling salesman who despite his brash manner was really cowardly, a reluctant hero. But Hope was that no more.

Now that he was known for taking sides, that he could speak out in favor of one party's program (much as Will Rogers had done in the thirties), Hope had lost some of his ability to wield an influential nationalistic voice.

Now, as he took the stage in Oklahoma City, he laid it all out for everyone to see. Simply, eloquently, he called upon the nation to reunite; he evoked traditional values; he was trying to induce confidence at a time when confidence in all the important American institutions was faltering or failing. Because he had written so much of it, this was as genuine a Bob Hope message as Americans were likely to hear:

This land of mine. You know, it isn't really mine or yours except by special arrangement. We only have it by lease for our lifetime, and we have the responsibility to handle it with care and leave it better than we found it, keep it clean so life can renew itself, and our children can hand a torch to the next generations waiting to run. Our forefathers knew we'd become a great nation, with millions of people, industry, manufacturing, traffic. They must have known we'd even have smog. Why else would they start our national anthem, "Oh, say can you see . . ."? No, America is more than a place to love. It's a way to love. It was conceived in freedom and born in freedom, and freedom is still our most important product. We know there are places in the world where these freedoms can't be taken for granted because they simply don't exist. And there are millions behind fences who envy our ability to speak out. . . .

This is about the only place left on the earth where the impos-

sible dream has a chance of making it. This country was founded
on impossible dreams—the Pilgrims at Plymouth Rock, the signing of the Declaration of Independence, the walk on the moon,
Lee Trevino beating Jack Nicklaus, and a foreigner by the name
of Canonero II coming over here and winning the Kentucky Derby. The impossible dream. Where but in America can a man like
Johnny Cash make a million dollars singing about a railroad that
went bankrupt. This really is the land of opportunity. Did you
know that fifteen years ago Elvis Presley couldn't spell Tennessee
and now he owns it? What opportunity! . . . Man finds cure for
diseases so we can live longer, then builds freeways to prevent
overpopulation. Believe me, it's a wonderful world. It may destroy
itself, but you'll all be able to watch it on TV. . . .

There are confusing times. These are very confusing. Some of
the people seem to be down on that dream called America today.
They view Vietnam and they call it a shame—a dirty war. And it
is. No one ever invented a clean one in the history of man-
kind. . . . I can remember when kids grew up thinking their
mothers and fathers were the greatest. And the funny part of it
was the adults tried harder to be the greatest when they had all
that love thrown at them. . . .

A lot of people knock the kids of today. Sure, there are a few
kooks, there always have been. But I get around a bit and I think
the majority of this generation of young people is the most aware,
the most intelligent and the most promising we've ever had, and
they better be, with the world they're facing! . . .

They say this is a difficult time to be young. In my memory,
there never was a time when things weren't rough. Certainly the
men who started this whole thing, who put this great country in
business, lived in up-tight times. But they did one smart thing—
they fashioned a wonderful tool for coping with it. It's called our
Constitution. Not that it has always been absolutely right. But
those good men who fashioned it knew that the need for change
would arise and they built in a mechanism for that change. It's
not done with violence. It's done with peaceful dissent and the will
of the majority . . . a pathway spoken of with pride as the
American Way.

The newspapers are now busy trying to prove who caused the
war. They like to give it names like "It's President A's war," or
"President B's War." Well, the fact remains that it is our war. It's
our kids who are fighting in it. Those bullets hurt just as much
whether a Democrat or a Republican started it. I don't like war—
I think it stinks. I know it stinks. . . . I've smelled it in the burn
wards of combat hospitals. I've seen the kids who would have
loved to shake hands with me if they still had that hand. I hate
war with all my guts. But I admire the guys with guts enough to
fight them when they have to be fought. . . .

But it's gone a long way, this Vietnam conflict, in disrupting
our country. Perhaps somewhere along the line we could have

withdrawn with grace and honor on our part. I don't know. I don't know if anyone knows. But we were committed, and bred in our very bones is the tradition or integrity that makes us keep on helping the little guy. The tide seems to be turning and our troops are coming home, and in our haste to heal our wounds, to bridge the chasms, and to reunite our nation, we must remember our heritage that we always have and always will answer a call for help. As a young nation we were helped. We said it was man's right to be free and since then we've tried to help other young nations. That is why President Eisenhower sent advisors to South Vietnam and President Kennedy sent in troops. History will record their decisions were made in the interest of freedom.

This Fourth has been a great day to count our blessings. But do remember, the love of country, the myriad of expressions of loyalty we lump into one big bag and call patriotism is not a cloak to be put on one day a year. It's a mantle for all seasons. . . .[13]

British pop culture scholar John Fisher, in his perceptive study of a group of world-sized entertainers, *The Legends*, sums up his careful assessment of Hope this way:

It would have been the ultimate irony of the Vietnam war if it had succeeded, as it threatened to do, in bringing about the downfall of the entertainer with greatest claim to be styled Mr. Sandman of the American Dream, the most decorated civilian in American history. But if Hope had proved he was not untouchable, he came through the ordeal with his optimism intact, a politically neutral quality characteristic of the American spirit which, if his television ratings are to be believed, may well have led people other than those who merely want their right-wing prejudices confirmed to forget the immediate past and to identify with him still.[14]

And I'm such a ham. Somebody said if I was in a blizzard and two Eskimo dogs walked by, I'd do ten minutes for them. But I'm not the kind of guy who's on all the time either. I don't wanna be on all the time.[1]

43. The Last Christmas Show

If Hope had been successful in his bid to free the POWs in December 1971, he would have been at the top of Gallup's list of men that Americans admire most. As it was, Hope finished ninth in the Gallup poll behind Richard Nixon, Billy Graham, Ted Kennedy, Lyndon Johnson, Hubert Humphrey, Spiro Agnew, Ralph Nader and Pope Paul VI. Hope's appearance in the top ten, after an absence of a few years, was in part a reflection of his attempt to free the prisoners.

On December 19, shortly after arriving in Bangkok during his around-the-world Christmas tour, Hope telephoned Ambassador Leonard Unger to seek his help in meeting with the North Vietnamese to discuss the comedian's going to Hanoi to entertain the POWs. Unger contacted his counterpart in Laos, Ambassador G. McMurtrie Godley. On December 22 word came from Laos that Hope would be received in Vientiane.

Shortly after dawn the next day, a U.S. Air Force general escorted Hope and his PR man to the airport and a small unmarked CIA airplane for the 90-minute top-secret flight to Vientiane.

In flight, word came that Hope's appointment had been canceled. But Hope continued the flight, so he could at least entertain the American Embassy employees in Vientiane.

Upon his arrival, Hope was met by Ambassador Godley, embassy prisoner-of-war specialist Richard Rand and missionary Edward Roffe of the Christian Alliance Church, and was ushered into an unbearably hot mobile office at the airport for a briefing. Godley and Rand informed Hope that the meeting was on again. The Reverend Roffe was to be his interpreter, and he escorted Hope and his PR man to the North Vietnamese Embassy, a modest French colonial house surrounded by a tall iron fence on a tree-covered street on the outskirts of the city. Hope was nervous when they entered a small living room and met First Secretary Nguyen Van Tranh, a young man in his early thirties.

After exchanging pleasantries, Hope reminded Van Tranh that he had requested a visa to visit Hanoi. Van Tranh told Hope that he could not make a decision until he contacted his foreign minister.

Over tea and cookies, Van Tranh said, "Our country has been at war for 26 years and our people are suffering, especially our children."

Hope, who confessed later that he was "winging" the entire interview, took out his wallet and turned to a photograph of his grandson Zachary (Tony and Judy's). "Wouldn't it be great if the children of our country could help the children of your country, in exchange for the release of the prisoners?"

Van Tranh said quickly, and for the first time in English, "Your President could get the prisoners of war released tomorrow if he would listen to the seven points of our peace talks in Paris."

"I don't know anything about those seven points," said Hope. "All I know is that the children of this war on both sides are the real victims. I would like to see the children of America contribute their nickels and dimes to help your children and get the prisoners released."

"Nixon knows well the prisoners will be released when your government agrees to a withdrawal date."

"Nevertheless I hope you will think about this idea of a children's relief fund, a children-to-children program to rebuild homes and hospitals and schools," Hope said quickly, realizing the word "prisoners" had already altered the tone of their meeting.

Van Tranh said he was grateful for Hope's interest in the Vietnamese children. He understood Hope's compassion for his countrymen who were detained. He could not say anything definite about Hope's visa request, but he did say that he hoped one day the comedian would entertain in Hanoi.

Outside on a veranda, Hope and Van Tranh shook hands and a hundred yards away the Associated Press photographer snapped a picture of the handshake. Hope refused to speak to the reporter, pending an embassy debriefing. Later, Hope entertained 400 employees in the embassy compound.[2]

Hope had planned to say nothing to the press, but when he walked into the lobby of the hotel he was met by a mob of local newsmen and foreign correspondents. They came up to his suite and crowded in.

"Did you discuss this with anyone before coming to Bangkok?"

"No," said Hope. "I had been thinking of trying to visit Hanoi for some time because of my many talks with relatives of the prisoners wherever I go. They stop me at shows and airports and ask if I can do something."

"Does the President know?"

"By now he must," answered Hope. "But this was my idea."

"You talked money with the North Vietnamese."

"I told them I thought I could make a proposition to raise a lot of money."

"How much?"

"I don't know. I was thinking in the neighborhood of ten million." Hope had never mentioned an amount to Van Tranh. "I think we could do that. We could put on shows in addition to the money the kids raised."

"Ross Perot offered ransom—"

"This is not ransom," snapped Hope. "That's a bad word. I don't think they'd buy that at all. This has to be a children-to-children agreement. Tomorrow I intend to send a formal proposal of my idea to Van Tranh."

On December 24, the AP confirmed that President Nixon did not know about Hope's intentions but welcomed it as a private gesture. On December 25, the AP filed from Vientiane a story that quoted a North Vietnamese official as saying Hope would most likely be denied a visa and that only "courtesy" had kept Van Tranh from saying so. But Hope was not daunted.

He finished the world tour at Guantánamo Bay and received the sad news that Rosy O'Donnell had died. Hope took the entire troupe to Colorado Springs for a final tribute to his friend at the military funeral. Back home, Hope readied his documentary account of the Christmas tour and fell in stride with his schedule of personal appearances and engagements. He even found time to take Dolores, Tony and Judy, Linda and Nat, Nora and Sam, Kelly and all the grandchildren to Acapulco for a five-day "delayed Christmas" celebration. But through it all he maintained a constant vigil on his chances of obtaining a visa.

Hope made four trips to Washington in a six-week period to talk with either President Nixon, Secretary Kissinger or Secretary Rogers. On his last visit, Secretary Rogers told Hope of the Nixon–Kissinger plan to offer $2.8 billion in relief aid to the North Vietnamese. To which Hope quipped, "How did I know I was offering them a tip?"[3] Hope backed off, assured from these Washington briefings that everything possible was being done to effect the POW release.

It seemed the country was in good hands. Nixon was riding high, his trips to China and to Russia were labeled a success, the war was winding down, and there were more troop withdrawals. Hope was telling the media that there might not be any reason for him to go overseas anymore. His jokes were less war-ridden. His March television broadcast was devoted to Nixon winning the New Hampshire primary and his trip to China:

> . . . President Nixon's trip was an international success. A new poll shows he had a better-than-even chance to be re-elected President in this country . . . and a forty percent chance of being elected President of China . . . Some conservatives feared Mr. Nixon lost his shirt in China but that's not true. Kissinger found the ticket and he's going back for it. . . .[4]

Sitting in that audience, while Hope did his monologue and a sketch with Sammy Davis, Jr., and Juliet Prowse, was writer C. Robert Jennings, on assignment from *Today*, a widely circulated Sunday supplement. Jennings was asking: "What can you say about a sixty-nine-year-old legend that refuses to die?" He decided that you could treat him as a "pukka folk-hero," or perhaps do the "Old Star Interview" with plenty of jokes, or

> . . . you can take the current tack, which is to misquote him ("War is beautiful"—*Life*); denigrate him ("The funny thing about Bob Hope is that he's not very funny"—*Look*); or make scurrilous references to his politics and sex life (*The New York Times*). But any way you go, it just won't fly.
> . . . So you observe, try to capture something of sinew and feeling, even indulge in a little Indian wrestling of egos—trusting that in the accretion of the details of Hope's daunting business, the flying shards of colloquial speech, the geegaws of personality at odd points of time and pressure, there might emerge some mosaic of the true man, if even a smudged one.[5]

Jennings felt he could not find his story focus in a series of publicist-supervised interviews, so he asked if he could go on the road, as Joan Barthel had done, to watch the moving target. The comedian sized Jennings up and said, "Good idea." And it was a good idea. Jennings had the acuity to perceive what Mort Lachman and a few others close to Hope could also perceive; that this recent talk about how much Bob Hope had changed was so much "twaddle." Hope had not changed. The world may have changed but not Bob Hope. That mutual admiration between Hope and his adopted country, manifested so particularly in his relationship with the GI, in peace and war, and more generally in his assiduous pursuit and realization of the American Dream, was too fixed, too pervasive for any major disruption.

"Bob," said Jennings, "you're staring at the sunny side of seventy. What about it? Isn't it time to think about quitting?"

"Hell, no. You belong to the public. You got nine people writing for you, eight people publicizing you, a large group, uh, that keeps me moving, including the Red Cross."

"But you will quit?"

"Never. Listen, I only do the things I want to do."

And in the next few weeks—next few months—next few years—he illustrated that last sentence clearly. In April he joined Jack Benny on a platform at Jacksonville University where they received twin honorary degrees. He flew to Palm Springs to play in the Dinah Shore golf tournament and then back to Los Angeles where he and Benny and cellist Gregor Piatigorsky clowned through an evening of gags for a Wellesley College benefit (chaired by Judy Hope), flew to Washington for the White House Press Photographers Dinner and back to Toluca Lake for one of the most publicized fund-raisers of the year. Hope allowed himself to be photographed, caricatured, cartooned, satirized in a dozen ways as Packy East, the fighter coming out of retirement to face Sugar Ray Robinson in what was billed as the "Fight of the Century."

A boxing ring was set up in Hope's backyard. Attending were celebrities: Cary Grant, Debbie Reynolds, Milton Berle, Chuck Connors, Lorne Greene, Nancy Sinatra, Jonathan Winters and neighbor Dorothy Lamour plus a generous collection of Hope's affluent friends and associates. Chasen's catered the buffet; Les Brown produced the music and at the end of the evening Hope handed Sugar Ray a check for $100,000 for his Sugar Ray Youth Foundation.

But sometimes Hope, shrewd as he was in choosing events he would favor, misjudged the promoters. A case in point was "La Semaine de Sportif à Paris" (Sports Week in Paris), a promotion by a young Georgia boy named Ramar "Bubba" Sutton to raise money for the Eisenhower Wing of the American Hospital in Paris. Sutton's credentials were not blue ribbon but the program he had lined up in Paris—and the overall conception—was impressive. Besides, Bob and Dolores had been invited by Ambassador Arthur Watson to be his guests at the official residence. Sutton had also enticed several of Hope's Palm Springs and Palm Beach friends to join them in Paris as host-sponsors if they could ante up $10,000. There were elegant luncheons, cocktail parties and dinners thrown for the American athletes and very wealthy American and Parisian patrons of the American Hospital.

The social events went well, but financially things went from bad to worse. Sutton's expenses were swallowing up funds that might go to the hospital. Sutton had already hired a French film crew to cover some of the events, but now he hired them to cover the entire thing as a documentary that he could sell to a United States television network. Otherwise, the American Hospital would have to stand some of Sutton's losses.

Hope had agreed to play the golf tournament at St.-Germain with Billy Casper and headline the gala variety show at the Théâtre de la Musique. By this time he realized that everything depended on the success of the television documentary.

When the week was over Bob and Dolores flew to Ireland to spend a weekend with some Palm Springs friends and then on to New York for an overnight before Hope went to Wilberforce University to receive another Honorary Doctorate of Humanities. He then flew back to New York for an appearance at West Point's graduation.

Three days later, Hurricane Agnes slammed into Florida and worked her way through the Carolinas, Virginia, Maryland, Pennsylvania and, finally, New York. Before it was over and the property toll would be assessed, 226 people were known dead and another 124 were missing.

The Red Cross was heartened to hear that Hope had agreed to headline a benefit at Baltimore's Civic Center. Within a few days, Trans World Airlines had offered a plane, the Baltimore Hilton offered free accommodations to any and all stars who would come and the old Mechanic Theater was opened at no charge by the Nederlanders.

Hope called Zsa Zsa Gabor, Jimmy Stewart, George Jessel, David Janssen, Steve Allen, Fess Parker, Janet Leigh, Forrest Tucker and Joe Namath. His staff made contact with Gisele MacKenzie, James Darren, Linda Bennett, Gloria Loring, George Maharis and Tige Andrews. Altogether there were 28 stars. Hope had not forgotten another offer and called Dick Gregory, who said he would be honored to appear with Hope for this cause.

The stage was set and the cameras were rolling but all was not smooth. Zsa Zsa expected, after her first appearance, to make a second and went to her dressing room to change. When she came back and was informed that she was not needed, her temper flared. She grabbed up her Lhasa Apso, Genghis Khan, called for her car and went back to the Hilton. Hope sent some Red Cross administrators to the hotel to talk with her and get her to come back. Zsa Zsa made a second appearance.

George Jessel was also miffed when he found out that time might not allow him to appear at all. However, he was a little more enterprising than Zsa Zsa. He went to his dressing room and, disguising his voice, made repeated calls to the telethon number demanding that Jessel make an appearance. And by "popular demand" George Jessel made an appearance.

And Hope's 1972 campaign stumping for the Republicans paid off that night in a surprise visit from the First Lady. Pat Nixon spoke to the audience and then answered calls from donation viewers for half an hour. That evening, efforts raised $2,105,000.

When Hope returned from the east he viewed the Paris Sports Week film. He was so appalled that he flew to Paris at the end of July to reconstruct the documentary and make it marketable. He hired Louis Jourdan to do the narration and some on-camera comments and reshot a number of continuity scenes. A month later he was back in Paris for a final editing. And, so all would not be lost, he filmed several acts for his own television special.

By late summer, the Sports Week special had lost its immediacy and its interest for potential sponsors, despite the charitable connection.

Meanwhile, Ramar Sutton was circulating among Hope's friends trying to promote more money for the American Hospital. Naturally, Hope had already emptied his friends' pockets for the Eisenhower Medical Center in Palm Desert.

Adding fuel to the fire, Sutton was running up hotel bills, restaurant tabs and car-leasing expenses to the tune of three and four figures, all in Hope's name. Eventually Martin Gang was forced into court to face several creditors on Hope's behalf.

All in all, Hope had spent thousands of dollars trying to salvage a property which was never shown; a charity was stuck with enormous bills and nothing to show for all the effort.

Annoyed as Hope was, he was able to transfer his attention to the release of his most recent movie, *Cancel My Reservation*, which he made in the fall of 1971 with Eva Marie Saint, Ralph Bellamy, Keenan Wynn and Ann Archer.

The film was to have its initial run at Radio City Music Hall. This was the first Hope picture to ever have a screening at this famous showplace. Although it was nothing like getting an Oscar, Hope was thrilled.

The film was a disappointment, an anachronism. Hope must have known then that he would not continue making movies, because almost at once he huddled with Bob Thomas about coauthoring a book about his forty-year "love affair with the movies," a kind of wrap-up of that part of his life.

In October, amid his usual appearances around the nation, he slipped into Washington the same day Henry Kissinger flew in from Paris between sessions of the Peace Talks for executive briefing. Rumors flew about the city that peace was at hand. Hope told the guests at the Army dinner how relieved he was that his forthcoming tour of Southeast Asia would be his "last Christmas show."

In Mid-November, one of the most touching moments of Hope's advancing years occurred. In San Antonio, Texas, the comedian stood surrounded by giggling, screaming, adoring youngsters who had voted, from a range of possible national heroes, "the Bob Hope Elementary School" as the name of their new school building. That little ceremony swelled the list of monuments and memorials bearing his name in various parts of America: a bronze bust in a park in Oklahoma City; another in the Patriots Garden in Florida; his name on a wing of the Parkinson's Disease Hospital in Miami, on a halfway house for delinquent boys in Cincinnati, a facility at Columbia University Medical Center, a theater at Southern Methodist University, a main thoroughfare in Rancho Mirage that passes the Eisenhower Medical Center, and countless rooms in hospitals the country over.

Two days before Hope left with his 75-member troupe for what he called his "last Christmas show," Louella Parsons died at the age of ninety-one. As a reigning gossip queen of Hollywood, she had been an unfailing booster of Bob and Dolores Hope since their 1938 arrival. Hope attended her funeral at the Good Shepherd Church and was shocked to find so few stars paying their last respects. Apart from Jack Benny, George Burns, Danny Thomas, Jack Warner, David Janssen and Earl Holliman, the only mourners were press agents who had yearned for space in her Hearst column and on her national radio show.

The two weeks that ended 1972 also ended the national spectacle of Hope's overseas tours for the GIs. He took with him for this highly emotional finish comedian Redd Foxx, dancer Lola Falana, Rams quarterback Roman Gabriel, Dolores Reade Hope (who wanted to be in on the finale) and a group of young beauty contest winners and Hollywood hopefuls called the "American Beauties," and, of course, Les Brown and his band plus several media people.

Because it was well known that this was a farewell tour, the crowds were emotional and appreciative. Hope was cheered and presented with plaques, awards, trophies, citations and honors from the Korean government, the Japanese government, and what was left of the government of South Vietnam. Through an unfortunate misunderstanding concerning some of Hope's jokes

about Thai people, the Thai government awarded no special honor to
Hope.)

Covering Hope's last Christmas show for the Knight Newspapers was
veteran reporter Shirley Eder who wrote in the *Detroit Free Press* on
December 28, 1972:

> With difficulty I'm trying to choose the one standout moment
> of the entire trip—there were so many. When we started out on
> the plane, Hope's producer, Mort Lachman, told me there is
> usually one thing or one spot during a performance that grabs you
> more than any other. He was right! . . . it was when Dolores
> (Mrs. Hope) came out just before the finale that it all really got to
> me. Six thousand boys and men stood up when she made her
> entrance, then sat down again and were very still while she sang
> "White Christmas."
>
> I looked around at all those young men, many of them with
> their head lowered trying to hide their emotions. Hundreds sat
> with tears streaming down their faces, especially when Dolores
> ended the song, "And may all your Christmases be home."
>
> At this point, I looked away from them, as they tried to look
> away from their shipmates, because the tears were streaming
> down my face, too.

The accustomed 90-minute documentary of the two-week trip followed in
color on NBC–TV. It drew the expected large viewing audience and, perhaps
less expected, critical acclaim from columnists and editors the country over.
Of course, it must be said that the program followed, by two days, Nixon's
suspension of all bombing of North Vietnam and his deactivation of the
mines in Haiphong Harbor, which relieved even the one-time hawks.

Hope flew to Washington on an American Airlines plane designated as
The Inauguration Special because it was full of entertainers headed for performances at Nixon's second inaugural.

Later in the spring of 1973, with the help of Pete Martin, Mort Lachman
and NBC's Betty Lanigan, Hope began to write his fifth book, already titled
The Last Christmas Show. Hope dedicated the book to the Men and Women
of the Armed Forces, and pledged the royalties to the USO. In the final
section of the book, he commented on why time and circumstance had dictated an end to his Christmas tours:

> . . . you can imagine what emotions those words stir in me. I
> guess the strongest feeling is gratitude—gratitude that the pain-
> ful war was winding down to the point where the trips were
> becoming less necessary, gratitude that my strength and the need
> for me were coming out about even . . . I felt the last Christmas
> trip was almost more important than the previous ones, if only
> because our troops were so aware of the mixed feelings back
> home. They had read about the anti-war protests in the papers,
> and they'd heard about them in letters from home. A lot of them
> had started to wonder whether they were headed in the right
> direction, whether they were really fighting for their country,

whether what they were doing was right. They began to wonder whether all the political fighting back home had cost their country the strength and unity it needed to support their fighting in Vietnam. Because of this, it was clear to me that those kids needed a Christmas show more than ever.[6]

During the Christmas seasons of 1973, 1974, and 1975, Hope visited military hospitals in various parts of the nation. Reflecting on these visits, Hope said, "Everytime we'd walk up to a bed a kid would stick his hand out and say, 'Long Binh,' or 'Da Nang.' For most of us the war is over. For many of these kids it will never end."

The Statesman Years

1973–

This is the grandmother I sleep with. . . . She's so Catholic, she thinks Oral Roberts is a dentist, and Norman Vincent Peale is a stripper. . . .[1]

44. A Night with "Pops" in Boston

"One of my writers, Larry Klein, looked at me one day and said, 'You know, if you had your life to live all over again, you wouldn't have time to do it.'[2] I wouldn't want to live it over again. It's been pretty exciting up to now. The encore might not be as much fun."

Hope's 1954 autobiography opened with those lines. He was then fifty. He was now a durable seventy. Those intervening decades had seen him matching (and sometimes surpassing) the energy of his salad days. One of his favorite responses was: "I'd rather wear out than rust out." To most observers he showed little sign of wearing out, and no inclination to retire.

This is how he struck Bill Murray of *Playboy* during the hours they talked:

> Hope bounces as he walks, hums little tunes to himself, seems to vibrate quietly in his chair, as if he's consciously, like a trained athlete, working all the time at keeping himself loose. For a man his age, he's in superb condition, the jowls of his famous profile firm and his flesh tone that of a man in his early fifties. His tongue is still in great shape, too. . . .[3]

Playboy, which had developed a reputation for incisive interviews with interesting people, had waited months to break into Hope's crowded schedule, and when the comic finally agreed to meet with Murray, he warned he didn't have much time. The subjects were predictable: his Mount Rushmore image, his conservative politics, the youth scene, Vietnam, his GI tours, and his supposed half-billion dollars in wealth. But some new notes were struck. One was Watergate. Murray wanted to know how Hope felt about the opinion polls that questioned Nixon's honesty.

"I think he has a tremendous record, I really do. What he's done with the Russians and the Chinese has taken a lot of the heat off. It was a great job. That and the fact he has brought back 500,000 of our men from Vietnam are enough to make me like him very much."

Hope felt that the Justice Department ought to be handling the investigation rather than Congress.

"Don't you think the Watergate Committee has served a legitimate function?" Murray asked.

"Hell, yes, but it's dragging on and on and it's not good for the country." Of course, that conversation took place in August 1973. A full year would pass, almost to the day, before the oval office tapes and the Woodward and Bernstein reporting would reveal such complicity in the highest office that Nixon would resign. And throughout Watergate Hope did not avoid joking about Dean, Haldeman, Erlichman, Liddy—even the "mysterious" tape erasures—although he never seriously impugned Nixon. (In fact, after both Agnew and Nixon had been disgraced, when talk show host Lou Gordon demanded to know, "How can you remain friends with a thief and a scoundrel?" Hope replied, "Lou, if you were my friend in the same position, I would still be your friend.")

Those subjects aside, there was something else refreshing about this *Playboy* interview. For the first time in months Hope was being asked about his life's work:

"What is the secret of your comedy?"

"Material has a lot to do with it, but the real secret is timing," said Hope, "not just of comedy but of life. It starts with life. Think of sports, even sex. Timing is the essence of life and definitely of comedy. There's a chemistry of timing between a comedian and his audience. If the chemistry is great, it's developed through the handling of the material, and the timing of it—how you get into the audience's head."

"But you couldn't get along without your writers."

"Every comedian needs writers, because to stay on top you always need new material. It's like getting elected if you say the right things, but only if you say them right. The great ad libbers are the ones with the best timing, like Don Rickles. I showed up in the audience one night at NBC where he was cutting everybody up on *The Dean Martin Show*. I walked in after the show had started and the people in the back saw me and started applauding, and then the audience in the front turned around, and they applauded, and I was taking it big. Rickles backed away to the piano and when everything quieted down, he walked up to the mike and said, 'Well, the war must be over.' It was just magnificent timing and it hit very large. Timing shows more in ad libs than anything else."

"Do any of the younger comics make you laugh?"

"God, yes. Mort Sahl and Woody Allen, they're great. But my favorite was Lenny Bruce. The last time I saw him was at El Patio in Florida. I'd seen everybody else on the Beach and I just saw a little ad saying LENNY BRUCE AT EL PATIO and I said, 'We've got to go.' We went out there and I sat in the back. In those days planes were falling going from New York to Miami for some reason or another and so he walked to the mike and he said, 'A plane left New York today for Miami and made it.' That was his opening—not 'Hello' or anything. And then he told the audience I was there and he shouted, 'Hey, Bob, where are you?' And I said, 'Right here, Lenny.' And he said, 'Tonight I'm going to knock you right on your ass.' And he did.

"He had so much greasepaint in his blood it came out in his act. That's what I loved about him. He talked our language."

Murray asked, "What are your aspirations now?"

"To keep working," said Hope. "I'm going to do a movie based on the life of Walter Winchell, either a movie or a two-episode television thing. I'm in love with the idea. I knew Winchell. I went through that whole era. I'll really enjoy that."[4]

Those *Playboy* sessions represented a turning point in Hope's media relations. Like other journalists in the early seventies who interviewed with Hope to illuminate his politics, Murray found himself respecting the artist in the man. Even though the story labeled Hope as "proselytizingly patriotic" and "dangerously simplistic" about politics, and called him "out of touch" with both minorities and America's youth, there was also the assessment that Hope proved "time and time again—entertainingly—that he doesn't need his writers around to sound like a comedian, and a great one, too."

Naturally there were some unmentioned subjects that might have given the interview more dimension. One subject avoided was Hope's relationship with the Vietnam POWs. Possibly Murray did not know that Hope was national chairman of the POW–Wives' bracelet campaign, but he must have known about Hope's efforts to free the prisoners and to visit them in Hanoi. Surely he read that Bob and Dolores were part of the entertainment at Nixon's White House homecoming celebration for the POWs. But probably only Dolores knew the depth of Bob's feelings about the length and conditions of their internment in North Vietnam. The day the POWs came home, Hope was sitting on the end of his bed facing the television set and watching prisoners set foot on home soil. When he heard their stoic and tired voices speaking their love for America, he began to weep.

Another event of 1973 that underscores the Hope concept of family, which ranged in his mind from the visionary "family America" down to the more tangible "family Hope," was the manner in which he spent his Fourth of July. On July 2 he had flown to Oklahoma City to pretape the annual *Stars and Stripes Show* for Lee Allen Smith, but he arrived home on July 3 in time for the largest gathering of family in Hope history. Bob had invited every living member of the clan (including Dolores' family) to gather in Los Angeles at his expense for a monster reunion. The children alone, when all were assembled in and around the Moorpark Street estate on July 3, numbered 50. The grandchildren, grandnieces and grandnephews, from Ohio and Illinois and California, were everywhere, running and exploring the grounds, swimming with Uncle Bob, raiding the cookie jars that lined the counter of the formal pantry.

For a full week Bob and Dolores joined the mob on a rented school bus to Disneyland, and the pair were tugged and hugged through half the attractions at the park. Without Bob the gang went to Knotts Berry Farm, the San Diego Zoo, Universal Studios and finally to Olvera Street for an enchilada feast where Dolores sang to them. All in all it was an extraordinary Hope outing. Not the least remarkable part was the fact that Hope knew all their names.

Another indication of Hope's reaching out to family was the time he now spent with Dolores. They were relaxing together in the desert, and Dolores was making more appearances with him than ever before.

What had finally reached Hope's consciousness was the necessity to spend enough "down" time to avoid recurrences of the hemorrhaging blood vessels which would certainly lead to blindness. But that didn't mean he was sitting still. As he said to UPI's Vernon Scott:

"You can't do *that*, when you're living, you've got to live it your way. You just can't say 'I'm going to slouch it out' for the next ten years. I take it easy. I only work about 200–250 days a year out of 365. That's not too much. I have an awful lot of free time."[5] It was more a matter of scheduling; the total time on stage hadn't changed.

But people around him were getting older and wearing out. One of the

most difficult adjustments was forced on him when one of the two women in
his life who kept him glued together decided it was time to quit. His personal
secretary, Marjorie Hughes, had more than earned her retirement. Petite,
seemingly frail and astonishingly efficient, Marjorie Hughes had worked
unstintingly for 31 years as discreet custodian and manager of his private
affairs, guardian of his comedy vaults, sometimes bookkeeper, sometimes
governess to the children as they were growing up.

At her request, the retirement party, held in the living room of the Hopes'
home, consisted of only the people she wanted to see (except a couple of
reporters and a photographer or two). One of the newsmen asked Hope if he
would stand beside her and give her a farewell squeeze.

"This is not my squeezing secretary," Hope said. "I've never even called
her Marjorie—it's always been Miss Hughes and Mr. Hope, like Russia and
China talking together. But seriously, no man's had a better secretary."[6]

Hope had to adjust to her absence, but his pliability, the vaudevillian's
ability to accept any conditions, was well ingrained. After Miss Hughes
there was a disordered succession of secretaries and not one of them could
measure up to Marjorie's conception of how to take care of the man. One of
the successors took a pile of correspondence off her desk one night and
shoved it into a cabinet where it remained for two years. In that correspondence were letters from the White House and from Governor Rockefeller.
But mostly the equilibrium of Miss Hughes' office systems was maintained.

As for the out-front equilibrium, that was a question put to him by Neil
Hickey of *TV Guide*. Hope was asked if he felt that his "consistent candor"
in expressing his personal views had hurt him professionally. Hope said, "I
don't really know. It might. But all you can judge is your popularity. I still
play all the places I always did, and do as good or better than ever. My TV
shows are still one-two-three in the ratings and I'm getting offers that are
unbelievable. So I can only judge it on that."[7]

One of these offers came from Texaco in the fall of that year and he
accepted it gratefully. For the past several years, since the dissolution of his
long-term Chrysler exclusive contract, Hope's comedy specials on TV had
been underwritten in a magazine concept with different sponsors for each
special, and he missed the exclusive product identity and sponsor caressing
he was used to. He was delighted to sign with Benton and Bowles in behalf of
their client, Texaco, Incorporated, to provide seven hours of programming a
year (a minimum of four and a maximum of five comedy specials) for three
years at $3,150,000 a year, plus $250,000 more to do commercials. He was
to be the company's chief spokesman.

Not long after Hope signed the Texaco contract, he was compelled to
share a sad blow with many other Americans. Jack Benny died unexpectedly
of pancreatic cancer. A chapel full of Benny's friends, including some of the
world's most recognized people, mourned him: Henry Fonda, Raymond
Massey, Irene Dunne, Edgar and Candice Bergen, Rosalind Russell, Merle
Oberon, Dinah Shore, Johnny Carson, Danny Thomas, Groucho Marx,
George Jessel, as a sampling, as well as Governor Ronald Reagan, Senators
George Murphy and John Tunney, and all of Jack's radio gang. Mary Benny
had asked Rabbi Edgar Magnin to conduct the service and she asked both

George Burns and Bob Hope to say a few words. Hope was as eloquent as he had ever been:

> How do you say goodbye to a man who is not just a good friend, but a national treasure? It's hard to say no man is indispensable. But it is true just the same that some are irreplaceable . . . Jack had that rare magic—that indefinable something called genius. Picasso had it. Gershwin had it. And Jack was blessed with it. He didn't just stand on the stage . . . he owned it.[8]

A few weeks later Hope had reached the decision that his long-standing co-ownership with NBC of Hope Enterprises ought to end. There had been some differences of late with the network over the corporation's management and concern over its profitability. After negotiations, Hope became sole proprietor. His new independence immediately gave him the opportunity to listen to offers from CBS and ABC, and that leverage resulted in the biggest contract he ever negotiated with NBC—$18 million for the next three years—when the renewal time came up in March 1975.

But it was not all roses. Part of Hope's sales pitch to Texaco and NBC for this big money was a "new look." He would remain as executive producer of very "special specials," each one the product of a different creative mind. Wonderful, Texaco said, and advised Hope to clean house, to fire everyone. This, to the man whose loyalty was as unquestioned as his wealth, was nearly unthinkable. Yet he did it.

Jimmy Saphier was no longer around. A relatively new face in Hope's business life, Bill Eliscu, put the comic and Texaco together; Saphier had been ill.

Hope knew that he should be the one to tell Mort Lachman (with Hope for 28 years), or Lester White (with Hope since vaudeville days) or Norman Sullivan (who was part of the original Pepsodent gang) that they were victims of Texaco's housecleaning. But by the time he got around to saying something to each of them, the news had leaked out and they all heard from other sources. As expected, there was some bitterness. How could Hope break up the old gang? Hope reasoned, "It had to be done, because I thought that, after 25 years, it was time to get a fresh format, some new ideas, a new style." What did Hope mean by a new style? "I mean they'll be all new productions. We'll be changing our format so that each show revolves around a total idea rather than unrelated sketches. They'll be done more in a spectacular style, with different producers for each show. About the only thing that won't change is myself."[9]

At the same time, Hope laid off both his New York and Hollywood publicity offices, Kalmus and Liberman, because he had acquired new publicity support connected with the Texaco deal. (Both Kalmus and Liberman returned to him in 1976, however.) The only person in the Hope organization not replaced at that time was Ward Grant, his personal media relations man, who was handed the thankless task of being the "punching bag" for those Hope veterans on the way out the door, and the "information booth" for all the new people being hired.

Meanwhile, Hope's life was consumed by such a busy schedule that it kept him immune to the turmoil within his organization. He was busy promoting his new book, *The Last Christmas Show*. He was also involved in running his own Desert Classic golf tournament, playing in a dozen other charity tournaments, doing his usual paid personal appearances and benefits. He picked up his twenty-sixth through thirty-first honorary degrees from Florida Southern, Northwood Institute, Norwich University, Bethel College, University of Scranton and Utah State. He also picked up the "Comedian of the Century" award from the National Entertainment Council in Washington, D.C., and the "Best Male Performer" at the People's Choice Awards, by popular vote of television viewers.

One of the smartest things Mort Lachman did for Hope, before he cleaned out his desk and moved over to become producer of *All in the Family*, was to advise the comedian not to tamper with Ogden Nash. Tony's wife, Judy, who was putting together a Wellesley College Building Fund benefit, had arranged for Arthur Fiedler to do a Boston Pops night as a fund-raiser, and got a "yes" from her father-in-law to make an appearance with the venerable maestro. When Hope asked, "What'll we do?" Fiedler sent him by return mail a copy of the Ogden Nash lyrics to Saint-Saëns' *Carnival of the Animals*. Fiedler expected Hope would want to have his writers punch up the Nash verses to his own personal specifications. Hope sent the manuscript over to Lachman and Mort said, "Leave 'em alone. You can't improve on the best."[10]

So on May 5, Hope arrived in Boston with Dolores, Nora and Kelly. Judy arrived with her two tots, Zachary, six, and Miranda, three. Miranda was scheduled to make her theatrical debut with her grandfather in a musical number, "You Must Have Been a Beautiful Baby."

To plug Hope's new commercial backing, and because Hope knew that Fiedler collected fireman's hats, Ward Grant called Chuck Gouret of Benton and Bowles and asked them to find an old Texaco firechief's helmet worn by Ed Wynn. What they came up with was the one worn by Steve McQueen in *The Towering Inferno*.

That night turned out to be pure Hope gold. "I don't know how long Arthur Fiedler's been conducting," Hope told the audience just after his entrance, "but his first job was the victory party after the Battle of Bunker Hill."[11]

For the narration Hope sat on a high stool behind a music stand. He seemed to be enjoying it; he rolled the Nash word-play like "totally turtlely torpor" off his lips with relish. That it was not taped for television—because of Hope's specific request—is unfortunate, and Hope later regretted that stipulation. It was, however, audiotaped and has been broadcast more than once on Public Radio stations.

After the Saint-Saëns piece, there was a Fiedler medley of songs from Hope movies and Broadway shows and then Hope introduced Dolores. "This is the grandmother I sleep with. She's so Catholic she thinks Oral Roberts is a dentist and Norman Vincent Peale is a stripper."[12] Dolores graciously acknowledged the huge welcoming applause and then sang in her appealingly throaty style "On a Clear Day You Can See Forever."

The family affair continued when tiny Miranda came out of the audience to sit next to Bob on the steps leading to center stage. The three-year-old said, "I don't want to win any beauty prizes. I just want to be like you."

Hope's double take fanned the audience's roar. Several times she interrupted her grandfather to ask if she was going to be paid for this appearance. When he didn't respond, she said calmly, "I'm not worried. Both my parents are lawyers."

The next morning, looking over the Boston newspaper coverage of the Pops event, he noticed there were several photos of Miranda and only one of himself. He turned to Ward Grant and said, "Remind me not to work with *her* again."[13]

On October 24, 1975, Hope's first show for Texaco was aired. In keeping with his contract it was a formidable beginning. It was a two-hour show of segments from 25 years of Hope's television shows presenting 97 stars on black-and-white film and color tape, and live studio appearances by Bing Crosby, John Wayne and Frank Sinatra.

Hope said: "When you do a show like this it kills you to leave stuff out but you must. I spent two weeks reading through the old scripts and looking for the best of the 800 or so sketches we've performed over the years. Then, after we made the selections there was the whole matter of clearances. I had to pay every writer and all the performers received a minimum salary."[14]

And what performers he had—legendary stars like Chevalier, Bea Lillie, Ethel Merman, Jimmy Durante, Ernie Kovacs, Jack Benny, Gloria Swanson, Jimmy Cagney and Ed Wynn; enduring stars like Dinah Shore, Rex Harrison, Mickey Rooney, Martha Raye, Betty Grable, Lana Turner, Joan Crawford, Lucille Ball, Steve Allen, Jack Paar, Barbra Streisand, William Holden, Phil Silvers, James Garner, Ginger Rogers, Fernandel, Ken Murray, Shirley MacLaine, Shelley Winters, Natalie Wood, Perry Como, Danny Thomas, Gina Lollobrigida, Fred MacMurray, Andy Williams, Sammy Davis, Jr., Milton Berle and Carol Burnett.

The risky part of such an historical parade is that it inevitably invites comparison. NBC was pleased that both the press notices and the critical reviews of the show were generally positive. Against NBC's wishes but with the blessing of Hope, "A Quarter-Century of Bob Hope on Television" was authorized for advance viewing (minus the last-minute monologue) by the New York media. John J. O'Connor of *The New York Times*, in his October 27, 1975, review, was as insightful as any critic in his appraisal of the message that Bob Hope had assembled to speak for himself as a representation of his contributions to television. After stating bluntly "By any yardstick, Mr. Hope is an extraordinary figure in American show business," O'Connor lamented the fact that the comic's "open courting of the establishment status quo" had blunted his ability to produce more pungent comedy:

> Some proof of this is on display, ironically in tonight's tribute. Almost invariably the material from the earlier TV years is superior stuff. It has more energy, zaniness and pure sass. His familiar routines with Bing Crosby are still marvelous. Too frequently, the later skits rely heavily on extraneous gimmicks, on silly drag costumes, on the mere presence of celebrity.
>
> Still, it can hardly be denied that Bob Hope is a performer of immense stature, an outstanding humanitarian and a very, very funny man. Tonight's highlights are dreadfully uneven, but there

are enough good moments scattered throughout the two hours to
demonstrate splendidly what all the fuss is about.

*I'm pretty sure I'm seventy-five. . . . But I've lied to so
many girls . . . Of course, they find out about one
A.M. . . . That's a joke, Dolores! . . .*[1]

45. A Capital Affair

At age seventy-two, Hope finally got his high school diploma. The comedian
already had 32 honorary degrees "from places I couldn't get into legitimate-
ly," and earlier in 1975 he had been made honorary chancellor of Florida
Southern College in Lakeland. But somehow no one had ever thought of
awarding him an honorary secondary school degree.

Of course, said Hope, "I had to help build the high school." Texaco executive Jack Williams was a long-standing supporter of the Hughen Center for
Crippled Children in Port Arthur, Texas. After he had successfully persuaded Hope to give a benefit concert to raise money for construction of the
nation's very first high school for crippled teenagers, the Hughen officers
and directors decided to name the new facility The Bob Hope High School
for Crippled Children.

The morning after the benefit, Hope was pushing the ceremonial gold-
plated shovel into the site of the new building, when the center's president
Claude Brown surprised him with the school's first diploma. He turned to the
crowd and offered, "Now that we've got a high school for these kids, how
about a college. Could we make these shows an annual affair?"[2] He got a
tremendous hand from his audience but the more skeptical among them
frankly doubted they would ever see him again. They were wrong.

Hope returned to help Hughen three times. The first was to do another
benefit show. Next he organized a regional telethon and conducted it from a
Houston TV station, which netted over a million dollars for the new high
school. Then Bob and Dolores went back to Port Arthur to do a joint concert
at which time the Center broke ground for the Dolores Hope Library.

Hope treasures that high school diploma, but when asked to name the
most prestigious honors of his long career, Hope lists three: the Congressional Gold Medal that Jack Kennedy handed him, the Sylvanus Thayer Award
from West Point, and the Order of the British Empire (CBE) approved by
Queen Elizabeth in the spring of 1976. The Insignia of the Honorary Commander of the Order of the British Empire was conferred on the comedian at
the British Embassy in Washington on July 1, a few days before the culmi-
nation of America's Bicentennial. Standing next to Hope in the formal
reception hall was his friend and former ambassador to the Court of St.
James, Walter Annenberg (receiving a Knight of the British Empire honor),
Dr. Wallace Sterling, chancellor of Stanford University, and Eugene
Ormandy, conductor of the Philadelphia Orchestra. It was a simple ceremo-

ny. The British Ambassador, Sir Peter Ramsbotham, made the presentation, saying that the comedian was "regarded with enormous affection in Britain. His services to British troops around the world during the Second World War, in particular, have never been forgotten by the British people. He has often appeared at Royal Command performances in Britain and is known to be a favorite of the Royal Family."[3]

The next day Hope introduced Gerald Ford at the Kennedy Center gala which was the Capital's official start of the Bicentennial. Hope had initially declined Ford's request because of a conflicting personal appearance. But the President offered to have an Air Force jet standing by to whisk Hope off in time for his concert if he would agree to open the gala.

In fact, Hope was flown all the way back to Los Angeles after his appearance so he could make a fast turnaround—a shower, a change of clothes, pick up Dolores—and back to Washington for two State dinners. The first was the outdoor dinner party Gerald and Betty Ford were hosting for Queen Elizabeth and Prince Philip, and the second, the following night, was the Queen's own dinner party for the Fords at the British Embassy.

That White House spread in the Rose Garden was, according to all media reports, the most elaborate of the Queen's American appearances, with guests like Lady Bird Johnson, Alice Longworth Roosevelt, Telly Savalas (star of the Queen's favorite American TV show), Nelson Rockefeller and Olympic skater Dorothy Hamill. Hope was the Queen's personal choice as entertainer.

The remainder of that Bicentennial year for Hope was fairly standard except for a few favorite events on his schedule, like his personal appearance at the Calgary Stampede in Alberta, or being guest ringmaster at the Ringling Brothers Barnum and Bailey Circus the night of a big Project Hope benefit.

In the fall, when the Thalians asked Hope, Crosby and Lamour if they would consent to be the honored guests at their charity ball in Los Angeles, it seemed a good time to confirm persistent rumors that the three would be reunited in their first movie since 1962. Ben Starr had delivered them a script called *Road to Tomorrow* which called for shooting locations in England, Saudi Arabia and Moscow. At the time Hope said, "I prefer the title *Road to the Fountain of Youth*—but in any case we play ourselves. It starts out with Bing and I taking our grandchildren to the airport, and meeting each other again after all these years. We tell each other how good we're looking at our age, and before you know it, we're on a plane to London and off on another mystery. Of course, along the way we bump into mother, Lamour." Crosby interjected, "We've got to get more lunacy into that script, Rob. When you've got two old guys you've got to do something wild."[4]

Lamour was cautious about all this. She remembered what happened the last time, but now she was better prepared. She and Bill Howard had moved back to Los Angeles, and Dorothy was making a good living again as an actress. Plus, she was being consulted from the start on this project.

There were signs that the new *Road* would be shot in mid-1977 in England, produced by Sir Lew Grade. Crosby had already arranged a summer tour of Europe, kicked off at the London Palladium. Meanwhile Hope agreed to help Bing celebrate his 50 years in show business at a gala tribute televised at Pasadena's Ambassador Auditorium in March. Twelve hundred friends of Bing were seated in the audience watching him sing his final song alone on the stage. He bowed as the crowd gave him a standing ovation. Hope and Crosby's other guest star, Pearl Bailey, had retired to their dressing rooms, letting it be "Bing's night."

As Crosby started to leave the stage, he lost his footing and sagged into a prop wall which masked a twenty-five-foot orchestra pit. Bing's weight was too much for the flimsy retainer and he crashed through to the pit below. Kathryn gasped and rushed to him; Bing was trying to get up, blood dropping from his cut forehead. Neither of them realized that his injuries were more profound than they appeared. From his Huntington Hospital bed the next day, Crosby told Hope, "I gotta change the act and get a new finish."[5]

Bing's accident pushed the prospects of a *Road* filming further into 1977, and because his recovery was so much slower than expected, the picture had to be postponed indefinitely. Hope filled in his schedule with golf and benefit golf tournaments, and interviews and guest television appearances he had been putting off. He picked up his thirty-seventh, thirty-eighth, thirty-ninth and fortieth honorary degrees from St. Anselm's, Benedictine, Western State, and Baldwin-Wallace. In August his seventh book, *The Road to Hollywood*, coauthored with AP's Bob Thomas, was published, and a fat promotion schedule followed.

At every appearance Hope made in August and September, he found some way to plug *The Road to Hollywood*. Inevitably his media encounters focused on his relationship with Crosby. So his mind was full of Bing that October 14 when the telephone rang in his suite at the Waldorf Towers, and he was told that Bing had suffered a heart seizure following a golf game at Madrid's La Moreleja Club and was dead. Hope was stupefied.

He said to Bob Thomas, who asked him for a comment: "I'm supposed to go out to Morristown, New Jersey, tonight to do a show in memory of Hugh Davis, my old friend who died a year ago, also of a heart attack. But I can't do it. I'm going to have to cancel. Do you know that this is the first time I've ever had to do that? I just can't get funny tonight. It's just not in me. I'm going home."[6]

That may have been the first time anyone ever heard Bob Hope say the words, "I'm going home."

He flew to Burbank's Lockheed Airport that afternoon in a private jet. He asked Bill Cosby to replace him at a Tucson, Arizona, engagement the following night. At home he was inundated by requests for a statement. At nearly two o'clock on Saturday morning, striding the periphery of his Toluca Lake estate under the stars, with his dogs "Steele" and "Shadow" trotting along and Ward Grant at his side, Hope searched for words that might convey his impression of Bing. Finally, Hope stopped, turned and headed toward his office. He dictated to Grant:

> The whole world loved Bing with a devotion that not only crossed international boundaries, but erased them. He made the world a single place and through his music, spoke to it in a language that everybody understands . . . the language of the heart. . . .

No matter where you were in the world, because of Bing, every Christmas was white. And because we had him with us . . . it will always seem a little whiter.

The world put Bing on a pedestal. But somehow I don't think he ever really knew it. Bing asked the world, "Going my way?" and we all were. . . .

Yesterday, a heart may have stopped, and a voice stilled, but the real melody Bing sang will linger on as long as there is a phonograph to be played . . . and a heart to be lifted.[7]

Bob and Dolores were two of the thirty people Kathryn Crosby invited to mourn her husband at private services held in St. Paul the Apostle's rectory chapel at six o'clock in the morning of October 18. Kathryn told them Bing was emphatic in his instructions that only the closest of family and friends were to be asked. Although Bob and Bing had drifted apart somewhat after the singer's remarriage and move to Hillsborough in northern California, their closeness had been rekindled in recent years. Bing's will, signed in June 1977, was specific about wanting Hope at his burial service.

In less than ten days, Hope was scheduled to present as part of his Texaco "special specials," a show called "The Road to Hollywood" designed to plug his new book and to present highlights of his movie career from 1938 to 1972. It occurred to him that he ought to do a show dedicated to Crosby's memory, so he scrapped the format, which was nearly complete, and substituted another script that focused on the *Road* pictures and Bing's contribution to movies and television. It was called "On the Road With Bing" and, quite predictably, it turned out to be one of the most endearing and popular television specials Hope ever produced.

When one world-famous figure dies, there is always an urgency to make sure that other living legends are shown adequate appreciation before it's too late. Almost every organization that Hope was connected with expected to celebrate his seventy-fifth birthday in May of 1978 in some very special way. But the prize must go to a man in Wampum, Pennsylvania, who had a different kind of dream. He couldn't afford to throw a birthday party for Hope because he was too poor; but he had a plan to inform the nation about Bob's seventy-fifth birthday. His one claim to fame was that he was, according to the *Guinness Book of Records,* the "world champion hitchhiker." His name was DeVon Smith and in 1974 he had criss-crossed the nation getting signatures on a huge "Happy Birthday America" card which he presented to President Ford at the White House on the Bicentennial. His *Guinness* record claimed he traveled 11,000 miles to amass the 21,868 signatures for that Bicentennial card.

In the early fall of 1977, Smith had appeared one day in the editorial offices of the *Daily Trojan,* on the University of Southern California campus, and announced he would begin his signature collection for the Bob Hope birthday card then and there. The newspaper staff thought him a bit odd, but he spoke sensibly. He resembled a modern Johnny Appleseed, they thought, and so they gave him some publicity to help him to get the 1,106 signatures at USC and launch his tour.

"I'll be traveling about 17,000 miles a month for the next few months to 49 states. I hitchhike and sleep on Greyhound buses and eat one meal a day—breakfast—so I can get 100,000 signatures for Bob's birthday."

DeVon proved to be resourceful. Before he left Los Angeles he found his way into several film studios where he got 35 movie and television personalities to be the first celebrities to sign Hope's birthday card.[8]

Some of those same stars had been signed up to take part in a special birthday salute on April 3, 1978, this one for Oscar. Howard Koch, president of the Motion Picture Academy and producer of the Oscar ceremony, asked Hope if he would return to the role he had played so adroitly for so many years, as single master of ceremonies of a whopping 50th Anniversary celebration of the Academy Awards.

The stage setting for this gala at the Dorothy Chandler Pavilion was a multi-leveled gold staircase emblazoned with the names of previous Oscar winners. As the curtains parted, standing at various levels of those stairs were some of the outstanding recipients of gold statuettes through the years.

As Hope's name was announced, and he stepped gingerly down the steep staircase, he passed Fred Astaire, Michael Caine, Kirk Douglas, Joan Fontaine, Greer Garson, Mark Hamill, Goldie Hawn, William Holden, Walter Matthau, Jack Nicholson, Gregory Peck, Eva Marie Saint, Maggie Smith, Barbara Stanwyck, Cecily Tyson, Jon Voight, Raquel Welch and Natalie Wood. Hope said:

> Hey, can you believe this group . . . All on the same stage at the same time . . . It looks like a clearance sale at the Hollywood Wax Museum . . . All Oscar winners. I'm the only one who had to show my American Express Card to get on stage . . . Anyway, good evening and welcome to the real *Star Wars*. . . .[9]

Vanessa Redgrave caught the sidebar headlines that night because she used her moment in the spotlight to blast "militant Zionist hoodlums," and to espouse her political views. Hope held his tongue. There was no need to say what the audience also felt. But all in all it was a night of rich sentiment and memories.

A little less than two months later, another birthday party—Hope's seventy-fifth—was getting under way in Washington, D.C. It happened there because the USO wanted to salute Bob on his birthday on behalf of the armed forces. Hope liked that idea, providing the occasion could become a benefit for the building fund of the proposed USO World Headquarters in the Capital. Of all the seventy-fifth birthday proposals Hope had listened to during the previous year, this one made the most sense. Besides, the new headquarters would bear the name "The Bob Hope U.S.O. Center" and part of the new complex, other than office space and a theater, would house a museum area displaying a segment of Hope's vast collection of GI memorabilia.

From that point on the birthday concept mushroomed. Hope, NBC and Texaco immediately saw the production potential of a black-tie gala at the Kennedy Center. They envisioned a roster of big-name talent entertaining the comedian, who would sit back and enjoy it all as a spectator. James Lipton and Gerald Rafshoon were executive producers, and Bob Wynn was signed to produce and direct a three-hour animated birthday card headlined by Pearl Bailey, Lucille Ball, George Burns, Sammy Davis, Jr., Redd Foxx, Eliott Gould, Alan King, Dorothy Lamour, Carol Lawrence, Fred MacMurray, the Muppets, Donny and Marie Osmond, Telly Savalas, George C. Scott, Elizabeth Taylor, Danny Thomas and John Wayne, plus a dozen other variety acts. Both Kathryn Crosby and Dolores Hope would have segments all their own, and the evening would have a national blessing in the person of Jimmy Carter (on film).

But that serenade by the nation's superstar entertainers at the Kennedy Center was only one part of the proceedings. The two-day affair officially began at noon on May 24 when Bob and Dolores were honored at a luncheon hosted by a large contingent of Congressional wives. Later that afternoon they were limousined to the White House to join a five o'clock reception in the East Room, where 500 guests from Washington and Hollywood upper circles were gathered. Jimmy Carter, his wife Rosalynn and daughter Amy were waiting to greet them. When Bob and Dolores were escorted in, the President asked them to stand at his side and then took over as top banana.

> I've been in office 489 days . . . In three weeks more I'll have stayed in the White House as many times as Bob Hope has . . . Bob has a second career, making commercials. But it's not true that he sold Pepsodent to George Washington . . . We all know *he* had wooden teeth . . . He was a Lemon Pledge man. . . .[10]

Carter commended Hope for his patriotism, his "healing sense of humor," and for his caring about the GI. Hope thanked Carter and cautioned him about being "too funny," then said:

> I've never seen so many freeloaders in my life . . . What a kick it is to shake hands with the President and the First Lady . . . Thank you, President and Mrs. Carter, for loaning us your house . . . God knows, we paid for it. . . .[11]

The *Washington Star*, used to covering its fair share of political and entertainment celebrities, felt constrained to comment on the mega-power of the patrons and patronesses associated with the two-day Hope birthday tribute. Some of the names on that long and impressive list were Vice President and Mrs. Mondale, former President and Betty Ford, Mrs. Bing Crosby, General Omar Bradley, Mamie Eisenhower (who sent a glowing telegram to Bob), Averell Harriman, Henry Kissinger, George Meany, the Nelson Rockefellers, W. Clement Stone and Cyrus Vance. The *Star* pointed out with particular relish that conservative Barry Goldwater's name was immediately followed on the list by less-than-conservative newspaper publisher Katharine Graham. It was so mixed a group of bedfellows that no one could call it a Republican birthday party.

Media people were in close pursuit as Bob and Dolores left that White House reception for Alexandria, Virginia, where the Hopes were throwing their own party to thank the crowd of celebrities appearing in the three-hour gala the next night. Bob had arranged to take over Peter's Place, a fashionable dining spot owned by Dolores' sister's son, Peter Malatesta, a former aide of Spiro Agnew.

Dolores' original list of 30 or 40 close friends had grown and grown. The Hopes kept adding people until it reached a tightly packed 210 "close friends and family" to be seated in the main room for an Italian meal. Hope invited the media people to sit down with them, too. There was something warm and godfatherish about the scene, a marvelous clan gathering with all the love and the deference for the patriarch.

Murphy and Fred MacMurray were probably the only ones in the room besides Dolores who remembered Bob's cocky arrogance in those early Broadway days. Dorothy Lamour went back a long way with Hope, too. She had come to Washington, despite the recent death of her husband, because "nothing could have kept her away."

A five-star general, Omar Bradley, sat on the sidelines in his wheelchair with General William Westmoreland, reminding him how fast Hope had charged through Europe and North Africa during World War II.

Carrot-haired Lucille Ball and raucous Phyllis Diller were discussing Hope as their leading man as only two comediennes could. And the presence of people like Senator John Warner and his wife, the beauteous Elizabeth Taylor, emphasized Hope's intimacy with shakers and movers along the Potomac.

One of Bob's favorite comedians, Mark Russell, the only pre-planned entertainer at that party, said it best when he got up to face the group. "Bob, somewhere tonight in Hollywood there is a tourist from Alexandria, Virginia, wondering where all the stars are."[12]

At the close of the dinner party, when Hope stood up to acknowledge all the love that was being radiated for his benefit, he could not bring himself to be serious. Pearl Bailey had sung special lyrics that began "Hello, Bobby" to the tune of "Hello Dolly"; Dolores had sung "S'Wonderful"; Mayor Mann had presented Hope with the keys to Alexandria (to join the 500 other city and town keys on display in the Hope Museum), and Bob was asked to cut the first of a number of special cakes presented to him in the next 24 hours. "I'm pretty sure I'm seventy-five. But I've lied to so many girls. Of course they always find out about one A.M.—Dolores!—that's a joke!"[13]

It was the following morning that turned the trick, that caused tears to well up and roll down to his famous jaw. And it was an event, scheduled for ten o'clock, that he thought was too early. "Can't we make it eleven?" he asked Ward Grant, who had been coordinating his Washington schedule. But Grant just looked at his boss, thinking that when Congress decides to pay an unusual tribute to an entertainer on the floor of the House, it's a rare event; but when they plan to devote a full hour to this tribute, then somehow, Bob, ten o'clock is not too early.

Just before ten, Bob and Dolores, Linda and Nora (without their husbands because both were in the process of legal separation), Tony and Judy, Kelly, four grandchildren, his one remaining brother, Fred, with LaRue, were ushered into VIP seats in the House of Representatives gallery. He fully expected to hear a resolution passed commending his humanitarian acts, because that is what he had been told. He was certainly not prepared for the unconventional behavior during the next 50 minutes.

After the morning prayer, Speaker "Tip" O'Neill recognized Congressman Paul Findley of Illinois who said in a stentorian, congressional voice: "Mister Speaker: Today is the seventy-fifth birthday celebration of Bob Hope, the greatest humorist of this century. But we are not celebrating just Mister Hope's humor today. Instead, we are taking time to express our deep gratitude on behalf of the American people for his consistent willingness over the years to contribute countless hours serving his country and worthy charities." In his gallery seat Hope listened quietly to Findley's rhetoric:

> He is a great physician. He has eased the pain of inflation and taxes, something no member of this House has ever done.
> He never hurt anyone, except when we laughed too hard.
> Christmas away from home, whether in the cold reaches of Germany during World War II, or the sweltering heat of Vietnam years later, was still enjoyable and memorable to millions of American men and women because Bob Hope was there. . . .[14]

Findley finally yielded the floor to Congressman Schulze of Pennsylvania who compared Hope to Adlai Stevenson's definition of patriotism which is "the tranquil and steady dedication of a lifetime." Schulze yielded to Jim Wright of Texas:

> I would not want to suggest Bob Hope has been entertaining American troops a long time, but it seems only fair to report that there is no other entertainer who has fan letters from Lexington and Concord. . . .
> We in Congress especially thank you for helping us laugh at ourselves. We had darned well better. If we did not, we would be the only ones in America who were not.[15]

Wright yielded to Guyer of Ohio who struck a more serious note:

> While we were lighting our Christmas trees, Bob was on the other side of the world, lighting the hearts, faces and spirits of thousands of scared, lonely homesick servicemen and women who often wondered if anyone cared. . . .
> When others were down on America, Hope was up on it. . . .[16]

Guyer yielded to majority whip Brademas of Indiana who paid tribute to the *Road* pictures as "one of America's great contributions to modern humor." From Brademas to Congresswoman Pettis of California who lauded the extraordinary fund-raising efforts of the Hopes.

From Pettis the floor went to Congresswoman Oakar of Cleveland, who got laughs by thanking Hope for sticking by the Cleveland Indians through thick and thin.

Findley then recognized Wydler of New York who electrified the proceedings with this remark: "I am going to violate the House rules and address a comment to our distinguished guest."

O'Neill spoke up quickly: "The gentleman is aware of the rules?"

"I am aware of the rules," replied Wydler. "On behalf of the people in my district, Bob, and of the people of America, just this one sentence sums up our feelings toward you, and that is, 'Thanks for the Memories.' "[17] Sustained applause.

When it was quiet, Wydler yielded to Moakley of Massachusetts who said, "It is against the rules to sing in the House, so I would just like to take the song 'Thanks for the Memories,' and recite a parody I have written around it, and just address it to our guests today. In doing so, I am saving the Members, I am sure, a little bit of strain on their ears." The best of his lyrics came near the close:

> Thanks for the memories
> Of golf with Tip and Ford,
> None of us ignored,
> It sure took guts to sink those putts
> Which showed how well you scored
> How lovely it was.

> With the Republicans at the White House
>   you've feasted,
> With the Democrats at the White House
>   you fasted,
> Now Carter's here
> Serving Billy Beer.
> And thanks for the memories
> Of road trips that were fun
> That kept Bing on the run,
> We're very glad you got to make
> The road to Washington,
> We thank you so much.[18]

There was a long stretch of applause. Hope was laughing.

Claude Pepper of Florida inspired sounds of "Hear—Hear—Hear!" when he looked up at the gallery and said, "Bob, if you want to endear yourself further to everybody in the House, just assure us before you leave that you will not run against any of us."[19]

And so it went; to Congressman Wylie of Ohio, to Sikes of Florida, to McClory of Illinois, Harkin of Iowa, Montgomery of Mississippi, Rousselot of California, Glickman of Kansas, and Stratton of New York.

Congressman Boland of Massachusetts reminded his colleagues that Dolores had a birthday two days before Bob and everybody applauded her.

The penultimate member to be recognized was minority whip Robert Michel who broke the second and probably most stringent House rule by singing:

> Thanks for the memories,
> Of places you have gone
> To cheer our soldiers on,
> The President sent Kissinger
> But you sent Jill St. John
> We thank you so much!

Seventy plus five is now your age, Bob,
We're glad to see you still upon the stage, Bob,
We hope you make a decent living wage, Bob,
For the more you make—
The more we take![20]

The applause was interrupted by Findley's request that the House recognize Speaker O'Neill, and O'Neill's utter amazement at the infraction of the time-honored custom in one of the nation's oldest institutions, was perhaps, one of Hope's finest accolades:

> I explain to our guests, particularly, that singing in the House, and speaking in a foreign language, are not customary in the House.
>
> Also, you may be interested to know that in my 25 years in Congress, and I know there are members senior to me here, never before have I ever witnessed anything of this nature.
>
> The rules say that nobody can be introduced from the gallery, and that rule cannot be waived. Presidents' wives and former Presidents merely sit there. I have seen distinguished visitors, who have come to the House, sit in the galleries, but never before have I seen anything compared to what is transpiring on the floor today.
>
> It is a show of appreciation, of love and affection to a great American, and I think it is a beautiful tribute.[21]

O'Neill ended his remarks with "He is a fine American, he is a great American, he is an all-American. Happy birthday, Bob Hope." The members stood and sang "Happy Birthday," and when they finished they continued to stand, looking up at him, applauding. Hope was standing too, and his eyes glistened. Dolores at his side faced him applauding. Both Linda and Nora were crying, too. But they all were applauding, Kelly, Fred, LaRue and the grandchildren. All in all, it isn't offered any citizen to have much better than that.

I watched Paleface *on television the other night. Sometimes I get a feeling I've a son I never met.*[1]

TAG
One More Time

When Congress has risen to its feet for you in an unprecedented, rule-shattering "happening" on the House floor; when the President of the United States, Jimmy Carter, has sanctioned your national birthday party; when 24 of your colleagues like John Wayne, Elizabeth Taylor, George

Burns, Lucille Ball, Pearl Bailey—and even Miss Piggy—have come to sing your praises, when Gerald and Betty Ford, Rosalynn Carter and the cream of Washington society give you a standing ovation for your 75-year life on the road—what do you do for an encore, Bob?

You could walk on the moon, except you know the moon shuttle hasn't started running yet, and moon rocks don't applaud. You could always direct a film—you frequently tell media people it's one of your lifetime goals. You could finally achieve that important recognition for your cinematic art which you and others feel is overdue. Or, you could break yet another barrier and set yet another record by being the first American performer allowed to create an entertainment special for television in the People's Republic of China. You can't decide between the last two choices—so you pick both.

A little less than a year after his birthday salute in Washington, Hope was invited to be the honoree of a tribute to his film career sponsored by the prestigious Film Society of Lincoln Center in New York City. It was the dream child of Film Society director Joanne Koch who got the idea as she was watching a Dick Cavett–Woody Allen interview on the Public Television Service one night. About that show, Cavett said: "I steered the conversation to Hope and recalled a private conversation with Woody years earlier, in which he had done an appreciative cadenza on Hope's greatness as a screen comic. Carefully separating his adulation of Hope's screen work from Hope's TV shows (and political views) Allen praised him again in immaculately worded encomia, allowing how it would be fun to edit the body of Hope's film work into segments illustrating his admiration of Hope's screen talent in its many parts."[2]

At Koch's urging that is exactly what Allen did. He edited and narrated a 63-minute compilation of clips from 17 Hope films of the 1938–1954 period, including cuts from five *Road* pictures and generous portions of *The Lemon Drop Kid*, *Monsieur Beaucaire*, *My Favorite Brunette*, *Son of Paleface*, and *Fancy Pants*. Allen titled his tribute, *My Favorite Comedian*.

Cavett, as master of ceremonies of the event, welcomed nearly 3,000 show business, financial and political celebrities to Lincoln Center's Avery Fisher Hall, and explained that although Woody had been happy to create the film tribute and narrate it, he could not come to the theater because such big events made him "break out in a rash."

But Allen's voice was there, and during a Hope–Crosby camel scene from *Road to Morocco*, he said, "I saw this film in 1941 when I was only seven years old, but I knew from that moment on what I wanted to do with my life."[3] When a scene from Hope's 1947 film *Where There's Life* came up, Woody was heard saying, "a woman's man, a coward's coward and always brilliant." Allen added to his tribute a scene from one of his own films, *Love and Death*, to show specifically how Hope's style had influenced his own.

Cavett said it was time to rectify a "slight artistic wrong" done to Hope by neglecting his talents as an actor. He suggested that Hope had been taken for granted because, like Rex Harrison, he "makes what is terribly difficult look so easy that it is underrated."[4]

Hope was truly pleased as he took the stage to say a few words, and there was a wisp of nostalgia in his voice: "I enjoyed it. I'd forgotten—we did so much ad-libbing."[5]

This event inspired a number of reevaluations of Hope's movie career including one by *The New York Times* critic Jeffrey Couchman who esteemed Hope as a "first-rate comic actor and a man worthy of a respected place in film history," but felt the reason Hope never received the same critical acceptance afforded other movie comics like Chaplin, W.C. Fields and Groucho Marx was that Hope "never created a consistent character of grandiose proportions."[6] One could argue successfully that except for Chaplin, Fields and Marx, no other film comic has sustained (through at least 30 films of his golden period) such a unified comic persona. Hope spoofed the same things they did—lechery, cowardice, vanity, greed and the other common targets of sterling comedy—but he did it without a duck-walk, painted-on moustache or funny hat. No tricks of voice, no dialects or ethnic characterizations—he was always Bob Hope.

His dumb wise guy, his reluctant hero, his bragging coward are all parts of the genus "wise fool," the oldest and most persistent comic type in American humor. When he brags about his courage, or his looks, or his sexual powers, or his brains, we laugh because we see our own braggadocio in him. When he takes a pratfall we know we're in for the same thing. His appeal, his averageness is the reason in the forties and fifties people flocked to see his movies. That's also why television stations across the country still program them so frequently. And why youngsters continue to send mail to "Bob Hope, Paramount Studios, Hollywood." It's also probably why China's Ministry of Culture asked Hope to conduct an acting seminar and to bring some of his middle-period films when the comedian paid his historic visit there in 1979.

The Road to China was not the last *Road* that Hope would present to an American viewing audience, but it was one of his most memorable. He waited longer for official sanction to take this road than he had for his trip to Russia in 1957, and he paid more money ($1,700,000) for the privilege of making this show than his or any other production company had paid for a television variety show.

Hope began badgering Henry Kissinger at private gatherings as early as 1973 about wanting to be the first entertainer to do a variety show in China, and he offered to improve his Ping-Pong game if that would help.

Hope persevered quietly for six years before he was finally granted permission to tape a show in China for American TV. "The only way I could get the green light," said Hope, "was to agree to give them world rights after we had shown it the first time."[7]

When that green light flashed in 1979, Hope recognized the enormity of the undertaking and asked Jim Lipton, who had put together the complex three-hour Washington birthday salute, and his own daughter Linda, whom he believed ready for her big production break, to act as co-executive producers, and asked Bob Wynn to produce and direct at the line level.

Saturday, June 16, 1979, Bob and Dolores, Jim and Hedakai Lipton, two Hope writers, Gig Henry and Bob Mills, Hope's masseur Dale Hofstetler, makeup man Don Marando, and a few other technicians stepped off the plane at Peking's airport. It was not your typical Hope airport arrival with eager crowds, a brass band, pom-pom girls and a big news conference.

"There was a group of Japanese diplomats on our plane when we got off," said Dolores, "and we were pushed aside as the diplomats were greeted.

While they were bowing, we kind of sneaked around and I turned to Bob and said, 'How does it feel to be ignored?' It was the first time in many, many years that I have been with Bob and nobody looked at him. We had a lot of laughs about it."[8]

Hope's anonymity continued, at least for the entire next week while Hope scouted locations in Peking and Shanghai, while he was entertained at luncheon by Ambassador Leonard Woodcock, went shopping along Liu Li Change—a winding alley of ramshackle shops with lace-curtained windows—while he took a stroll through Tian An Men Square swinging his golf club, and certainly when he was driven the fifty miles northwest of Peking to see the Great Wall.

But once his American cast had arrived, one that included ballet superstar Mikhail Baryshnikov, mimists Robert Shields and Lorene Yarnell, country music singer Crystal Gale, soul singers Peaches and Herb, and Big Bird from *Sesame Street*, and they began taping at various landmarks around Peking, crowds gathered to gape and to follow them.

It was a rich and varied experience for Hope and what he showed Americans on that three-hour telecast reflected it. One particular segment, taped at famous Democracy Wall, was censored by the Chinese government. That piece of tape was smuggled out but never used on the show. Hope respected the Ministry's explicit caution that Hope make no political references in his jokes. "In my monologue at the Wall," Hope said, "I had one Mao-Tai and my head felt like the Gang of Four, but the Ministry asked me to take it out. So we changed it to 'I felt like my head was going through a cultural revolution' but they snipped that for being too political."[9]

The Hopes remained in China a month, the longest trip Bob and Dolores had been on together in many, many years. They were thrilled with almost everything they saw and did except the banqueting. "This place is a front for Alka-Seltzer," he said as he and Dolores would head for a quiet evening of bread, butter and milk in their hotel room.[10]

Los Angeles Times television critic Cecil Smith who, through 30 seasons of Hope TV specials, had been one of the comedian's severest and most perceptive arbiters, wrote an exceptionally long and detailed review of "Bob Hope on the Road to China." He described the show as a "huge sprawling vaudeville" and was impressed with Hope's vitality. He observed that not all of Hope's topicality delighted the Chinese and said tellingly:

> Hope with that tentative grin on his face waited for the interpreter to finish like a little kid waiting for a balloon. When the audience laughed, he moved right on, when it didn't, he seemed at a loss. Eager as a young comic facing his first audience. At 76! With his money![11]

To say that with so much surprise is not to really know the quintessential Bob Hope for whom applause was the simplest of motivations. At seventy-six! at sixty-six! at eighty-six! the same. To tell more jokes (even though the writing quality seemed inferior recently), to win new votes (China, for example, or the fact that teenage readers of *Seventeen* magazine in 1979 voted him their most admired personality), to sell more products in 1979 (reengaged by Texaco as national spokesman, and hired by California Federal Savings as its local credibility figure on radio and television), to win more awards (in a single week in 1980 Hope was honored by the Catholics, Jews, Salvation Army, Motion Picture Pioneers, the USO and the Air National Guard), to be remembered (the Bob Hope Museum which would house the memorabilia of a lifetime), to freshen his continuing love affair with the American public (in the May 27, 1981, issue of weekly *Variety* Hope's 30-year Nielsen national audience ratings were published and he was declared the all-time champion, an "unparalleled record of ratings achievement for a man of any age and none the less astonishing despite the fact that his appeal has begun to slide a bit in the past decade").

To characterize the staying power one last time, to illustrate his sheer physical stamina which comes purely from attitude, one has to look at the events of September 1980:

—On Labor Day night, in Universal Amphitheater, which usually features rock stars, the comedian made his first hard-ticket live appearance in Los Angeles since he did *Roberta* at the Philharmonic in 1939. Les Brown and Diahann Carroll warmed up the huge crowd, which rose to its feet when Hope entered, and stayed up long enough for Hope to see who had shown up. There was Ken Murray, who had helped bail him out that first Sunday night at the Palace in 1932; there was Fred MacMurray, Eve Arden, Martha Raye, Lamour, and several other former leading ladies plus a guest list of contemporary movie and TV personalities three pages long. Two new generations of Hopes watched Grandpop cavort and Grandma Dolores make her local stage debut. The show ran for five nights, drawing respectable crowds each night.

—On September 8, Bob and Dolores, together with their friends the Clark Cliffords, the Stuart Symingtons and the Alex Spanos, took off on a significant "road" to Moscow; to St. Andrews, Scotland and Eltham, England. Bob had been asked to entertain the American community in Moscow because U.S. diplomats and their families were feeling a bit "hangdog and lonely" because of the recent strain in United States–Soviet relations. Ambassador Tom Watson threw a party at Spasso House for 380 people with Bob and Dolores providing the entertainment. Because it was an election year the Carter–Reagan jokes were perhaps the crowd favorites:

> . . . Jimmy Carter is hoping Billy is born again, and he comes back as Ronald Reagan's brother. . . .
> . . . I was hoping Reagan would pick Charlton Heston for his vice presidential running mate . . . we need a miracle. . . .[12]

—On September 22, Hope got a very special feeling when he arrived back in England for the opening at Epsom, Surrey, of the Bob Hope British Classic—a golf tournament that would be an annual event to benefit spastic children—and for a new performing arts center in his birthplace, Eltham.

When he drove up to the front door of the south London row house, at 44 Craighton Road, his arrival had been pre-announced and there were media and a gallery of fans in the street. He went inside and had tea with the current residents, John and Florence Ching.

Later Alex Spanos asked Hope if at any time as a child he had dreamed about being anything like what he had become.

"Sure. When I went to the movies. I even wrote a poem as a kid about a dream I had about the circus."

"Do you remember it?"

"No. It turned up a few years ago in Cleveland when Ringling Brothers asked for circus memorabilia to be put into a time capsule that would be opened in 2075. I must have written it at Fairmount Grammar School as a class project."

Later that day the famous Hope memory was pushed to come up with a close approximation of the original:

I dreamed I was a circus clown
I wore a funny suit
My shoes were blue, my nose was red
I had a horn to toot.

But when I tried to take a step
My feet refused to move.
I looked down to see the cause
A lion held me in his paws.

I asked him please to let me go,
He growled and moved away
"I'll let you free to do a show,
And come again another day."[13]

Afterwords and Acknowledgments

The debt owed many people who helped shape this biography of Bob Hope is sizeable. Although 20 years of association with Hope made researching his life easier, it would have not been possible without help from his family, his lifelong friends, and numerous associates who shared impressions and supplied anecdotes.

As I sifted through thousands of bits of data concerning this most public of men, I encountered more than one version of certain episodes in his life, and when variance appeared I allowed conversations and interviews with Hope to predominate.

When I credit beginnings, it was my late mother Winnie who used to say, "You ought to write a book," and more recently my father Lloyd reminded me.

But more concretely, these are my tributes:

To three University of Southern California colleagues, Professors Walter Fisher and Kenneth Owler Smith and Professor Emeritus Theodore Kruglak, for guiding the doctoral thesis from which this book grew.

To Mildred Rosequist Brod, who shared most generously her memories and memorabilia of the early Cleveland years; Mrs. Bill Howard (Dorothy Lamour) for being such a wise "girl in the middle" on all those "Roads"; Marjorie Hughes, whose sage counsel and acute perception improved my judgement; Mildred MacArthur Serrano, for her sensitive observations about the Hope family; dear Marjorie Thayer who gave so unstintingly her editorial skills and her encouragement.

To these among Hope's close professional associates: producer-writer Mort Lachman, and veteran Hope writers Lester White and Charlie Lee, who offered incomparable portraitures of the man; Ward Grant, for insightful guidance through Hope's public and media relationships; Howard Miller, for sharing 20 years of Hope's USO activities; Alan Calm, for recalling Hope's early Broadway years; Charles Cirillo, for reliving life on the vaudeville circuit.

Special thanks to Fred Hope for illuminating early family years, and to Wyn Hope for a rare perspective and for sharing her late husband's book, *Mother Had Hopes*.

To Eve Arden, Paul Bailey, Herb Ball, Les Brown, Norma Brown, Sil Caranchini, Frank Carrall, Ann Charles, Jerry and Flo Colonna, Mary Davis, Fred de Cordova, Nancy Gordon, Gig Henry, Robert Hussey, Allan Kalmus, Sam Kaufman, Maggie Klier, Betty Lanigan, Frank Liberman, Barney

379

McNulty, Joe Morella, Onnie Morrow, Gary Null, Johnny Pawlek, Paul Pepe, Jerry Raboy, Earline Richmond, Henry Rieger, Joe and Barbara Saltzman, Dee Shidler, Bob Thomas, Sandra Tonsing, Lady Carolyn Townshend and Earl Ziegler.

Finally, to my friend Gil Parker for his vision; Robert Lescher for his confidence; Nancy Perlman at Putnam; and Diane Reverand, a superb editor.

Filmography

SHORT COMEDIES

Going Spanish (Educational Films, 1934) Cast: Bob Hope and Leah Ray. Directed by Al Christe. Screenplay by William Watson and Art Jarrett.

Paree, Paree (Warner Brothers, 1934) Cast: Bob Hope (as Peter Forbes), Dorothy Stone, Charles Collins, Lorraine Collier, Billie Leonard. Directed by Roy Mack. Screenplay by Cyrus Wood (based on a musical *Fifty Million Frenchmen* by Herbert Fields, E. Ray Goetz and Cole Porter).

The Old Grey Mayor (Warner Brothers, 1935) Cast: Bob Hope, Ruth Blasco, Lionel Stander, Sam Wren, George Watts. Directed by Lloyd French. Screenplay by Herman Ruby.

Watch the Birdie (Warner Brothers, 1935) Cast: Bob Hope, Neil O'Day, Arline Dintz, Marie Nordstrom, George Watts. Directed by Lloyd French. Screenplay by Dolph Singer and Jack Henley.

Double Exposure (Warner Brothers, 1935) Cast: Bob Hope, Johnny Berkes, Jules Epailley, Loretta Sayers. Directed by Lloyd French. Screenplay by Burnet Hershey and Jack Henley.

Calling All Tars (Warner Brothers, 1936) Cast: Bob Hope, Johnny Berkes, Oscar Ragland. Directed by Lloyd French. Screenplay by Jack Henley and Burnet Hershey.

Shop Talk (Warner Brothers, 1936) Cast: Bob Hope. Directed by Lloyd French. Screenplay by Burnet Hershey and Jack Henley.

FEATURE FILMS

The Big Broadcast of 1938 (Paramount, 1938) Cast: Bob Hope (as Buzz Fielding), W.C. Fields, Martha Raye, Dorothy Lamour, Shirley Ross, Lynn Overland, Ben Blue, Leif Erikson, Grace Bradley, Rufe Davis, Kirsten Flagstad, Tito Guizar, Lionel Pape, Dorothy Howe, Russell Hicks, Leonid Kinskey, Patricia ("Honey Chile") Wilder, Shep Fields and his orchestra. Directed by Mitchell Leisen. Produced by Harlan Thompson. Screenplay by Walter De Leon, Francis Martin and Ken Englund, based on a story by Frederick Hazlitt Brennan, adapted by Howard Lindsay and Russell Crouse.

College Swing (Paramount, 1938) Cast: Bob Hope (as Bub Brady), Gracie Allen, George Burns, Martha Raye, Edward Everett Horton, Florence George, Ben Blue, Betty Grable, Jackie Coogan, John Payne, Cecil Cunningham, Robert Cummings, Jerry Colonna, Tully Marshall. Directed by Raoul Walsh. Produced by Lewis Gensler. Screenplay by Walter De Leon and Francis Martin, adaptation by Frederick Hazlitt Brennan of an idea by Ted Lesser.

Give Me a Sailor (Paramount, 1938) Cast: Bob Hope (as Jim Brewster), Martha Raye, Betty Grable, Jack Whiting, Clarence Kolb, Nana Bryant, Emerson Treacy, Kathleen Lockhart, Bonnie Jean Churchill, Ralph Sanford, Edward Earle. Directed by Elliott Nugent. Produced by Jeff Lazarus. Screenplay by Doris Anderson and Frank Butler, based on a play by Anne Nichols.

Thanks for the Memory (Paramount, 1938) Cast: Bob Hope (as Steve Merrick), Shirley Ross, Charles Butterworth, Otto Kruger, Hedda Hopper, Laura Hope Crews, Emma Dunn, Roscoe Karns, Eddie "Rochester" Anderson, Edward Gargan, Jack Norton, Patricia ("Honey Chile") Wilder, William Collier, Sr. Directed by George Archinbaud. Produced by Mel Shauer (associate). Screenplay by Lynn Starling, based on Albert Hackett and Frances Goodrich's play *Up Pops The Devil*.

Never Say Die (Paramount, 1939) Cast: Bob Hope (as John Kidley), Martha Raye, Ernest Cossart, Paul Harvey, Siegfried Rumann, Andy Devine, Alan Mowbray. Directed by Elliot Nugent. Produced by Paul Jones. Screenplay by Don Hartman, Frank Butler and Preston Sturges, based on the play by William H. Post.

Some Like It Hot (Renamed *Rhythm Romance*) (Paramount, 1939) Cast: Bob Hope (as Nicky Nelson), Shirley Ross, Gene Krupa and Orchestra, Una Merkel, Rufe Davis, Bernard Nedell, Wayne "Tiny" Whitt, Harry Barris, Frank Sully, Clarence H. Wilson, Dudley Dickerson, Richard Denning, Pat West, Lillian Fitzgerald, Sam Ash. Directed by George Archinbaud. Produced by William C. Thomas (associate). Screenplay by Lewis R. Foster and Wilkie C. Mahoney, based on the play by Ben Hecht and Gene Fowler.

The Cat and the Canary (Paramount, 1939) Cast: Bob Hope (as Wally Hampton), Paulette Goddard, John Beal, Douglass Montgomery, Gale Sondergaard, Nydia Westman, George Zucco, Willard Robertson, Elizabeth Patterson. Directed by Elliot Nugent. Produced by Arthur Hornblow, Jr. Screenplay by Walter De Leon and Lynn Starling, based on the John Willard play.

Road to Singapore (Paramount, 1940) Cast: Bob Hope (as Ace Lannigan), Bing Crosby, Dorothy Lamour, Anthony Quinn, Charles Coburn, Jerry Colonna. Directed by Victor Schertzinger. Produced by Harlan Thompson. Screenplay by Frank Butler and Don Hartman, based on a story by Harry Hervey.

The Ghostbreakers (Paramount, 1940) Cast: Bob Hope (as Larry Lawrence), Paulette Goddard, Richard Carlson, Anthony Quinn, Paul Lukas, Willie Best, Pedro De Cordoba. Directed by George Marshall. Produced by Arthur Hornblow, Jr. Screenplay by Walter De Leon, based on the play by Paul Dickey and Charles W. Goddard.

Road to Zanzibar (Paramount, 1941) Cast: Bob Hope (as Fearless Hubert Frazier), Bing Crosby, Dorothy Lamour, Una Merkel, Eric Blore, Luis Alberni, Joan Marsh, Douglas Dumbrille, Iris Adrian, Noble Johnson. Directed by Victor Schertzinger. Produced by Paul Jones. Screenplay by Frank Butler and Don Hartman, based on the story "Find Colonel Fawcett" by Don Hartman and Sy Bartlett.

Caught in the Draft (Paramount, 1941) Cast: Bob Hope (as Don Bolton), Dorothy Lamour, Lynne Overman, Eddie Bracken, Clarence Kolb, Paul Hurst, Phyllis Ruth, Irving Bacon, Arthur Loft, Edgar Dearing. Directed by David Butler. Produced by B.G. DeSylva. Screenplay by Harry Tugend with additional dialogue by Wilkie C. Mahoney.

Nothing but the Truth (Paramount, 1941) Cast: Bob Hope (as Steve Bennett), Paulette Goddard, Edward Arnold, Leif Erikson, Helen Vinson, Willie Best, Glenn Anders, Grant Mitchell, Catherine Doucet, Clarence Kolb. Directed by Elliott Nugent. Produced by Arthur Hornblow, Jr. Screenplay by Don Hartman and Ken Englund, from the play by James Montgomery based on the novel by Frederic S. Isham.

Louisiana Purchase (Paramount, 1941) Cast: Bob Hope (as Jim Taylor), Victor Moore, Vera Zorina, Irene Bordoni, Dona Drake, Raymond Walburn, Maxie Rosenbloom, Phyllis Ruth, Frank Albertson, Donald MacBride, Jack Norton, Barbara Britton, Margaret Hayes, Jean Wallace, Dave Willock. Directed by Irving Cummings. Produced by Harold Wilson (associate). Screenplay by Jerome Chodorov and Joseph Fields, from the musical comedy by Morrie Ryskind based on a story by B.G. DeSylva.

My Favorite Blonde (Paramount, 1942) Cast: Bob Hope (as Larry Haines), Madeleine Carroll, Gale Sondergaard, George Zucco, Victor Varconi, Edward Gargan, Dooley Wilson, Isabel Randolph, Monte Blue, Minerva Urecal. Directed by Sidney Lanfield. Produced by Paul Jones (associate). Screenplay by Don Hartman and Frank Butler, based on the story by Melvin Frank and Norman Panama.

Road to Morocco (Paramount, 1942) Cast: Bob Hope (as Turkey Jackson), Bing Crosby, Dorothy Lamour, Anthony Quinn, Dona Drake, Mikhail Rasumny, Laura La Plante, Yvonne De Carlo, Monte Blue. Directed by David Butler. Produced by Paul Jones (associate). Screenplay by Frank Butler and Don Hartman.

They Got Me Covered (Goldwyn–RKO, 1943) Cast: Bob Hope (as Robert Kittredge), Dorothy Lamour, Lenore Aubert, Otto Preminger, Eduardo Ciannelli, Florence Bates, Marion Martin, Donald Meek, Walter Catlett, Philip Ahn, John Abbott, Mary Treen. Directed by David Butler. Produced by Samuel Goldwyn. Screenplay by Harry Kurnitz, based on the story by Leonard Q. Ross and Leonard Spigelgass.

Let's Face It (Paramount, 1943) Cast: Bob Hope (as Jerry Walker), Betty Hutton, Zasu Pitts, Phyllis Povah, Eve Arden, Dave Willock, Raymond Walburn, Marjorie Weaver, Dona Drake, Arthur Loft, Joseph Sawyer. Directed by Sidney Lanfield. Produced by Fred Kohlmar (associate). Screenplay by Harry Tugend, based on a musical play by Herbert Fields, Dorothy Fields and Cole Porter suggested by a play by Norma Mitchell and Russell G. Medcraft.

The Princess and the Pirate (Goldwyn–RKO, 1944) Cast: Bob Hope (as Sylvester the Great), Virginia Mayo, Walter Brennan, Walter Slezak, Victor McLaglen, Marc Lawrence, Hugo Haas, Maude Eburne, Mike Mazurki, Bing Crosby (guest bit). Directed by David Butler. Produced by Samuel Goldwyn. Screenplay by Don Hartman, Melville Shavelson and Everett Freeman, adapted by Allen Boretz and Curtis Kenyon from a story by Sy Bartlett.

Road to Utopia (Paramount, 1946) Cast: Bob Hope (as Chester Hooton), Bing Crosby, Dorothy Lamour, Hillary Brooke, Douglas Dumbrille, Jack LaRue, Robert Barrat, Nestor Paiva, Robert Benchley (narrator). Directed by Hal Walker. Produced by Paul Jones. Screenplay by Norman Panama and Melvin Frank.

Monsieur Beaucaire (Paramount, 1946) Cast: Bob Hope (as Monsieur Beaucaire), Joan Caulfield, Patric Knowles, Marjorie Reynolds, Cecil Kellaway, Joseph Schildkraut, Reginald Owen, Constance Collier, Hillary Brooke, Mary Nash, Douglas Dumbrille. Directed by George Marshall. Produced by Paul Jones. Screenplay by Melvin Frank and Norman Panama, based on Booth Tarkington's novel.

My Favorite Brunette (Paramount, 1947) Cast: Bob Hope (as Ronnie Jackson), Dorothy Lamour, Peter Lorre, Lon Chaney, Jr., John Hoyt, Charles Dingle, Frank Puglia, Ann Doran, Willard Robertson, Bing Crosby (guest bit). Directed by Elliott Nugent. Produced by Daniel Dare. Screenplay by Edmund Beloin and Jack Rose.

Where There's Life (Paramount, 1947) Cast: Bob Hope (as Michael Valentine), Signe Hasso, William Bendix, George Coulouris, George Zucco, John Alexander, Denis Hoey, Joseph Vitale, Harry Von Zell. Directed by Sidney Lanfield. Produced by Paul Jones. Screenplay by Allen Boretz and Melville Shavelson, based on a story by Shavelson.

Road to Rio (Paramount, 1948) Cast: Bob Hope (as Hot Lips Barton), Bing Crosby, Dorothy Lamour, Gale Sondergaard, Frank Faylen, Joseph Vitale, Frank Puglia, Nestor Paiva, Jerry Colonna, The Wiere Brothers, The Andrews Sisters, Tan Van Brunt. Directed by Norman Z. McLeod. Produced by Daniel Dare. Screenplay by Edmund Beloin and Jack Rose.

The Paleface (Paramount, 1948) Cast: Bob Hope (as Painless Peter Potter), Jane Russell, Robert Armstrong, Iris Adrian, Robert Watson, Jack Searl, Joseph Vitale, Charles Trowbridge, Clem Bevans, Jeff York, Stanley Adams, Iron Eyes Cody. Directed by Norman Z. McLeod. Produced by Robert L. Welch. Screenplay by Edmund Hartmann and Frank Tashlin, with additional dialogue by Jack Rose.

Sorrowful Jones (Paramount, 1949) Cast: Bob Hope (as Sorrowful Jones), Lucille Ball, Mary Jane Saunders, William Demarest, Bruce Cabot, Thomas Gomez, Tom Pedi, Paul Lees. Directed by Sidney Lanfield. Produced by Robert L. Welch. Screenplay by Melville Shavelson, Edmund Hartmann and Jack Rose, based on the Damon Runyon play.

The Great Lover (Paramount, 1949) Cast: Bob Hope (as Freddie Hunter), Rhonda Fleming, Roland Young, Roland Culver, Richard Lyon, Jerry Hunter, Jackie Jackson, Karl Wright, George Reeves, Jim Backus, Sig Arno. Directed by Alexander Hall. Produced by Edmund Beloin. Screenplay by Edmund Beloin, Melville Shavelson and Jack Rose.

Fancy Pants (Paramount, 1950) Cast: Bob Hope (as Humphrey), Lucille Ball, Bruce Cabot, Jack Kirkwood, Lea Pennman, Hugh French, Eric Blore, Joseph Vitale, John Alexander, Norma Varden, Colin Keith-Johnston, Ida Moore. Directed by George Marshall. Produced by Robert Welch. Screenplay by Edmund Hartmann and Robert O'Brien, based on Harry Leon Wilson's novel *Ruggles of Red Gap*.

The Lemon Drop Kid (Paramount, 1951) Cast: Bob Hope (as The Lemon Drop Kid), Marilyn Maxwell, Lloyd Nolan, Jane Darwell, Andrea King, Fred Clark, Jay C. Flippen, William Frawley, Harry Bellaver, Sid Melton, Ida Moore. Directed by Sidney Lanfield. Produced by Robert L. Welch. Screenplay by Frank Tashlin, Edmund Hartmann and Robert O'Brian. With additional dialogue by Irving Elinson, adaptation by Edmund Beloin of the Damon Runyon short story.

My Favorite Spy (Paramount, 1951) Cast: Bob Hope (as Peanuts White), Hedy Lamarr, Francis L. Sullivan, Arnold Moss, Stephen Chase, John Archer, Morris Ankrum, Luis Van Rooten. Directed by Norman Z. McLeod. Produced by Paul Jones. Screenplay by Edmund Hartmann and Jack Sher.

Son of Paleface (Paramount, 1952) Cast: Bob Hope (as Junior), Jane Russell, Roy Rogers, Bill Williams, Lloyd Corrigan, Paul E. Burns, Douglas Dumbrille, Harry Von Zell, Iron Eyes Cody. Directed by Frank Tashlin. Produced by Robert Welch. Screenplay by Frank Tashlin, Robert L. Welch and Joseph Quillan.

Road to Bali (Paramount, 1952) Cast: Bob Hope (as Harold Gridley), Bing Crosby, Dorothy Lamour, Murvyn Vye, Ralph Moody, Peter Coe, Leon Askin; and as guests: Bob Crosby, Humphrey Bogart (in a clip from *The African Queen*), Jane Russell, Dean Martin, Jerry Lewis. Directed by Hal Walker. Produced by Harry Tugend. Screenplay by Frank Butler, Hal Kanter and William Morrow, based on a story by Frank Butler and Harry Tugend.

Off Limits (Paramount, 1953) Cast: Bob Hope (as Wally Hogan), Mickey Rooney, Marilyn Maxwell, Eddie Mayehoff, Stanley Clements, Marvin Miller, John Ridgely, Carolyn Jones. Directed by George Marshall. Produced by Harry Tugend. Screenplay by Hal Kanter and Jack Sher.

Here Come the Girls (Paramount, 1953) Cast: Bob Hope (as Stanley Snodgrass), Tony Martin, Arlene Dahl, Rosemary Clooney, Millard Mitchell, William Demarest, Fred Clark, Robert Strauss. Directed by Claude Binyon. Produced by Paul Jones. Screenplay by Edmund Hartmann (his story) and Hal Kanter.

Casanova's Big Night (Paramount, 1954) Cast: Bob Hope (as Pippo Poppolino), Joan Fontaine, Audrey Dalton, Basil Rathbone, Arnold Moss, John Carradine, Hope Emerson. Directed by Norman Z. McLeod. Produced by Paul Jones. Screenplay by Hal Kanter and Edmund Hartmann, based on a story by Aubrey Wisberg.

The Seven Little Foys (Paramount, 1955) Cast: Bob Hope (as Eddie Foy), Milly Vitale, George Tobias, Angela Clarke, Richard Shannon, Billy Gray, Lydia Reed, Linda Bennett, Jimmy Baird, James Cagney (as George M. Cohan). Directed by Melville Shavelson. Produced by Jack Rose. Screenplay by Melville Shavelson and Jack Rose.

That Certain Feeling (Paramount, 1956) Cast: Bob Hope (as Francis X. Digman), Eva Marie Saint, George Sanders, Pearl Bailey, David Lewis, Al Capp, Jerry Mathers, Florenz Ames. Directed by Norman Panama. Produced by Norman Panama and Melvin Frank. Screenplay by Norman Panama, Melvin Frank, I.A.L. Diamond and William Altman, based on the play *King of Hearts* by Jean Kerr and Eleanor Brooke.

The Iron Petticoat (Metro–Goldwyn–Mayer, 1956) Cast: Bob Hope (as Chuck Lockwood), Katharine Hepburn, Noelle Middleton, James Robertson Justice, Robert Helpmann, David Kossoff, Alan Giggord, Alexander Gauge. Directed by Ralph Thomas. Produced by Betty Box. Screenplay by Ben Hecht.

Beau James (Paramount, 1957) Cast: Bob Hope (as Jimmy Walker), Vera Miles, Alexis Smith, Paul Douglas, Darren McGavin, Joseph Mantell, Jimmy Durante (as himself), Walter Catlett. Directed by Melville Shavelson. Produced by Jack Rose. Screenplay by Jack Rose and Melville Shavelson, based on *Beau James,* the biography of James Walker by Gene Fowler.

Paris Holiday (United Artists, 1958) Cast: Bob Hope (as Robert Leslie), Fernandel, Anita Ekberg, Martha Hyer, Preston Sturges, Andre Morell, Alan Gifford. Directed by Gerg Oswald. Produced by Robert Hope. Screenplay by Edmund Beloin and Dean Riesner, based on a story by Robert Hope.

Alias Jesse James (United Artists, 1959) Cast: Bob Hope (as Milford Farnsworth), Rhonda Fleming, Wendell Corey, Jim Davis, Gloria Talbot, Will Wright, Mary Young; and as guests: James Arness, Ward Bond, Gary Cooper, Bing Crosby, Gail Davis, Jay Silverheels, Hugh O'Brian, Fess Parker, Roy Rogers. Directed by Norman Z. McLeod. Executive Producer, Bob Hope. Produced by Jack Hope. Screenplay by William Bowers and Daniel D. Beauchamp, based on a story by Robert St. Aubrey and Bert Lawrence.

The Facts of Life (United Artists, 1960) Cast: Bob Hope (as Larry Gilbert), Lucille Ball, Ruth Hussey, Don Defore, Louis Nye, Philip Ober, Marianne

Stewart, Peter Leeds, Louise Beavers, Robert F. Simon, Mike Mazurki Directed by Melvin Frank. Produced by Norman Panama. Screenplay by Norman Panama and Melvin Frank.

Bachelor in Paradise (Metro–Goldwyn–Mayer, 1961) Cast: Bob Hope (as Adam J. Niles), Lana Turner, Janis Paige, Jim Hutton, Paula Prentiss, Don Porter, Virginia Grey, John McGiver, Florence Sundstrom, Clinton Sundberg. Directed by Jack Arnold. Produced by Ted Richmond. Screenplay by Valentine Davies and Hal Kanter, based on a story by Vera Caspary.

Road to Hong Kong (United Artists, 1962) Cast: Bob Hope (as Chester Babcock), Bing Crosby, Dorothy Lamour, Joan Collins, Robert Morley; and as guests: Peter Sellers, Frank Sinatra, Dean Martin, David Niven, Zsa Zsa Gabor, Dave King, Jerry Colonna. Directed by Norman Panama. Produced by Melvin Frank. Screenplay by Norman Panama and Melvin Frank.

Critic's Choice (Warner Brothers, 1963) Cast: Bob Hope (as Parker Ballantine), Lucille Ball, Marilyn Maxwell, Rip Torn, Jessie Royce Landis, Jim Backus, Rick Kellman, Dorothy Green, Marie Windsor, Jerome Cowan, Lurene Tuttle, Stanley Adams. Directed by Don Weis. Produced by Frank P. Rosenberg. Screenplay by Jack Sher, based on the Ira Levin play.

Call Me Bwana (United Artists, 1963) Cast: Bob Hope (as Matt Merriwether), Anita Ekberg, Edie Adams, Lionel Jeffries, Percy Herbert. Directed by Gordon Douglas. Produced by Albert R. Broccoli. Screenplay by Nate Monaster and Johanna Harwood.

A Global Affair (Metro-Goldwyn-Mayer, 1964) Cast: Bob Hope (as Frank Larrimore), Lilo Pulver, Michele Mercier, Elga Andersen. Directed by Jack Arnold. Produced by Hall Bartlett. Screenplay by Arthur Marx, Bob Fisher and Charles Lederer, based on a story by Eugene Vale.

I'll Take Sweden (United Artists, 1965) Cast: Bob Hope (as Bob Holcomb), Tuesday Weld, Dina Merrill, Frankie Avalon, Jeremy Slate, Rosemarie Frankland. Directed by Frederick De Cordova. Produced by Edward Small. Screenplay by Nat Perrin, Bob Fisher and Arthur Marx.

Boy, Did I Get a Wrong Number! (United Artists, 1966) Cast: Bob Hope (as Tom Meade), Elke Sommer, Phyllis Diller, Cesare Danova, Marjorie Lord, Kelly Thordsen, Benny Baker, Terry Burnham, Joyce Jameson, Harry Von Zell. Directed by George Marshall. Produced by Edward Small. Screenplay by Burt Styler, Albert E. Lewin and George Kennett, based on a story by George Beck.

Eight on the Lam (United Artists, 1967) Cast: Bob Hope (as Henry Dimsdale), Phyllis Diller, Jonathan Winters, Shirley Eaton, Jill St. John, Stacey Maxwell, Kevin Brody, Glenn Gilger, Debi Storm, Michael Freeman, Austin Willis, Peter Leeds, and Hope's grandchildren—Avis and Robert Hope. Directed by George Marshall. Produced by Bill Lawrence (associate). Screenplay by Albert E. Lewin, Burt Styler, and (also story) Bob Fisher and Arthur Marx.

The Private Navy of Sgt. O'Farrell (United Artists, 1968) Cast: Bob Hope

~~(as Master Sergeant Dan O'Farrell)~~, Phyllis Diller, Jeffrey Hunter, Gina Lollobrigida, Mylene Demongeot, Henry Wilcoxon, William Wellman, Jr. Directed by Frank Tashlin. Produced by John Beck. Screenplay by Frank Tashlin, based on a story by John L. Greene and Robert M. Fresco.

How to Commit Marriage (Cinerama, 1969) Cast: Bob Hope (as Frank Benson), Jane Wyman, Jackie Gleason, Maureen Arthur, Tina Louise, Leslie Nielsen, Paul Stewart, Irwin Corey. Directed by Norman Panama. Produced by Bill Lawrence. Screenplay by Ben Starr and Michael Kanin.

Cancel My Reservation (Warner Brothers, 1972) Cast: Bob Hope (as Dan Bartlett), Eva Marie Saint, Ralph Bellamy, Forrest Tucker, Keenan Wynn, Doodles Weaver, Betty Ann Carr, Henry Darrow, Chief Dan George, Anne Archer. Directed by Paul Bogart. Executive Producer, Bob Hope. Produced by Gordon Oliver. Screenplay by Arthur Marx and Robert Fisher.

APPEARANCES, CAMEOS, DOCUMENTARIES

Don't Hook Now (Paramount, 1938) Filmed golf tournament. Bob Hope as himself with Bing Crosby. Directed by Herbert Poleise.

Star Spangled Rhythm (Paramount, 1942) Feature film. Cast: Bob Hope (as himself, Master of Ceremonies), Eddie Bracken, Victor Moore, Betty Hutton, Anne Revere, Walter Abel, William Bendix, MacDonald Carey, Walter Catlett, Jerry Colonna, Bing Crosby, Gary Crosby, Edgar Dearing, Cecil B. De Mille, Dona Drake, Katherine Dunham, Edward Fielding, Paulette Goddard, Eddie Johnson, Johnny Johnston, William Haade, Susan Hayward, Sterling Holloway, Maynard Holmes, Alan Ladd, Veronica Lake, Gil Lamb, Dorothy Lamour, Fred MacMurray, Mary Martin, James Millican, Ray Milland, Ralph Murphy, Lynne Overman, Dick Powell, Marjorie Reynolds, Eddie "Rochester" Anderson, Betty Rhodes, Preston Sturges, Franchot Tone, Arthur Treacher, Ernest Truex, Walter Whal, Vera Zorina, the Golden Gate Quartet, Slim and Sam. Directed by George Marshall. Produced by Joseph Sistrom (associate). Screenplay by Harry Tugend.

Welcome to Britain (Strand–M.O.I., 1943) A guide to British institutions and behavior for U.S. troops stationed in England. Cast: Bob Hope (as himself), Felix Aylmer, Carla Lehmann, Beatrice Lillie, Burgess Meredith, Johnny Schofield, Beatrice Varley. Directed by Anthony Asquith with Burgess Meredith.

All Star Bond Rally (20th Century-Fox, 1945) One-reel variety show for the U.S. Government—War Activities Committee and U.S. Treasury Department. Cast: Bob Hope (as himself, singing "Buy Buy Bonds"), Jeanne Crain, Bing Crosby, Linda Darnell, Betty Grable, Harpo Marx, Frank Sinatra, Fibber McGee and Molly, Harry James and his orchestra. Directed by Michael Audley.

Hollywood Victory Caravan (Paramount, 1945) Two-reel variety show for U.S. Government. Cast: Bob Hope (as himself), Robert Benchley, Humphrey Bogart, Bing Crosby, William Demarest, Dona Drake, Betty Hutton, Alan Ladd, Diana Lynn, Franklin Pangborn, Olga San Juan, Barbara Stanwyck, Carmen Cavallaro. Directed by William Russell. Screenplay by Melville Shavelson.

Variety Girl (Paramount, 1947) Feature film—Variety Show in tribute to the Variety Clubs of America. Cast: Bob Hope (as himself), Mary Hatcher, Olga San Juan, DeForrest Kelly, Neila Walker, Torben Meyer, Jack Norton, Bing Crosby, Gary Cooper, Paulette Goddard, Alan Ladd, Veronica Lake, Dorothy Lamour, Burt Lancaster, Ray Milland, Robert Preston, Gail Russell, Barbara Stanwyck, Billy De Wolfe. Directed by George Marshall. Screenplay by Edmund Hartmann, Frank Tashlin, Robert Welch and Monte Brice.

The Greatest Show on Earth (Paramount, 1952) Feature film. Bob Hope (unbilled—cameo as part of the audience in one scene). Directed by Cecil B. De Mille.

Scared Stiff (Paramount, 1953) Feature film—remake of *Ghostbreakers*. Bob Hope (unbilled walk-on—cameo). Directed by George Marshall.

Showdown at Ulcer Gulch (*Saturday Evening Post*, 1958) Promotional film. Bob Hope (unbilled—cameo).

Five Pennies (Paramount, 1959) Feature film. Cast: Bob Hope (as himself, as guest), Danny Kaye, Barbara Bel Geddes, Tuesday Weld, Harry Guardino, Louis Armstrong, Bob Crosby, Susan Gordon, Ray Daley, Richard Shavelson. Directed by Melville Shavelson. Screenplay by Melville Shavelson and Jack Rose.

The Sound of Laughter (Union Film Release, 1963) Feature-length documentary of comedy scenes from early talkies. Bob Hope and Leah Ray in scene from *Going Spanish*. Directed and compiled by John O'Shaughnessy. Narration by Fred Saidy, spoken by Ed Wynn.

The Oscar (Paramount, 1966) Feature film. Bob Hope (as himself) in one scene as Master of Ceremonies of Academy Awards presentation. Directed by Russell Rouse.

The Muppet Movie (Sir Lew Grade, 1979) Feature film. Bob Hope in cameo as the ice cream man. Created by Jim Henson. Directed by James Frawley.

NOTES

In addition to personal interviews and conversations with Bob Hope; interviews and conversations with many people who have been and are now associated with him; quotations and notations from the comedian's autobiographical writings, and hundreds of media accounts, there are three essential sources of data underpinning this life story that are referred to frequently during these end notes: They are:

The Bob Hope Joke Files (BHJF), stored in two vaults in the comedian's Toluca Lake estate office, include comedy material dating from vaudeville, radio, film and numerous personal appearances and benefits of the 1920s and 1930s, and continuing through the most recent television and personal appearances of the 1980s, filed chronologically by show, and cross-filed by subject matter.

The Bob Hope Personal Files (BHPF), also housed in his Toluca Lake office, include his correspondence and his professional and business records covering half a century.

The Hope Enterprises Public Relations Files (HEPRF), located in a separate office in Toluca Lake, include fact sheets, biographies, correspondence, press clippings, scrapbooks and photographs that cover the comedian's professional and personal activities for a quarter of a century.

CUE IN: "This Is Your Life
Leslie Towns Hope!"

1. BHJF. Personal appearance routine. Circa 1969.
2. According to family records, this is the correct spelling of Bob Hope's maternal surname, and has been incorrectly spelled "Townes" since the comedian's childhood in Cleveland, Ohio.
3. BHJF, BHPF, HEPRF. Additional details about this five-day London trip derive from conversation and correspondence with Lady Carolyn Townshend, Alan Haire, Denis Goodwin and Mildred Rosequist Brod.
4. BHPF. Lord Louis Mountbatten had asked producer Mike Franko-

vich to help persuade Hope to do this benefit, and once Hope decided affirmatively, the comedian and Mountbatten corresponded directly.

5. Memorandum from Lady Carolyn Townshend, November 11, 1970. HEPRF.
6. Monologue, United World College Fund Benefit, Royal Festival Hall, London, November 16, 1970. BHJF, BHPF.
7. Telegram, Mountbatten to Hope, November 16, 1970. BHPF.
8. Mountbatten to Hope, November 17, 1970. BHPF.
9. *This Is Your Life* transcript. BHPF.
10. Monologue, Gala Cabaret, World

Wildlife Fund Benefit, London, November 18, 1970. BHJF
11. Sir Lew Grade to Hope, November 19, 1970. BHPF.
12. Monologue, Miss World Contest Finals, Royal Albert Hall, London, November 19, 1970. BHJF, BHPF.

1. 44 Craighton Road
1. Pete Martin. *Bob Hope's Own Story: Have Tux Will Travel: As Told To Pete Martin* (New York: Simon and Schuster, 1954), p. 11. Details about Hope's parentage and the family's early years in Wales and England were supplied by the comedian, various relatives on both sides of the Atlantic, and the efforts of Sue P. McKean and Kendall H. Williams, Research International, Salt Lake City, Utah.
2. James Hope. Unpublished manuscript "Mother Had Hopes." This lyric represents one of many recollections Avis Hope passed along to her son Jim during late night conversations in the kitchen of their Cleveland home between 1910 and 1915.
3. Interview with Jack Hope, September 1960.
4. "Mother Had Hopes."

2. Doan's Corners
1. *Have Tux, Will Travel*, p. 23. Hope's early Cleveland, Ohio, years are re-created through interviews with Hope family members, with Mildred Rosequist Brod, the recollections of several of the comedian's childhood friends, as well as the unpublished "Mother Had Hopes."
2. Letter from James Kier to James Hope, 1955 (included in "Mother Had Hopes").
3. Monologue, Boys Clubs of America benefit, May 4, 1967. BHJF.
4. *Have Tux, Will Travel*, p. 7.
5. *New York Herald Tribune*, July 10, 1938.

3. East Palestine, Lima and Brazil
1. *Have Tux, Will Travel*, p. 39.
2. Interview with Mildred Rosequist Brod, Summer 1979.
3. Ibid.
4. Ibid.
5. Ibid.
6. BHPF.
7. *Cleveland Press*, May 17, 1974.
8. Vaudeville scrapbooks, BHPF. Details depicting Hope's years with Tab shows and on various vaudeville circuits have been taken from the comedian's personal vaudeville scrapbook, and from two others kept by Frank Maley, manager of Hurley's *Jolly Follies*, and loaned to Hope by one of Maley's relatives, Don Matticks of Lubbock, Texas.
9. *Cincinnati Inquirer*, February 11, 1942.
10. *Springfield Daily Sun* (no date), reprinted in the 1925–26 edition of the Gus Sun Booking Exchange Company artist's catalogue. BHPF.
11. Interview with Hope, May 1981.
12. Ibid.

4. Sidewalks of New York
1. *Have Tux, Will Travel*, p. 56.
2. Interview with Hope, May 1981.
3. Hope vaudeville scrapbook. No exact date but certainly Autumn 1925. BHPF.
4. *Cincinnati Inquirer*, February 11, 1942.
5. Ibid.
6. Interview with Hope, May 1981.
7. *Have Tux, Will Travel* p. 50.
8. Interview with Mildred Rosequist Brod, Summer 1979.
9. BHJF.
10. Interview with Hope, May 1981.
11. *Have Tux, Will Travel*, p. 55.
12. *Reading* (Pa.) newsclip with no date but probably close to May 15, 1927. BHPF.
13. Interview with Alan Calm, Summer 1979.
14. BHJF.
15. *Have Tux, Will Travel*, p. 65.
16. Interview with Hope, May 1981.

17. Interview with Brod, Summer 1979.

5. Stratford to Proctor's 86th
1. *Have Tux, Will Travel*, p. 71.
2. Ibid, p. 67.
3. Interview with Hope, May 1981.
4. *Have Tux, Will Travel*, p. 69.
5. Ibid, p. 71.
6. Interview with Hope, May 1981.
7. *Have Tux, Will Travel*, p. 72.
8. Vaudeville material. BHJF.
9. Interview with Hope, May 1981.
10. *Have Tux, Will Travel*, p. 73
11. Vaudeville material. BHJF.
12. Interview with Hope, May 1981.
13. Ibid.
14. Interview with Charlie Cirillo, Summer 1979.
15. *Have Tux, Will Travel*, p. 75.
16. Ibid.
17. Ibid, p. 78.

6. Hollywood, Who Needs It?
1. *Have Tux, Will Travel*, p. 87.
2. Interview with Hope, May 1981.
3. Vaudeville material. BHJF.
4. Interview with Mildred Rosequist Brod, Summer 1979.
5. "Mother Had Hopes."
6. Ibid.
7. Vaudeville material. BHJF.
8. Ibid.
9. Interview with Hope, May 1981.
10. Ibid.

7. Heaven on 47th Street
1. Vaudeville material. BHJF.
2. *Have Tux, Will Travel*, p. 84.
3. Vaudeville material. BHJF.
4. Ibid. BHJF.
5. Ibid. BHJF.
6. Ibid. BHJF.
7. *Silver Screen*, March 1942.
8. *New York Times*, February 11, 1931. Marion Spitzer in *The Palace* (New York: Atheneum, 1969) writes: "Neither in the Palace record book nor in Bob's own book [*Have Tux, Will Travel*] is there a definite date given for his appearance there as a single. The only reference is to Bob Hope as part of *Antics of 1931*." Odd, because the reviews describe his single spot and his part in the *Antics* afterpiece, and the newspaper advertising of the week carries the name Bob Hope in the same size type as headliner Bea Lillie.
9. Interview with Hope, May 1981, and *Have Tux, Will Travel*, p. 96.

8. Benefits, Benchmarks, and Ballyhoo
1. Morella, Epstein and Clark, *The Amazing Careers of Bob Hope* (New York: Arlington House, 1973), p. 74.
2. Interview with Hope, May 1981.
3. *The Amazing Careers of Bob Hope*.
4. Richy Craig material. BHJF.
5. Milton Berle. *Milton Berle, An Autobiography with Haskel Frankel* (New York: Delacorte, 1974).

9. Gowns by Roberta
1. Interview with Hope, May 1981.
2. Barry Ulanov. *The Incredible Crosby* (New York: Whittlesey House, 1948), p. 153.
3. Interview with Lester White, Summer 1979.
4. Max Gordon and Lewis Funke. *Max Gordon Presents* (New York: Geis, 1963).
5. Interview with Hope, May 1981.
6. *Have Tux, Will Travel*, p. 108.
7. Ibid. Also material from Berle's autobiography.
8. Interview with Hope, May 1981.

10. Why Erie?
1. *Have Tux, Will Travel*, p. 112.
2. *Modern Screen*, November 1943.
3. *Have Tux, Will Travel*, p. 112.
4. Bob Thomas. *Winchell* (New York: Doubleday, 1971), p. 119.
5. George Murphy. *Say, Didn't You Used to Be George Murphy?* with Victor Lasky. (New York: Bartholomew House, 1970), p. 161.

11. Say When
1. *Have Tux, Will Travel*, p. 113.
2. Harry Richman. *A Hell of a Life*

(New York: Duell, Sloan and Pearce, 1956), p. 178.

3. Interview with Hope, May 1981.

4. *The New York Times*, November 9, 1934; *New York Evening Journal*, November 9, 1934; *The New Yorker*, November 15, 1934; *Daily Mirror*, November 9, 1934.

5. Radio monologue, January 4, 1935. BHJF, BHPF.

6. *Have Tux, Will Travel*, p. 118.

7. Radio monologue, November 9, 1935. BHJF, BHPF.

12. Ziegfeld Follies of 1935
1. *Have Tux, Will Travel*, p. 119.

2. Interviews with Eve Arden and Fred DeCordova, Summer 1979; Hope, May 1981. John Murray Anderson. *Out Without My Rubbers* (New York: Library Publishers, 1954). Jerry Stagg. *The Brothers Shubert* (New York: Random House, 1968).

3. Interview with Eve Arden, Summer 1979.

4. *Have Tux, Will Travel*, p. 121

5. Interview with Lester White, Summer 1979.

13. Red, Hot and Blue!
1. *Have Tux, Will Travel*, p. 128.

2. Interview with Hope, May 1981; Gene Fowler. *Schnozzola* (New York: Viking, 1951); Ethel Merman and Pete Martin. *Who Could Ask For Anything More?* (New York: Doubleday, 1955); George Eels. *Cole Porter, The Life That Late He Led* (New York: Putnam, 1967).

3. *Have Tux, Will Travel*, p. 123.

4. Ethel Merman. *Merman, An Autobiography With George Eels* (New York: Simon and Schuster, 1978). Interview with Hope.

5. *Daily Mirror*, October 30, 1936; *New York Post*, October 30, 1936; *Evening Journal*, October 30, 1936.

6. *Have Tux, Will Travel*, p. 126.

14. Hollywood, Take Two
1. Bob Hope. *They Got Me Covered* (Hollywood: Bob Hope, 1941), p. 42.

2. *Rippling Rhythm Revue*, radio monologue, May 9, 1937. BHJF.

3. Interview with James Saphier for feature story, 1969.

15. New Boy in Town
1. Monologue material. BHJF.

2. *Woman's Home Companion*, November 1953.

3. Conversation with Dolores Hope, October 23, 1971.

4. Hope interview in *The World Book Year Book*, 1979, p. 128.

5. Interview with Rita Millar Sigmund, Summer 1980.

6. Radio monologue, *Your Hollywood Parade*, January 4, 1938. BHJF.

16. This Is Bob (Pepsodent) Hope
1. Interview with Hope, May 1981.

2. Saphier to Hope, May 17, 1938. BHPF.

3. *New York World-Telegram*, June 24, 1938.

4. Interview with Mildred MacArthur Serrano, Summer 1979.

5. *Los Angeles Times*, August 28, 1938.

6. William French. "From Gags to Riches," manuscript. BHPF.

7. BHPF. Also conversations with Saphier at various times between 1965 and 1970.

8. Radio monologue, first Pepsodent show, September 27, 1938. BHJF, BHPF.

9. United Press wirecopy, June 19, 1939.

17. Family, Family, Everywhere
1. BHJF.

2. *Have Tux, Will Travel*, p. 234.

3. *New York Post*, July 31, 1939.

4. *New York Daily Mirror*, August 3, 1939.

5. Interview, Bob Hope, The Museum of the Sea, *Queen Mary*, Long Beach, May 13, 1970.

6. International News Service, August 25, 1939.

7. *Have Tux, Will Travel*, pp. 167–

68; also Museum of the Sea interview, May 13, 1970. BHPF, HEPRF.

18. Three for the Road
1. *The Incredible Crosby,* p. 157.
2. Radio monologue, September 27, 1939, BHJF.
3. Radio monologue, October 24, 1939. BHJF.
4. *Motion Picture Herald* (clipping, no date). BHPF.
5. Hope and Bob Thomas. *The Road to Hollywood* (New York: Doubleday, 1977), p. 31.
6. *New York Herald Tribune,* July 10, 1938.
7. Lamour, Dorothy. *My Side of the Road* (Englewood Cliffs, N.J.: Prentice-Hall, 1980).
8. *The Amazing Careers of Bob Hope,* p. 108.
9. *The Amazing Careers of Bob Hope,* p. 111.
10. Interview with Hope, May 1981.
11. *Where There's Life, There's Bob Hope.*
12. Lamour. *My Side of the Road.*
13. *The Incredible Crosby,* p. 154.
14. Academy Awards monologue, February 29, 1940, BHJF.
15. *The Amazing Careers of Bob Hope,* p. 106.
16. Interview with Hope, May 1981.
17. Ibid.
18. BHJF.

19. They Got Me Covered
1. Academy Awards monologue, February 21, 1941.
2. *Los Angeles Examiner,* February 22, 1941.
3. *The Merv Griffin Show,* January 3, 1972. Tape. BHPF.
4. *Sky,* November 1974, p. 20.
5. Interview with Hope, May 1981.
6. Radio monologue, March Field, California, May 4, 1941, BHJF.
7. *Time,* July 21, 1941.
8. Interview with Hope, May 1981.
9. *They Got Me Covered,* p. 22.
10. BHJF.
11. Opening serious speech, radio broadcast, December 16, 1941. BHJF.

20. Victory Caravan
1. *The Road to Hollywood,* p. 47.
2. Leonard Maltin. *The Great Movie Comedians* (New York: Crown, 1978), p. 188.
3. *The Road to Hollywood,* p. 47.
4. *The Merv Griffin Show,* January 3, 1972. Tape. BHPF.
5. *Variety,* May 5, 1942.
6. *Boston Globe,* May 1, 1942.
7. John Lahr. *Notes On a Cowardly Lion* (New York: Knopf, 1969), p. 249.
8. *Atlanta Constitution,* May 27, 1942.

21. Frozen Follies
1. Interview with Hope, May 1981.
2. Telegram from General Buckner to Hope. BHPF.
3. Bob Hope, *I Never Left Home* (New York: Simon and Schuster, 1944).
4. Alaskan monologue, September 1943, BHJF.
5. Bob Hope, "What I Saw In Our Alaska Army Camps," *Motion Picture,* November 1942.
6. Interview with Hope, May 1981.
7. *Woman's Home Companion,* November 1953.
8. Interview with Elza Schallart, 1943.
9. Ibid.

22. I Never Left Home
1. *I Never Left Home.* p. 3.
2. Overseas monologue, Summer 1943, BHJF.
3. Ibid.
4. Liza Schallaert, "Bob Hope—Soldier in Civvies," *Photoplay* November, 1943. HEPRF.
5. Bob Considine. "If There's A Hope—There's A Laugh," *Miami Herald,* October 3, 1943.
6. Ibid.
7. *I Never Left Home,* p. 3.
8. *This Week Magazine,* June 4, 1944.
9. *I Never Left Home,* p. 124.
10. Ibid, p. 161.
11. Ibid, p. 178.

23. Good Evening, Mr. President

1. White House Correspondents monologue, Washington, March 7, 1944. BHJF.
2. Carroll Carroll. *None of Your Business* (New York: Cowles, 1970), p. 192.
3. *I Never Left Home*, p. vii.
4. Charles Thompson. *The Complete Crosby* (London: W. H. Allen, 1978), p. 126.
5. Ibid.
6. Lamour. *My Side of the Road*, p. 140.
7. White House Correspondents monologue, Washington, D.C., March 7, 1944. BHJF.
8. Ibid.
9. Interview with Hope, May 1981. Also, "Hope Suspends Studio, Studio Suspends Hope," *Los Angeles Times,* November 12, 1944.
10. Hope serious message, Pepsodent broadcast, June 6, 1944.
11. *San Francisco Chronicle,* September 12, 1944.
12. King Feature columns. BHPF.
13. Publicity file, November 12, 1944. BHPF.

24. Back for More
1. Bob Hope, *So This Is Peace* (New York: Simon and Schuster, 1946), p. 92.
2. Academy Award monologue, March 15, 1945.
3. *Chicago Sun-Times,* May 13, 1945.
4. Interview with Hope, May 1981.
5. *Family Circle,* January 25, 1946.

25. So This Is Peace
1. *So This Is Peace*, p. vii.
2. "Bob Hope: A Self Portrait," publicity file. BHPF.
3. Publicity file. BHPF.
4. BHPF.
5. Interview with Wyn Hope, Summer 1980.
6. *Archbold Buckeye,* July 10, 1946.
7. *San Francisco Chronicle*, October 2, 1946.
8. Associated Press wirecopy, October 13, 1946.

26. King's Jester

1. *Have Tux, Will Travel,* p. 224.
2. *So This Is Peace,* p. 1.
3. Book promotion material. BHPF.
4. Bruce Torrence. *Hollywood: The First 100 Years* (Hollywood: Hollywood Chamber of Commerce—Fiske, 1979), pp. 228-29, 235.
5. Radio monologue, Pepsodent Show, April 22, 1947. BHJF, BHPF.
6. Closing tribute, Pepsodent Show, November 4, 1947. BHJF, BHPF.
7. *Have Tux, Will Travel,* p. 248.
8. Special scrapbook commemorating the marriage of Princess Elizabeth to Philip Mountbatten, the news clippings dated November 20–November 26. BHPF.
9. Transcript. BHPF.

27. Christmas in Berlin
1. Radio monologue, Swan Show, December 28, 1948. BHJF.
2. A.E. Hotchner. *Doris Day, Her Own Story* (New York: Morrow, 1976), p. 79.
3. Radio monologue, Swan Show, September 14, 1948. BHJF.
4. Radio monologue, Swan Show, November 9, 1948. BHJF.
5. Interview with Bob Thomas, May, 1981.
6. Radio monologue, Swan Show, December 28, 1948. BHJF.
7. Interview with Robert Kelso backstage at USO show, Long Binh, South Vietnam, 1970.

28. We'll Move Your Pin on the Map
1. *Doris Day, Her Own Story*, p. 110.
2. *New York Herald Tribune,* December 21, 1948; *The New York Times*, December 21, 1948.
3. *Doris Day, Her Own Story*, p. 110.
4. Ibid.
5. *Time*, October 10, 1949.
6. Open letter from Hope to Harry Ginsberg, BHPF.
7. Radio monologue, Swan Show, September 21, 1949. BHJF.
8. *Los Angeles Times*, September 19, 1949.

9. Bob Hope, *The Last Christmas Show* (New York: Doubleday, 1974); also interview with Mildred MacArthur Serrano, Summer 1980.

29. Easter Sunday
1. Television monologue, Frigidaire's *Star Spangled Revue*, May 29, 1950. BHJF.
2. *Have Tux, Will Travel*, p. 237.
3. *Los Angeles Times*, January 9, 1950; *Riverside Press and Enterprise*, January 9, 1950.
4. *New York Herald Tribune*, March 1, 1950.
5. Publicity file. BHPF.
6. Interview with Hope, May 1981.
7. *Tele-Views*, July 7, 1950.
8. Television monologue, Frigidaire's *Star Spangled Revue*, Easter Sunday, April 9, 1950.
9. *Journal-American*, April 11, 1950; *Daily News*, April 11, 1950; *World-Telegram and Sun*, April 11, 1950.
10. Television monologue, Frigidaire's *Star Spangled Revue*, May 29, 1950.
11. Interview with Hope, May 1981.
12. *Los Angeles Times*, June 9, 1950.

30. On the Beach at Wonsan
1. Korean tour monologue, September 1950. BHJF.
2. *The Road to Hollywood*, pp. 76–77.
3. *Have Tux, Will Travel*, pp. 205-6.
4. Manuscript in publicity files. BHPF.
5. Korean Tour monologue, October 1950. BHJF.
6. *Los Angeles Times*, October 27, 1950.
7. Closing tribute, Chesterfield Radio Broadcast, November 3, 1950.
8. BHPF.
9. Interview with Hope, May 1981.
10. British Amateur Tournament. BHPF.

31. Liking Ike
1. *Have Tux, Will Travel*, p. 248.

2. Truman joke file. BHJF.
3. *Have Tux, Will Travel*, p. 248.
4. Television monologue, April 26, 1952.
5. Vincent X. Flaherty column, *Los Angeles Examiner*, June 25, 1952.
6. Republican Convention monologue, July 1952. BHJF.
7. Daily Columns. BHPF.
8. Palladium monologue, September 1952. BHJF.
9. Quoted by Guild, *Where There's Life, There's Bob Hope.*
10. *The Complete Crobsy*, pp. 172–3.
11. Television monologue, October 12, 1952. BHJF.
12. Television monologue, November 9, 1952. BHJF.
13. Television monologue, December 7, 1952. BHJF.
14. Television monologue, May 24, 1953. BHJF.
15. Television monologue, February 16, 1954. BHJF.
16. Television monologue, May 11, 1954. BHJF.
17. Television monologue, November 9, 1952. BHJF.
18. Television monologue, April 19, 1953. BHJF.
19. *Have Tux, Will Travel*, p. 231.
20. White House Correspondents monologue, May 8, 1953. BHJF.
21. Television monologue, May 24, 1954. BHJF.
22. Eisenhower file. BHJF.
23. Television monologue, May 24, 1953. BHJF.
24. Television monologue, February 22, 1960.
25. Television monologue, February 15, 1961. BHJF.

32. Have Tux, Will Travel
1. Television monologue, October 20, 1953. BHJF.
2. "Hope for Housewives," *Newsweek*, December 15, 1952.
3. Radio monologue, Daily Jell-O broadcast, November 11, 1952. BHJF.
4. Weekly Jell-O broadcast, January 7, 1953. BHJF.

5. Closing tribute. Ibid.
6. Joey Adams. *Here's to the Friars: The Heart of Show Business* (New York: Crown, 1976). pp. 167-70. Also a voluminous file of letters, telegrams, memorabilia of the event in BHPF.
7. Friars monologue, February 27, 1953. BHJF.
8. *Los Angeles Times* stories of May 4, 1942; June 15, 1942; January 30, 1943; February 3 and 5, 1943.
9. Interviews with Majorie Hughes, Summer 1979.
10. *Los Angeles Times*, June 8, 1949.
11. *Los Angeles Times*, June 28, 1950.
12. *Los Angeles Times*, November 17, 1950.
13. Leo Rosten. "Gags to Riches," *Look,* September 24, 1953.
14. *Confidential,* 1956.

33. The Hard Road to Russia
1. Russia telecast monologue, April 5, 1958. BHJF.
2. Robert Osborne. *50 Golden Years of Oscar: The Official History of the Academy of Motion Picture Arts and Sciences* (La Habra: ESE California, 1978).
3. Ibid.
4. Academy Awards monologue, March 19, 1953. BHJF.
5. *The Road to Hollywood*, p. 83.
6. Interview with Hope, May 1981.
7. *The Road to Hollywood* p. 83.
8. Publicity file. BHPF.
9. Interview with Saphier, 1965.
10. *New York Herald Tribune*, October 20, 1954.
11. Publicity file. BHPF.
12. *Washington Star*, December 8, 1954.
13. Interview with Bob Thomas, Spring 1981.
14. *The Road to Hollywood*, p. 85; *The Amazing Careers of Bob Hope*, p. 163.
15. *The Road to Hollywood*, p. 86.
16. *Hollywood Reporter*. BHPF.
17. *The Road to Hollywood*, p. 87.
18. Bob Hope. *I Owe Russia $1,200* (New York: Doubleday, (1963), p. 221.
19. Ibid. pp. 228-29.
20. Russia trip file. BHJF.
21. Russia telecast monologue, April 5, 1958. BHJF.
22. *I Owe Russia $1,200*, pp. 252-54; interview with Mort Lachman, Summer 1979.
23. Russia telecast tribute, April 5, 1958. BHJF.

34. The Eye
1. *The Last Christmas Show*, p. 72.
2. Ibid.
3. Greenland–Labrador Christmas tour monologue, January 9, 1955. BHJF.
4. *The Last Christmas Show*, p. 79.
5. Ibid, p. 81.
6. *New York Herald Tribune*, July 22, 1957.
7. Interview with Frank Liberman, Summer 1980.
8. Bayonet Bowl monologue, Christmas 1957 tour. BHJF.
9. *The Last Christmas Show*, pp. 101–2.
10. Ibid, p. 111.
11. "The Future Still Hopeful," *TV Guide*, May 23, 1958.
12. Ibid.
13. *New York Post*, March 2, 1959; *New York Journal-American*, March 3, 1959.
14. *Family Weekly*, April 4, 1959.

35. Facts of Life
1. Alfalfa Club monologue, Washington, January 21, 1961.
2. Conversation with Saphier, 1964.
3. Cantor to Saphier, March 22, 1958. BHPF.
4. Persons to Knowland, March 17, 1958. BHPF.
5. This writer was assigned by NBC in August 1959 as publicist for *The Bob Hope Show* and his association with the comedian began with this trip to Alaska.
6. *San Francisco Chronicle*, October 29, 1980.
7. *The Last Christmas Show*, p. 131.

8. Television monologue, April 20, 1960. BHJF.
9. *The Last Christmas Show.*
10. Television monologue, April 17, 1961. BHJF.
11. Television monologue, May 13, 1961. BHJF.
12. Interview with Hope, May 1981.
13. *The Road to Hollywood*, p. 87.
14. *The Complete Crosby*, pp. 208-9.
15. *My Side of the Road*, pp. 198–201.
16. Interview with Rapp, December 1965. HEPRF.
17. Personal appearance file. BHJF.

36. The Rose Garden
1. *Washington Post*, September 13, 1963.
2. *Evening Star*, June 5, 1963.
3. Georgetown University monologue, June 4, 1963. BHJF.
4. *Los Angeles Times*, August 7, 1962.
5. Interview with Wyn Hope, Spring 1981.
6. *The Last Christmas Show*, p. 177.
7. Okinawa monologue, 1962 Christmas tour. BHJF. HEPRF.
8. Associated Press and United Press International wire stories, *Washington Post, Washington Star*, September 13, 1963. HEPRF.
9. Children's Hospital news bulletins, December 6–December 12. BHPF. HEPRF.
10. *The Last Christmas Show*, p. 166.
11. Ankara monologue, 1963 Christmas tour. BHJF. HEPRF.

37. Operation Big Cheer
1. Bien Hoa monologue, 1964 Vietnam Christmas tour. BHJF.
2. NBC News conference, January 12, 1965. HEPRF.
3. Vinh Long monologue, 1964 Vietnam Christmas tour. BHJF, HEPRF.
4. Hope–Bill Mauldin interview, *Bob Hope Show*, March 26, 1965. BHJF, HEPRF.

5. Commencement address file, BHPF, HEPRF.

38. Hope for President
1. Bob Hope, *Five Women I Love, Bob Hope's Vietnam Story* (New York: Doubleday, 1966) p. 249.
2. Vietnam monologue, 1966 Christmas tour. BHJF.
3. *Five Women I Love*, p. 127.
4. Ibid.
5. USO Silver Anniversary monologue, March 31, 1965. BHJF, HEPRF.
6. Author's personal notes and observations.
7. *Family Weekly* manuscript. BHPF.
8. *New York Post*, June 11, 1966.
9. Interview with Allan Kalmus, Summer 1980.
10. KVI news releases, January 19, 1967. HEPRF.
11. *Five Women I Love*. pp. 249-255
12. Interview with Hope, May 1981.
13. *The New York Times*, December 23, 1966.
14. *New York Times Magazine*, October 4, 1970.
15. *The Last Christmas Show*, p. 180.
16. Vietnam monologue, 1967 Christmas tour. BHJF.
17. Vietnam monologue, 1968 Christmas tour. BHJF.

39. Father of the Brides
1. Agnew file. BHJF, HEPRF.
2. *Los Angeles Times*, January 12, 1969.
3. *The New York Times Magazine*, October 4, 1970.
4. Agnew file. BHJF, HEPRF.
5. *Los Angeles Times*, June 15, 1969.
6. *Los Angeles Times*, June 22, 1969.
7. *Los Angeles Herald-Examiner*, August 17, 1969.
8. *Dallas Times Herald*, October 10, 1969.

40. You Can't Walk Away

1. Bradley University personal appearance routine, November 8, 1969. BHJF.
2. Marvin Kalb and Bernard Kalb. *Kissinger* (Boston: Little, Brown, 1974), p. 143.
3. Eisenhower Birthday Dinner monologue, October 14, 1969. BHJF.
4. *Greenville News*, October 25, 1969.
5. Ibid, October 27, 1969.
6. *Boston Sunday Advertiser*, November 9, 1969; *Boston Herald Traveler*, November 13, 1969. HEPRF.
7. *Peoria Journal Star*, November 8, 1969; *Bradley Scout*, November 14, 1969. HEPRF.
8. *Kissinger*.
9. *Peoria Journal Star*, November 9, 1969.
10. *Variety*, November 13, 1969.
11. *Seattle Times*, November 15, 1969.
12. Ibid.
13. Associated Press, United Press International, *Washington Post, Washington Star*, December 15, 1969. HEPRF.
14. Transcript, "The Bob Hope Christmas Show," December 1969. BHJF.
15. *The Last Christmas Show*. p. 290.
16. *St. Louis Globe-Democrat*, December 23, 1969.

41. Some Rain on the Fourth
1. Excerpt from a letter Hope wrote to newspaper editors and publishers asking them to support "Honor America Day" July 4, 1970.
2. Eisenhower benefit file. BHJF, BHPF, HEPRF.
3. "Five Stars for a Five-Star Man" NBC telecast, January 27, 1970. Also HEPRF.
4. Letter from Hope to Lucius Lee. BHPF.
5. *Houston Chronicle*, May 15, 1970.
6. *The New York Times*. June 5, 1970.

7. News conference, Washington Press Club, June 29, 1970. HEPRF.
8. *Washington Star*, July 4, 1970.
9. Honor America Day monologue, July 4, 1970. BHJF, HEPRF.
10. Letter from Dick Gregory to Hope. BHPF.

42. A Partisan Voice
1. *Life*, January 29, 1971.
2. *The New York Times Magazine*, October 4, 1970.
3. *Washington Post*, November 29, 1970.
4. Interview with Frank Liberman, Spring 1981.
5. *The New York Times Magazine*, October 4, 1970.
6. Ibid.
7. *Life*, January 29, 1971.
8. Interview with Bob Thomas, Spring 1981.
9. *New York Daily News*, March 18, 1971.
10. Telegram from Hope to Potter, Associated Press wirecopy, March 18, 1971.
11. Ibid.
12. Ibid.
13. Remarks for "Stars and Stripes" telecast, Oklahoma City, July 4, 1971. BHJF, HEPRF.
14. John Fisher. *Call Them Irreplaceable*. (New York: Stein and Day), p. 165.

43. The Last Christmas Show
1. C. Robert Jennings "On the Road with the All-American Funnyman," *TODAY*, The Philadelphia Inquirer, July 2, 1972.
2. *The Last Christmas Show*, pp. 326–30; also this writer's personal notes and observations.
3. Ibid.
4. Television monologue, March 6, 1972.
5. Jennings, *On the Road*, July 2, 1972.
6. *The Last Christmas Show*, p. 343.

44. A Night With "Pops" in Boston

1. Boston Pops monologue, May 4, 1975.
2. *Have Tux, Will Travel,* p. 1.
3. *Playboy*, December 1973.
4. Ibid.
5. Vernon Scott. "What Makes Bob Hope Run?" United Press International feature, November 17, 1973.
6. *Los Angeles Times*, September 13, 1973.
7. Neil Hickey. "The Comedian Turns Serious," *TV Guide*, January 19, 1974.
8. Jack Benny eulogy, December 29, 1974. BHJF. Also Irving Fein. *Jack Benny, An Intimate Biography* (New York: Putnam, 1976).
9. Hope to Bill Barrett, *Cleveland Press*, August 21, 1975.
10. Interview with Mort Lachman, Summer 1979.
11. Boston Pops monologue, May 4, 1975. BHJF.
12. Ibid.
13. Interview with Ward Grant, Spring 1981.
14. *Dallas Times Herald*, October 24, 1975.

45. A Capital Affair

1. *Washington Star*, May 25, 1978.
2. *Port Arthur* (Texas) *News*, November 10, 1975.
3. Citation accompanying the CBE. BHPF, HEPRF.
4. *Chicago Tribune*, August 24, 1975.
5. Interview with Hope, May 1981.
6. Interview with Bob Thomas, Spring 1981.
7. Hope tribute to Crosby. October 14, 1977. BHJF.
8. Interview with DeVon Smith, Summer 1980. HEPRF.
9. 50th Anniversary of Oscar telecast monologue, April 3, 1978. BHJF.
10. Michael Bandler. "Mr. Hope Goes To Washington," *Modern Maturity*, November 1978.
11. *Washington Post*, May 25, 1978.
12. *Washington Star*, May 25, 1978.
13. Op. Cit.
14. Congressional Record, May 25, 1978. BHPF, HEPRF.
15. Ibid.
16. Ibid.
17. Ibid.
18. Ibid.
19. Ibid.
20. Ibid.
21. Ibid.

Tag: One More Time

1. *The New York Times*, July 1, 1980.
2. *Film Comment*, May–June, 1979.
3. *Los Angeles Times*, May 9, 1979.
4. Ibid.
5. *Variety*, May 16, 1979.
6. *The New York Times*, May 6, 1979.
7. *Youngstown (Ohio) Vindicator*, September 9, 1979.
8. NBC News feature, September 5, 1979.
9. *Youngstown Vindicator*, September 9, 1979.
10. Associated Press wire story, June 18, 1979.
11. *Los Angeles Times*, September 14, 1979.
12. American Embassy in Moscow monologue, September 10, 1979.
13. BHPF.

Index

Hobley, McDonald, 262
Hoff, June, 49
Hofstetler, Dale, 375
Hogan, Charles (Charlie), 15–16, 19, 25, 56–58, 60
Hogan, Pat, 15–16
Hohenlohe, Prince Alec, 244
Holden, William, 270, 363, 368
Holland, Jack, 195
Holliman, Earl, 351
Hollywood Victory Caravan, 159–65, 388–89
Holtz, Lou, 92, 101
Honors and awards, 377
  Al Jolson Memorial Medal, 255
  "Best Male Performer" award, 362
  Bob Hope Day (Philadelphia), 191
  "Bob Hope Day at the Fair," 135
  "Comedian of the Century" award, 362
  Congressional Medal of Honor, 281, 288–90, 292–93, 364
  Distinguished Service Medal, 203
  Eleanor Roosevelt Memorial Award, 308
  Emmy nomination (1963), 291
  Family of Man Award cancelled, 341–42
  Friars' Club testimonial dinner (1953), 253–54
  Golden Globe Award (1963), 291
  Grand Marshal of Roses Parade, 205
  on his 75th birthday, 362, 367–71
  honorary degrees, 288, 307, 319, 321, 341, 348–49, 364, 366
  on last Christmas show, 351–52
  "Leading Entertainer" and "Leading Comedian" awards (1941), 159
  Medal of Merit, 241
  Milestone Award, 286
  monuments and buildings bearing Bob Hope's name, 293, 307, 351, 364, 368, 370, 377
  My Favorite Comedian, 374
  National Association of Broadcasters Distinguished Service Award, 292
  Order of the British Empire, 364–65
  Peabody and Sylvania merit awards, 269
  SAG Award, 307
  Silver Lady Award, 312
  Special Oscar (1941), 148, 159
  Splendid American Award, 307
  Sylvanus Thayer Award, 317, 364

  among ten most admired men (1971), 345
  "This Is Your Life" tribute, 12–13, 18–22, 340
  TV Guide Award (1963), 291
  from U.S. Air Force, 225
  USO award, 310–12
  USO citation, 238
Hood, Gail, 47, 49
Hoover, Herbert, 77
Hoover, J. Edgar, 203
Hope, Alice (aunt), 36
Hope, Anthony (Tony; son), 11, 22, 23, 147, 198, 206, 213, 214, 221, 243, 288, 292, 301, 347, 370
Hope, Avis (Avis Towns; mother), 31–37, 39, 49, 54–55, 60, 70–72, 74–75, 78, 84–88, 91, 92, 202
Hope, Bob (Leslie Towns Hope), 34, 65, 147, 250–51
  adolescence of, 40–42
  as AGVA president, 244, 253
  attends royal wedding, 208–10
  Benny's death and, 360–61
  at Bicentennial opening gala, 365
  birth of, 33
  career of
    as author, *see specific works*
    Crosby and, *see* Crosby, Bing
    early, 42–60
    as journalist, 190, 192, 225, 244
    1946 national tour, 199–202
    1951 European tour, 236–37
    1952 European tour, 244–47
    O'Donnell's influence on, 61–62
    university tours (1960s), 300, 324–27, 340–41
    See also specific aspects of career; for example: Film career
  childhood of, 34–35, 37–40
  childhood poem of, 378
  at Eisenhower Birthday Dinner, 323–24
  golf playing by, 73, 103, 121, 206, 213, 263, 276, 294, 319, 320, 322
    for benefits, 159, 160, 165, 193, 200, 287, 307, 377
    in Britain, 237
    with Crosby, *see* Crosby, Bing
    Desert Classic, 305, 362
    with Eisenhower, 248–49, 255
    in 1951 European tour, 238
  at Gridiron Dinner, 184–85
  health problems and accidents of, 184,